HOMO
TRANSFORMANS

HOMO
TRANSFORMANS

THE ORIGIN AND
NATURE OF THE SPECIES

MARY ELIZABETH AMES

Print information available on the last page.

Rev. date: 03/29/2018

To order additional copies of this book, contact:
Xlibris
1-888-795-4274
www.Xlibris.com
Orders@Xlibris.com
764002

CONTENTS

Illustrations

Tables

Boxes

Figures

PREFACE

To the reader,

Modern medicine is advancing its use of genetics to prevent inheritable diseases, correct genetic defects that lead to disease, and treat or even cure a disease known to have an underlying genetic defect. Thus, medicine is trying to target its treatment to the specific genetic makeup of the individual (personalized medicine) rather than to a population of people.

The intent of this book—and the story embedded in it—is to introduce the reader to genetics. To this end, the author has tried to blend a review of genetics with a fictional story that illustrates several gene functions. Hopefully, it will provide the reader with an understanding of how genes work, how they are inherited, the complexity of how they interact, and the role they play in both health and disease. (Note: The devil is in the details, and the details are in the supplemental notes.)

The author has attempted to make the content regarding the genetics of *Homo sapiens* scientifically accurate as of the time the book was written. The reader is encouraged to consult the Genetics Home Reference (https://ghr.nlm.nih.gov) for additional information about genetics in general and for specific genetic diseases in particular.

Please be advised that any reference to *Homo transformans*, fire-breathing dragons, and genetically engineered human and animal hybrids is pure fantasy. Even though the biology that supports metamorphosis in humans may be present, the genes are missing. Should the reader find the story altogether too improbable, he or she is encouraged to read about the duck-billed platypus (*Ornithorhynchus anatinus*). Its genome has been mapped and found to contain genes from several classes of animals: mammalian, reptilian, avian, amphibian, and fish.

Finally, the astute reader who attends to his or her reading of this book will realize that the author has not disclosed a key relationship in the story. The author has provided for the reader's consideration all the evidence needed to discern the relationship. (Proper attention to the pedigrees should prove enlightening.)

Carneiro B. A., Costa R., Taxter, T., *et al.* (2016.) Is personalized medicine here? *Oncology* (Williston Park), 30(4), 293-303, 307.

Marson, F. A. L., Bertuzzo, C. S., Ribeiro, J. D. (2017.) Personalized or Precision Medicine? The Example of Cystic Fibrosis. *Front Pharmacol*, 8, 390. doi: 10.3389/fphar.2017.00390.

Warren, W. C., *et al.* (2008.) Genome analysis of the platypus reveals unique signatures of evolution. *Nature,* 453(7192), 175–183. doi:10.1038/nature06936.

Acknowledgments

I wish to express my gratitude to Ms. Nancy Renfro, BSFS, MA, for her dedicated review of the narrative and for editing its grammar, punctuation, and composition (and my arithmetic). I am also very grateful to Mrs. Suzanne Smith Sundburg, BA, Phi Beta Kappa, for her expertise as a copyeditor, and to Ms. Esther Ferington for her expertise as a developmental editor.

I am indebted to Dr. Catherine Kopac, RN, PhD, DMin, GNP-BC, for reviewing the genetics of both *H. sapiens* and *H. transformans*. I also wish to thank Dr. George Crossman for his review of the story and how it illustrates the concepts of genetics.

I wish to acknowledge Mr. Ross Cuippa, art director, and Mr. Carl Cleanthes, creative director, and the graphic artists and illustrators of Epic Made who provided the dramatic scenes and vivid renderings of hybrid creatures featured in the narrative.

Finally, I wish to acknowledge Mr. Travis Black, senior publishing consultant, and Mr. Louie Anderson, submissions representative, both of Xlibris, for their guidance and support in the publication of this manuscript.

PART I

The Rise of H. transformans

CHAPTER 1

Dragonensis dragonis rubra

A young woman had spent most of the day scouting for grasses and grains in the open prairie at the base of a southwestern mountain range. As she neared the woodlands on her way home, she transformed into a white-tailed deer. As a deer, she had a much wider visual field, heightened senses of smell and hearing, greater agility, and could reach a speed of thirty to forty-five miles per hour in short bursts. Thus, she would have greater ability to detect predators once she entered the woods. She could have chosen to fly back to her village as a prairie falcon, which can reach speeds of up to ninety miles per hour; however, she had seen eagles over the area. Eagles prey on falcons.

The Hunt

In transforming into a deer, the young woman made a critical error. She thought she was alone and did not take sufficient precautions to cover her metamorphosis. A party of four hunters saw the young woman stoop down and disappear into the grasses. Intrigued, the hunters also hunched down in the grass where they waited and watched. Several minutes later, a white-tailed deer rose up from the place where the young woman had disappeared. The hunters knew at once that the young woman, now a white-tailed deer, was a female *Homo transformans* (*H. transformans*) and a spectacular find. Females had greater abilities to transform than males did, hence female genes were in high demand. Two major organizations were vying for female *H. transformans* and would pay a handsome price for one, especially if captured alive.

The hunters quickly devised a plan to capture the deer. With the breeze in their favor, three of them circled widely around the deer, staying low to avoid being seen. When they were in place, the fourth hunter abruptly stood up and began running toward the deer. The deer saw the hunter and immediately bolted toward the forest. Suddenly, she saw three bowmen stand up along an arc in front of her, aiming their arrows at her. Certain she would not escape without being struck by at least one arrow, she suddenly transformed into a prairie falcon. She would take her chances with the eagles. In doing so, she revealed herself to be an *H. transformans* with extraordinary ability. This only fueled the hunters' desire to catch her.

The falcon did not get far. The transformation had delayed the bird's ability to achieve flight speed rapidly. The lead hunter, a strong bowman and skilled archer, was able to strike her left wing with an arrow. The hunters watched the wounded falcon fall to the ground and disappear into the tall grass. They rushed to achieve the bird and were shocked when they encountered a wounded cougar in its place. She had chewed off the arrow's shaft from her foreleg and launched a violent but brief attack on the hunters. Then she faded quickly into the grasses. Caught completely off guard, the hunters barely escaped with their lives and had no chance to draw their bows before the cat disappeared.

The cougar headed for a rocky escarpment where she knew there was a complex large cave. As the hunters chased after her, the lead hunter directed one of them to get reinforcements. "We need more men and more weapons," he said. "Bring nets, heavy ropes, and the catapult. For all we know, that cougar may become a four-hundred-pound grizzly next."

The three remaining hunters, now mindful of their own safety, tracked the cougar to the cave. There they waited just outside, barring the cave's entrance. In the meantime, the fourth hunter was on a mission to get men and materiel, including a catapult that could launch a large spear with great force.

A Defiant Stand

Meanwhile the cougar took advantage of the time they gave her. Trapped inside the cave, she scouted out its features and characteristics. There were many places where one could hide or launch a sudden attack. So she waited.

With the arrival of reinforcements, the hunters invaded the cave to capture the cougar. They found neither a cougar nor a grizzly bear. Instead, they were met by a red dragoness that was waiting for them. She immediately unleashed her fire, consuming the nearest hunters—nets, bows, arrows, and all. Those not in the dragoness's line of fire fled the cave, except for the lead hunter, who held his ground to allow his comrades to escape. Sheltered by rocky outcroppings in the cave, he targeted the dragoness. One arrow found its mark, striking her in her right side and seriously wounding her. The dragoness unleashed her fire once more. Even though rocks blocked the dragoness's fire, its intense heat finally drove the hunter from the cave.

Unable to transform again and no longer able to hide, the dragoness knew her fire would soon be spent. In one last effort to drive the hunters away, the dragoness took the fight to them. Unbeknownst to her, the hunters had set their catapult on a rise with its spear in line with the entrance to the cave. It was just beyond the reach of a red dragon's fire. One hunter manned the catapult, with the lead hunter standing guard, while other hunters fled toward the rise or hid behind large boulders. All were both anxious and excited at the prospect of killing a dragoness. Her carcass would bring a great bounty, especially her eggs, and they were eager for the reward. They did not know that this dragoness would have no eggs.

When the dragoness emerged, the hunters released the spear from the catapult. It struck the dragoness on the left side of her chest. Mortally wounded, she unleashed a firestorm upon her attackers (illus. 1). Then, in a final act of defiance, she turned her fire upon herself. When the flames finally died down, no trace of the dragoness remained—not even her ashes.

An Unlikely Story

The hunters that survived their encounter with the red dragoness returned with a tale that few would believe. First of all, they described a female *H. transformans* who could undergo multiple transformations from one animal into another. Although their listeners could believe they saw a woman become a deer and even a cougar, most were skeptical of the number of transformations the original hunters claimed they saw. The presence of a red dragon so far from its mountain aerie was unusual but certainly possible. The notion that anyone could transform into a dragon was ridiculous and the source of much amusement and belittlement.

3

Illus. 1. Defiance.

Two organizations, however, were not amused. They were concerned the story was true. To their dismay, no trace of evidence remained from which either one of them could extract the genes that allowed an *H. transformans* to undergo metamorphosis into a red dragon. Nevertheless, both organizations remained on high alert to identify and capture any other *H. transformans* who possessed such capability. At a time when their once highly advanced civilization had been blasted back into the fifteenth century, such power was both terrifying and eagerly sought.

CHAPTER 2

A New Species

A pair of foxes—a male (Edvar H'Aleth) and a female (his wife, Ruth)—were sunning themselves temporarily on top of a grassy knoll. After a while, they both departed together and resumed their patrol over their territory, H'Aleth (map 1). As they traveled, they kept a careful watch on the skies, listened to sounds, and sniffed for scents in the air and on the ground. They were searching for any sign that creatures not native to the region had entered it. If any such indicator was found, Edvar would investigate it on the ground while Ruth transformed into a peregrine falcon and followed him in the air. In this manner, the fox, with his sensitive nose, and the falcon, with her powerful sight, worked together to discern potential invaders. Both knew it was only a matter of time before their adversaries discovered where they were. Eventually, their House and its members would come under siege.

Map 1. The Territories.

A New Characteristic

Both Edvar and Ruth were *H. tranformans* and were born with the ability to undergo metamorphosis. The species name *transformans* was derived from the word *transformation*. Transformation was a radical change in structure, form, and function. Metamorphosis was transformation in a living organism. It occurred most commonly in insects (e.g., from a caterpillar to a butterfly) and amphibians (e.g., from a tadpole to a frog). Normally, other animals did not undergo metamorphosis. They matured through gradual growth and development while maintaining their basic structure and form throughout life. In some members of *Homo sapiens* (*H. sapiens*), however, this process was amended after a massive stellar eruption in the galaxy released a powerful gamma ray burst that struck Earth (box 1).

Box 1. *Stella Ignis.*

Stella Ignis

Stella Ignis (SI) was a massive supernova in the galaxy that released a gamma ray burst and caused a geomagnetic storm several times greater than that of a coronal mass ejection from the sun. Earth's geomagnetic field was temporarily overwhelmed, disrupting it down to and including the ozone layer. Earth's distance from the supernova, its orbit around to the far side of the sun and away from the blast, and its rotation helped minimize the extent of gamma radiation exposure over the planet.

Loss of the ozone layer led to a mass extinction similar to the Ordovician. Life forms sensitive to radiation damage were also lost unless they were protected deep underground or were resistant to the effects of gamma radiation. Since humans are not resistant to radiation, people went deep underground into caves and caverns and took with them as many plant and animal species as they could muster and support. As Earth gradually recovered over the next 150 years, humans along with plants and animals reemerged as environmental conditions allowed.

Human society and knowledge had been preserved, albeit under severely constrained environmental conditions. When humans reemerged, they found that most building structures had decayed due to the effects of weathering or the effects of gamma radiation on construction materials. In contrast, some machines that had withstood weathering could be refurbished and reused provided they did not rely on electronic components.

Box 1

Humans and other organisms who escaped exposure to gamma radiation were unaffected by it. Those who were exposed to nonlethal doses of it were able to recover from its effects. Some members of *H. sapiens* might have been resistant to the adverse effects of gamma radiation and had no ill effects even at higher levels of exposure. Thus, those who were not exposed to gamma radiation and those who were exposed to nonlethal levels or were resistant to it survived the burst and produced offspring.

A new characteristic began to arise in some humans about 175 years after Earth was struck by the gamma ray burst. After many generations, a few humans appeared who were capable of transforming into another species of animal, which, with rare exceptions, was another species of mammal. Prior to this time, metamorphosis had not been observed in humans. Perhaps the exposure to gamma radiation triggered the capability in some members of *H. sapiens* to undergo metamorphosis.

When instances of human transformation first appeared, they seemed to be random and entirely spontaneous. Initially, only a few individuals showed the ability to transform successfully, including the ability to reverse their transformation and resume their human form. Those who were unsuccessful became a contorted mass of flesh that could not survive. As more individuals demonstrated the ability to transform successfully, patterns of inheritance could be seen in their offspring.

Once members of *H. sapiens* recognized that some of its members could transform into other species reliably and their progeny could do the same consistently, a new species called *Homo transformans* was declared. Although *H. sapiens* and *H. transformans* had the same human form and function, the distinction was clear. Those who were *H. transformans* had the ability to transform. Members of *H. sapiens* did not. Thus, humans who could transform were classified with other humans under the same genus (*Homo*) but designated as a different species (*transformans*) (table 1).

Year (SI)	Table 1. Chronology of Events Post-*Stella Ignis*
0	*Stella Ignis*
150	Recovery and resurgence of plant and animal life, including humans
175	First appearance of individuals with transforming capabilities
325	*H. transformans* declared a new species within the genus *Homo*

Edvar H'Aleth could transform within the canine family. His alternate species were the red fox and gray wolf. Ruth could transform into both mammals and birds. Her mammalian alternate species were the gray wolf and gray fox, cougar and lynx, and river otter. Her avian alternate species were the peregrine falcon, Cooper's hawk, and long-eared owl. Edvar's capabilities were relatively common among *H. transformans*. Ruth's capabilities were rare and extraordinary.

Many organizations arose with the intent of identifying the source of *H. transformans's* ability. The Biogenetics Company, managed by a board of directors, and the Cassius Foundation, owned by Angus Cassius, were the two largest organizations conducting research into the genetics of *H. transformans*. Both organizations acquired scientists and geneticists to find out why some people could transform and others could not. The researchers in both groups reported the same problem. "We can't tell the difference between *H. sapiens* and *H. transformans* simply by looking at them," a spokesman said. "We need subjects who are known *H. transformans* in order to study and compare their genetic profile to that of *H. sapiens*." In time, their research revealed that the new species had far more genes arrayed across multiple chromosomes than did the average *H. sapiens*.

Cracking the Code

Like other *H. transformans*, Edvar's and Ruth's ability to transform was limited to those species of animals whose genes they possessed. For any species to display its physical characteristics, there had be an underlying genetic code directing how each characteristic should be formed. Genes contained the instructions (the code) to make the physical structure of a living organism. This code was handed down from parents to offspring and reflected the memory (inheritance) of how physical structures were made in the past.

In any species, deoxyribonucleic acid (DNA) was the building block of genetic material. Genes, comprised of DNA, represented a functional unit of DNA (illus. 2, box 2). There were two broad categories of genes: (1) coding genes, which provided the instructions for building a physical structure, and (2) noncoding genes, which regulated the activity of other genes, including the coding genes. The total genetic makeup (the genome) of *H. sapiens* included about three million pairs of genes, of which approximately twenty thousand were coding genes. The genome of *H. transformans* far exceeded this number. In addition to their *H. sapiens* genes, their genes coded for the form and function of their alternate species as well. This was the case for both Edvar and Ruth.

Illus. 2. Genes and DNA.

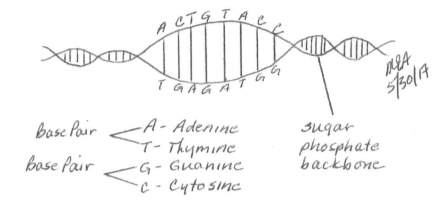

Base Pair — A - Adenine
            T - Thymine
Base Pair — G - Guanine
            C - Cytosine

sugar
phosphate
backbone

Box 2. Genes and DNA.

> Genes and DNA
>
> Illustration 2 shows a portion of DNA stretched out. Essentially, a strand of DNA is an extremely long staircase that is kept wound up most of the time. The staircase consists of a series of base pairs that form the steps. The base pairs are anchored in place on the two banisters (the sugar phosphate backbone). A segment of the staircase (DNA) is unwound only when it is needed. When that portion of the staircase is not being used, it will be kept wound up and compressed.
>
> Box 2

The question of how individual genes worked and where they were located had been a matter of investigation for geneticists long before *Stella Ignis*. With the rise of *H. transformans*, there were many more questions regarding how the genes of alternate species arose or became embedded into the genome of *H. transformans*. Were these genes always present in an inactive or suppressed state, or were they added somehow to the existing genome? For Angus Cassius, these were mere academic questions. "I need to know now," he thundered, "which genes cause transformation, what chromosomes they are on, and exactly where on the chromosome they can be found." He needed this information to manipulate and possibly modify the new species for his own purposes.

A chromosome was simply an extended strand of DNA that was bunched up and compressed into a microscopic package so that it would fit inside an individual cell (illus. 3, box 3). When arrayed in their proper order along their assigned chromosome, individual genes provided the plans for building an organism and directing how other genes would be used in building it. This included the instructions for making the building materials (e.g., proteins and other substances), assembling them into a form, and directing how the organism will function.

Illus. 3. Chromosomes and Genes.

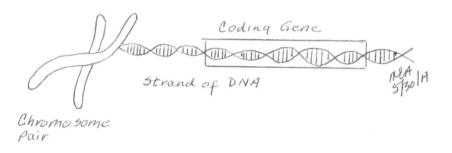

Coding Gene

Strand of DNA

Chromosome Pair

Box 3. Chromosomes and Genes.

Chromosomes and Genes

Illustration 3 shows a generic pair of chromosomes. A chromosome consists of a long strand of DNA with large numbers of genes clustered together in a predetermined sequence. Portions of the DNA strand that are not being used are bundled up and compressed to form the chromosome.

A strand of DNA has been teased out of one of the chromosomes. A segment of the strand has been isolated to show a portion that represents a gene.

Box 3

Normally, all *H. sapiens* had a full complement of twenty-three paired chromosomes for a total of forty-six (illus. 4, box 4). For each pair of chromosomes, one was donated by the mother and the other was donated by the father. With the exception of the reproductive chromosomes, the two strands in each pair were identical and were aligned with each other so that the same (or almost the same) genes from each parent were also paired together.

Illus. 4. Chromosome Pairs.

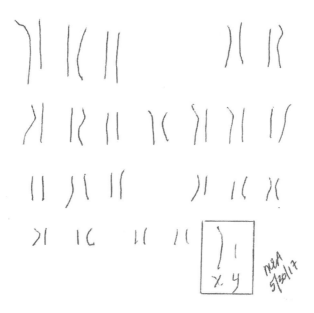

NORMAL MALE KARYOTYPE

Box 4. Chromosome Pairs.

Chromosome Pairs

Illustration 4 shows a normal complement of twenty-three pairs of chromosomes for a total of forty-six chromosomes. They are arrayed as they would be seen in a standard karyotype.

A karyotype reveals the number and appearance of chromosomes as seen under a microscope. The karyotype seen in illustration 4 has an X and a Y chromosome for a male. A female would have two X chromosomes.

Box 4

In *H. transformans*, the size and number of chromosomes increased depending upon the degree of difference in the individual's baseline genome (*H. sapiens*) and that of the other species into which the individual could transform. Additional chromosomes could be needed to support the DNA required for transformation into multiple species, especially if the species were not mammalian. Fortunately, multiple genes shared across different classes significantly reduced the genomic burden that an *H. transformans* had to have in order to transform into another species.

Edvar likely had an expanded number of gene pairs across multiple chromosomes to support his two canine alternate species. This could have resulted in an increase in the size of the affected chromosomes without necessarily increasing their number. Ruth, however, likely had additional chromosomes to support her avian alternate species.

Serendipity

The origin of the genes for transformation was unknown. They could have been present all along and activated by exposure to intense gamma radiation. Alternatively, they could have been the result of multiple mutations triggered by the gamma ray burst. If the mutations conferred a selective benefit to an individual (e.g., survival), the genes were likely to be passed on through successive generations of progeny. Perhaps human metamorphosis arose from a combination of these factors.

As a fox, Edvar H'Aleth had keener eyesight, hearing, and smell than any human. As a wolf, he had greater strength and endurance, as well as powerful jaws that could break large bones. As either one, he was stuck on the ground. As a raptor, Ruth had the power of flight, nearly telescopic vision, a sharp curved beak, and talons that could rend flesh. Together, Edvar and Ruth could fend off a much larger adversary.

Unfortunately, there were no records of either Edvar's or Ruth's lineage. Their parentage was lost to history, as was the source of their abilities, especially those possessed by Ruth. During the time in which they lived, the lineage and genetic profiles of *H. transformans* families were not recorded. Most families hid their capabilities and their status to avoid being persecuted as freaks or captured by bounty hunters and sold to organizations that wanted their genomes. There were too many reports of *H. transformans* disappearing, especially women. Those who disappeared were never seen again.

Consequently, how Ruth acquired her capabilities was unknown. It could have been from a series of random mutations over multiple generations or the serendipitous matching of two compatible genomes—her parents—in one generation. Most likely, it was a combination of both.

Supplemental Notes and Citations

General references for *Homo sapiens* in this section are from Beery and Workman (2012), Brooker (2009), Carroll (2009); Jorde (2014a, 2014b), Guyton and Hall (2006); Porth (2009). Additional citations are as noted. Although the concepts below have been applied to *Homo transformans* as well, the reader is reminded that any reference to *H. transformans* is pure fantasy.

Transformation and Metamorphosis

Metamorphosis occurs in an organism that has already undergone growth and development and then transforms into another organism with a completely different structure. In contrast, morphogenesis is the development of structure and form through typically gradual changes that occur during normal growth and development (Reddi, 2000). Obvious changes in form and function occur as an embryo develops into a fetus. Changes in growth and development continue, albeit less dramatically, as the fetus develops into a fully formed newborn baby and the infant develops into an adult.

Effects of Gamma Radiation

Gamma rays are high-energy electromagnetic particles released from radioactive atoms (ionizing radiation). These particles significantly affect cellular structures, including DNA (Hada and Georgakilas, 2008). Gamma rays that strike subatomic particles can cause a change in the structure of atomic nuclei (Konevega and Kalinin, 2000; Tisljar-Lentulis et al., 1983).

A gamma ray burst can deplete the ozone layer leading to excessive ultraviolet radiation on Earth's surface (Thomas, 2009). The Ordovician extinction was one of five mass extinction events on Earth. It may have been triggered by a gamma ray burst (Melott et al., 2003). Some organisms have cellular processes that protect DNA from damage or have DNA repair mechanisms capable of reconstructing the genome or both (Jayakumar et al. 2015; Pavlopoulou et al., 2015; Sekhar and Freeman, 2015). Several species of bacteria are known to be resistant to radiation, including gamma radiation (Raddadi et al., 2005; Rainey et al., 2005, Yu et al., 2015). Some organisms that have countermeasures against the effects of ionizing radiation may actually benefit from the exposure (Gabani and Singh, 2013).

Gamma rays also evaporate water in construction materials and degrade concrete (Soo and Milian, 2001; Vodak et al., 2011; William et al., 2013).

Genes

A gene—deoxyribonucleic acid (DNA)—is a unit of heredity that contains the instructions (code) for how and when to make a physical structure (e.g., a protein). Since genes consist of DNA, the two terms are often used interchangeably. Genes consist of three sets of nucleotides. A nucleotide is a molecule of DNA composed of a sugar (deoxyribose), a phosphoric acid molecule, and one of four nitrogenous bases—thymine (T), cytosine (C), guanine (G), and adenine (A). The sugar and phosphoric acid form the backbone of the DNA strand that supports the bases. It is the different combinations of the four nitrogenous bases—T, C, G, A—that create the genetic code. The code itself is comprised of up to sixty-four different combinations of three out of the four available bases (otherwise known as a triplet).

Coding genes direct the production of proteins. They provide the instructions for building twenty of the twenty-two amino acids that are the building blocks of proteins. A multitude of noncoding genes regulate if, when, and how other genes—both coding and other noncoding genes—are actually used. The total gene complement of an individual organism (e.g., bacterium, virus, human, frog, etc.) is called its genome. The reader is referred to the National Center for Biotechnology Information (http://www.ncbi.nlm.nih.gov/genome) for additional information on the *H. sapiens* genome.

Chromosomes

A chromosome is a continuous linear strand of genetic material (e.g., DNA), with genes linked together in a predetermined sequence, twisted around each other, and bundled together to form a single, compact structure that will fit in the nucleus of a cell. The nucleus of the cell is a microscopic organelle that houses the cell's DNA as well as other types of genetic material. The reader is referred to the Genetics Home Reference (https://ghr.nlm.nih.gov/primer/mutationsanddisorders/genemutation) for additional information about cells and the functions of organelles inside the cell, including the nucleus.

With the exception of the reproductive cells (ovum and sperm), all other cells normally possess a full complement of the individual's DNA, including a full set of paired chromosomes. Reproductive cells have only a single copy of each chromosome. Thus, an individual ovum and sperm will have only one reproductive chromosome coding for either the female gender (an X chromosome) or the male gender (a Y chromosome). The two reproductive chromosomes bear no resemblance to each other whatsoever and share few genes.

Different species may have different numbers of chromosomes. The normal complement of chromosomes for *H. sapiens* is forty-six. In contrast, the duck-billed platypus has fifty-two chromosomes (Warren et al., 2008). Regardless of the differences in numbers of chromosomes, animals have many genes in common. These genes were conserved during evolution from a common ancestor and continue to be used across many classes of animals (Shorey-Kendrick et al., 2015).

Gene Mutations

Gene mutation is a permanent change in the structure of a gene. A mutation may or may not result in a change in the gene's function. Changes in function, if any, could be beneficial or harmful. Mutations can be spontaneous (random) or induced (man-made). Many agents (mutagens) are known to cause a change in gene structure and/or increase the frequency of mutations (Jorde, 2014a). Cosmic radiation (e.g., gamma rays and ultraviolet sunlight) are naturally occurring mutagens and are sources of random mutation. Radiation produced by nuclear power plants, radiation therapy, selected cancer chemotherapy agents, and toxic chemicals (e.g., nitrogen mustard) are man-made mutagens (Ikehata and Ono, 2011).

Mutations can affect an individual gene or a gene pair. Point mutations occur at the level of an individual gene. It may involve a single gene (e.g., sickle cell anemia) or several discrete genes across multiple chromosomes (e.g., cancer, diabetes). Pair substitution occurs when one gene pair is replaced by another gene pair.

If the cell can reproduce itself (mitosis), then mutations can be passed on from parent cell to daughter cells. If the change occurs in a reproductive cell (ovum, sperm), then the change can be passed on from parent to child. The reader is referred to the Genetics Home Reference (https://ghr.nlm.nih.gov/primer/mutationsanddisorders/genemutation) for additional information on gene mutations.

CHAPTER 3

The X^T Factor

When people first discovered that some humans could transform into another species, they began to wonder if everyone could do so. When most people tried, however, nothing happened. It seemed that only a few people possessed the ability.

An independent research company, Biogenetics, discovered that two distinct sets of genes were required. The first one conferred the capability to transform, and the second one contained the genes that coded for the characteristics of the species. The director of research and development at Biogenetics briefed his board of directors accordingly. "Both are essential for transformation," he told them. "But even if people possess the genes of another species, they cannot transform without the genes that provide the capability." The chairman recognized the implications immediately. "If we can control the capability, then we can control the process." He directed the research department to refocus its efforts. "Identify the genes that confer the capability and find where they are located," he ordered.

Biogenetics became intent on discovering the genes that regulated transformation. This knowledge would put the company in a powerful position. Accordingly, it had no intention of sharing their discovery with anyone else, especially Angus Cassius. "Figure it out for yourself," its chairman told their rival, knowing full well the latter's intentions.

Angus was furious but not dismayed. *I will have your discovery*, he thought to himself. *My spies will bring it to me.*

The X^T Chromosome

The genome of *H. transformans* was built on the genome of *H. sapiens*. The ability of *H. transformans* to transform into another species was determined entirely by genetic changes to the *H. sapiens* genome. There were several factors that affected the process of transformation. These included (1) the individual genes involved (which could add millions more to the genome), (2) their specific functions, (3) how and in what order they were paired on their respective chromosomes, and (4) the degree to which they were expressed as characteristics in the individual. Even in *H. sapiens*, these factors governed how genes operated and how they interacted with other genes. In *H. transformans*, however, these factors also determined the extent to which a human may or may not be able to transform into another species.

The ability to transform at all was governed by multiple genes found only on a transforming X chromosome (X^T). In both *H. sapiens* and *H. transformans*, the reproductive chromosomes (X and Y) determined the gender of the individual and the corresponding gender characteristics. The remaining nonreproductive chromosomes (autosomes) housed the genes that governed the rest of their physical characteristics. Since males had one X chromosome and females had two, both had the potential to possess an X^T chromosome. Thus, the ability to transform into an alternate species was governed by having both (1) an X^T chromosome, which, if present, conferred the capability, and (2) the genes of an alternate species found on the rest of the chromosomes, which provided the characteristics.

Pushing the Envelope

As *H. transformans*, both Edvar and Ruth had become quite adept at transformation. Edvar could change into a wolf over several minutes. Changing into a fox required more time. In either case, he would have to be in human form before becoming either a fox or a wolf. He could not transform directly from one alternate species into the other one. He found this situation rather annoying, especially since his wife suffered no such constraints.

Ruth had greater facility in transforming. She could change into any of her alternate species in only a few minutes. In addition, she could transform directly from one alternate species into another alternate species without first resuming her human form. She could accomplish this feat even if the two species were from different classes (e.g., from a fox [mammalian] to a falcon [avian]).

As a male, Edvar had one X^T (X^T, Y). By virtue of being a female, Ruth could have had one X^T (X^T, X) or two X^T chromosomes ($2X^T$). Given Ruth's extraordinary capabilities, there was no doubt she had two X^T chromosomes. Clearly, there were limits on how much transformation a single X^T chromosome could support. Having one X^T provided Edvar with the capability to transform; however, it limited the scope of his capability. This likely explained at least some of the corrupted transformations that occurred among *H. transformans* who tried to force a transformation that their genes could not support.

Even if an individual had the capability to transform (possessed an X^T chromosome), the individual still needed to have the genetic code (genotype) underlying the other species' visible characteristics (phenotype). Genotype limited the individual's options to assume the phenotype of another species. This was clearly evident in the number of alternate species Ruth could assume compared to those available to Edvar. Both had the basic genome of *H. sapiens*, and both had the capability to transform. Both had the complete genotype for a species of fox and for the gray wolf. Ruth, however, also had the complete genotypes for additional species and a second X^T chromosome to support the transformations.

A Playful River Otter

Occasionally, Edvar and Ruth would go to a local freshwater pond fed by a stream. There, Ruth would indulge herself and transform into a river otter. She would frolic in the water while Edvar stood guard as a gray wolf. A native wolf would not hesitate to prey on an otter. So on occasion, Ruth would tease Edvar with an otter's rendition of a come-hither look and then dare him to try to catch her (illus. 5).

Illus. 5. Come Hither.

Although wolves were fairly good swimmers, Edvar knew full well there was no chance he could catch Ruth in the water. Swimming underwater, a river otter could reach speeds of nearly seven miles per hour. Nevertheless, Edvar would accept the challenge and jump in to chase after her. Once they emerged on land, however, the tables were turned. Edvar would pounce on Ruth.

Edvar often wished he could become an otter and race through the water alongside Ruth. Alas, his genotype did not permit it. Still, both of them had the genotypes for a wolf and a fox, so both could transform into a wolf or a fox to travel together.

To Be or Not to Be

In *H. sapiens*, not all genes needed to be visible in the phenotype. Some genes were not active because they were suppressed (e.g., by another gene) or because they were inactivated. It was also possible for a gene to be partially active or visible. The same conditions existed in *H. transformans*. An *H. transformans* who had only a partial genotype of another species could not transform into that species. That individual could, however, get some benefit from a partial genotype if some of the genes were expressed. If so, those genes could provide enhancements to native human characteristics (e.g., greater muscle mass, better eyesight, longer canine teeth, etc.).

Neither Edvar nor Ruth could transform into a red wolf. Yet, two of their children could—H'Ophelia and Edmond. "How did that happen?" Edvar had asked Ruth.

"Both of us can transform into a wolf," Ruth answered. "I wonder . . ." she mused and then added, "My grandmother had red hair and could become a red fox. Was there anyone like that in your family?"

"Not exactly," Edvar replied. "I had an uncle who had red hair, but he was an *H. sapiens*." Unbeknownst to the two of them, both carried a single gene for red coloring. A single gene was not sufficient for either parent to have red hair or fur. Two of their children, however, inherited that single gene from both of their parents, which allowed them to display red hair.

There was no record of Edvar's and Ruth's genotypes. It was entirely possible that the genomes of one or both of them carried a partial set of genes for other species. If so, these genes would not have been expressed unless they conferred an enhancement to an existing ability. Thus, neither

Edvar nor Ruth would be aware they possessed a partial set of genes for other species. Yet they could still pass them on to their offspring.

In *H. sapiens*, many of the gene pairs inherited from parents were exactly alike. It was quite common, however, to have slight variations in the structure of a gene without incurring any change in its function. Many of these differences were the result of naturally occurring random mutations. Gene variations that coded for the same function might be paired with each other on their respective chromosomes. As long as the genes were native to the species (e.g., *H. sapiens*), their differences may have resulted in no change or caused only subtle changes that went unnoticed.

In contrast, for a transformation to occur, all genes in gene pairs that support transformation needed to be exactly alike and arrayed in exactly the same way on their respective chromosomes. These genes were tightly linked. Any variability within a gene pair would derail the process of transformation. Consequently, there were many more *H. transformans*—individuals with an X^T in their genotype—who could not transform than there were those who could. This made the H'Aleth family all the more remarkable.

Family Matters

Edvar and Ruth had five children, two sons and three daughters, all of whom were *H. transformans*. As long as *H. transformans* were in human form, they had the same reproductive capabilities as did *H. sapiens*. When transformed into an alternate species, however, the reproductive capability of *H. transformans* was suppressed. This was not due to any action by the X^T chromosome. It was a result of the stresses placed on individuals when they transform. The process of transformation was a major physiologic stressor that required significant energy resources to support and maintain the transformation. As a result, abundant amounts of stress hormones were released while undergoing transformation and while in a transformed state.

In both *H. sapiens* and *H. transformans*, the primary purpose of these stress hormones was to support those physiologic functions needed to survive in the moment. Reproduction was not one of them. When *H. sapiens* was under sustained levels of stress, hormones that supported pregnancy could be suppressed. It was no different in *H. transformans*. Yet once a transformation was reversed and the human form was resumed, the state of stress subsided and fertility was restored.

All five of Edvar and Ruth's children shared their parents' abilities. Like their mother, H'Anna, H'Ophelia, and H'Elena could transform into a variety of mammals and birds. Both sons, Edvar Jr. and Edmond, could transform into a wolf and fox, as did their father. This was a powerful family.

Supplemental Notes and Citations

General references for *H. sapiens* in this section are Beery and Workman (2012), Brooker (2009), Carroll (2009), Jorde (2014a, 2014b), Guyton and Hall (2006), and Porth (2009). Additional citations are as noted.

Reproductive Chromosomes and Autosomes

The X and Y chromosomes are the two reproductive chromosomes. In *H. sapiens*, the X chromosome codes for multiple functions essential for life and for the female gender and the characteristic features and physiology seen in the female of each species (Ross et al., 2005). The Y chromosome codes primarily for male gender and the characteristic features and physiology seen in the male of each species. Autosomes are any chromosomes that are not a sex chromosome. They are a balance of the remaining (nonsex) chromosomes in a species and code for all the remaining features and functions characteristic of the species.

Genotype and Phenotype

Genotype is an individual's overall genetic composition, whether or not it is expressed as an observable characteristic. Phenotype is an individual's observable characteristics as dictated by his or her genotype (e.g., eye color, gender, metabolism, etc.) (Devlin and Morrison, 2004). Efforts are underway to identify the relationships governing the influence of genotype on phenotype (Bush et al., 2016). For now, phenotype cannot be used to predict genotype, nor can genotype be used to predict phenotype. There are far too many variables affecting the influence of genes on phenotype.

There are many internal and external influences on gene activity, including if and when a gene is active. An active gene may be exerting its effects, yet not be seen (expressed) in the phenotype. When expressed in the phenotype, the gene has a visible effect that is displayed in physical characteristics.

Genetic Polymorphisms

These are naturally occurring variations in the structure of a gene. Two different versions of the same gene may be paired together. Most of these differences are benign and cause no change in function; however, they are a significant source of variation among individuals in a species and provide the basis of genetic diversity within the species. In *H. sapiens*, there are four different versions of the genetic code for valine (an amino acid), all of which provide the same standard valine (Liu et al., 2015). In contrast, there are multiple gene variations in liver enzymes responsible for degrading chemical compounds, including drugs (the CYP 450 system). Some of these variations may affect the *rate* at which drugs are degraded, thereby altering the duration of their effect.

Gene Expression

Not all genes need be expressed. There are many situations affecting whether or not a gene is expressed in the phenotype. Expression may depend upon whether a gene pair is homozygous or heterozygous, one gene is dominant and the other is nondominant (recessive), and the gene is active or inactive. As a result, some genes may be repressed or only partially expressed.

Homozygous versus heterozygous. If both members of a gene pair have exactly the same genetic code, they are homozygous. If the genes in a gene pair are not identical and each one is a variation of the gene, then they are heterozygous. This variation may or may not cause a change in the gene function. In the case of valine, a heterozygous gene pair causes no change in the production of valine. In contrast, there are many different variations in the *BRCA1* and *BRCA2* genes (tumor suppressor genes). Some but not all these variations inactivate the genes' tumor suppressor functions, thereby increasing the risk of developing certain types of cancer (e.g., breast, ovarian).

Dominant versus recessive. When paired with a dominant gene, a single nondominant (recessive) gene will not be expressed. If both parents harbor a single recessive gene for red hair and a dominant gene for brown hair, the red hair gene would not be expressed (Zdrojewicz et al., 2016). Both parents would have brown hair because the gene for red hair is suppressed by the more dominant gene for brown hair. If both parents passed their one gene for red hair to their offspring, then that offspring would inherit two red genes and be able to express red hair. There would be no brown gene to overpower a single red gene.

Active versus inactive. Not all genes are active continuously. There are genetic mechanisms (on/off switches) for turning on (activating) genes when their products or actions are needed and turning them off (inactivation) when they are not needed. Genes can be inactivated either by another gene or by an external (epigenetic) agent acting on the gene.

Penetrance. Partial expression is the extent to which a specific genotype is expressed in an individual's phenotype. An individual may have the gene but does not express it fully (incomplete penetrance, e.g., sickle cell trait), or the gene may not be expressed until later in life (age-dependent penetrance, e.g., Huntington's chorea). The reader is referred to the Genetics Home Reference (https://ghr.nlm.nih.gov/primer/howgeneswork/geneonoff) for additional information regarding mechanisms for regulating gene activity in *H. sapiens*.

Stress Hormones

Several hormones are released during a stressed state. These include adrenaline, cortisol, glucagon, and others. In *H. sapiens*, prolonged release of glucocorticoid hormones (e.g., cortisol) during a stressed state results in the inhibition of several hormones involved in both fertility (e.g., follicle-stimulating hormone, which promotes the development of ova and sperm) and sustaining a pregnancy (e.g., luteinizing hormone and progesterone, which promote development of the uterus to support pregnancy) (Geraghty and Kaufer, 2015; Tsutsui et al., 2012; Whirledge and Cidlowski, 2010, 2013). Suppression of ovulation via central nervous system control mechanisms can also cause cessation of menses (hypothalamic amenorrhea) (Genazzani et al., 2010; Kalantaridou et al., 2004; Latham, 2015).

Conditions of physiologic stress are seen among professional female athletes who may cease to ovulate and menstruate (Orio et al., 2013; Scheid and De Souza, 2010). Conditions of starvation whether enforced (e.g., humanitarian crises) or self-afflicted (e.g., anorexia nervosa) will have the same results (Misra and Klibanski, 2014).

CHAPTER 4

First, Do No Harm

Among social creatures of many species, including *H. sapiens*, subgroups were formed based on common interests, needs, and relationships. With the recognition of *H. transformans* as a new species, factions within *H. sapiens* developed based on different points of view and intentions. Some viewed *H. transformans* as a higher level of evolution, whereas others saw it as a freakish act of nature. Some viewed *H. transformans* as simply an extension of *H. sapiens* with additional abilities, whereas others viewed it as a subspecies to be controlled and manipulated.

Some factions sought to understand the nature and evolution of *H. transformans* in the hope that it would improve the human condition. Others hoped to exploit *H. transformans* as a powerful resource for their use. If they could control the process of transformation, their dominance would be assured. Given those differences, several factions established organizations that represented their particular beliefs. The desire to discover and use the capability to transform spurred the allocation of resources to reestablish genetics research and development facilities that could discover—and possibly engineer—human metamorphosis. In the meantime, one common goal was to expand the number and capability of *H. transformans* within their own ranks.

Given the relative rarity of the genetic ability to transform, several organizations initially established programs in an effort to identify what changes in *H. sapiens* conveyed this ability. These organizations took a variety of different approaches toward transformation. Several relied on breeding programs and specialized in matching males and females with the same desired characteristics. Others relied on manipulating the genome to achieve the desired result. The Biogenetics Company and the Cassius Foundation were at the forefront of these research efforts.

An Opportune Discovery

The Biogenetics Company focused on the science of transformation. Its members sought to identify the genome and biogenetic factors influencing and controlling the process. If they could identify both the genes and the genetic factors regulating their expression, then they could control the process—or so they thought.

The Biogenetics Company discovered several mutations in the X chromosome that led to the capability to transform. They also discovered that only one transforming X chromosome (X^T) was needed to transform into species in the same class (e.g., mammals), provided the X^T has the required genes arrayed in the proper order. The ability to transform successfully across families (e.g., canine and feline) within the same class required the presence of two X^T chromosomes.

Since females could inherit two X^T chromosomes, the capability and ability to transform across families were found almost exclusively in females. Finally, the ability to transform successfully into species that were outside one's class (e.g., from mammal to bird) required a $2X^T$ female who was descended from a specific founding ancestor. Unbeknownst to them, Ruth was one of only two females first known to transform across classes and the only one known to have progeny. History would recognize her as a founding ancestor.

Since X chromosomes did not need to carry any genes for transformation, the likelihood of receiving an X^T from both parents was low. Consequently, the Biogenetics Company initiated breeding programs to increase the number of X^T chromosomes in their subjects.

Breeding programs attempted to promote desired genotypes (e.g., X^T) by matching individuals who possessed similar phenotypes with one another (e.g., *H. transformans*). There had been many attempts among several species (e.g., show dogs, milk cows) to develop breeding lines that would engender the desired characteristic in subsequent offspring. This often meant pairing two individuals who were already closely related to each other and had the same or similar genomes. These programs relied heavily on inbreeding to achieve their goals.

Inbreeding led to a more homogenous genome. As genetic variability declined, pairs of relatively rare (recessive) genes increased. Many of these genes had not been visible in the past because they were paired with another (dominant) gene, which trumped them. If the same two relatively rare genes—one from the mother and one from the father—were matched with each other, then the characteristic they supported would be expressed in the phenotype. Depending upon the characteristic expressed and the influence of other genes on that characteristic, the outcome could be good, bad, or mixed (e.g., cows that produce small amounts of sweet milk or cows that produce large amounts of sour milk).

Even when the desired genotype was achieved, it was often overwhelmed by the number of gene defects that led to a vast array of physical deformities, mental deficiencies, emotional lability, psychological instability, metabolic abnormalities, and other derangements. As the genome became more constrained, the number and severity of these disorders became progressively greater. Many proved to be incompatible with life.

Testing the Limits

The Cassius Foundation took a much darker approach to the new species. Angus Cassius intended to use the abilities of *H. transformans* to gain control over all the regions and establish himself as the sole leader over both *H. sapiens* and *H. transformans*. He was not a patient man. Consequently, the ability of some *H. transformans* to become an apex predator drew his attention. He envisioned developing even more powerful subjects by combining some of their traits. Thus, he aggressively sought out any *H. transformans* who could become a powerful and aggressive animal.

Angus also used genetic engineering to amend an individual's genetic code so that it would support transformation, at least in subsequent progeny if not in the parent. He also used a variety of methods, including mutagens and other agents, to speed up the process of transformation. As the rate of transformation increased, so did the number of errors in the process. Consequently, Angus's use of accelerants increased the incidence of disrupted and aborted transformations, which in turn led to a sharp increase in the prevalence of corrupted creatures.

As a result, Angus's genetic engineering programs fared even worse than Biogenetics's breeding programs. Both organizations had similar outcomes—creating diseased or deformed offspring or corrupted creatures, most of whom did not survive.

Last but not least, a third organization, the Eugenics Corporation, adopted a businesslike approach to the situation. Their executives wanted to capitalize on the research of other organizations to produce and market *H. transformans* capable of transforming into a specific species, as requested by their clients. In this manner, they could control the number, availability, and price (at least at retail) of *H. transformans* based on their range of species.

Social Values

With its focus on scientific discovery, the Biogenetics Company took a practical approach to solving the mysteries of transformation. Discovering the X^T chromosome represented a good outcome, provided Biogenetics could control access to this knowledge for its own profit and status. This ethic did not preclude any benefit to others; however, any harm done to humans or animals was justified by the result.

Cassius, motivated solely by his desire for power, was never troubled by the rights or welfare of any of his subjects. He never thought to modify or adjust his methods to prevent harm or suffering to anyone—human or animal. Many of his test subjects suffered greatly at his hands unless they were fortunate enough to die quickly.

Eugenics, with its strictly business approach, did not consider itself at odds with social values at all. It was willing to trade with anyone for a price. In acting as an intermediary, it was providing a service to its business partners. It was not involved with any of the methods they used and, therefore, felt no responsibility for them.

Thus, conflicts with social values were not a consideration for any of the three organizations. With the intense competition for both resources and results, any notion of ethical practices was dismissed (box 5).

Box 5. Deontological Principles of Ethics.

Deontological Principles of Ethics

The decision to act is based on a duty to do no harm or, if unavoidable, to do the least harm.
Autonomy—to allow self-determination (without harm to others)
Justice—to be fair and equal, to be impartial
Beneficence—to do good, to provide for the welfare of others
Nonmalfeasence—to do no harm, to prevent harm to others

Box 5

Adversaries

Angus immediately began devising plans to wrest control of smaller organizations and use their resources to expand the number, if not the capability, of *H. transformans* under his control (map 2). In this manner, he sought to achieve dominion over any society he could reach. This did not go unnoticed by Biogenetics and Eugenics, and they became suspicious of Cassius. Their respective governing bodies met and decided that their mutual survival would be more assured if they merged. They did so, creating the Biogenics Corporation, a symbolic merger of the two company names (map 3). Their combined assets rivaled those of the Cassius Foundation in both size and resources and put them on an equal footing with it.

Angus flew into a rage when his spies reported the merger. Then he decided on yet another path. "I will build an army of *H. transformans*—boars, bears, wolves, and wolverines—that will be so formidable that no one will dare stand against me," he fumed. *I may even create a few of my own*, he mused to himself.

Ironically, the Cassius Foundation and the Biogenics Corporation had similar goals and objectives. As noted above, however, their relationship was less than collegial. Both were aggressive in promoting their own agendas and competed with each other for power and influence. Consequently, they were each other's primary adversary.

Map 2. Cassius Territory.

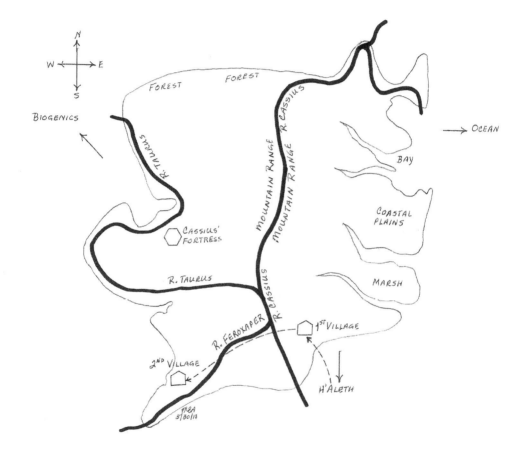

Map 3. Biogenics Territory.

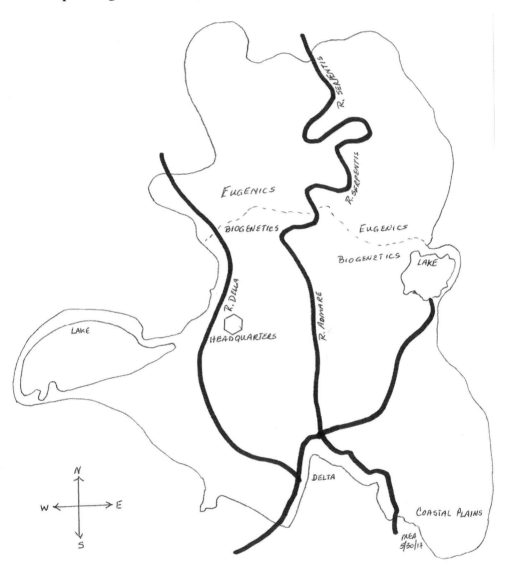

Both Cassius and Biogenics used inbreeding and genetic engineering in an attempt to increase the numbers of *H. transformans* within their own ranks. Both sought to design more powerful specimens with greater abilities. Angus relied heavily on genetic engineering. To keep pace with him, Biogenics incorporated genetic engineering into its breeding programs. Thus, both used inbreeding and gene manipulation to alter genomes. Both used accelerants to speed the transformation process. Neither was concerned about poor outcomes in their test subjects. Biogenics considered such outcomes regrettable, whereas Angus dismissed them altogether. When an adverse effect resulted in a subject with useful if deformed features, both made every attempt to breed or clone it. This was accomplished with some degree of success; however, cloning was expensive, and inbreeding eventually led to lethal conditions that limited the number of subjects.

In their desire to outmatch each other, the two organizations also competed to absorb smaller, weaker factions. This provided them with additional, albeit limited, resources, including more subjects (genomes) to use in their experiments. In this manner, both were able to increase their range of influence and control.

Most independent small factions were relatively short-lived when the outcomes became apparent. Three to four generations had passed without successfully breeding or inducing reliable transformation. Most importantly, none of the individuals who were born with the genetic ability to transform across multiple classes had been bred or engineered. Consequently, the majority of breeding and engineering programs either merged with Biogenics or the Cassius Foundation or shut down. In the end, the number of programs remained few, and the two organizations were at a stalemate—until a female *H. transformans* appeared who could change into a red dragoness. Then the race was on to identify and recreate the genome that could convey such power to a single individual (table 2).

Supplemental Notes and Citations

Founding Ancestor

A founding ancestor (founder) is the individual in whom a particular characteristic was first noted and from whom the genes conferring the characteristic can be traced and followed through subsequent generations (Araujo et al., 2016; Lammela et al., 2016; Yancoski et al., 2009). A founding ancestor may or may not be the ultimate origin of the genes underlying the characteristic. This term simply represents how far back the gene and its trait can be traced.

Table 2. Chronology of Socioeconomic Events Post-Recognition of H. transformans.

Year (SI)	Table 2. Chronology of Socioeconomic Events Post-Recognition of *H. transformans*
0	*Stella Ignis*
335	Biogenetic Company's discovery of transforming X chromosome (X^T)
335–395	Development of *H. transformans* biogenetics industry and its subsequent decline. Merger of Biogenetics Company and Eugenics Corporation to form Biogenics Corporation. Consolidation of industries by Biogenics Corporation and Cassius Foundation.
395	Identification of an *H. transformans* with dragon as an alternate species
395–455	Resurgence of biogenetics industry with intense competition between Biogenics Corporation and Cassius Foundation

Genetic Admixture and Consanguinity

Genetic admixture refers to genetic variability that is introduced through progeny that arises from two unrelated parents (Busby et al., 2015; Fernandez et al., 2013). This provides the means for introducing new genetic material into a line of progeny. Not all the genes on their paired somatic chromosomes (autosomes) may be exactly alike. Thus, genetic differences between the chromosomes provided by the mother and the father introduces a different combination of genes into an offspring. This mixture leads to genetic variability and limits the likelihood of inheriting the same recessive gene from both parents.

Consanguinity refers to breeding among closely related individuals. Inbreeding recycles the existing gene pool. This leads to recurrent patterns of genetic inheritance, which decreases variability and increases the likelihood of inheriting recessive genes. If a pair of recessive genes is benign (e.g., red hair), this poses no risk to progeny. If a pair of recessive genes code for the same genetic defect, then offspring will inherit a genetic disorder.

For example, in *H. sapiens*, the *HEXA* gene codes for an enzyme that breaks down a substance toxic to the brain and spinal cord. A defect in this gene allows the substance to accumulate, leading to death at an early age (Tay-Sachs disease, https://www.ncbi.nlm.nih.gov/gene/3073). Both genes in the individual must be defective for the individual to develop the disease. In this case, the defective gene is recessive. If even one of the two genes is normal, the disease will not be expressed. The normal gene is dominant and codes for an enzyme that functions normally. The incidence of inheriting recessive genes becomes progressively higher as breeding lines narrow.

In contrast, the *HTT* gene codes for a protein involved with the function of nerves in the brain. A defect in this gene leads to dementia and uncontrollable abnormal limb movements (Huntington's chorea). If an individual has even a single *HTT* gene with this defect, the individual will develop the disease. In this case, the defective gene is dominant.

Genetic Engineering

Genetic engineering is the manipulation of genes in order to change an organism's genome (for better or worse) and synthesize the gene's product for other uses (e.g., medical research and therapy, pharmaceuticals, etc.). There are numerous tools for identifying genes and their locations, especially for purposes of identifying defective genes, identifying parentage, and obtaining forensic evidence.

Cloning

Cloning refers to both artificial and natural production of genetically identical DNA and organisms (Carroll, 2009). Nonreproductive cells that divide naturally (mitosis) reproduce identical copies of themselves (clones, otherwise known as daughter cells) to produce a colony of identical cells, which are used to build tissue. The birth of identical twins represents a natural process for producing two identical organisms (at least at the time of birth) from the same fertilized ovum (monozygotic twins). Fraternal twins develop from two ova fertilized by two different sperm (dizygotic twins) and are not genetically identical.

CHAPTER 5

Predators and Prey

An Ever-Increasing Threat

Over time, the Biogenics Corporation and the Cassius Foundation became ever more adversarial as they searched for the genome that supported transformation into a dragon. The one who could gain this advantage would achieve dominion over the other—and everyone else. This presupposed, of course, that the *H. transformans* who could transform into a dragon could and would be dominated by someone who could not. In their single-mindedness, neither organization considered the possibility that this assumption might not be correct.

As Biogenics and Cassius competed with each other, they became increasingly aggressive in their pursuit of *H. transformans* with capabilities they could use to strengthen their positions. Both knew that the greatest capability lay in an adult female with two X^T chromosomes. Both organizations had males and females with one X^T chromosome. As of yet, neither organization had females with two. In an effort to acquire the latter, both Biogenics and Cassius enlisted the services of bounty hunters.

In turn, the bounty hunters preyed upon anyone identified as *H. transformans*. They would capture and sell an *H. transformans* to the highest bidder. Since female *H. transformans* brought the best price, even *H. sapiens* females were being kidnapped. Women who were $2X^T$ looked the same as those who had one X^T or none at all. Their base genome was still *H. sapiens*. Bounty hunters did not hesitate to claim that an *H. sapiens* woman was an *H. transformans*, if they could get away with it. Fraud was rampant in the bounty hunter business.

Scions of H'Aleth

Ruth's capabilities had rarely been seen in anyone else. Since Ruth had two X^T chromosomes ($2X^T$) and her husband had one (X^T, Y), all their sons would have one X^T chromosome (X^T, Y) and all their daughters would have two ($2X^T$). Like their mother, Ruth's daughters had similar capabilities. H'Anna could become a red fox, gray fox, cougar, peregrine falcon, and great horned owl; H'Ophelia a red wolf, gray fox, cougar, peregrine falcon, and long-eared owl; and H'Elena a red fox, gray wolf, lynx, Cooper's hawk, and great horned owl. If they were discovered, their inheritance would make them targets for a legion of bounty hunters.

Patterns of inheritance were critically important for breeding programs. These programs attempted to manipulate genotype by matching parents with similar phenotypes in order to obtain desired characteristics in the offspring. This concept relied on the notion that phenotype predicts genotype. Yet even in *H. sapiens*, the outcome of matching just two physical traits, the male and female gender, could not be predicted (fig. 1). For each pregnancy, there was a 50% chance that an offspring would be male or female.

Similar patterns of inheritance occurred in *H. transformans*. There were four possible patterns of inheritance for an X^T. The likelihood (probability) of inheriting one or two X^T chromosomes depended upon which egg and which sperm did or did not have an X^T and which two matched up (fig. 2 and fig. 3). The inheritance pattern for Edvar and Ruth (fig. 3) was the one most eagerly sought by Cassius and Biogenics and shows why both were desperate for a $2X^T$ female.

Fig. 1. Probability of Male or Female Offspring: *H. sapiens.*

Fig. 1. Probability of a Male or Female *H. sapiens* Offspring

	Mother	
	Ovum with X	Ovum with X
Sperm with X Father Sperm with Y	X X Female	X X Female
	X Y Male	X Y Male

This pattern shows four possible combinations of X and Y. Each pregnancy has a 1 in 4 chance—or a 25% probability—of inheriting one of the four combinations. The table also shows that *each* pregnancy has a 1 in 2 chance (50% probability) that the offspring will be either a male or a female.

Fig. 2. Pattern No. 1: Maternal X, X^T with Paternal X, Y.

Fig. 2. Probability of Male or Female *H. transformans* Offspring: Pattern No. 1—Maternal X, X^T with Paternal X, Y

	Mother	
	X	X^T
Father X	X X	X X^T
Y	X Y	X^T Y

H. sapiens   H. transformans

Key: X^T = transforming X chromosome
    X = maternal or paternal nontransforming X chromosome
    Y = male chromosome

In pattern no. 1, the mother has only one X^T. For each pregnancy, there is a 50% probability the child will have an X^T and be *H. transformans*—25% that a female child with have an XX^T and 25% that a male child will have an an X^TY. There is a 50% probability that a child will not inherit an X^T at all and will be *H. sapiens* (25% chance each for males and females).

Fig. 3. Pattern No. 2: Maternal X^T, X^T with Paternal X^T, Y.

Fig. 3. Probability of Male or Female *H. transformans* Offspring: Pattern No. 2—Maternal X^T, X^T with Paternal X^T, Y

Mother (Ruth)
$X^T X^T$

Father X^T (Edvar)	$X^T X^T$	$X^T X^T$
Y	$X^T Y$	$X^T Y$

H.transformans

Key: X^T = transforming X chromosome
Y = male chromosome

In pattern no. 2, the mother has two transforming X chromosomes ($2X^T$) and the father's sole X chromosome is an X^T. For each pregnancy, there is a 50% chance that the child will be a female with $2X^T$ and a 50% chance the child will be a male $X^T Y$. There is a 100% chance that a child will have at least one X^T chromosome.

A Narrow Escape

Edvar and Ruth were acutely aware of the risks associated with being identified as *H. transformans*. They built their first home south of the junction between the Feroxaper and Cassius rivers, in an area of mixed woodlands and grasslands as the mountains gave way. The site was well beyond any town or village. The nearest village was several miles away, unincorporated, and without any formal governance. It supported a few small industries—primarily farming, animal husbandry, crafts (furniture and pottery), and hostelry. It hosted a marketplace, where people could come to trade their wares, and a small inn.

Edvar and Ruth were self-sufficient and very discreet. They had built a house of wood taken from a nearby forest and fashioned a thatched roof from stalks of wild grasses and reeds. They tended their own vegetable and herb gardens, egg-laying hens, and a nanny goat, which provided a little milk. They made or repaired most of their own clothes and wicker furnishings. There was a freshwater stream nearby, and the surrounding forest abounded with oak trees that provided a plentiful supply of acorns in season.

In an effort to protect themselves and their children, Edvar and Ruth presented themselves as *H. sapiens*, as did any of their friends who were also *H. transformans*. "You must do the same," they told their children. "Make no mention of your true species. It is too dangerous. Always present yourselves as *H. sapiens*," they admonished. When members of the family did transform, it was usually for the purpose of conducting surveillance in and around the immediate area where they lived or for providing security. Despite their efforts to remain unobtrusive, an attempted abduction showed them that their efforts were not enough.

There were times when the family needed supplies they could not grow or make for themselves. So they would have to travel to one of the villages scattered about the region. There they could trade some of their goods for the supplies they needed, usually grains, honey, cheese, and cloth. During these trips, family members knew they were at their greatest risk, so they never traveled alone.

Ruth and her daughter H'Anna had traveled to one such village as *H. sapiens* to shop and trade with the people there. H'Ophelia, another of Ruth's daughters, and her husband, Daniel, accompanied them to provide a measure of safety. During the trip, H'Ophelia had transformed into a

Cooper's hawk to keep watch from the air. Daniel had transformed into a gray fox to conduct surveillance on the ground. For all appearances, Ruth and H'Anna seemed to be traveling unescorted. They were among many human visitors that came to the village that day. Migrant workers, farmers, and mercenaries also came there. Some came for bargaining and trading, some for selling their wares, and others looking for work or seeking food and lodging.

A foursome of visitors to the village, three men and a woman, eyed the two women. One of them mentioned, "The older woman might not be of much value, but the younger woman could bring a handsome price."

"This might be our best chance to capture two females that we can claim are *H. transformans* and sell to the highest bidder," another member offered. So they watched and waited.

When Ruth and H'Anna finally left the village to return home, they were followed at a discreet distance by the four bounty hunters. Two of the men were armed with bow and arrows. All four assailants carried knives. Yet it was not their intent to hunt down and kill the two women. There was no profit in that outcome. Once the women were surrounded, however, the assailants would use their weapons to threaten the women into submission. If necessary, the older woman could be sacrificed to gain the younger one.

Once Ruth and H'Anna reached the boundary of the village and entered the woodlands, Ruth said, "We are being followed."

"I noticed," H'Anna replied.

From her vantage point in the trees, H'Ophelia also had spotted the furtive movements of the four people tracking Ruth and H'Anna. Daniel, who had gone ahead to conduct surveillance on the ground, was not yet aware they were being followed. When the four hunters increased their pace to close the distance between themselves and the two women, H'Opheila called out a warning and dived in the direction of the danger. Everyone heard the warning call. The four assailants immediately charged toward the two women, who were still some distance ahead. The older woman (Ruth) suddenly broke away and disappeared. Daniel promptly set up an ambush for the runners he could hear approaching. H'Anna, who had no time to transform, ran away while still allowing the assailants to keep her in sight. This could buy precious time for her mother and keep the assailants distracted. H'Ophella continued to fly above the assailants, diving at them to mark their progress. She dodged skillfully through the trees, foiling their attempts to shoot her down.

Then the hawk's call suddenly changed its character. H'Anna abruptly stopped running and turned to face her attackers. She appeared to be out of breath and completely exhausted. Not so. While the assailants celebrated that they had achieved the younger and most valuable of the two women, H'Anna was drawing them into the trap the hawk had signaled. As they approached H'Anna, the hunters became the hunted.

Suddenly, a gray mountain wolf erupted from the woodland underbrush and slammed into the largest male. The gray fox attacked another male while the Cooper's hawk assailed the head, face, and eyes of the third male, easily dodging his attempts to battle her with a knife. H'Anna faced off with the sole female in the foursome. She, along with her brothers and sisters, had been trained in martial arts for purposes of self-defense. When the battle ceased moments later, the largest male lay mortally wounded. The second male was incapacitated by multiple debilitating bite wounds to his body. The third male was blinded in one eye and bloodied with gashes all over his head, face, and neck. The female assailant lay defeated upon the ground—with no life-threatening injuries. The four assailants had been caught off guard and were unprepared for a counterattack. The forces they faced had overwhelmed them, despite the weapons they carried.

After the incident, Edvar and Ruth and their extended family abandoned their home as quickly as possible. The assailants who survived undoubtedly would report what had happened, and more bounty hunters would follow. Thus the family departed to find a new home in a far more remote location, where they could live and raise their families. Several of their friends, most of whom were also *H. transformans*, recognized the danger and left with them.

Supplemental Notes and Citations

Euploidy
This is the normal number of chromosomes in a cell for a given species. As previously noted, all nonreproductive cells in the human body should have a full set of twenty-three paired chromosomes, including an XX or an XY, for a total of forty-six chromosomes. Only reproductive cells, the ovum and sperm, should develop with a single set of twenty-three unpaired chromosomes.

Patterns of Inheritance
Whereas inheritance of a particular characteristic cannot be predicted with accuracy, its probability can be estimated if the genotype is known. Inheritance

can be inferred retrospectively through the use of pedigrees that identify who did and did not have a particular characteristic, provided this information is known. Pedigrees can be used subsequently to identify breeding pairs.

Mendelian Inheritance

This is a straightforward pattern of inheritance based on the concept that a particular gene can be identified and traced from generation to generation (Brooker, 2009; Gayon, 2016). It typically reflects the patterns of dominant versus recessive genes. This allows an assessment of the likelihood (probability) that offspring will or will not inherit a certain characteristic (or disease condition). Sickle cell disease is a common example of Mendelian inheritance in which the mutated gene causing the disease is inherited from the parent (Habara and Steinberg, 2016).

Not all genetic traits can attributed to the transmission of a specific gene from parents to offspring. Mendelian inheritance of Parkinson's disease is very rare (Hernandez et al., 2016). Most cases of Parkinson's disease are attributable to a combination of predisposing genetic and nongenetic factors, resulting in a familial tendency to develop the disease.

Chapter 6

Minor Details

When *H. transformans* first appeared, those who were affected did not know what was happening to them or how to control it. Many of them suffered aborted, incomplete, or misaligned transformations. Few survived the distorted forms that emerged from these disasters. Over time, those who had successful transformations and those who survived corrupted transformations began to learn what did and didn't work to control it. They gleaned from experience the rules governing transformation without understanding the reasons. Eventually, these rules were handed down to offspring, but not before hundreds of *H. transformans* had died.

As transformations became increasingly successful, what was once viewed as a curse came to be seen as a benefit. When Edvar and Ruth patrolled the grasslands in their new territory, Edvar would transform into a fox and Ruth into a falcon. When they patrolled the nearby woodlands, Edvar would transform into a gray wolf and Ruth into a Cooper's hawk. If threatened by an intruder, both could transform into gray wolves and chase it off. If necessary, their adult children could join them and form a wolf pack.

Often when Edvar and Ruth would go on patrol, Edvar would become a gray wolf and Ruth a gray fox. The wolf had more muscle and speed to confront an intruder. The fox could maneuver through much smaller spaces to spy on one. At these times, they needed to be especially vigilant. Should any human be heard nearby, Ruth would dart under cover among the rocks and underbrush. Edvar would blend into the forest or lie low in tall grasses. The pair would not have time to transform back into humans, and they could not be seen together. A native wolf would not hesitate to prey on a fox. Any bounty hunter who saw a gray wolf and a gray fox sniffing noses would know immediately that they were *H. transformans*.

A Delicate Balance

Edvar's abilities represented the conditions humans encountered most commonly when transforming from a human to a nonhuman species. The most basic transformation consisted of a member of one species (e.g., *H. transformans*) changing into a member of a similar species with different characteristics (e.g., *H. australopithicus*). In these instances, the two species already shared over 99% of the same genes (genus *Homo*). As the differences between species increased (e.g., from a member of the human family into a member of the canine family), transformations became increasingly more complex. The sheer size and complexity of the genome significantly increased the risk of disruption and damage to the genotype. The size differences between some species also complicated metamorphosis.

The process of transformation required the delicately balanced and tightly coordinated efforts of all the genes of transformation. Under the influence of the X^T chromosome, the native genome (*H. sapiens*) was normally active and the genome(s) of other species were suppressed until such time as a stimulus triggered a transformation. Thus, on a day-to-day basis, an *H. transformans* looked just like an *H. sapiens*. They shared the same base genome. The stimulus to transform usually involved an emotional or physical condition that invoked a strong desire or need to change species. The researchers at Biogenics found that hormones served as the chemical triggers for transformation and growth factors mediated the changes needed (box 6). They hypothesized that the X^T chromosome either lifted the restrictions on the set point for size or reset it based on the species.

Box 6. From Tadpole to Frog.

From Tadpole to Frog

Frog eggs are released and fertilized in freshwater ponds. They become an embryo in about three days. Subsequently, the free-floating embryo develops a mouth, external gills, and a tail. At this point, the embryo has become a tadpole and can feed and propel itself through the water. Subsequently, the tadpole develops an outer skin, which grows over the gills. At the same time, the hind legs begin to form and grow, and the front legs follow suit. During this phase of development, the tail is gradually shrinking, and lungs are developing. Once the lungs are fully developed and the tail has been resorbed, the result is a fully formed adult frog.

The developmental changes seen in the frog are driven by the thyroid hormone. It acts as an agent to change form (a developmental morphogen) and triggers activation of genes that direct the changes (a trophic signal). In effect, it directs the remodeling of the amphibian's phenotype from a tadpole into a frog. In order to do so, effects of the thyroid hormone vary with the tissue involved and where the tissue is located. For example, the thyroid hormone triggers the development of the leg muscles at the same time it directs the resorption of the tail.

Box 6

Once transformation was triggered, regulatory genes on the X^T chromosome (which conferred capability) activated and deactivated the appropriate genes. During transformation from human form into another species, the expression of native genes that would not be used—especially those affecting phenotype—were suppressed while genes of the other species were activated. Autosomal (nonreproductive) genes induced the majority of the structural changes. Only the individual's gender (as dictated by its native reproductive chromosomes) and intellect were maintained across transformations. This assumed that the transformation was successful and had not been corrupted in some way.

Finally, unless the individual wanted to remain a member of the other species indefinitely, he or she needed to have the capability to change back into his or her native form. Fortunately, the genes on the X^T chromosome did not discriminate in this matter. After transformation into another species, an *H. transformans* still retained his or her own native genome. When the individual triggered the resumption of human form, the X^T chromosome reexpressed the native genes and suppressed the genes of the other species. Some outward manifestations could be shed immediately (e.g., hair, fur, scales). Structural changes took longer. There were cellular processes inherent in *H. sapiens* to remove any nonnative cells that did not support the human form.

Patience

The process of transformation required a significant change in an individual's physical structure and form. It took time for genes to be activated and deactivated; for proteins to change their structure; for cells, tissues, and organs to realign; and for the organism as a whole to adapt to these changes. The time required to make a transformational change depended upon the novelty of the change and its complexity, including significant differences between the sizes of both species. Thus, the easiest and most successful transformations would be expected among similar species within the same family (e.g., dog to wolf in the canine family) and were almost always restricted to members of the same class (e.g., mammal to mammal). These transformations were only possible because a considerable amount of genetic code was shared among the different classes (homology). This vastly facilitated transformations.

The wolf, the dog, and the fox were all members of the canine family. The fox branch of the family broke off long before the dog became distinct from the wolf. Hence, the wolf and the dog were more closely related than the wolf and the fox. The genome of *H. sapiens* was found to share a significant proportion of the same genes found in the dog (about 80%). So *H. sapiens* was genetically closer to the wolf than to the fox. Consequently, Edvar could transform into a wolf with greater ease and less time than a fox. It was the degree to which different species shared the same genes that made transformation into another species feasible.

When the member of one species (e.g., human) changed repeatedly into the same member of another species (e.g., a wolf), the genetic mechanisms for that specific transformation became more readily activated. The phenotypic changes were more easily accommodated as well. As the frequency of a specific transformation increased, it could occur more rapidly. Over time, these transformations could happen fairly quickly.

During the attack by four assailants, H'Anna had lured them away from the place where Ruth disappeared in order to give her mother time to transform. Fortunately, Ruth's transformation into a gray wolf was well practiced. It did not take long.

The patience required to undergo a successful transformation was not instinctive. It had to be learned. Those who rushed or forced a transformation risked being corrupted and even killed. This was why so many *H. transformans* initially did not survive. These lessons were handed down to later generations by parents and friends who did survive. Edvar and Ruth were successful because they were careful. They knew under what circumstances they could and could not transform. Their children were successful because their parents taught them the rules and supervised them as they learned to transform.

Supplemental Notes and Citations

General references for *H. sapiens* in this section are Beery and Workman (2012), Brooker (2009), Carroll (2009), Jorde (2014a, 2014b), Guyton and Hall (2006), and Porth (2009). Additional citations are as noted.

Genetic Homology

Many gene sequences are derived from a common ancestor and are conserved, shared, and reused among nearly all classes within the animal kingdom and even a few across kingdoms (e.g., the animal and plant kingdoms). They include genes that code for structure, function, and regulation of gene activity (noncoding genes). A bat's wings, a cat's front leg, and a human's arm all evolved from the same ancestor and therefore are homologous structures. Genes that regulate basic biologic functions such as metabolism are found in all living organisms.

Hormonal Triggers and Growth Factors

In *H. sapiens,* hormones are produced in response to internal and external stimuli (Ranabir and Reetu, 2011). Stress hormones (e.g., adrenaline, cortisol, glucagon, etc.), sex hormones (estrogen, progesterone, testosterone, etc.), and hormones that regulate energy metabolism (e.g., thyroxine, growth hormone) are likely to be involved in either triggering or supporting growth and development, including transformation in those species known to undergo metamorphosis (Cheng et al., 2010). Growth factors, also called trophic signals, direct cell growth, proliferation, and differentiation into specific cell types and regulate a variety of cellular processes. Many hormones are growth factors.

Apoptosis and Autophagy

Apoptosis is a programmed cell death that occurs when a cell has reached the end of its natural lifespan (Fogarty and Bergmann, 2015). Red blood cells, which carry oxygen to the tissues, have an average life span of 120 days. Platelets, which play a major role in blood clotting, have an average life span of seven to ten days.

Autophagy is the process by which dead cells and their components are broken down. The components may be destroyed, recycled for use by other cells, or used in building new cells (You et al., 2015).

CHAPTER 7

Custom Designs

There were some members of both *H. sapiens* and *H. transformans* who were impatient with the process of transformation and sought out means to accelerate it. From a strictly business perspective, the faster the better. This presupposed, of course, that the transformation was successful.

Angus Cassius decided on a different approach. Given the capability of what even one X^T could do, he sought to implant the genes for creatures of his own design in an *H. transformans*. Then he would leverage the X^T to bring his creations into being, or so he thought.

Designing a Hybrid

In order to manipulate a genome (for good or ill), one first had to identify which genes are already present and where they were. Gene typing could identify what genes were present. Gene mapping identified where specific genes were located. The Biogenics Company, which specialized in breeding programs, used these tools to identify *H. transformans* with matching genes that would lead to capabilities the company deemed highly desirable. They also used them to screen out subjects with defective genes.

Gene sequencing identified specific combinations of genes that governed a characteristic or function and where they were located. Angus took advantage of sequencing to manipulate the genome. Through gene splicing, genes could be excised and, if desired, reinserted at a different location. Gene editing offered the best means for changing gene sequences.

Both procedures could be used to transfer genes from one species into the genome of another; however, it came with a caveat. Whenever individual genes were manipulated, their actual effect on other genes—and, therefore, on genotype and phenotype—could not be predicted. Even when genes from an individual were transferred somewhere else in the *same* individual, there was no assurance that the intended changes would occur.

Ironically, some genes had the ability to move themselves from one place to another place (transposable elements). In changing their location, these genes altered gene expression. Biogenics's geneticists hypothesized that transposable elements were utilized in the transformation process. "Their activity is strongly influenced by the presence and number of X^T chromosomes," their researchers reported. "We believe that these genes move and realign with other genes to support a transformation, then return to their original location to support resuming the human form. We think they could be a major factor in the speed of transformation as well."

The Cassius Foundation used gene splicing extensively to add the genes of other species to an *H. transformans*. Angus insisted on using this method to alter the genomes of an *H. transformans*, despite warnings from his staff, "There is no guarantee that these transplanted genes will work as intended, even if they do anything." Generations later, Rafe [rāf] Cassius, the great-great-grandson of Angus Cassius, would learn this lesson all over again when he used genetic engineering to design the phenotypic characteristics he wanted in a hybrid. Often his creatures bore no resemblance to the design he had in mind. He would end up with bizarre creatures that were not what he expected, not what he wanted, and often not viable. Nevertheless, if they survived and could function in some capacity, he would use them as a source of manual labor.

A Pilot Test

One of Angus's designs was the cercopithursid [*cer*-co-*pith*-ur-sid] (illus. 6), an *H. transformans* that had the genes of a baboon and a bear spliced into his genome and then was forced into a transformation he could not reverse. Cassius engineered these and other hominids for purposes of performing hard labor in the villages under his control. He also intended to use them to attack and kill an enemy.

Illus. 6. Cercopithursid.

By:

Cassius often tested the fighting capability of his hybrids. He would infiltrate Biogenics's territory to release a newly minted hybrid to see how it would react to a threat. One day, he transported a cercopithursid that he had not fed in a few days and released it just outside a Biogenics town. When it entered the town looking for food, the townspeople were terrified. The residents were shopkeepers, farmers, and merchants. There were no soldiers. Nevertheless, a group of townspeople armed themselves with knives, pitchforks, shovels, and hatchets. They accosted the beast in an attempt to drive it away or kill it.

The cercopithursid, who was still an *H. transformans*, had no intention of harming the townspeople despite his ferocious appearance. The townspeople had no way of knowing this, and the cercopithursid could not tell them. He no longer had the ability to speak. The townspeople were certain the creature belonged to Cassius and was a deadly threat to them. When they attacked him, the fight was entirely one-sided. The cercopithursid fought back in self-defense, killing some of them and seriously injuring others. Then he fled from the village with injuries of his own before he could be attacked again.

Angus considered the incident a successful pilot test. His creature had demonstrated its ability to engage in a violent assault and successfully kill or incapacitate his attackers. He recovered the cercopithursid by offering him shelter and food. Subsequently, Angus returned the cercopithursid to his village to resume working as a laborer there.

Haste Makes Waste

Both the Cassius Foundation and the Biogenics Company used accelerants to increase the rate of transformation in subjects with desired characteristics. Unfortunately, this also increased the rate of incomplete and skipped steps in the process. Forcing or accelerating a transformation often damaged chromosomes and, therefore, the integrity of gene sequences. Genetic errors expressed in the phenotype become ever greater and more extreme. Thus, the use of accelerants led to disrupted transformations and the disasters that resulted. An *H. transformans* with a single X^T chromosome had the highest risk. Often, the scope of the change was simply too great for one X^T to support.

The risk of chromosome breakage and gene disruption also increased as the genomes of human and other animal species diverged. The greater the differences in their genomes, the less homology they had. Fortunately, there were genetic mechanisms that could repair some of these breaks.

Still, care had to be taken even with previously successful transformations. If the transformation was too abrupt or was aborted before it was complete, the process could be corrupted. This would leave the individual stranded in a state of partial transformation with no ability to complete or reverse it. Genetic derangements and physical deformities invariably resulted unless the transformation was between members of the same or very similar species. Thus, even Ruth needed a little time to transform.

Corrupted transformations also occurred when an individual's native genome could not accommodate a physical change or only partially supported the genome of the desired species. Invariably, the attempt resulted in serious derangements and was almost always fatal.

Demanding Changes

Even successful transformations came at a cost. The energy requirements were high for even a single transformation. They were even higher for multiple transformations. As complexity increased, so did the metabolic demands that drove the need for more oxygen and energy. It could take days for an individual to complete a complex transformation, and the effort could leave the individual exhausted, weak, and vulnerable. For this reason, most members of *H. transformans* that could change into more than one alternate species first had to change back to human form for recovery before transforming again.

Not even Ruth could undergo complex transformations without being at risk. Direct transformations between two animals could be taxing, especially if done on an emergency basis. This was a real possibility since some of her alternate species were prey animals for native wolves and other apex predators. Sometimes Ruth would have to rest afterward before she could transform again—even back into human form. If necessary, she could reverse a transformation fairly expeditiously if it proved more advantageous.

With the complexity of the genome and the enormous risk of errors, it was not surprising that the number of *H. transformans* who could undergo transformation successfully was quite low. Even rarer were those *H. transformans* who could transform above and beyond their own class (e.g., into birds, reptiles, fish, etc.). Not only could Ruth and her daughters accomplish these feats, they also could transform from any one of their alternate species directly into another one. Had their abilities become known, they, too, could have disappeared. Hence, the family kept their abilities a closely guarded secret.

Supplemental Notes and Citations

General references for *H. sapiens* in this section are Beery and Workman (2012), Brooker (2009), Carroll (2009), Jorde (2014a, 2014b), Guytgrimon and Hall (2006), and Porth (2009). Additional citations are as noted.

Gene Typing, Sequencing, and Mapping

Gene typing can be used to determine genetic compatibility and the degree of genetic variability between two organisms. It is also a means of identifying individuals with genes that code for a disease or disability.

Gene sequencing identifies the order in which genes are arrayed on a particular strand of DNA or a chromosome (Bentley et al., 2008). Genes coding for a particular trait need not be colocated. They can be on different segments of the same chromosome and on different chromosomes. Once genes are sequenced, numerous techniques are available for modifying a gene sequence.

Gene mapping identifies the linear order and sequence of genes and their physical location on one or more chromosomes across the genome (Carroll, 2009; Jorde, 2014a). The reader is referred to the National Human Genome Research Institute (https://www.genome.gov/10000715/genetic-mapping-fact-sheet/) for additional information on gene mapping and its uses.

Gene Splicing and Genome Editing

Gene splicing connects one or more genes into a sequence in such a manner that the gene is functional (Jorde 2014a). This could include the removal or insertion of genes at a given location. This can be accomplished through the use of enzymes (recombinases) to modify DNA (Gaj, Sirk, Barbas, 2014). Sequences may be added using enzymes (integrases) to insert the gene(s) (Craigie and Bushman, 2012; Fogg et al., 2014).

Genome editing uses a relatively new technology known as clustered regularly interspaced short palindromic repeats (CRISPR), which facilitates editing an existing gene sequence by excising or adding a sequence (Hille and Charpentier, 2016; Mitsunobu et al., 2017; Shen et al., 2017; Shuang et al., 2017; Tolarová et al., 2016; Yin et al., 2017). This technology uses an enzyme (endonuclease) to edit a gene sequence by repairing, replacing, or inactivating a gene. The gene may be native to the organism (e.g., a normal gene replacing a damaged gene), or it may be a transfer from one species to another species (e.g., a viral gene). (Note: The Cassius Foundation would have reveled in this technology.)

Methods of Manipulating the Genome

Genetic engineering incorporates the use of natural and man-made agents to alter genetic code by changing (mutating), inactivating, or deleting an existing gene. A variety of organic (e.g., viruses) and inorganic (e.g., radiation) agents can be used.

Viruses (viral vectors) can be used to insert or facilitate the introduction of foreign genes into a native genome (Brown and Hirsch, 2015). When introduced into autosomal (nonreproductive) genes, the change affects the individual. It is not inheritable, so offspring are not affected. When introduced into reproductive genes, the change may or may not affect the individual; however, it is inheritable and can be passed down to offspring. In *H. sapiens*, viral vectors have been used in gene therapy. These genes can carry the genetic code for a critical substance an individual lacks. One example of a viral vector is the human immunodeficiency virus (HIV). This virus has a genetic code consisting of nine genes. In *H. sapiens*, the virus invades and integrates its genes into human DNA. The virus then redirects human genes to reproduce millions of copies of the virus, which ultimately kill their host (Faulhaber and Aberg, 2009). In a complete turn of events, the genes of the HIV virus that do *not* code for its reproduction are being used to transport other genes that treat disease or correct deficiencies into human DNA (Nayerossadat, 2012; Pluta and Kacprzak, 2009).

Ionizing radiation (e.g., x-rays, gamma rays) can induce genetic changes, including gene mutations and chromosomal rearrangements (Asaithamby and Chen, 2011; Daley et al., 2013; Kim et al., 2006; Suzuki et al., 2003). When reproductive cells are affected, some of these changes can be inherited by offspring. In somatic cells, many of the changes lead to derangements of cell function and result in cell death. This is the basis for the use of radiation therapy to treat cancer.

Mobile Genes

Also known as transposable elements (TEs), these are small DNA sequences that can change their location in the genome in a cut-and-paste fashion. They are estimated to comprise about 44–46% of the human genome (Belancio et al., 2009; Mills et al., 2007; Morales et al., 2015; Vand Rajabpour, V. et al., 2014). Many of these elements are homologous with other mammalian species (Britten, 2010). Transposable elements are considered a major source of genetic diversity. If not tightly regulated, however, they can have adverse effects as well (e.g., chromosome breakage, gene mutation, gene inactivation) (Britten, 2010; Mills et al., 2007). Note: Hormones may be one of the agents that stimulate transposable elements to move to another location (Brooker, 2009).

Chromosome Breakage

Chromosome breakage is not uncommon in *H. sapiens*. Breaks that are not successfully repaired invariably disrupt the normal structure of the chromosome and sequence of genes along with it. This results in the misalignment of genes (at best) or genes that are lost altogether. The extent of the damage often leads to severe genetic defects, most of which are incompatible with life. For example, in *H. sapiens*, a chromosome break that deletes the short arm of chromosome 5 results in an infant with defects in the heart and mental retardation (cri du chat syndrome).

The broken segments of the affected chromosome, with its genetic material, can be (1) reattached upside down (inverted), (2) relocated to a different place within the chromosome, (3) relocated to a totally different chromosome (translocation), (4) left unattached to any chromosome, or (5) deleted altogether. Any one of these will disrupt the function of genes on the affected chromosome. Translocation also disrupts the operations of the receiving chromosome.

CHAPTER 8

The Three Houses

As the Biogenics Corporation and Cassius Foundation competed with each other, they became increasingly aggressive in their pursuit of power and resources. Their antagonism toward each other had grown to the point of open hostility. Through subsequent generations, the heirs of Angus Cassius continued to encompass more territory and strengthen the foundation's army to enforce their will. Biogenics, in turn, countered by building an army of its own in order to defend its properties. Multiple skirmishes between the two had shown that their powers were equally matched. Neither one was able to overpower the other. It was then that their attentions turned to the three Houses.

The House of H'Aleth

The House of H'Aleth was the first of the three Houses to be established. It traced its origin back to the marriage of Edvar H'Aleth to his wife Ruth (ped. 1). After the attempted abduction of Ruth and one of her daughters, the family, with their relatives and many friends, fled their homes in secret. They relocated in another region, which was remote from their original home and sparsely inhabited. It was bound by extensive grasslands to the west, hardwood forests to the north and northwest, an expansive river to the east, and coastal plains and inland waterways to the south (map 4). There, Edvar and Ruth and their extended family settled and built an estate.

Ped. 1. Pedigree for Descendants of Edvar and Ruth H'Aleth: First, Second, and Third Generations.

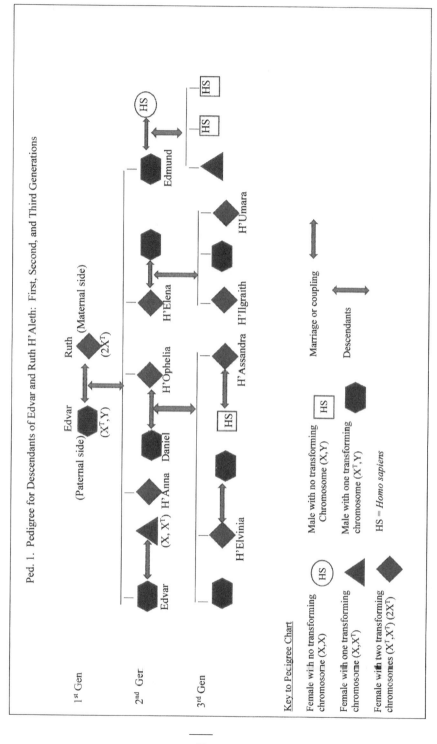

Ped. 1. Pedigree for Descendants of Edvar and Ruth H' Aleth: First, Second, and Third Generations

Map 4. H'Aleth Territory.

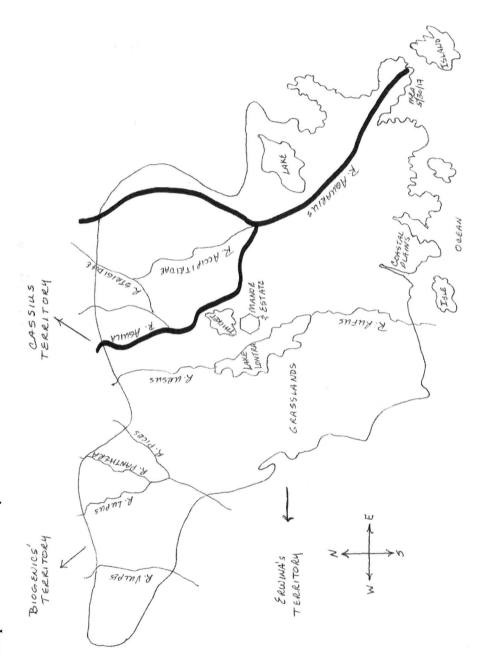

The immigrants reestablished themselves once again as *H. sapiens*. They were careful never to transform when strangers—*H. sapiens* or *H. transformans*—were nearby. Over time, the family and their friends became well established, and gradually, a village grew around them. Eventually, it became the seat of governance.

Smaller villages were established in the territory now known as H'Aleth, as more *H. transformans* fled the conflicts between Cassius and Biogenics. As Edvar and Ruth's younger children intermarried with other families in the region, their household expanded with new members, including grandchildren. It became evident that nearly all the offspring were *H. transformans* with varying degrees of capability. This put them at risk for discovery by Cassius and Biogenics, as the latter expanded their areas of influence and control.

To cover their true identities, the extended family and friends organized into a faction of their own. The House of H'Aleth was chartered under the leadership of the original family. Edvar and Ruth consulted with their children, their spouses, and with friends who had fled to the new territory with them. "All of us are *H. transformans*, as are our children and grandchildren," began Edvar. "If we are going to organize ourselves into an independent community, we should formalize the rules which we already follow. In this way, others who seek to join us can learn our ways before they decide to adopt them."

Ruth made her position clear. "I want this community to represent a place of refuge for any *H. transformans* who has been hunted or persecuted," she said. "And I want it to welcome any *H. sapiens* who bears no malice toward those of us who are *H. transformans*, especially any of them that have been persecuted for supporting us."

So the group formulated a charter, which included a mandate to use family histories only to screen for genes that would lead to disease, deformity, or death. If any were found, the information would be used to advise family members and potential spouses of the likelihood of passing on the gene and the risk of disease in their progeny. Family histories would not be used to breed *H. transformans* for their abilities. The charter also included a covenant forbidding the use of inbreeding. Finally, members would accept the natural ability of anyone who was able to transform. In honor of Ruth and Edvar, who had led their escape to the new territory and had fostered so many newcomers to the territory, the members added a provision to the charter that named their community the House of H'Aleth.

Subsequently, members built an organization that focused on the welfare and protection of *H. transformans* and offered a haven for any who were being hunted for their abilities. Sympathetic members of *H. sapiens* were welcomed among their ranks. These members often served as the board of directors so that *H. sapiens* would appear to be at the head of the organization.

Edvar became a proponent for studying and recording the natural history of *H. transformans*. "We should follow the progression and development of our species over time," he advocated. To this end, members of the House of H'Aleth began to keep careful and complete records of the family history of their members, including the species into which they could transform.

Family Lineage

Ruth was the first Mistress of the House of H'Aleth. As her family grew through the marriage of her children, she became its matriarch. When the House of H'Aleth was formerly chartered, Ruth assumed the role and title of Mistress. Her daughters became known as Sisters of the House. In subsequent generations, all daughters who were direct descendants of Ruth were considered Sisters of the House of H'Aleth (app. A).

As the role and title of Mistress was passed down through the generations, the descendant who became the next Mistress was one who could trace her lineage directly back to Ruth and possessed the greatest capability and experience. This was always through the female line as reflected in the detailed records and pedigrees the family kept.

Pedigrees for all the families were graphic representations of their family history, which served many purposes. These included (1) establishing lineage and determining social relationships (e.g., for genealogy purposes), (2) identifying a pattern or mode of dominant or recessive gene inheritance (e.g., for genetic counseling), (3) calculating the probability that offspring might inherit a particular gene and be a carrier or express the gene (e.g., to identify the risk of disease), (4) making reproductive decisions (including whether or not to have children), (5) making treatment decisions (e.g., use of gene therapy), and (6) for genetic research. Prior to the availability of gene sequencing technology, pedigrees were based on family history that traced relationships among family members. These reflected patterns of inheritance though multiple generations (fig. 4 and fig. 5).

Fig. 4. *BRCA* Gene Inheritance Pattern.

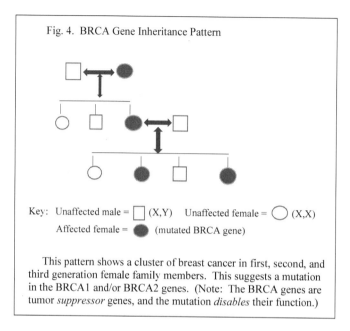

Fig. 4. BRCA Gene Inheritance Pattern

Key: Unaffected male = □ (X,Y)   Unaffected female = ○ (X,X)
     Affected female = ● (mutated BRCA gene)

This pattern shows a cluster of breast cancer in first, second, and third generation female family members. This suggests a mutation in the BRCA1 and/or BRCA2 genes. (Note: The BRCA genes are tumor *suppressor* genes, and the mutation *disables* their function.)

Fig. 5. X^T Chromosome Inheritance Pattern.

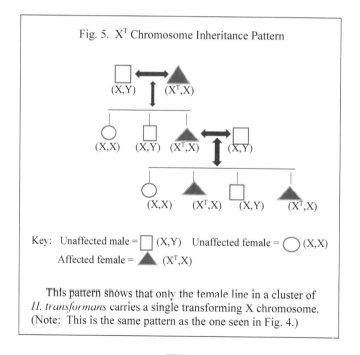

Fig. 5. X^T Chromosome Inheritance Pattern

Key: Unaffected male = □ (X,Y)   Unaffected female = ○ (X,X)
     Affected female = ▲ (X^T,X)

This pattern shows that only the female line in a cluster of *H. transformans* carries a single transforming X chromosome. (Note: This is the same pattern as the one seen in Fig. 4.)

Sister Houses

For a while, H'Aleth's geographically remote location buffered it from the attentions of the Biogenics Corporation and the Cassius Foundation. H'Aleth's scouts, *H. transformans* who could take the form of animals native to the areas they watched, were embedded throughout its territory and patrolled it regularly. They could roam throughout H'Aleth and conduct surveillance missions without being discovered or identified.

Over many years, as family members interacted with people from other villages, they may have betrayed themselves inadvertently. Rumors of a clan of *H. transformans* in the region began to creep into the towns and villages. Sometime later, rumors of a stronghold of *H. transformans* eventually reached Cassius and Biogenics. Many members of H'Aleth grew concerned that one or both of these organizations would learn where they were and seek to overpower them.

An increasing number of H'Aleth's members wanted to expand the use of pedigrees to include selective breeding. "This could increase both the capability to transform and the scope of transformation among our members," a spokesman said. "We believe this step can strengthen our ranks and is essential to provide for our defense against future attack." Such a practice, however, would violate a covenant. In addition, other House members expressed concern that family members would pressure other family members or even their own children to engage in a breeding program with the intent to advance the status of the family. Furthermore, there were no guarantees that progeny would possess the desired characteristics. "What then would be the fate of such a child?" asked these members.

To counter this legitimate concern, the subgroup conferred among themselves and proposed a solution. "Genetic counseling will be included as an integral component of any decision to mate based on capabilities and abilities," a spokesman said. "Counseling will provide both guidance regarding any potential genetic risks and an assessment of any duress to participate. We can establish an ethics committee to review any cases in which the rights and welfare of the participants—and any offspring—are in question." Despite these provisions, many House members thought that too many of the original covenants were being breached. Over time, differences in philosophy and breeding practices led members who supported selective breeding to separate and establish a new House, the House of Erwina [Er-*wĭn*-a].

Despite their differences, the two Houses remained closely aligned. Neither House condoned genetic engineering. The House of Erwina continued to follow the same protocols and procedures for maintaining and screening the pedigrees of their members. In addition, its members carefully screened the pedigrees for genes that, when paired, might enhance selected characteristics while screening out those that might be deleterious. They also established strict policies prohibiting inbreeding or forcing couples to breed against their will or prohibiting a union between two unrelated members who might be better matched genetically with someone else.

Not long after, subgroups within both H'Aleth and Erwina advocated for the judicious and prudent use of genetic engineering. Mapping genomes would permit the identification of specific gene sequences that would allow some manipulation of genetic code. Gene therapy was already available to prevent or treat some genetic disorders by adding genes that were missing, repairing a defective gene, or even replacing a defective gene. Hence, proponents argued, "The science of genetics has progressed to the point where we can correct some genetic errors. We can add a covenant that would forbid any manipulation intended to create a specific genotype or to complete a partial genotype. Any changes made to an individual's genetic code would be to the benefit of that individual or to their offspring." They also vowed that genetic engineering would not be imposed without the individual's consent and would not be used to create superhumans or hybrids.

Subsequently, a third sister house, the House of Gregor [Gre-gor], was formed. Its members established a genetics review board to provide oversight and approval of any plan to use genetic engineering. Although selective breeding was entertained, most reproduction would be natural and no inbreeding would be allowed. In order to protect its resources, Gregor was established in the distant north, where snow and ice most of the year provided an effective barrier against invasion. It, too, remained closely aligned with the other Houses.

Although the three Houses had some philosophical and methodological differences, they still had much in common. They were able to reconcile their differences, which allowed them to share knowledge and resources for their mutual benefit and to combine resources to meet a common need. They joined together to establish an education center, a medical center, and a research center. The Houses agreed to sponsor one center each, with all

Houses participating in the establishment of each center. The House of H'Aleth continued to sponsor research on the biology and natural history of *H. transformans*, while the House of Gregor supported medicine and genomic research. The House of Erwina supported education (app. B) and housed the archives of all three Houses, including all their research. Members from all the Houses could access and use the resources of any House as needed.

All throughout this time, the people of H'Aleth became increasingly concerned that bounty hunters would try to kidnap their children. They were especially concerned about hunters in the service of the Cassius Foundation. There had been a precedent, and H'Aleth's borders were no longer as remote as once they had been. Angus Cassius's heirs had engulfed much of the territory between them. H'Aleth's people had learned, however, that neither Biogenics nor Cassius were interested in young *H. transformans* children. An *H. transformans* child was only useful when he or she could both reproduce and transform. Apparently, neither organization was disposed to kidnap any children they had to raise. The House of H'Aleth had a solution that took advantage of their adversaries' disinclination to foster children.

H'Aleth sent their children to the House of Erwina at an early age, where they would receive a formal education. Geographically, Erwina was much farther away from the territories controlled by Cassius. In addition, Erwina was better protected by natural barriers, and H'Aleth's territory would serve as a buffer.

Thus, it was in the House of Erwina that most children, including those from the House of Gregor, would be taught the science underlying the process of transformation, learn its risks and limitations, and develop the skills needed to transform successfully within their own limitations.

Supplemental Notes and Citations

Genetic Counseling
This is a consultation with geneticists and/or medical professionals with expertise in genetic diseases regarding (1) the likelihood of having a gene and/or transmitting a gene or a genetic disease to offspring based on family history, (2) testing for the gene and the implications of positive or negative results, and (3) options and recommendations for addressing any issues found (GA-NEPHGEC, 2010a).

Tracing and Pedigrees

Medical tracing seeks to identify family members who have or had a disease (if known), their cause of death (if known), and their age (if known) (Wattendorf and Hadley, 2005). Most diseases result from an interaction between genetics, lifestyle, and environmental factors that may predispose an individual to a disease; however, some diseases are caused directly by gene mutations, which lead to disordered function. Identifying family members who have had the same disease provides a pedigree that can suggest the level of risk a descendant has for developing it too. The study of Alzheimer's disease and discovery of genetic factors associated with the disease began with family histories (Guerreiro and Hardy, 2014.) The closer the family relationship, the higher the risk for a close relative.

Geneticists prepare a pedigree from family history and conduct an analysis to determine (1) if there are multiple instances of a disease clustered in that family, (2) if there appears to be a pattern of inheritance, and (3) what that pattern may be (GA-NEPHGEC, 2010b; Hinton Jr., 2008; Lynch and Lynch, 2006; Rodrigues et al., 2016.) If the pedigree (family history) suggests a hereditary predisposition to a particular disease, then genetic testing is recommended (if available). The Office of the Surgeon General has an online tool at https://familyhistory.hhs.gov/FHH/ html/index.html that can assist members of the general public in preparing a family health history. The reader is encouraged to prepare one for yourself and your family.

Gene Therapy

Gene therapy uses genes to prevent or correct a disease caused by an underlying genetic defect (e.g., if someone is missing the gene for an enzyme essential for life, inserting that gene into a living cell will induce the cell to make that enzyme) (Brown and Hirsch, 2015).

PART II

In the Realm of Cassius

CHAPTER 9

Rafe

Rafe Cassius was an *H. transformans* and a fourth-generation descendant of Angus Cassius, the original founder of the Cassius Foundation (ped. 2). Rafe was well established in the foundation and, as a direct descendant of Angus, was in line to assume control of it. He was naturally a large man, well-built, muscular, and once quite handsome. He had been very athletic in his youth and had become skilled as a swordsman. His features and abilities once made him a prime candidate for breeding programs, in which he participated.

More importantly, Rafe could transform into three large and powerful mammals, one of which was a great horned boar. The boar was his preferred alternate species. It was built like a battering ram with powerful neck and shoulder muscles, and it could reach a charging speed of thirty miles per hour. Its massive head had tusks that extended four to five inches and curved outward to the side. These tusks gored many opponents. All these attributes, both human and animal, made Rafe arrogant and overconfident.

A Corrupted Transformation

As noted previously, one of the greatest dangers associated with transformation was one that was incomplete. Transformations that were too abrupt, aborted, or otherwise disrupted before they were completed would be corrupted and were almost always irreversible. Genetic derangements and physical deformities invariably resulted and often led to death.

Ped. 2. Pedigree for Descendants of Angus Cassius.

Ped. 2. Pedigree for Descendants of Angus Cassius

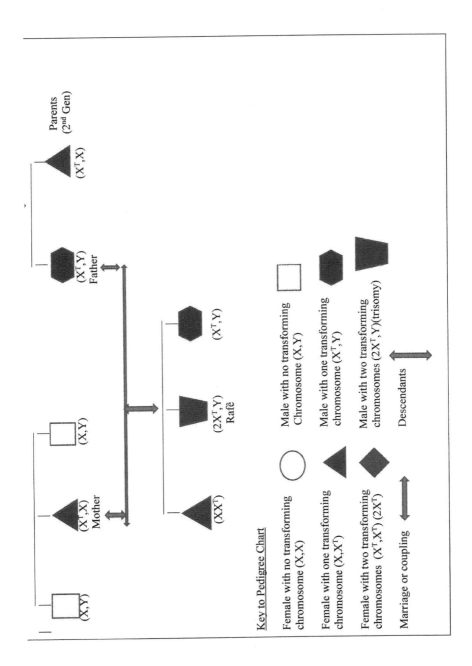

Parents (2nd Gen)

(X^T,X)

(X^T,Y) Father

(X^T,Y)

$(2X^T,Y)$ Rafë

$\overline{(XX^T)}$

(X,Y)

(X^T,X) Mother

(X,Y)

Key to Pedigree Chart

Female with no transforming chromosome (X,X)

Female with one transforming chromosome (X,X^T)

Female with two transforming chromosomes (X^T,X^T) $(2X^T)$

Marriage or coupling

Male with no transforming Chromosome (X,Y)

Male with one transforming chromosome (X^T,Y)

Male with two transforming chromosomes $(2X^T,Y)$(trisomy)

Descendants

One day, Rafe attempted to transform too rapidly from a great horned boar back to human form and became trapped, unable to complete the transformation. This left him partially but permanently disfigured and deformed and unable to transform again (illus. 7).

The right and left sides of his body were affected disproportionately. Most of his facial features on the left side were enlarged but not misshapen. Most of his facial features on the right side were contorted. A jagged remnant of a horn protruded from his forehead between the right eye and ear. His right eyelid was stretched down and to the side, narrowing his field of vision on the right side. His right naris was flared, and the bony bridge of his nose was enlarged, flattened, and thickened on that side. Both the upper and lower lip were fleshy, with the upper lip drooping over the lower one. The left side of his tongue was much larger than the right, and his teeth on the left were larger and shaped like molars. There were no canine teeth on either side. His larynx and vocal chords on both sides were enlarged. These changes made his voice deeper, coarser, and guttural.

The left shoulder was misaligned and allowed only minimal movement. The left arm and hand were grossly enlarged. The arm was contracted at the elbow and at the wrist, which were frozen into place. The left hand was misshapen. Except for the fourth and fifth fingers, which deviated outward, the rest of the hand looked like a cloven hoof. The thumb was grossly enlarged, and the second and third fingers were fused together. Both were topped by thickened bony nails. His right shoulder, arm, and hand appeared normal for an *H. sapiens* man. So he could still wield a sword. The left leg was hyperextended backward, as would be the hind leg of a boar. A cloven hoof could be seen where the foot and toes should have been. The right leg was hyperextended to a lesser degree and much larger than the left; otherwise, the right leg and foot appeared normal in shape. Rafe maintained his balance using a wide-angle stance.

His back and spine were arched into a convex shape, giving him a humped back. His thoracic spine curved to the right to accommodate the increased size of the left chest wall. His chest on the left side was broader and deeper, and both his heart and left lung were enlarged. His lumbar spine curved to the left, causing his abdomen to bulge out. The right side of his abdomen was enlarged to accommodate the intestines and colon that had shifted to that side.

Illus. 7. Rafe Cassius.

The skin on his left side was a dark brownish-black color, thick and leathery, and covered with a thick coat of animal hair. It was chronically infested with mites, ticks, and other parasites, which left open, festering sores on that side of his body. The skin on the right side of his body appeared to be normal human skin. Even so, it, too, was infested by parasites that had migrated from his left side.

The Spice of Life

Fortunately for Rafe, there was no need to have a unique gene for every function or location where a gene might be used. Some genes could be reused in multiple locations and even serve different purposes depending upon where they were active and with what other genes they interacted (pleiotropy). Thus, the same gene could have effects that were quite different from one place to another.

This genetic feature decreased the genomic burden significantly in *H. transformans* with their expanded genomes. Genes that served multiple purposes likely streamlined the change from one form into another. This was an enormous advantage to *H. transformans* during the normal process of transformation.

Since the expression of these types of genes could be highly variable, predicting what one would or would not do when inserted at a different location in the genome was a risky proposition. The results were unpredictable. This was a major problem for both Biogenics and Cassius in their genetic engineering programs. Even when they inserted or rearranged genes in a controlled fashion and at a predetermined location, the outcomes often did not meet expectations. In a corrupted transformation such as Rafe's, genes could be rearranged in an uncontrolled manner with dire consequences. They could lead to broken and scattered gene sequences, displaced or destroyed genetic material, and other genetic aberrations in a random and unpredictable fashion. Under such conditions, the influence of even one gene with many different effects could be profound, especially in an expanded genome. Hence, the effects of a disrupted transformation were disastrous and usually lethal.

This had been Rafe's fate. Although he had survived his aborted transformation, he was left with multiple grotesque malformations, some of which were quite disabling. This once handsome man was left permanently disfigured with a physical form that was frightening to behold. It was a wonder he survived. Such a disaster would have killed a lesser man. It might have been pleiotropy that both saved him and deformed him.

Serendipity

It was rare for Rafe to leave the security of his fortress. He rarely allowed his full visage to be seen unless he intended to frighten and intimidate a subordinate or an adversary. An incursion into Biogenics territory offered one such occasion. While on the march, he encountered an injured and exhausted Great Gray dragoness (app. C). She had broken her wing and could not fly. Repeated efforts to drag herself over the ground resulted in multiple abrasions and deep lacerations. The broken wing rendered her unable to hunt, so she could not feed herself. Fortunately, she had a devoted mate (illus. 8) who stayed with her and only left to hunt. Although the gray dragon could bring his mate food to eat, he could not bring her water, and she could not travel to get it. Thus, the dragoness continued to weaken despite her mate's efforts.

The gray dragon was away hunting when Rafe and his men found the dragoness in a debilitated state. She could not generate any fire, her breath was weak, and she couldn't move. She was unable to defend herself and could be either killed or captured. Rafe chose the latter.

The dragoness could give Rafe a major advantage over the Biogenics Corporation. Since he couldn't breed the dragoness herself, perhaps he could use the genetic composition of her eggs to create another dragon via genetic engineering. His geneticists would extract genetic code from her eggs and splice segments of it into the genomes of both *H. sapiens* and *H. transformans* embryos. Then they could observe the embryos as they developed for expression of dragon characteristics.

Since the dragoness was alone, Rafe was not aware she had a mate. It took almost an army of men with their machines and hybrids as beasts of burden to move the dragoness to an abandoned tower in a village under his control. When the task was accomplished, the dragoness was confined and chained in the inner chamber, which once had been used as a silo. Although it had a set of huge doors at its base, the interior of the silo was barely large enough in diameter to house the dragoness. The tower was nearly sixty feet high with two small windows at the top—one facing east and one facing west. Light from the sun only filtered into the top of the chamber.

Illus. 8. *Dragonis fuscus magna.*

When the gray dragon returned from hunting a day later, he found his mate missing. He also found the scent of men and other creatures where she had lain. Since he saw no signs that she had been killed, he tracked their scent on the ground just long enough to determine the direction in which they were headed. Then he sought his mate by air.

Dragon eyesight is keen. Even in deep woods, he would be able to see her. Yet he did not. When he began to fly closer to the ground, the wind brought her scent to him again, and he could follow it.

Once the dragon found his mate's location, he still could not see her. When he called to her with a sound humans heard only as a deep and barely audible rumble, she was able to answer him. Then the dragon knew his mate was imprisoned in the tower. Now, he faced a quandary. If the dragon used his strength or fire to breach the tower, it might collapse upon his mate and kill her. Even if freed from the tower, the dragoness still could not flee.

Rafe saw the dragon and noted his hesitation at the tower. He now knew the dragoness had a mate who wanted her back. Rafe knew that none of his men or machines could withstand the dragon's attack. But he had an offer that might keep the dragon's wrath at bay. Alone, Rafe approached the dragon and stood directly in front of him.

A Secret Weapon

Rafe knew he would have to be very careful in what he said when he addressed the dragon. Dragons were very perceptive. "I will provide the dragoness with food and water and treat her wounds," he announced to the dragon. He said nothing about healing her broken wing. "I will keep her alive in return for your services."

"My territory is under attack," Rafe continued. [This was not true—yet; however, it was definitely looming in the future.] "Even now, my enemy is mobilizing its forces and will soon be on the march, if not already. [This was true.] If I cannot stop them, they will descend upon all the villages in this area, bombard them with their cannons, and destroy everyone and everything in them, including the dragoness. [This was a possibility. Biogenics was preparing to march toward H'Aleth, as was Rafe.] I am mobilizing my own forces in a counterattack. I can be victorious and keep them from ever reaching this village if I have your support. [This was true.]"

The dragon listened to Rafe's proposal with suspicion. He had discerned that Rafe was quite capable of deceit, and he sensed many half-truths in what he said. Outright lies, however, were difficult to detect. His corrupted transformation had caused distortions in the architecture of his larynx resulting in a harsh, distorted, and throaty voice.

The dragon considered this offer briefly and countered with a few conditions of his own. "I will fight for you if an enemy force enters this region," he replied with the following caveat. "If my dragoness continues to decline or dies, this agreement will be null and void as will you and your men."

Rafe was unconcerned about this amendment and agreed to it. The men were expendable, and Rafe himself would not be here. He wanted the power and destruction a dragon could bring to an attack on the Biogenics Corporation and, possibly, for his own assault on the House of H'Aleth. So Rafe planned to keep the dragoness alive, if in poor condition. The dragon knew well that Rafe would provide little relief for his mate; however, it would give the dragon time to formulate an alternative plan of his own.

The dragon's conditions precluded any preemptive strike on Biogenics before they could fully mobilize. Rafe would have to delay engaging them until they were closer to H'Aleth. Still, H'Aleth's borders were only a few days' march from the village. *That should be close enough,* he reasoned. Rafe agreed to the dragon's terms. If his forces readily overcame those of Biogenics, he might withhold the dragon and keep it a secret. But should Biogenics's forces prove to be formidable, *then I will unleash my dragon to wreak destruction upon them,* he thought. So focused was he on defeating Biogenics, he didn't consider what defenses H'Aleth might mount. Even if he had done so, he would have dismissed them as insignificant. He had a dragon and the misconception that it was under his control.

Supplemental Notes and Citations

Pleiotropy

Pleiotropy is the ability of the same gene to exert different effects on multiple traits (Brooker, 2009; Paaby and Rockman, 2013; Price et al., 2015; Sivakumaran et al., 2011; Zheng and Rao, 2015). A pleiotropic gene may exert its effects by acting on biologic pathways that are completely independent and/or by affecting a single trait that subsequently affects multiple traits downstream from it (Gratten and Visscher, 2016). Consequently, a single pleiotropic gene can serve many purposes. It can affect many physical traits and have multiple variable effects on different organ systems (Paaby and Rockman, 2013; Zheng and Rao, 2015). Consequently, the effects of changing a pleiotropic gene are often unpredictable.

Pleiotropy is a common characteristic in genes that are widespread and present among several cell types. Although it does not inherently cause disease, this feature was discovered through the study of gene mutations known to cause disease (Louvi and Artavanis-Tsakonas, 2012; Pasipoularides, 2015; Sivakumaran et al., 2011; Solovieff et al., 2013). For example, collagen is a compound found in nearly all body tissues. It has a vast range of uses in many different tissues. Assuming the gene for collagen functions normally, it is quite helpful to have a gene adjust its function to support different tissue types that need its product. Unfortunately, in *H. sapiens*, a single gene mutation in the genetic code for collagen also results in a wide variety of phenotypic defects.

CHAPTER 10

Prelude to War

In their pursuit of dominance, both Cassius and Biogenics expanded their respective territories as much as possible. In deciding which territory to annex next, both Biogenics and Cassius considered the House of Gregor, with its genetic engineering capability, to be the most desirable of the Houses to acquire; however, it was also the least accessible (map 5). It was the farthest away and surrounded by imposing natural barriers and a hostile environment. These factors made approaching Gregor far more difficult than that of the other two Houses.

The House of H'Aleth was the next most desirable because of its detailed pedigree records, which identified the capabilities and abilities of each member, most of whom were *H. transformans*. In addition, H'Aleth had focused on the biology and natural history of *H. transformans*. If both the people of H'Aleth and their pedigrees could be captured, the victor would achieve dominance over his archrival. The wealth of resources, especially the $2X^T$ females, would assure it. H'Aleth was also the closest of the three Houses to both organizations. Surrounded by grasslands, woodlands, and rivers, it was the most accessible and, therefore, the most amenable to attack. Even its inland waterways were accessible by ship.

Map 5. Gregor Territory.

The House of Erwina was not under consideration—yet. It was farther away than H'Aleth, although not as far as Gregor. Its natural barriers could be overcome, albeit not readily. Lastly, although Erwina's breeding programs and archives might provide useful information, neither Biogenics nor Cassius considered Erwina's resources particularly important. This assessment later proved to be a serious miscalculation.

The Balance of Power

Given their adversarial relationship and competition for resources, both the Biogenics Corporation and the Cassius Foundation had established armies that were well equipped with archers, swordsmen, catapults, and cannons. Fortunately for the populace of contested territories, sparse mineral deposits of sulfur, coal, and potassium nitrate limited their supply of gunpowder. Nevertheless, both armies were capable of mounting an effective offense. Thus, there had already been many skirmishes over acquisition of territory and resources.

In their rush to absorb the Houses, both Biogenics and Rafe Cassius inadvertently targeted the same House to acquire first—the House of H'Aleth. Spies enlisted by both organizations brought this news to their attention. Once the two entities realized they were after the same resource, both mobilized in an attempt to reach H'Aleth first. If either organization was going to acquire this jewel, it would have to get past the other one to do so. Once again, this put them in direct conflict with each other—this time on a much larger scale.

In contrast to the Biogenics Corporation and the Cassius Foundation, the House of H'Aleth did not have an army. It had a security force that monitored and patrolled its territory, including its villages and the estate, which served as H'Aleth's seat of government and housed their research facility. These people were skilled archers and swordsmen in their own right and quite capable of accosting and removing most intruders—by force, if necessary. In addition to archery and swordsmanship, most of its members could transform into animals, many of whom were apex predators that would become ferocious if attacked.

An Imminent Threat

As Cassius and Biogenics extended their reach, their skirmishes grew ever closer to H'Aleth. H'Osanna, Mistress of the House of H'Aleth, had prepared for the possibility that her House and all its land would be engulfed by their war. She had learned long ago that the conflict between the two long-standing adversaries might spill over into H'Aleth's territory. When scouts reported that both Biogenics and Cassius were planning a major offensive, she knew this would be no skirmish. She also knew that H'Aleth's defenses could not stop an army with cannons.

When the fight between Cassius and Biogenics crossed into H'Aleth's territory, H'Osanna ordered the evacuation of the eastern villages closest to their territories. The villagers would take refuge at her estate. "Bring them here," she ordered. "Tell them to bring as many of their resources as they can. Only their scouts should remain to keep watch." Even though the estate was well supplied and had a source of fresh water, H'Osanna knew that more supplies would be needed during a long siege. The scouts, *H. transformans* who could take the form of animals native to the areas they watched, would continue to maintain surveillance.

Long ago, the people of H'Aleth had fortified her family's estate with an eight-foot stone wall (illus. 9). The estate hosted the manor house, which served as H'Aleth's seat of government, and the adjoining research facility. Initially, the wall was meant to provide a measure of security and prevent encroachment by strangers onto the estate. Subsequently, as Cassius and Biogenics extended their reach, it became a bulwark in the event of an attack. Yet neither the wall nor the structures within it were built to be a fortress. Cannon fire would bring down its stone wall and its buildings. Nevertheless, with villagers seeking refuge there, H'Ossana ordered the wall surrounding her estate and the manor itself reinforced, including means to repel any attackers.

A Looming Battle

As the battle between Cassius and Biogenics moved closer, ever greater numbers of people from other outlying villages fled from the encroaching armies and sought refuge at the estate. When H'Aleth's scouts alerted H'Osanna that the enemy's forces were only two or three days away, H'Osanna decided it was too dangerous for the villagers to remain there. She ordered those who could not or should not assist with H'Aleth's defense to leave immediately and seek sanctuary in the sister Houses. "All those who can mount a defense and whose children have reached the age of adulthood may remain if they choose to do so," she said. "All others will leave."

Illus. 9. H'Aleth's Estate and Manor.

Those people strong enough to attempt the more arduous journey to Gregor went there for greater safety. The rest, including those with young children, went to Erwina. Erwina was the closer of the two Houses, and travel to it posed the least hardship. It was also where their children would go normally for schooling, and many members of H'Aleth already had children in school there. Small young children would ride on horseback with an *H. sapiens* adult. In this way, the adults could travel quickly, taking themselves, children, and horses to safety. Most *H. transformans* would transform into their alternate species to make the journey. In this way, they could travel faster than they otherwise would in their human form. Those who could transform into deer or other large mammals would carry older children on their backs. Thus only H'Aleth's defenders, including H'Osanna, remained when Cassius and Biogenics reached the outer borders of the estate.

Most of the Sisters, along with many men and women—*H. sapiens* and *H. transformans* alike—stayed to defend their home. H'Ossana was the great-granddaughter of Edvar and Ruth H'Aleth, who founded her House. As Ruth's direct descendant through the maternal line, H'Osanna was $2X^T$. Like her mother and grandmother before her, she could transform across mammalian and avian species. All the Sisters who remained to defend their House had the ability to transform into animals known to be aggressive and powerful. Both H'Osanna and her mother, H'Elvinia, could transform into a cougar. Her aunt H'Assandra and her cousin H'Igraith [hil-*grāy*-ĭth] could transform into a lynx. All of them could transform into some species of raptor. Hence, even in human form, all the Sisters had enhanced strength and endurance and exquisite visual acuity—gifts of their cougar, lynx, and raptor genes.

When Biogenics and Cassius first encroached on H'Aleth's territory, H'Aleth's security forces planned an offensive effort of their own. As the sounds of battle approached, H'Aleth's chief of security deployed the majority of his security forces to the wall. They were bolstered by villagers who volunteered to stay and defend their land. Many of these people could transform into wolves and a few into bears, a boar, and a buffalo.

Jointly, the security forces and the villagers formed an offensive force to defend the wall and prevent a breach. If that effort failed, they could retreat and join others to defend the manor itself and the people within it. The wall would not be breached, nor would their House fall without a fight. Still there was hope. H'Aleth's forces could yet prevail if Cassius and Biogenics exhausted their own resources first in their assault against each other.

H'Ossana was certain that Cassius and Biogenics wanted the genealogical records and research housed in the manor and research building. She was equally certain they would want to capture as many of her people as possible to have access to their genomes. Thus, it seemed unlikely that either enemy would release a barrage of cannon fire to destroy the buildings and burn everything in them.

In order to prevent Cassius or Biogenics from possessing any of H'Aleth's records, H'Osanna sent all of them to the sister House that could best use them. "Give all the pedigrees and natural history studies to families going to Erwina," she ordered. She issued a similar order for all of H'Aleth's research, including gene samples and karyotypes from all their members, and sent them to Gregor. Finally, if H'Aleth's defenses were overrun, then the defenders themselves would flee to avoid capture.

No one doubted that the enemy would do all in its power to conquer their House and take possession of all its resources, including its people. Alas, this proved not to be the case.

CHAPTER 11

The Fall of H'Aleth

When Biogenics's and Cassius's armies converged on their mutual target, they found themselves in the position of fighting on two fronts: the House of H'Aleth, which their respective armies were expected to overwhelm, and each other, where the outcome was less certain. The animosity between them was so great that neither organization entertained for a moment the notion of dividing up the prize. Thus, the initial clash was between the forces of Biogenics and Cassius when each one tried to stop the other one from reaching H'Aleth.

H'Ossana and her people could hear the sounds of mayhem and cannons closing in on their village. They braced for an attack on the estate as two mortal enemies vied for the resources housed there.

The Battle for H'Aleth

Whereas Biogenics's commanders were grimly determined, Rafe Cassius was confident of victory. He had a secret weapon and would use it, if necessary, to destroy Biogenics's army and anyone else that got in his way.

During the battle, a branch of the Biogenics's forces broke off. They skirted the field of battle and headed toward the east wall surrounding H'Aleth's estate. This field position afforded Biogenics significant advantages over Cassius. Firstly, Biogenics would be in a position to attack Cassius on his flank. Secondly, once the wall was breached, Biogenics would reach the manor quickly, well in advance of Cassius. This plan was contingent upon Biogenics's main force holding off Cassius's army long enough and on H'Aleth's forces failing. Rafe had prepared for this possibility. *If I cannot have the House of H'Aleth,* Rafe thought angrily, *then no one will.*

H'Aleth's defenders and Biogenics's forces were fully engaged at the wall when what appeared to be a massive machine of war in the distance suddenly took flight and swept down upon them. Cassius had unleashed his secret weapon, a Great Gray dragon, with orders to destroy all combatants inside and outside the wall. Both defenders and attackers were stunned. Neither of them had any idea that Cassius possessed such a creature or how he could have acquired one. Had he finally engineered an *H. transformans* that could transform into a dragon? The question was moot.

First, the dragon attacked H'Aleth's and Biogenics's forces where they were fighting at the wall. Dragon fire encompassed the entire area. So intense was his fire that it killed everyone and destroyed everything in a matter of moments. Then, the dragon turned his attention to the manor and bore down directly upon it.

The defenders at the manor recognized the scope of the disaster. They all saw the firestorm at the wall, which lasted only a few minutes, and realized they could not save the manor nor could they flee. They had no defense against a dragon. None of their people had the genetic ability to transform into a dragon and challenge the one bearing down upon them.

Dragon fire quickly engulfed the manor (illus. 10). Although the defenders sought refuge first within the manor and then in the cellars below, it was to no avail. The heat of the dragon's breath and his fire melted the mortar that held the stones in place and supported the walls of the cellars. The manor crumbled into a cavern created when its cellars collapsed. It was completely destroyed. Everyone still within it was killed— if not from the dragon's fire, then from the collapse of the building.

Then the dragon turned on the rest of the estate, destroying every remaining structure and burning all the land encompassed within its walls. While the dragon's attention was on the estate, the remainder of the Biogenics's forces rapidly withdrew. Cassius had won the day.

Thus, it appeared to the two combatants that all of H'Aleth's resources were lost—its people, its history, and its pedigrees. Not so. Most of the people of H'Aleth had already fled to the other Houses and took their capabilities and abilities with them. The knowledge gained from their study of the biology and natural history of *H. transformans* was saved in

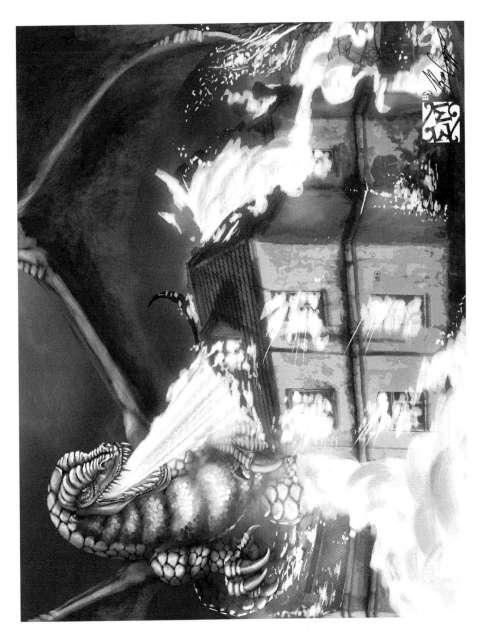

Illus. 10. Firestorm.

the archives of Erwina. Their research was safe in the House of Gregor. As long as these two Houses remained, the House of H'Aleth would be remembered, as would all those who died defending it (table 3).

Table 3. Chronology of the Three Houses.

Year (SI)	Table 3. Chronology of the Three Houses
0	*Stella Ignis*
325	*H. transformans* declared a new species within the genus *Homo*
365–380	Marriage of Edvar and Ruth H'Aleth (founding generation) followed by the birth of 5 children—3 daughters and 2 sons (2nd generation)
385	Emigration of Edvar and Ruth and other families
389	House of H'Aleth established
387–419	Birth of Edvar and Ruth's grandchildren (3rd generation)
407	House of Erwina established
407–435	Birth of Edvar and Ruth's great-grandchildren (4th generation)
415	House of Gregor established
417	Natural history and research center formally established under the aegis of the House of H'Aleth for the study and protection of *H. transformans*
422	Establishment of education center at Erwina
427–470	Birth of Edvar and Ruth's great-great-grandchildren (5th generation)
428	Establishment of genetics and medical centers at Gregor
433	Death of Edvar H'Aleth (age 86)
461	Death of Ruth H'Aleth (age 114)
481	Destruction of the House of H'Aleth

Through the Wormhole

Yet two did not die in the conflagration. They had fled the manor and were not within it when the dragon attacked it. Both of them were direct descendants of Ruth and Sisters of the House of H'Aleth. One was an old woman who had recognized long ago that an attack on her House was inevitable. "As do we," her Sisters agreed, "and we are watching for it."

Not well enough, the old woman thought. Several months before the attack, she had begun preparing a means of escape should the estate be overrun.

In the oldest and deepest cellar, the older Sister found a break in the masonry of a wall on the northeast corner of the manor. She transformed into a badger and began to dig. Over time, she excavated a deep tunnel, which ran toward the northern end of the estate. She made the diameter large enough for an adult human to crawl through it on his or her belly or a small child crawling on hands and knees.

After some distance, a thick clump of roots barred her way. She realized she had reached the dense thicket just beyond the northern wall. The thicket served as a barrier between the grounds of the estate and the forest beyond and well deserved its attribution. Its shrubbery was comprised of thick, leathery intertwining branches and dark-green serrated leaves. The plant was well defended, with sharp long spines on its leaves and clusters of poisonous red berries. Its fibrous roots were twisted and even thicker than the branches, and the roots burrowed deep into the ground. They proved to be a challenge even for a badger. So at that point, the badger was forced to turn toward the east and gradually slope the tunnel upward to reach the surface. There, the tunnel ended just beyond and behind an arm of the thicket that extended eastward. At this point, the thicket would provide cover from any forces attacking the manor behind it.

A Blanket of Fire

When the attack was launched against H'Aleth and before the dragon's conflagration began, the old woman stayed to defend her House. When she saw the dragon and the firestorm at the wall, she knew she had but a moment to act. She abruptly left her station and retrieved the only child remaining at the manor. "Come with me," she barked as she snatched a satchel she had kept prepared, "and hurry. We are leaving now." At a brisk pace, she headed for the second cellar with the child running after her. They reached the entrance to the narrow tunnel she had prepared just as the gray dragon turned his attention toward the manor.

"Get into the tunnel now," she snapped, then transformed into a badger and followed the child into it. A few minutes later, the earth shuddered, causing chunks of dirt to fall into the tunnel as the two crawled through it. Fortunately, the badger was capable of clawing through them or creating a bypass around any obstruction. Unbeknownst to them, the manor had collapsed into its cellars below. In doing so, it obstructed the entrance to the tunnel and obliterated any sign of it.

When the old woman and child reached the tunnel's end and climbed to the surface, the melee was well behind them. Enemy forces were transfixed on the manor and the sight of a Great Gray dragon hovering over it. Fires blanketed the grounds and obscured the old woman and child from view as they crept toward the forest. Thus did the two escape unseen and reach the forest beyond. When they disappeared into it, they passed out of all knowledge of their enemies and of their people.

CHAPTER 12

Into the Boar's Den

Just as a gray dragon descended upon the manor house at H'Aleth, an old woman and a child fled from the manor and the conflagration in secret. The old woman knew it was imperative that the child be hidden from both Biogenics and Cassius. So when one wants to avoid discovery by one's enemies, what better place to hide than in their midst?

Once more in human form, the old woman led the child through the forest. "Stay silent," she commanded the child, even as thorns and underbrush tore at them. During the night after H'Aleth's destruction, she led the child across a bridge over the nearby river Aguila [*ah*-gī-la]. They continued to travel for several days through a forested region, where they encountered the river Accipitridae [*ak*-cī-*pit*-rī-dī], which did not have a bridge. Although badgers prefer not to swim, they can and will when necessary. So once again, the old woman transformed into a badger. With the child holding onto her, she swam to the other side. They continued their trek through a forested region until they reached the river Arcturus [ark-*tur*-us]. Once they crossed the bridge over the river, they were in Cassius territory. When the trees began to thin, they were well inside the enemy's domain. Eventually, they came upon a village.

In Hiding

The village was one of many others just like it scattered throughout the region. The people and other beings living there were not an uncommon or unlikely mix for a village in Cassius territory. They lived in poverty with little food, no clean water, and scant or no shelter. The mortality rate was high for anyone who became ill or injured. They had little charity toward one another because they had nothing to give. Into just such a village did the old woman bring the child.

When the old woman and the child arrived, they looked just as wretched and decrepit as the villagers. The old woman knew she could be of use and saw an opportunity for her and the child to disappear inside an unremarkable village within enemy territory. One of the first priorities was to find a location away from contamination where she could build a shelter to house herself and the child.

The old woman did not want the villagers to perceive the two of them as invaders. So she identified a suitable site just outside the village's boundary. Then both she and the child began to gather supplies to build the shelter, start and maintain a fire, and gather food and medicinal herbs from the surrounding area.

With the child's help, the old woman built a shelter made of stones and set in mortar (app. D, illus. 33). It was six by four by four feet in size with a narrow doorway about two feet high and two feet wide—barely large enough for them to squeeze inside the shelter. The interior was about twenty-four square feet, which was enough room for her, the child, and some storage room for food and fire supplies. Most of the shelter was darkened, even in broad daylight. The small doorway was the only source of light for the interior of the structure and the only opening into it. There were no windows.

During one night, the old woman transformed into a badger. Just outside the shelter, she dug a shallow pit for a fire. It was close enough to the shelter's entrance that both she and the child could tend the fire from the doorway and protect it, if necessary. It also would be close by during the winter when they would need to heat hearthstones for warmth. Next, they fashioned a covering over the pit to shelter it and the fire from rain and snow.

It took months to build the shelter and fire pit. The old woman and the child had barely enough time to collect and store supplies for the winter—herbs, acorns, seeds, edible tubers and mushrooms, wild berries, and onions for food; twigs, pieces of bark, acorn hulls, and dried grasses, which they would bind into tight small bundles for a fire. These items were small enough to stash inside their shelter and keep them dry. The acorn hulls occupied one back corner and provided bedding for the storage of food items. The twigs and bark occupied the other back corner. The grass bundles were kept on the floor to provide a little bedding until they were used for fuel. A shallow area was scooped out in the middle of the hut just large enough to hold a heated hearthstone. They finished their labors just in time for the start of winter.

Once the shelter was erected, both the old woman and the child could retire into it at night. "Stay in the back," she ordered, "and stay behind me." The child would settle toward the back of the shelter, and the old woman would settle toward the front, near the doorway. The child was allowed to sleep first for several hours while the old woman kept watch. During these times, she would transform into a badger, which by nature, is a nocturnal animal with keen night vision. Toward daybreak, the old woman would resume her native form. She would rouse the child to keep watch. "Remain watchful and keep the fire low," she admonished her. "If the fire becomes too low, then throw a few acorn hulls, twigs, and bark into the pit. Do not leave the shelter and always stay behind me." If an intruder or attacker appeared, the old woman could transform quickly into a badger. The badger's reputation for aggressiveness was renowned. It could fend off predators much larger than itself, especially from the cover of its den.

Homo deformans

There were few people in the village who belonged to *H. sapiens*. The majority of villagers were corrupted *H. transformans*, known sarcastically as *Homo deformans*. They were failed attempts to breed or engineer someone with a particular set of desired characteristics. A vast array of genetic malformations were represented in the villagers. Most were structurally defective in some way, and many were mentally deficient as well. The scope of malformations ranged from mild (e.g., partial or total loss of a limb or an eye) to grotesque (e.g., badly deformed and disfigured). Yet their deformities and limitations were not so severe that the affected individuals could not be put to work.

When nonnative DNA became mixed into *H. transformans's* native genome (*H. sapiens*), there was a risk it could disrupt the native gene sequence. Whether the gene was native or nonnative, if its sequence was incomplete (e.g., a partial gene sequence), fractured (e.g., broken in one or more places), or otherwise damaged, then it would not function correctly, if at all. If the structure coded by a damaged gene sequence can even be made, it would be defective. In addition, there were great risks for fragmentation of both native and nonnative genomes during transformation. Since transformation was forced in many of Cassius's creatures, their risks were much higher. These factors accounted for the majority of the deformed beings seen in a Cassius village and further exemplified why individuals who could transform successfully were relatively rare.

Fortunately, *H. transformans* possessed the same processes for correcting errors and mending breaks in DNA as did *H. sapiens*. These processes either repaired the gene sequence, which would allow the characteristic to be expressed, or removed it. Unfortunately, if the processes that would normally clean up and correct DNA errors were corrupted themselves, then they could not perform their functions. Even if unaffected, these repair mechanisms evolved to correct defects and breaks in otherwise normal gene sequences. Many of these repair mechanisms could not engage with genes damaged by a corrupted transformation. This all but ensured the outcome would be permanent, if not lethal.

An Unsuspecting Predator

There were both human and animal hybrids in the village. These hybrids were not corruptions. They were genetically engineered by Rafe to serve as laborers and guards. The latter were imbued with characteristics that would make them aggressive fighters. The majority of them were animal-animal hybrids in which the genes of one species were mixed with those of one or more other species. This was usually accomplished in the embryo stage, after which the embryo was allowed to grow and develop into an adult hybrid animal, if it survived.

There were a few human-animal hybrids in which Rafe used viral vectors to insert selected animal genes to the genome of an *H. transformans*. Then the victim was forced into a transformation, rendered unable to transform again, and left permanently in his hybrid state. The crocutalupoid [*cro*-cu-ta-*lup*-oid] (illus. 11) was one such hybrid. It was created when the genes of a hyena and wolf were spliced into the genome of an *H. tranformans*. It was engineered to hunt large prey and fight an enemy.

Illus. 11. Crocutalupoid.

The Cassius Foundation would send the hybrids to villages that had a mine, a factory, or other industrial activity that needed laborers, beasts of burden, and guards. Those who had greater strength and ability often dominated and abused those less fortunate. If not mentally deficient, the human hybrids often became guards. They were given greater access to food, water, and shelter in return for protecting the Foundation's resources—which did not include the villagers.

The old woman knew that many of hybrids seen in the village had been tormented. "Some but not all of the creatures you see here are dangerous," she told the child. "Most of the animal hybrids are. Still, as long as we do not come too close to their cages or to where they are kept chained to guard buildings or supplies, we are less likely to antagonize them." During the day, the risk of an attack by one of the human hybrids was lower as long as she and the child did not appear to be a threat to them. At night, however, the risk was much greater.

One night, a crocutalupoid crept stealthily toward the shelter as if he were stalking prey. He was. This was how he viewed the two slight humans living together without any protection. As he crept closer, he heard no sound and saw no movement from the shelter. He paused as he approached the entrance. His prey seemed unaware of any danger. When he lunged to go inside, he was met with a violent attack from a ferocious animal with huge curved claws on its forepaws and powerful jaws that could crush bones.

Part hyena, the crocutalupoid had a bite force of nearly 1,100 pounds per square inch, one of the most powerful of any mammal. He was unable to leverage it. His head and neck fit into the opening to the shelter; however, he couldn't get his shoulders through the doorway. Meanwhile, his head, eyes, and snout were being ravaged by a badger defending its den.

Bloodied and injured, the crocutalupoid soon backed out of the doorway. He had been unable to overcome the defender and opted to forgo any further attempts to get a meal there. As he departed, he glanced back to see if he was pursued by the animal that had attacked him. If so, the tables would be turned; however, the animal did not follow. Only the slight glow of two greenish-yellow eyes at the entrance served notice not to return again.

Surcease

The old woman was skilled in the preparation of potions such as soups and salves. Indeed, she had extensive knowledge of all manner of concoctions: soups, syrups, elixirs, liqueurs, teas, and sauces for consumption; emollients, salves, plasters, pastes, and tinctures for application to wounds and sores. She also had extensive knowledge of a vast array of herbs, barks, seeds, minerals, fruits, vegetables, flowers, mushrooms, and berries and the properties they possessed (app. E). She knew which ones were edible and which were poisonous, hallucinogenic, and sedating.

On foraging trips outside the village, the old woman and the child would pick dandelion plants, which grew wild and were plentiful in the region. The old woman used the leaves in soups. Occasionally, she would find small patches of lippea alba, peppermint, oregano, and basil—probably the remnants of an old herb garden. These she could use to treat infected wounds and provide some relief from misery.

The old woman also knew how to cleanse fouled water by clarifying it, boiling it over the fire, and then allowing it to cool. Then, she would use the local vegetation and what little food was available to make soups and other potions for herself, the child, and the villagers. She also used the medicinal herbs and essential oils the two had carried with them to make medicinal potions. The old woman taught the child how to prepare all these mixtures.

None of the potions could reverse or correct malformations in the villagers; however, they did provide some nutrition that otherwise would not have been available. In this way, the old woman, with the child as her apprentice, was able to provide the villagers and their guards with some relief from suffering. Thus did the two integrate themselves into a small village deep in Cassius territory and survive there.

Mistress

All the while, the old woman continued to convey her knowledge and skills to her apprentice. While living in H'Aleth, the child had learned all the recipes and potions commonly used there. Now, the child was obliged to learn many more—some of which were quite exotic—and was admonished to say nothing about them to anyone. The child also learned to search in fields, forests, caves, and streams for ingredients not found in the village. At the same time, she also learned the effects of each one.

The child was already fluent in two languages: the common language used across the regions and Rμηeîc. Now she was obliged to learn the local dialect where they were living. She was admonished to speak only in the dialect of the village and never read or write where villagers might observe it. "The villagers have no knowledge of written language," the old woman told the child. "To use writing would arouse suspicion about our origin." Excursions away from the village—ostensibly to find herbs and other plants—offered the child an opportunity to speak the other languages and to practice reading and writing in them.

Since nothing could be written down, the child had to learn everything by memory. Fortunately, this was something she had been obliged to do in the past. Making the potions and recipes for the villagers kept her memory of these recipes refreshed. Eventually, these mixtures and their preparation became ingrained. Secret potions were made much less frequently and were less practiced. To keep the child's knowledge of these potions fresh, the old woman required her to recite and mime the preparation of these recipes.

The old woman also taught the child how to prepare a potion of fluorescent phosphorus by mixing minerals (nitrate, potassium, phosphorus, magnesium) with charcoal and sulfur in water and adding starch from taro roots to form a paste. A writing instrument would be dipped in the paste and then allowed to dry. When lit with a spark or a match, the paste will ignite and burn. Then one could write on the air until the source of fuel in the paste was consumed. The letters and words would stay visible for a few seconds and then fade away, leaving no trace that anything had been written. This obliged the child to become a fast reader, since the writing would fade almost as fast as the words were written. The old woman also taught the child how to select and modify quills, pine needles, and twigs to become a writing instrument.

As the child grew well practiced and competent, both she and the old woman gained confidence in her abilities. Nevertheless, the child was never allowed to practice without the old woman nearby. Instead, the old woman would direct her to prepare one recipe independently while the old woman prepared another. In this way, the child gained independence in preparing most of the recipes they used.

Throughout her life, the child only knew the old woman as Mistress and addressed her as such. The old woman only addressed the child as Child and never spoke of her given name, her age, her date of birth, or her parents.

Supplemental Notes and Citations

Congenital Defects

Congenital defects are the result of gene and chromosome disruptions (Sun et al., 2015; Webber et al., 2015). These are defects that could not be fixed by repair mechanisms *in utero*. Examples include congenital heart defects, which are primarily gene disorders (Webber et al., 2015); amelia, which is the congenital absence or failure to fully develop part or all of one or more extremities (Bermejo-Sánchez et al., 2011); and cyclopia, which is the presence of a single eye and primarily a chromosomal defect (Orioli, 2011). Note: Unlike Mendelian inherited gene defects, congenital gene defects are not inherited.

DNA Repair Mechanisms

Genes may be embedded within one or multiple DNA strands and across one or more of the original 46 chromosomes. There are processes that can facilitate the integration of gene sequences, the excision of damaged genes, or the attachment of genes to the end of a chromosome.

DNA polymerase represents a group of enzymes that can replicate an exact copy of a DNA strand, then proofread and edit it for errors, making corrections along the way (Brooker, 2009; Carroll, 2009).

DNA ligase is an enzyme that attaches or reattaches DNA gene segments, including broken edges (Brooker, 2009; Carroll, 2009).

Integrase is an enzyme that helps insert genetic code. In *H. sapiens*, it is an enzyme used by the HIV virus to insert its genetic code into a human DNA strand. There are several drugs that treat HIV infection by inhibiting the action of this enzyme (Cragie and Bushman, 2012; Faulhaber and Aberg, 2009).

Endonuclease is an enzyme that can cut out damaged DNA and repair the strand. It permits editing of a single base pair in a DNA strand (Carroll, 2009; Kuraoka, 2015). Gene editing uses nucleases to correct mutated genes that cause disease (Tolarová et al., 2016.)

Recombinase is an enzyme that reattaches genes and chromosomes (Daley et al., 2014, 2013). In *H. sapiens*, interference with the function of a recombinase enzyme (*RAD*51) is implicated in the *BRCA2* gene associated with breast cancer (Jensen, 2013).

CHAPTER 13

Unexpected Encounters

One day, the old woman received a summons to go to another village and attend to the people there. She was not surprised that word of her work had spread. Gradually, over time, living conditions in the Cassius village improved under her influence. She would entice the villagers to clean themselves—at least, partially—in return for soup. Her soups and medicinal potions alleviated enough suffering that the villagers were willing to comply. Enticing them to clean the village, however, proved to be a bridge too far. Nevertheless, travelers to the village noted that the conditions of its inhabitants were better than those of other villages. Even so, the old woman was surprised at being summoned and wondered who issued the orders. This concerned her and caused a major dilemma. Should she leave the child to stay alone in their present village or take the child with her?

Being summoned suggested a ranking person was involved. If the summons was issued by an agent of Rafe Cassius, which was possible, then the child could be in danger. Conversely, once she was away, there was a risk that the child could be threatened by the villagers, especially the guards. Then there was the matter of the unknown demands of the village to which she had been summoned. The old woman might need the child's assistance to deal with them. Finally, she decided that bringing the child with her was the lesser of the available evils. Fortunately, at this time, there was no indication that the child could transform. So the two of them gathered up the supplies they would likely need and left the village with the escort sent to fetch them.

The Dragoness

When the old woman and her apprentice arrived at the village, they were told they would not be tending to the villagers. Instead, they were taken to a tower. When its silo doors were opened, allowing light to flood into the chamber, both were taken aback by the sight of a gray dragoness. The dragoness did not react to their presence and made no motion toward them. She was a weak, malnourished, and apathetic creature riddled with sores and other lesions that had not been treated. The injured wing was limp and deformed where the break occurred. There was barely any room within the narrow chamber to move at all, so she could not stretch or flex her other wing. She could not have taken flight even if she had the strength to break free. The old woman sensed the pain and anguish the dragoness felt.

During her capture, the dragoness had refused to eat the rodents brought to her as food. She was becoming progressively weaker and, more importantly, was not producing any eggs. Rafe was at risk of losing both a potent weapon—her mate—and a source of dragon eggs. He had heard of an old woman in an outlying village with some skill in treating wounds and ailments. So he ordered the old woman brought to the village to tend to the dragoness.

The old woman took advantage of this extraordinary situation. Not only did she treat the dragoness's wounds, she also taught the child all she knew about dragons: their characteristics and abilities (app. C) and the different species (app. F). "Dragons are mammals, as are we," she explained. "They are among the oldest of the mammals. They hatch their young from eggs, yet they nurse their young with milk, as we do. They communicate with one another by sounds that typically fall below our hearing. These sounds can travel long distances and echo through the aeries. Sometimes you may hear rumblings." The old woman paused for a moment and then added, "When dragons speak to humans, they raise their pitch to just within our range if you know how to listen to them." When the child asked how dragons breathe fire, she replied, "They don't. They generate their fire from glands in their throat. Enough questions for now." The old woman had to be careful. Guards must not hear their conversation.

There was a substantial risk associated with caring for an injured dragoness—not the least of which was being so close to one. The old woman had demanded that the silo doors be left open so she could see to treat the dragoness's wounds. This also provided a means of escape, if needed. As the dragoness's condition improved and she gained strength, at some point she would become physically able to attack both her captors and her benefactors. The old woman hoped to achieve the former while avoiding the latter.

The old woman and the child first prepared several ointments and salves for the wounds by adding melted beeswax to an essential oil of selected herbs. The old woman prepared a salve with zizyphus and aloe to be applied daily to any open wounds. The child prepared a nutritious gruel, which included crushed acorns and meat from the dead rats the jailors provided. The old woman added St. John's wort to the gruel twice daily to ease the dragoness's stress and anxiety. Before applying treatments, the old woman would administer a tincture of belladonna, which allowed the dragoness to slip into a twilight sleep. During these times and with the child's help, the old woman would attempt to flex and extend the dragoness's wings and release their frozen joints. The break was too old to be repaired; however, the old woman created a splint for the affected wing segment and applied it in a manner that would allow the rest of the wing to fold and unfold around it.

There was another risk—possibly a far more serious risk—posed by treating the dragoness. Whoever had summoned them (Rafe) might learn of the old woman's abilities and, in doing so, become suspicious of her origin. So her ministrations to the dragoness had to appear to be only just enough to keep her alive with the possibility of restoring her egg-laying capacity. As it turned out, the dragoness proved to be a willing coconspirator in this effort.

Another Unexpected Encounter

Indeed, it was Rafe that had sent for the old woman. *If the old crone proves able to treat the dragoness*, he thought, *then I will keep her for myself.* Once he learned that the old woman was having some small degree of success, he left his fortress and traveled to the village by a little known path and entered it unannounced.

Rafe crept into the storeroom where many supplies, including medicinal herbs, were kept. The storeroom was almost filled with barrels of nuts and seeds, bags of grain (wheat, rice, corn), kegs of wine, wooden boxes of fruit (apples, pears, peaches), rolls of cloth materials, shelves with jars of preserves and vials of liqueurs, and cured meats hanging from the ceiling. This arrangement provided many crevices in which to hide from curious eyes. Near the entrance to the room, there was space for a small worktable.

Rafe preferred darkened settings with little light—shadows created by drapes, walls that provided barriers, darkened corners. He also knew that the storeroom would be closely guarded, by his order, to prevent its resources from being raided by the village folk. So there he waited, unseen in the shadows, for the old woman to appear. She never did. Instead, it was a child who had been dispatched to retrieve ingredients the old woman had requested. Rafe watched as the child moved about the storeroom selecting the items required. Eventually, she came into the storeroom's dimmer regions to look for items that were less commonly used.

The child sensed a being hiding nearby and prudently decided to give no sign that she knew someone else was present. There were many frightened creatures in the village who wished to remain in hiding. When the location of a required ingredient obliged the child to get too close, a half human–half animal hybrid suddenly appeared. It had a disfigured face and a fierce visage. The being was closer than the child had anticipated.

The child froze and waited. Although this being's physique was quite striking, it was no worse than some others she had seen in Cassian villages. The child simply had not seen one quite like him. Clearly, he was deformed and disfigured by some mechanism. The child noted also the draining sores on the deformed arm and hand. Some were ulcerated and bleeding, and others were purulent. "You have many wounds," the child said in a quiet voice. "Would you like them treated?"

Rafe looked intently at the offeror. The child was a human female and appeared to be about twelve years of age. Her species remained to be determined.

"You believe there is a treatment?" he uttered quietly.

"It is possible," the child replied. "Wounds and sores such as these are not uncommon."

"How would you treat them?" Rafe asked.

"I can prepare and apply salves that may be effective," the child replied.

Rafe lunged forward to be face-to-face with the child. "Can you cure them?" His question was a demand, and when his voiced was raised, it was mixed with sounds of a snarl.

Startled, the child promptly stepped back yet still maintained her composure. "I think not," she replied. "The salves may soothe your wounds and treat infection. They cannot cure the condition that caused them."

Rafe looked at the child thoughtfully. "How do you know this?" he asked, quiet again.

"My mistress taught me these things," she answered.

The old woman, Rafe thought to himself. *This child has been well trained. I would know more about the old one she calls Mistress.* "Prepare your salve," he commanded.

The child complied. Rafe watched as she selected and measured each ingredient; prepared those that needed to be chopped, ground, or boiled; mixed them in their proper order; and then rendered the preparation down until it was an emollient. When the salve had cooled, the child stood before Rafe and waited, as she had done many times before while her mistress judged her potions. Rafe looked at the child and considered for a moment whether or not to accept it.

"Apply your salve," he ordered, and she did.

A Dangerous Situation

When the child returned with the ingredients her mistress had requested, she relayed her encounter with the being in the storeroom. The old woman found her report disturbing.

"Describe the features of the creature you treated," ordered the old woman.

The child gave a careful and detailed description of the features she observed. "He appeared to be a hybrid—part man, part horned animal. He was intelligent and could speak in the common language. His voice was very coarse, yet he spoke clearly enough for me to understand every word he said." The old woman stood quite still. She had heard of these features through guards' idle talk. Now she was deeply concerned that this *H. transformans* was Rafe Cassius. *Why is he here?* she wondered. *What does he know? Does he suspect—or at least question—our origin?*

"What did you prepare for him, and how did he respond?" asked the old woman.

The child replied, "I prepared an antiseptic salve from essential oils of oregano and menthol, then added aloe in its preparation. As his wounds absorbed these agents, there was gradual lessening of the tension in his features, and he leaned back against a crate. Shortly thereafter, his eyes closed. Yet I'm certain he remained fully awake. When he did not stir, I left him and returned with the ingredients you requested."

Now, the old woman had a sense of foreboding. Unwittingly, the child may have benefited the one being who posed the greatest threat to her. She may have given this hybrid a reason to kidnap her—not because she might be able to transform, but because she could treat his wounds. The old woman knew the two of them needed to leave the village undetected as soon as possible. This meant freeing the dragoness as well.

Chapter 14

A Diversion

Under the care of the old woman and her apprentice, the dragoness's condition gradually improved and with it her energy level. She was less lethargic and appeared favorably disposed toward her caregivers. The old woman knew that the dragoness's breath had been restored. She had seen it and had exposed the child to it in limited doses. Whether or not the dragoness could breathe fire was unknown. If not, the old woman was certain her mate could—and, undoubtedly, would.

An Alliance

The dragoness had long been aware of the old woman's thoughts through the latter's discussions with the child. Thus, she was aware also of the nature of the old woman's species (*H. transformans*) and sensed not only a high capability to transform but also a high level of ability. In contrast, the dragoness sensed no such capability or ability in the child. Once the dragoness was certain of the old woman's intentions, she began to communicate with her. At a pitch just barely audible to humans, she relayed why she was still alive. "The human known as Cassius wants to use my eggs—my genes—to create a dragon of his own making. This I cannot allow. Cassius will destroy them to get my DNA. So I have been eating them. Even though I destroy my own eggs, they provide me with some food. If I am discovered, Cassius will know the real reason he has no eggs."

Both the old woman and the dragoness knew the implications if Cassius learned of the dragoness's deception. Even if he did not kill her because her mate remained nearby, he might prevent them from ever being together again. Thus, the dragoness and the old woman forged an alliance that might free all of them.

The dragoness was bound by three chains—one at each back leg and one at her neck. Each chain was attached to an iron collar around each leg and her neck. The other end of each chain was embedded at equal distances around the tower's walls and was sealed. If the dragoness ever pulled the chains out, the tower would collapse upon her. One of the solutions the old woman prepared—ostensibly to treat the dragoness's wounds—was, in truth, to treat her heavy chains. It was a dilute solution of sulfuric acid (H_2SO_4), a highly corrosive agent, which would dissolve the iron from which the chains were forged. Due to the narrow confines of the chamber, a concentrated solution could not be used. There was too great a risk that the dragoness's scales would come in contact with the corrosive and be seriously damaged.

The old woman carefully assessed the links of each chain. Each link was large and heavy, so it would be best to leave as little length of chain as possible. Too many links could prevent the dragoness from taking flight. Yet the links could not be so close to her that her scales would come in contact with the solution. Some links were not as thick as others and would wear down more quickly. Yet the changes made to the chains also needed to be sufficiently subtle to fool the guards. If they noticed anything at all, they would think the changes were little more than dirt, grime, and rust. Finally, the old woman identified the most suitable links to treat with the acid.

The old woman and child stayed and treated the dragoness and her chains for several more days. During this time, the old woman was devising a strategy to flee from the village and escape to Erwina. It was urgent that they leave as soon as possible. Coming to this village had put her and the child in danger; however, it had also put them considerably closer to Erwina's territory. There were two major problems to overcome: how to leave without being seen or missed and how to set the dragoness free. If the latter could be accomplished, then the resulting excitement—and turmoil—would create a diversion that would cover their escape.

As fate would have it, a different diversion was in the offing.

Assault on the Village

After Rafe's attack on their forces at H'Aleth, the co-owners of the Biogenics Corporation did not let the assault go unanswered. They reassembled their remaining forces, resupplied, conscripted additional troops, and plotted their revenge on Rafe. Since Rafe had denied them the assets they could have gained from H'Aleth, they determined to recoup at least some of their losses by draining Rafe's resources. Thus, Biogenics's commanders had been launching sudden skirmishes—hit-and-run attacks—on multiple fronts at once and then quickly retreating to hide, only to launch others elsewhere. Not even a dragon can be in two places at once, much less three or four. The commanders had recognized that some their attacks triggered the dragon's response whereas others did not. So far, they had not discerned any pattern. So it was by chance alone that Biogenics decided to attack the village where the old woman and the child were treating the dragoness. They had no idea it was protected by a dragon.

The dragoness's mate was away on a hunt when he saw a troop of armed men in the distance. They were traveling on a trajectory that would take them to the village where his mate was imprisoned, and they did not have far to go. Suddenly, he heard the sound of cannon fire. Alarmed, he ceased his hunt immediately and flew back—intent upon driving the attackers away. When he arrived, the village was already under attack. Yet his attention was drawn not to the attackers but to the tower. It was listing and shedding stones from its outer walls—especially from the top of one side. In advance of entering the village, Biogenics's forces had unleashed a bombardment upon it. One of the tower's walls was damaged by a stone missile. This weakened the structure, which had not been maintained for many years. Its collapse seemed inevitable.

Frantic, the dragon began clawing at stones at the top of the tower and pushing them away from it. If the tower was going to fall, he would remove as many of the stones as possible first. In this manner, he might lessen the impact of its collapse upon his mate. The tower was about fifteen feet taller than he was. In order to work from the top down, he had to stand up on his back legs. His size was too large and heavy to sustain a standing position for long. So he alternated between standing upright and hovering to pull the stones away. Yet he could only hover for a moment lest his wing beat shatter the damaged tower and it collapse on his mate.

The old woman and the child had been tending to the dragoness's wounds when the assault on the village began. They were in the tower when it was struck by the missile. The old woman knew that she and the child had to get out, as much to avoid detection and capture as to avoid being killed themselves. The old woman was determined to free the dragoness before the tower collapsed, but she feared for the child's safety. "Leave the tower now," she ordered. "Run toward the nearest copse of trees and hide there." To the old woman's surprise and consternation, the child refused.

Both of them immediately ceased applying medicinal salves and began applying as much corrosive as possible to the chain links they had been working to break. If the dragoness could be freed from her chains, she might be able to break free of the tower. If not, the tower would collapse, raining tons of rock and mortar down into the silo, killing her and possibly the old woman and child. When the dragoness's mate began his assault on the tower, the danger from falling debris became even greater.

As the attack on the enclave become more intense, the tower walls were reverberating. More of its stones were loosening. The guards had already fled the tower—and the dragon—and were trying to escape the onslaught as well. The dragon held his fire. If his mate could not fly, he did not want to start a raging fire from which she could not escape.

Since there were no guards to confront the old woman, she prepared a much stronger corrosive solution to use on the chains. "Get one of their axes," the old woman ordered, "and strike at the links where they are weakest." The child took an ax left behind by one of the guards and began striking the treated links. Where a fracture appeared, the old woman applied more corrosive. In this manner, the chains started to degrade quickly.

In an attempt to break the weakened links, the dragoness began to pull against the chains with as much force as she could muster. In doing so, her body struck against the walls of the tower. This only served to loosen its stones even more. As conditions deteriorated, the dragoness became more aggressive in her attempts. When the dragon saw his mate thrashing about in the chamber, he bade her be still while he continued to remove stones from the top down.

There was a lull in the bombardment as the attackers entered the village. Then, they saw a Great Gray dragon clawing at the tower, and he saw them. As he reared back in a fury to spew his fire directly upon them, the attackers fled in a rout. The dragon returned to removing stones from the tower. There would be little time before the attackers would unleash their bombardment again, aiming directly at him. As the dragon clawed away at the tower, more chunks of stone and mortar were raining into the chamber. The dragoness was not the only one being pelted by these fragments. She reared up as far as she could to shield the old woman and child from the fragments while they worked to free her. This served to keep her still, as her mate had directed.

Escape

Finally, a link in one of the chains split open. Moments later, another one gave way. Only one remained—the one about the dragoness's neck. This had been the most difficult and dangerous to treat. One had to stand directly in line with the breath of a dragoness. Still, the old woman had found an accessible link that was more rusted than the others. It, too, had to be treated with the stronger corrosive. The dragoness turned her head aside to allow the application of the corrosive.

By this time, the dragoness's mate had rendered the side of the tower struck by the missile down to about thirty-five feet high. The rest of the tower was beginning to crumble in earnest. The dragoness's head was now just above the wall of the damaged side. The dragoness told the old woman to leave with the child. She and her mate were about to make a final assault together on the tower walls in an effort to bring them down around her—not upon her.

The old woman and child fled the tower. When they looked back, they saw the dragoness whip her head and neck around to one side, breaking the chain on her iron collar. The old woman was surprised. *Appearances can be deceiving*, she thought. *The dragoness is much stronger than she seemed.*

Then the dragoness and her mate both pushed against the weakened section of the tower—she from within pushing directly outward and he pushing at an angle to direct the remaining wall away from her. The section gave way, tearing a gaping hole in the side of the tower. The dragoness was free. Although she still had chains dragging from her neck and legs, she tried to hover. After a few practice attempts, she was light enough and had strength enough to lift off the ground and become airborne. Her splinted wing helped her stay aloft, but it would prevent her from achieving much altitude or speed.

Before the two dragons departed, the old woman turned to the dragoness and requested, "Cast your breath in a golden glow over the child." The old woman knew that a dragon's breath was a potent accelerant both for activating a transforming X chromosome and the genes of any alternate species an *H. transformans* might have. This was the primary reason why the old woman had exposed the child to the dragoness. To prevent damage or injury, she had gradually increased the amount of time the child spent in the presence of the dragoness and, therefore, the amount of time she was exposed to the dragoness's breath. Now, it was imperative that the child come of age as quickly as possible.

The dragoness did as the old woman requested—knowing full well her intent. Thus the genes of other species within the child were activated. The old woman could not know this yet, for it takes time for such changes to occur even with the use of an accelerant. *Was it enough?* she wondered. She had no way to test the child for the effects, if any, until the child attempted a transformation. There was no question that the child had the genetic capability to do so. Her lineage assured it.

As the dragon lifted off with his mate to return to their home range, he turned to seek out the forces that had bombarded the village. Spotting them with their machines of war, he flew over them with a searing flame, destroying all their machines and anyone in them. He would do the same to Cassius if he ever encountered him again.

Now, the old woman and the child must slip away and disappear as quickly as possible. In setting fire to Biogenics's war machines, once again a Great Gray dragon provided the old woman and the child with cover for their escape.

CHAPTER 15

Flight to Erwina

The old woman immediately set forth with the child to Erwina. It was critical that she deliver her there and, in so doing, return her to her kinsmen. Many of them had fled to Erwina before H'Aleth was attacked. It was also the nearest sanctuary and a place where the child could develop her abilities.

When the old woman had been summoned to the village, she and the child had traveled on horseback, which made the journey far less arduous. Now, they would have to travel on foot again. Since they could not risk being seen, they could not use any of the bridges across the river Pices [*pī*-cēs]. Fortunately, this river was relatively narrow and its waters much calmer than those of the Aguila. Even so, it proved taxing for an old badger to cross with a child who could not swim. The old woman was exhausted when they reached the far shore (map 6). It was the last river she would cross.

Map 6. Flight to Erwina.

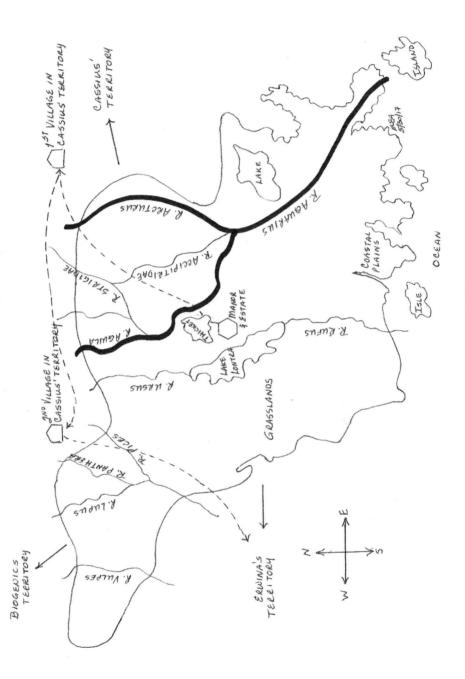

Geographically, the Houses of H'Aleth and Erwina had been the closest of the three Houses. Erwina was situated to the west of H'Aleth. Gregor was much farther away in the north-northeast and was quite remote. Erwina's region was bordered by mountains to the north, extending east and west, and by open areas of territory to the far northeast, typically claimed by the Biogenics Corporation, and to the east claimed by the Cassius Foundation. Both organizations contested the east-northeast region, claiming it for their own. With the destruction of H'Aleth, Cassius also claimed the southeast. When the old woman and the child fled toward Erwina, they traveled in a west-southwest direction. By this route, they traveled through territory claimed by Cassius that was largely unoccupied and, thus, avoided the contested areas where skirmishes between Biogenics and Cassius were common.

Watchful Waiting

As they traveled, the old woman kept watch over the child—both for signs she could transform or signs that she had been damaged. The old woman had taken a great risk. The dragoness's breath would have altered the normal timeline for transformation. Once the genes of other species were activated, the outcome could be disastrous.

The old woman was uncertain how soon the child would be able to transform. Thus, she could not know for certain into which species the child could transform. She knew well which alternate species her mother possessed; however, she knew nothing of the sire. So the old woman exposed the child to the many mammals they encountered along their way—fawns, *foxes*, dogs, horses, deer, *wolves*, goats, sheep, milk cows, *cougars*, lynx, *river otters*, badgers, beavers, and many others both small and large. She also pointed out *falcons, hawks*, eagles, osprey, *owls*, and vultures seen along the way. She did this to see if the child showed any inclination to transform. The old woman noted with some resignation that the child wanted more to be with an animal than to become one. The old woman could not see the significant effect this exposure truly was having. Unbeknownst to her, the child already possessed the capability to transform. Now the genes of other species that she had inherited were awakening rapidly.

Well before the House of H'Aleth fell to dragon fire, the old woman had told the child that she, too, would be able to transform. Barring some genetic mishap, her lineage assured it. When the child would be able transform and into what species remained to be seen. Since the child was only eight years old at the time, these questions would not be answered for a few years yet.

In the meantime, the old woman had taught the child about the process of transformation, the dangers involved, and the consequences of trying to force one. To emphasize the latter, the old woman described cases of corrupted transformation that she had seen. Most of the consequences had been dire, and some were quite gruesome.

When the child asked how she would know what her alternate species were, the old woman replied, "You will sense a kinship with the animal regardless of its species." The old woman then warned the child, "Do not confuse a sense of kinship with caring for or loving another animal or being attracted to another animal because of its characteristics. These feelings represent an attraction to the animal rather than a sense of being the animal."

Yet it required experience and guidance to distinguish kinship from attraction. Hence, nearly all children would mistake an attraction to a particular animal and a longing to become that animal for a sense of kinship. So when a child was physically able to transform, they were taught to wait quietly—perhaps even sleep—to see if a transformation gradually took place. Children were admonished never to force a transformation.

The children of H'Aleth learned these lessons in the House of Erwina. There, they attended school and received formal instruction in transformation and were closely supervised when learning to transform. The old woman had not sent the child to Erwina. The child learned all she knew about transformation from her mistress, who now was tiring and could no longer keep watch over her. The child knew she would have to be very careful if she sensed a transformation. Waiting proved to be a useful tactic.

Kinship

The journey to Erwina on foot proved to be longer than anticipated. The old woman was moving more slowly—especially when walking up a steep incline or over rough terrain. She needed to stop more frequently to rest and catch her breath. The child assumed more and more of the tasks that must be done to sustain their trip—making a shelter, starting a fire, preparing food, and removing any trace of their passage. She also prepared potions from plants she found in the area to help ease her mistress's distress when she could no longer walk or catch her breath. One of these was a weak tea made from leaves of the foxglove and dandelion plants (app. E). This would strengthen her heartbeat and ease her labored breathing. She would prepare a potion from the roots of valerian to help her mistress rest.

The child's greatest difficulty was in finding and preparing soups that would entice her mistress to eat. Despite the exertions of travel, the old woman had no appetite, and she had lost weight. A small amount of lentil soup, where lentils could be found growing in the wild, was most successful. Lentils provided a good source of vegetable protein and carbohydrates, B vitamins, and minerals (iron and zinc).

Where possible, they camped among trees—preferably with dense underbrush and near rapidly flowing streams. The trees and underbrush kept them hidden, and the streams provided fresh water for drinking and cooking. As her mistress rested, the child would scout out their surroundings looking for herbs, nuts, berries, and other sources of food. During these times, she transformed into species that were kin to her and would help her find these resources with greater efficiency. She could survey the area for other creatures too, including humans. As a Cooper's hawk, she could scout the area quickly and silently. As a red fox, with its exquisite sense of smell, she quickly located herbs and berries and could detect other animals in the area. As a river otter, she could search for crustaceans to add to soups—and have a nice swim in the process. She was careful never to leave her mistress alone or unobserved for long. As a hawk and a fox, she could look in on her mistress often without disturbing her.

Like Begets Like

Evolution from a common ancestor still left descendants with a large proportion of genes that were closely aligned (homologous). Even after species diverged from that ancestor, the genes for many useful physiologic processes were conserved and passed on to many different branches of descendants. They arose from the same ancestral gene and continued to be used across many classes and species. Many of the physiological processes that underlie life itself (e.g., oxygenation) had a common genetic origin.

Even though different species had different genes coding for their specific phenotypic characteristics, many of their genes and the processes for regulating their expression were quite similar from one species to the next. The genes that coded for muscles and bones were essentially the same. How they were arranged may have been different, resulting in a much different form. The wings of bats and arms of primates were homologous structures derived from the same common ancestor, despite differences in their appearance.

Genetic homology was a saving grace for *H. transformans.* It facilitated the expression of the phenotypes seen in alternative species because gene expression relied largely on the same genetic processes used by all species. Thus, the efficient process of transformation relied fundamentally on not only a transforming X chromosome but also on the conservation and sharing of genes, especially those that regulated gene functions and facilitated gene expression across alternate species. Coupled with the complete genome of another species, it was the percentage of genes that the different species shared that allowed the child to transform into a fox, an otter, and a hawk.

The Passing of H'Ilgraith

After several days of travel, the two finally reached the outskirts of a village well inside Erwina's territory. While still some distance away from the village, they stopped. The old woman decided not to enter it. Her labors not quite done, she lay down for the last time in the shade of a large tree. She knew she would go no farther, and so did the child.

Although the old woman had always been somewhat aloof, seldom had she and the child been separated even while they lived in H'Aleth. Since fleeing to a Cassius village, separations were rare, and the old woman was always close by. Other than brief encounters with other people at H'Aleth and the villagers, the child had known no one else. Now faced with the inevitable loss of her mistress, she was becoming overwhelmed with grief and felt lost.

Just then, the old woman commanded the child's attention. She spoke in short phrases, punctuated by the need to breathe. "Listen, Child, for I must tell you who we are and what you must do when I am gone.

"I am H'Ilgraith, Sister of the House of H'Aleth and a direct descendant of Ruth, its first Mistress. You are H'Ester, also a direct descendant of Ruth and a Sister of the House of H'Aleth. Now, you are its Mistress. All those who would have been Mistress before you are gone—lost when H'Aleth was destroyed. Just before it fell, I stole you away and hid you to keep you safe until your abilities could mature. And now, I cannot finish my task.

"When I am gone, you must travel without delay to the House of Erwina. There you will learn the history of your House and what will be required of you as its Mistress. You must not reveal yourself to anyone until your abilities are fully developed and are at your command. When the time comes, you may yet restore the House of H'Aleth."

H'Ilgraith further commanded H'Ester to tell no one of her past. She should say only that she was a foundling who had been raised by an old woman alone. She should not reveal what she has been taught except to say she was taught how to speak, read, and write in the common language. She should never speak the dialect used in the village where they had lived unless she found herself in the midst of those who use it. She should acknowledge that she had been taught how to prepare basic potions that any child would be taught at home—soups, soaps, and antiseptics. She should not reveal her knowledge of the healing potions except upon need or reveal those she learned in secret. If necessary, she should act ignorant of these things and ask for instruction, even if she already knew how to prepare them. She must continue to recite in her mind and practice unobserved all the potions she had learned to keep her memory of them sharp.

By the end of H'Ilgraith's instructions, H'Ester had regained her composure. "What would you have me do when you are gone? Where shall I bury you?" she asked.

"You must not bury my body!" H'Ilgraith admonished. "Burn it! Leave no trace of it! No one must ever gain access to my DNA for their own design."

"Yes, Mistress," H'Ester replied. She understood what that meant and how it would have to be done.

H'Ester remained beside H'Ilgraith and tended to her until she died the following day. Once again, H'Ester was nearly overcome by sorrow and a sense of being completely alone. Yet she knew she had one last service to perform for her mistress. She regained her composure and waited. By the next day, she had transformed into a red dragoness. With her fire, she burned her mistress's body until there was no trace of it. Not even ashes were left. Once her task was finished, she waited where her mistress had lain until she returned to her human form. Two days after the death of her mistress, H'Ester left the site and turned toward the village. She had decided to enter it to see what she could learn there.

Supplemental Notes and Citations

Phylogenomics

Phylogenomics is the evolutionary history of a group of organisms based on genetic profiles. With the ability to identify and map genomes of many species in multiple classes, efforts to trace the origin of species has changed from an examination of their skeletal features to an analysis of their genetic codes.

A clade is a group of organisms that includes all descendants with a common ancestor. Birds, dinosaurs, and crocodiles all have a common egg-laying ancestor. The monotremes (e.g., duck-billed platypus, etc.) also lay eggs; however, they have a different ancestor. The monotremes are mammals. Within the mammalian class, there are three subclasses. Placental mammals are by far the largest subclass. Marsupials and monotremes comprise the other two much smaller subclasses.

Gene Conservation and Homology

All multicellular organisms, including *H. sapiens,* are comprised of an advanced type of cell, the eukaryotic cell. These cells contain specialized organelles not found in more primitive organisms (e.g., prokaryotes). One of these is the nucleus in which DNA is organized as chromosomes. Among many others are the mitochondria, which provide approximately 95% of a eukaryotic cell's energy requirements. They have genes of their own and are thought to be adapted from bacteria that became integrated into eukaryotic cells.

Many useful genes and gene sequences have been handed down from a common ancestor and reused across many classes and species (Manda et al., 2016; Nitta et al., 2015; Ohta and Flajnik, 2015; Shorey-Kendrick et al., 2015; Wells et al., 2015). The genes for the renin-angiotensin-aldosterone system, a critical system in the regulation of fluid balance in vertebrates, including humans, has been conserved for millennia (Fournier et al., 2012). The genetic code for the amino acid tryptophan (UGG) is the same in bacteria, plants, and mammals, including humans. These genes and others like them serve to show to what extent different classes of animals share a common genetic background.

Approximately 92% of all mammals are genetically similar. The genetic homology within *H. sapiens* is approximately 99.9%. Among other members of the genus *Homo*, it is approximately 99.5%. The degree of genetic homology between humans and other primate species is very close (approximately 95% with chimpanzees). The degree of homology between humans and other mammals decreases as differences between families increase (approximately 90% with cats, 80% with dogs, 60%–70% with mice and rats). There is even some homology between humans (mammalian class) and other classes such as birds (approximately 50–60% with chickens), insects (approximately 60% with the fruit fly), and even fish. Zebrafish have been found to have high genetic homology to humans (Goldsmith and Jobin, 2012).

PART III

In the House of Erwina

CHAPTER 16

A Chance Encounter

As H'Ester approached the village, she compared its setting with that of her village in H'Aleth. There would be no comparison with the Cassius village.

A Rustic Setting

The village appeared to be rural and located in an agricultural setting (app. G). It had a marketplace and a single building of modest size made with wood. There were no stone buildings or any complex of buildings. There were several small structures scattered not too far away. These appeared to be made primarily of thatch and were likely the villagers' homes.

With one singular exception, the villages in Erwina were small and rustic. This was quite deliberate. Erwina's people decided it would be prudent to keep their lives as simple and unobtrusive as possible, especially in those regions closest to H'Aleth. These areas were also closest to Biogenics's and Cassius's territories and so were at great risk of becoming encompassed by the rivalry between them. After the conflagration at H'Aleth, the people of Erwina shifted their emphasis to saving lives and not possessions should a dragon come to call.

As H'Ester approached the village, she noted that everyone appeared to have normal features. She could not tell who was an *H. sapiens* or an *H. transformans* (if anyone). She found this situation striking. Given where she had lived for the past year, it seemed almost surreal. H'Ester stood for a while and studied the people as they moved about the streets—their appearance, what they were doing, how they acted toward each other, and their speech patterns. She would emulate these patterns and behaviors as much as possible. Given the suspicions that can attend a stranger, H'Ester did not want to appear too alien to the village people. Unfortunately, she could do nothing about being dressed in a smock made from a grain sack.

Deja Vu

Many of the villagers seemed hurried—as if time were of the essence. She watched as an older woman shepherded several children toward one of two horse-drawn covered wagons. Although of mature age, the woman was still younger than H'Ester's mistress. She was clearly in charge of the group of children, who represented a wide range of ages and included both boys and girls. Two of them—a boy and a girl, both about H'Ester's age—were helping the woman guide the rest of the children to the wagon.

While H'Ester was observing this activity, the older woman noticed her. For a moment, they looked at each other. To H'Ester, the woman's countenance and manner seemed vaguely familiar—perhaps not unlike that of her mistress, although not nearly as stern or taciturn. To the woman, H'Ester, too, seemed strangely familiar yet completely unknown—perhaps, it was her demeanor as she stood quietly and observed their activities.

Then one of the woman's younger charges called out, "Matron, are we leaving now?" With the woman's attention drawn to the youngster, H'Ester turned away. She still had not learned in which direction from the village her destination lay—south or west—and needed to learn more before she could choose her path. Once again, she was feeling the loss of her mistress, who always seemed to know what to do and which way to go.

In the meantime, the two older children in the group H'Ester had been watching were helping the younger ones into the wagon. This allowed the matron, Matron Trevora [trĕ-vōr-ah], to turn her attention once again to H'Ester. She was concerned. Clearly, the girl was a stranger in town, unattended and without provisions. Her attire was a long dress, simple and undecorated, and made from a coarse material that was not native to Erwina. *Who is this girl, and what is she doing here?* she wondered and decided to inquire.

Although H'Ester had turned away, she could still see the woman approach her. H'Ester turned toward the woman and waited. When the woman was six feet away, a proper distance between strangers, she stopped and stood still. In the common language, she remarked in a polite but formal tone, "You are not from this region. May I be of assistance?"

H'Ester had been considering the woman as she approached. "Thank you," H'Ester replied, also in the common language and in a formal tone. "Can you tell me in what direction lies the House of Erwina?"

"Yes," the woman replied. "May I ask first why you wish to know?"

"My mistress bade me go there," H'Ester replied.

H'Ester sensed the woman grow very still, although her countenance did not change. Matron Trevora had not heard the title Mistress spoken since the fall of H'Aleth. Could this girl be a spy sent by Biogenics or Cassius? This seemed unlikely. Surely, both would know that students in the House of Erwina addressed their teachers as matron, madam, or master. Could she have come from Gregor? This was even less likely. The House of Gregor would have sent notice to Erwina that they were sending a new student. Furthermore, they would never have sent one of their members on such a trek alone and without provisions. This situation was quite unusual. The girl standing before her was a mystery. Still, Matron Trevora did not sense a threat. So she introduced herself without stating her origin.

"I am Matron Trevora. May I ask your name?"

H'Ester had to think quickly. She reverted to the name her mistress had always used. "I am called Child," she replied.

"Do you not have a formal name?" Matron Trevora asked.

"It is the only name my mistress used when she called me," H'Ester replied, quite truthfully.

"May I speak with your mistress?" Matron Trevora asked.

"No," H'Ester replied quietly. "My mistress is gone. She died two days ago." Once again, a sense of profound sadness crept over her. She stilled it quickly, but not quickly enough. The woman who called herself Matron Trevora recognized it, and empathy helped her to make her decision.

"I and my charges travel to the House of Erwina," she stated. "Would you like to join us?" If the girl agreed, it would provide an opportunity to observe her at length. By covered wagon and with small children, the trip would take four days. Should the girl reveal herself to be a threat, there would be time to address the matter before they arrived at their destination.

Even so, Matron Trevora was taking a significant risk in allowing this stranger to travel with her and her charges.

H'Ester also decided to take the risk. She, too, had sensed no threat from Matron Trevora. Although it was possible that the woman was stealing children to take to Cassius, this seemed unlikely. The children did not appear stressed or fearful, and most were much too young to have come of age. Unless Cassius and Biogenics had changed their modus operandi, there were only two in the group that might be of interest to them and only if they were *H. transformans*.

CHAPTER 17

Ruwena

The older girl who had helped Matron Trevora get her charges on the wagon clearly was quite capable of accepting responsibility. Hence, Matron Trevora allowed her to proctor the younger girls. The older boy shouldered the same responsibility for the younger boys in the group. When H'Ester joined the children, who were on the first covered wagon, the older girl promptly assumed responsibility for H'Ester as well. She had been briefed by Matron Trevora to keep a watchful eye on the newcomer and why.

Ruwena

The older girl approached H'Ester directly and announced, "My name is Savannah. I will be your guide on the trip back to the manor." Savannah was a slender girl, with shoulder-length blond hair and an effervescent personality. "What is your name?" she asked.

This time, H'Ester was prepared for the question. "My mistress called me Child. She used no other name for me."

Savannah was surprised at this revelation; however, she recovered quickly and declared, "Well, there are too many children here—and even more where we are going—to call you Child. We—meaning you and I—need to give you a name, preferably one that no one else has. That way, your name will be unique to you. Do you have any ideas?"

H'Ester didn't have the slightest idea. It had never occurred to her to devise a name for herself. Furthermore, all the names she knew were

131

either those of people in H'Aleth, which could reveal her origin, or in the dialect of the village she had left. Even if there had been a name she liked, she could not use it. "What name would you suggest?" she asked of Savannah.

Savannah suggested several names. H'Ester stopped her when she spoke the name Ruwena [roo-wē-nah]. H'Igraith had told H'Ester that she was descended from Ruth—a name H'Ester knew intuitively she should not use. So she selected Ruwena as a surrogate.

"Ruwena," H'Ester said to Savannah. Thus, as Savannah introduced H'Ester to the others traveling with the wagon, H'Ester became known as Ruwena. Even Matron Trevora seemed to find the name suitable.

An Urgent Departure

The two wagons were joined by an escort of four horsemen. Ruwena (née H'Ester) could discern that the men were armed, albeit discreetly. She had observed one of the men, Barrow, speaking to Matron Trevora earlier. He had heard rumors that Biogenics had bombarded a Cassius village not too far from Erwina's border with H'Aleth. Moments ago, one of his fellow scouts confirmed the attack had occurred. It was likely that Rafe had already launched his counterattack. Thus, there was an urgency to return home with the children in case the quid pro quo between Cassius and Biogenics spilled over the border into Erwina's territory, as it had at H'Aleth.

Erwina's territory was sliced into uneven sections by rivers coming down from the mountains and passing through its territory (map 7). At one time, Erwina shared open territory with H'Aleth. After H'Aleth's fall, Cassius claimed H'Aleth's territory and a portion of the open territory west of it. Biogenics contested this claim, especially the northwestern reaches of H'Aleth. Hence, the two adversaries battled for possession of what had once been H'Aleth's territory.

"We need to leave quickly," Barrow said grimly. "Now, if possible."

Matron Trevora had been aware of the rumors and had planned to leave as soon as possible. "We are ready to go now," she replied. *Could the unknown girl we now know as Ruwena be a refugee from this fight?* She wondered. This, too, seemed unlikely. The girl had been taught proper manners by someone, most likely her mistress—another unknown.

Map 7. Erwina Territory.

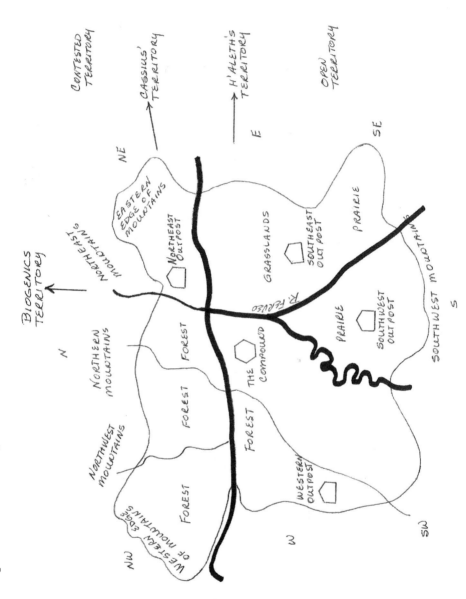

As the wagon with its passengers left the village, the second wagon fell in behind it. Ruwena noticed that the second wagon was packed full of supplies—sacks of grain (oats and barley) and peanuts, wooden crates of fruit (oranges, lemons, and grapefruit), rolls of cloth woven from cotton and wool, and stacks of tightly rolled and compacted stalks of reeds and dried grasses.

There were no roads leading out of the village. The terrain was flat and covered with thick grasses over which the wagon and horses traversed without difficulty. Tracks left by their passage were quickly erased when the grasses, briefly pushed down by wheels and hooves, sprang back into place. Based on the direction the wagon was going, it was clear the company was headed away from the territories occupied by Cassius and Biogenics.

There was little to do during the ensuing four days. Ruwena had not been assigned to any tasks, so she offered her assistance. Savannah took advantage of the offer. If Ruwena proved helpful, it would ease some of the workload on Savannah while providing an opportunity for her to observe Ruwena. In the same manner, Ruwena used the opportunity to learn more about Erwina and its people. Ruwena remained mindful of H'Ilgraith's admonitions that she act ignorant of practices that perhaps she should not know. This proved to be quite a balancing act. Ruwena had to decide on a moment's notice what Savannah expected her to know. She discovered that there were many things Savannah thought Ruwena should know, which she did not, and many others that she shouldn't know and did.

While they traveled across the plains, Ruwena observed several mammalian and bird species—some of which she recognized. In order to avoid revealing what she knew, Ruwena asked Savannah about all of them. They spotted a red fox taking quick short hops in the grass—clearly after something it was trying to catch. They watched a small group of mule deer, who, in turn, were watching them from a distance. At one point, a red-tailed hawk soared in the southern sky. Later, they watched a peregrine falcon in a dive for an unseen prey animal—probably a mole or a mouse. Savannah was also on the lookout for a red wolf and a brown bear, but she didn't see either one on this trip. Savannah was careful not to mention that some of these animals could be Erwina scouts who had transformed into their alternate species for purposes of surveillance. Savannah also pointed out the different types of grains—wheat, rye, and barley—that were scattered throughout the plains grasses. Ruwena found Savannah well-informed about plants, animals, birds, and other natural species within Erwina's territory.

The Angry River

Eventually, Ruwena noted changes in their terrain as they began to go up a ridge. The area was becoming forested with trees that grew denser as they ascended the ridge. It was along this ridge that they spotted a Cooper's hawk. The ground became progressively more littered with rocks as the number of rocky outcroppings and boulders increased.

There was no road over the ridge; however, there was a faint trail where wagon wheels had left their mark on the forest floor. The trail guided the drivers through the forest and up the ridge. As they crested the ridge, Ruwena could see the valley below and a wide river that coursed through it. As they came nearer to the river, Ruwena could see the water flowing at a very rapid rate.

"That is the Ferveo [fĕr-vē-o] River," Savannah told her. "We will cross it here."

Ruwena was surprised. "Here?" she asked, mindful of the other rivers she and her mistress had crossed.

"Yes," Savannah answered. "Below here, the riverbed falls steeply toward dangerous rapids farther down."

"How do we cross it?" Ruwena asked. Clearly, the river was too deep and the water was flowing too fast for a wagon to cross and she could see no bridge.

"We will ferry across it," Savannah replied.

Across that river? Ruwena thought to herself. She could see no signs of a ferry, dock, or boats anywhere. She would learn later that the Erwinians built no physical means for crossing any of the rivers. After the destruction of H'Aleth, they had destroyed the bridges that had once supported traffic between Erwina and its sister House. Where there were no such structures, they could not be used by an enemy or burned by a dragon. All crossings required small flat-bottomed barges, rowboats, canoes, or kayaks that could be hidden in dark crevices, shallow caves among the rocks, or under rocky ledges at the waterline. Entrances were either too small to be noticed or could be camouflaged by rocks and river debris.

The men on horseback rode ahead of the wagon and down to the river where they disappeared from view. A short time later, a wide flat-bottomed barge came into view. The wagons with their horses and the men with their mounts moved onto the barge, which had been secured temporarily against a rock formation that jutted out into the river. After the wagons with their

135

passengers and goods and the horses were secured, the barge was released from its mooring. Three of the men, the older boy Erik, and Savannah all grasped poles and pushed the barge into the river. Barrow took the tiller as the barge's helmsman. Matron Trevora and Ruwena had secured the younger children inside their wagon and remained with them to keep them calm and reassured. Although Ruwena maintained her composure, she was anything but assured. She copied the manner in which Matron Trevora braced herself for the river crossing and held on.

The river swiftly pulled the barge downstream while Barrow steered the craft at an angle toward the opposite side of the river. The barge heaved first one way, then another, as the current raced toward the rapids. Those manning the poles struggled to keep the craft away from the rocks and boulders jutting out of the riverbed. The children in the wagon struggled to keep from being tossed around as the wagon heaved with the barge. It was a tumultuous ride, to say the least. From one moment to the next, Ruwena thought the barge would crash on the rocks or overturn. It was an entirely new and altogether harrowing experience for her.

The actions of those keeping the barge away from the rocks also helped propel it toward the opposite bank of the river. Barrow steered the barge toward another large boulder that jutted out into the river. There, a shallow eddy swirled on its near side. As the barge reached it, the waters became much calmer. The craft was poled to the shore and secured without further ado. Finally, Ruwena could take a breath.

The landing place was a small stretch of sandy beach well below the top of the riverbank. Once again, there was a narrow path with faint wagon tracks leading to the top. The children, Ruwena, and Matron Trevora disembarked from the wagon and the ferry. Then Matron, Savanna, Ruwena, and Erik helped the smaller children up the side of the bank using whatever hand- and footholds they could find. This allowed the horses to pull the wagons up the narrow path to the top of the bank. Meanwhile, the men with their horses had pulled the barge into the shadows of the rocks, camouflaged it so it would not be seen from the far shore, and erased all signs of the landing. Then the horsemen followed the wagon up the path. As they did so, the last horse dragged behind it a large hardwood shrub that was leafless and dead. The shrub's sharp, broken branches scraped away the marks left by the wagon's wheels and the horses' hooves. The shrub was left in place at the top of the path to block it.

CHAPTER 18

Another World

The remainder of the trip to Erwina's main village occurred without incident. The travelers had encountered no adversaries along the way, and Ruwena had seen no hybrids or corrupted creatures of any kind. Nevertheless, there was no dawdling on this trip. After the destruction of H'Aleth, the prolonged quid pro quo skirmishes between Biogenics and Cassius had kept the two adversaries occupied. For a while, this had brought a time of relative quietude to Erwina's settlements to the south and west—if not to its northern and northeastern villages. Still, the people of Erwina knew that they were the next target for acquisition. So Erwinians were cautious when newcomers arrived.

The Manor House

As the wagon approached a much larger village, Ruwena saw the northeastern mountains and forests that formed its backdrop. The village itself was quite extensive and was laid out like a compound (illus. 12). Even though it was fortified, the permanent residents chose to keep the fortifications unobtrusive. They wanted their home to appear friendly and familiar to the young children who had left their families to live in Erwina. This also kept their fortifications more secure. Although visitors were uncommon, any who did come would not be able to report on Erwina's defenses—willingly or otherwise.

Illus. 12. The Compound.

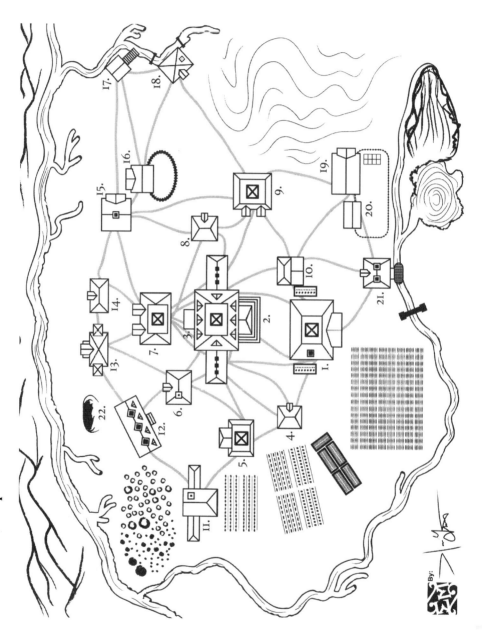

As they entered the village grounds, Savannah pointed out small grain fields where the residents grew wheat and rye. "We really can't grow much grain here," she said. "The fields are for teaching us about grains and how to grow them." She also pointed out the granary and mill. Ruwena noticed many gardens to the west and groves of trees to the northwest. "We can grow plenty of fruits and vegetables," Savannah reported.

Ruwena saw Barrow ride ahead to a large stone structure—the first of many other stone structures laid out behind it. One in particular towered above all the others. As the children's wagon halted in front of the first stone building, Ruwena asked Savannah, "What is this place?"

"This is the manor house," replied Savannah. "It is where everyone comes who has been away from the village and where all visitors come first. Since we are returning home and you are a visitor, all of us will be greeted here before we go any farther."

Indeed, the manor house was where everyone came upon returning from an expedition or a trading mission or any other activity that took them outside the compound. Here, they would be met by family and friends and given refreshments before giving an account of their adventures to others who expressed an interest in them, especially security. Hence, the manor served as both a welcome center and a security checkpoint without appearing to be the latter.

So it was at the manor house where Matron Trevora recounted to Head Matron Aquina [a-*quī*-nah], head of the House of Erwina, and Headmaster Morenavik [mōr-*rein*-ă-vĭk], dean of the schoolhouse, and Master Titus [*tĭ*-tus], chief of security, what had happened in the southeastern outpost. Subsequently, Matron Aquina summoned Savannah to join them.

Savannah did not need to be told why she was being summoned. She was well prepared to engage with them. She had decided that Ruwena was not a threat and definitely needed to be educated. "Ruwena is behind for someone her age," she announced to the faculty.

A member of the manor house showed the children, including Ruwena, where they could refresh themselves before having afternoon tea. Then, Ruwena and the other children entered a room with a table set for tea. It was almost exactly like the teas her mistress had taught her to set up. To Ruwena's dismay, some of the food appeared to be made with meat. Her mistress had forbidden her to eat anything made of meat since there was no way of knowing whether its source was corrupted. Eggs from birds and milk and cheese from cows and goats were acceptable alternatives.

So she deferred selecting anything until a plate of muffins and bread was passed around the table. She would learn later that no meat was used in the preparation of any of Erwina's food.

A New Home

Shortly thereafter, Matron Trevora returned with Savannah. Matron Trevora dismissed the younger children and directed Erik to take them back to their living quarters. Then she spoke to Ruwena, "We do not know who you are or who your mistress was. Still, we invite you to stay in Erwina, if you wish to do so. Be advised, however, that there are rules for living here. You will be expected to comply with them. In addition, we will expect you to attend school as would any other child in Erwina so that you can become a responsible adult. In return, we ask the same of you as we do of all our members. Do everything in your power to protect and defend your new home and everyone who lives here with you—especially the children. What would you like to do?"

I could have a new home, Ruwena thought to herself. "I would like to stay," she replied, "and I will do my best, as my mistress would expect me to do." Ruwena heard nothing in the arrangement that would not have met with her mistress's approval, and it allowed her to follow her mistress's bidding. She would still need to be careful lest Matron Trevora disapprove of some of the things her mistress had taught her.

Savannah was pleased with Ruwena's decision. Matron Trevora directed Savannah to continue mentoring Ruwena while she became acclimated to the compound, in general, and to the school, in particular. In fact, Ruwena needed to learn almost everything a four-year-old child needed to learn upon arriving at Erwina, especially the House rules (box 7). "The rules are intended to keep students safe," Savannah explained. "As you advance from one form to the next, you will have more flexibility to come and go both inside and outside the compound."

Box 7. House of Erwina Rules.

House of Erwina Rules

1. Students in Forms I–III are not allowed to leave the compound without the escort of a faculty or staff member or a Form IV student authorized to escort students.
2. Form IV students may leave the compound unescorted with permission of the faculty.
3. Students in Forms I and II are not allowed to be outside the schoolhouse at night without an adult escort. Form IV students may serve as adult escorts to students in Forms I–II.
4. Senior Form II students may be allowed outside the schoolhouse at night without an escort with permission of the faculty.
5. Form III and IV students are allowed out of the schoolhouse at night; however, they may not leave the compound at night.
6. Form III *H. transformans* students may transform into their alternate species once they have been certified by faculty to do so; however, they must have someone with them in the event of an adverse transformation. Certified Form IV students may transform at will.
7. Form IV students may be assigned to patrol the compound at night accompanied by a member of the security force.
8. If a student observes anything that seems unfamiliar or anyone they do not recognize, the student will report it to a faculty member or security as soon as possible. When in doubt, ask.
9. In the event of an enemy attack, students are not to engage their attackers unless they have no other option for escape.

Box 7

"What is a form?" asked Ruwena.

"It's the level of schooling in which a student is enrolled at Erwina," Savannah replied. "Form I is the beginning level where we learned to read and write, do basic arithmetic, and learn basic skills needed for everyday life. Almost everyone starts school as a freshman in Form I. I was five years old when I started. Forms II, III, and IV continue with more advanced topics. This will be my senior year as a Form II student. When I graduate, I will return to school as a Form III freshman. Everyone is expected to attend school through Form III, and many of us will go on to Form IV." Thus began Ruwena's first remedial lesson.

The Courtyard

Before taking Ruwena to the schoolhouse, where her quarters still needed to be assigned, Savannah decided that the first order of business was to show Ruwena the rest of the buildings near the manor and the schoolhouse (app. H). Ruwena would need to know which ones they were and how to get to them almost immediately.

"It is important for you to learn your way around so you can find your classes without getting lost," Savannah said. "Students are expected to arrive on time. I will show you most of the buildings today since they are in the courtyard. Then tomorrow, we can tour the grounds and the buildings outside the courtyard."

Most of the buildings were clustered around the schoolhouse, which served as the centerpiece. They stepped briefly inside each building as Savannah identified what it was and its purpose. Moving clockwise from the manor house (which stood at VI on the sundial), Savannah and Ruwena arrived first at the archives, where all the records from the three Houses were stored and referenced. The adjacent natural history and research building (at IX on the sundial) was established in honor and in memory of the House of H'Aleth. Here, many of the people of H'Aleth who had fled to Erwina continued their research on and documentation of the natural history of *H. transformans*.

Next, they entered the medical infirmary where staff treated common injuries and illnesses in humans as well as the adverse effects of transformation. "There is a veterinary clinic also, where veterinarians treat sick and injured domestic and wild animals," Savannah remarked. At the athletics center (XII on the sundial), Savannah showed Ruwena where students participated in sports and learned the skills they needed to protect themselves. Then, they went into the rectory where meals were cooked and served to both students and faculty. The two girls snatched a muffin on their way out.

Then they passed the faculty quarters (III on the sundial). Savannah noted, "They are off-limits to students except in an emergency." Before going to the schoolhouse, they stepped inside the botanical gardens. It housed plants that could not tolerate cold northern temperatures, and it provided a place for seedlings to become established. "It's wonderful," said Ruwena, who wanted to stay longer. Savannah had to pull her out.

During the tour, Ruwena observed several people who worked in the buildings. Conditions appeared to be the same as those at H'Aleth. She saw no one with any deformities, and everyone appeared to be healthy and well nourished. Ruwena began to wonder if her mistress had sent her to Erwina because everyone here belonged to *H. sapiens*. She would be hidden here just as she had been hidden in the Cassius village. Ruwena would learn later that this was not the case.

As the two girls toured the compound, Savannah described how people communicated with one another. Within any given village, including the compound, people usually spoke to one another directly either at a planned time or on an impromptu basis. "If someone in the granary wants to speak with someone in the armory, the person in the granary simply walks over to the armory," she explained. If people couldn't leave their station, they could use a courier, usually a staff member or a student, to carry documents or a message across the village. Communication between villages was a different matter. The long distances precluded methods used within a village. Small messages could be sent via winged couriers trained by staff in the aviary or falconry. If messages needed to be secured or documents needed to be transported, then couriers would be used. Savannah didn't mention that the courier would transform into his or her alternate species for greater ease and speed of travel. The alternate species would be outfitted with a satchel or pouch containing documents or other items.

Savannah also pointed out the five bell towers in the compound: one each on the manor house (the south bell tower), the natural history building (the west bell tower), the athletics building (the north bell tower), the faculty quarters (the east bell tower), and the schoolhouse (the central bell tower). Each bell pealed three times once per day to signal the hour: the south bell tower at 9:00 a.m., the west tower at 12:00 noon, the north tower at 3:00 p.m., the east tower at 6:00 p.m., and the central tower at 9:00 p.m.

Savannah explained, "Each bell tower has a different tone, and you will be expected to learn the tone for each bell tower. This is how you will know when you are late for school or late returning to the dorm at night. Too much tardiness gets you into trouble." Savannah made no mention of the role these bells played in providing a warning system should the compound come under attack.

The last building Savannah showed Ruwena was the schoolhouse. There, they spent the rest of the day.

CHAPTER 19

The Schoolhouse

The schoolhouse was the largest building on the grounds and a very imposing building from Ruwena's perspective. She had never seen a building that large. Prior to coming to Erwina, the tower that imprisoned the dragoness was the tallest building she had seen. The center structure was five stories high. There were two wings connected directly to the school's central building, and they extended at least a hundred feet. As one faced the front of the building, the east wing (on the right hand side) and the west wing (on the left hand side) were two stories high. As Savannah took Ruwena on a tour of the schoolhouse, she briefed her on the schoolhouse rules (box 8). "These are the rules for living in the dormitory. They also tell you what to do in case of an emergency," Savannah remarked and then added, "They can be stifling at times."

A Brief Tour

Savannah described the layout of the schoolhouse as she and Ruwena walked through it (app. I, part 1). "The first floor is mostly faculty offices and conference rooms," she said. "The dormitories are upstairs. Each form has its own dormitory, starting with Form IV on the fifth floor." Both girls were looking at a large and striking center staircase that ascended to all five floors and split all the dormitories in half. "As you graduate from one form to the next, you get to climb more stairs," Savannah added dryly.

Box 8. Schoolhouse Rules.

Schoolhouse Rules

1. Dormitory rooms are to be left unlocked at all times unless students are directed to lock them by faculty or a dormitory supervisor.
2. Since all doors must remain unlocked unless otherwise directed, students will always knock before entering a dormitory room—even their own. If requesting entry to another student's room, the student(s) will wait to be invited to come in before doing so.
3. Students will retire to their rooms promptly at their designated evening hours or when so directed by faculty or a dormitory supervisor.
   Form I—7:00 p.m.
   Form II—freshmen, sophomores—8:00 p.m.; juniors, seniors—10:00 p.m.
   Form III—11:00 p.m.
   Form IV—12:00 midnight unless on a nighttime assignment.
4. Students will follow faculty instructions in classroom laboratories, field practicums, and field expeditions. Be careful and stay alert.
5. Students in Forms II and III will make potions only under the direct supervision of a faculty member.
6. Students in Form IV may make potions independently once certified to do so by a faculty member.
7. In the event of an emergency or evacuation, all students will follow directions given by faculty or a dormitory supervisor or a Form IV student.
8. In the event of an emergency or evacuation, senior Form III students and Form IV students will assist all other students.
9. In the event of an evacuation, all students in each form will exit the schoolhouse via their designated evacuation routes unless otherwise directed by faculty, a dormitory supervisor, or a Form IV student.
10. In the event of a fire or explosion, evacuate the area immediately and sound the alarm.
11. In the event of a small fire (e.g., trashcan or laboratory sink), sound the alarm immediately. Students who are Form II seniors and above may extinguish the fire, if feasible. If not feasible, evacuate the area.
12. Qualified Form II seniors and Form III students may serve as mentors or tutors for students in Form II, upon the recommendation of faculty.
13. Qualified Form IV students may serve as mentors or tutors for students in Forms II and III, upon the recommendation of faculty.

Box 8

Savannah and Ruwena walked up the staircase to the third floor. Behind the center staircase on each floor was the commons, where students from the form could mingle and where they convened at the direction of faculty. "If there is an emergency, this is where we gather to get information and directions for what to do," Savannah said.

On either side of the commons was a corridor leading to the right and left wings. "The boys' rooms are on the right-hand side. Our rooms are on the left," Savannah told Ruwena. "At the end of each wing, there is a staircase that descends from the fifth floor all the way down to the second cellar. This is really important," Savannah emphasized. "The second cellar leads to tunnels on each side of the schoolhouse. We can use them to evacuate the building. You will need to learn where each tunnel goes and how to get to each one."

When Savannah and Ruwena entered the schoolhouse library, Ruwena was astounded. It was enormous, comparatively speaking. H'Aleth's manor house had a small library that housed history, literature, geography, and other resource materials. The natural history building had a large science library. Ruwena had been allowed go to the library in the manor house; however, her mistress forbade her to go to the science library. H'Ilgraith did want not to draw any unwanted attention from the researchers. They were likely to ask questions about the child's parentage. Instead, she would bring some of the texts back to their living quarters, where Ruwena was expected to read them.

There were no books, papers, or writing materials of any kind in a Cassius village. The inhabitants could neither read nor write—not even the guards. It was not allowed. While living there, both Ruwena and her mistress had to behave as if they could not read or write. The fluorescent writing tools proved to be quite useful for teaching and learning lessons when they were away from the village.

Schooling

After Savannah and Ruwena finished their tour of the schoolhouse and library, Madam Wilhelmina [wĭl-hĕl-mē-nah], assistant dean and curriculum chair, met with both of them. Matron Trevora had arranged an interview with her to determine at what point of study Ruwena should be admitted. Madam Wilhelmina would assess Ruwena's current level of schooling, if any, and decide what remedial classes she would need. In turn, this would determine into which form Ruwena would be admitted and, therefore, where her quarters would be.

Madam Wilhelmina asked Ruwena, "What schooling have you had?" Ruwena recited the lessons her mistress had told her to acknowledge. She had been taught how to speak, read, and write in the common language; how to count; how to add, subtract, multiply, and divide what she had counted and how to calculate proportions; how to cleanse fouled water; how to prepare soups, soaps, and antiseptic potions; how to identify edible plants including fruits, vegetables, and cooking herbs; how to clean and dress simple wounds; and how to make and mend her own clothes. Ruwena made no mention that most of the humans she tended in the Cassius village were deformed and said nothing of the dragoness.

Then Madam Wilhelmina asked, "Who taught you your lessons? Did you go to school?"

"My mistress taught me these things," Ruwena replied. Over time, this would become one of her stock replies when asked how she knew something.

Madam Wilhelmina decided that Ruwena should be evaluated by each of the teachers who taught classes in Forms I and II (app. B, tables 6 and 7). This would allow Ruwena to meet them and allow each teacher to assess Ruwena's proficiency. "Each faculty member will assign tasks for you to complete, which will test your knowledge and skills," said Madam Wilhelmina. "In that way, the faculty will be able to evaluate your performance and determine at what level you should be enrolled."

"For the time being, you are assigned to Form II," said Madam Wilhelmina. This was based in part on Ruwena's apparent age and because it was likely that she had mastered all the lessons presented in Form I and most of those presented in Form II.

Living Quarters

At the end of the meeting with Madam Wilhelmina, Savannah showed Ruwena her assigned dormitory room. Savannah explained that all dormitory rooms were laid out in the same manner and were outfitted uniformly. Although the accommodations were rather plain, Ruwena noted that they were not as Spartan as her living quarters at H'Aleth. There was certainly no comparison to the shelter she lived in at the Cassius village. Most importantly to Ruwena, the room had windows.

Ruwena was amazed at the amount of space and furnishings provided. Savannah told her, "These rooms are set up to accommodate as many as four students, and two more could be crammed in, if necessary. It can get really crowded," she cautioned. "Most of the time, there are two or three students in a room."

"The center of the room must be kept clear at all times," Savannah admonished. "If there is an evacuation, we have to get out of our rooms, get to the stairs, and get out of the building or into the tunnels in less than a minute." Ruwena saw that the door to the hallway was wider than any doorways she had seen at H'Aleth. Savannah also pointed out that all doors could be locked from the inside or the outside, whereupon she instructed Ruwena in schoolhouse rule number one. "All students are to keep their doors unlocked unless a faculty member tells you to do otherwise." The door to Ruwena's room would be no exception.

For now, the room was empty except for Ruwena. She would remain by herself until more was known about her. Matron Aquina would not risk having an unknown individual in a room where other students would be talking among themselves and could inadvertently offer information that a stranger should not hear. Ruwena was relieved. She welcomed the opportunity to have some time to herself. Later that evening, she opened the largest window and looked outside. Shortly thereafter, a woodland owl rose up on silent wings and flew out (illus. 13).

Illus. 13. On Silent Wings.

CHAPTER 20

Wine, Wind, and Water

The next morning, Savannah took Ruwena on a tour of the grounds within the boundaries of the perimeter (app. H). "You will need to learn these locations so that they are second nature to you," she advised. There were no maps or schematics of the compound to aid a visitor or an intruder.

The Gardens

Savannah and Ruwena began their tour by walking through the flower gardens on both sides of the manor house. They reminded Ruwena of the ones at the manor house in H'Aleth. She saw many of the same flowers she had seen there and several new ones as well. Master Ferronas [fer-ōn-as], the master gardener, pointed out, "Many of these flowers attract pollinators—bees, butterflies, hummingbirds, and even moths—which we need to pollinate the vegetable and herb gardens." Ruwena was familiar with bees and butterflies, which were common in H'Aleth; however, she had not seen hummingbirds there. There were no pollinators in a Cassius village due to its lack of vegetation. When Master Ferronas pointed out a hummingbird, Ruwena became enthralled watching it. It was an exquisite creature. Sadly, it would have been killed in a Cassius village—either for food or for its beautiful plumage.

Savannah and Ruwena also passed by the herb gardens. Ruwena noted that Savannah did not point out the medicinal herbs and said nothing about them. Clearly, Ruwena should not know about these plants—at least, not yet.

In the vegetable gardens, Ruwena saw many foods that she had eaten at H'Aleth—root vegetables such as potatoes (white and yams) and carrots and onions, legumes such as beans and peas (several varieties), acorn squash and cucumber, green peppers, tomatoes, lettuce and cabbage, and green leafy vegetables such as spinach and collard greens. She also saw vegetables that were new to her such as beets and turnips, mustard greens and kale, gourd squash, and chili and red peppers. "Many vegetables are the source of essential nutrients we all need to be heathy," said Master Ferronas. "Some of these nutrients even influence the function of our genes."

"How?" asked Ruwena

"Ah, an excellent question," replied Master Ferronas. "Genes provide the codes that determine how we look and function," he explained. "The environment provides several substances that influence the functions of our genes, including vitamins that we get from the food we eat."

Ruwena would learn much later in her schooling that these environmental agents would not change a gene's structure or composition. Instead of being part of the gene, they would be attached to it (epigenetic). Through their interaction with a gene, these epigenetic agents would affect how or even if it functioned. They could be found throughout the genome and could affect phenotype without ever changing the genotype. Environmental factors that strongly influenced gene function included access to adequate nutrition (e.g., vitamins) and exposure to toxic agents (e.g., smoking, alcohol, heavy metals, etc.).

One agent in particular, which could be found throughout the genome, played a key role in turning off genes. Virtually all cells used the same housekeeping genes to maintain normal cellular functions. Consequently, these types of genes were not normally turned off. A specialized cell would need only its housekeeping genes and those genes that supported its particular specialty. Those that didn't support the cell's operations could be turned off. For example, genes that coded for proteins critical to the function of a muscle cell would be turned off in a nerve cell. Genes that coded for the substance critical for insulating a nerve would be turned off in a muscle cell. Often, an epigenetic agent would be used to turn off the genes a cell did not need.

Adequate nutrition was essential for the production of some important epigenetic agents. The B vitamins, especially folate and B_{12}, were essential components of one such agent that regulated growth and development.

A diet deficient in these vitamins during pregnancy would lead to birth defects in the brain and spinal cord.

Nutrition was not an issue for any of the three Houses. There were plenty of gardens with vegetables, groves of fruit trees, and many fields of grain to provide essential nutrients. Resources were sufficient to provide for the welfare of the population, which, as a whole, was quite healthy. Since infant mortality and birth defects were low, most families chose to have two or three children. This birth rate kept the population stable without creating an additional strain on resources.

Conditions were exactly the opposite in a Cassius village, where nutrition was virtually nonexistent. There were no gardens in or around a Cassius village. The only vegetable found in the surrounding area was a wild onion. Although many villages had a storeroom stocked with food, those resources were not put there for the benefit of the villagers. They were intended solely for Cassius's army and armed guards. Thus, these storerooms were closely guarded, mostly by hybrids, who would be fed in return. Fortunately, there could be no infant mortality or birth defects in a Cassius village. The hybrids were sterile.

The Winery

In the winery, Ruwena saw baskets full of grapes and berries—blackberry, blueberry, strawberry, and raspberry. There were crates of oranges, peaches, pears, and melons imported from other villages. These fruits were the primary sources of sweet confections. Most of them were used as fresh fruit, fruit juice, or prepared as jams and jellies. The winery's main purpose was to produce these products. Madam Wallenexis [*wal-ĕn-ex*-is], chief enologist and master winemaker, explained how fruit was processed into juices, jams, and jellies. She also explained how wine was made when the juice of grapes and other fruits was allowed to ferment. She kept small supply of various wines in a locked closet in the winery.

Ruwena was allowed to sample many of the products the winery made, including a sip of wine. The juices were prepared without added sugar and were delicious. The jams and jellies tasted good, although they were perhaps a bit too sweet. She had sampled many of these at H'Aleth, yet her mistress rarely allowed sweets and never offered her wine. So the wine was completely new and completely awful. After sampling juices and jellies, it tasted bitter and burned her throat. She asked Savannah, "Why would anyone want to drink this?"

"Wine is an acquired taste," Savannah replied, "one that I have yet to appreciate."

A Perennial Debate

As Ruwena and Savannah were about to leave the winery, Master Gaius [gī-us], the potions master, came by to reengage Madam Wallenexis in a discussion regarding the preparation of wines and where they should be kept. They disagreed on the latter point.

Master Gaius reminded Madam Wallenexis of his opinion regarding her delving into the realm of potions. "Wines fall under the potions category, as do soups," he asserted. "Therefore, wines fall under my purview." Furthermore, the preparation of wine required the same attention to detail as did his potions. "The ingredients must be prepared properly, measured accurately, and mixed in their proper order before fermentation can begin," he argued.

Madam Wallenexis reassured Master Gaius that she knew far more about preparing wines than he did. Furthermore, she asserted, "You know perfectly well that the preparation of soups is intended to train beginning students for the preparation of medicinal potions." Most importantly, however, students should not be exposed to alcohol on a recurring basis. "It is a toxic agent that can cause considerable damage with too much exposure," she reminded him.

"Exactly," responded Master Gaius. "Since wine contains alcohol and its use is limited, it should be treated as other restricted agents in my lab and kept secured."

"It is secured," responded Madam Wallenexis firmly, "in my wine cupboards. Since wine is never used in your potions, there is no need to keep it in the potions lab. Besides, I'm not about to have my wines blown up in your lab every other week."

"It's not that often!" retorted Master Gaius.

From time to time, students rotating through the winery would witness these exchanges. The staff would reassure the students that all was well, saying, "Those two have been debating that subject for decades."

Wine was served primarily at celebrations. It was not used as a daily beverage. Alcohol was another environmental agent that interfered with growth and development. Its use during pregnancy was a major concern. It turned off some of the genes involved in fetal growth and brain development.

These were not alcohol's only effects. Intoxication from any source—fermented fruit, euphoria-inducing plants, or hallucinogenic plants—was avoided due to the dangers it posed. Transformations under the influence of alcohol and other intoxicants could easily become corrupted. This threatened not only the welfare and possibly the life of the affected *H. transformans* but also of anyone who was nearby. Given the risks of a corrupted transformation from intoxication, the three Houses strongly advised their members to avoid drinking fermented beverages in excess and never when they might transform.

In theory, the use of alcohol in a Cassius village was not an issue. It was forbidden there. This was not out of any concern for the welfare of the villagers. Intoxication interfered with productivity. In reality, wine could be found in a Cassius village. It often crept its way into a village when the guards would trade storeroom supplies for a cask of wine. So it was not unusual for guards to imbibe spirits of fermenti when they could get it. One of the greatest threats in a Cassius village was a hybrid who became intoxicated. Ruwena knew this all too well. The effects had been illustrated dramatically late one afternoon.

A Deadly Indulgence

One of the crocutalupoids assigned to guard the storehouse in the Cassius village had decided to sample some wine stored there. The hybrid soon became inebriated and disoriented. Subsequently, he developed an unsteady gait and uncoordinated movements. He lost his balance and crashed into several barrels, crates, and storage bins as he tried to regain his balance.

One of the other hybrids, a cercopithursid, responded to the ruckus thinking the storehouse was being raided. Instead, he encountered an agitated and aggressive crocutalupoid that turned and attacked him. A violent fight broke out between the two hybrids (illus. 14).

Illus. 14. A Deadly Indulgence.

Suddenly, signs of distorted features beyond those due to wolf and hyena began to appear in the crocutalupoid. These signs heralded the onset of a corruption of his original transformation. He began to have seizures. Startled by this development, the cercopithursid abruptly broke off his attack. His hesitation lasted just long enough for him to realize that his adversary was incapacitated, whereupon the cercopithursid quickly ended the crocutalupoid's life.

The crocutalupoid's seizures could have been triggered by alcohol intoxication or by changes engendered by the onset of a corrupted transformation. Most likely, it was both.

Wind and Water

After watching how fruits were processed in the winery, Savannah and Ruwena walked past the tree groves to the northwest. In one of the groves, Ruwena noted a bizarre structure that had the trunk of a tree with four extensions that looked like the spokes of a wheel without the rim.

"What is that?" Ruwena asked Savannah.

"It's a windmill. They are quite common in this region," answered Savannah. "The windmills are another source of power for us," Savannah said without further explanation. Windmills and their tunnels were hidden for a reason. The structure was connected by an underground tunnel to one or more buildings in the compound. Thus, it was also part of the escape route if the village came under attack. Although Ruwena's mistress had told her about windmills, Ruwena had never seen one. The manor house where she was raised had a steam generator that supplied energy to its village.

Savannah and Ruwena stopped briefly at the armory (app. H, illus. 35), the falconry, and the aviary on the north. At each location, Savannah gave a brief description of their purpose. "You will get a chance to rotate to these locations as part of your schooling," Savanna told Ruwena. The two girls continued around the perimeter of the compound to the boathouse and fish hatchery on the northeast. Savannah showed Ruwena the different types of boats. "You will be expected to master rowing a rowboat and paddling a canoe," Savannah said. At the fisheries, Savannah pointed out which fish were trout and which were bass and how to tell one from the other.

Then, they walked through an open field along the eastern border and past the pond, where Ruwena saw another structure she did not recognize. It was built across a freshwater stream.

Once again, Ruwena asked, "What is that?"

"It's a water wheel," answered Savannah, who was surprised that Ruwena didn't know. "It works like a windmill, except that waterwheels require briskly flowing water to power them," she explained.

Ruwena was fascinated by wind- and watermill structures. The granary was adjacent to the waterwheel and had a gristmill of its own. When Savannah and Ruwena stepped inside, Ruwena was transfixed by the gears and how they moved the heavy blocks of stone used to grind the grain. It was amazing. Ruwena wanted to stay and watch; however, Savannah cautioned that they needed to return to the schoolhouse. There were several tasks that they had yet to do. After a short walk, they finally returned to the manor and then the schoolhouse.

Savannah said nothing about the steam generators. Ironically, it was one power source with which Ruwena was most familiar. Although the steam generators were common knowledge to everyone who lived in the compound, Savannah was not certain how much information she should give Ruwena. The compound was the only place in Erwina that had them. Since the generators relied on coal for fuel, their use was limited to supporting those activities that required power twenty-four hours a day. The medical infirmary, the vet clinic, and the science laboratories in the natural history and research building needed an uninterrupted power source.

During the tour, Savannah made no mention of the Erwina's defenses in the event of an attack. One of these defenses was a camouflaged mound of stones that completely encircled the compound beyond its perimeter. Savannah also made no mention of the hemp ropes threaded into the tree canopy. They and the tunnels were means of escape should the compound come under attack. Ruwena noticed, however, that many of the trees appeared to be laden with some form of vine.

After the tour, Savannah advised Ruwena that she must not leave the compound without permission. Students in Forms I through III were not allowed to leave without the escort of a faculty or staff member or an adult family member. "It's not always safe outside the compound," Savannah said. Ruwena knew this all too well.

Supplemental Notes and Citations

Epigenetic Agents

These are nongenetic biochemical agents that attach to DNA. Epigenetic agents play a critical role in the regulation of gene expression and are essential for normal growth and development throughout the life cycle. They are present across many species and can be modified by the environment (Champagne, 2013). They are derived from environmental substances such as vitamins, caffeine, alcohol, and other substances. (Lee, 2015; Wright and Saul, 2013). Once absorbed into the body, these substances are used to produce the epigenetic agent. Ultimately, environmental conditions can affect gene expression and lead to different phenotypes in the presence of the same genotype (Duncan et al., 2014).

The epigenome refers to agents that are attached to genes but not a part of the genetic code itself. Technically, they lie outside the genetic code. They affect a gene's activity without incurring any change in the gene's structure (Delcuve et al., 2009; Jin et al., 2011; Merkle, 2009b). The entire genome is subject to epigenetic factors, including reproductive cells (ova and sperm). Consequently, epigenetic factors (e.g., DNA methylation) that affect reproductive cells can be inherited by offspring and can persist across generations. Epigenetic inheritance is a stamp or tag that is passed on to progeny (genetic imprinting). It is possible that inheritable epigenetic factors may account for the reason why some families are predisposed to developing a particular type of disease (e.g., heart disease) (Pacchierotti and Spano, 2015; Sarkar, 2016).

Methyl Groups

These are common biochemical agents that regulate gene activity. When a methyl group attaches to the DNA associated with a particular gene (DNA methylation), it effectively turns off that gene (Jin et al., 2011; Jones et al. 2015). DNA methylation is a major epigenetic mechanism for controlling the activity of genes, including those that are implicated in the development of cancer.

Excess activity (hypermethylation) is associated with decreased activation of genes, some of which inhibit the development of cancer (e.g., tumor suppressor genes such as *BRCA1/BRCA2*) (Jin et al., 2011; Kazanets et al., 2016; Luczak and Jagodzinski, 2006; Mummaneni and Shord, 2014; Ning et al., 2016). Drugs that interfere with DNA hypermethylation are being developed to treat cancers in which hypermethylation is a factor (Hamm and Costa, 2015).

Inadequate activity (hypomethylation) is associated with increased activation of genes, some of which can induce the development of cancer (e.g., oncogenes) (Jin et al., 2011; Luczak and Jagodzinski, 2006; Mummaneni and Shord, 2014; Ning et al., 2016).

Specialized Cells

These are cells that develop to perform specific functions. All somatic cells contain twenty-three paired chromosomes and a full complement of DNA. As cells differentiate and become specialized, they only need the genes for their specialty and their housekeeping genes to be active.

In a muscle cell, actin and myosin are functional protein elements that make muscles contract. Genes that code for these proteins will be active in a muscle cell. In a nerve cell, myelin is a substance that supports and promotes the conduction of electrical impulses. Genes that code for this substance will be active in a nerve cell.

Nutrition

Foods are the source of several essential biochemical elements that regulate gene activity. The B vitamins, in particular, affect the levels of substances from which methyl groups are derived, and their levels vary with diet (Beaudin and Stover, 2007; Mentch and Locasale, 2016; Park, 2012; Selhub, 2002). Folate (folic acid, vitamin B_9), cyanocobalamin (vitamin B_{12}), and pyridoxine (vitamin B_6) participate in the regulation of DNA methylation (Khandi and Vadakedath, 2015; Mentch and Locasale, 2016; Su et al., 2016).

Deficiencies of folate and vitamin B_{12} during pregnancy are known to cause defective development of the brain and spinal cord (the neural tube) in the fetus. Failure of the neural tube to close during embryonic development during the third to fourth week of pregnancy leads to congenital defects such as spina bifida (Beaudin and Stover, 2007; Salih et al., 2014). There is strong association between these deficiencies and improper DNA methylation of certain genes (Green and Marsit, 2015; (Safi et al., 2012; Salih et al., 2014; Stolk et al., 2013). Consuming foods rich in B vitamins can have a protective effect. Folate supplements during pregnancy have reduced significantly the incidence of neural tube defects.

The primary sources for most B vitamins are fruits, vegetables, and whole grains. Whole grains are rich in folate. Fish, poultry, and other meats are rich in B_{12}. Eggs and milk products, such as cheese, are other sources of B_{12} for those who do not eat meat. Dark-green leafy vegetables and some fruits (e.g., oranges, cantaloupe, and berries) are sources of B_6. The reader is referred to the National Institutes of Health Office of Dietary Supplements Vitamin and Mineral Supplement fact sheets for additional information (https://ods.od.nih.gov/factsheets/list-VitaminsMinerals/).

Teratogens and Toxins

Teratogens are agents (typically toxins) that cause developmental defects and malformations in the embryo or fetus, which persist after birth. Alcohol is a known teratogen (Gupta et al., 2016; Khalid et al., 2014; McCance and Grey, 2014). It affects the same pathways used by folate and interferes with DNA methylation (Fowler et al., 2012; Kalhan, 2016; Kruman and Fowler, 2014). Alcohol also affects noncoding genes that initiate gene activity (promoter genes) (Gupta et al., 2016). Noncoding genes are involved in regulating function of other genes, both coding and other noncoding genes (Jones et al., 2015; Long and Miano, 2007).

In fetal alcohol spectrum disorders, alcohol induces hypermethylation of genes found in chromosomes 2, 16, and 18. Consequently, the DNA in those genes is turned off. This causes a range of abnormalities in the infant including effects on brain development. The effects can cause growth retardation and cognitive and behavior deficits (Gupta et al., 2016; McCance and Grey, 2014; Porth, 2009; Resendiz et al., 2013; Ungerer M. et al., 2013). The type and extent of deficits depends upon the amount of exposure (light to heavy alcohol use), at which point(s) in the pregnancy the exposure occurred, and how long it lasted (acute or chronic). Increased consumption of foods rich in folate and vitamin B_{12} may mitigate some of these effects (Khandi and Vadakedath, 2015).

CHAPTER 21

Protocol and Etiquette

Over the next few days, Savannah continued to orient Ruwena to the routines of the compound and the schoolhouse. Several matters had to be addressed as expeditiously as possible.

"When in doubt, address everyone as master or madam," Savannah advised Ruwena, "Even if it is not their proper title, it is considered a courtesy. Do try to get the matrons right. It is also important to learn who are the chiefs and heads of operations." Ruwena realized she had many names and titles to learn at Erwina (app. J). In a Cassius village, she only needed to know who the guards were—and not by name.

Proper Attire

The next afternoon, after touring the grounds, Savannah announced, "I'm taking you to see Madam Fredrika [frĕd-rē-ka]. You need new clothes. You can't keep wearing that same smock forever and ever." Savannah didn't say what she thought of it, and Ruwena didn't ask. She didn't bother telling Savannah that she had been wearing the smock—and one other just like it—for over a year.

So Savannah and Ruwena visited Madam Fredrika, head seamstress, for Ruwena to be fitted for clothes. Madam Fredrika worked in the schoolhouse in the first cellar near the laundry. After introductions were made, she asked Ruwena if she had any other smocks, clothes, or robes. When Ruwena replied that she did not, Madam Fredrika offered to make

Ruwena two sets of clothes—one pair for warm weather (spring and summer) and one pair for cold weather (fall and winter). She could have one of the items ready by the end of the day. The rest would be ready within two to three days at the most. She then set about taking Ruwena's measurements.

Madam Fredrika asked Ruwena if she preferred any particular colors for her clothes. "Typically, light colors are used for spring and summer, and darker colors for fall and winter," she counseled. Ruwena had become accustomed to wearing only one color in the Cassius village—brown, as in a grain sack. She knew, however, that she needed to respond promptly. "Brown," she replied on reflex. This would allow her to blend into the forest and with many of the buildings in the compound.

Savannah just looked at Ruwena. Then she announced, "You need three more colors. You can have green, rose, or yellow for spring and summer. You can have wine red, dark blue, or dark purple for fall and winter."

Ruwena just looked at Savannah. *You can't blend into the forest— or anyplace else—dressed in such colors,* she thought. Then, she quickly reminded herself that she was no longer in a Cassius village. "Green," she said and then added on impulse, "wine red and dark blue." Green would allow her to blend in with many grasses and plants during the growing season. Dark red and dark blue would help her blend into the night. Once again, she was envisioning how she could remain unseen in a Cassius village. So Madam Fredrika fitted Ruwena for two light smocks—spring green and light tan for spring and summer. Later, she would fashion two smocks from heavier materials—wine red and dark blue for fall and winter. Before leaving, Madam Fredrika gave Ruwena a nightgown. "All nightgowns are made with the same pattern. Only the sizes are different," she told Ruwena.

Afterward, Savannah took Ruwena to Master Androv [*an*-drŏf], head tailor and shoemaker. He was located adjacent to Madam Fredrika. The two shared the same storeroom for their supplies. There, Ruwena was fitted with one pair of sandals for warm weather and one pair of leather boots for cold weather and snow. The boots were made from the hides of uncorrupted animals that had died of natural causes. The hides protected feet from the cold and from rain and snow. She was given two pairs of cotton socks as well.

A Quandary

With the fitting for her clothes, Ruwena knew that none of them would support a transformation readily. Of necessity, clothing for *H. transformans* had to be loose fitting to accommodate changes in size and shape with transformation. Often, clothing would be a flowing robe or a loose tunic that could be tied at the waist. If there were sleeves, these, too, were made with ample material and often had ties at the wrists. The length of a robe's skirt varied according to the alternate species; however, they were almost always below the knee to ensure sufficient cover when transforming. The necks of the robes were scooped. For winter, there was extra material in the form of a collar, which could be pulled up around the neck and closed with a tie for warmth.

Loose, flowing robes were essential for transformation. They allowed room for the change to occur and for the alternate species to exit the clothing with little or no impediment. In reverse, they allowed the alternate species to return to the clothes and settle or even shelter inside the robes while changing back to human form. Consider the river otter. Slipping one's arms out of the sleeves before transforming would allow the otter to back out of a robe easily or, if there was enough room, to turn around in it. Later, the otter could slip back into the robe and poke its head through the neck. Once transformed into a human again, the individual could slip his or her arms back into the sleeves. The amount of cloth needed could be a bit problematic for those whose alternate species was quite large. For a brown bear or an elk stag, one needed enough cloth in the robe to pitch a tent. Robes of this size tended to be rather cumbersome to wear.

Fortunately, people who were *H. transformans* were not obliged to wear such apparel all the time. If there was no intent or plan to transform, they could dress in conventional clothing like any other *H. sapiens*. If an urgent need to transform arose while dressed in conventional clothes, then the *H. transformans* might need to disrobe. For this reason, many *H. transformans* would wear conventional clothing that was at least two sizes too large.

Ruwena kept the robe she had worn in the Cassius village. This proved to be advantageous later on when she wanted to transform. When Ruwena had the opportunity, she would make another one. *Surely there are grain sacks somewhere in Erwina I can use,* she thought to herself. Even at H'Aleth, her mistress had obliged her to learn how to make her own robes and smocks so that she could continue to clothe herself when she grew out of them.

Echoes of a Cassius Village

For the first few days, Savannah had been Ruwena's sole companion at the compound. Savannah finally decided it was time for Ruwena to meet the rest of her classmates. "Introductions are in order," she said. So Savannah began dragging Ruwena out of her solitude and into the commons to engage with other Form II students.

Classmates were a new experience for Ruwena. While living at H'Aleth, she had been tutored alone by her mistress and had little contact with other children—most of whom had been sent to school in Erwina. When present among other adults, she rarely spoke. Her mistress had admonished her that children should be seen and not heard and should speak only when given permission or when a response was expected. Hence, Ruwena was quite uneasy around people she did not know, including her classmates.

"You need to learn who your classmates are, and they need to at least recognize you," Savannah said. "It's really important."

Students were expected to account for each other in the event of an evacuation. Thus, all students within a form needed to know their comrades and recognize them both on sight and upon hearing their voices. Since students nearly always moved forward together from one form to the next, this was not a problem. In fact, most of the children lived in the compound, so they already knew one another. When women in the outlying villages became pregnant, many of them moved to the compound for the added protection afforded their unborn child and newborn infant. Once their infants were about a year old, most of the mothers from the southwestern villages would move back with their infant to be with the rest of their family. For mothers from the northeastern and southeastern outposts, arrangements were usually made for their husbands to join them in the compound. It was too unsafe to raise small children in those regions.

At times, a few people from Biogenics and Cassius territories would come to Erwina seeking asylum. Most, but not all, would have young children they were trying to protect. Sometimes, it was only the children who reached Erwina. Consequently, it is not entirely out of the ordinary to have a brand new student join the ranks of an existing cohort.

In the Cassius village, Ruwena's mistress had required her to recognize all the villagers who lived there so that she could recognize when a stranger appeared. In addition, her mistress insisted she know every guard and every hybrid, human or animal, and where they were stationed. Since this was likely to change every day, it was something that had to be learned anew every day. So Ruwena understood the need to recognize every student. There were far fewer students than villagers, guards, and hybrids. *This will not be a difficult task,* she thought.

Eventually, Savannah rounded up the students who, with Savannah, would be Ruwena's immediate classmates as seniors in Form II (app K). There were eleven seniors—twelve, including Ruwena. There were four girls—now five—and seven boys. The three additional girls included Avelynda [a-věl-ĭn-da], Marianna, and Samiya [sam-ī-ya]. The boys were Deven, Ervan, Hendrik, Javier, Qwincy, Salwen, and Erik. Of the twelve students, Deven and Qwincy were *H. sapiens*. Ruwena quickly memorized each student's name and just as quickly learned to recognize each student both by sight and by the sound of his or her voice—just as she did for the guards in the Cassius village.

Social Life

At H'Aleth and in the Cassius village, Ruwena's mistress had directed that she not mix socially with the villagers. She should not become friendly or engage in idle chatter with anyone in either location. The risk of a careless remark was too great. At H'Aleth, she might be cornered by questions she could not answer, thereby raising suspicions. In the Cassius village, it could betray their origin and put them in danger of being discovered. At Erwina, exactly the opposite conditions were the norm. Not only was Ruwena expected to learn who everyone was and to which room they were assigned, she was expected to engage with them socially. Ruwena paled at the thought. This was almost as frightening as the barge ride. Savannah, of course, saw no problem at all. She was raised in Erwina.

It could have been worse. Student numbers were generally low. In addition to the twelve seniors, there were eleven juniors, fourteen sophomores, and nine freshmen in Form II. Fortunately for Ruwena, not all forty-six students converged on the commons at one time. Students would come and go all day long. Younger students were required to retire to their rooms earlier in the evening, leaving the commons to older students who could stay up later. Seniors in Form II could stay up as late as 10:00 p.m. before retiring to their rooms. Finally, not everyone came to the commons. Many students visited in each other's rooms.

"We'll get around to all of them," Savannah remarked confidently—much to Ruwena's dismay.

To her surprise, Ruwena found some social engagements quite pleasant and almost relaxing. Many of the students and faculty were accomplished musicians. Almost every evening, music was being played somewhere in the compound. String and wind instruments were most common. Even a rare drum could be heard. Ruwena had never seen her mistress play a musical instrument, nor was Ruwena taught to play one. Her mistress had admonished her that it was much more important to learn the songs of each animal and bird species she encountered. This had proved to be invaluable in the Cassius village.

Children in Erwina first learned to play the instruments and music, if any, their parents played. Subsequently as students, they honed their talents by playing in ensembles with the faculty, staff, and other students. These sessions provided a welcome respite from the work and stress of the day and soothed many frazzled nerves, including Ruwena's. Students who did not know how to play an instrument and expressed an interest in doing so could almost always find a willing fellow student or faculty member who would tutor them after school hours.

There was one precaution everyone needed to observe when making music (and merriment). Music carries on the wind. If the tone of the music is not tempered, then its source could be found by a skilled and attentive listener. Such a listener might be an enemy spy or scout transformed into his or her alternate species with heightened senses. Hence, music could be lively but not loud.

CHAPTER 22

Chaos and Gravity

Cleanliness and Tidiness

Unlike H'Aleth and Erwina, there was no bathing or laundry in a Cassius village. Water in the village was contaminated as were any nearby streams or ponds. When Ruwena and her mistress went searching for herbs, nuts, and other food sources, they also looked for a freshwater stream. Most of these streams originated in the mountains, so the water was quite cold. When one was found, they would scoop water out of the stream to bathe and wash their clothes. These were the only times they could really feel clean. In between such times, they would use some of the clarified and boiled water they prepared to rinse their face and hands daily and wipe off the rest of their body every few days. At least this water could be warmed over a fire in the winter.

Given the vegetation used to build their shelter and kept inside it, Ruwena would clean it daily. She removed all the contents and checked them for any denizens that had also sought shelter there overnight. Then, she swept out the inside with a handmade broom and put the contents back where they belonged. This was just one of her daily chores. She was accustomed to doing them when she lived with her mistress in H'Aleth. In the Cassius village, however, harsher conditions made these tasks more difficult and burdensome.

At the schoolhouse, students were expected to attend to their own cleanliness on a daily basis and as needed (depending upon practicums).

They were expected to keep their rooms clean and tidy also. "Normally, roommates share these duties," Savannah told Ruwena. "One will sweep, another will dust, and a third will straighten up," she added. As the sole occupant of her room, Ruwena would need to do these chores for herself. Savannah further cautioned Ruwena to keep her room tidy. "Each form has a dormitory supervisor who will conduct spot inspections of students' rooms." Woe betide the students of a disheveled room who faced Matron Patrina [pa-*trē*-nah], the supervisor for Form II. Her alternate species was a wolverine.

Chaos

Students were expected to change their own bed with fresh linen every week and take their dirty clothes and linens to the laundry room housed in the first cellar. Students washed their own clothes and linens under the watchful eye of Madam Gannett [*gan*-net], the head laundress, and her staff.

Ruwena's first trip to the laundry (under the watchful eye of Savannah) revealed a chaotic scene. The laundry room was enormous. The girls were scattered about various stations and running back and forth from one station to another. Standing at the doorway into the laundry, Savannah explained how the room was organized and how it was supposed to operate (app. I, part 2). This rational arrangement survived the students in Form I, who were under the tutelage of the laundry staff. It did not survive Forms II through IV. "It's chaos, really," she admitted.

"We are restricted in how much water and soap we can use," advised Savannah. "It conserves water and keeps the amount of soap suds in the wash to a minimum." Students boarding in the same dormitory room often would combine their laundry to wash and rinse their clothes together. In this way, they were able to conserve soap and water and speed up the process, freeing themselves from laundry duty much sooner.

Gravity

In a Cassius village, filth was everywhere and with it contagion. Upon arriving at the village, one of the first orders of business for Ruwena's mistress was to find a patch of ground on the outskirts of the village that could be cleaned up. Then, whenever she approached or walked through the village, she would have a broom she made from a dead hardwood bush she tied to a slender tree branch. She would use the broom to sweep away everything in her path down to clean dirt. In this manner, she could minimize exposure to the filth of the village. When she was done with it, she would burn the dead bush and find another one. Dead bushes were everywhere around the village. Later, Ruwena assumed this duty.

At the schoolhouse, the dormitories on each floor had two baths—one for the girls and one for the boys. Bath was a polite misnomer. There were no bathing facilities in any of the baths. Despite the name, they more closely resembled latrines. There were six private toilets in each one. Each toilet had two flushes. Water to flush the toilets was supplied by a cistern on the roof. "Do not drink the water from any of the flushes," Savannah admonished. "Drink only the water that comes from the hand pump in the commons."

Ruwena was curious about the toilets and their flushes. Even though she had used something similar at H'Aleth, her mistress had never told her anything about how they worked. "How do they work?" she asked Savannah, who always seemed to know everything.

For once, Savannah could not answer this question. How toilets flushed and what happens to the stuff deposited in them had never been a point of interest for her. Although she really didn't want to know, she suggested, "Perhaps Master Heroditus [her-ŏd-ī-tus], the chief engineer and builder in Erwina, might be able to answer your question." Whereupon Savannah, with a sigh, resigned herself to learning about toilets.

When approached, Master Heroditus was surprised by the students' interest. Only the staff who managed the facilities usually discussed these matters with him. "The flushes actually control trap doors," he explained. "When the lever is pulled, the trap door opens, allowing the toilet to empty into the proper channel and, at the same time, allow water to flow from the cistern to flush the system. Gravity does the rest," he said. He described how the human waste was then filtered and treated with bacteria, which broke down the constituents, microalgae, which used the nitrogen and phosphorus for growth, and sunlight that killed potentially dangerous organisms. Once the waste was treated, it was released back into the environment to enrich the soil. Then Master Heroditus asked, "Would you like to go to the roof and see the cistern?"

Both Savannah and Ruwena eagerly accepted his offer. Savannah was thrilled. She had never been up on the roof. To her knowledge, students were not allowed up there. Master Heroditus took them to the fifth floor of the schoolhouse, though a locked door, up a steep flight of narrow stairs followed by an even steeper hand-over-hand ladder, and finally, through a latched trapdoor onto the roof. Master Heroditus then described how the cistern worked. Both students listened politely, but what really impressed them was the spectacular view of the compound from the roof of the schoolhouse. "The roof is a great place to have a picnic in the spring and fall, and it also serves as an outlook post," said Master Heroditus, smiling. This last nugget of information would prove to be quite useful.

PART IV

A Sound Education

CHAPTER 23

Proficiency and Potions

Prior to coming to Erwina, Ruwena's mistress tutored her in most of the subjects children were taught at school. In addition, her mistress stressed certain skills and knowledge most children did not receive until they were much older, including the rules of transformation. In doing so, her mistress omitted any subjects she thought of little practical use. Her duty was to ensure the child could survive on her own, transform safely, and execute her duties as the mistress of her House.

Certain Inconsistences

At H'Aleth and in the Cassius village, Ruwena had contact with many wildlife species. Thus, she was familiar with most wild animals—including mammals, birds, reptiles, amphibians, and a few fish. Master Pasterov [*păs*-ter-of], chief biologist and zoologist, found her knowledge of native animal and bird species more than sufficient. In contrast, Ruwena had little experience with domestic animals. She had seen goats, milk cows, and chickens on H'Aleth farms. At the manor house, however, she had little contact with any of them. Although her mistress taught her the purpose of each one, Ruwena gained no experience caring for them. Thus, Madam Varentova (*vār*-en-*tō*-va), chief of animal husbandry, remarked, "It is odd that this child knows nothing about the care and feeding of farm animals." Consequently, Master Pasterov and Madam Varentova concluded that Ruwena knew many things about wildlife she wasn't expected to know and knew next to nothing about domesticated animals, which she was expected to know.

It was the same thing for plants, fruits, and vegetables. Madam Ocala [o-*sa*-la], chief botanist, found that Ruwena could distinguish edible from nonedible plants in the wild and knew which ones were poisonous. She was familiar with most fruits, vegetables, grains, and herbs; however, she had little knowledge of agriculture. Most of these products had been brought to the manor house in H'Aleth. In a Cassius village, there were no fruits, vegetables, or nuts. On field trips, she and her mistress would occasionally find berries—especially wild strawberry, wild grape, and blackberry—which were their only sources of fruit. There were no fruit trees. Oak trees and their acorns were plentiful, and occasionally she and her mistress would find a hickory tree while on a field trip into the forest.

Madam Bernarda [bur-*nar*-da], assistant dean, found Ruwena fully proficient in reading and writing in the common language. "She can even spell accurately and use proper grammar and punctuation," she remarked. Madam Carawan [*cāre*-a-wăn], chief statistician, had found Ruwena fully proficient in arithmetic; however, she had little knowledge of advanced mathematics such as algebra or geometry. Ruwena's mistress had taught her many things. Algebra and geometry were not among them.

Master Stuvidicus [stu-*vĭ*-dĭ-cus], a physician, found Ruwena quite capable of clarifying and purifying water. When asked about medicinal potions, Ruwena responded, "My mistress would often make these recipes." She was careful not to acknowledge that she could do so herself and could recognize medicinal herbs. She would learn about these plants when she attended the appropriate class or was told what they were. In contrast, Master Ignatius [ig-*nā*-cē-us], chief geologist, was surprised at how many minerals Ruwena recognized. As for soils and rocks, she knew only what she could and couldn't walk on.

When asked by Madam Kavarova [ka-var-*o*-va], specialist in martial arts, Ruwena knew nothing about any defensive measures. She had not seen weapons where she lived in H'Aleth. The guards at the Cassius village carried a variety of arms—swords, knives, axes, bows and arrows, and spears; however, she made no mention of it. She simply stated, "My mistress did not teach me the use of weapons," which was true. *Perhaps, her mistress thought her too young at the time,* Madam Kavarova thought.

Despite Ruwena's best efforts to maintain a consistent level of knowledge, the faculty recognized that there were gaps in what she had learned. Basically, she knew little of what most children of Erwina knew from life in their villages. Those things that she did know, however, she knew very well. The faculty wondered how someone could be so well prepared and yet be so ignorant at the same time. Nowhere was this more apparent than in the preparation of potions.

The Potions Laboratory

When Savannah showed Ruwena the potions lab on her tour of the schoolhouse, she saw row after row of ingredients filling up shelves that were mounted on the front and back walls (app. I, part 3). As Ruwena looked at them, she found many she did not recognize. She determined that she would read about these agents later in the library to learn their actions, in which potions they were used, in what proportions or amounts, how they were prepared, and the reason for using them. She learned later that students were expected to use library resources to learn about each ingredient in a recipe before using it.

"Master Gaius, the potions master, will ask students at random about the ingredients that will be used in class that day," Savannah warned. "He will expect you to know its uses, its effects, in which types of potions it is used, the correct amount to be used in the potion, and so on." Woe betide the students who could not provide this information or provided an incorrect answer. Those students were invited to help scrub down the lab at the end of the school day. It should be noted here that students were not given detention per se. They were issued an invitation to participate in an after-school activity, which they were expected to attend.

Ingredients were shelved in alphabetical order—not in accordance with the recipe books. It was incumbent upon the students to read the labels on the containers and select the correct ingredient. This did not always happen. Hence, there were four windows on the back wall that could be opened to air out the lab, if necessary.

A Tale of Two Sulfurs

Savannah recounted an episode that happened not too long ago. A student was preparing a potion that used ground sulfur clover as one of its ingredients. This ingredient was made from a species of clover plant whose yellow-colored flowers were dried and then ground into a powder. The student inadvertently retrieved sulfur from the shelf. This was a bright-yellow powder prepared from sulfate mineral crystals. The student proceeded to add the sulfur powder in accordance with the directions for sulfur clover. After adding water to the ingredients, the student heated the solution as the recipe directed. Almost immediately, the smell of rotten eggs began to fill the potions lab. It was the unmistakable pungent odor of sulfur dioxide (SO_2). Eyes began to water, noses to run, and some students began coughing. The student, Master Gaius, and the rest of the class quickly recognized the error. Students flew to open up the windows while Master Gaius covered the potion with a lid, took it off the fire, and immersed it in cold water.

The hapless student who made the error spent the next week after school reading every label of every ingredient on all the shelves in the potions lab (except the restricted ingredients). Master Gaius periodically grilled the student on the difference(s) between ingredients that looked alike or sounded alike.

Poisons

Restricted ingredients (toxic agents, hallucinogenic, sedating, hypnotic, etc.) were kept in a locked supply closet along with the recipe books for potions VIII and IX. These agents were kept locked up not only because of their actions and potential for toxicity but also because of their interactions. Most were used in medicinal potions and often combined with other agents.

Another type of transformation, a biochemical transformation, occurred in the liver of both *H. sapiens* and *H. transformans*. The liver had enzymes that acted on (metabolized) a wide variety of substances to fundamentally change their character. Most of these biochemical actions were benign and either produced substances that were helpful (e.g., nutrients) or degraded substances that were harmful (e.g., toxins).

Medicinal agents were strongly influenced by liver enzymes. To complicate matters, however, some medicinal agents could stimulate these enzymes whereas others could suppress them. When one agent affected the liver's ability to transform another agent, the latter could become less effective (as if a smaller amount had been taken) or more toxic (as if an overdose had been taken). Sometimes an agent that posed no danger in its native form would become quite toxic when it had been transformed by the liver. As a result, students who took the medicinal potions classes were taught that all medicinal agents were poisons if taken in sufficient quantity or with another agent with similar effects or with another agent that changed its effect. This tenet was stressed throughout the students' classes.

In yet another twist, there were multiple naturally occurring variations in the structure and function of the liver enzymes responsible for transforming many substances, including medicinal agents. Hence, their level of activity was highly variable from one individual to another. The basis for this variability was in the different versions of the genes that coded for these enzymes. Although these variations resulted in liver enzymes that accomplished the same task, there were differences in how slow or fast the enzymes functioned.

This was especially problematic in *H. transformans*. Both the human and the alternate species were likely to be affected by any given agent. The sensitivity to the agent and the reactions to it may be very different in the human versus the alternate species. Thus, an agent that was safe for one may be toxic to the other. Reactions that caused serious illness in one also threatened the well-being of the other. Reactions that triggered unexpected and uncontrolled transformations were life-threatening.

Only advanced students who understood these potential interactions and reactions and their dangers were allowed to take the advanced preparation of potions classes X and XI. They had to learn the dose and interactions of each restricted agent and the effects it had on *H. sapiens*, *H. transformans*, and the species into which the latter could transform. Most of the students who took these classes planned to attend medical school at Gregor and specialize in either human or veterinary medicine.

Unfortunately, there were always a few unwary and unwise students tantalized by what exotic agents might be in the restricted closet. Invitations to clean and restock the supply closets, including everything stored in them, kept most students from dabbling in restricted agents without faculty permission. Of course, there were exceptions.

Wayward Students

One evening, three students gained unauthorized access to the restricted ingredients closet in the potions lab. They were after dried *Psilocybe semilanceata*, a common species of wild mushroom. Back at their commons, they prepared a soup to which they added the mushroom. Once the soup had cooled enough to eat, the three students sampled their concoction several times. Time slipped by as they waited to see if the mushroom had any effects. Finally, one of them said, "I don't feel a thing." Another said, "I haven't noticed any effect either." The third student admitted, "I'm feeling a little giddy."

The three students debated why two of them felt no effect and one did. All three had eaten the same amount of soup. Their deliberations were suddenly interrupted by a commotion behind them. Another student had come into the commons and decided to try some of their soup. This student became increasingly anxious and began to transform unexpectedly and unintentionally. He started to panic, which only served to accelerate his transformation.

The original three students were horrified. They recognized immediately that this was a medical emergency. One tried to calm and reassure the affected student. Another raced to find any dormitory supervisor or faculty member. The third flew to the school bell tower and rang it repeatedly. The bell alerted everyone in the compound to an emergency and its location and activated security and the medical team.

When the medical team arrived, the three students who had mixed the soup immediately informed Dr. Stuvidicus of the restricted ingredient they had added to their soup. Dr. Stuvidicus sedated the fourth student and took him to the infirmary.

To everyone's relief, the student recovered fully. Subsequently, all four students were tested for their ability to degrade the biologically active agent in *P. semilanceata*. Matron H'Osanna reported her findings to Matron Aquina. "The first two students were found to be fast metabolizers. In them, the active agent was rapidly degraded. The third student, who had felt giddy, was found to be a slow metabolizer." As the three students continued to have more of the soup, the active agent was accumulating in the third student. Matron H'Osanna admitted to being a little puzzled by the fourth student. "He was found to be an intermediate metabolizer of the agent and should have been able to degrade it in a timely, if not rapid, manner." When Master Navarov [năv-ar-ŏf] learned of the incident, he informed Matron H'Osanna that the latter's reaction was due to a toxic effect the agent had on the student's alternate species.

The three wayward and remorseful students were summoned to appear before Matron Aquina, Master Morenavik, and Master Gaius. Matron Aquina deemed the endangerment of the fourth student an accident. "The breach of the restricted ingredients closet and the unauthorized use of a restricted agent was intentional and willful," she declared. As discipline, she revoked the majority of the students' privileges. "In lieu thereof, you will have the privilege of maintaining the orderliness and cleanliness of the potions lab for the remainder of the current term," she said, "and all of the next term."

The Potions Master

Before a student was allowed to begin the potions classes, the student had to demonstrate to Master Gaius his or her ability to measure solid, liquid, and powdered substances accurately and calculate amounts used in a recipe accurately. A student who could not demonstrate proficiency in measurements was not allowed to enroll. Instead, they were required to attend remedial instruction.

Ruwena had demonstrated her competency in arithmetic earlier. So prior to undergoing proficiency testing in potions, Matron Trevora gave Ruwena the recipe books for the potions I–IV courses. "Do not prepare any potions that are not in these texts," she admonished Ruwena. "Students in the past have been known to experiment with potions beyond their ability with serious consequences, including one student who died."

Ruwena recognized all the ingredients used in the four texts. Most of the recipes were either nutritional or contained agents designed to soothe common complaints such as an upset stomach (peppermint), irritated skin (aloe), minor cuts (honey), and bruises (menthol). None of the recipes used medicinal plants, and none contained herbs or minerals known to be toxic to humans or animals. All the recipes were relatively simple, from Ruwena's perspective. Ruwena found only five recipes that were completely new, and she memorized them readily. As her mistress had taught her, Rowena mimed the preparation of these potions until she was confident she could do them successfully. Other recipes had slight variations on those she already knew. These, too, she memorized easily.

When Ruwena appeared before Master Gaius, he selected potions from all four texts. He mixed the order in which he asked Ruwena to prepare them. He watched as she selected and prepared the ingredients for each one, mixed them in the proper sequence, and rendered them or not in accordance with the recipe. She had no need to refer to the recipe books. Thus, Ruwena readily passed the proficiency exams for potions I through IV.

Master Gaius quickly recognized Ruwena's ability. He suspected, also, that she knew more complex potions—not just those at levels I through

IV. *She is far too capable,* he thought to himself. So he devised one more test. He gave her a recipe from one of the restricted classes (potions IX, offered the senior year of Form III). It was a solution that contained a dangerous component, sulfuric acid. When Ruwena read the ingredients, she recognized it immediately. Without revealing what she knew, Ruwena declined to prepare the potion.

"Why not?" demanded Master Gaius.

"Matron Trevora instructed me to make no potions that were not in the recipe books she gave me," replied Ruwena.

"I am also faculty here and the potions master," Master Gaius reminded Ruwena. "I am directing you to prepare the potion."

Ruwena considered him for a moment. She was fairly certain he was testing her. "I will prepare this recipe with Matron Trevora's permission," she replied. With this, the potions master dismissed her. *She has been well trained,* he thought. *But by whom?* Ruwena was excused from potions I through IV. *And probably won't need V or VI either,* thought Master Gaius.

Supplemental Notes and Citations

Biotransformation

This is the conversion of one agent into another by biochemical processes in the body. The liver is the primary organ that breaks down (metabolizes) foreign agents, including alcohol, and, essentially, makes them biodegradable. Most agents are rendered inactive and made disposable either through the kidneys or the intestinal tract (Lynch and Price, 2013; Nebert et al., 2013). Some drugs, however, are activated by liver enzymes.

Acetaminophen is a common analgesic (pain-relieving drug) in many over-the-counter and prescription medicines. Used as directed, it poses little risk unless an individual has liver damage. Taken in amounts that exceed recommended doses, however, the drug can overwhelm even a healthy liver's ability to metabolize it. The drug is then redirected to another metabolic pathway that transforms it into a toxic compound.

Liver Enzymes

These are proteins responsible for both the production and/or metabolism of an enormous range of substances including nutrients, therapeutic drugs, and poisons. The cytochrome P450 family of enzymes is the main group degrading foreign compounds (xenobiotics), including drugs. Three subfamilies account for about 70% to 80% of the enzymes used to metabolize drugs. Most of these enzymes inactivate the compounds they encounter; however, some can convert a drug from an inactive to an active form. The reader can learn more about these enzymes and their influence on drug metabolism at the Genetics Home Reference (https://ghr.nlm.nih.gov/primer/genefamily/cytochromep450).

Inducers are agents (drugs) that lead to an increase in the amount of a liver enzyme which, in turn, increases the rate of metabolism of a particular agent. In most cases, this means that the agent is degraded faster and, therefore, becomes inactive sooner.

Inhibitors are agents (drugs) that lead to a decrease in the amount of a liver enzyme, which, in turn, decreases the rate of metabolism of a particular agent. In most cases, this means that the agent is degraded more slowly and, therefore, is active longer.

Genetic Polymorphism

As noted previously, it is quite common to have slight variations in the structure of a gene (e.g., the four gene combinations that code for valine) without incurring any change in its function. When there are variations in gene sequences that code for the same product or function and these differences occur commonly in a population, they are called polymorphisms (instead of mutations). Some variations, however, can have significant effects on function (Quiñones et al., 2017; Zanger and Schwab, 2012). These include the gene variations that code for the CYP450 family of liver enzymes responsible for metabolizing many agents, including drugs.

For example, an individual's ability to metabolize alcohol depends upon the effectiveness of the liver enzymes to degrade it. There are genetic polymorphisms among these enzymes that affect this ability and, in turn, the likelihood of developing a dependency on alcohol (Jangra et al., 2016; Wall, et al., 2016).

Note: There is a fine line between a polymorphic gene and a mutation. Both can be considered normal or abnormal depending upon their effect (Karki et al., 2015).

Dosage

Dosage is the amount of a substance administered to achieve a specific effect. Typically, for any given medicinal agent, there is an average rate of metabolism in the general population for that agent. Some individuals will degrade the agent more slowly (slow metabolizers) whereas other individuals will degrade it much faster (fast metabolizers). This alone accounts for the wide range of responses among individuals who receive the same agent in the same amount. Without knowing which type of polymorphism an individual has and to which enzyme(s), determining the right amount of an agent to give someone can become an exercise in trial and error.

CHAPTER 24

Prudent Decisions

Ruwena was having many experiences in the House of Erwina that were completely new to her. Most of them were fascinating, some were surprising, others almost overwhelming—such as the wild ride she had on the barge—and yet none were truly perilous. According to Savannah, the barge trip across the river was a routine crossing. As far as Ruwena was concerned, the next time she needed to cross that river, she was flying over it.

One of Ruwena's new experiences would be attending class with other students. When Savannah learned that Ruwena had never attended school, she instructed her remedial student in classroom rules (box 9). Originally developed for young children first entering the school (Form I) to govern their behavior in the classroom, the rules were carried forward to all classes regardless of Form.

Ruwena's Program of Study

Collectively, the faculty had no doubt that Ruwena would be ready to enroll as a senior in Form II in the fall. Based on their assessment of Ruwena's proficiencies, she would be excused from most of the formal courses in Forms I and II, except senior year. "You will need to be tutored in mathematics, general biology and botany, and general geology during your senior year," Matron Tevora advised her. "Madam Wilhelmina will tutor you in family matters," she added. This was considered essential since Ruwena had been raised alone.

Box 9. Classroom Rules.

Classroom Rules

1. Students will arrive at their assigned stations on time.
2. Students will arrive prepared for class (readings and assignments completed).
3. During class, students will remain quiet and speak only when so directed by faculty.
4. During class, students will attend to faculty presentations and demonstrations and listen carefully to explanations.
5. During class, students may raise their hands whenever they have a question for the faculty.
6. During class, students may speak in normal tones when assigned to a small group or during open classroom discussion.
7. Written compositions will be legible and demonstrate evidence of proofreading for proper grammar, spelling, and punctuation (Form II and above).
8. In the laboratory, students will maintain a clean and organized work space.
9. At the end of a laboratory session, students will clean the equipment they have used and return equipment, reagents, and other materials to their proper places.
10. During exams and quizzes, students will work independently. A student may seek help quietly from a faculty member.
11. During exams and quizzes, students will remain seated and quiet until all students have finished or time up has been declared by faculty or a faculty member has dismissed them from class.

Box 9

Courses in the history of the three Houses and of the Biogenics Corporation and the Cassius Foundation were deferred to provide the academic time needed for these subjects. Savannah would continue to be Ruwena's mentor for the sake of consistency. Savannah was more than willing to do so. She considered Ruwena her protégé.

Until the start of fall term, Ruwena would engage in proctored studies for the remainder of the summer concurrent with the following practicums: (1) animal husbandry, including pasture, barn, henhouse, and stable animals; (2) the fishery; (3) gardening, including vegetable, flower, and nonmedicinal herb gardens, which would include soil types as well; (4) tree husbandry in the fruit and nut groves; and (5) wildlife, in the gardens (pollinators), at the pond (fish, small reptiles, and amphibians), and in the aviary (birds and small mammals). Faculty expected these practical experiences to fill in the gaps in her knowledge prior to enrolling as a senior in Form II. They would orient her to the compound as well. Ruwena would not be allowed to go on expeditions outside the compound unless faculty thought it was safe for her to do so. Hence, regional geography classes were deferred. Thus, Ruwena (under the close supervision of Savannah) spent her first summer in a series of practicums. She found most of them benign and refreshing, as the majority allowed her to be outside.

Gardens and Arbors

Ruwena was eager to work in the gardens where she could escape the confines of the schoolhouse. She spent as much time as possible tending them. Each day, when she had finished her tasks in one or the other garden, she was allowed to pick some flowers for her room or select a vegetable she wanted for a snack. Ruwena selected several different vegetables she already knew she liked—tomatoes, cucumbers, carrots, potatoes—as well as ones that were completely new to her. Squash, pumpkin, and any of the melons all had pleasant flavors. After sampling chili peppers and mustard greens, Ruwena decided to avoid these food items assiduously.

Ruwena had practicums in both the tree nursery and in the fruit and nut tree groves. Like all students on a practicum in the tree groves, she was allowed to pick a fruit or some nuts of her choice each day she worked there. In the tree nursery, Ruwena learned how to tend to young sprouts. If a tree needed to be harvested for some reason, Madam Davidea [dah-vĭ-dē-ah], the chief arborist, would take several cuttings or harvest seeds from the tree before it was cut down. She would plant them in her tree nursery and tend to the shoots that grew over the next few years until they could be transplanted. In this manner, the forest would be sustained over time. Only the compound housed a tree nursery. This was the safest place to have one.

Once the nascent tree sprout grew into a sapling, Madam Davidea would recruit arbor staff and students to transplant the tree in a location where trees were needed. If one of the outer villages had requested a tree, some of the saplings would be taken to that village. One such outing occurred during Ruwena's summer practicum.

Madam Davidea took several Form II students on a field exercise to transplant some saplings in the southeast region. The trees would be planted along the banks of a stream, where they would thrive, provide shade for wildlife, and protect the streambed from the hot summer sun. Ruwena was invited to go on the expedition. As part of their experience, students would learn how to dig up the trees, bind their root balls for transport, and transplant them at their new location.

Madam Davidea was accompanied by Sala, a Form IV student, who would serve as a proctor for the students. During the outing, one of the students noted an unusual animal crouched on the limb of an older tree near the stream. It appeared to be some type of lizard. He spotted another lizard just like it floating in the stream. The student pointed out both animals to Madam Davidea and his fellow students and asked, "Do you know what kind of lizard this is?"

"No, I do not," replied Madam Davidea. Sala stooped down to get a closer look at the one in the stream. She had taken the comparative anatomy course and was trying to identify it. "These animals have physical features consistent with lizards that can glide from tree to tree except they are much larger than typical tree lizards," she remarked. "Some type of lizards can swim, although they usually have webbing only in their feet, not between their front and back legs." She thought for a moment and then stood up to speak to Madam Davidea, "This could be a hybrid species given the physical characteristics and apparent capabilities. These animals could be the result of an interspecies mating or genetic engineering," she said. "Most lizards will not attack unless they are threatened," she added. "We should move away." Too late.

Suddenly the lizard in the tree leaped into the air (illus. 15). It spread out its four limbs to reveal the folds of skin that allowed it to glide. They almost looked like bat wings. The lizard was targeting one of the students. Its mouth was open to deliver a bite, and its fangs were clearly visible.

Horrified, Sala quickly drew her knife and struck the animal, causing it to fall to the ground. Her blow killed it. Now the students were horrified, and Madam Davidea was startled. "Why did you kill it?" she asked.

"Lizards don't have fangs," Sala replied. "Vipers do. This is definitely a genetically engineered hybrid, and it is probably venomous."

Illus. 15. A Close Call.

Sala carefully wrapped up the dead lizard-like creature. When the expedition returned to the compound, she took it to Master Pastorov for examination. Master Mikalov [*mĭk-ă-lŏf*] would conduct a genetic analysis from tissue samples he received from Master Pastorov. When the dissection and genetic typing were done, the two faculty members provided their findings to Matron Aquina and Master Titus.

"The lizard is a viperoperidactyl [*vī-*per-o-perĭ-*dăc*-tyl]," reported Master Pastorov. "It is a genetically engineered lizard-viper hybrid, and it does carry a deadly venom." The faculty had little doubt it was one of Cassius's creatures. Sala had made a prudent decision.

The Pond

While Ruwena lived in H'Aleth, her mistress had insisted they conserve potable water. It was a precious resource. Ruwena learned just how precious it was when they fled to the Cassius village. All its water was fouled. What little fresh water Ruwena had seen in Cassius territory came from fast-flowing streams well away from the village. Her mistress would take her to such locations on a search for roots and herbs. Coming from a Cassius village that had no fresh water, it seemed to Ruwena that there was an abundance of it in Erwina.

The water in the pond was fairly clear and would be relatively easy to prepare as drinking water for the compound but for one small detail. Although it was quite large and had an underground source of water, it was not a lake. There was not enough water in the pond to supply all the fresh water Ruwena saw being used. "We have access to water from several fresh water streams in our area," said Madam Kendorra, Erwina's chief engineer.

Ruwena soon learned that people in Erwina's villages would collect rainwater in wooden cisterns. They also could dip water from aquifers where accessible from the surface. Where ground water was relatively close to the surface, the villages would have a well.

The pond was teeming with a wide variety of wildlife and vegetation that lived in and around it. Ruwena saw species that were completely foreign to her, and she was utterly fascinated by them. She had seen frogs, dragonflies, and a few fish in H'Aleth's decorative water lily pond. Master Nemenicus [nĕ-*mĭn*-ĭ-cus], chief ichthyologist and herpetologist, described the different species found in and around the pond at Erwina.

Ruwena longed to dive into the pond and swim around in it—just not as a human. Alas, the vegetation around the pond would not provide sufficient cover for a river otter. An otter would be too large and readily spotted, and the people in the compound were vigilant. On the other hand, water lilies are rooted in the mud beneath the pond. The pond also had elodea, a common aquatic plant that stayed submerged. *Perhaps, if I stayed submerged,* Ruwena wondered. Except for her nose from time to time, she could swim in the pond and hide among the elodea and waterlilies. But the moment she stuck her head above water, she would stand out like a sore thumb. *Perhaps, if I swim at night,* she thought. Unfortunately, an aquatic mammal cannot fly out a window, so this would require multiple transformations. Then, there are the faculty and scouts who patrol the compound at night. Their alternate species were nocturnal mammals with excellent night vision. If they espied a river otter in their pond one night, they would insist on learning how it got there. *Perhaps not,* Ruwena thought.

To Milk or Not to Milk

On their original tour around the compound, Savannah had pointed out the cows and goats in the fields. There were no milk cows or goats at H'Aleth's manor house. Milk and milk products were imported from other villages. Had any such animal wandered into a Cassius village, it would have been eaten.

"You will learn how to milk a cow," Savannah remarked.

Ruwena eyed Savannah suspiciously. She had learned how to milk juices from various plants to use in potions, but milk a cow?

"You must be joking," Ruwena asserted.

"Not at all," Savannah replied.

During her practicum in animal husbandry, Ruwena observed how cows and goats were milked. Although the technique was different from that of milking a plant stem, the principle was the same. Ruwena had no difficulty learning this new skill. She quickly became immersed in how the milk was churned and processed into butter, cream, and cheese, which she was allowed to sample. She liked all these products and decided that milking cows and goats was not so bizarre after all.

As Ruwena progressed through her summer practicums, faculty found her progress quite satisfactory. Finally, she rotated to the practicum she most eagerly awaited: the aviary.

CHAPTER 25

Rescue and Release

The Aviary

The aviary introduced Ruwena to many of the native species of birds in the northern reaches of Erwina. Scouts who had interned here and in the falconry had been taught how to capture injured birds and bring them back to Erwina for care and rehabilitation. Both adult birds, who had recovered from their injuries, and fledgling birds, who had graduated from the nursery, needed a place to hone their flying skills prior to being released into the wild. Most of the birds were rescues.

Ruwena was surprised that birds were not the only rescues in the aviary. Other denizens who were common in the forest and not carnivorous spent their prerelease days there as well. There were small mammals including an abundance of baby squirrels, a few rabbits, and a few reptiles such as turtles.

Prior to releasing the fledgling birds and young squirrels, the faculty would take students on field trips to put up nests for the squirrels and birdhouses for the fledglings. When a rehabilitated bird was ready for release, the faculty, staff, and students would travel to a remote location to release it and watch it fly away on its own. Unfortunately, not all the rescued birds could be released. Although they had recovered from injury, some could no longer fly. Their role was to teach the children of Erwina and Gregor about their species, how to observe them in the wild, and how to protect them.

The Falconry

Ruwena's strong kinship with the raptors drew her to the falconry. When she requested permission to visit it, Master Xavier (zā-vǐ-er), chief falconer, allowed her to observe the different raptor species, including falcons, owls, hawks, and eagles. She was not allowed to interact with the raptors directly. This would have to wait until she successfully completed the falconry course in Form III, where she would be taught how to handle raptors safely. Master Xavier invited Ruwena to witness the release of a rehabilitated golden eagle. "What happened to it?" Ruwena asked. Master Xavier recounted the bird's story.

Rachel, one of Erwina's scouts, had seen the eagle soaring over territory that had once belonged to H'Aleth. When the eagle banked to change direction, a group of men running in formation also saw it. Suddenly one of them, an archer, drew his bow. Although the eagle abruptly changed direction, the archer's arrow struck one of its wings. Fortunately, the arrow did not fracture a bone; however, it prevented the eagle from sustaining controlled flight. It glided on thermals until it was forced to land at the edge of Erwina's southeast outpost.

Rachel had been on patrol as a scout and had witnessed the incident. She saw the eagle descending too rapidly in a poorly controlled flight. She raced to the place the eagle landed and saw where the arrow had pierced its wing. She had to be careful and make sure she was not seen by any of the men. The archer did not break formation to collect his trophy, and the group stayed on their trajectory.

The bird's fall had only aggravated the wound. Rachel knew that Master Xavier would be able to treat the bird; however, trying to take the eagle to the compound could damage the wing further. So when the men were out of sight, Rachel lifted the eagle as carefully as she could and took it into the village. The villagers would protect and care for the bird until Master Xavier arrived.

Rachel then transformed into a red wolf and set out for Erwina's compound. Even with frequent bursts of speed, it would take at least two days to reach it. When she reached the Ferveo River, she sought out a hidden kayak and transformed back into a human to cross the river. Once Rachel reached the west bank, she concealed the kayak. Then she transformed once again into a red wolf to go the rest of the way to the compound.

As a former student at Erwina, Rachel knew the layout very well. While still a red wolf, she stopped at the boathouse. Master Salinas [sal-en-us] was only slightly surprised to see a red wolf trot inside, snatch an unoccupied robe, and slip into it. When Rachel resumed human form, she alerted Master Salinas of the need for urgent transport to the east bank of the river. She abruptly turned and raced across the compound to find Master Xavier. Once Rachel told him about the eagle, he prepared a pouch of supplies. In the interim, Master Salinas and his staff had a readied a canoe to take the two rescuers across the Ferveo as rapidly as possible. Once across the river, Master Xavier transformed into a gray wolf and Rachel strapped the pouch to his back.

Even with the urgency of the situation, both Master Xavier and Rachel needed to be careful once both of them transformed on the east side of the river. Native red and gray wolves were competitors and did not share the same territory graciously. Hence, they should not be seen together. This problem was solved when Master Xavier transformed first and left as soon as Rachel strapped the pouch to his back. An hour or so later, a red wolf could be seen leaving the east bank.

Master Xavier, as a gray wolf, took the most direct route to the outpost and set a pace to get there as quickly as possible. The red wolf took a circuitous route. Thus, the two wolves did not cross paths on their way to the village. Once Rachel saw that Master Xavier had arrived safely, she resumed her patrol over the southeast territory.

"I was able to remove the arrow from the eagle's wing, splint the wing to its body, and transport it back to the falconry," said Master Xavier. "Like many other injured raptors, the eagle underwent convalescence and rehabilitation in the falconry. Now that it can resume flight, it will be released back into the wild."

Ruwena joined several other students to watch the bird's release. Since they would be traveling well beyond the compound's boundary, they were accompanied by security and joined by a few scouts. While the bird was in his care, Master Xavier had trained it to perch on his outstretched arm and to tolerate a cover on its head. While they traveled to a nearby glade, Master Xavier had put a cover over the eagle's head to keep it quiet. Once they arrived, he took the cover off. The eagle took perhaps a minute to view her surroundings. Then she took flight and came to rest on a branch high up in a tree bordering the glade. It was a thrilling sight.

"She will soon find her way back to her native territory," Master Xavier told the students.

Ruwena knew then that the falconry was the one place she needed to be most careful. Of all the raptors, she was closest to the hawk, falcon, and owl. When she first looked upon these birds long ago during trips away from the Cassius village, she knew they were kindred to her, just as she had sensed her kinship with other species when her mistress had exposed her to a wolf cub, a fox kit, a cougar cub, a playful river otter, and a winged mammal that was not represented in the falconry. As much as Ruwena wanted to stay with the raptors, she thought it best to return to the aviary. There she was much less likely to betray herself.

At no point during any of Ruwena's practicums was the topic of human metamorphosis addressed. Nevertheless, she saw the transformation class on the curriculum for senior Form II students and knew she would be taking that class. Until then, she should know nothing about the processes or practices of transformation.

CHAPTER 26

Practice Makes Perfect

Since Ruwena was new to Erwina, brief tours of duty in several of the institutions were arranged. These were designed to acquaint Ruwena with the services they provided and how they operated. Thanks to Savannah, Ruwena had already received an introduction to the archives, natural history building, and the school library. She had seen also the gristmill and winery and how they operated. All that remained was the rectory, the armory, and the gymnasium. These experiences would put her on an almost equal footing with her classmates who were born at Erwina or had come there at an early age. It was during some of these practicums, however, that Ruwena had a few (mis)adventures.

The Rectory Kitchen

Ruwena thought that her introduction to the rectory and its kitchen would be little more than learning what was required to prepare soup potions. This she already knew how to do. When she walked into the kitchen, she was nearly overwhelmed by the vast array of utensils that lined the walls and were stacked in cupboards and drawers. The number of ways and variety of tools to measure something was almost dizzying.

Ruwena had first learned how to make potions in the sparsely-outfitted small kitchen in the house where she and her mistress lived at H'Aleth. Under her mistress's tutelage, she learned how many pinches, grains, leaves, florets, or petals to use and which size of spoons or ladles or portions thereof to use. So she recognized only a few of the cooking utensils hanging from the walls and kept in drawers and cupboards in Erwina's rectory kitchen.

She could guess how some of the items might be used, but *why would anyone want a spoon with holes in it?* she wondered as she picked up a slatted spoon.

Savannah saw Ruwena staring at the spoon she had picked up. For someone who was almost always composed, Ruwena was almost wide-eyed. "It's for straining pasta," she said. Savannah had been mentoring Ruwena for some time now, and she had learned how to recognize when her protégé was puzzled by something.

There were many mouths to feed in Erwina—especially schoolchildren, who liked muffins. At H'Aleth, Ruwena had learned to bake bread as she had learned how to make potions. She could prepare fruits and vegetables as well. Her mistress, however, did not approve of confections. Certainly, there were none in a Cassius village. Those ovens baked only bricks. Until she came to Erwina, she had no idea how muffins, cakes, and pies were made—even though she had enjoyed eating them since coming to the compound.

Savannah tried to reassure Ruwena. "You will be shown how to use the most common utensils and how to bake, broil, and grill," she said. *Grill?* Ruwena thought, suppressing a mental groan. The only grilling she had ever known was when her mistress tested her knowledge of potions.

The Armory

Ruwena had seen no weapons of war until she arrived at the Cassius village. Her mistress had told her that the war between Cassius and Biogenics had been waged for many years. H'Aleth had been a casualty of that war. At the armory, once again Ruwena saw many weapons of war—swords, shields, spears, bows and arrows, and others. Although weapons were commonly seen in hunters, Ruwena had already learned that Erwinians did not hunt animals for food or sport. When she saw the array of weapons, she asked, "Are we at war?"

Master Chernavich [*churn*-a-vĭch], the chief armorist, was surprised and concerned at this question. "No, we are not," he replied. "There are two warring factions to the north and east of us. Their war could spill over into our territory. So we need to be prepared." This had already happened once.

"There are many strange and unnatural creatures roaming throughout our territory," he added. "Most of them will attack without provocation and often on sight."

Ruwena did not mention the creatures she had seen in the Cassius village that met his description. The lupucercopith [*lu*-pu-*cer*-ko-pĭth] (illus. 16) was one such a creature. Her mistress had told her that it was a hybrid created by Cassius. He had spliced the genes of a baboon into the genome of a wolf in an attempt to create an aggressive wolf-baboon hybrid to serve as a guard animal. Cassius intended for his creature to have the long snout and fangs of a baboon with the body and speed of a wolf. It was a disappointment. It had an uneven gait caused by disjointed hips and forelegs that were longer than its back legs. It had neither speed nor agility; however, it did meet Cassius's other requirements. It looked like a wolf except its snout was deformed, and it had long upper canines protruding from its mouth like those of an extinct saber-toothed tiger.

The lupucercopith was a violent hybrid. It would attack anyone or anything within its reach and lunged at any passerby. One day, one of them broke loose and went on a rampage in the village. A rusted link in its chain had finally given way under the constant strain the animal had put on it. Once freed, it attacked and killed or badly mauled several villagers who were defenseless against it. It turned on the guards as well until the latter, who were armed, finally killed it. The guards also suffered losses in the attack.

Ruwena and her mistress had been away from the village foraging for herbs, nuts, berries, and other resources they could use to prepare soups. Thus, they did not witness the incident. When they returned, evidence of the slaughter was all around them. Even now, Ruwena could see the horrible scene as if it had just happened. The memory of it made her sick, and she quelled it as quickly as possible.

During her practicum in the armory, Ruwena learned about each type of weapon and its purpose, how to hold one without injuring herself or anyone else, and observed how they were made. Accompanied by Master Chernavich, she was allowed to take one of the wooden staves outside and try to wield it. It was almost as tall as she. As Ruwena attempted to manipulate the stave, its height and weight threw her off balance. Master Chernavich caught her and the stave before she could knock herself out with it. At that point, Ruwena decided it was a good thing she had no plans to develop her skills with a stave.

Illus. 16. Lupucercopith.

The armory also made and repaired a wide variety of other tools and equipment used throughout the compound; however, there were limits. Master Chernavich, who was also the chief heraldist, drew the line at making kitchen and tableware for the rectory—much to the annoyance of Master Ratorovic [ră-*tor*-o-vĭk]. Fortunately, the artisans were quite willing to make pottery and glass items and even flatware for use in the kitchen.

Ruwena watched with fascination as master artisans created glassware using blowpipes and molds. The glass was formed by heating sand until it became fluid. Then it was allowed to cool until it could be molded. The glass could be colored by adding various minerals. After cooling, the artisan could paint the glass or etch designs on the surface. One of them showed her how to blow glass and let her try it for herself. It was much harder than it looked. She also watched as master potters molded clay into many shapes and fired them in the kilns.

Although there were no art classes per se in the curriculum, the artisans provided many opportunities for students to learn art and artistic design. Students would learn how to sketch designs that later would be etched into glassware or painted on pottery. Later, if students chose a summer practicum or internship with the artisans, they would be taught how to etch the glassware and paint the figures and patterns on pottery. Many of these designs depicted major events in the history of *H. transformans*— *Stella Ignis*, the many legends surrounding Ruth and her family, and the destruction of H'Aleth. In their own way, the artisans were recording the history of both *H. sapiens* and *H. transformans* and keeping it alive for the current generation.

Swimming Lessons

The barge and kayak were the primary means of navigating the rivers that bordered the most populated regions of Erwina. Thus, all students were taught how to swim and how to navigate rivers using barges, rafts, canoes, and kayaks. Ruwena had already had all the rafting experience she wanted. The faculty, however, insisted that she learn how to row a boat alone and in a team, how to paddle a canoe, and how to pole a barge. Ruwena could not participate in any of these activities until she could demonstrate proficiency in swimming. "You need to learn to swim," Savannah told her. Ruwena sighed silently, *I'm already a good swimmer.*

Ruwena was introduced to Madam Merena [mer-ā-nah], a specialist in swimming and diving, who would evaluate her swimming prowess. When asked if she could swim, Ruwena answered, "Yes." Then Madam Merena asked Ruwena to swim across the indoor pool using her preferred swimming style. It suddenly dawned on Ruwena that her preferred swimming style was river otter, which she couldn't demonstrate while masquerading as *H. sapiens*. Nevertheless, swimming as an otter had come naturally to her. *Surely I ought to be able to swim as a human as well,* she thought. So Ruwena slipped off the side of the pool, into the water—and promptly sank like a rock. River otters have a thick water-repellant coat of fur, an insulating layer of fat that provides buoyancy, and webbed feet. As a human, Ruwena had none of the above.

As Ruwena struggled to get back to the surface, Madam Merena dived in and pulled her up. Clearly, swimming lessons were in order. She asked Ruwena, "How did you learn to swim?"

Ruwena did not know how to answer this question. In reality, her ability to swim as an otter was instinctive. "It just happened," she answered.

Not finding Ruwena's answer particularly helpful, Matron asked, "Who taught you to swim?"

Ruwena had never been taught to swim. The manor house at H'Aleth did not have a swimming pool, and there were no streams nearby deep enough for swimming. Certainly, there was no swimming in the fouled waters around the Cassius village. Her mistress had forbidden her to even wade in them. The water could cause deadly illness. "I just did on my own," she replied, another technically correct answer.

Feeling a bit frustrated, Madam Merena asked, "Where did you learn to swim?" She was hoping to get some degree—any degree—of insight into Ruwena's past swimming experience. If she knew in what setting—pond, river, pool—Ruwena had tried to swim, she might have a better understanding.

Ruwena was at a loss. "In water?" she ventured.

Madam Merena was astounded by this reply. "Of course, it was in water! You can't swim on land!"

"River water," Ruwena answered quickly.

Madam Merena stood looking at Ruwena. Ruwena found it reminiscent of how her mistress would stand when she was about to criticize one of her potions.

"You really don't know how to swim, do you?" said Madam Merena sternly.

"Apparently not," Ruwena replied lamely. *Not as a human,* she thought.

Whereupon Madam Merena decided that swimming lessons should begin immediately—starting with how not to drown in standing water.

Ruwena quickly learned to float and tread water. Afterward, some swimming strokes were relatively easy to learn. Paddling with both arms and hands while kicking with both legs and feet underwater seemed natural. She could easily hold her breath for two minutes. The sidestroke on the surface of the water was not unlike what an otter could do. More sophisticated swimming strokes—breaststroke, butterfly stroke, even freestyle—seemed awkward.

Diving off the side of the pool also seemed quite natural to Ruwena. She could reach the bottom of the deepest part of the pool easily. At first, diving off a high platform seemed unnatural. Then she realized that hawks and falcons dive from great heights—just not into water; however, sea eagles and osprey do. When using the springboard, she could leap up and out, spread her arms as if they were wings, and then assume a diving position to enter the water. This seemed more natural to her, and it might prove a useful means of escaping an aerial predator over water. Once she dived into the water, she could transform into an otter and swim away. She did not mention this to Madam Merena.

CHAPTER 27

Zebrafish

With Savannah as her guide, Ruwena joined the cohort of students entering the fall term—the start of their senior year in Form II. Ruwena progressed through her customized program of study without incident. She did, indeed, pass the proficiency tests for potions V and VI. As a Form II senior, however, she was careful not to take the test for potions VII (app. B, table 7).

Although somewhat tedious, the formal classes were not difficult. Ruwena was surprisingly well versed in human anatomy and was able to help Savannah with this subject. Ruwena needed to do so very carefully. Her knowledge was backward engineered by her mistress, who would tell her which features and systems were distorted in the hybrid or corrupted creatures that they encountered in the Cassius village. Then, her mistress would describe how these features and systems should look and function.

Ruwena found the customized study of biology and botany with their associated practicums the most interesting of all her classes. During her proctored study of general biology with Master Pastorov, Ruwena first learned about morphogenesis. Zebrafish developed very quickly from an egg to an embryo stage in three days. Since the body of a zebrafish was transparent, she could literally watch its growth and development. If its genotype was modified while it was still in the egg stage, the phenotypic changes could be observed in as little as three days.

Building Form and Function

Master Pastorov described morphogenesis as the gradual changes in structure, form, and function that occurred as an organism grew and developed into adulthood. As an example, he described the development of a fertilized ovum into an embryo and then a fetus during pregnancy. "Even though the human embryo undergoes significant physical changes, these changes reflect stages in normal growth and development," he explained. Even after reaching adulthood, changes would continue to occur (e.g., increasing muscle size, growing taller, etc.). Although shape might be amended somewhat, the adult still maintained his or her basic shape, form, and function.

Ruwena recalled when a young varanhieracta [*var*-an-hī-ĕr-*ac*-tah] was brought to the Cassius village. It had been hatched from a Komodo dragon egg after the genes of an eagle had been spliced into the genome of the egg. It seemed that Cassius was trying to genetically engineer a dragon that could fly. This young hybrid had the head and torso of the komodo with feathers blended in among its scales, but no wings—yet. It was let loose in the village to forage on whatever it could find, which included some of the villagers, and to see if it would continue to grow and ultimately develop wings.

Master Pasterov then contrasted morphogenesis with metamorphosis, which is the transformation of an organism into an altogether different shape, form, and function. In *H. transformans*, metamorphosis was quite apparent in the transformation from human into a different species and its reversal. Despite the varanhieracta's features, Ruwena realized it was not undergoing metamorphosis. It was simply growing in accordance with the genome it had been given artificially.

Ruwena learned that for any changes to occur—whether by morphogenesis or metamorphosis—there had to be an underlying genetic code (a plan) directing the changes. Master Pasterov explained, "Deoxyribonucleic acid is the blueprint or master plan for how an organism is formed because it contains the gene sequences for building form and function. These sequences contain not only coding genes for how to create building materials such as proteins, they also contain noncoding genes for how to assemble them into muscle and bone and other tissues. Ultimately, all these genes direct the final shape and form an organism will have."

The same regulatory genes that directed the expression of the human phenotype were also likely to direct the expression of any alternate species phenotypes in *H. transformans*. "Consider the duck-billed platypus," said Master Pasterov. "Its genome reflects genes found in mammals, reptiles, birds, amphibians, and fish." Indeed, the phenotype of the duckbill consisted of a rubbery snout shaped like that of a duck, a torso and webbed feet with claws like those of an otter, a tail like that of a beaver (only slightly more elongated), and a spur on the male's foot that injected venom like that of a reptile. The females laid eggs like a reptile and lactated like a mammal. The platypus represented a true hybrid (with thanks and a tip of the hat to genetic homology).

Developing Form and Function

Master Pasterov explained further that growth referred to the development and differentiation of tissues and organs. Growth was stimulated by chemical substances that activated the genes that coded for the formation of proteins and other constituents. These substances included growth factors and hormones (trophic signals) that directed how cells, tissues, and organs would develop and what their final form and function would be. "These same factors are active during transformation," said Master Pastorov. "You will hear about them again when you take the transformation class."

In *H. sapiens*, there were a large number of growth factors and hormones that directed and supported growth. Many of these were thought to play a significant role in transformation. One large family of growth factors (TGFβ) included chemical signals that directly affected embryonic development. In *H. transformans*, these and other growth factors likely facilitated the change in shape and function during transformation. Both Angus and later Rafe Cassius tested this hypothesis repeatedly by using growth factors to increase the size and strength of their genetically engineered hybrids. Both were pleased with the effects initially until they realized that these factors also accentuated the hybrids' deformities, which often accelerated their demise. This was the fate of the varanhieracta. It continued to grow in size and weight consistent with a Komodo dragon. Unfortunately for the animal, the bones of its legs were hollow, consistent with the bones of a raptor. Eventually, they were unable to support its weight.

Finally, if the underlying genetic code directing the production and actions of these factors was corrupted, then the factors would not function normally and might not be produced at all. Whether the individual is an *H. sapiens* or an *H. transformans*, neither one would grow or develop normally in their human form. An *H. transformans* who had both the capability and the complete genome of an alternate species would not be able to transform if a hormone or growth factor critical to the process failed to function properly.

Making Alterations

By nine to ten weeks of age, the human embryo would have formed all its organ systems with the exception of the central nervous system, which would continue to develop throughout pregnancy. In effect, *H. sapiens* changed from a single-celled entity into a developing fetus within ten weeks. "This extraordinary feat of development still amazes me," said Master Pasterov.

The means by which the embryo achieved these changes was by having embryonic stem cells with the ability to change into any cell type the developing embryo needed. Even in adulthood, specific types of tissues (e.g., muscle, nerve, etc.) continued to maintain a supply of adult stem cells. These cells could repair and replace their specific tissues if necessary; however, they could not do so for any other tissue type.

In order for *H. transformans* to undergo the extensive changes required to transform into another species, it was hypothesized that their embryonic stem cells remained active throughout the life of the individual. These stem cells provided the ability and flexibility (plasticity) required at the cellular level to change into any cell type supported by the individual's genome.

Finally, in both *H. sapiens* and *H. transformans*, there were several mechanisms by which cells, tissues, and the organs comprised of them could modify some of their characteristics depending upon conditions. Although these changes could affect cell and tissue functions and even modify their form, they did not reorganize internal structures or transform shape. Some changes occurred commonly and often were driven by an organism's internal or external environment. These changes could be helpful or harmful. An example of a helpful change was when cells and the tissues they comprise enlarge to enhance functionality. "Gymnastics is a good example," said Master Pasterov. "Both heart and skeletal muscles enlarge to support the extra workload. This is called conditioning," he explained. "In deconditioning, the process is reversed when the reason for it no longer exists."

Sequelae

Ruwena thought back to the many hybrids she had seen in a Cassius village. Rafe Cassius's misuse of genetic engineering had caused terrible deformities. Nearly all the hybrids were distorted and disfigured in some way, and the varanhieracta was no different. As it grew larger and heavier, the hollow bones of its legs shattered under its weight. Afterwards, it could no longer hunt or feed and did not survive. It never developed wings. It sickened Ruwena to think how the Cassian hybrids must have suffered.

Still, Rafe considered his experiment a success. He proved that he could develop a hybrid from an embryo—at least in a reptile—and would come to rely heavily on this method for the production of animal hybrids. His major constraint was the time needed for the embryo to develop into an adult. Hence, his use of this technology was limited to those species that would develop in a few months. He was not going to grow a human hybrid quickly. So he still had to rely on forced transformation in those *H. transformans* whose alternate species had characteristics he wanted.

Supplemental Notes and Citations

General references for the synthesis of proteins from DNA in this section are Beery and Workman (2012), Carroll (2009b), Jorde (2014a, 2014b), and Guyton and Hall (2006). Additional citations are as noted.

Growth

Morphogens are agents that exert control over growth, development, and morphogenesis (Mehlen et al., 2005; Tabata and Takei, 2004). These agents can induce cell division, govern the migration of cells to their assembly site, and influence the shape and pattern of cell differentiation (Bellas and Chen, 2014; Zhou et al., 2015). Some agents can initiate a change in gene expression. Note: The reader is cautioned not to confuse morphogen with mutagen.

Trophic signals are chemical agents and proteins (e.g., hormones, growth factors) that promote cell growth, differentiation, migration (of cells to their assembly sites), and survival. Hormones coordinate a vast array of physiologic functions. They are produced and secreted into the blood by their respective endocrine glands and are distributed throughout the body. Some hormones are used by virtually every cell, whereas others target specific cell types. Several hormones (e.g., growth hormone, thyroxine) exert a direct effect on genes to exert their influence, either to direct the production of proteins and other compounds or to direct how these components would be used.

In an adult *H. sapiens*, an abnormal increase in the production of the growth hormone (usually caused by a benign pituitary tumor) can lead to increase in the size of bone and soft tissues (acromegaly) (Scacchi and Cavagnini, 2006). This is most visible in the face and hands; however, it affects internal organs as well (Abreu et al., 2016). So structural changes in size can occur in a fully grown adult over a long period of time.

Transforming growth factor β (TGFβ) is a family of morphogens and growth factors directly involved in the development of many different types of tissues such as blood vessels (vascular epithelial growth factor), bone and cartilage (bone morphogenic proteins), nerve, heart, and tissues of other organs of the body (growth and differentiation factor) (Chen et al., 2004; Nana et al., 2015; Reddi, 2000). TGFβ1 is a subgroup of factors that control cell growth, proliferation, differentiation, and survival (Kajdaniuk et al., 2013; Gordon, and Blobe, 2008).

Adaptation

Changes in cell structure and/or organization occur in response to direct stimulation and changes in the environment. Cellular changes lead to corresponding changes in tissues and organs, affecting their structure and function.

Adaptive changes are normal physiologic changes that enhance functionality and prevent loss of function. Hypertrophy is an increase in functional cell size (not the number of cells) resulting in an increase in tissue size. Muscle building is an example. Hyperplasia is an increase in the number of cells also resulting in an increase in size.

Maladaptive changes are pathologic and are usually the result of disease or lead to dysfunction or disease. Dysplasia is cell growth that results in abnormal changes to mature cells. Changes in size, shape, and organization vary from one cell to another, often leading to a loss of the tissue's normal function. This type of change is considered deranged growth. A high grade of dysplasia is strongly implicated as a precursor of cancer.

Gene Activation

The gene sequence below describes the steps in the production of a protein. The process is not unlike making a cake from a recipe.

Step 1—locate the master recipe (at the location of the desired gene sequence, unwind the strands of DNA, which are loosely bound for ease of separation).

Step 2—make a copy of the master recipe (transcription is the process of making an edited copy of a DNA gene sequence, called mRNA, for use in the production of a protein. RNA polymerase is a group of enzymes that isolates and separates the desired segment of DNA and makes the mRNA. Note: The edit is substituting uracil for thymine in forming mRNA.)

Step 3—using the copy of the recipe (mRNA), read the directions and identify the ingredients (translation is the process whereby mRNA interprets the directions for synthesizing a protein, including identifying the ingredients, e.g., which amino acids to use and in what order).

Step 4—fetch the ingredients and line them up in the order in which the recipe states they will be used (transfer RNA [tRNA], another subtype of RNA, retrieves the correct amino acids and assembles them in the sequence dictated by mRNA).

Step 5—add the ingredients and bake as directed by the recipe (ribosomal RNA [rRNA], another subtype of RNA, serves as a matchmaker between mRNA and tRNA so that the ingredients, amino acids, can be assembled in their proper order as dictated by the original gene sequence in DNA).

Only about 1.5% of the human genome is used to code for proteins. The remainder consists of noncoding genetic material that serves a variety of purposes, including separating coding sequences and controlling the entire process for accessing and activating other genes.

Stem Cells

Embryonic stem cells are cells with an unlimited ability to reproduce and the ability to change into any cell type the embryo needs (pluripotency) (Borsos and Torres-Padilla, 2016; Daley, 2015; Findlay, 2007; Melcer and Meshorer, 2010; Mitalipov and Wolf, 2009; Na et al., 2010; Seymour et al., 2015). Within three to four days after fertilization, a hollow ball of cells forms (the blastocyst), which subsequently develops into an embryo. Under the influence of pluripotent stems cells, the embryo begins to form tissues (e.g., cardiac muscle tissue), which subsequently become organs (e.g., the heart) and organ systems (e.g., the cardiovascular system). Within these different types of tissues, a subset of specialized stem cells (multipotent stem cells) can differentiate into the kinds of cells used by a specific type of tissue (e.g., bone, muscle, skin, etc.).

Adult stem cells have the property of tissue regeneration and replacement (Dulak et al., 2015; Peng et al., 2012). Unfortunately, in *H. sapiens*, many tissues (e.g., the heart) do not have stem cells and cannot regenerate tissue that is lost. When heart muscle is destroyed in a heart attack, it cannot be replaced by new heart muscle. Instead, the affected tissue is replaced by scar tissue, which provides structural support but cannot participate in pumping blood.

Plasticity refers to the ability of one type of (stem) cell to change into another type of (stem) cell (Blanpain and Fuchs, 2014). This usually occurs under the influence of growth factors that (re)direct the cells development (Stachowiak and Stachowiak, 2016; Terranova et al., 2015). Note: The reader is cautioned not to confuse plasticity with pleiotropy. Pleiotropy is the ability of a gene to have multiple and varying effects depending upon where it is active without any change in the gene itself.

Cell Death

Apoptosis is programmed or planned cell death. It is a normal, orderly process for removing unwanted cells that are too old, too many, too cranky, and are no longer needed (Merkle, 2009a). The cell releases its own digestive enzymes, which break down its structures and shrinks it. Then, the remains of the dead cell are engulfed by another type of cell (a phagocyte) that will dispose of it. In *H. sapiens*, millions of cells normally die each day as they are replaced by new ones (e.g., skin, intestines, blood cells).

CHAPTER 28

From Caterpillar to Butterfly

Ruwena's ability to transform mirrored that of her great-great-grandmother's. Her metamorphosis into any of her alternate species was smooth, streamlined, and timely. She had never given any consideration to how she was able to transform. It just happened. Her mistress never offered any explanation other than kinship with another species. Master Pastorov rectified this discrepancy.

Transcending Evolution

Master Pastorov used the manner in which a caterpillar changes into a butterfly as a representative example of metamorphosis. "Within a caterpillar's chrysalis, enzymes break down most of its structures," he explained. "The core of some structures remain, and specialized cells that are still alive drive the change into a butterfly." He paused for a moment and then added, "This radical change in structure, form, and function is truly extraordinary." *Just as it is with us,* he thought, mindful of his own metamorphosis into one of the largest land mammals, a polar bear.

The transformation from caterpillar to butterfly (or a tadpole to a frog) reflected a complete and permanent restructuring of these organisms. Neither one could reverse their transformations. In *H. transformans*, however, transformation reflected a temporary restructuring of form and function. The presence of an X^T chromosome continued to support metamorphosis throughout life and remained active regardless of what form an *H. transformans* took.

The changes in physique from human form to that of another mammal seemed extraordinary. Yet there were underlying processes to accomplish this feat, just as there were for the butterfly. In *H. transformans*, embryonic stem cells could become any type of cell needed. Growth factors and hormones, which influenced what form and features the tissues would have, remained active and allowed reprogramming in vivo of both structure and function. Transposable elements supported the expression of alternate species genes through temporary genetic remodeling. As long as a complete set of genes dictating phenotype were present, processes supporting tissue plasticity permitted the changes.

Even in *H. sapiens*, factors in a cell's external environment, such as mechanical forces, and its internal environment, such as oxygenation, could lead to changes in cell characteristics, including the number of cells and their orientation within tissues. Some tissues could be rebuilt and renewed. Under the influence of trophic signals, bone had the capacity to regenerate and rebuild (remodel) itself. It was continually being resorbed and replaced even under normal conditions. New blood vessels (angiogenesis) could be built to support tissue needs. Even the outer layer of skin was continually replacing itself as dead skin cells were sloughed off. These same processes were at work in *H. transformans*.

Specific hormones had a direct influence on the rate and extent of growth, development, and size. In *H. sapiens*, growth rate slowed after puberty until a certain body and organ size is reached at which time growth in size ceased. This set point could vary considerably among members of the same family. In *H. transformans*, these limits were reset during transformation to be consistent with those of the alternate species.

Hidden Traits

It was winter term when the first transformation class was offered. During this class, Ruwena learned that the majority of the inhabitants of Erwina were *H. transformans*. The species of each member—*H. sapiens* or *H. transformans*—was determined at birth when genetic testing revealed whether or not the infant possessed an X^T chromosome and, if so, how many. Testing also revealed whether or not the child possessed a full complement of genes for an alternate species. Afterward, the birth of each child was entered into the family pedigree for that child demonstrating his or her lineage, with annotations for gender, species, the number of X^T chromosomes, and the potential ability to transform into a specific alternate species (box 10). *Do I have a birth record somewhere?* Ruwena wondered.

Box 10. Birth Record.

Record of Birth

Last name: Devveni   First name: Evan
Date of birth: SI466:0617:1832.42   House: Erwina
Gender: Male   Live birth: Yes
Species: *H. transformans*   Genotype: X^T, Y
Genome mapped: Yes
Alternate species genome found: gray wolf, red fox
Additional annotations: paternal grandfather's alternate
species was a red fox

Last name of father: Devveni   First name: Will
Date of Birth: SI423:1122:0936.12   House: Erwina
Species: *H. transformans*   Genotype: X^T, Y
Alternate species: gray wolf

Last name of mother: Devveni   First name: Edrea
Date of Birth: SI435:0905:1325.36   House: Erwina
Species: *H. transformans*   Genotype: X^T, X
Alternate species: gray wolf, red fox

Name(s) of attendant(s) at birth: H'Umara
Signature certifying birth: H'Umara
Date: SI466:0617:1841. 12

Box 10

Yet not all *H. transformans* possessed the ability to transform. Thus, both students and their parents needed to be reminded that having the capability to transform (an X^T) by no means conferred the ability. Everyone who was born into Erwina or married into it was tested, even people who were *H. sapiens*. An apparent *H. sapiens* could be unaware that he/she possessed a full complement of genes for an alternate species. Without an X^T, however, those genes could not be expressed.

In contrast, some people could have inherited an X^T chromosome without a complete genotype for an alternate species. As a result, they possessed the capability but lacked the ability to express the phenotype of an alternate species. This was not uncommon. It was one of the reasons why there were many people with an X^T who could not transform and were classified as *H. sapiens*. Nevertheless, two such parents could produce an *H. transformans* child, provided the child also inherited a complete genome for an alternate species (figure 6 and figure 7).

Fig. 6. Patterns of Inheritance for *H. sapiens* to *H. transformans*: Pattern No. 1.

Fig. 6. Patterns of Inheritance for *H. sapiens* to *H. transformans*: Pattern No. 1

Maternal X, X^T (*without* a full complement of genes for an alternate species)
Paternal X, Y (*with* a full complement of genes for an alternate species)

		Mother X	Mother X^T
Father	X	X X	X X^T
	Y	X Y	X^T Y

In pattern no. 1, the mother has one X^T but does not have a full complement of genes for an alternate species. The father does not have an X^T but does possess a full complement of genes for an alternate species. (Note: Genes for alternate species are found on autosomal chromosomes.)

For each pregnancy, there is a 50% probability the child will have an X^T—25% that a female child will have an XX^T and 25% that a male child will have an X^T, Y—thereby conferring the capability to transform. There is a 50% probability that a child will not inherit an X^T at all (25% chance each for males and females). There is a 50% probability that a child will inherit a full complement of genes from the father and, therefore, will have both the capability and the ability to transform (25% chance each for males and females).

Fig. 7. Patterns of Inheritance for *H. sapiens* to *H. transformans*: Pattern No. 2.

Fig. 7. Patterns of Inheritance for *H. sapiens* to *H. transformans*: Pattern No. 2

Maternal X, X (*with* a full complement of genes for an alternate species)

Paternal X^T, Y (*without* a full complement of genes for an alternate species)

	Mother	
	X	X
X^T	$X^T X$	$X^T X$
Y	X Y	X Y

(Father is labeled on the left: X^T / Father / Y)

In pattern no. 2, the mother does not have an X^T but does possess a full complement of genes for an alternate species. The father possesses an X^T but does not have a full complement of genes for an alternate species.

There is a 50% probability that female offspring will have both the capability and ability to transform, and a 50% probability that male offspring will possess a full complement of genes without the ability to transform. Nevertheless, sons can still pass on the ability to transform into that species to their offspring who could mate with a female X^T (see figure 6, pattern no. 1).

These inheritance patterns were discovered first by the researchers at H'Aleth. After conferring with one another, the three Houses agreed that anyone possessing an X^T chromosome should be considered an *H. transformans*, regardless of his or her ability to transform. All three Houses also agreed that any *H. sapiens* who possessed a full complement of genes for an alternate species should be protected as well. Those individuals who possessed an X^T without the complete genotype of an alternate species or possessed the genotype but not the X^T were still sought out by Biogenics and hunted down by Cassius. If caught, they could be forced into breeding programs in which someone with a complete genotype could be mated with someone with an X^T chromosome, even if the latter could not transform. Their mating could produce offspring that would have both and be able to transform.

Transformation I—Basic Rules

Regardless of their pedigrees, children of both species grew up with one another. Thus, both *H. sapiens* and *H. transformans* students attended all classes together, including those directed at transformation. Since the process of transformation could be very dangerous, *H. sapiens* people needed to know as much about the process and its dangers as did *H. transformans* people.

Most of the *H. transformans* students had not yet come of age and, therefore, had not yet developed the capability or the ability to transform. They would soon do so, however, and needed to learn the rules before they started transforming. Consequently, the rules of transformation were pounded into the students (box 11). "Failure to comply with these rules could result in a student being assessed as unsafe, a potential threat to others, and forbidden to transform," admonished Matron H'Umara [*hu*-mar-a], who was backed by Matron Aquina. (This was extremely rare.)

Most students were compliant—if only because they were eager to be certified by the faculty, which would allow them to transform without faculty supervision. They could test their limits later. This notion was addressed as well. To illustrate the risks involved and the rationale for the rules, faculty recounted two past cases of corrupted transformations in students. One of them proved deadly.

Box 11. Rules of Transformation.

Rules of Transformation

1. When students first develop the capability and ability to transform, they may do so *only* under the direct supervision of faculty or another supervising adult.
2. Students must not attempt to transform outside their abilities.
3. Students must not attempt to transform without sufficient time to do so safely.
4. Students must complete each transformation fully and successfully before transforming again.
5. *Uncertified students* may not transform without approval of the faculty *except* in an emergency.
6. In the event of a confirmed attack, students with the capability and ability may transform to *escape* an enemy, if necessary, without approval of the faculty.
7. Students are not to engage an enemy or a predator as a human or as his/her alternate species *unless* they have no other means of escape.
8. *Certified* Form II seniors and Form III students may transform without direct supervision of faculty *as long as they are accompanied by another certified student or an adult.*
9. Certified Form II seniors and Form III students who transform must remain inside the campus perimeter.
10. Certified Form IV students may transform at will, without an escort, and may go beyond the *perimeter*; however, they may not go beyond the *boundary* of the compound without faculty permission.

Box 11

The Challenge

In anticipation of the summer games, two Form III freshmen, who were good friends, decided they wanted to see which one of them was the faster sprinter in their alternate species, the gray fox. Both had passed the transformation class and were allowed to transform with permission of the faculty. Neither of them was certified.

Early one morning, after their roommates left for breakfast, the two transformed in their rooms and met on the athletic field. There they lined up together on the track. As previously arranged, both tapped a front paw in unison three times. Ready, set—as their paws struck the ground for the third time, they both took off racing. When one nosed out the other, both trotted back to the starting line and raced again. The result was the same.

Then, the loser trotted over to the starting line for the track with hurdles. The challenge was obvious. Both foxes lined up. The same starting rules were used, and they took off. The two foxes—rather, the two students—were having a grand time when they heard the south bell tower peal. Uh-oh.

Now they were in a race of a different kind. One of the two students realized he was going to be late for class and accepted the fact. So he went to his room and waited until he had resumed his human form. He then reported to class with his apologies for being tardy. As the class progressed, he became increasingly worried about his classmate who had not yet arrived. Perhaps his friend had opted to skip class. Although he knew this was possible, he also knew it was highly unlikely.

The student abruptly excused himself from class to seek out his friend. He looked in his dorm room, back on the athletic field, and in some of his friend's favorite haunts without success. Now deeply concerned, he sought out the first faculty member he could find in the schoolhouse, Master Pastorov. The worried and anxious student reported, "Both Franz and I had transformed into foxes and were racing each other on the track when we heard the bell sound for class. We both ran back, but he never showed up for class. Now I can't find him."

Master Pastorov promptly alerted Master Titus, who dispatched security to seek out the missing student. Master Pastorov also alerted the infirmary of the possibility that a student may have suffered an injury, possibly one due to transformation. Security found the second student still on the athletic field, hidden by some stationary equipment. The scout recognized the symptoms of an aborted transformation and carried him immediately to the infirmary. Franz was treated successfully and survived; however, he was left with a permanent convex curvature of his lumbar spine and hyperextension of both legs at the hip. He could no longer transform. Later, he admitted to his friend, "I thought I could beat the clock and transform fast enough to make it to class on time."

A Deadly Decision

Long ago, another student with the complete genome of a red fox and a partial genome of a gray wolf was able to transform into a red fox. Most of his friends, however, could transform into gray wolves. When they traveled together in their respective alternate species, the wolves could outpace him in a sprint and often did. Frustrated with this situation, the student who could become a fox thought he had the solution. Since both wolves and foxes are members of the same family, *Canidae*, he assumed there was enough similarity between the two species that his fox genome would supplement his wolf genome so that he could transform into a gray wolf. The student did not consult with anyone about this notion.

One day, when the student was about to join his gray wolf comrades, he began his transformation into a fox. Partway through the transformation, he attempted to invoke his gray wolf genes. The effect was terrible. Between the aborted fox transformation and an incomplete wolf genotype, neither transformation could be completed. The contorted result was incompatible with life, and the student died. This was the incident that led to the requirement for certification. From that time forward, students had to be certified before they could transform without supervision.

Even after listening to these past events, sometimes a student would be careless or disregard one of the rules. In so doing, the student would become very ill with signs suggestive of an impending corruption. This was a medical emergency. It also provided a real-life example to the rest of the student body of what could happen. The student providing this lesson would have his or her certification postponed or rescinded, provided the student recovered and still retained the ability to transform.

As her mistress had commanded, Ruwena did not reveal that she, too, was an *H. transformans* and had learned the rules and risks of transformation from her mistress. So Ruwena attended, listened carefully for any new information, and only spoke if addressed by the faculty. By the end of the winter term, Ruwena recognized that she was $2X^T$. The class rules had served her well.

Coming-of-Age

Periodic testing for activation of the X^T was conducted on *H. transformans* students until their X^T was found active. Approximately three to four months later, the genes of their alternate species would be activated. Prior to that time, the autosomal genes of other species (if any) remained dormant.

In both *H. sapiens* and *H. transformans*, the hormones that stimulated puberty were the same. Children from both species underwent puberty for their reproductive systems to mature. It was during this time that they developed the secondary sex characteristics of their gender and achieved reproductive capability. In *H. transformans*, these hormones also triggered the capability to transform. Thus, both sexes must first undergo puberty, in which their native gender is established, before the genes for transformation would be activated. For those with one X^T chromosome, the age at which the X^T was activated usually fell between ages of twelve to thirteen for females and thirteen and fourteen for males. For females with two X^T chromosomes, the average age of activation was eleven to twelve. Hence, these children could undergo precocious puberty. Thus, girls who were $2X^T$ were able to transform earlier than the rest of their classmates.

It took time for the changes associated with puberty to develop. It also took time to make the changes associated with the capability to transform. In both cases, genes needed to be activated, anatomy needed to develop, and physiology needed to adapt to the changes triggered first by puberty and then by activation of an X^T chromosome. Once transforming genes on an X^T chromosome were fully activated and the individual had developed the capability to transform, the genes of other species (if any) were activated. The ability to transform typically developed over a four- to eight-month period of time, unless an accelerant was used. At that point, an *H. transformans* child was considered to have come of age. Then students could begin practicing transformation under close supervision.

Supplemental Notes and Citations

General references for the actions of hormones are Matfin G. (2009) and Brashers and Jones (2012). Additional citations are as noted.

Growth Factors and Hormones

Trophic signals such as growth factors can trigger intracellular signals that direct (reprogram) growth in a cell via interaction with its DNA (Poser et al., 2015). The integrative nuclear fibroblast growth factor is one example of a growth factor that can change a cell's identity, which allows for reprograming of structure and function (Stachowiak and Stachowiak, 2016; Terranova et al., 2015). Some of these agents can (re)direct genes and trigger the development of tissues and organs though their signaling pathways (Evans and Mangelsdorf, 2014; Grimaldi et al., 2013; Sirakov et al., 2013, 2014).

In *H. sapiens*, bone remodeling refers to the normal turnover of bone constituents and the process of repairing bone after a fracture (Crowther-Radulewicz, 2014). Bone morphogenic protein is a growth factor that belongs to the transforming growth factor beta group (Chen et al., 2004; Reddi, 2000). It also influences the development of heart, brain, and cartilage tissues (Chen et al., 2004).

Several hormones also trigger intracellular signals that directly affect the growth and maturation of tissues. Some target specific tissues (e.g., reproductive hormones), while others affect all cells (e.g., thyroxin). Growth hormone stimulates growth and maturation of many tissues, including bone. The parathyroid hormone acts to mobilize the mineral resources needed to build or remodel bone.

Stem Cells

Multipotent stem cells present in the walls of blood vessels can generate many of the cell types that comprise a blood vessel (Psaltis and Simari, 2015). The development of new blood vessels is needed to support growth and repair of tissues. Collateral circulation is one example of the development of new arteries (arteriogenesis) and capillaries (angiogenesis) to support blood flow to tissues.

Transposable Elements (TE)

The Alu family of transposable elements is the primary variety in *H. sapiens* (Wang and Huang, 2014). They can also affect recombination and activation of genes (Rowold and Herrera, 2000).

External and Internal Influences

External forces can cause changes in shape, pattern, and differentiation (Heisenberg and Bellaiche, 2013). For example, exercise can lead to an increase in muscle size (hypertrophy). Other factors that can effect changes include hormones that can increase the number of cells (hyperplasia) and changes in environment (e.g., oxygenation, level of acidity) that can lead to a change in cell type (metaplasia).

Conditions inside the cell, physical and biochemical actions, can cause changes in cell characteristics. In *H. sapiens*, growth factors can trigger the activity of certain intracellular enzyme systems (e.g., Abl kinases), which, in turn, can reorder the structure (morphology) of the affected cells (Hernandez et al., 2004).

Tissue Plasticity

The ability of some cells to change their characteristics and become a different type of cell (plasticity) can lead to a different tissue type and, therefore, divergent phenotypes (Champagne, 2013). Trophic signals are often shared across species and influence plasticity during development (Champagne, 2013). Epigenetic processes also can affect gene expression without changing the gene itself.

Keratinocytes are a type of skin cell that changes its cellular structure as it migrates to the surface of the skin. Its internal structure is completely reorganized in order to form a protective barrier against the environment (Simpson et al., 2011).

Features

Homo sapiens carries genes that, when (over)expressed, resemble features found in some alternate species. These include enlargement of bones (gigantism, acromegaly); excessive amounts of thick hair covering the body (hypertrichosis); thickened, dried scales for skin (ichthyosis); and thickened black velvet skin (acanthosis nigrans). In *H. sapiens*, most of these changes are associated with hormonal (trophic) disorders or genetic mutations.

Set-point is the maximum size a body can achieve. The body size in mammals is a highly variable, complex, multifactorial trait affected by a wide range of factors including genes and genetic mutations (Kemper et al., 2012). In *H. sapiens*, internal regulation of body and organ size occurs through suppression in growth of cell numbers or size or both, which may be triggered by mechanisms or signals intrinsic to each organ and tissue type (Lui and Baron, 2011; Rosello-Diez and Joyner, 2015; Stanger, 2008; Tumaneng et al., 2012). Organ size tends to be proportional to body size. Insulin and TOR kinase are two signaling pathways in *H. sapiens* that can alter organ size (Gokhale and Shingleton, 2015; Leevers and McNeill, 2005).

CHAPTER 29

The Winter Games

In her new life, Ruwena found she was under a much different kind of stress than what her mistress and life in a Cassius village had imposed. In Erwina, she was surrounded almost constantly by highly sociable and intelligent people, both in and out of the classroom. Savannah would introduce her to classmates she had not yet met and drag her to social activities, which Ruwena found stifling. The only place that offered any solitude and surcease from the presence of others was her dormitory room at night, and there she was confined to the schoolhouse. So while she was still the sole occupant of her room, Ruwena indulged in her favorite avenue of escape. She opened the large window and flew out.

In the trees not far from the falconry, Master Xavier had observed an owl he had not seen previously. He knew most of the raptors that frequented the area. This bird was new and not native to the region. It was a woodland owl with dark tufted ears; grayish-brown speckled feathers on its back, wings, and tail; and breast feathers that were white. These birds normally inhabited forests in the southeastern territories that were once under the auspices of the House of H'Aleth and now fell under the Cassius Foundation.

What are you doing here? Master Xavier wondered. Had it been driven out of its territory by predators or war? Had its food source dwindled, driving it farther afield to find prey? The owl seemed to be considering him as well. After a few moments, the bird took flight and flew farther into the woods.

The falconer would see glimpses of the owl from time to time, sporadically, and always late at night. He looked for its daytime roost but could find no sign of one. On those nights when he patrolled the perimeter as a gray wolf, he would catch glimpses of other nocturnal birds. Glimpses of the woodland owl remained brief and infrequent until a sudden thunderstorm late one night. High winds and hail drove several raptors—along with Master Xavier—into an open roost at the falconry for refuge. The birds were scattered among the rafters. One of them was the woodland owl.

The owl and Master Xavier watched each other for a few moments. As if the bird could understand what he was saying, Master Xavier asked, "Where are you from?"

The owl seemed to listen to the question, but made no reply. Master Xavier made no attempt to approach the bird out of concern he might drive it out into the storm. The hail and high winds could cause serious injury to any bird. So he approached and spoke to another owl that he knew well. This owl had been injured and brought to the compound for treatment and rehabilitation. It had made a full recovery and was released back into the wild. So this owl knew Master Xavier well and stepped onto his outstretched arm (illus. 17).

After a few minutes, the bird returned safely and unharmed to its place in the rafters. Once the storm passed, all the birds who would not be roosting there for the night flew away—including the immigrant owl.

As fall became winter, Master Xavier no longer saw the woodland owl. It may have migrated back to warmer climates.

Kindred Spirits

Although Ruwena was relieved to know that she was among others like herself, she did not reveal that she already had the ability to transform. Given her mistress's past admonitions, Rowena was uncertain how to proceed. So she continued in the role of an *H. sapiens* and supported her classmates who were learning how to transform and how to control the process. She was always close by when Savannah underwent transformation into her alternate species, a gray wolf. In this manner, Ruwena protected and supported Savannah just as Savannah had done for Ruwena since coming to Erwina. Once Savannah became proficient at transforming, she spent more time roaming about the compound as a wolf.

Illus. 17. The Immigrant Owl.

Ruwena often wished she could join her and, at times, was sorely tempted to reveal her own abilities. Still, she remembered her mistress's warning. At some point, Ruwena would have to let Savannah and the faculty know her true species.

Until then, Ruwena would need to be more cautious. Her last encounter with the chief falconer clearly raised questions—at least in Master Xavier. So while the weather still allowed, she transformed into her alternate species only when she could range deeper into the forest at the outer borders of the compound. Few humans went there, especially at night. Even so, she would encounter other nocturnal mammals and birds and wonder if they, too, were transformed. She knew that many sentries patrolled the borders of the compound and kept watch over it. None of them were in human form.

A Contrast of Winters

When winter term began, the compound was covered in snow. For once, Ruwena was glad she did not have to go outside. Winter in the Cassius village had been brutal. It lay farther north, so the cold temperatures and the wind had made a life of hardship even worse. Snow was common, and snowstorms would bring inches to a few feet at a time. If enough snow fell, Ruwena and her mistress used it to build a wind break against northeasterly winds, thus protecting both the fire and their doorway. Without protection from winter weather and a fire for warmth, mortality from hypothermia was high for both humans and hybrids. The village hybrids whose alternate species was a furred animal would develop an extra thick coat to protect them. Yet even they would die if left exposed to severe cold or winter storms for too long.

Wood fires were the only source of heat in a Cassius village; thus, wood was a precious commodity. Most of the villagers' huts were built of dried grass, so keeping a fire inside or even near one was extremely hazardous. The huts were little more than tinderboxes. If a cinder took hold, a hut would become rapidly engulfed in flames. The resulting conflagration would destroy everything in it, including anyone inside, and would spread to other structures nearby. Even if the residents escaped the fire, they would no longer have shelter against winter weather.

During the winter, Ruwena's mistress had co-opted an idle oven to provide a communal fire. She showed the villagers how to harvest dried grasses, bind them into bundles, and use them to supplement wood for the fire. She also showed them how to heat stones in the fire, retrieve them without getting burned, and use them as a source of radiant heat in their huts. These activities required something new from the villagers—cooperation—at least, from those who could understand what needed to be done. From gathering wood, acorns, and dried leaves and grasses, the villagers learned that they could have heat in their huts without the risk of fire. Heat would radiate from the stones, and this source of heat was renewable as long as there was one fire in the village that everyone could use. The roasted acorns provided a nutritious supplement to a meager diet made even more deficient by winter.

In contrast, there were hearth fires on every floor of the schoolhouse except for the second deepest cellar. Students could fill a kettle with water and heat it over the fire. The hot water could be used to warm bathwater, brew a cup of tea, or make soup. There were hearthstones for every dormitory room, and each room had a bed warmer that was brought out of storage. Students could put small stones, kept near the fireside, in the bed warmer and heat it over the fire. Then, they could warm their bed linens and bedclothes at night and wearing apparel in the morning. Blankets and comforters from the wooden chest were layered on the beds.

Ruwena learned about most of these comforts in the middle of one night. It was particularly cold—too cold for Ruwena to sleep in her room without heat. So she left it for the commons, where she lay down close to the fire. Born of necessity, Ruwena was a light sleeper. She awoke when Matron Patrina came into the commons.

"What are you doing here?" Matron Patrina asked sternly.

"I was too cold and couldn't sleep in my room," Ruwena answered.

"Good heavens, child. Come with me." Whereupon Matron Patrina turned and took Ruwena back to her room. Matron Patrina had been apprised of her new student's history—or lack thereof—and why she was in a room alone. She took a comforter out of the chest for Ruwena to put on her bed. Then, she took the bed warmer and a hearthstone from the chest and said, "Follow me."

Both of them went back to the commons, where Matron Patrina instructed Ruwena to put the hearthstone on the rack above the fire. Then she held the warmer open while Ruwena took a small hand shovel and put in it several small stones that had been roasting in the fire. This reminded Ruwena of how she had kept some warmth next to her body during the winters in the Cassius village. She would put several small warmed stones down the front and back of her smock, where they would fall to her waist and be held there where her smock was tied. She could use the stones from the bed warmer to do the same once they had cooled enough.

They both returned to Ruwena's room where Matron Patrina instructed Ruwena in the use of a bed warmer to warm her bedclothes and wearing apparel. Then Matron Patrina took this opportunity to inspect Ruwena's room. She found it clean and tidy. *My mistress would never have allowed otherwise*, Ruwena thought to herself and realized that Matron Patrina reminded her of H'Ilgraith. Afterward, they both returned to the commons to retrieve the heated hearthstone. Since Ruwena was the sole occupant of her room, Matron Patrina instructed her to put the hearthstone under her bed.

"Now get in bed," she ordered. Ruwena complied and pulled the covers over her. "Better?" Matron Patrina asked.

"Yes," Ruwena replied emphatically as she nestled under the warmed comforter. It felt luxurious. "Thank you."

"You are welcome," Matron Patrina replied. "Now go to sleep," she commanded as she left the room and closed the door behind her. Later, Ruwena awoke to a sharp knocking on her door and the sound of the south bell tower.

"Ruwena. Are you there?" It was Savannah and the 9:00 a.m. bell.

Ruwena flew out of bed, figuratively speaking. She had overslept. Her mistress would be chastising her now. "Come in," she called to Savannah.

Savannah came in and began tidying up the bed while Ruwena donned her winter smock. "What is your hearthstone doing under the bed?" Savannah asked.

"Matron Patrina told me to put it there," Ruwena replied.

"She was here?" Savannah asked, wide-eyed. It was an academic question.

Sound Battle Stations

During the winter, it was not uncommon for snow to blanket the compound due to its proximity to the northern mountains. The arrival of snow was greeted with delight by most of the students—especially those that had come from villages farther south where snow rarely fell. Alas, classes never needed to be canceled since they were held in the same building as the dormitory. Most winter practicums were indoors at other buildings and could be reached by walking. So older students (Form II seniors and above) would be drafted along with the faculty to assist staff in clearing walkways to all the buildings around the courtyard. It was during such times that the students needed to be wary.

One day, after over a foot of snow had fallen overnight, students and faculty were engaged in clearing the walkways within the courtyard. Suddenly, a Form IV senior was struck in the back by a carefully aimed snowball. This was followed immediately by a salvo of several more snowballs—some of which hit their target (a student) and some of which didn't. Across the courtyard behind the students, several faculty members had furtively built an arsenal of snowballs behind one of the snowbanks created when a walkway was cleared.

Someone shouted, "Take cover!" Savannah immediately grabbed Ruwena and ran with her and several other students behind the nearest opposing snowbank. Ruwena was startled and quite concerned. She had no idea what was happening and feared the compound was being attacked. She immediately began looking around for the source of the attack when Savannah pulled her back and shouted, "Stay down, and start making snowballs." Savannah was in the middle of making one herself.

This was not what Ruwena expected to hear—or see. Students on both sides of her were doing the same thing. Everyone was in a high state of excitement, yet they were laughing and enjoying themselves. Clearly, this was not an enemy attack.

Then, Ruwena spotted several older students who had taken cover behind another snowbank to their right. This group was more experienced and able to react quickly. They were already heaving snowballs back at the faculty, forcing the latter to duck for cover.

"What is going on?" she shouted at Savannah over the surrounding din.

"It's a snowball fight." Savannah shouted back.

Ruwena was astonished. "We're in a fight with the faculty?"

"They started it." Savannah replied. "Now start making snowballs," she ordered again.

Ruwena saw that students in her group were already throwing snowballs at the faculty. Her mistress would have been appalled by this behavior. *Oh well*, she thought and promptly joined in the fray.

The snowball fight lasted about ten minutes or so when the faculty realized they couldn't keep up with the volume of snowballs the students could produce. Now they were getting pelted from two angles. So they finally surrendered. "Just wait until the summer games," they whispered among themselves, conveniently forgetting they had started the fight.

As it turned out, these were not the only snowball fights. Sometimes, it would be one form against another. Other times it would be boys versus girls, usually from within the same form. Any student walking outside after it had snowed was in peril. As Ruwena joined in more snowball fights, others began to notice that her aim was pretty good. They did not know that her keen eyesight was a courtesy of her raptor genes.

CHAPTER 30

Chasing Dreams

Spring was a welcome relief. It foretold the end of the school year and heralded relief from the tedium of classes. Some of the classes had been less than riveting. The Transformation I class had been the most eagerly awaited class by all the Form II students except for one. It was spring term, and the veterinary first aid class was the one Ruwena was most eager to attend.

The Veterinary Clinic

In a Cassius village, wild animals were never rescued. If the villagers encountered an injured animal, they killed it. The animal's death was a blessing to them. They ate the meat (usually raw), used the hide for clothing, and used the bones that they didn't eat for tools (usually weapons). Ruwena had learned from her mistress which salves and potions would bring relief to the malformed and corrupted creatures in the Cassius village. In many cases, the same potions could treat both animals and humans. So Ruwena would need to exercise caution in the vet first aid class lest she reveal what she should not know.

Although the class addressed both domestic and wild animals, it was here that Ruwena really learned about domesticated animals. Master Navarick [nav-ar-ĭk], chief veterinarian and doctor of veterinary medicine, described their physical structures, mental capabilities, and what they could and could not do.

In the vet clinic, Ruwena helped provide care for both domestic animals and injured wildlife. Her passion, however, was the care and treatment of wildlife brought into the clinic. Many young birds and mammals were orphaned. While conducting surveillance, the scouts would keep watch over nests in their areas. If they noted that no parent had been seen for more than a day, it was possible that the parent had been killed by a predator. So the scouts would bring in the babies. "Once baby birds are old enough, they will graduate to the aviary," Master Navarick told the students. "If they are raptors, they will be moved to the falconry when they are ready to fledge," he added. Baby mammals and reptiles were raised in the infirmary, providing valuable experience for students until the animals could be released into the wild or to the pond.

There were pets in Erwina as well—mostly dogs and a few cats. The compound at Erwina did not keep sheep, so the only dogs were guard dogs. In truth, they were village pets kept primarily by individual families and were known to everyone. The village was their home too, and they would defend it. Caring for injured or sick dogs and cats provided Ruwena with insight into her canine and feline alternate species.

Boating Lessons

Unfortunately, Ruwena also faced the class she dreaded the most after swimming—boating. Since Ruwena had finally demonstrated an adequate ability to swim in calm waters, she was eligible to learn how to row a boat, which she found cumbersome. There was nothing otter-like about a rowboat. It seemed very awkward and difficult to steer. Ruwena's slight build was to her disadvantage. Although her muscle tone and strength were quite good, she simply didn't have a great deal of coordination as a human in using the oars. When sitting across from a team member, however, she had no difficulty using both arms to stroke a single oar and maintain a rhythm.

After the rowboat, canoeing was entirely different. She could navigate this craft easily and found it quite refreshing. Here, at least, she could be on the water—if not in it—and could do so in full daylight. Furthermore, if necessary, she could transform in the space afforded by a canoe with more privacy than a rowboat. She was relieved to be excused from kayaking. This was for more experienced swimmers and boaters than she.

Thankfully, Master Salinas taught students how to pole a barge on calm waters—initially on the pond and then in a section of the river where the current was mild. Here, again, skill proved to be Ruwena's major limitation. She would be able to assist with poling a barge as Savannah had done; however, it frightened her to think of managing a barge on her own. To her relief, Master Salinas told her that this would not happen. "Even if an individual is strong enough to pole a barge alone, it is not allowed," he said. "It is an unsafe practice."

When spring term ended, the ensuing summer sessions offered a large number and wide variety of activities. As Form II graduates, Ruwena and her classmates were allowed to engage in activities of their choice provided they had passed the corresponding courses and demonstrated proficiency in any associated practicums. Students had the opportunity to hone their skills in areas of interest to them and be of service at the same time. By working in these areas, students gained more insight into what was required as well as developing greater proficiency in the areas they selected. Since winters tended to be harsh, most outdoor activities had to wait until spring.

Woodworking

Woodworking was one of the most popular summer activities for many students. Summers were very busy for the shop staff. Nearly everyone needed something built or repaired—furniture, nesting boxes for the vet clinic, oars for the boathouse, and the list goes on. This area afforded students a wide variety of activities including making and repairing wicker products, building birdhouses and nests, and even hollowing out wood for a new canoe or kayak. Sumiya, Ervan, and Javier volunteered for duty in the woodworking shop. They would work under the supervision of Master Yacobon, master carpenter. Experienced Form III students, who also provided additional support for the woodworking staff, would serve as their preceptors.

A practicum or internship in the woodworking shop provided students with another opportunity to engage in artistic endeavors. They could create novel shapes and designs for many items—especially in wicker and wood. They could work with master artisans in preparing sketches for artistic designs that would be engraved in wood. Finally, those students who proved to be very precise in their work were invited to train with artisans who crafted many of the musical instruments available to Erwinians.

Boatmanship

Avelynda and Erik zeroed in on the boathouse. Both loved boating and didn't mind which kind of watercraft they used. So they enjoyed learning how to maintain them, assisted in building some of them, and gained additional experience in boatmanship under the supervision of Master Salinas. Slowly but surely, they were becoming a couple.

One afternoon, both Avelynda and Erik were invited to row with team that was practicing for a regatta. They joined five Form III students and two Form IV students to form a team of eight rowers and a coxswain. The crew would be practicing on the Ferveo River in relatively calm waters, not far from the riverbank and well upstream of the rapids. While underway, Avelynda spotted a bird circling overhead not far from them. "It looks like a small vulture," she said. "Perhaps a fledgling."

As the bird circled nearer and lower over the crew, it became evident that it was not a native vulture (illus. 18). Its head looked like that of a bat except it had a vulture's beak. Its wings were oddly shaped and looked almost scalloped. Suddenly it strafed the boat, barely missing one of the students. Since the crew carried no weapons, they used their oars to harass the creature and drive it away from the boat. With their focus drawn to the bird, the river's current pulled the boat into the center channel, where the flow was much faster.

Now they were being propelled downstream at a perilous rate. The aerial predator that had attacked them was left behind. The students were now in a desperate race to regain control of their boat and steer it back toward the riverbank. Four of the students used the handles of the oars to parry away from the rocks while four paddled toward the shore. The coxswain, turned helmsman, guided the boat. They were nearing the narrows, where the boat would be shattered on the rocks. The flow was now too fast and turbulent for even a strong swimmer to break out of the current. With an enormous effort, the students herded their boat toward a large boulder jutting out into the river from the riverbank. It was a landing site for a barge. The boat slammed into the boulder and cracked but did not shatter.

The students, wet and bedraggled but alive, climbed out and onto the riverbank. Their training and experience in boatmanship had stood them in good stead. As they watched their boat sink into the water, the coxswain remarked wryly, "I can't wait to explain this to Master Salinas."

Illus. 18. Aegyroptera.

"I think we should thank him," said Avelynda.

When the students came ashore, they were well outside the confines of the compound. After nearly being swept away, they now had to find their way back. Once they arrived at the compound, they reported the loss of their boat to Master Salinas and then sought out Master Titus. Once they recounted their experience, he called in Master Pasterov. Based on the students' description of the creature they saw, Master Pasterov identified it. "It is an aegyoptera [ā-gē-ŏp-tĕr-ah]," he said, "and one of Cassius's creatures." This and other such incidents served as a reminder that Cassius was not far away.

Sweet Rewards

Gardening was another popular area of service. Many students would work in the gardens if only for some of the delicacies they could find there. Both Savannah and Marianna elected to intern in the gardens. Both students knew they would be expected to remember all the ingredients they had used in the past when they took their next potions classes. Working here provided an excellent opportunity to reinforce their knowledge of the ingredients used in many recipes—and to sample some of the more desirable ingredients used in those recipes.

Salwen decided to intern in the winery. He was very fond of the jams and jellies made there and planned to make them in his home village. He wanted to learn how to prepare the fruit and how to operate the equipment used in preparing jams and jellies. He also assisted in harvesting (and sampling) the fruit to learn how to tell when it was ripe enough to pick.

Henrik chose to work in the armory. He wanted to become a scout and needed to learn about weaponry. Although he was already proficient as a bowman, he also used the opportunity to fine-tune his archery skills. One of the ways he did so was to shoot apples from their trees for target practice, which provided him with a tasty snack as a reward.

A Treasure Trove

Qwincy had an older brother who had moved to Gregor to study genetics. Qwincy had learned from his brother how important pedigrees were to a geneticist. So he elected to intern in the natural history and research center as an assistant to staff members who were preparing or researching a pedigree. He practiced interviewing willing subjects for their pedigrees, which were already on file. Then he would compare his documentation with the official pedigree to see what he missed—or might have discovered. Thus, his internship took him to the archives as well (app. H). While in the archives, Qwincy learned how to make and preserve parchment documents. Everyone had access to paper-based documents. Access to parchment documents was restricted in order to preserve them.

Wishful Thinking

Ruwena's first choice was the falconry; however, she was not yet eligible to intern there. In the meantime, her second choice was the vet clinic. Even though she thought the bulk of her experience would be caring for domestic animals, she would still have opportunities to care for wildlife, which was her preference. Since Ruwena had done well in the veterinary first aid class, she was eligible to intern there.

As it turns out, Deven was interested in the vet clinic also. His primary interest was caring for domestic animals. His family had a small herd of milk cows and raised chickens in the southwestern region. Knowing how to care for these and other domestic animals would be a great benefit to him and his family and several of their neighbors. So Ruwena and Deven were able to focus on their species of choice. Master Navarov was pleased to have both of them. The vet clinic was a twenty-four-hour operation every day of the year.

Ruwena's third interest—which she knew was beyond her reach—was to become a scout. She longed to roam outside the boundaries of the compound and to explore the surrounding territory. Although life in a Cassius village and her years of training under her mistress had prepared Ruwena for life on her own, she could not acknowledge this experience—at least not yet. In addition, the learning curve for a scout was steep. All scouts were required to be skilled in the martial arts and be expert archers. They also needed to be strong swimmers, skilled in boatmanship, and able to take a kayak over grades IV and V rapids. Ruwena could do none of the above. So she dismissed any notion of becoming a scout, officially.

Although *H. sapiens* could serve as scouts, they were at a significant disadvantage. They had to be very careful not to be seen. Scouts who were *H. transformans*, however, had to able to transform into at least one species native to the area where they were serving as a scout. Ruwena knew she would have no problem meeting the latter requirement. She knew, when she became a Form IV student later on, she would be taking a class in scouting and surveillance (app. B, table 9). Once she learned the rules of scouting, her ability to transform into alternate species should relieve her of some of the other requirements—not the least of which was swimming.

A Visitor in Good Standing

Both Ruwena and Savannah had completed their senior Form II studies successfully, as did their classmates. All would be moving forward to become Form III freshmen in the fall. Ruwena's first full year at Erwina had passed fairly quickly. As she grew accustomed to living there and meeting people, she became a little more at ease. Unwittingly, she had slipped back into an old habit—calling Matron Trevora Mistress. Matron Trevora did not correct her. "I hope at some point Ruwena will reveal more about herself if she thinks of me in the same way she once did her former mistress," she told Matron Aquina.

Ruwena's origin was still unknown. Even her age was an estimate, since not even she knew when she was born. Faculty had not been able to ascertain if Ruwena simply had no memory and, therefore, no knowledge of her past or if she were holding back. Those who worked more closely with Ruwena suspected the latter, and they understood that her tale might have to wait until she was as sure of them as they wanted to be of her. There was one source of reliable reassurance. "None of the animals or birds or other natural inhabitants on the compound have shied away from her," reported Master Pasterov. "If she were a corrupted human, the animals would have sensed it and shunned her."

Ruwena had good reason to be cautious. She had come to Erwina at her mistress's behest. To Ruwena's knowledge, however, H'Ilgraith had not had contact with Erwina or with any of its people during the year the two of them had spent in Cassius territory. In that village, the threat of danger and tension was constant. H'Ilgraith had always admonished her, "No place is safe. You must be alert for danger wherever you are."

When H'Ester, as Ruwena, first came to the compound, she had no way of knowing if it would be any different. Although Ruwena soon learned that danger wasn't everywhere in Erwina, she knew it was not far away. Older students were instructed to be alert for danger and to watch over the younger children. Even the youngest children were taught to be observant, report anything that seemed unfamiliar, be wary of anyone they did not know, and report their observations to faculty or security.

Despite Ruwena's cautiousness, she and Savannah became very close. When Savannah decided to take Rµηeîc as an elective, Ruwena elected to take the classes with her. She had learned Rµηeîc long ago from her mistress. Since she had not had any opportunity to use it after her mistress died, the classes proved to be a useful review. In a reversal of roles, Ruwena helped Savannah conquer an ancient language. Often, both of them would speak in Rµηeîc not only for the practice but also for the camaraderie that sharing a common language provided. Ruwena also taught Savannah how to prepare the fluorescent phosphorus mixture for writing in the air. Thanks to the presence of so many different bird species, quills were plentiful and made the best writing tools. Savannah was delighted and asked Ruwena, "Where did you learn how to make fluorescent ink?" As always, Ruwena answered, "My mistress taught me this."

As she entered Form III, Ruwena was accepted as a visitor in good standing and was allowed to move about the compound freely, including outside the perimeter. As a Form III student, however, she was still not allowed to leave the compound without the escort of faculty or staff.

PART V

Decisions

CHAPTER 31

A Raid on the Compound

Red Alert

Early one morning, just after dawn, Matron Patrina rushed down the girls' corridor rapping sharply on each door and ordering students to get up and get dressed. "Erwina is under attack," she barked. Evan, a Form III senior, was doing the same thing on the boys' corridor. Matron Patrina immediately designated Savannah as the proctor for Form II girls since she had already had experience proctoring younger students. She told Evan to designate Erik as the proctor for the boys for the same reason.

Savannah and her counterpart, Erik, immediately leaped into action. Savannah accounted for every student in her charge. "Make sure your windows are shuttered and be sure you dress warmly and wear your leather boots," she directed. It was still cool, and they could be traveling over rough terrain. "If you have any food or water in your nightstand, you should bring it with you," she added. She also directed students with empty water carafes to bring them and fill them from the pump in the commons. Then Savannah mustered all students in her corridor—accounting for each one and reminding them to be quiet.

"Is this a drill?" asked one of the sophomores in a whisper.

"I don't know," answered Savannah. She brought her charges to the Form II commons, where they were joined by Erik and his fellow students. Matron Patrina, Evan (Form III), and Sala (Form IV) met them there.

Matron Patrina informed her charges that hostile forces were nearing the compound. "Our security forces, scouts, and many of the faculty are trying to prevent these forces from entering the compound," she said. "In the event their efforts fail, everyone must evacuate immediately. I leave now to join them." At this point, Matron Patrina departed leaving Sala and Evan to give further direction to the Form II students.

Sala briefed the students on the situation and on the current known whereabouts of the enemy forces. "Some of our scouts spotted an enemy raiding party sneaking through the forest on the western border of the compound. They saw a group break off from the main force, which has reached the compound's western perimeter," Sala announced. "It is imperative that all students evacuate in a north-northeast direction. All students are to rendezvous at the boathouse. There, you will get into boats or on barges, travel downstream, and eventually cross the river."

The students were given no further information about the situation. Older students knew from past experience what actions they were expected to take, which included guiding younger less experienced students. Ruwena fell into this latter category. She did not know what to do. Unlike her classmates who had practiced evacuations in the past, she had no prior experience fleeing with a large group of people. She and her mistress had fled alone, and her mistress had always guided her.

Ruwena also lacked training in most of the athletic and defense skills her classmates had learned. In her disguise as an *H. sapiens*, she could not transform into another species. Nevertheless, she did have some advantages. She had keen eyesight even in the dark (an enhancement from her raptor genes) and a sharp sense of smell (a benefit of her fox and wolf genes). She could climb over rough terrains and rubble without losing her footing (a gift from her cougar genes), and she could twist, turn, and dodge quickly (a gift from all her alternate species, including the otter). She just couldn't swim worth a hoot. So she dreaded the thought of another boat ride over the Ferveo River. Over the past year, she had learned about the tunnel network and had memorized it, as her mistress would have demanded.

The Plan of Escape

Given the total number of students in Form II, they needed to be divided into smaller groups. This allowed for greater flexibility in determining escape routes and would prevent the raiders from assaulting and capturing a large group of students all at one time. The main disadvantage would be in accounting for all students at their rendezvous point and the need to find—and possibly rescue—any students that did not reach it.

"Freshmen students in Form II will join students in Form I," announced Sala. "These students will be paired with Form I students in a buddy system to provide support and reassurance." The freshmen were immediately dispatched to join Form I students in their commons for their briefing. Sala explained to the remaining Form II students, "This action puts the more vulnerable students together. The majority of the Form IV students will muster with them and guide their groups." Equally important, the transfer reduced the size of Form II from forty-six students to thirty-seven students, enabling their groups to be smaller. The smaller the number, the more easily they could account for one another.

Sala directed that three groups be formed with an equal mix of senior, junior, and sophomore students. Seniors with prior supervisory experience—Savannah, Erik, and Henrick—would lead their groups. Each group would have one *H. sapiens* student. The remaining *H. transformans* students were allocated randomly to one of the three groups (table 4).

Table 4. Initial Form II Groups.

Table 4. Initial Form II Groups for Obstacle Course			
	Group A	Group B	Group C
Senior leaders	Savannah	Erik	Henrik
	Javier	Samiya	Marianna
	Avelynda	Ervan	Salwen
	Deven	Qwincy	Ruwena
Juniors	4	4	3
Sophomores	5	4	5

Sala then laid out multiple potential escape routes to the north and northeast. Some of these routes had been designated for the Form I students, which now included the freshman Form II students. When she was finished, Sala informed the Form II students that Evan would be rejoining Form III as one of their group leaders, and she would be joining the Form IV students in support of Form I. Form II was completely on its own now. "Good luck," she said, in parting.

Options

The three groups immediately set to deciding which routes to take for their evacuation. Avylenda spoke up first, "Erik and I interned at the boathouse with Master Salinas. He mentored us in boatmanship too. We should get there as soon as possible to help set up the boats and man the barges."

Both Savannah and Henrik agreed. "Take the tunnel from the library [bldg. 3] past the gym [bldg. 7] and the vet clinic [bldg. 15] to the boathouse [bldg. 17]. This is the shortest and most direct route. Get there as fast as you can."

Then Erik reminded everyone, "We both shouldn't take the same route. I can take an alternate route through the aviary [bldg. 14]."

"Wait," said Ruwena. "Most of the routes Sala presented converge at the vet clinic. There is only one tunnel from the vet clinic that leads directly to the boathouse. It will be jammed if too many students take that tunnel."

Henrik added, "Form I with most of Form IV will end up there too, except they will leave from the east wing and travel via the rectory [bldg. 8]. If that happens, the route from the stables [bldg. 16] may be jammed as well."

Then Savannah made a decision. "Avylenda, switch into Erik's group. That way both of you can take the most direct route and reach the boathouse as quickly as possible. Leave now," she ordered.

Ervan moved quickly to even up the two groups. "I'll take Avylenda's place with Savannah," he said, as group B headed out at a brisk pace.

"Now we must decide quickly which route the rest of us will take," said Savannah.

Henrik considered the remaining options. "One of us can go via the aviary. It will take longer and allow more time for others to get through the vet clinic. But I think whoever goes that way will still end up in the same bottleneck." Then he proposed taking the tunnel from the east wing of the schoolhouse to the faculty quarters [bldg. 9] then to the fish hatchery [bldg. 18]. From there they would have to travel above ground to reach the boathouse. That was risky; however, it was a totally different approach that did not go through the vet clinic or use the stables. It was unlikely to be used by anyone else, so it was possible that both groups could go that way. "The main problem is that its initial heading is southeast. Without knowing where the enemy is, we could be heading toward them."

Ruwena and Savannah immediately looked at each other. Both knew one way to find out. "We can survey the entire compound from the roof of the schoolhouse," Savannah announced. "All of you, head down to the second cellar of the east wing, and be quiet. Start toward the faculty quarters. Henrik and I will go to the roof. We will catch up with you. Depending upon which way we see the enemy headed, we can turn back toward the rectory or continue on to the fish hatchery."

Ruwena reminded Savannah that it had taken several minutes to reach the roof of the schoolhouse. "That was from the first floor, and we were not in a hurry." Savannah replied. "It won't take nearly as long this time, and we will run to catch up with you." As Savannah and Henrik bolted away, Javier and Marianna took charge and led their two groups down the side staircases on the east wing to the second cellar, into the tunnel system, and headed toward the faculty quarters.

When Savannah and Hendrik reached the roof, they could see at least twenty individuals coming through the vineyards and the herb and vegetable gardens. They were all converging on the schoolhouse. A small group was going past the winery [bldg. 11] toward the natural history building [bldg. 5], possibly headed toward the rear of the schoolhouse. Another larger group was going around the archives [bldg. 4] toward the west wing and the front of the schoolhouse. They watched as a third small group broke away from the larger group and headed toward the east wing, which was not far from the faculty quarters.

"We've got to get out of here," urged Henrik.

"Look," said Savannah. "Over by the armory. There is some kind of animal going past it."

"I see it," replied Henrik. "It looks like a bear." It appeared to be headed toward the falconry [bldg. 13] when it disappeared into dense underbrush. The falconry was on the way to the aviary.

As they both fled from the rooftop, Henrik said, "We need to catch up to our groups. Going via the faculty quarters may be the best route after all despite its heading."

"We should warn the Form III students about the bear," said Savannah. "They were planning to evacuate via the aviary." *I wonder if that was a faculty member*, Savannah thought to herself. *If so, this is a drill.* In case she was wrong, she said nothing to anyone about her suspicions.

Savannah and Henrik ran down the stairs along the west side, which was the nearest access to the second cellar. As they reached the first floor, they heard footsteps on the main staircase. They froze, motionless and soundless. As they listened, they heard the footsteps heading up the stairs. Faculty and students would be evacuating down the stairs and would not be using the main staircase. *Are these raiders,* wondered Savannah, *or faculty members looking for students who failed to evacuate in a timely manner?* Once their footsteps faded, Savannah and Henrik continued down the stairs quietly until they reached the door to the second cellar. It was pitch-black, yet both students knew from past experience where to find the door to the tunnel and how to open it without making any sound. Deep underground, they could at last whisper to each other.

Henrik drew the well-oiled bolt closed then used one of his ties to hold it in place. Then Savannah handed one end of her long sash to Hendrik while she gripped the other end in her hand. Together they trotted down the tunnel on opposite sides. The sash kept them in contact and running abreast of each other while they hugged their side of the tunnel. If they met anything or anyone even half their size, they would snag it with the sash. If that happened, both would let go of it and run as fast as they could while whatever they encountered untangled itself.

A Surprise Encounter

They reached the east wing of the schoolhouse and found the door to the second cellar already secured from the tunnel side. From there, the tunnel branched to the left (toward the rectory) and to the right (toward the faculty quarters). Savannah used the sash to cross over to the right-hand side to join Henrik in searching for the entrance to the right-hand tunnel. They had not quite reached it when they heard soft footsteps at a brisk pace coming toward them. With the footsteps came a light held up high. Quickly, Savannah and Henrik saw their tunnel, ducked into it, and flattened themselves against the left-hand wall, motionless. If the enemy had gained access to the tunnel system, hopefully they would continue toward the schoolhouse.

It was not the enemy. Raphael, a form IV senior, walked past them. He was holding a hurricane lamp. Henrik stepped out and announced himself and Savannah. "You cannot go back into the schoolhouse," he whispered. "Raiders have already entered it."

Raphael was clearly surprised by this encounter. "Then we all need to head toward the faculty quarters," he said as he motioned them to follow him. As they moved down the tunnels, Raphael told Savannah and Henrik, "The tunnel from the rectory to the vet clinic is jammed. It is completely blocked. We heard reports that two large animals, a jaguar and a wolverine, had escaped from the vet clinic and had entered the tunnel system. Students were scrambling to evacuate through both the gym and the aviary. I am looking for another way to get through the tunnels to the boathouse."

Just as I suspected, thought Savannah. There was only one jaguar in the compound, Madam Merena, and only one wolverine, Madam Patrina.

Nevertheless, Savannah whispered urgently, "We have to warn them. We saw raiders passing the natural history building headed for the back of the school. They would be close to the gym by now. We also saw a wild bear passing the armory and heading toward the falconry. It could have reached the aviary by now."

Once again, Raphael was surprised to hear this information from two Form II students. "It is probably too late to warn them," he said, "and we cannot go back. They will have to deal with the situation."

Savannah was shocked by this statement. "Isn't it better to warn them and give them a chance to escape rather than try to rescue them later?"

"Yes, it is," Raphael replied patiently. "The two of you also have a duty to escape. It is entirely possible that you may be among the very few who do escape. You cannot go back. It is too dangerous."

"I can," said a voice. Savannah recognized Ruwena's voice at once. They had met up with their Form II comrades. Ruwena knew how to navigate the entire network of tunnels. Her mistress would have demanded it. As an owl, she could fly though them unseen by anyone and reach the aviary in a few minutes.

"Absolutely not!" Savannah whispered adamantly. "You have never been involved in an evacuation, and you would probably get caught. You stay with the group."

Ruwena made no reply.

CHAPTER 32

Best Laid Plans of Bears and Boars

Raphael did not join the students as they continued on their way. He headed back toward the schoolhouse. This raised Savannah's index of suspicion even more. "Perhaps he changed his mind about warning the Form III students," Henrik suggested. In any case, Form II was on its own once again.

The two groups were still together when they approached the faculty quarters. They planned to pass under it and take the left-hand tunnel to go to the fish hatchery. They never got that far.

As military strategists learned long ago, no plan survives its first encounter with the enemy. The students ran into a thick, heavy mist with the smell of smoke, as if fires were burning above them. Although the tunnels were deep underground with nothing in them to burn, smoke and burning ash could still get into them via entrances from other buildings. The students knew they had to avoid any smoke-filled tunnel. Extremely hot toxic gases could burn their airways and lungs and cause poisoning and suffocation. These gases would be concentrated in an enclosed space, such as a tunnel. Thus, the tunnel leading under the faculty quarters to the fish hatchery was effectively blocked.

Plan B

"We could take the tunnel to the botanical gardens [bldg. 10]," suggested Samiya. "From there, we can reach the barn [bldg. 19]. At least it is on the east side of the compound." Once they reached it, however, the only way to go straight to the boathouse was above the ground. It was a long way. No one thought for a minute that so many students could reach the boathouse without being detected.

Salwen had a bold idea. "We could go back to the schoolhouse. It's risky, but from there, it's a straight line under the schoolhouse to the medical infirmary. Since the schoolhouse is not on fire, there should be little smoke or ash. From the infirmary, we can turn and go to the falconry or the armory. From either one, we can reach the forest and use the hemp highway to escape."

This plan meant cutting across the center of the compound, under the noses of the raiders, before heading north by northwest to the forest. Savannah's first reaction was "Are you out of your mind?"

"It might be possible," Henrik mused. Even though both he and Savannah now strongly suspected this activity was an unannounced evacuation drill, they still did not want to get caught by the faculty.

"We were all taught how to climb trees and rock formations, ascend into the canopy, and move through the forest using the hemp highway. If we can reach it without getting caught, we stand a good chance of getting away."

Silent Running

Once more, the girls' sashes and the boys' ties were deployed and robes and smocks were allowed to flow freely. The students formed two lines—one for the right side and one for the left side of the tunnel. Savannah and Henrik took one sash between them, as did Ervan and Marianna, who were the last students in each line. Each remaining student in a line held a sash or tie in each hand connecting them with the student immediately in front and in back of them. After a head count and name check, the students headed back through the tunnel toward the schoolhouse. They moved as quickly as they could, half walking and half trotting in tandem and in total darkness.

"I wonder how long our luck can hold out," Savannah whispered to Henrik. Then Savannah remembered. "Ruwena," she whispered. "You can see in the dark better than any of us. Take my place—I will be right behind you—and follow Henrik's lead." So the change was made as Ruwena moved from Henrik's line to Savannah's line. As ties were adjusted accordingly, Ruwena looked ahead into the tunnel and slipped back in time to when she lived in a Cassius village. She remembered well her mistress's admonitions. *Stay alert. Make no sound and remain unseen.*

The trip back to the schoolhouse occurred without incident. They heard no sound and made none—except the slightest of footfalls—and encountered no other persons or beings.

By the time the students had reached the schoolhouse, they had become well practiced at keeping up and maintaining a pace on their march. Now, Savannah and Henrik picked up the pace in an effort to get past the schoolhouse as quickly as possible. The tunnel system to the infirmary was on a north-by-northwest heading. It would take them directly under the schoolhouse and past the library, which had multiple branches to other buildings and, therefore, multiple doors. The longer they lingered under the schoolhouse—or anywhere near it—the greater their risk of discovery. As they neared the schoolhouse, the students began to see hints of smoke; however, it faded as they rushed past it.

Both Savannah and Henrik were deeply concerned about being discovered. They did not know if the tunnel doors from buildings within the courtyard had been secured. Given the report that two apex predators had escaped from the vet clinic, the Form II students could not count on anything being secured on the north side of the compound.

The students had cleared the schoolhouse and reached the point at which the tunnel branched—right toward the gym and left toward the infirmary. Suddenly, Ruwena froze and jerked sharply on the ties in her hands—the signal to stop. Savannah, Henrik, and every student beyond them did the same to pass the message along. Everyone remained still and quiet. They assumed the enemy was near. They needed to be quiet and motionless to avoid detection.

Neither Hendrik nor Savannah could see or hear anything. Ruwena could. She gave her sashes to Savannah, including the one to Henrik, and whispered to Savannah to head down the tunnel to the infirmary. Ruwena could feel Savannah's hair flowing as she shook her head in refusal. Ruwena gave Savannah a gentle push toward the infirmary and then disappeared. She had moved silently into the tunnel toward the gym.

A Duel of Sight and Sound

Ruwena had heard a low growl and had caught the scent of a big cat—the jaguar. Although she did not know the scent of a wolverine, there were no other unknown scents emanating from the tunnel. Silently, she transformed into a woodland owl and flew along the ceiling of the tunnel. As she neared the gym, dim light filtered into the tunnel from its entryway. At that point, her keen nocturnal vision spotted the glow of the jaguar's eyes without the cat seeing her. She flew over the cat, who felt a slight ripple in the air and heard the slightest rustle of feathers. Unable to see the bird, the cat turned to follow the sound. The owl continued to lure the cat back toward the gym. When the cat seemed to lose interest and turn away, she flew back to tease it. The cat was ready. This had been a ploy to trick the bird—suspected of being a transformed student—and capture it. Had it not been for her mistress's training, Ruwena might have been caught. She, too, was prepared and dodged the cat's lunge and outstretched paw as she flew past it. Turning quickly, she strafed the cat from behind and deliberately flapped her wings, gaining speed as she flew toward the gym. The cat immediately followed the sound but never heard the bird again. Having gained sufficient speed, Ruwena turned around once more and glided silently over the cat.

Ruwena continued down the tunnel, picking up her smock along the way. When she was close to the other students, she became *H. sapiens* once again and ran the rest of the way. When she reached Ervan and Marianna, she whispered to them and ducked under their sash. Then she rejoined Savannah, who was relieved to know Ruwena was back.

"I'm going to murder you!" whispered Savannah vehemently.

In the meantime, the jaguar was left with a few puzzlements. *How did the bird avoid my attack and get away?* wondered Madam Merena, who rarely failed to capture a wayward student. More importantly, *which student can transform into a bird?* To her knowledge, none could. She needed to find out before she could scold the student who had faced off with a predator instead of fleeing from it—unless, of course, it was one of the faculty members who had interceded.

Plan C

The students reached the medical infirmary without incident, or so most thought. The next decision was where to go next.

"We can still try to reach the boathouse via the aviary and the vet clinic," said Henrik. "This will get us to the boats and keep anyone from searching for us."

Still, there was the minor problem of a wolverine on the loose. If the jaguar had taken the tunnel from the vet clinic to the gym, it was a good bet that the wolverine would have taken a different path. But which one? The tunnels to the boathouse and the aviary seemed the most likely.

"Don't forget about the bear," Savannah cautioned.

"Wouldn't that bear have moved on by now?" asked Devan.

"A native wild bear probably would have kept moving," answered Henrik. "Any attempt to catch a bird would have been met with disappointment. The raptors would have made their way to the top rafters and been well out of the bear's reach. The same is true for the birds in the aviary." *A faculty member, on the other hand, would remain—waiting to ambush a student*, he thought to himself.

Finally, Henrik said, "We have an obligation to escape, and it is our first obligation. We also have an obligation to try to reach the boathouse. If we can reach the hemp highway, we can take it as far to the east as it goes, which is just past the vet clinic. Then it will be open field the rest of the way. At that point, we will have to make a run for it—literally. We will head toward the falconry and avoid the aviary."

The decision had been made. The students proceeded to the tunnel heading to the falconry. They traversed it without incident. All hints of smoke had disappeared after they had passed underneath the schoolhouse. They encountered no other students, raiders, or apex predators. Everything was going smoothly as they neared the exit from the tunnel system into the falconry. Henrik went ahead while the rest remained back in the tunnel, where the light from the falconry did not reach. As Henrik peered cautiously around the edge of the tunnel entrance, he saw a wild boar standing in front of it, staring right at it and at him, not more than a hundred feet away. "Uh-oh," he said and ducked back inside the tunnel.

The students knew what that meant and ran back deep into the tunnel with Henrik right behind them. Doorways into the tunnel system were made wide deliberately to allow large numbers of people to pass through them. Hence, the boar could easily enter the tunnel system. Once inside, however, its eyesight was poor, and it would not be able to see well. This did not stop boar from charging the entrance and anyone coming through it. So it did.

The students had no chance of outrunning a boar that could reach a charging speed of thirty miles per hour. Thankfully, it did not pursue them past the point in the tunnel where all light was lost. So they paused again while Henrik reported what he found. Although he was certain the evacuation was a drill, he said nothing to the other students. "If we try to go through the falconry, the boar is going to get someone and probably more than a few of us. We will have to retrace our steps and take the tunnel to the aviary, where, no doubt, a wolverine will be waiting for us," he ended with a sigh.

"Or we can head for the armory," offered Salwen. "From there, we can make a dash for the bat cave, which is just inside the forest's edge. If we make it that far, we should be able to reach the hemp highway."

"We keep moving farther away," said Devan. He was becoming worried. "We will reach the boathouse by the time everyone else has sailed. How will we get away?"

"We won't go to the boathouse," said Marianna. "We will head for the northeast outpost."

"We should be able to get a good view of the compound from the hemp highway," remarked Henrik. "If we see it is overrun by the raiders, we will stay on the highway and try to reach the northeast outpost."

We'll probably get reprimanded for doing it too, Henrik thought to himself.

CHAPTER 33

Better Late than Never

The two groups moved rapidly through the tunnel to the armory. There they exited cautiously into the building, alert for telltales signs that anyone or anything else was in the armory too. It was empty. Twenty-five students breathed a sigh of relief.

A Brief Respite

"Can we rest here for a while?" asked one of the sophomores.

Savannah and Hendrik looked at each other. "Yes," answered Savannah, "for a short while." She asked the seniors to look for any small weapons they could carry, now that they could resume using their sashes and ties for their clothes. She tasked the juniors to make sure all the doors were latched and locked from the inside while the sophomores looked for any food or drink. This would give everyone something to do while she and Henrik conducted surveillance of the area before traveling above ground.

Savannah, Henrik, Ervan, and Marianna cautiously looked out the windows as far as they could on three sides of the armory that had windows. Savannah kept Ruwena with her. "I'm not letting you out of my sight," she said.

Ruwena also looked up. She pointed out the trapdoor in the ceiling. If accessible, a rooftop view might be more informative—especially since they could not see out one side of the armory at all. There were two steep, narrow ladders leading to the loft and two ladders leading to the trapdoor. Savannah, Henrik, Ervan, and Ruwena ascended both ladders and then

252

went through the hatch onto the rooftop of the armory. The students lay down flat on the roof to avoid being seen. Hopefully, no one would think to look up at the roof.

Four pairs of eyes were able to see the entire area over a 360-degree range. They had an excellent view of the compound similar to the view from the schoolhouse roof, only from a different perspective. They could also see far into the distance over the forest to the northern mountains. Unfortunately, not even Ruwena's sight could penetrate the forest canopy once it was leafing out. The students could see no immediate threat to them. It appeared that no one suspected where they were.

When the four seniors returned from the roof, Henrik announced, "We have to leave—now. We have a window, where no one seems to be looking in our direction. We must try to reach the boathouse well before dark, and it is nearing noon now."

In the meantime, the other students had found a cache of fruit and bread rolls and carafes of water. They also found several weapons stowed in the armory. None of the Form II students were weapons qualified. Henrik was the best bowman among them. For a moment, he considered taking a bow and a quiver of arrows. If they had to head toward the northeast outpost, it would take them several days to get there. A bow and arrows could provide some measure of protection. Then Henrik reconsidered the idea. Both the bow and the quiver were likely to become entangled while traversing the hemp highway. So he decided against it. Subsequently, each of the seniors took a knife with a sheath that they could secure safely on their person.

Then everyone grabbed a bite to eat and drink and some food items to take with them. When everyone was ready, the two groups banded together once again and quickly filed out the back door. They ran the distance over open ground to the edge of the forest. Seniors ran ahead to conduct surveillance from the forest floor and plot their route to the hemp highway. Everyone needed to get off the ground as quickly as possible. They were at great risk of being spotted while they stayed on the ground.

An Unexpected Encounter

They reached the forest and headed north by northwest to the hemp highway. Everyone was alert for raiders and large carnivores as they moved inward. Although they were trying to be quiet, walking on the forest floor was not conducive to stealth. Too many dead, dried leaves from the fall and winter were still littering the forest floor.

The students were within sight of the hemp highway when Javier saw something move to the southwest of them about one hundred yards away. With its back was to him, it looked like a large brown bear. It might be the same one Savannah and Henrik had seen from the schoolhouse rooftop. He caught up with Savannah and Henrik to let them know.

Although brown bears are common in the northern woods, they tend to avoid human habitation. The students were still within the boundaries of the compound. *Master Heroditus most likely,* thought Savannah. In any case, the students needed to be careful. If caught, Master Heroditus wouldn't kill them, but a wild brown bear might.

Ervan and Marianna were instructed to take the rest of the students into the hemp highway as quickly as possible while Javier led Henrik and Savannah (with Ruwena in tow) to where he saw the bear. They would keep watch on the bear's movements from a discreet distance while the rest of the students kept on. If the bear spotted then, they should be able reach the highway in a matter of minutes and begin their ascent into the trees.

As the four seniors caught sight of the bear, it seemed to be ambling away on all four feet. It appeared awkward as it walked. Ruwena knew immediately something was wrong. For its part, the bear seemed to sense the students' presence. It turned its head toward them and looked in their direction.

"That's a really strange-looking bear," remarked Javier in a whisper.

It was a cercopithursus [cer-ko-*pith*-ur-sus] (illus. 19), a hybrid creature that Cassius made from splicing genes of a baboon into those of a brown bear. It had the size and shape of a brown bear with the face and fangs of a baboon, a baboon's slender longer forearms, and hands with opposing thumbs and sharp long claws. It was aggressive and easily aroused. Ruwena recognized it right away. "It's not a bear," she whispered urgently. "We have to leave now."

The four students knew they needed to retreat as quietly as possible so the bear would not be alarmed. They must not run—the bear might be tempted to give chase. They kept a low posture and backed up slowly. As they saw the bear rise up on its hind legs, they stopped and froze. If they didn't move, the bear might miss seeing them through the trees and underbrush. Although the near vision of a bear was quite good, its distance vision was relatively poor. On the other hand, bears had a very good sense of smell and an acute sense of hearing. It was the breeze that betrayed the students. It had shifted, and they saw the bear raise its snout and sniff the air.

Illus. 19. Cercopithursus.

"Get out of here now," Ruwena whispered urgently. "Stay as low to the ground as you can and still run. We have to get into the trees and warn the compound," she added.

Savannah tried to calm Ruwena. "Don't worry," she whispered back. "We're leaving. It's probably Master Heroditus made up to look more frightening."

Ruwena was even more alarmed by Savannah's response. Savannah seemed to be operating under the assumption that this was a drill and they were not really in any danger. Ruwena looked directly at Savannah and spoke calmly and deliberately, "No, it isn't. I have seen this creature before." Just then, the creature bared its fangs and let out a guttural snarl as it dropped back down onto all four legs. The students realized immediately this was no faculty member. It seemed to be looking directly at them. Suddenly it charged. The students bolted for the hemp highway with Ruwena bringing up the rear. She knew she would have to transform to protect her friends. At little more than one hundred yards away, they had no chance to outrun the creature.

Just as suddenly, the natural history center's bell tower rang out an alarm. It was quickly joined by the other bell towers. The combined sound of all five bells carried readily beyond the armory and drew the creature's attention. It turned toward the compound and bellowed back with a savage and unnatural sound. Its distorted features were seen clearly in profile. Distracted by the persistent ringing of the bells, the creature had turned away. In doing so, it may have lost the scent of the students. It did not turn back to pursue them.

Aftermath

Savannah and Henrik's suspicions were confirmed. The raid was an evacuation exercise that was terminated abruptly with the discovery of a hybrid creature near the armory. The faculty and staff were relieved that the exercise had taken the majority of students well away from the threat. They were still concerned that most of the students in Form II were still missing in action.

Form II group B had arrived at the boathouse well ahead of most other students and had begun preparing the boats and barges. Avelynda and Erik had taken charge and directed other students who had arrived and could assist. Master Salinas had observed their actions from a discreet distance.

"I am very pleased with how they handled themselves and the situation," he reported. "They were well prepared."

Raphael reported his meeting and subsequent departure from Form II students at the faculty quarters. "I thought the Form II students had decided to head for the infirmary," he said.

Madam Merena, who had prowled the tunnel between the vet clinic and the gym, reported rounding up several students from both Forms I and III; however, she did not encounter any Form II students. "At one point, I encountered a bird that had gotten into the tunnel," she mentioned briefly. *A smart bird*, she thought to herself. She was still suspicious that the bird had not merely wandered into the tunnel.

Master Iranapolis reported seeing Henrik at the mouth of the tunnel into the aviary. He saw no other students. Since Henrik was the leader for Form II group C, the rest of that group may have stayed back in the tunnel—a wise decision. When Henrik disappeared and did not reappear, "I thought he would head toward the aviary," said Master Iranapolis.

Some of the Form III students who had reached the aviary without being caught did not see any Form II students. Those who had reached the hemp highway reported seeing other Form III students there, but no Form II students.

The scouts who had spotted the hybrid bear and sounded the alarm had not seen any students or evidence that anyone had been attacked. The scouts did find a partially eaten carcass of a native red deer. While monitoring and tracking the beast, the scouts saw it rise up on its hind legs, as if alerted to something. Then the bells sounded. The scouts heard the creature bellow and then saw it move away.

Somewhere between the infirmary and the aviary, two groups of Form II students had disappeared. The search was on to find them until a bedraggled group of students were spotted racing from the forest to the boathouse—better late than never. Matron Patrina went to the boathouse and waited for them. She was relieved to see all her remaining charges arrive safely. She appeared before the students looking very stern. "You are late," she admonished. "Now get cleaned up. Supper is waiting." Ruwena thought, *How like my mistress she sounds.*

Alarm Bells

More than bell tower alarms were going off at the compound. The faculty in general and security in particular were alarmed by the presence of an extremely dangerous creature inside the compound. With faculty and students absorbed in the evacuation exercise, thankfully the scouts were keeping watch. Madam Lindenova [*lĭn*-dĕn-*o*-va] tasked her staff to begin working immediately to identify what type of creature it was. Master Josephus [*jo*-ĕ-fŭs] would perform an autopsy, while Master Mikalov would perform genetic testing. Master Titus would dispatch security and scouts to scour the compound and the region immediately around it for other signs or evidence of the creature's passage—or that of any other hybrid animal.

Faculty would learn from the students what they might have seen. This could be accomplished without creating undue anxiety. It was customary to meet with the students of each form the day following an exercise. Students would describe the decisions they made and the rationale underlying them, the actions they took, the results—or, in some cases, consequences—of their decisions and actions and identify what they would do differently. During these sessions, faculty would advise students of the hybrid bear that had been seen in the compound and ask what, if anything, the students had seen. The session with Form II proved informative.

Matron Trevora and Matron Patrina led the assessment of Form II. In evaluating the students' actions, the two faculty members found most of their actions justifiable, if not recommended. They gave an excellent rating to the decision to move Avelynda to Erik's group and dispatch them forthwith to the boathouse. They deemed the decision to go by the faculty quarters valid; however, the decision to backtrack under the schoolhouse was deemed a high risk. "That was a dangerous thing to do," said Matron Trevora sternly. "If raiders had penetrated the tunnel system, you could have been captured." Given that decision, the faculty approved the student's decision to get to the boathouse via the armory and the hemp highway.

Then Matron Trevora asked the students in groups A and C, "What would you have done if you had arrived at the boathouse after everyone else had left?" Savannah and Erik had to admit they hadn't considered what they would do. Both agreed that they would take any remaining craft and cross the river.

"What if all the remaining craft had been burned to prevent an enemy from pursuing us?" asked Matron Trevora. The river was quite wide at the boathouse. Although its waters were not especially turbulent there, it still had a relatively strong current in its main channel. A strong swimmer—a scout and, perhaps, a Form IV student—could swim the distance at that point on the river. Younger students would not have the endurance, even if they had the skill.

"We would have to get back to the forest," said Henrik. "We could take the hemp highway as far as it goes and head to the northeast outpost."

"We would wait for you," said Avelynda. "We could hold back one barge until you arrived."

"And if the enemy appeared on the horizon first?" asked Madam Trevora.

The students hesitated. "I will be waiting with you," said Matron Patrina. "We will leave when we must. As you have heard, your comrades have an alternate plan."

The students in groups A and C did receive kudos for surveillance—both from the roof of the schoolhouse and the roof of the armory. Still, the faculty thought it unwise to stay so long at the schoolhouse.

With the arrival of Master Titus, the conversation turned to the hybrid creature. He was concerned about the bear Savannah and Henrik saw from the roof of the schoolhouse. To his relief, he learned that it was Master Chernavich, who had transformed into his alternate species, a black bear. Thus, the hybrid bear near the armory was the only sighting by any student. "You do know that native bears are dangerous," he said sternly.

"Yes," answered all the students almost in unison.

"We were staying low and backing away slowly," said Henrik. "Whenever it looked toward us, we stopped and froze. When the tower bells rang, the creature turned away, and we bolted for the highway." *Not quite in that order,* he thought to himself.

Savannah added nothing more. Later, when the students had returned to their dormitories, she confronted Ruwena in her room. "What do you mean you have seen one before?" she demanded.

Ruwena realized immediately she was at risk of exposing her past. She recovered quickly and provided her standard response. "My mistress showed me," she replied. This was quite true. Ruwena and her mistress had seen many different hybrids in the Cassius village and, over time, had learned what they were.

CHAPTER 34

The Scent of Flowers

The years spent in Form III were uneventful for Ruwena. During one summer in Form III, she had interned in the falconry. There, Ruwena felt she had the best of both worlds. She could work with rescued raptors recovering from injuries and with fledgling chicks. In addition, both falconry and aviary staff often worked together, so there would be opportunities to work with other birds as well.

Savannah, on the other hand, had not decided what area of work she wanted to pursue when she graduated. She loved working in all the gardens. It didn't matter which one, so she was considering working as a gardener, like her father, or becoming a botanist. Yet she sensed that she wanted something more. It seemed that her alternate species, the gray wolf, had zero interest in gardening.

Savannah reconciled this discrepancy by deciding that a wolf could range farther in search of plants and bring them back to the compound in a satchel or pouch. She decided that once she found a plant of interest, she could dig it up using her front paws, scoop it up in her mouth—roots, soil, and all—and drop it into a pouch. Then, she could resume her search carrying the pouch in her mouth. If necessary, she could resume her human form to dig up the plant. She had become quite proficient in changing from human to wolf and back again. All the while, she could do double duty and conduct surveillance while she was on a mission to find herbs or flowers.

Imagine a wolf smelling flowers (illus. 20). Ruwena wondered what else Savannah had been sniffing. Ruwena cautioned Savannah about her plan. "A wolf seen looking for flowers or herbs could arouse suspicions," she offered.

260

Illus. 20. A Wolf Sniffing Flowers.

"I'm tracking a scent," Savannah retorted.

Master Titus also cautioned Savannah that any animal seen toting a handmade backpack or satchel likely would be labelled a courier. Savannah sighed and said, "I'll ask Master Androv if he would make a satchel that looks like a dead rabbit."

Destiny

Savannah's yen to roam and work in the gardens may be a natural byproduct of both genetics and her environment. Both of Savannah's parents could transform into gray wolves. Her father was a master gardener and was content to keep large tracts of flowers, vegetables, and herbs. In contrast, Savannah's mother had a restless spirit and often ranged as a scout throughout Erwina's territory. As a small child, Savannah enjoyed being outside and would spend a great deal of time roaming throughout her father's gardens, as if she were on the prowl. As she grew older, she enjoyed tending the gardens with him.

Given that each parent donated one set of twenty-three chromosomes to their offspring and the identical (or almost identical) genes associated with them, the individual really only needed one of the two genes invoked. As a general rule, either gene could be used unless one was dominant and the other was recessive. There were other circumstances, however, in which only one of the two genes would be destined to be invoked while the other was destined to remain silent even though both of them were identical and equal. The gene destined to be active—either the mother's or the father's—was the one that would be expressed in the phenotype. The gene that was destined to be silenced was marked with a stamp (an imprint) and would not be expressed.

If the mother's gene carried the stamp, it would be silenced. The paternal gene would always be reflected in the offspring (regardless of gender). The reverse was true if the father's gene carried the stamp. Thus identical maternal and paternal genes were no longer functionally equivalent if one of them carried the stamp. The lineage of the stamped gene—maternal or paternal—was significant. Both affect growth and development in different ways. Thus, genetic imprinting could have a significant effect on phenotype without affecting the genotype.

Normally, any maternal or paternal gene could be imprinted at random unless one of the two was singled out during embryogenesis and stamped at that time. An embryonic imprint was permanent and affected growth and development throughout the individual's life.

Savannah's paternal wolf genes could have been imprinted during embryogenesis. If that had happened, her maternal wolf genes would be expressed and her paternal wolf genes silenced for the rest of her life. Her mother would be the parent of origin for her wolf genes. Perhaps Savannah's love of gardens came from spending so much of her childhood working with her father in his gardens. Perhaps her sense of restlessness—her desire to roam far afield as a wolf—came from her mother.

A Medicinal Inclination

Although Savannah enjoyed working with all plants, her favorites were flowers and cooking herbs. She had no particular interest in focusing on medicinal plants. This began to change during a summer internship in Form III. She brought several medicinal herbs and berries to a Form IV junior, Stefan, who was interning in the medical infirmary that summer. Some of the medicinal potions used in the clinic were in short supply. He was going to prepare more of them to replenish the infirmary's stock.

Savannah had done very well in the potions VIII classes, which focused on recipes containing medicinal herbs, and she was quite proficient in preparing both medicinal and nutritional potions. She had interned in the rectory kitchen in a previous summer internship. She explained this to Stefan and asked, "Could I stay and watch and, perhaps, even assist in the preparation of medicinal recipes? I would like to learn more about the potions that are made using the herbs I tend in the garden."

Stefan was glad to oblige Savannah's request. He asked, "Have you ever done any summer internships in the medical infirmary?"

Savannah replied, "No, I have not."

"You might want to consider it," Stefan said. "You will be able to see the effects of the medicinal plants we use after they have been administered." This idea intrigued Savannah; however, she had reservations. She had as much interest in learning about diseases—in humans or animals—as she had in learning about sanitation measures a few years ago. She had learned what she needed to know about first aid and the treatment of injuries, which was more than she wanted to know. "The class was fine until faculty brought out the moulage," she told Stefan.

Stefan grinned. He told Savannah, "You need not be exposed to serious illnesses or injuries unless an emergency arises. Your first aid training was just that—first aid. I want to know much more about treating illnesses and injuries." He added, "I want to become a physician. I'm working under the supervision of Matron H'Umara and Dr. Stuvidicus, and with their recommendations, I hope to study medicine at Gregor."

So Savannah transferred to the infirmary for the rest of the summer. She worked beside Stefan, providing him with the herbs and plants he needed and helping him make the soups, salves, and other potions for patients in the clinic. Savannah became quite proficient in preparing these recipes. She also worked up enough nerve to visit the patients, ask how they were feeling, and observe how they were progressing.

Over the rest of the summer, Savannah and Stefan found that they enjoyed working together. Without realizing it at first, they were becoming a couple. One day, Savannah asked Stefan, "How would you like to look for some of the wild plants, herbs, and berries that you use in your potions?" It would be Stefan's turn to be mentored. Late one afternoon, the two of them transformed into their respective alternate species to go afield. Stefan became a handsome elk stag, and Savannah transformed into her customary gray wolf. Native wolves preyed on elk; yet, this was not an issue. For a moment, the wolf could only stare at the elk. He was magnificent. Savannah was completely smitten.

Supplemental Notes and Citations

Genetic Imprinting

This is an epigenetic process, often via DNA methylation, that silences one gene, allowing the other gene to be expressed, effectively making the stamped gene inactive (Jirtle et al., 2000; Kappil et al., 2015; Lawson et al., 2013; Moore et al., 2015; Pfeifer, 2000). This process does not involve gene mutation (Tycko, 2000).

Embryonic imprinting is a process whereby imprinted genes are established in the embryo (after fertilization) with the parent of origin for each imprinted gene also established (Brooker, 2009; Kappil et al., 2015; Monk, 2015; Pacchierotti and Spano, 2015).

In genomic imprinting, a segment of DNA (versus a single gene) may be stamped (Brooker, 2009).

Parent of Origin

This describes the parent who provided the gene that is being expressed (Kalish et al., 2014; Kappil et al., 2015; Lawson et al., 2013; Moore et al., 2015; Pfeifer, 2000). This type of inheritance follows a non-Mendelian pattern of inheritance because marking (stamping) the gene causes offspring to differentiate between maternally and paternally inherited genes (Brooker, 2009).

CHAPTER 35

The Summer Games

The games were held each summer. They provided a measure of excitement and entertainment for all the villagers who could attend—largely proud parents and other family members—and served to release pent-up energy in the students. They were an opportunity for students to compete with one another and see who was best—at least, for the current year. Yet even these games had an underlying purpose. They provided opportunities to hone skills (individual events) and increase both strength and endurance (combination events).

By the summer of her junior year in Form III, Ruwena had gained enough proficiency to participate in a few of the individual events and team relays for *H. sapiens*. She could run very fast in a sprint and maintain a moderate pace for long-distance relays, and she was quite agile over uneven terrain and obstacles. As an *H. sapiens* student, she could not acknowledge the source of these traits and, really, should not have been competing with other *H. sapiens* students. Yet her classmates insisted she participate in something "If only to be sociable," Savannah remarked.

Ruwena ducked swimming and boating, and her teammates could not insist otherwise. Madam Merena was quite emphatic. "There is no chance I will clear Ruwena to participate in a swimming event. Period." This automatically ruled out boating. Although relieved, Ruwena was also a little disappointed. As a river otter, she could flirt with Erwina's best swimmers, and they would never catch her. *One day,* she sighed to herself. Until then, she would shout encouragement to her Form III teammates.

Standard Games

There was a wide variety of individual and team sports. The *H. sapiens* students could participate in all standard sporting events. Since not all alternate species could participate in the games, *H. transformans* students in their human form could also participate in standard events. Since the genes of their alternate species offered them an advantage even in their human form, they competed separately from *H. sapiens* students.

Form II seniors and Form III freshmen and sophomores could participate in biathlons. Form III juniors and seniors and Form IV students could participate in triathlons. Students interested in scouting often competed in the biathlons and triathlons.

Scouts who were not on active duty could participate in the games. Their competitions were separate as well, since nearly all of them were *H. transformans*, and their experience gave them an advantage over the students. Nevertheless, Form IV students were allowed to challenge experienced scouts in the same events. Faculty often would compete in these games as well. Sometimes it was to challenge one another and sometimes to be challenged by another younger and experienced scout.

Predators versus Prey

Predator-versus-prey games were for *H. transformans* students only and primarily for those who were certified to transform and were functioning independently on field expeditions. Form III juniors and seniors and Form IV students who were *H. transformans* were eligible to participate in these games. Scouts also joined in these games to compete with one another and occasionally with faculty, in the hopes of outwitting some of the latter. The compound and the northeast, southeast, and southwest outposts provided the venues for these games.

Predator-prey games had two underlying purposes. Firstly, in the real world, both scouts and students traveling as their alternate species (e.g., a fox) could encounter a natural predator (e.g., a wolf). Many apex predators in the *Canidae* and *Felidae* families have to accelerate rapidly to their top speed in order to catch prey. Their prey, which may be foxes and deer, need to do the same to escape. Hence, students also needed to develop the skills of their alternate species in order to avoid or escape a natural predator.

The *H. transformans* faculty and staff whose alternate species included an apex predator and students who would be their prey competed in these games to see who got caught and who escaped. Faculty whose alternate species did not include an apex predator would transform to keep watch over the participants, especially the students. They also conspired with other faculty to distract a student's attention away from a faculty member stalking the student. Although one might think this unfair, many social predators work as a team to bring down a prey animal (e.g., wolves, lions, hyenas, etc.).

Secondly, in the event of an attack by Cassius or Biogenics, the people of Erwina knew they couldn't escape quickly to Gregor. It was too far away, and travel was too arduous—especially for young children. They needed another solution—one that would take into account a fire-breathing dragon and allow them to escape to the southwest or into the mountains and caves. So they embedded their outer defenses into the natural barriers provided by the geography of the region. Everyone needed to know where these barriers were and how to traverse them and where camouflage was the best tactic versus where speed and agility would make the difference.

For these games, faculty members would transform into an apex predator somewhere in the area designated for the contest. Then a student, whose alternate species was a prey animal for that predator, would have to get across the designated area and reach their destination or complete a task without getting caught. If the predator so much as touched the prey with a paw or a whisker, the prey was caught. Deafening roars and intimidating growls were permitted (to the faculty's delight). Biting and clawing were not allowed. If used, the offender was automatically disqualified, and the win was awarded to his or her opponent.

Scenarios for the Form III students usually involved only one predator; however, the student wouldn't know what kind of predator he or she would be facing. The student also would not know whether or not he or she may have encountered a native predator. Given this real possibility, additional faculty in their alternate species kept watch over a student and would intervene should the student encounter a natural predator. Most often, faculty were dual-hatted as both predator and protector. As Form III students, Ruwena's classmates would be participating in the predator-prey games.

Scouts and Form IV students desiring to become scouts could expect an attack from more than one predator or enemy if not both. On rare occasions, a former student—usually a scout—would enjoy turning the tables on a faculty member. From time to time, faculty members couldn't resist the temptation to chase down other faculty.

Top Gun

Samiya was tasked to locate and identify an animal that had been seen around the main compound. It was not thought to be native to the territory. She transformed into a white-tailed deer and began her search. Her height and eyesight would allow her to see over a wider area. Her size also made her more visible; however, her coloring would help camouflage her location. Although her hearing and eyesight were very good, her sense of smell could detect a predator or an alien animal even before she could see or hear it. As she toured the compound and the mound around it, she spotted a place where something had broken through the top of the mound. There she caught the scent of a brown bear. *An animal that size should be easy to spot,* she thought.

As she continued her search for the brown bear, she caught another scent. When she looked around, she saw a red wolf leap from its place atop the mound some distance away. It was headed straight for her. She bolted and quickly accelerated to a speed that roughly matched the speed of the wolf. To her advantage, Samiya could leap over obstructions easily, whereas the wolf had to scramble over them. In this way, she was able to increase her lead and eventually get away.

She had no doubt that the wolf would continue to track her. So she found a dense thicket where she could lie down and hide, as a fawn would do. There she waited until she transformed back into a human. She waited still longer until she could transform again. Then she left the seclusion of the thicket and headed for a rocky outcrop.

In the meantime, the wolf continued on the trajectory the deer had taken. Much to his annoyance, he had lost the scent of the deer. As he approached the same rocky outcrop, a lynx suddenly lunged at him from above. The wolf bolted only to be chased by an aggressive—and apparently angry—lynx. The lynx broke off its attack when it reached another steep, rocky slope that it could navigate without difficulty and which the wolf could not. The lynx had turned the tables on the wolf and escaped. Sometimes, the best defense is a good offense.

Samiya never did find the bear. She did receive high marks for strategy. The faculty reminded her, however, that even one lone wolf can overpower a lynx. Samiya reminded the faculty that the lynx can climb trees. Later, Master Navarov admitted he almost jumped out of his skin when the lynx flew at him. For a moment, he thought he would have to defend himself against a native lynx when it suddenly broke off its attack. Then he realized why he had lost the scent of the white-tailed deer.

An Aerial Attack

Javier was in the southeast outpost. He had been tasked to alert the southwest outpost that an armed force was seen crossing the territory once inhabited by the people of H'Aleth. It appeared to be headed on a trajectory that would reach the southwest outpost in a little over a day. The villagers must be alerted to evacuate as quickly as possible. Javier transformed into his alternate species, the badger, and set out to warn the villagers. Unfortunately, his stocky short legs and long front claws were built for digging, not running.

The southwest outpost was just over sixty miles from the southeast outpost. Javier wasted no time setting off for it. At a steady, brisk trot interspersed with short bursts of speed, he estimated he might be able to average eight to ten miles per hour. At that rate, it would take him six to seven hours to reach the village outpost—provided he has no distractions. That would give the villagers only sixteen to eighteen hours to evacuate.

Javier had no doubt there would be at least one distraction. To his advantage, badgers are built low to the ground, and their coats are a mix of brown, black, and white colors. Both of these attributes provided camouflage in the grasslands. The need for speed, however, might mark that something was moving in the grass. This could betray his location and his heading.

The armed force (faculty and staff members) had stirred up many native species during its march—birds, mammals, and insects. Some of these natives were predators seeking to take advantage of distracted prey. One of them was a cougar that, presumably, came down from the southwest mountains. The cougar caught the badger's scent and began tracking him. Fortunately, badgers have a strong sense of smell too. Javier picked up the scent of the cougar when the wind shifted. He knew that a cougar was a large apex predator and likely would overpower him. He didn't know if it was one of the faculty or a native predator. This was more than an academic question. He needed to find an existing burrow or a stream where his scent could be lost.

Why did they ask a badger to make this run? he asked himself. Then it dawned on him. The cougar was hunting a badger. They often avoid humans. If Javier could find a burrow, he could excavate a den deep enough and large enough to accommodate a human his size. Then, he would curl up in a ball and transform. The cougar might be confused—even dismayed—by the scent of a human emanating from the den. *I'm certainly not going to outrun it,* he sighed. A cougar could reach top speeds of forty to fifty miles per hour.

Javier immediately began his search for a burrow. His sense of smell led him to a nearby abandoned prairie dog colony and the entrance to a burrow. He quickly excavated and enlarged the burrow, then ducked inside it. Once inside, he decided not to transform. Instead, he continued to excavate along one of the channels dug by the former inhabitants until he reached another entrance remote from the first one. This would break his scent trail. He poked his head above the ground just far enough to look around. Sure enough, in the meantime, the cougar had located the entrance he used. Javier would have to wait, but not for long.

A pair of burrowing owls with chicks in another nearby burrow had raised the alarm and began strafing the cat. A native cougar would have tried to catch the birds; however, this one did not. It left the burrow and resumed its patrol away from the birds and their burrow. Javier watched the cougar until it left the area. Although he was certain the cat was a faculty member, he remained alert. He did not want to get caught by any other predators, native or otherwise.

Javier completed his journey without further incident. It took him nearly ten hours to reach the village, and he was worn out when he arrived. *They really need to pick another species for this exercise,* he moaned to himself.

Sumo Wrestling

Galan, a Form VI senior, was one of three couriers tasked to take a secret message from the main compound to the southeast outpost. His task was to carry it over the ridge from west to east. Another courier had brought it over the river to the western edge of the ridge, where Galan had transformed into a black bear. The courier strapped the pouch containing the message to the bear's back. The first courier alerted him to sightings of enemy forces nearby, some of whom were *H. transformans*. The enemy had spies patrolling the area as their alternate species, and some of them were apex predators. Galan must reach the eastern edge of the ridge, where it merges into the grasslands, in time to meet a third courier, who would take the message the rest of the way.

Galan began his trek up the western side of the ridge. Although an apex predator himself, he had to be alert for those species that could attack a young-adult black bear. Larger black bears, wolves, and cougars were known to inhabit the ridge. A lone wolf likely would avoid a contest; however, a wolf pack might attack him. If he invaded the territory of another bear, it would attack. Then, there were humans, who, if armed, might attack him—some out of fear, others for sport. Fortunately, even adult black bears were good climbers. Galan threaded his way across the ridge as quietly as he could. His hearing was his most acute sense. Although his near vision was good, his distance vision left something to be desired.

Then Galan spotted a fully grown male black bear not far from him. The larger bear also saw him. Although Galan would have liked to think the bear was one of the faculty, he could not be sure. If the bear was a faculty member, a confrontation with it could jeopardize his mission and result in failure. Confrontation with a native bear could get him killed.

Galan faced a quandary. He could launch himself up a tree; however, so could the other bear. Conversely, the other bear could simply wait for Galan at the base of the tree, stranding him there. In either case, Galan would miss his rendezvous with the third courier. As another option, Galan could try to outrun the bear. A smaller, lighter, and somewhat nimbler bear might be able to outpace a heavier larger bear—especially running up the ridge. If the larger bear gains on him anyway, he can always get up a tree. The ridge was forested with suitable trees all through it. Finally, Galan could try to bluff the larger bear by roaring and posturing; however, that would risk a confrontation with it—not a good idea.

Having no good options that would allow him to complete his task, Galan decided to make a dash up the ridge in hopes of outrunning the larger bear. Unfortunately, the latter was fully capable of running up the ridge too. In addition, his longer stride gave him an advantage, and he quickly gained on Galan. Galan switched to plan B and aimed for a tree he could climb quickly. He never reached it.

Suddenly, a large brown bear erupted from the trees with an enormous roar to challenge the black bear chasing Galan. The two squared off to battle for supremacy. With much roaring and snarling, body slamming and pushing—but no biting or clawing—the two bears contested with each other. Then Galan knew that the two bears were likely faculty or scouts sparring with each other.

Galan really wanted to stay and watch the contest between these two behemoths. He knew, however, that he must take advantage of the brown bear's intervention and rendezvous with the other courier. He raced up the rest of the ridge and charged down the eastern side of it. This proved to be unwise.

About a third of the way down the eastern side of the ridge, Galan suddenly saw a gray wolf farther down the slope and off to his left. For a second, they both looked at each other. Then the first wolf was joined by a second, followed by a third and a fourth wolf. A lone wolf does not pose a significant risk to an adult black bear. A wolf pack is another matter altogether. When Galan saw the lead wolf crouch and hunch up his shoulders, Galan immediately resurrected plan B and made a dash for a nearby tree that would support his weight. As the wolf pack launched after him, he launched up the tree. Now he was trapped, and wolves were patient. If the wolves were faculty, they would wait until the exercise was over and then leave. If they were native wolves, Galan would be parked in the tree all night or until the wolves decided to hunt for other prey.

Fortunately for Galan, a small group of mule deer appeared at the crest of the ridge. Their keen eyes did not miss the wolves surrounding a tree. Their appearance, however, had alerted the wolves to their presence. This prey species would be irresistible to native wolves. If the wolves were faculty, faculty would know this and be obliged to pursue the deer. In either case, Galan was off the hook. The deer bolted back down the western side of the ridge with the wolf pack in hot pursuit.

Galan finally succeeded in making his rendezvous with the third courier. He learned later that the mule deer were faculty (Madam Lindenova, Matron Trevora, Master Morenavik, and Master Neminicus) as was the wolf pack (Master Xavier, Matron Aquina, Madam Patrina, and Master Gaius). The black bear was Master Chernavich, and the brown bear was Warren, an experienced scout. Warren had won the contest and was quite satisfied with the outcome. After all the predator-prey games when he was a student, the payback was sweet.

CHAPTER 36

Ascent into the Clouds

All senior Form III graduates were preparing to join the rest of the Erwinian community as adults. As part of their Form IV experience, they would be assuming the roles and responsibilities of adulthood for which they had been prepared. Consequently, most of the students had selected a summer internship in the arenas where they wished to practice after graduation. Savannah's experience interning with Stefan in the medical infirmary cemented her desire to become a botanist specializing in medicinal herbs and the preparation of medicinal potions. In this manner, she could augment Stefan's medical knowledge and support his practice as a physician. They planned to marry after she completed her Form IV studies.

Ruwena still wanted to be a scout; however, she found working with wildlife very satisfying as well. She decided she wanted to specialize in wildlife studies, which would allow her to work in the falconry, the aviary, and the vet clinic and even roam about the territory observing and studying the different species.

A Field Expedition

The summer after graduating from Form III, Ruwena and Savannah were delighted when they and two more Form III graduates, Erik and Henrik, were selected to go on a summer field expedition to the northeast outpost. All of them were considered advanced students with greater maturity and higher levels of proficiency, including the ability to transform (except for Ruwena).

The northeast outpost was situated on the flanks of a high mountain range that lay to the north and extended to the northeast and the northwest. It lay not far from where the northeasternmost reaches of Erwina almost touched the northwestern head of what had once been H'Aleth. This was the territory most hotly contested by Biogenics and Cassius.

Savannah, Erik, and Henrik—all *H. transformans*—would be mentored by three experienced *H. transformans* scouts, Rachel, Evan, and Warren. They had just returned from surveying the southeastern region of Erwina. They were on their way to survey the northeastern region. The troupe was joined by five faculty members, two of whom were *H. sapiens* faculty members. Madam Nadina [na-*dēn*-ah], an expert gymnast and instructor in gymnastics, would mentor Ruwena as the sole *H. sapiens* student. Master Leonid [*lē*-o-nĭd], the chief meteorologist, wanted to evaluate weather conditions and patterns in the northern mountains. He had observed that winter temperatures had been dropping in the northeast over the past three years and wanted to measure atmospheric conditions in these mountains. Master Vikarov [*vik*-ar-ov], whose alternate species was a bighorn sheep, wanted to observe two stars in the constellation Ursa Major. He wanted to see if either of them showed any changes in their luminosity. Master Xavier and Matron Kavarova, both of whom could transform into a large mountain wolf, would serve as guides on the expedition. Master Xavier would remain in human form. For additional protection, Matron Kavarova became a gray wolf and would remain in that form until they reached the outpost. In either form, both of them were quite capable of fending off one or more attackers.

The troupe would be traveling through the mountain forests and passes, crossing rivers, and traversing limestone caves to reach a mountain forest glen where a small outpost was hidden. The students were warned that the mountain was known to be restless from time to time. "There have been cave-ins, and some cavern chambers have collapsed," Master Xavier told them. "One must listen to the mountain before deciding to shelter in a cave or traverse a cavern," he cautioned.

The students couldn't help but notice that Master Xavier, the *H. sapiens* staff, and the scouts all carried weapons. Ruwena remembered the armed guards that had accompanied the horse-drawn wagon and its occupants when she first journeyed to the compound. This expedition would take them near the borders contested by Cassius and Biogenics. Surveillance reports had noted the presence of an aerial hybrid, a lyvulfon [lī-*vul*-fon] (illus. 21), in the region. This creature was Cassius's attempt to recreate the gryphon by splicing the genes of a vulture into the genome of a lynx. Given its presence in the northeastern region, it was likely that Cassius released it against Biogenics. Most of the skirmishes between the two factions, however, were taking place farther to the northeast than the expedition planned to go. Nevertheless, the troupe would have to exercise caution.

As they headed north by northeast, they traversed the dense hardwood forest at the foot and lower slopes of the northern mountain range. There were no defined paths through the region as a precaution against potential invaders. Master Xavier and Matron Kavarova knew the area very well as they had scouted and traveled through it many times in the past. So they threaded their way through the trees and vegetation without difficulty. The students were instructed to pay close attention to their surroundings at all times, both for safety and the ability to identify their surroundings in the future. This was their first exercise in surveillance and in finding their way back home again.

The nearest mountain peak was about seven thousand feet high. The trek would take the troupe up to about 1,500 feet by gradually winding their way up the slopes. Savannah was paired with Evan. Both of them could transform into gray wolves. Henrik, who could become a mountain goat, was paired with Rachel, who could transform into a lynx. Both of these alternate species were sure-footed in rocky terrain. Erik, who could transform into a raccoon, was paired with Warren, who could become a brown bear. The notion of a twenty-pound raccoon being paired with a seven-hundred-pound bear was a source of considerable amusement. "I think it's great," remarked Erik. "I'll just climb onto Warren's back and ride the rest of the way."

"Think again," Warren countered.

Within the troupe, there should be plenty of sharp eyes, ears, and noses. This would prove essential as the troupe ascended higher on the mountain's slope. They would encounter more mist and low-lying clouds, limiting visibility.

By:

Illus. 21. Lyyulfon.

Starting with the second evening and every other evening thereafter, the *H. transformans* students and their mentors would alternate between being in human form and transforming into their respective alternate species. In this manner, the students would become acquainted with the terrain and learn how to traverse it both as humans and as their alternate species. They would experience how it looked, smelled, sounded, and felt from both perspectives. It was critical that they learn in both forms how the terrain should be when no invader was present. So Erik did not get to climb onto Warren's back. Erik needed to learn about the territory from the perspective of a raccoon.

Long ago, when Ruwena first came to Erwina, she had learned her way around the compound by doing exactly the same thing that her classmates were now tasked to do. Only she did so as an owl. Late at night, she would watch from within the compound and for a short distance outside it (breaking a house rule). Alas, on this expedition, she could participate only in her human form.

Of Whistles and Rumbles

Since gender and intellect were maintained during transformation from one species into another, the students' capacity to learn remained even in their transformed state. Intelligence was an excellent example of a polygenic, multifactorial trait. There were no specific genes that determined intelligence in any species. Approximately 50% of the differences in intelligence among *H. sapiens* was attributed to genetics. The other 50% was attributed to environmental factors or diseases that adversely affected intellectual function.

Intelligence was assessed based on the presence of a number of capabilities that included problem-solving, communicating and cooperating with others of the same species, learning and remembering, recognizing one's self and others, and counting. With the exception of counting by numbers, most classes of animals including mammals, birds, and reptiles had these capabilities, some to a greater extent than others.

Decision-making was a complex interaction among factors affecting intelligence, the ability to recall what had been learned in the past, and behavior. The coordination of these functions was affected by an extraordinary array of chemical interactions in the brain. Genetic variability (polymorphisms) in the genes that code for chemical agents (neurotransmitters) that trigger these interactions could affect both cognitive and emotional behavior. Derangements in some of these agents were associated with psychosis.

Communicating via spoken and written language and counting by numbers were largely but not exclusively human behaviors. These behaviors could be mimicked in other species that have the physical structures (phenotype) to accommodate them. For those species that do not, many could learn to understand human language but not have the inherent ability to speak or write it. Similarly, humans could learn what certain vocalizations meant when uttered by another species (e.g., differences in the bark of a dog greeting its owner versus a stranger). Consequently, when humans transformed into another species, their ability to communicate was limited by what their physical form would allow and the manner of communication normally used by their alternate species. In no way did this diminish their intelligence. A human transformed into a mammal with claws or a bird with talons could still scratch out a written message on the ground. Similarly, a human could learn to recognize the different growls and snarls from a colleague who had transformed into a wolf.

Supplemental Notes and Citations

Intelligence

Level of intelligence is assessed based on the presence of a number of capabilities: (1) problem-solving, which can lead to innovation, use of tools, and adaptation to a new environment; (2) communication among other members (e.g., language in humans, whistles in whales and dolphins, rumbles in elephants); (3) memory (e.g., spatial and time); (4) ability to learn from experience or be taught by another (e.g., how to use a tool); (5) recognition of self and other members; (6) ability to cooperate and coordinate with others; and (7) ability to count.

Genetic Component of Intelligence

The estimate that 50% of intelligence is genetic is based on studies in twins (Deary et al. 2009). The environmental factors that can have a significant effect on intelligence include socioeconomic conditions, health and nutrition, and educational opportunities (Junkiert-Czarnecka and Haus, 2016; Plomin and Deary, 2015). Disorders that can affect intelligence include congenital diseases (e.g., Down syndrome, fragile X syndrome), inherited diseases (e.g., Huntington's chorea), and diseases that cause degenerative changes in the brain (e.g., Alzheimer's disease).

Neurotransmitters

Specialized cells in the brain produce an array of biochemical agents that affect both cognitive and emotional responses. These include dopamine (excitatory), norepinephrine (excitatory), serotonin (inhibitory), gamma-aminobutyric acid (GABA, inhibitory), and a host of others (Logue and Gould, 2014). Many pharmacologic agents that both emulate and inhibit these agents are used to treat emotional (e.g., depression, anxiety) and physical (e.g., seizures, diabetic nerve pain) disorders.

CHAPTER 37

Descent into the Depths

The trip through the mountain terrain continued for three days and nights. As the troupe reached about fifteen hundred feet in altitude, they came to the entrance of a cave. The entrance led downward about five hundred feet until they reached an underground river. Here they followed the river in human form until they reached an enormous cavern.

Iridescent Caverns

The cavern was spotted with stalagmites and stalactites, pools of clear water that had been filtered through the limestone layer, and several types of minerals including iridescent and fluorescent crystalline formations. It was beautiful. The temperature was cool at an even fifty-five degrees Fahrenheit. Ruwena had never seen such a fabulous place, nor had any of the other students. Nonetheless, the exercise was still the same: learn their way around the cavern as humans and as their alternate species.

The students were allowed to transform and, in pairs, explore the cavern under the watchful eye of Matron Kavarova. There were many nooks and crannies in which they could get lost. Ruwena longed to slip away, transform into a bat, and fly all around and through the cavern; however, she could not. She knew this intuitively as she sensed no kinship with them. *Why not?* she wondered. *I can transform into a dragon.*

Dragons, bats, and humans are mammals and, as such, share a certain amount of genetic homology. All three inherited their forelimbs from a common ancestor (homologous structures). As such, they share many of the same genes and signaling pathways for growth. Both bats and dragons—but alas, not humans—developed specialized forelimbs that gave them self-sustained flight under power (versus gliding). Birds also developed a type of forelimb that became wings; however, their wings evolved from a different ancestor (analogous structures). Ruwena could not transform into a bat because she lacked the specific genotype that would allow her to do so. Without the genotype, she could not replicate the phenotype.

An Intruder

The trip through the mountain took almost a day before they began to ascend out of the series of caverns and narrow ravines they encountered. It was here that Matron Kavarova encountered the scent of a hybrid animal. She immediately snapped a deep growl to Master Xavier. Her abrupt change and aggressive posture startled the students; however, Master Xavier knew exactly what it meant. Matron Kavarova had detected another being—a potentially dangerous one. As she sniffed the area and followed the scent, she drew Master Xavier's attention to its direction and path. It was perilously close to their own.

Master Xavier immediately turned to the troupe. "Move away now at a ninety-degree angle from our current path," he ordered, pointing to his left, opposite of the location of the scent. "Students who have transformed will remain in their alternate species. Do not attempt to resume human form." He knew that they would be better able to navigate the change in direction and have more agility to scramble up the rock formations. "Students who have not transformed should not do so. We have no time to waste and, therefore, no time to transform safely," he added.

Master Xavier, with Rachel and Evan, both of whom had resumed human form, made their weapons ready. The troupe traveled about 150 feet to one side until the footing was too poor for the *H. sapiens* members to go any farther. At that point, the troupe turned and resumed their ascent. The climb was now much harder and more perilous. It required considerable effort and more time to climb over and around rock formations, and it proved difficult for everyone. Even so, the rocks provided additional cover for them as they moved upward. It was not enough.

A large creature suddenly appeared and lunged at them. It looked like it was part wolf and part boar, with the snout and horns of a boar and the body of a wolf except for its short legs and hooves. The animal was too far away to reach the troupe and, in poor footing, slid downward away from them. This did not stop the beast, which was clearly deranged. It scraped, stumbled, and slipped on the rocks in an attempt to assault anyone it could reach.

Ruwena knew this kind of creature. It was a lupuseroja [*lu*-pu-ser-*o*-ja] (illus. 22), a violent wolf-boar mix of Cassius's design. Ruwena had learned from her mistress that these hybrids were genetically engineered. Cassius had spliced the genes of a boar into the genome of a wolf in an attempt to create an aggressive animal to guard the storerooms and weapons depots in his villages. They were kept chained and hungry to induce the desire to attack anyone who came too close and should be pitied, not hated. Nonetheless, they were dangerous and must be avoided. If they detected any other species but their own masters, they would attack.

Master Xavier ordered all the students to continue their climb as quickly as they could. "Master Leonid and Madam Nadina will guide you," he said. "Warren will be your guard." Master Xavier, Rachel, and Evan stayed back as a defensive barrier between the creature and the retreating students and faculty. They held their fire, hoping it would stumble into a deadly fall. It would be best not to leave any evidence of their presence—especially their weaponry. Matron Kavarova challenged the hybrid directly.

The lupuseroja found itself facing a ferocious large mountain wolf. Yet it seemed not to care. It continued to lunge forward as the wolf fought to drive it back. Ruwena saw this and slipped away from the others. She was almost certain the mountain wolf would be badly injured, if not killed, by this creature. This she could not and would not allow. Ruwena also knew that Master Xavier was right. There might not be enough time to transform safely. Nevertheless, she took the risk.

The wolf's back leg lost its footing on a slope. She slipped and fell on the rocks, sliding toward the lupuseroja. As she scrambled to get up, Master Xavier ran from his post and shouted to the creature to draw its attention to himself. He was too late. The lupuseroja had seen its chance for a kill and leaped toward the wolf. It never reached its quarry. Out of nowhere, a tawny-brown cougar, going for a kill of its own, leaped over the wolf and collided with the creature head-on.

Illus. 22. Lupuseroja.

By:

As muscular and powerful as the lupuseroja was, it was thrown backward. Both combatants fell downward over the rocks. The surprise attack and the cougar's agility gave the cat an advantage. The cougar's large padded feet provided better footing on the rocks. Powerful neck and shoulder muscles pulled down its prey. Its powerful jaws gripped the creature's throat while its claws sunk into its flesh. Even though the latter was heavyset and had the thick, muscular neck of a boar, the cougar's long canines reached their target. The lupuseroja fell farther downward, dragging the cougar with it until both disappeared.

During the fight, Master Xavier had reached the wolf to help her regain her footing. Both then ran to the edge of a rock formation near where the cougar and the creature had disappeared. There was no sign of them. *Where did the cougar come from?* Master Xavier asked himself. He knew that cougars were native to these mountains, so the cat could have come into the cave seeking a place to rest when it heard the commotion. Since cougars use stealth to hunt their prey, it might have used the ruckus to mask its approach in the hopes of catching its prey by surprise or to raid someone else's kill. If so, the cougar might have recognized the creature as another apex predator and a rival.

"It should not have been a student," said Master Xavier as both he and the wolf abruptly ascended the rocks as quickly as they could. The wolf advanced more rapidly and was already engaged in sniffing each and every person, students and staff alike, to account for everyone. Only one person was missing: the *H. sapiens* student Ruwena. Both faculty members, along with Evan and Rachel, began to search for her. Before long, Evan spotted Ruwena lying between two rock formations. When he reached her, she could not get up. She was shaking, cold, exhausted, and looked beat up. It appeared that she, too, had slipped and fallen upon the rocks. Fortunately, Evan was a powerfully built young man and very strong (a benefit of his wolf genes). He lifted Ruwena without difficulty and was able to carry her the rest of the way up to the egress from the cave. There, everyone rested and remained until all had resumed their human form.

After they exited the cave on the side of the mountain, the students asked Master Xavier what kind of creature had attacked them. He replied, "It was either a genetically engineered hybrid or a failed transformation event. I suspect the former." Then he admonished the students, "If I am correct, then do not fault the creature for what someone else made it."

What was it doing here, and how did it get here? he mused. If the creature had simply escaped to run free, it could have traveled here completely on its own. In that case, its absence would have been noted long ago and been forgotten. This would not be the case if Cassius had moved into the area. This was cause for considerable concern. *Where Cassius has moved in, Biogenics will not be far away,* he thought to himself.

Master Xavier had another lingering question. *Where did the cougar come from?* None of the *H. transformans* students had any feline genes. Ruwena was the only unknown in the group, and she was the only missing person after the fight with the creature. Although the majority of her injuries were consistent with a fall, several of her symptoms were suggestive of someone who had forced a transformation too quickly. The cougar had also fallen on the rocks, and it was not found. *I wonder,* he thought. Yet he also thought Ruwena was too young to have transformed so quickly. Only an experienced *H. transformans*—one who is well practiced—could transform so quickly and do so successfully.

CHAPTER 38

A Daring Rescue

The troupe continued on its journey as it had done before, this time with a heightened degree of alertness and a greater sense of awareness. Both Master Xavier and Matron Kavarova were anxious to confer with their colleagues in the northeastern outpost. Perhaps their scouts knew of movements by Cassius and Biogenics.

The Grotto

The northeast outpost was a small sunken grotto hidden among several large boulders at the base of the mountain (illus. 23). It was inside the forest that formed a boundary with the mountain. The area was dense with hardwood trees, especially oaks, which provided a canopy overhead. Several interconnecting caves had been excavated where crevasses had formed between the rocks. The caves served as storage areas, shelters, barren living quarters for their scouts, and meeting places. The connections between them were narrow passageways, some of which were natural formations between large boulders. Others were tunnels that had to be carved out deep underground.

There was a single wooden structure embedded between the two largest oaks. It was the outpost's main house. It blended so well with the trees that it could not be detected from outside the grotto. Underground tunnels connected the main house to nearby caves. These had to be excavated around the roots of the two oaks in order to keep from damaging the trees' root systems. The trek through those tunnels was interesting. No wonder the students had to take courses in gymnastics.

Illus. 23. The Grotto.

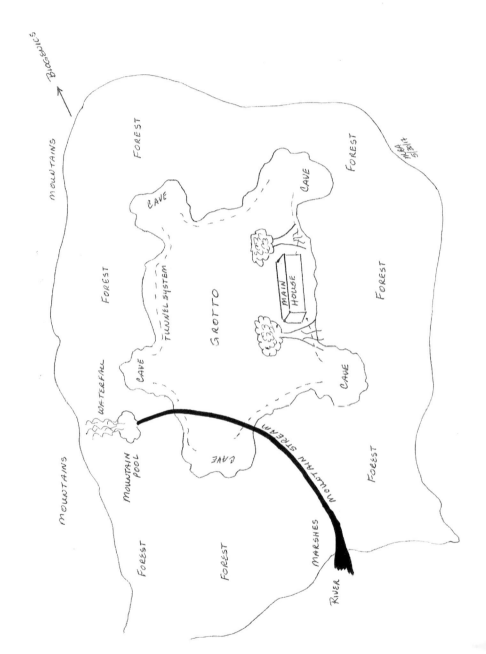

Water flowed down a crevice in the face of the mountain, creating a waterfall. In turn, the waterfall fed a deep pool from which a brisk mountain stream flowed through the grotto. Later, the stream joined others that flowed into a river. There were plenty of freshwater fish including trout, reptiles such as turtles and frogs, and other freshwater denizens.

The surrounding forest supported a wide variety of wildlife—birds, including raptors; beavers; raccoons; and other small mammals. Woodland deer could be seen early in the mornings and at dusk. The beavers had built their lodge and dam on a small feeder stream, creating a pond nearby, which supported a variety of amphibians, including frogs. Farther down from the pond, the stream also supported a family of river otters that had a burrow near it. There, they fed on fish and other tasty stream inhabitants. The pair were very content to stay where they were and rarely ventured far beyond the grotto except to find food. They were friendly to the scouts, who often gave the otters fish. The pair had two pups together and were raising them in the safety of the grotto.

After their travels, the troupe—especially the students—felt they had entered a paradise. It was beautiful, peaceful, and friendly, and there was hot food. As in the compound, students were allowed to roam freely throughout the grotto but not beyond its boundaries.

"Hybrid creatures have been seen in this region," explained Master Crocius [*crō*-ce-us], chief of the outpost, "and they are often deranged. Since they almost always attack on sight, many of our scouts remain in human form armed with bows and arrows. The scouts are skillful and can bring down most of these creatures with a single lethal shot. Then the creature and the arrow that killed it are burned." Master Crocius paused for a moment and then offered a warning. "Despite what you see here, it is a dangerous place."

This explains the hybrid creature we encountered in the cave, thought Master Xavier. Then he asked Master Crocius, "How common are cougars in the area?"

"Not uncommon," replied Master Crocius, "although we rarely see them. They will come down this far to hunt for prey but usually avoid contact with humans—another reason our scouts do not transform into mammals this close to the mountain."

The students were allowed to transform at will as long as they followed the rules of transformation and someone else was close by in case the student got into trouble. In fact, transformation was encouraged. Here they could gain greater facility as their alternate species. The students (including Ruwena) took advantage of their newfound freedom and began exploring the grotto. Ruwena promptly headed for the stream to look for the river otters. Not long afterward, a third river otter joined the resident pair and their pups. Ruwena knew she could not be away for long. She could not be seen as missing again.

Later that evening, the students were reminded that this was a field expedition. Erwina maintained close surveillance on its borders with Biogenics and Cassius. This outpost kept watch over the northern and northeastern regions between Erwina and Biogenics. The scouts at the outpost were very skilled in surveillance and would often slip over the border to expand their range of view. All of them could transform into a mammal native to the area they were watching. Students would be given opportunities to pair with a scout on a routine patrol around the grotto. This was the only time they were allowed outside its boundaries and not farther than a hundred yards away from it.

Students also received real-world reports of scouting and surveillance from well outside the grotto's boundaries. In their surveillance reports, scouts reported on activities in bordering Biogenics's villages—especially any indications that Biogenics was preparing to mobilize its forces. The scouts would report also on changes in the patterns or behaviors of native wildlife, if any. Sightings of any apex predators (e.g., bears, cougars) remote from the grotto would be noted during a routine report. Any evidence or sighting of a hybrid or a gray dragon was reported immediately. Much to Ruwena's dismay, one of the scouts reported seeing a third otter downstream cavorting with the other two adults. This was greeted as pleasant news. If the third otter had been a corrupted creature or a hybrid, the two adults would have chased it off. Still, Ruwena would need to be more careful.

Students also had assigned duties within the grotto itself to help keep it maintained and in good repair. The mountain seemed uneasy. At times, the students felt the ground shudder and then debris would rain into the grotto. Master Crocius explained that this was likely caused by seismic activity along a fault line under the mountain range. Many years ago, under stress from tectonic forces, one side of the fault moved upward while the other side slipped downward. This caused a major earthquake. One of their scouts on patrol in the area was killed. The tunnels and connections between the caves in the grotto were especially vulnerable to tremors.

They needed to be kept clear at all times in the event an invader found and attacked the outpost or there was a bad storm.

Still, for an hour or so each day, the students were freed from their lessons and duties and could roam wherever they pleased—and as whatever type of animal their genome supported—as long as they remained inside the grotto's boundaries. Thus, Ruwena could spend some time each day with the river otters.

A Duel in Midair

The area of the stream the otters occupied coursed through dense brush and trees, which helped conceal the location of their den. The brush also provided cover where they could hide from the few aerial predators—specifically, hawks and eagles—that also hunted near the stream and the river into which it flowed. The adults were not at risk for they were too large and heavy. Their pups, on the other hand, would make a fine snack. This meant the parents were always on high alert for predators on the ground or in the air. So it was a welcome relief for the parents to have a third adult to help watch over the pups. It proved to be a blessing.

One afternoon, when Ruwena was visiting the otter family as an otter herself, she spotted one of the outpost's scouts, Alan. This time, she saw him before he spotted her. She promptly ducked under the water and headed for dense underbrush overlying the stream. There she raised her head above the water just enough to watch the scout and breathe. The scout was not looking in her direction. He was looking toward the sky. Suddenly, the female otter barked several warning calls to her pups and anyone else who would listen. She, too, was looking up at the sky. Ruwena did the same and saw a strange creature, a lyvulfon, in flight overhead. She had never seen this hybrid, nor had her mistress ever described such a creature to her.

Suddenly, it dived toward the stream and snatched one of the pups. The pup's mother frantically grabbed the pup in her mouth and tried to pull it back down, but she couldn't. In the water, she had no traction, and the father was too far away to help. Alan saw immediately what was happening, drew an arrow, and took aim. He couldn't fire—the mother was between him and the lyvulfon as it struggled against the mother. He could bring the creature down and would do so. But he would have to wait until it broke free of the mother and hope it would not be too late for the pup.

The lyvulfon did break free and, with the pup in its claw, was rising into the air when Alan saw another otter launch itself upward out of the water, toward the creature, and in midair, transform into a Cooper's hawk. Alan watched in utter amazement as the hawk attacked the lyvulfon with its talons fully extended (illus. 24).

The hawk began to rip at the lyvulfon's head with its beak. The lyvulfon could not ascend any farther with the hawk on top of it, and it could not defend itself and hold onto the pup. So it dropped the pup and turned on the hawk. Then the aerial battle really began. The creature dwarfed the hawk in both body and wing span; however, it lacked the hawk's agility. The hawk was far more aerodynamic. Even though the lyvulfon could tuck its back legs under its body, its shape created significant drag during flight and limited its maneuverability. Nevertheless, with the two locked in battle, the creature's size and weight was to its advantage.

The hawk was in trouble when Alan finally had a clear shot. He brought down the creature, and when it fell, it separated from the hawk. At first the hawk appeared to be in a free fall itself. Then it recovered enough flight capacity to breaks its own fall. It fell into the dense underbrush, which served to cushion it. The lyvulfon crashed into the stream. Alan raced to get the creature out of the stream before it could contaminate the water. Then, he ran over to the mother otter trying to revive her pup. The pup was still alive but badly injured. He would have to get the pup to the grotto immediately if there was going to be a chance to save it. He picked up the pup and moved quickly to where the injured hawk had fallen. He didn't find the bird or any sign of it, not even a feather, and he was certain of where it had fallen. Given the pup's injuries, he couldn't take time to look for the hawk. So he turned away and ran to the grotto as fast as he could. The pup's mother followed after him.

Ruwena had transformed back into an otter just as she fell into the dense underbrush. While Alan dealt with the dead creature and collected the otter pup, she slipped back into the stream and hid among the vegetation and tree roots along the bank. She was heartbroken. The pup was completely limp and looked dead.

Illus. 24. A Duel in Midair.

In an act of desperation to save the pup, Ruwena had exposed her abilities to one of Erwina's scouts. Although the scout did not know who he saw transform in midair, he would not fail to report what he had seen. Now she had to get back to the village as quickly as possible to avoid being missed. This she could not do at first. She was exhausted and needed to remain an otter for a while longer. So she threaded her way back slowly through the underbrush, carrying her robe with her, until she was able to resume human form.

When she arrived at the main house, there was enough excitement and attendance at one of the caves that she could slip into the students' quarters unseen and get cleaned up. Then she joined everyone else at the cave where the pup had been taken. To her relief, the pup was still alive and would survive. Her risk had paid off, and for once, in all the commotion, she had not been missed. Although she was somewhat battered in the fight and the fall, her smock was sufficient to hide any signs. Compared to a hawk, the lyvulfon was clumsy in flight. The hawk had been buffeted by the creature's large wings; however, she had not been bitten or clawed.

Later that day, the creature's body was picked up by another scout. After the body was examined and a specimen of its tissue taken, it was burned with the arrow that had killed it. That evening, there was a briefing to which the students were not invited. There were two matters to discuss. First and foremost were the two hybrids who had appeared so close together—both in time and location. The faculty and staff were deeply concerned that Cassius was becoming more aggressive in releasing his abominations. Whether his target was Biogenics or Erwina or both was unknown.

The second matter was Alan's sighting of an otter—most likely the new arrival—that could transform directly into a bird. This level of capability had not been seen in many generations. Neither the hawk nor the otter were seen after the incident, so its fate was unknown. Master Xavier noted to himself that the third otter first appeared after their arrival. *Coincidence?* he asked himself. *I wonder.* All the faculty, scouts, and students—even Ruwena—were well-known. *It's not impossible that a single H. transformans could be living alone,* he thought. *Just unlikely. Biogenics is not that far away.*

It had become clear that the skirmishes between Biogenics and Cassius were intensifying. Furthermore, an increasing number of deformed creatures—products of Cassius's genetic engineering experiments—were coming into Erwina's territory. Given the recent incidents with the lupuseroja (at the cave) and the lyvulfon (at the river), the field trip was cut short. The region was far less safe than originally thought when the trip was planned. It was time to bolster surveillance and defenses in the immediate region, and this was not a task for students. The students were very disappointed. Nevertheless, preparations were made to leave the next day and return to the compound. There was much to report to the leadership there.

A Field Exercise in Readiness

Upon their return, the four students rejoined their fellow classmates. Since classes would not resume for a few more weeks, they would participate in strengthening Erwina's defenses. In order to avoid undue anxiety in all the students, faculty treated this as an impromptu field exercise for the entire student body. Much of this work resembled typical duties: keep tunnels clear of debris and look for decay and leaks, test the hemp ropes for strength and stability and look for fraying, and check the stocks of supplies and report any that have degraded or are missing.

Form IV students were tasked to assist in the armory since all of them had had a practicum there as part of their training in swordsmanship. They checked the weapons supply and took an inventory of what was available. Matron Aquina spoke privately with Master Heroditus. "I believe it would be prudent to increase production of weapons in the armory," she said. Master Heroditus concurred.

The Form III students who had been on the expedition traveled with other adults to check provisions in the caves along the man-made ridge that bordered the compound. They also checked on a series of stone formations on both sides of it that were actually designed to create a landslide if a keystone was loosened. During these trips, students were allowed to transform while traveling to and from these caves. These trips were treated as surveillance exercises as well. This made up, in part, for the opportunities lost at the northeast outpost.

If war came to Erwina, both Form III and Form IV students needed to be prepared. The adults would take the fight to their attackers. The older and more experienced students would be left to defend the compound, get all students to shelters, and help them flee through the tunnels. Few, if any, adults would remain behind to assist them. The students' knowledge, training, and practice throughout their schooling would be put to a real and possibly final test.

PART VI

Revelations

CHAPTER 39

H'Ester

When the fall term began as Form IV students, Savannah suddenly realized that Ruwena had never taken the two history courses, one that focused on the three Houses and one that focused on the Biogenics Corporation and the Cassius Foundation. She immediately impressed upon Ruwena the importance of their histories. "Read the history texts in the library," she urged. "They will help you understand the fighting between Cassius and Biogenics and what it could mean for us. You will be better prepared for what might come," Savannah warned.

Ruwena took Savannah's advice. She felt she knew enough about present day Erwina to defer Erwina's history to a later time. She knew almost nothing about Gregor; however, it was remote and seemed less germane to the situation. Cassius and Biogenics, however, were close at hand and were potential threats to Erwina. So Ruwena began her study of history with the Biogenics Corporation and the Cassius Foundation.

An Invitation

Matron Trevora approached Head Matron Aquina and Headmaster Morenavik with a proposal. She felt it was time to invite Ruwena to become an *H. sapiens* member of the House of Erwina, even though her lineage was still unknown. If either Cassius or Biogenics attacked Erwina, she would be in as much danger as anyone, and she could help with the younger students. Matron Trevora had consulted with faculty who had taught and observed Ruwena over the past five years. They were unanimous in their recommendations that Ruwena join their House. With the approval of Master Titus, Matron Aquina and Master Morenavik agreed. Matron Trevora approached Savannah with the news and asked her to bring Ruwena to the manor.

Savannah was thrilled. She knew exactly where to find Ruwena. The latter had been spending most of her spare time reading up on history in the library. Savannah raced to the library, where she found Ruwena in the history section, as expected. Savannah was very excited when she told Ruwena, "You've been invited to join our House."

Ruwena did not move or speak. Once she had finished reading the histories of Cassius and Biogenics, she had turned to the history of the three Houses. It began with H'Aleth. As she read its history and the description of its destruction, Ruwena realized why her mistress had hidden her in a Cassius village and remembered the mission her mistress had laid upon her. It suddenly struck Ruwena that she had lingered far too long in the comfort of the House of Erwina. She had spent nearly five years under its tutelage and supervision and had become immersed in it, as if she were a part of it. She had forgotten her purpose—to restore the House of H'Aleth—and felt she had done nothing to fulfill it. When she thought back on the sacrifices her mistress had made, she felt sick with remorse.

"Didn't you hear what I said?" Savannah asked. "It's official." she exclaimed. "You are one of us now."

Ruwena, despondent and weary, did not look up. "I cannot join your House," she said quietly.

Savannah was shocked. "What?" It was plain that something was terribly wrong. "Why not?"

"I have been remiss in my duty and now must do as my mistress bade me," Ruwena replied quietly and then looked up from the history book. "Please find your mistress, Matron Trevora. Tell her that H'Ester of the House of H'Aleth bids her greeting and would speak with her as soon as she may."

Savannah immediately looked around for this person. She could see no one else in the library. Ruwena still had not moved. So Savannah ran as fast as she could back to Matron Trevora, who was still speaking with Matron Aquina and Master Morenavik. She described to them what had transpired with Ruwena. "Ruwena said she could not join our House— something about being remiss in her duty," Savannah reported and then she gave Matron Trevora Ruwena's message. "She told me to tell you that H'Ester of the House of H'Aleth bids you greeting and would speak with you as soon as she may."

H'Ester

The three faculty members were dumbfounded. Could this be true? They all but flew to the library. On the way, Matron Aquina flagged a student to fetch Master Titus to the library at once. When they arrived, H'Ester stood up before them, as she would have done for her mistress. As Ruwena's current mistress, Matron Trevora spoke in a formal tone, "What is your true name?"

"H'Ester," H'Ester (Ruwena) replied.

"Who gave you that name?" Matron Trevora asked.

"My mistress told me this was my given name," H'Ester replied.

Matron Trevora then asked, "Who was your mistress?"

"My mistress told me her name was H'Ilgraith," H'Ester answered.

Matron Aquina left immediately to research the pedigree records for anyone by that name. It did not take her long to find it (ped. 3). H'Igraith was a third-generation descendant of Ruth through the maternal line. She was presumed to have been killed with all the others at H'Aleth.

When asked, H'Ester did not know her lineage. "My mistress had said only that I was a direct descendant of Ruth. She did not tell me when or where I was born or my parents' names." Her mistress had not told her these things in case she was discovered. If she did not know, she could not say—even if drugged.

If this were true, the three faculty members knew it was going to take a while to find H'Ester's pedigree. She could be descended from any one of Ruth's three daughters. Each line would have to be examined. Given the difference between H'Ilgraith's age, which could be calculated, and H'Ester's estimated age, H'Ester would be a fifth-generation descendant. If H'Ester was truly of H'Aleth, then both she and H'Ilgraith would have escaped the conflagration together.

Matron Trevora then asked, "How did you come by your mistress?"

H'Ester's did not know the answer to this question. "My mistress raised me alone," she replied.

"Where did you live?" Matron Trevora asked.

Ped. 3. Lineage of H'Ilgraith.

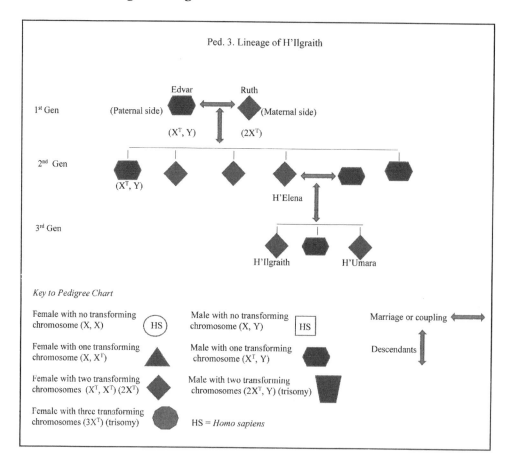

Ped. 3. Lineage of H'Ilgraith

1st Gen (Paternal side) Edvar Ruth (Maternal side)
(X^T, Y) $(2X^T)$

2nd Gen (X^T, Y) H'Elena

3rd Gen H'Ilgraith H'Umara

Key to Pedigree Chart

Female with no transforming chromosome (X, X) — HS

Male with no transforming chromosome (X, Y) — HS

Marriage or coupling

Female with one transforming chromosome (X, X^T)

Male with one transforming chromosome (X^T, Y)

Descendants

Female with two transforming chromosomes (X^T, X^T) ($2X^T$)

Male with two transforming chromosomes ($2X^T$, Y) (trisomy)

Female with three transforming chromosomes ($3X^T$) (trisomy)

HS = *Homo sapiens*

"In H'Aleth," H'Ester replied.

"Describe it," ordered Master Titus. He had slipped in quietly and now received a stern look from Matron Trevora.

"I was raised in a village not unlike this one, except it was built in open country," H'Ester replied. "It was surrounded by a tall stone wall. My mistress had a small dwelling near the manor house, a large stone building similar to your manor house. There was nothing in our village like the schoolhouse."

Then Matron Trevora asked, "Why did you and your mistress leave the village?"

"It was attacked," H'Ester replied.

"By whom?" asked Master Titus.

"My mistress did not say," responded H'Ester. "We went to the manor house when the alarm was first raised. Soon afterward, my mistress took me to a cellar. She transformed into a badger and led me through a tunnel, which ended at a thicket of thorns beyond the stone wall. From there, we ran into the forest." H'Ester remembered that experience all too well.

Both Master Titus and Matron Trevora recognized H'Ester's description of the stone wall, the manor house, the thicket, and the forest beyond. Both of them were originally from H'Aleth and had emigrated to Erwina long before H'Aleth was destroyed.

Matron Trevora struck her most official academic pose and approached H'Ester directly. "Who directed you to come to Erwina?" she inquired. She had asked a similar question of H'Ester at their first encounter.

"My mistress," H'Ester replied.

"For what purpose?" asked Matron Trevora.

H'Ester thought back to what her mistress had commanded. "She told me to learn the history of my House and what will be required of me as its Mistress. When the time comes, I may yet restore the House of H'Aleth."

Matron Trevora spoke in a firm voice, as a faculty member toward a student, "Then you have done as your mistress bade you, and you have not been remiss—except, possibly, for not telling us sooner. Why did you wait?"

H'Ester replied, "My mistress commanded me to tell no one who I was until my abilities were fully developed."

"Are they?" asked Matron Aquina quietly. She had returned with Master Gaius and Master Xavier.

"All the creatures I have attempted, I have done," H'Ester answered.

Then Master Xavier spoke, "By any chance, do these creatures include an owl, a cougar, an otter, and a hawk?"

"Yes," H'Ester replied.

H'Ester said nothing about the other creatures she could become, least of all a dragoness.

CHAPTER 40

Heritage

Matron Aquina and the others knew that if Ruwena, now known as H'Ester, could transform into both mammals (cougar, otter) and birds (owl, hawk), she would be an *H. transformans* $2X^T$ and fully capable. This could not be confirmed until H'Ester was observed transforming into a mammalian and an avian species. This requirement was easily satisfied.

A Startling Transformation

H'Ester, the faculty, and Savannah left the library and went to a field in a remote area of the compound. There H'Ester readily transformed into a red fox. The faculty were startled when H'Ester abruptly turned and bolted away at top speed. She raced to the top of a nearby rise and launched herself into the air. Then she twisted her body around and, as she did so, transformed in midair into a falcon in flight. *Now, Master Xavier, you can add fox and falcon to the list of my species,* H'Ester thought. Both Matron Aquina and Matron Trevora knew that only *H. transformans* who were direct descendants of Ruth through the female line were known to accomplish this feat.

In the absence of a pedigree, H'Ester's lineage could not be confirmed. Although it was almost certain that she was a direct descendant of Ruth, it was still possible she received her capability from other parentage. So Matron Aquina enlisted the assistance of Madam Florenza [flŏr-ĕn-za] and Madam Lindenova in the search for any other pedigree that might match Ruwena's capabilities. If any were found, Madam Lindenova would perform an analysis to see if there were any significant relationships that warranted further investigation.

While the search for a pedigree was underway, the faculty knew they needed H'Ester's genetic profile as well. As a presumed *H. sapiens* with no known relationship to anyone at Erwina, Ruwena's profile would have been irrelevant unless she married into their House. Now it was a matter of urgency.

H'Ester agreed to have her DNA analyzed at the natural history and research center for the number and shape of chromosomes in her cells and the location of genes along individual chromosomes. Master Mikalov advised Matron Aquina that the karyotype could be done by the next day. The remainder of the requested analyses would have to wait. They would be put in the queue along with all the other analyses the research center had put on hold. Their top priority was conducting an analysis of the genomic structure of the lyvulfon from the tissue sample Master Xavier had brought back.

By the next day, the center's staff had two top priorities. H'Ester did not have two X^T chromosomes. She had three.

On Unequal Footing

As previously explained, the reproductive cells of both *H. sapiens* and *H. transformans* should have had only twenty-three chromosomes—one copy of each chromosome including the reproductive chromosome, either a single X or a Y. If a chromosome pair failed to separate properly during development of a reproductive cell, then one ovum or sperm would receive both copies of the chromosome, whereas its twin egg or sperm would receive none at all (aneuploidy). With one singular exception, the absence of any chromosome would be lethal to the embryo. In contrast, an additional chromosome over the normal complement of forty-six could result in a live birth as long as the associated defects were not incompatible with life.

In *H. sapiens*, the most common example of an extra nonreproductive chromosome was Down syndrome. In this condition, the individual would be born with an extra chromosome 21 (trisomy 21) leading to a total of forty-seven chromosomes. This was usually a congenital abnormality associated with increased maternal age. The most commonly encountered examples of an extra reproductive chromosome involved duplication of the X chromosome (e.g., trisomy X [47, XXX] in female offspring and Klinefelter's syndrome [47, XXY] in male offspring). Abnormalities increased in both males and females with each additional X chromosome.

In an *H. sapiens* female, normally only one of the two X chromosomes inherited from the parents was active. The second X chromosome would be inactive to put males, who inherit only one X chromosome, on equal footing with females. Yet not all the genes on the silenced X chromosome were inactive. In *H. transformans*, the genes that support transformation remained active on any X^T chromosome, which enhanced the individual's capability to transform. That was why females had greater capability than males. An *H. transformans* male could have two X^T chromosomes (trisomy 47, $X^T X^T Y$) as well and with the same benefit. Thus, in *H. transformans*, an extra X^T chromosome would be advantageous.

Matron Aquina already knew that no prior *H. transformans* pedigrees from any of the three Houses demonstrated a trisomy X^T ($3X^T$) in females or a trisomy 47, $X^T X^T Y$ ($2X^T$, Y) in males. These genomes would have been flagged immediately. Thus, it seemed certain that if H'Ester were descended from Ruth, her father had to be $2X^T$, Y from another lineage.

H'Eleanora

Matron Aquina realized immediately that Erwina would certainly be attacked if either Cassius or Biogenics learned of H'Ester's trisomy $3X^T$ genotype. They would not hesitate to destroy all Erwina to get to her. Erwina's fate could be that of H'Aleth. Hence, this knowledge must be closely guarded and shared only with a very few people in Erwina and Gregor.

Matron Aquina quickly called together all those who had been at the library—Master Morenavik, Matron Trevora, Master Titus, Master Gaius, Master Xavier, Savannah, and H'Ester. To this assembly, she added Master Mikalov. "Your mistress was wise to hide you," she told H'Ester, "and now we must do the same." Then she addressed Master Mikalov, "The research center staff who know the results of H'Ester's genetic tests must say nothing to anyone save those who are present here. They must secure H'Ester's test results so that no one else can see them. Now you must send H'Ester's DNA to Master Ewan [*you*-wăn], chief geneticist at Gregor, for further analysis, and he must take the same precautions."

Matron Aquina turned to H'Ester. "Until we can find your lineage, we will say nothing more of the matter. You will remain Ruwena, an *H. sapiens*, and we will accept you into the House of Erwina until such time as you take your place as the Mistress of the House of H'Aleth or decide to remain as a member of the House of Erwina."

Matron Aquina returned to her search for a family pedigree in which a direct descendant of Ruth was mated with an unknown male, possibly as part of a breeding program. This she could not find in H'Aleth's records. She did find in Gregor's records a report of a pregnant woman, H'Eleanora (*hĕl-ĕ-an-or*-ah) from the House of H'Aleth, who had developed complications early in her pregnancy. Accompanied by an older female companion, she had gone to Gregor for management of her pregnancy and delivery of her infant. The medical center at Gregor was better equipped to manage complicated pregnancies, premature births, and infants born with inherited or congenital defects.

Sadly, H'Eleanora had died of complications shortly after delivering a live, full-term female infant in good condition. As soon as the infant was cleared to travel, the older woman left, taking the infant with her. The people of Gregor did not question that the infant had not had her genome mapped at their facility. They assumed that H'Aleth would do this and document the infant's pedigree with those of her family in her birth record. This assumption proved to be incorrect.

The Search for a Map and a Match

Matron Aquina wondered, *Could H'Ester be this infant?* She found H'Eleanora's pedigree. H'Eleanora was a direct descendant of Ruth through the female line and a Sister of H'Aleth. Her husband was an *H. transformans* from a well-respected family that was descended from another *H. transformans* lineage. She and her husband had two sons, both of whom were X^TY as well. All these family members had birth records and established pedigrees. Matron Aquina could find no pedigree record for a daughter. She would have to wait for H'Ester's DNA to be mapped before it could be compared with that of H'Eleanora, her husband, and her two sons.

Matron Aquina sent orders to Erwina's research center to conduct the gene mapping of H'Ester's DNA immediately and notify her as soon as the results were available. If H'Ester's genes display enough homology with H'Eleanora's, it could confirm a mother-child relationship. Regardless of whether it does or it does not, *why is there no record of this child?* wondered Matron Aquina.

At that time, it was common for many breeding programs to focus on increasing the number of X^T chromosomes in offspring by pairing a male and female *H. transformans*, each with an inheritance pattern that included an X^T, in the hope they would conceive a daughter with two X^T chromosomes. Other programs focused on the use of genetic engineering to excise an X chromosome and insert an X^T chromosome into a reproductive cell. When joined with its counterpart in an *H. transformans* (e.g., via in vitro fertilization), the combination could engender a female offspring with $2X^T$. There were programs that combined these two initiatives.

Supplemental Notes and Citations

General references for aneuploidy in *H. sapiens* in this section are Carroll (2009) and Jorde (2014a). Additional citations are as noted.

Aneuploidy

Euploidy is a normal number of chromosomes in a cell—forty-six for *H. sapiens*. Aneuploidy is an abnormal number of chromosomes for a given species (MacLennon et al., 2015). This could be the loss of one or more chromosomes (e.g., forty-five instead of forty-six) or gain of one or more chromosomes (e.g., forty-seven instead of forty-six).

In monosomy, one member of a chromosome pair is missing. In *H. sapiens*, the 45,XO genotype (Turner's syndrome) is a monosomy in which there is only one reproductive chromosome, an X, and no second reproductive chromosome. This results in a complement of forty-five (instead of forty-six) chromosomes. The offspring inherits the sole sex chromosome from the mother and none from the father. This genotype is the only monosomy compatible with life, and the offspring is able to grow into adulthood. Since there is no Y chromosome, the phenotype will be female. *Partial* chromosome deletions can be compatible with life; however, congenital defects will be present. Note: There is no 45,YO phenotype. The absence of any X chromosome is incompatible with life.

Trisomy is another form of aneuploidy in which one pair of chromosomes has an extra member. In *H. sapiens*, additional chromosomes often lead to defects and disability but are not necessarily lethal (Devlin and Morrison, 2004; Loane et al., 2013; Sato et al., 2017). In *H. sapiens*, the incidence of trisomy 21 (Down syndrome), trisomy 13 (Patau syndrome), and trisomy 18 (Edwards syndrome) increases with maternal age (Loane et al., 2013). Paternal age is implicated in most instances of trisomy 47,XXY (Eichenlaub-Ritter, 1996). The most common trisomy in *H. sapiens* is Down syndrome.

Down Syndrome (trisomy 21)

Down syndrome is a congenital anomaly. It is a structural and functional *abnormality* that develops during pregnancy and is compatible with life. It is caused by failure of chromosome 21 to divide and separate during the development of an ovum. The offspring inherits an extra chromosome 21 (Devlin and Morrison, 2003; MacLennon et al., 2015). Note: Research is underway to identify a means to remove an extra chromosome from embryonic cells, thereby averting the adverse effects of trisomy (Sato et al., 2017).

X Inactivation

There should be only one active X chromosome in *somatic* cells (Gribnau and Grootegoed, 2012; Migeon et al., 2008). In *H. sapiens* females, one of the two X chromosomes is tightly bound up (compacted into a small ball called a Barr body) to prevent its genes from being exposed and transcribed (X inactivation). This equalizes the number of X-linked genes in males and females. As a rule, additional X-linked genes are associated with adverse effects in *H. sapiens* (Pessia et al., 2012). Some genes on the second X chromosome may remain active and may be specific to a particular tissue (Berletch et al., 2011).

Trisomy X

In *H. sapiens*, a female has three X chromosomes (XXX genotype), which may lead to mild mental retardation and sterility. This is the most common female X chromosome abnormality with an incidence of approximately one in a thousand births (Afshan, 2012; Otter et al., 2010; Tartaglia et al., 2010). Note: In both male and female members of *H. sapiens*, increasing numbers of X chromosomes will lead to worsening outcomes.

Klinefelter's Syndrome

In *H. sapiens*, males receive two X chromosomes (XXY genotype) from the mother because the maternal pair of X chromosomes failed to separate properly, so the male progeny receives both copies instead of one. This is the most common male X chromosome abnormality with an incidence of about one in five hundred births. This disorder presents with a male phenotype, sterility, and other phenotypic characteristics depending upon the number of X chromosomes and whether or not they are inactive (Rocca et al., 2016; Visootsak and Graham, 2006).

In Vitro Fertilization

A set of procedures in which ova and sperm are collected, the ova are fertilized, and a fertilized ovum is implanted into the uterus (reproductive technology).

CHAPTER 41

Fragments

A Gap in Family History

Over time, H'Eleanora had become estranged from her husband. He was otherwise engaged in numerous activities inside and outside H'Aleth's borders and was rarely at home. Her two sons were old enough to attend school at Erwina, where they spent most of their time. When they did come home during the short breaks between semesters and summer sessions, they spent the majority of their time interning with their father. They, too, were rarely at home.

Thus, H'Eleanora decided she wanted another child, a daughter, who would be her own. So without consulting with anyone else, she decided to participate in a breeding program with the specific goal of becoming pregnant with a female offspring. Since all breeding programs focused on developing *H. transformans*, she knew that any female offspring would be a $2X^T$. This would ensure her daughter's standing in the House of H'Aleth, if not within her own family. H'Eleanora would deal with the latter situation later and defend her daughter accordingly.

To keep her planned pregnancy a secret, H'Eleanora selected the TransXformans Company, a relatively small and little known business specializing in breeding programs. Unbeknownst to her, its owners were in negotiations with both the Biogenics Corporation and the Cassius Foundation to get the highest purchase price for their small company. They were eager to have a female $2X^T$ in their program. This would bolster their

311

sale price. The company wanted to keep any unused embryos produced during in vitro fertilization. H'Eleanora refused; however, she would allow them to harvest one nonviable ovum. Begrudgingly, the TransXformans Company agreed to H'Eleanora's conditions. Although they would not be able to fertilize the immature ovum and develop an embryo, they might be able to retrieve enough genomic material to be valuable. H'Eleanora remained very suspicious of their intentions and sought out one of her Sisters, H'Ilgraith, to serve as midwife. There should be only one embryo developed, a female, and only one immature ovum harvested.

As a third-generation descendant of Ruth, H'Ilgraith was much older than H'Eleanora. She was very experienced as a midwife and highly skilled in the preparation of potions. Her knowledge of nutritional and medicinal herbs was extensive. Although she could transform into a red fox and a lynx, her preferred alternate species was the badger. Few people trifled with her.

Under the pretense of being unwell, H'Eleanora stayed with H'Ilgraith to hide her pregnancy. This was actually the case. H'Eleanora developed severe nausea and vomiting early in pregnancy and, subsequently, developed signs of toxemia later in her pregnancy. H'Ilgraith recognized the seriousness of this condition, which can lead to the death of both the mother and the fetus. She immediately took H'Eleanora to the House of Gregor for medical care. With H'Ilgraith accompanying her, H'Eleanora's pregnancy remained hidden from her House.

H'Eleanora was a potential Mistress of H'Aleth. H'Ilgraith would have protected H'Eleanora with her life, if necessary. Sadly, neither Gregor nor H'Ilgraith could save her. As H'Eleanora's condition deteriorated, both knew she would not live to care for her daughter whom she named H'Ester. H'Eleanora insisted that her husband and sons never know about the child. Her husband came from a well-respected family in H'Aleth, and he was a proud man. She was certain that if he learned that the infant was sired by an unknown male, he would reject the child as not his own. Without H'Eleanora to defend her daughter, the child would be shunned by her immediate family. So H'Eleanora entrusted the care of her infant to H'Ilgraith.

Thus, H'Ilgraith returned to H'Aleth with a foundling infant she had encountered along the way (which was technically true). Upon her return to H'Aleth, H'Ilgraith reported that H'Eleanora had died of shock (which was true). As was the case for most *H. transformans* of H'Aleth and certainly for any Sister, H'Eleanora's body was cremated.

At H'Eleanora's direction, her daughter's DNA did not undergo analysis at Gregor. This was not considered unusual since all three Houses could conduct their own basic DNA analyses. Thus, the child had no pedigree, and H'Ilgraith ensured that none was done at H'Aleth. When asked about the child's species, she simply replied, "Human." She knew that this would be interpreted as *H. sapiens*. There would be no need to provide a pedigree unless the child married into the House.

H'Ilgraith became the child's sole caretaker, teacher, and her mistress. Together, they lived a rather Spartan life. H'Ilgraith could not risk sending the child away to Erwina for her education, nor would it provide sufficient training and preparation. Over the intervening years, H'Ilgraith taught the child everything she would need to know to live on her own and all she should know as a Sister whose lineage made her eligible to become Mistress of the House of H'Aleth. Eventually, when the child came of age, her heritage would have to be revealed. H'Ilgraith had no idea how she was going to explain all this to her fellow Sisters or to H'Osanna, then Mistress of the House of H'Aleth.

Closing the Gap

When Master Mikalov mapped Ruwena's DNA, he found it showed a high probability that H'Ester and H'Eleanora were related. "They both have the gene sequences coding for the same mammalian and avian species," he told Matron Aquina. "Even more significantly, they both have what appears to be a fragment of an extra chromosome, and the gene sequences for this fragment are the same in both of them." He also reported that H'Ester had partial genomes of other mammalian species—elk, moose, boar, and bison—scattered throughout her genome that were not found in H'Eleanora's genome or in those of her husband or two sons. These incomplete gene sequences were too fragmented to be transformed and likely represented genes inherited from the biologic father. "The biggest difference between their genomes was the number of X^T chromosomes," said Master Mikalov. "H'Ester has three, whereas her mother, H'Eleanora, had two."

It seemed certain that H'Ester was the daughter of H'Eleanora by another *H. transformans* male. If the child and father ever had pedigrees done at H'Aleth, they were never sent to Erwina.

When Master Mikalov's staff initially examined H'Ester's karyotype, they found that most of H'Ester's chromosomes were larger than those in *H. sapiens*, implying that there was additional genetic material. This would happen when the genomes of multiple species were also present. Traditional karyotyping could not discern what these additional genes were or exactly where in the chromosome they were located. Hence, the staff conducted additional testing to identify the genes and where they were located. They were able to do this using the genes from other species for which they had a matching code for comparison.

Master Mikalov discovered there were some genes he couldn't match with any of the species for which he had a genome. This was not surprising. Erwina's genome database was not exhaustive. The laboratory had codes for all the common species of mammals, birds, and reptiles. Hence, they could identify the genes for all the species H'Ester's genome was now known to support. In H'Ester, however, there were other gene sequences for which they had no matching probe—specifically, there were no matches for the chromosome fragment that both H'Ester and H'Eleanora carried. Thus, Master Mikalov could not map the chromosome fragment to any gene sequences he had in his database. *Perhaps Gregor will identify what genes are in the fragment,* he thought.

Gregor housed the center for genetic research, so it held a vast database of DNA, including those from H'Aleth and Erwina. It also conducted analyses on the DNA of any member who had a corrupted transformation and of any hybrid or corrupted creature encountered by the other Houses. Since Gregor's primary missions were genetic research and medical treatment of genetic disorders, it had facilities for advanced genetic testing. Gregor could detect genetic changes even smaller than those Erwina could detect. Gregor's geneticists could identify abnormal gene sequences, detect a change in a single component (nucleotide) of a gene, and find point mutations. They could conduct whole genome sequencing or sequencing of a subset of the genes that code for proteins and do detailed genotype-phenotype correlations. Advanced testing should verify whether or not H'Eleanora was H'Ester's mother. Perhaps it could identify the parent of origin for the third X^T chromosome, which could either be the mother or the father.

It should be remembered, however, that genotype did not predict phenotype. Many factors precluded a straightforward cause-and-effect relationship between genotype and phenotype. Some genes would only be partially expressed or not expressed at all. Interactions among several genes could have been involved in the final expression of a phenotype, and external influences (e.g., use of an accelerant) could affect gene expression. Thus, different phenotypes could come from the same genotype. Appearances could be deceiving.

Confirmation

Master Mikalov carried the DNA samples to Gregor himself. He met with Headmaster Ewan and gave him the samples with an urgent request for analysis. "We have done all that we can," he told Master Ewan. "Based on our analysis, we think that H'Eleanora and H'Ester are mother and daughter. We need confirmation of our findings, if possible. In addition, there is an extra gene fragment that we cannot identify." As requested, Headmaster Ewan made an analysis of H'Ester's and H'Eleanora's DNA specimens his top priority. He, too, was curious about an extra chromosome fragment and investigated it as well.

First, the staff at Gregor repeated the DNA analyses already done at Erwina and confirmed the latter's findings. Then they used DNA fingerprinting to identify differences. These confirmed the same scattered gene sequences attributed to additional species that were found in H'Ester but not in H'Eleanora.

Whole genome sequencing revealed that the size of H'Ester's genome was significantly increased. It was likely that it could only be expressed because of the third X^T. Thus, Gregor's researchers expected H'Ester's level of ability to have extremely high energy requirements. They found evidence of these requirements being met in the increased number and concentration of mitochondrial genes. When Gregor compared H'Ester's mitochondrial DNA with those of H'Eleanora's, they were the same. There was no longer any question that H'Ester was the daughter of H'Eleanora (ped. 4).

Whole exome analysis of the chromosomal fragment was proving difficult. Gregor's geneticists had no gene sequences in its standard *H. transformans* DNA data bank that matched those found in the fragment. The regulatory genes could be matched and were consistent with those normally seen in other species demonstrating the degree of genetic homology expected in *H. sapiens* and *H. transformans*. Subsequently, they compared the fragments with DNA from their data bank of hybrid and corrupted human and animal specimens. They found no match.

Ped. 4. Pedigree for H'Eleanora and H'Ester.

Pedigree for H'Eleanora and H'Ester

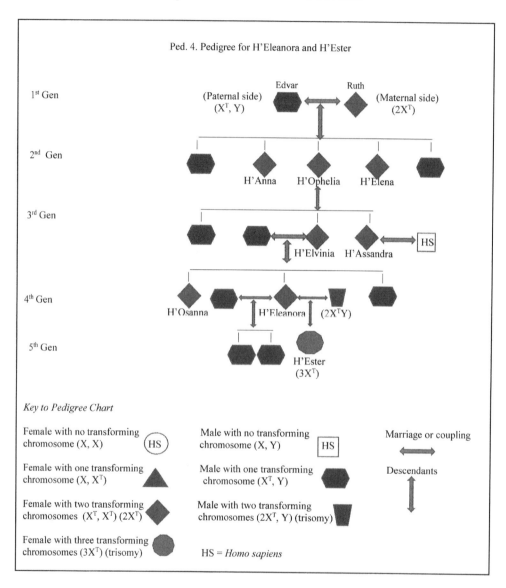

Ped. 4. Pedigree for H'Eleanora and H'Ester

Key to Pedigree Chart

Female with no transforming chromosome (X, X)   (HS)

Male with no transforming chromosome (X, Y)   HS

Marriage or coupling

Female with one transforming chromosome (X, X^T)

Male with one transforming chromosome (X^T, Y)

Descendants

Female with two transforming chromosomes (X^T, X^T) ($2X^T$)

Male with two transforming chromosomes ($2X^T$, Y) (trisomy)

Female with three transforming chromosomes ($3X^T$) (trisomy)

HS = *Homo sapiens*

Gregor had one other small DNA database, which they kept separate from the other data banks. *I wonder,* mused Master Ewan. *Is it possible? It had happened once before.*

Dragon Seed

Gregor had no samples of DNA from the only *H. transformans* known to have become a dragon. This had occurred long ago, presumably from a random mutation. The female who had this capability was hunted down and killed, but not before she had transformed into a dragon and turned on her attackers. Nonetheless, dragons are mammals—not immortals. The dragon was killed while she still had fire within her. Consequently, her body was consumed by its own fire. That fire was so intense that nothing was left, not even ashes.

Gregor did have DNA from samples from all three species of native dragons. Most of the samples from gray dragons had come from those who had died of natural causes or unintentional injury. The samples from the red dragons had come from those that had been killed for their decorative scales before they came under the protection of the House of H'Aleth. Humans were their only known predator. The DNA for arctic dragons came from eggs that had been lost and had frozen under arctic temperatures. Subsequently, Gregor's geneticists had developed DNA probes specific for each subspecies of dragon. In this manner, they could identify subsequent samples and recognize when a new species had been discovered.

On a hunch, Master Ewan tested the two fragments—one from H'Ester and one from H'Eleanora—against the DNA probes from each species of dragon and found a near match. He immediately went back one generation and reexamined the DNA from H'Eleanora's mother (H'Ester's maternal grandmother). He had no recollection of such a fragment in other descendants of Ruth, and indeed, he found no such fragment in H'Eleanora's mother. To his surprise, he found the fragment in H'Eleanora's father (H'Ester's maternal grandfather), who was an X^TY (ped. 5).

Ped. 5. Lineage of Fragment.

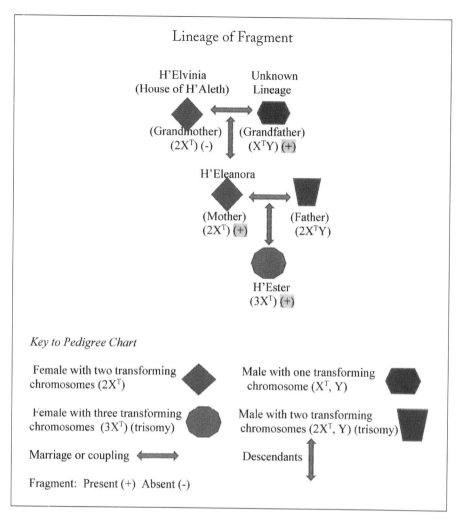

Lineage of Fragment

H'Elvinia
(House of H'Aleth)
(Grandmother)
$(2X^T)$ (-)

Unknown
Lineage
(Grandfather)
(X^TY) (+)

H'Eleanora
(Mother)
$(2X^T)$ (+)

(Father)
$(2X^TY)$

H'Ester
$(3X^T)$ (+)

Key to Pedigree Chart

Female with two transforming chromosomes $(2X^T)$

Male with one transforming chromosome (X^T, Y)

Female with three transforming chromosomes $(3X^T)$ (trisomy)

Male with two transforming chromosomes $(2X^T, Y)$ (trisomy)

Marriage or coupling

Descendants

Fragment: Present (+) Absent (-)

H'Eleanora had inherited the fragment from her father. As a male *H. transformans*, he could not have expressed this genotype. If H'Eleanora $(2X^T)$ could express it, she kept it hidden. Given the threat H'Aleth faced from Biogenics and Cassius, this seemed unlikely. The ability to express this genotype, however, might have been limited to someone with trisomy X^T. Since H'Eleanora's father came from a different lineage of *H. transformans*, one outside the House of H'Aleth, Master Ewan could not trace the fragment back any further. Its origin would remain unknown.

As for the fragment, it shared a 99.5% homology with the DNA of the gray dragons, a 99.2% homology with the arctic dragons, and a 99.8% homology with the red dragons. The difference could represent another subspecies closely related to the red dragon or an interspecies mating between a red and gray. To date, the latter had not been known to occur.

Now the question arose—could this fragment support transformation into a dragon? "I cannot say," Master Ewan told Master Mikalov when he reported his findings. "This fragment may only be a segment from another species, which is not represented in our database."

"What if it were the complete genome of some kind of dragon? Could the rest of H'Ester's genome support transformation into the dragon?" asked Master Mikalov.

Master Ewan thought about this for a moment. "I don't know," he replied. "I would not recommend she risk her life in the attempt," warned Master Ewan.

Notes and Citations

General references for genetic testing are Brooker (2009), Carroll (2009), Jorde (2014a), and Porth (2009). Additional citations are as noted.

Nonviable Ova

Multiple nascent ova begin to develop within follicles in the ovary in accordance with the menstrual cycle. Most of the time, only one ovum becomes the dominant ovum and reaches full maturity at which time its chromosomes are fully formed. The other immature ova then regress and degenerate. The mature ovum carries a single copy of the maternal genome.

Genetic Testing

Karyotyping detects large chromosome abnormalities including any abnormal number of chromosomes (e.g., trisomy) or configuration of a chromosome (e.g., a translocation). Specific genes and their locations cannot be seen. It cannot detect very small abnormalities that affect small segments of DNA within a chromosome. It is further constrained by a requirement to have living cells that can still divide, during which time their chromosome structure becomes clearly visible under a microscope. Illustration 3 depicts a standard karyotype.

Cytogenetic gene mapping can identify the general location of a gene along its chromosome. Each chromosome has a unique banding pattern, which is revealed when the chromosomes are stained. Genes can be mapped according to the band where they are found.

Fluorescence in situ hybridization (FISH) analysis can detect the precise location of a gene on a chromosome. It can also detect much smaller submicroscopic rearrangements and deletions than can conventional karyotyping (Carroll, 2009b; Peters et al., 2015).

DNA probe is a set of complementary genes for a known protein sequence. When added to a solution containing the genes that actually code for that protein sequence, the probe will form a paired DNA sequence and thus identify the gene sequence in question (Carroll, 2009b; Peters et al., 2015).

Chromosomal microarray analysis (CMA) has a very high resolution, greater than FISH. It can detect the abnormalities at the level of gene sequences (Botkin et al., 2015; Peters et al., 2015). It can also detect long segments of homozygous genes, which indicate a lack of genetic diversity and are associated with inbreeding.

Single nucleotide polymorphism (SNP) microarray can detect a difference in a single nucleotide (e.g., swapping C for T). SNPs are the most common type of genetic variation and provide the basis of genetic diversity both within groups and across populations. Like CMA, the SNP microarray can identify long segments of homozygous genes focusing on identification of paired homozygous recessive genes, which could cause hereditary genetic diseases associated with inbreeding (Benn et al., 2013). It also looks for the frequency of known alternative gene sequences (polymorphisms) to see if they have the expected degree of variability (Budowle and van Daal, 2008; Ochiai, 2015). Note: All but one of the amino acids have at least two different genetic codes—and some have as many as six.

Sanger sequence can detect point mutations (single gene mutations), which cause genetic diseases (Botkin et al., 2015).

Whole genome sequencing (WGS) examines the entire genome (Botkin et al., 2015).

Whole exome sequencing (WES) specifically examines genes that code for protein synthesis, where most genetic defects are found (Bently et al., 2008; Peters et al., 2015).

DNA fingerprinting analyzes the differences, if any, in DNA sequencing (Samuelsson et al., 2010). The more closely related two individuals are, the less variability there will be in gene sequences that are typically highly variable across a population. Hence, fingerprinting can be used for both identification and for establishing the closeness (or remoteness) of a relationship. SNP microarrays may be used to fingerprint DNA (Budowle and van Daal, 2008).

Mitochondrial DNA is inherited exclusively from the mother (Bettinger and Wayne, 2016; Sato and Sato, 2013).

CHAPTER 42

Mistress and Matron

With the revelation that H'Ester was a direct descendant of Ruth and the last surviving Sister of the House of H'Aleth via the maternal line, two actions needed to be undertaken. First, H'Ester (now Ruwena again) should complete her studies through Form IV as had the mistresses of H'Aleth before her. "Your mistress would expect you to complete your education," advised Matron Trevora. Ruwena realized she needed the last two years of formal schooling to prepare for the task of restoring the House of H'Aleth. Although she was willing to complete them, she was not willing to delay further in taking action on the task her mistress had given her. Matron Aquina agreed. "I see no reason why you cannot not begin preparing for your role as Mistress at the same time you are completing your studies," she said. The courses in civics and governance would serve as cover for Ruwena to work with department heads. She was excused from the advanced science courses to provide more time to learn her new duties.

Matron Aquina asked Matron Trevora to mentor Ruwena in learning the responsibilities she would have as Mistress of the House of H'Aleth. Matron Trevora ($2X^T$), also a descendant of Ruth, was born into the House of H'Aleth. Although once a Sister of H'Aleth and eligible to be its mistress, she had relinquished that role when she married into the House of Erwina. She was approaching seventy years of age when she first encountered Ruwena in an outpost village. Ruwena's deportment, learned in the House of H'Aleth, might have been why Matron Trevora sensed something familiar about her. Matron Trevora's bearing, also learned in the House of H'Aleth, and her age were likely the reasons why Ruwena sensed something familiar in the woman who first greeted her after the death of her mistress.

"Tails" of a Venerable Age

Most members of the three Houses were long-lived and remained active and robust well into their eighties. Once they reached their nineties, they tended to slow down although many continued to be in good health and served as advisers and mentors. Their life span, however, rarely extended past one hundred and ten years of age. Trauma was the primary cause of premature death.

Sisters of the House of H'Aleth and their descendants often lived well over one hundred years of age. Yet they rarely reached 120 years old before they died. H'Ilgraith was seventy years old when she assumed the care and raising of H'Ester. Thus, she was in her eighties when they both fled from the destruction of H'Aleth. Although a senior among the Sisters still living at the time, she was by no means the eldest. H'Ilgraith might have exceeded the venerable age of one hundred had it not been for the hardships of living in a Cassius village. The burden of survival under those conditions aged her physically and shortened her life span accordingly.

There was no single factor that accounted for why some people lived longer than others. A study of the genomes of *H. sapiens* who were one hundred years old did not identify any specific genes leading to a longer life span. Yet there seemed to be a familial tendency to long life. Offspring of parents who were long-lived also tended to be long-lived. This would suggest that there were some genetic factors that may extend life. Longevity also could have been affected by factors that either slowed biologic aging or protected against age-related diseases. Certain inherited diseases expressed later in life typically resulted in an early death.

There were still limits to life span even in otherwise healthy populations. With the exception of stem cells, cells that can still replicate themselves were limited in the number of times they could do so. Their DNA strands had a tail, which protected them for as long as it persisted. This tail was shortened each time a cell divided. When the tail was gone, the cell would age. Eventually, it would die naturally. This limit decreased the likelihood that errors would occur after DNA had been copied too many times.

The geneticists at Gregor could not identify a specific genetic reason for the apparent limit on a life span of 120 years in *H. transformans*. Ironically, the extended life span did not appear to be due to having an X^T chromosome. Researchers did find a strong correlation between their life span and those who could trace their lineage back to Edvar and Ruth H'Aleth. Both Ruth and Edvar were long-lived. The researchers found that their descendants had substantially longer tails, which could have been the source of their greater longevity in the absence of disease or injury.

Mission and Purpose

Matron Aquina had excused Matron Trevora from some of her teaching duties to allow time for her to mentor Ruwena. Matron Trevora arranged for Ruwena to intern with each of the department heads and chiefs at Erwina, beginning with security. These were set up as practicums under the pretense of preparing her to join their House. Master Titus worked with Ruwena first and emphasized the importance of surveillance and security for everyone at Erwina, including her. Ruwena knew this all too well from the year she spent in a Cassius village. She also knew if she were to reestablish H'Aleth, she would need to know how to protect its people.

A significant part of the discussions above included what H'Aleth's purpose would be. H'Ilgraith died without telling Ruwena what she should do once H'Aleth was restored. From H'Aleth's history, Ruwena learned that H'Aleth had focused on the natural history of *H. transformans*. She also found that her great-great-grandparents had established H'Aleth as a refuge for *H. transformans*.

Matron Aquina asked, "Would you want H'Aleth to resume its work on the natural history of *H. transformans* and move the natural history and research center under its umbrella again?" Ruwena thought better of this. Erwina had not allowed H'Aleth's legacy to be lost and had built an institution to support it.

"I think it would be much safer if it stayed in Erwina and remained aligned with the archives," Ruwena replied. Matron Aquina agreed with this decision.

None of the Houses had ever used their resources for colonization. After the destruction of H'Aleth, the two remaining Houses had bolstered their offensive capabilities strictly for their own defense. Would the Houses of Erwina and Gregor be strengthened if the House of H'Aleth was restored? Master Titus suggested, "Perhaps H'Aleth could be established as a military outpost." Ruwena was concerned about this direction. This was not part of H'Aleth's heritage. Under the auspices of Ruth and Edvar, it had become a safe haven where *H. transformans* who were being hunted or persecuted could live. Now, both Erwina and Gregor had assumed this role.

Ruwena remembered the pitiful creatures she saw in the Cassius villages. Most of the villagers who lived there were disabled as a result of deformities caused by Cassius's genetic experiments. Perhaps H'Aleth could be reestablished to provide a safe haven for the impoverished villagers under Cassius's yoke. Ruwena decided to plead their case.

"I would prefer that H'Aleth become a sanctuary once again," Ruwena replied. "Perhaps I can help the villagers who live under Cassius, as my mistress once did. They are not monsters," she told the faculty. "If we can help them and give them a decent place to live, then they may help us defend it." Many of the hominids like the serojabovids [*ser*-o-ja-*bōv*-id] (illus. 25) were engineered specifically for performing hard labor in Cassius villages and were quite strong. "They could become even stronger if well-nourished and their deformities treated to the extent possible," suggested Ruwena.

Ruwena did not mention the cercopithursids, crocutalupoids, and cercolupoids [cer-co-*lu*-poids]. These hominids were engineered specifically for purposes of guarding Cassius's supply depots and villages. Although not all of them were inherently violent, many of them were treated violently and had learned to react in kind.

"How do you know this?" asked Master Titus.

"Before coming here, I lived in one of the villages for nearly a year," Ruwena replied. "My mistress changed fouled water into potable water, prepared potions to feed the villagers, and treated their wounds and sores with salves, even though we could not treat their deformities. It is from living in this village and another like it that I learned all I know about the people and hybrids living in Cassius villages."

Matron Aquina nodded. "So this was H'Igraith's plan when H'Aleth was destroyed," she mused thoughtfully. "She thought that Erwina would be next, as did we. So she hid you, H'Aleth's last surviving Sister and future Mistress, where Cassius would never look for you."

Illus. 25. Serojabovid.

After a moment, Master Titus said, "It might work." Yet Ruwena knew this would not restore the House of H'Aleth as her mistress and others had known it. Just as importantly, who would help her establish a place inhabited primarily by Cassian hybrids?

Restoration

Most of the inhabitants of Erwina and Gregor would be *H. transformans*, and many would be fourth- and fifth-generation descendants of Edvar and Ruth. They would have traveled with their children, who now would be about Ruwena's age and would have spent most of their lives in Erwina or Gregor. After many years, most of the immigrants from H'Aleth, especially their children, would consider Erwina and Gregor their homes. In all likelihood, so would their parents. Only a few people of the third generation would still be living. Like H'Ilgraith, most of them would be elderly. They should not be asked to reestablish their House, even though they might be willing to do so. Whether or not any of them would want to join a new Mistress in her quest was another matter. Ruwena asked herself, *Should I reestablish H'Aleth as a separate house or allow it to live on in Erwina and Gregor?* Of one thing she was certain. A House cannot have two mistresses.

When Ruwena discussed her dilemma with Matron Aquina and Matron Trevora, Matron Aquina had a different suggestion. "Instead of looking only to those people whose heritage was H'Aleth, open the opportunity to anyone who might be interested in establishing a new House," she suggested. "Many of the young adults in Erwina might be intrigued by such an adventure."

People in Erwina and Gregor were long-lived. This was due, in large part, to healthy living conditions, as well as their lineage. Thus, there was little opportunity in either of the two remaining Houses for the adventurous to do anything different. Ruwena might find many young men and women who might be excited by the opportunity—and some by the danger—of establishing a new House of H'Aleth. If so, then Ruwena would have a young House. *Could this work?* Ruwena wondered.

Master Titus cautioned Ruwena about the dangers she would likely encounter. "It is unlikely that you will be able to reclaim H'Aleth's ancestral territory without inciting a war with Cassius," he counseled. "War with Biogenics is less certain. They may sit back and wait to see the outcome. If Cassius has to expend his resources to retain the territory, it might give them an advantage. This assumes, of course, that Cassius does not produce another dragon."

Ruwena stated outright, "I do not want to risk a war." It was unthinkable to ask the young or the old to die in what could be a futile battle to reestablish the House of H'Aleth. From what Ruwena had learned, H'Aleth had no effective natural barriers. Even if she could reclaim the territory, it was unlikely that there would be enough people from Erwina and Gregor to hold it against Cassius's or Biogenics's armies. Without providing some meaningful relief for the proposed inhabitants, she could not rely on receiving any help from them. Based on her experience living in a Cassius village, it was highly unlikely they could provide any support.

Master Titus acknowledged that these were valid concerns and risks. He thought it curious, however, that Ruwena did not react to the threat of a dragon. *Perhaps the issue is moot,* he thought. *If you cannot withstand an army, then you won't prevail against a dragon.*

One thing was certain. Things could not go back to the way they were before Cassius attacked H'Aleth. Out of necessity, many changes had taken place in the interim. People throughout the remaining two Houses had to adapt to them. Yet Ruwena felt an obligation to do all she could to reestablish her House. Her mistress had sacrificed so much to protect her in the hope of preserving it. Now, Ruwena felt it was her responsibility to restore it.

Ruwena had another problem. She knew relatively little of her House before she was forced to leave it as a young girl. Her mistress had kept her secluded. It was not enough simply to read about it.

"Speak to those people who once called H'Aleth home," suggested Matron Trevora. "This can be done under the pretext of a class project. The civics course will provide excellent cover for you to interview many of the former inhabitants." Since Ruwena would take the civics course in the fall, Matron Trevor advised her to interview the oldest members of H'Aleth first. For some of them, their lives were coming to a close.

Supplemental Notes and Citations

Aging

Humans age at different rates (Milman and Barzilai, 2015). This is due, in part, to the difference between chronological and biological age (Milman and Barzilai, 2015). In biologic aging, physical changes associated with aging may appear earlier or later than expected for an individual's stated chronological age. Factors that accelerate aging are often associated with chronic physical stressors, including diseases that lead to disability and debilitation. Genetic factors promoting aging include damage to DNA with loss of its integrity, less effective DNA repair mechanisms, fewer protective mechanisms (e.g., anti-oxidants), and shorter telomeres (Franzke et al., 2015; Pan et al., 2016; Pusceddu et al., 2015; Shadyab and LaCroix, 2015).

Age-related diseases are diseases that usually develop over time. (Age-related diseases should not be confused with age of onset diseases.) Although there may be a familial tendency to develop these diseases, there are often multiple underlying factors including lifestyle, genetic predisposition, and epigenetic influences. Two common examples are (1) atherosclerosis (excessive fatty deposits narrowing and occluding arteries), which leads to hypertension, heart attack, and stroke, and (2) type 2 diabetes mellitus. In contrast, familial hyperlipidemias are inheritable genetic disorders in which high levels of lipids lead to a heart attack in a young adult. There are also genetic factors that provide protection from disease. These include tumor suppressor genes, genes that decrease harmful types of cholesterol (e.g., low density lipoproteins) and raise beneficial types of cholesterol (e.g., high-density lipoproteins).

Age-of-onset diseases are hereditary diseases (often autosomal dominant) that tend to be expressed once a certain age range is reached (e.g., Huntington's chorea and amyotrophic lateral sclerosis, also known as Lou Gehrig's disease).

Longevity

Telomeres are segments of genetic code at the end of a gene sequence. This tail is shortened with each division of a cell—one telomere at a time—until it is lost through attrition (Jones et al. 2015; Oeseburg 2010; Shay 2016). At that point, the cell can no longer undergo mitosis and ages. A study of *H. sapiens* who lived to be a hundred years or older revealed they had longer strands of telomeres, which were inherited by their progeny (Milman and Barzilai 2015).

Recent research suggests that mitochondrial DNA (mtDNA), which is inherited from the mother, may be another factor in promoting greater longevity (Shadyab and LaCroix 2015).

The genome-wide association study (GWAS) examined genomes of people with a specific disease to look for genetic markers of that disease, if any. One such study, which looked for longevity genes, did not reveal any (Milman and Barzilai 2015); however, genes involved with cellular housekeeping and energy (e.g., mitochondrial genes) may support longevity (Moskalev et al. 2014). The reader may review similar studies for diseases of interest at https://www.genome.gov/20019523/.

CHAPTER 43

Scouting Lessons

Ruwena asked to travel to the lands that had once belonged to H'Aleth. She had never seen most of the territory that had once been her homeland. "Perhaps if I could see it, I could better understand the scope of the demands that must be met to reclaim it," Ruwena remarked. She had many alternate species at her command, and the trip would not take her long. "I can fly over the territory," she said.

"Absolutely not!" The faculty were unanimous and adamant in opposing this request.

First of all, the skirmishes between Biogenics and Cassius were unpredictable and often came much too close to Erwina's boundaries. Both contestants had archers that could bring down a raptor. Secondly, there was a significant risk of encountering violent hybrids and other corrupted creatures that wouldn't hesitate to kill anything or anyone they encountered. Thirdly, eagles prey on hawks, as does the great horned owl, which also preys on falcons and other owls.

Scouting and Surveillance

Master Titus had an alternative proposal to offer. "I can arrange additional field exercises in surveillance and security at selected outposts in the northeastern and southwestern territories that still fall under our auspices," he said. Scouting and surveillance was part of the program of study for both Form IV juniors and seniors. The study of flora and fauna of inland waterways (junior year, within Erwina's region of influence) and coastal plains (senior year, beyond Erwina's region of influence) would provide additional opportunities to learn and practice scouting techniques. "If Ruwena demonstrates proficiency as a scout, then she can go on a joint scouting expedition into the territory that was once under H'Aleth and is now under Cassius."

Matrons Aquina and Trevora looked very intently at Master Titus. It wasn't quite a glare. Master Titus promptly reassured them that Ruwena would always be partnered with an experienced scout. He reminded the faculty that Ruwena had already demonstrated her ability to protect others during the summer field trip to the northeast outpost. The faculty had to concede that point. (They never learned about Ruwena's encounter with a jaguar in the tunnels.) Then, he reminded everyone—Ruwena, in particular—that the purpose of these expeditions was for her to develop skills as a scout on a surveillance mission.

"I can barely swim," said Ruwena, "and I don't know how to kayak."

"You can become an otter and outswim any of us," acknowledged Master Titus, "and you won't be doing any kayaking."

The debate then turned to which region Ruwena should go first. The northeast region seemed to be the most perilous location, given the clashes between Cassius and Biogenics and the number of dangerous creatures already encountered there. In its favor were the many species of animals that live in the area. Many Erwinians can transform into one or more of the species and would not seem out of place. There may be an opportunity for Ruwena to watch an engagement between Cassius and Biogenics from afar and begin to learn about their strategies. Finally, if scouts were discovered or endangered, the northeast outpost had many hidden locations in the mountains. Scouts could hide for a short time or take refuge for weeks, if necessary. Although Ruwena had already been to that region, her experience there had been limited.

The southwestern region seemed somewhat less perilous, since scouts only occasionally reported sighting Cassius's forces or creatures. Its disadvantages were the wide-open spaces with scattered trees and few places to hide from keen eyes. Most of the alternative species used by scouts in that area had to be alert constantly for an attack from natural predators. While eagles prey on hawks, wolves and lynx prey on foxes and many other mammals.

The southeastern region posed similar problems. Its grasslands and prairies were wide open and provided little cover for predators or prey. It was also much too close to the boundary with H'Aleth's territory, now claimed by Cassius. Some of Cassius's creatures had been known to wander there.

Ruwena was not concerned about encountering *H. transformans* villagers who had wandered far afield from a Cassius village looking for food. She spoke their language and had not forgotten it. "These people are not violent," she said. "They are victims of Cassius's cruelty and have been left to suffer for it." Her greatest concern was encountering the hybrids Cassius had engineered to guard and protect the resources he stored in the villages. "Most of these creatures were bred to be aggressive and are often violent. Of all the ones I saw there, the ursuscro [ur-*sŭs*-crō] was by far the most dangerous," she said.

Master Titus was alarmed by this news. The ursuscro was a hybrid in which Cassius spliced the genes of a boar into the genome of a bear in order to create a bear-sized boar (illus. 26). Cassius wanted a weapon of war against an *H. transformans* opponent, especially one whose alternate species is a bear. "Where did you encounter an ursuscro?" Master Titus demanded to know.

Ruwena recounted a horrific incident involving an ursuscro at a Cassius village not far from the border with H'Aleth. She did not mention it was the village where she and her mistress were tending a dragoness. They were walking through the village on route to the tower when they were barred by guards. Several villagers, all corrupted *H. transformans* sent to the village as laborers, were gathered together in an enclosure. They had been given axes, clubs, knives, and a few shields. Then they were set against an ursuscro in a fight to the death.

Ruwena remembered the carnage wrought by the ursuscro. The villagers had no chance against the beast, nor was any intended. Her mistress had told her that Cassius was training the hybrid to attack people who were armed. He wanted the hybrid to encounter little resistance so it would attack Biogenic's armed forces without hesitation. "I wanted to leave," Ruwena said. "I did not want to see the villagers slaughtered. But my mistress bade me stay. She wanted me to learn just how deadly this creature was. She described it as a living weapon of war. Later, when we were alone, my mistress told me that the ursuscro can be killed by a strong, skilled bowman with a quiver full of arrows. It can also be killed by a large spear fired from a catapult."

With the knowledge that an ursuscro had been in a village near the border with H'Aleth, the matter of where Ruwena would go was settled. She would return to the northeast outpost.

The Art of Self-Defense

Before any future scouting exercises, Master Titus insisted that Ruwena be instructed in both defensive and offensive skills. Ruwena was in dire need of training in self-defense. Due to her point of entry into the schoolhouse, she had missed most of this segment of Erwina's educational program. Master Titus wanted Ruwena to have some means of self-defense as a human, in the event she could not transform or her alternate species could not overcome an attacker.

Master Titus arranged for Ruwena to be mentored by Rachel, an experienced scout, until Ruwena left for the northeast outpost. Rachel kept watch over the southeastern region. She was an expert archer and was tasked to teach Ruwena how to use a bow and arrow.

"Why do I need to use a bow and arrow when I can become a hawk?" Ruwena asked. "How is an arrow more effective than a hawk or falcon?"

Rachel explained, "When in human form, I can take aim and fire an arrow faster than I can transform into a red-tailed hawk and fly to my target or fly away." Ruwena wasn't certain she could thread a bow and arrow faster than she could transform.

"There are far too many dangerous hybrids in the world," Rachel said. "Some of them are very large, very violent, and can fly." Ruwena had to admit this point. She had already encountered one such creature that might have killed her had it not been for a skilled archer.

Both Rachel and Ruwena could transform into a raptor. Hence, both had keen eye sight and could spot a target equally well. The same could not be said for Ruwena's proficiency in aiming her bow and arrow. In the beginning, she would zero in on her target visually while pointing her arrow somewhere else. After a few practice sessions, Ruwena finally demonstrated that she could thread an arrow and aim it in the general direction of her target. At that point, Rachel informed Master Titus, "Ruwena could threaten an attacker by drawing her bow and arrow. But if her attacker freezes, she will probably miss him." Ruwena was much better at hitting a moving target—a gift of her raptor genes.

At the same time Ruwena was taking archery lessons, Master Iranapolis [ir-ăn-*a*-pōl-ĭs] was instructing her in the basic skills used in martial arts. She proved to be more proficient than expected and advanced quickly to an intermediate level. In developing these skills, her alternate species served her well. Her flexibility and agility were supported by her cougar, fox, and otter genes; her strength, stamina, and speed by the cougar, wolf, and dragon; and her balance and coordination by all her alternate species. She also owed her heightened awareness of sound and movement to them.

A few weeks later, Matron Kavarova and Ruwena journeyed back to the northeast outpost. Once they arrived there, Matron Kavarova reintroduced Ruwena to Evan. Evan was the scout who had found Ruwena in the cave and carried her out after the assault by the lupuseroja. He was a native-born Erwinian. Evan's alternate species—a red fox and gray wolf—were well suited to the northeast territory. Thus, Evan knew the territory very well. He was skilled in martial arts, swordsmanship, and archery, and he was a good swimmer—all the things Ruwena was not. As a human, she could barely thread a bow and arrow. She was a marginal swimmer who, according to Madam Merena, would not drown in a shallow pool. Ruwena often wondered, *Where are those genes?*

Matron Kavarova thought it best for Evan and Ruwena to pair up as scouts and survey the surrounding areas as a practicum for Ruwena. During this time, Evan would tutor Ruwena in the finer points of scouting in a relatively safe setting. At the same time, they would learn to recognize each other's mannerisms. Thus, they would work together as humans and as the two alternate species they both had in common: red fox and gray wolf.

A Pair of Foxes

During most of their initial scouting forays, both remained in human form. Evan would explain his role, describe a scouting practice or explain its rationale, and answer any questions Ruwena had. During this time, Evan noted how quiet and reserved she was. She spoke only when necessary. "No idle chatter," her mistress had commanded. There was too great a risk that a careless comment would betray and endanger them. Ruwena was very observant as well. This, too, her mistress had demanded in a region controlled by Cassius. Evan also noted that Ruwena would discern things around them that most new graduates would not notice. When he asked her how she knew these things, she would always answer "My mistress told me so" or "My mistress showed me this."

Finally, one day at the edge of some woods, a grassy field opened up before them. At this time, they were red foxes. As they stepped across the edge to view the setting, the two foxes sat down. It was a beautiful day—sunny, warm, and breezy—and there were no foreign sounds or smells. It was the first time Evan had seen Ruwena look almost serene as she sniffed the air and scanned the skies. *At last, she seems relaxed,* he thought, *at least a little.* Then he decided to try an experiment.

In fox fashion, Evan began to frolic. He leaped into the air, snatched a leaf in his mouth from a low-hanging tree branch, and shook it vigorously. Then, he spotted a soft patch of fallen leaves below the same tree and dived into it. He rolled around in the leaves, and when he came to rest on his back, he looked up at Ruwena. She was staring at him wide-eyed—the human equivalent of dumbfounded (illus. 27).

Initially, she was startled when he suddenly attacked a tree leaf. Now, all she could do was look at him in disbelief. Evan resumed rolling around in the leaves—which felt good. Then he got up, raced around the tree, through the underbrush, and back again. He even chased his own tail a few times.

Now Ruwena was really worried. She followed him—at a discreet distance—and watched as he cavorted with the shrubbery. *Had he lost his mind?* she wondered. Could he have encountered some psilocyabin, cannabis, or other hallucinogenic or euphoria-producing plants? Did he encounter the pheromones of a female fox? Ruwena had not seen or smelled any of these things in the area they had covered. *He's lost his mind,* she concluded.

Finally, Evan stopped. He sat upright and just looked at Ruwena. Slowly, she approached him. He did not move. When she got close to him, she began sniffing him all over—from the tips of his ears to the tip of his tail—searching for any sign or scent of something abnormal. Evan waited patiently while Ruwena vacuumed every inch of him. She found leaf litter in his fur—nothing more. She finally sat in front of him and looked at him, waiting, as she had done so many times in the past. *Perhaps he has regained his senses,* she hoped.

Illus. 27. A Woodland Frolic.

No. Suddenly, Evan pounced on the ground right in front of her. Ruwena must have leaped a foot up in the air when he did so. Evan couldn't help himself. In an uncharacteristic and nonfox fashion, he rolled over on his back and looked like he was laughing his head off—which, in fact, he was. That was when Ruwena realized what was going on.

So that's it, she thought. Whereupon she promptly pounced on top of him. They both began mock wrestling and rolling around in the leaves. Ruwena chased after Evan, who kept escaping from her. Finally, after a few more minutes of madcap racing and dodging around trees and shrubs, they settled down for a few minutes before resuming their patrol. *That was fun,* Ruwena thought to herself and then wondered how she would justify her behavior to her mistress. *Exercise,* she told herself. *Wrestling is a form of exercise, and so is running.* She knew perfectly well her mistress would have been shocked by her behavior and chastised her sternly.

CHAPTER 44

On Patrol

An Intruder

Ruwena and Evan were still enjoying their outing when both caught the scent of a wolf in the air. It was not one of their own members. This wolf was a stranger, and its odor seemed fouled. If they were to investigate this foreigner, they would have to be very cautious. Wolves prey on foxes. Ruwena also looked to the skies. Where there was one intruder, there could be others.

For a while, the two foxes followed the wolf's scent. When it became stronger, Ruwena transformed into a Cooper's hawk and began her search. She soon spotted a large black hybrid with a body shaped like a wolf. She recognized it instantly. It was a lupucercopith (illus. 16).

Ruwena immediately shrieked a warning call to alert Evan. Then she dived at it to point out its location. In doing so, Ruwena also alerted the wolf-like creature to her own presence. It immediately jumped and snapped at her. She avoided the attack easily and dived at it again. Ruwena engaged in a dangerous game of cat and mouse in an attempt to lead it away from Evan. When the hybrid wolf picked up the scent of fox in the air, it abruptly abandoned its futile effort to catch the bird and turned to search for the fox. When the creature began heading to Evan's direction at a steady if ungainly pace, Ruwena knew it was after Evan. She gave another shrill cry and accelerated her diving attacks on the creature in an effort to distract it and to alert Evan to the change in its direction. The trees were denser now. Their low-lying branches coupled with the hawk's agility and speed impaired the creature's ability to snatch her out of the air. She would disappear into the trees then go into a steep dive, strafing the wolf to harass it.

As a wolf, Evan could hold his own with a native wolf. As a fox, he was no match for one. He needed an escape. Evan immediately began searching for an outcropping or mound of rocks with an opening just large enough for him to fit inside it and too small for the wolf now tracking him. As yet, he did not know that the wolf hunting him was a hybrid. Evan looked back briefly to locate Ruwena when he saw her dive into the canopy and disappear into it. He did not see her soar above it again.

Evan knew that if the wolf caught the hawk, Ruwena would be killed. The only way he knew he could intervene was to change into a wolf himself as rapidly as possible. His transformations between human and fox and between human and wolf were well practiced and readily accomplished. He had forced a transformation from fox back to human once and gotten away with it (after being sick for two days). Now he was going to force a transformation from fox to human to wolf—two forced transformations, one on top of the other. Even if successful, he knew he might become corrupted and unable to transform again. He might die during the transformations, or he might be killed by the wolf hunting him because he was too weak to fight. Still, he had to do something to try to save Ruwena.

Saving Grace

As the wolf and fox evolved, their genomes diverged, as did some of their characteristics. Nevertheless, they continued to share many of the same gene sequences. As a result, *H. transformans* often would have multiple copies of the same gene sequences provided by the mixing of two or more different genomes. This was Evan's saving grace.

Theoretically, all animals would have two copies of every gene—one from the mother and one from the father. It was not uncommon, however, to have more than two copies. Additional copies of a gene segment could be caused by insertions, duplications, or trisomy. These additions could influence the functions of other genes depending upon what the genes do and where they were located (pleiotropy). They could accumulate over time if the affected cells underwent cell division (mitosis). If the affected cell was a reproductive cell, the additions could be inherited by offspring.

In *H. sapiens*, copy number variation accounted for about 10% of human DNA. It was a significant source of genetic variation among individuals and a common cause of genetic differences in the *same* individual. Given the multiple additional gene sequences typically seen in *H. transformans* (depending upon the number of alternate species), an even higher percentage of copy number variation would be expected. If these copies were associated with the genes they should affect, then this would streamline the process of transformation and improve its efficacy.

A Deadly Onslaught

The hybrid wolf was engaged with the hawk when he heard another animal behind him. The creature turned just as a large gray wolf rammed into it. The gray's assault was forceful enough to knock the hybrid wolf down. Nonetheless, the latter was able to counter the attack by biting into the wolf's body with his long fangs. Although the fight between the two animals lasted only a matter of minutes, it was fierce and vicious. The corrupted wolf was the larger of the two wolves; however, it lacked agility. Due to a deformity in its hips, it had trouble coordinating turns and changes in position. This proved to be an enormous advantage for the more agile gray wolf. The gray was able to outmaneuver the corrupted wolf and finally kill it—at a price. The gray was seriously injured and greatly weakened by the fight. It had several deep bite wounds and multiple lacerations from the hybrid creature's fangs and claws.

Ruwena was unable to do anything to help the gray wolf while the two animals were embattled. Had she tried to join the fight, she might have jeopardized the wrong wolf. She had no idea who the gray wolf was. Could it be another scout who had been alerted by her calls and responded? Where was Evan? She would have to find him later. The gray wolf struggled to its feet, tried to walk, and then collapsed. It needed help urgently. Ruwena flew above the canopy and began circling and shrieking. She was calling Evan, she thought, who could race back to the outpost and get help.

Fortunately, her original cries had already alerted Warren, another scout on patrol as a brown bear in the region. At the outpost, Master Crocius had also heard the hawk's persistent shrieks and was almost certain it was Ruwena. So he and two other scouts had set out immediately to find her and Evan. Hence, it was right after the fight ended that Master Crocius, his scouts, and a large brown bear converged at the site. The bear immediately had to dodge a hawk's razor-sharp talons before Ruwena realized who it was. They saw her land beside a badly injured wolf and saw the hybrid creature nearby. Master Crocius recognized the gray wolf immediately. "Evan!" he called sharply. The wolf did not respond. Ruwena was devastated. She knew then she would not need to search for a red fox.

Evan's wounds were bound quickly to minimize blood loss. Then he was carried back to the outpost—still as a gray wolf. The other two scouts hauled the corrupted wolf back for examination. They needed to know what kind of creature it was before destroying it. Ruwena remained a hawk and took flight to watch over the scouts and Evan as they returned to the outpost. Warren remained a brown bear and served as a guard during their return. Both the hawk and the bear were alert for any other intruders. They saw none.

Once back at the outpost, Ruwena resumed her form as a red fox. She followed Evan into the infirmary where his wounds were treated and steps were taken to support his transformation back to human form. Both Master Crocius and Dr. Jozefa [jō-zě-fǎ], the outpost's physician, treated Evan's wounds and examined him carefully for any signs of poisoning or corruption. They found no obvious signs. "Nonetheless, Dr. Jozefa will have to watch him for a few days," Master Crocius said to the fox. "He will observe Evan for any signs of internal corruption as well as any complications from his wounds."

Over the next few days, Evan was kept sedated to slow the process of transformation and allow it to be more gradual. This also provided relief from pain, reduced the stress he was under, and allowed time for his wounds to begin healing. Dr. Jozefa also kept watch over the slight red fox who, in turn, was keeping watch over Evan. Periodically, she would sniff the wolf—and later the human—from top to toe, alerting the medical staff if her sensitive nose detected any problem.

The sedatives were gradually withdrawn and finally stopped. To everyone's relief, Evan had returned to his human form with all systems functioning normally. When he finally woke up, it was because a cold moist nose was against his ear, sniffing it. He did not move as the nose sniffed its way from his head to his toes, down one side and up the other side. When the nose was finished, Evan stretched out his full length and faced the red fox behind the cold nose. "I'm fine," he said. He continued to recover without further medical intervention.

Evan learned soon afterward that Ruwena had remained a red fox and would not leave him until his transformation back into human form was complete and his wounds were healing. The staff had to bring her food and water if they wanted her to eat and drink. After Evan's recovery, the two remained close.

Supplemental Notes and Citations

Copy Number Variation

It is not uncommon to have more than the standard two copies of a gene (Mishra and Whetstine, 2016; Zhang and Lupski, 2015). This is most apparent in aneuploidy, when there is a duplication of an entire chromosome (e.g., trisomy); however, it can also occur in cells that can divide (mitosis). The parent of origin of the extra copy likely influences phenotype (Rocca et al., 2016).

Mosaicism

The genetic composition in some cells of an organism differs from the other cells in that organism (Campbell et al., 2015; Zilina, 2015). The change can occur during mitosis, at which time the change is inherited by daughter cells (clones) (Vattahil and Scheet, 2016). In turn, the clones will continue to propagate the change until mitosis in those cells ceases. Thus, mosaicism in nonreproductive cells may actually be quite common.

PART VII

Reckoning

CHAPTER 45

The Lyvulseroptera

After the destruction of H'Aleth, Cassius had every intention of using his dragon to assault Biogenics directly—especially after Biogenics began multiple concurrent hit-and-run attacks against him. When one of their attacks freed the dragoness, he blamed Biogenics for the loss of his dragon. He assumed it was their bombardment of the village and the tower, which set the dragoness free to join her mate. To some extent, that was true. Yet had Rafe examined the tower itself or the chains left behind, he would have found other clues to the dragoness's freedom. He did not, and the full force of his fury was turned toward Biogenics.

If Cassius couldn't have a naturally born dragon, "I will create one," he avowed to himself. *It shouldn't take too long,* he thought. Rafe had always used gene splicing, accelerants, and mutagens in his genetic engineering programs. He would do so again with the genomes of animals that he would use to create his dragon.

Lyvulseroptera

First, Cassius decided to recreate the legendary gryphon—the beast with the body, tail, and hind legs of a lion and the head, wings, forelegs, and talons of an eagle. From this exercise in frustration spewed forth many bizarre creatures. Some of these survived and were deliberately released into Biogenics's territory to terrorize their people and anyone else living there. If people fled the area out of fear, then it would be easier for Cassius to occupy it. One of those creatures was the lyvulfon, the hybrid that was killed attacking the otter pup.

The lyvulfon was a major milestone for Cassius. It had many of the characteristics he desired, not the least of which were life and flight. Since the lyvulfons did not breathe fire, Rafe continued to work on his masterpiece. To make his creature look more like a dragon, his next effort was to blend the genome of a bat into the lyvulfon. He already had some limited success mixing the genes of birds and bats. *Adding bat genes to the lyvulfon shouldn't be a problem,* he thought. Many a failed experiment corrected this misapprehension.

Finally, Cassius was able to generate bat-like wings on his creature that fell short of his expectations. They were inverted and could not support flight. None of the creature's features conveyed the ability to breathe fire or to fly. So he could go no further. He had no idea how to recreate dragon fire (a mixture of hydrocarbons, sulfur trioxide, and nitrogen), and this maddened him even more. Dragons were the only animals known to possess the ability to make fire biologically, and his past effort to acquire genes from the eggs of a dragoness met with failure.

Cassius decided on a different tactic. If his creature could not breathe fire, then it would spit poison. So his next exercise was to splice the genes of a spitting viper into his creature. This took a while. Still he persisted, until copious amounts of poisonous saliva drooled from his creature's mouth—not quite what he had in mind.

Cassius finally managed to architect a creature that could spit poison. He had not created the dragon he wanted; however, it would have to do. The lyvulseroptera [*lī*-vul-ser-*ŏp*-ter-a], a lyvulfon with the genes of viper and bat spliced into it, was a bizarre being (illus. 28). It had the sharp pointed nose and ears of a bat and a bat's forehead. It had the eyes of the lynx and the tongue and fangs of a viper. It retained the beak of a vulture. It also had a long slender neck, akin to the body of a snake, by which it could maneuver its head nearly 360 degrees to the right or the left. It still had the hind legs and tail of a lynx and the forelegs and talons of the vulture.

Unlike its predecessor, Cassius had given the lyvulseroptera's body a coat of armor made of thick keratin plates impregnated with calcium phosphate, which gave the plates a bony consistency. If necessary, it could tuck its legs, head, and useless wings underneath its body and curl up in a ball, like a pangolin, leaving only the surface covered by its plates exposed to an attacker. *Since it can't fly, it might as well be armored,* Rafe reasoned to himself.

Illus. 28. Lyvulseroptera.

By now, the lyvulseroptera's body was quite large and bulky. Its bat-like wings dragged on the ground, impeding its forward motion. Although it could lumber across the ground, its body was too heavy and the wings too misaligned to lift the creature off the ground.

Through no fault of its own, the lyvulseroptera was an ugly creature and might have been pitied were it not so deadly. Its venom was a potent mixture of agents including a neurotoxin that caused paralysis and digestive enzymes that would break down proteins. It could spit its poisonous venom for a distance of nearly twenty-five feet and inject it via its fangs. The rapid-acting venom would paralyze its prey as it was dissolving the victim's tissues and organs. The suffering would be intense but thankfully short. Any victim would be dead in a matter of minutes.

Descent into Madness

The notion of biogenetically engineering a fire-breathing dragon using the genes of other animals was completely irrational. Cassius needed the genes of a dragon, which the dragoness never provided. Over time, Rafe's aborted transformation was leading him into madness. He was developing a progressive thought disorder that caused his thinking to become deranged and his personality to change. This was not entirely unexpected. Even as Rafe's aborted transformation from boar back to human disrupted the architecture of his body, so too could it have disrupted the architecture of his brain.

Similar to the genetics of intelligence, the tendency to develop a psychosis was a polygenic, multifactorial trait. There was no direct link between any gene and psychosis; however, there were many genes that potentially increased the risk given the right environmental conditions. Since the risk of psychosis was found to be increased among first-degree relatives and decreased among more remote family members, this suggested that there could be a familial tendency. Many members of the Cassius family, including Rafe, were known to be ambitious, impatient, and aggressive. Even so, none had shown any sign of disordered thinking. Neither had Rafe before his aborted transformation.

There were several neurotransmitters that affected how information was processed and how the centers that process the information reacted to it. These neurotransmitters affected both physical and emotional responses and, consequently, personality. Dysregulation of the genes that coded for these substances could have led to an excess or a deficit of one or more of them, leading to an imbalance between those that were excitatory (e.g., dopamine) and those that were inhibitory (e.g., gamma-aminobutyric acid, GABA).

Cassius's aborted transformation could have caused traumatic injury to his brain. Damage to nerve cells and their connections could have affected brain function directly and altered or blocked the pathways used by neurotransmitters. Finally, failure to complete the transformation could have left nonnative nerve tissue within and between brain cells, which would disrupt the brain's architecture and interfere with its function.

What exactly led to Cassius's decline into madness was unknown. Regardless of the cause, his madness was accelerating, fueled by his rivalry with and antagonism toward Biogenics and by his frustrated attempts to create a dragon.

Supplemental Notes and Citations

Psychosis

This is a neurologic-developmental disorder influenced by genetic, environmental, and possibly social factors (Jonas et al., 2014; Pasch, 2009; Takahashi, 2014; Toth, 2015). It is characterized by a disorder of perception, emotion, memory, and judgment leading to disordered thinking, loss of touch with reality, thought disorders, and disorganized behavior. These disorders may be manifested as delusions (persistent belief in something that is not real) or hallucinations (sensory perceptions that are not real) or both.

Multiple genes, when present in the same genome, convey an increased risk of developing schizophrenia and bipolar disorder (DeRosse et al., 2012; Jorde, 2014b). Non-Mendelian inheritance of epigenetic influences (e.g., DNA methylation) may also be factors (Toth, 2015).

Neurotransmitters are chemical agents that can excite (e.g., dopamine), quiet (e.g., GABA), or soothe (e.g., serotonin) areas of the brain. In *H. sapiens*, hyperactivity of dopamine pathways can cause delusions and hallucinations. Disruption in dopamine pathways have been implicated in neuropsychiatric disorders (Jonas et al., 2014).

Traumatic Brain Injury (TBI)

Rotational and angular shearing forces disrupt nerve cells and their supporting structures, leading to nerve damage and, possibly, damage to the blood vessels that supply the brain (Boss, 2014; Shively et al., 2012; Washington et al., 2016). The damage could be limited to one or more small areas of the brain or be more global in extent. In *H. sapiens*, in the absence of recurrent episodes of TBI, mild TBI is transient, followed by complete recovery over a period of weeks.

Abnormal Brain Tissue

In *H. sapiens*, there are conditions in which deposition of abnormal matter disrupts brain function (e.g., multiple sclerosis, Alzheimer's disease, etc.). Alzheimer's disease is associated with formation of a substance (amyloid) that forms plaques in the brain that block and, therefore, disrupt nerve transmission (Pasch, 2009; Serrano-Pozo et al., 2011). It is also associated with another abnormal material that forms tangles inside nerve cells, interfering with their function. Similar changes have been noted after traumatic brain injury (Washington et al., 2016). These changes lead to progressive failure of cerebral functions associated with a decrease in cognitive function or behavioral disturbances (dementia) or both. Note: A specific form of inherited early-onset Alzheimer's disease is caused by an autosomal dominant gene mutation (*APP*, *PSEN1*, or *PSEN2*) (Cohn-Hokke et al., 2012; Loy et al., 2014).

CHAPTER 46

A Stitch in Time

After the destruction of H'Aleth, Erwina had expected to be the next target. It was simply a question of who would advance first, when, and with what armaments. So the leadership hastily prepared evacuation plans and preparations in anticipation of an attack. As fate would have it, Cassius and Biogenics were too busy sparring with each other to attack Erwina—the House they thought least valuable. It was during this interlude that Erwina developed its own defense strategy, which included a means of escaping dragon fire, and took the opportunity to test and refine their plans and preparations.

An Early Warning System

The southeast territory of Erwina east of the ridge was an open expanse of grassland that was essentially flat. It spanned about two hundred miles before merging into prairie toward the west. Most of its trees lined rivers and streams. Except for distance, there were no other natural barriers in this region. The grasslands would be no impediment to a capable army. People living in the plains would have little time, if any, for flight. Consequently, this region was sparsely populated.

The villagers and the scouts who watched and patrolled the grasslands and plains became Erwina's designated early warning system. Hence, there was a strong emphasis on surveillance in that region of Erwina. With all the defensive measures Erwina had in place, its strongest defense lay in constant vigilance.

Should suspicious activity be observed, someone would need to alert the nearest village and raise the alarm. An *H. transformans* who could transform into a bird was rare. Consequently, the villagers would have to rely on those *H. transformans* whose alternate species were fleet of foot, could blend into the environment, and could defend themselves against an attack. Fortunately, most of the villagers could transform into an animal that could race to other villages and to the compound. The summer predator-prey games provided the opportunity to train for this situation.

Plans and Preparations

If Cassius attacked Erwina, Master Titus advised Matron Aquina, "I am certain that the compound will be his primary target." Matron Aquina agreed.

The compound was almost four hundred miles west of its border with H'Aleth. After crossing the grasslands, Cassius would have to get his machines of war over the rough and steep terrain of the ridge and across the tumultuous and dangerous Ferveo River. These would pose no barrier to a Great Gray dragon, if Cassius still possessed one. At a top speed of almost 240 miles per hour, the dragon could cover the entire four-hundred-mile distance in less than two hours. "Cassius's army cannot move that fast," said Master Titus. "Even under a forced march, it will take his forces almost three days to reach the Ferveo River from the western edge of H'Aleth's territory." The ridge and the river would slow down his machines of war. He would have to move rocks and cut down trees to cross the ridge and then construct some means to cross the river. "We do not know how many of his creatures can swim. If not well trained, even those that can swim may be swept away and drowned."

Although Cassius could send his dragon ahead to destroy everything in its path, Master Titus thought it more likely that Cassius would keep it close. "I suspect strongly that Cassius will want to see the destruction of the compound and everyone in it—just as he did at H'Aleth," he said. "I estimate that the population of the compound will have no more than ninety-six hours to both evacuate and reach a minimum safe distance away from the compound," he continued. "The southeastern and southwestern villages will have far less time."

In conjunction with the faculty and operations chiefs, Master Titus developed an evacuation plan specifically for the compound. This plan could be modified depending upon the direction from which an attack came and in what direction the evacuation would be. The goal was to evacuate as many people as possible and reestablish their House in another remote—and hopefully unknown—location. The task was to determine how much could be done and how quickly and how long it would take to evacuate hundreds of people—possibly a thousand or more if those fleeing from the southeastern region evacuated to join the compound. This would be a herculean task that needed to be accomplished in less than seventy-two hours—leaving twenty-four hours to get as far away as possible. To this end, all chiefs, department heads, faculty, and their respective staffs needed to know what tasks they had to accomplish and how much time they had to do them. Last but not least, the students—Form II sophomores and above—needed to know to whom to report and where.

To Matron Kavarova, Master Iranapolis, and Madam Merena he said, "We will lead any defense against an attacker to give those evacuating as much time as possible to escape. I will assign members of my security force, including scouts, to provide an armed escort for the evacuation." The defenders would be joined by skilled archers and by those whose alternate species and weaponry skills or both made them a formidable adversary in close combat. Students in Form IV who were weapons qualified would supplement the security forces providing the escort. The remaining security forces and scouts would stay and defend the compound.

Matron Aquina declared, "Adults who are capable and wish to remain behind to assist in the defense may do so, provided their children have completed Form II and the adults themselves are not essential to reestablishing the House." All who planned to stay behind understood the risk they would be taking. The lessons from H'Aleth had not been forgotten. Unlike the estate at H'Aleth, however, the Erwinians had built many hidden avenues of escape.

All these preparations presupposed that there would be some advanced warning—even two hours—to fetch at least some food and water, medical supplies, and weapons. Even if there was barely enough time to run, nonperishable items were prepositioned at the terminus of tunnels that led out of the compound. Adults and older students could grab a backpack or satchel on their way out with the assurance that something useful would be in it. A stitch in time saves nine.

Chapter 47

Strategies

Erwina's southeastern scouts had infiltrated far enough into Cassius territory to hear rumors that Cassius was readying his forces for an attack. Where he would attack remained unclear; however, a clash with Biogenics seemed certain. If Cassius attacked Biogenics, then Erwina could follow the conflict before deciding to flee their territory. If Biogenics forces floundered or the conflict came too close to Erwina's boundaries, then Erwina would evacuate all but their defensive forces. Thus, the people of Erwina knew war was coming and with it the possibility of dragon fire. So they, too, made ready.

Cassius's Strategy

Cassius's strategy was to acquire Erwina's resources and then crush Biogenics—permanently. To this end, Rafe planned his march on Erwina. He had gathered three hundred or so villagers—*H. sapiens* and hominids alike—to supplement his fighting force. These people would form the first wave of his assault. Most of them—including the cercopithursids, serojabovids, and other hominids he had bred for work—had no training in martial arts or in the use of weapons. Cassius had never wanted them to learn how to fight. They might rebel against him. Now, he armed the villagers with weapons they did not know how to use. He knew they would not be an effective fighting force, and he didn't care. He still expected them to inflict some casualties on Erwina's paltry forces and distract them while his second wave—his real fighting force—was brought forward to annihilate all who were still standing.

The second wave would consist of multiple components: (1) a company of experienced archers; (2) humans who could man his cannons and animal hybrids who could haul them across the ground; (3) the *H. transformans* in his service who could change into large and fiercely aggressive wolves, bears, boars, hyenas, and baboons; (4) his geneticallyengineered human-animal hybrids (hominids), cercolupoids and crocutalupoids, bred for aggressiveness and strength; and (5) his genetically engineered animal hybrids, the cercopithurus, lupucercopiths, lupuserojas, ursuscros, and lyvulfons. He would even unleash a horde of aegyopteras to harass his enemy's forces and deplete their archers' supply of arrows.

Cassius would hold back his crowning achievement—the lyvulseroptera. This creature was by far and away his most deadly. "I will save it for the final destruction of Erwina's compound—combatants and noncombatants alike," he said, just as he had done at H'Aleth with a dragon. How he was going to get the cumbersome creature over the ridge and across the river was not a matter he had considered. The lyvulseropteras certainly were not going to fly across those barriers. Not for a moment did Rafe think back on the level of effort required to haul a dragoness a much shorter distance over relatively flat, if forested, terrain. It had been too long ago, and his memory had failed him.

Biogenics's Strategy

Commander Elisar [el-ī-*sar*] was a veteran of the battle for H'Aleth. He was well aware of Cassius's intentions toward his employer and suspected his intentions toward Erwina were the same. Based on his experience, he adopted a straightforward strategy: wait. Biogenics had continued to build up their forces. While doing so, they watched to see what Cassius would do next. He had been surprisingly quiet for a while. "If he marches on Erwina, we will bring our forces quietly and discreetly within range of the field of battle," Commander Elisar told his officers. "Then we will wait for an opportune time to attack his army, preferably from his rear."

Biogenics hoped Cassius had not acquired another dragon. They had not heard of one, but then, neither had they known of the first one before it appeared. It seemed likely that something had happened to his dragon; otherwise, Cassius would have continued using it to attack Biogenics.

Even if he still had one, it would be deployed at the front of the fight. Depending upon Erwina's resistance, it was possible that the dragon would expend much of its fire and Cassius most of his forces by the time Biogenics attacked. Cassius would be caught off guard and unprepared to deal with another fresher army.

Erwina's Strategy

Beneath the iron top of the ridge, there was a deep layer of limestone. Water running through this layer created caverns beneath the ridge. Some of these caverns were quite deep and had fresh water pools or underground rivers running through them. Many of the caves and caverns were too deep for a dragon's fire to reach. Erwinians had stowed supplies and armaments in caves and rock formations on both sides of the ridge. There they could mount an offense or defense or could retreat into them, away from dragon fire. If Erwina were to come under attack, it would be best to meet the enemy on the eastern side of the ridge, where they would have the high ground. If an enemy ever breached the ridge and reached the river, Erwina's fighters could mount a counterattack from the western side of the ridge. The enemy would be trapped against the river. This presupposes, however, that no dragon was involved in the conflict.

Matron Aquina met with Master Titus, Master Iranapolis, and Matron Kavarova. "We have two strategies," said Master Titus. "The first is to repel an invasion and prevail against Cassius, if possible." The compound's security forces and Erwina's scouts were well trained and experienced in the field and would form the backbone of their defense (absent a dragon). "The second and most likely strategy is to buy enough time for Erwina's people to evacuate the villages and flee into the mountains or to lands west of us." Erwina's forces would need to buy their people at least enough time to disperse into the wildernesses of the southwest and northwest. In either case, students would escape with as many elders as possible. They were the ones who had to survive to rebuild the House of Erwina.

Ruwena had insisted on being a part of these strategy sessions. If Erwina was destroyed or even scattered into the wilderness, any chances of restoring the House of H'Aleth would be lost. She felt compelled to prevent this from happening, if she could. Still unbeknownst to anyone, Ruwena knew she could become a force of reckoning against any enemy.

Red Alert

It was shortly thereafter that Rachel, as a red wolf, raced into the compound to meet with Matron Aquina and Master Titus. She carried on her back a report in a courier's pouch so that no one would have to wait for her to transform before receiving word that Cassius was on the march. He was headed in a westerly direction that would take him through the lands once held by H'Aleth into the grasslands of Erwina. Biogenics's forces had not been seen making any movement. "So it is Cassius's army that we will face," said Master Titus.

The communique also reported that scouts had seen large numbers of hybrids as well as humans, cannons, and a large unwieldy creature that looked like a corrupted ostrich. It was being toted on a cart. They saw no sign of a dragon; however, neither had H'Aleth until it was upon them.

Matron Aquina and Master Titus realized that villagers in the southeastern region needed to evacuate immediately. The southeastern outpost likely would come under fire first as Cassius marched toward the compound. Matron Aquina turned to Rachel and said, "The villagers must evacuate across the river without delay and join us here in the compound. Tell them to bring as many resources as they can carry. You will remain at the village and assist in their evacuation." She dispatched Rachel with a communique informing the villagers of this plan.

Barrow, a southwestern scout, was dispatched to the southwestern villages with a similar communique strapped to his back. As a red wolf, he, too, could travel quickly and hide among the grasses to avoid detection until he reached his destination. There, people were advised to begin their evacuation into the southwest mountains. This was a terrain their scouts knew well. Before his departure, Barrow was apprised of the location where Erwina's people hoped to resettle and would be able to guide people from the southwest to that area once it was clear that Cassius's forces were not headed their way.

Alan, as a gray wolf, was sent as a courier first to the northeast outpost. There, he apprised Master Crocius, Evan, and Warren of the impending attack on Erwina. From the northeast outpost, Alan traveled to Gregor to notify its people. Meanwhile, Master Crocius and his scouts prepared to receive refugees. The caves and caverns in the northeast territory could shelter several hundred people. These places were already stocked to harbor scouts. "Now we must bolster those supplies as much as possible," he told his staff. The entrances to most of these locations were isolated and hidden. If the people in them remained still and quiet, the enemy could walk right by an entrance and never see it.

With these arrangements made, Matron Aquina issued orders to all her chiefs, department heads, and the faculty. "Be ready to evacuate the compound within seventy-two hours." She sent a similar notice to all the private living quarters nearby. Master Titus, Master Iranapolis, and Matron Kavarova mobilized Erwina's defensive forces to meet Cassius.

CHAPTER 48

To Duty Stations

With the order to evacuate, Erwina's disaster plan went into effect. All five bell towers rang out at once, heralding danger and sending everyone to their appointed posts. All students returned to the schoolhouse and reported to their respective commons to await a briefing by their dormitory supervisors.

"Erwina is under attack," announced Madam Wilhelmina to her Form III students. "This time, the danger is real. This is not a drill, and it is not an exercise. Armed forces march against us, and we must evacuate. Gather your belongings and report to your duty stations."

"We are ready," replied Savannah. The students had recognized the presence of an imminent danger when they heard the five bells tolling. They did not know the nature of the danger or whether they were to shelter in place or evacuate. After returning to the schoolhouse, Savannah and Erik mustered their classmates, including Ruwena, as they arrived at the dormitory. This time, they would meet the challenge much differently. They would be separated and did not know when, or if, they would see each other again. As they left the dormitory, they wished each other well and promised to see one another again. All save one went to his or her assigned duty station. Ruwena slipped away to seek out Master Titus.

A Race against Time

As prearranged, Head Matron Aquina, Headmaster Morenavik, Matron Trevora, and Master Heroditus would lead the evacuation. Each one would be stationed at the head of a company of about 200 to 250 people who were evacuating. They were joined by Master Leonid, who advised them on weather conditions they would likely encounter depending upon their heading. They were joined also by Master Ignatius, who knew the geography of the regions, the location of water resources, and which caves and caverns were most resistant to dragon fire.

Madam Morenavik and her staff readied the horses for riding and for pulling wagons for people and supplies that could not travel any other way. Students who were experienced equestrians assisted with the horses. "Load as many bags of feed as possible into the wagons," she told her staff. Although the horses and other livestock could graze for food above ground, there was no grazing in caves and caverns.

Except dried herbs, most food supplies were perishable. Grains and root vegetables could be stored for longer periods, so stores of these food supplies were kept ready for transport, used periodically, and then replenished by fresh stores. Madam Ranicova [ran-ĭ-cō-va] directed the students assigned to the rectory, "Pack up as many ingredients and food supplies as you can in the time allotted," she said and then showed them which ones to pack up first. Master Ratorovic told the rectory staff, "Distribute any prepared food among the villagers, faculty, and students so they can have something to eat while they get ready to evacuate."

Matron H'Umara, Master Stuvidicus, and the infirmary staff assisted the two patients who could not travel unassisted to a covered wagon. "We will move out in advance of the rest of the company as soon as a wagon is ready," said Matron H'Umara. Although a supply of nonperishable medical supplies were prepacked and ready for transport, the staff packed up as many additional medical supplies as time permitted—especially medicinal potions. With the exception of essential oils, most potions were perishable. Some of these supplies would be carried on the medical wagon. Others would be distributed to the remaining companies. Master Gaius and his students packed up essential nutritional powders and medicinal potions available in the lab. Here, too, nonperishable ingredients were already packed for immediate transport. Once their tasks were done, Master Gaius and his staff and students joined the medical team.

Master Chernavich and his staff dispensed weaponry to those adults and students qualified to use the weapons available. In many cases, Form IV students and the majority of adults were qualified in multiple weapons—especially archery and swordsmanship—and would be heavily armed. (Erwina did not have cannons.) Master Chernavich also ordered, "All Form III students and Form II seniors who are certified in archery will receive a bow and quiver of arrows. Form IV students certified in swordsmanship will receive steel swords and shields." Students who had undertaken a practicum or an internship at the armory and knew its inventory assisted with dispensing weapons and with packing up as many bows and arrows and other small arms as time permitted.

Most of the materials used to set up shelters were already prepared and prepositioned for immediate transport. Depending upon the season, exposure to wind and rain and extreme temperatures could be as deadly as an enemy force. Given that the most likely evacuation route would be through the northern mountains, a winter evacuation could be deadly without adequate protection in tents. If the evacuation were to the south and west, canopies to provide shelter from sun and extreme heat would be needed. Master Heroditus told his staff and students, "Gather up both sets of materials in case our planned evacuation route has to change."

Madam Fredrika, Master Androv, and their staffs, with the assistance of Madam Gannett and her staff, gathered the materials they would need to repair and replace clothes. They also packed up any clothing and footwear already made, including any clean clothes in the laundry. These items could be used to supplement clothes, if needed, or be cannibalized to repair clothes. Madam Gannett also had preprepared packages of soap.

Master Yakobon [yak-ō-bŏn] and his carpentry staff provided the crates, boxes, and baskets needed for supplies not already packed up in advance. "These should be few," said Master Yakobon to his students. Most supplies were prepared so that they could be carried by an individual in a back pack. This meant that everyone physically able to do so carried some portion of the supplies in accordance with their abilities. "We will still need crates to transport the hens and their chicks," he explained.

Since the southeastern outpost needed a river evacuation, Master Salinas told his boathouse crew, "Mobilize as many boats, barges, canoes, and kayaks as possible to bring people from the outpost across the river. Any craft not needed to transport people will be used to transport supplies they bring with them." Canoes and kayaks stationed at the boathouse were loaded onto barges for transport across the river. He and his staff and the scouts knew where many were hidden along both sides of the river's banks. Once the southeastern villagers arrived on the river's western shore, people from the compound would be there to greet them and guide them to their point of departure in the evacuation.

Preserving Flora and Fauna

Several faculty, staff, and students converged on the botanical garden. Madam Ocala and Master Ferronas [fer-ōn-ăs] bundled up flowering plants that attract pollinators, herbs (nutritional and medicinal), and vegetable plants. Master Janislov [jan-ĭs-lof] bundled up seedling plants and grasses that produce grains. Madam Davidea selected a few seedling fruit and nut trees, which her staff bundled together. Madam Wallenexis and her staff gathered up some young grapevines. All these plants and seedlings would be used to restart gardens in another location. "If time permits, we will all go to the herb and vegetable gardens to harvest any produce that is ripe and get additional herb and vegetable plants," said Madam Ocala.

Master Navarov and his staff released into the surrounding forest any animals in the vet clinic capable of surviving. None would be released into the pond or stream behind the water mill. "If our village is struck down by a gray dragon, its breath and fire will evaporate all the water in the pond and the stream that supplies it," explained Master Neminicus [nĕ-men-ĭ-cus] to the students assisting him. "We will transport any reptiles and amphibians in the vet clinic and the aviary to the stream behind the fruit tree groves."

Master Xavier and the falconry and aviary staff released any raptors and birds capable of flight. "What about the raptors that can't fly?" asked one of the students. "We will take them with us," replied Master Xavier. "Even when they are unable to fly, they are still formidable predators in close quarters," he explained.

Farm animals that could sustain sufficient speed were herded for evacuation. Madam Varanitova [var-an-ĭ-tō-va] and her staff drove the rest of the farm animals with a supply of food into the tunnel systems that would not be used for the evacuation. "Most of these animals will not survive long in the wild, and most will return to the compound if driven away," she explained to her students. "Deep inside the tunnels, they could survive dragon fire." Cassius's forces were unlikely to enter the tunnels because of the heat at their entrances. If the animals survived in the tunnels, eventually they would find their way out and return to grazing on the land. If the land had been seared by a dragon, then they would need to travel to forage for themselves.

The hen house staff packed up as many hens as possible. Their eggs would be a major source of protein. So each company of people would carry hens. Here, there was a need for crates. The rest of the farm birds were taken into the tunnels with food.

Madam Phillius [$f\breve{\imath}l$-$\bar{e}$-us] and her staff drove the fruit bats to the rear chamber of their J-shaped cave and left a large amount of fruit to feed them. Hopefully, Cassius's dragon would ignore the bat cave. It was possible, however, that Cassius might assume people had taken refuge there and order his dragon to sear it with flames. She hoped that the absence of any human cries might shorten the firestorm if only to preserve the dragon's fire. Not even Great Gray dragons have an endless supply of the substances that fuel their fire. Any bats that had not ventured back into the front chamber might survive a dragon's onslaught.

Preserving Erwina's Heritage

Madam Florenza and the archives staff packed up all the parchments—pedigrees first. Madam Borislav [*bor*-is-lof], the chief cartographer, instructed the library staff and students, "Pack up all maps, atlases, and any other documents that describe Erwina's territory. They cannot be left behind to guide our enemy and give them direction," she explained. Madam Lindenova, Master Josephus, Madam Carawan, and the rest of the natural history staff collected all the history and research papers that documented *H. transformans* as a species. Most were already bound and were readily retrieved.

All the pedigrees and DNA analyses were given to Master Mikalov, whose alternate species, a caribou, would take them to Gregor with all speed. He was accompanied by Master Janislov, an arctic wolf, to provide support and protection. Even in winter, these two could travel to Gregor. The remaining documents had to be carried until they could be stowed in a safe dry location deep underground where they could be retrieved later (hopefully).

Most importantly of all, Madam Bernarda, Madam Patrina, and Madam Wilhelmina marshaled the students in Forms I, II, and III, respectively. All students were tasked to pack their clothes and fill their water carafes. Madam Bernarda ushered the Form I freshman and sophomore students to their evacuation points. "You will assist in readying materials and tending to small animals brought to the area," she told them. Junior and senior Form I students and students in Forms II and III reported to their assigned duty stations to assist in evacuating different areas of the compound. These included areas that needed substantial manpower to gather and pack supplies and materials that were perishable and could not be packed up in advance. Students assigned to these areas evacuated with their faculty and staff. With students among them, the faculty knew they could not linger at their own risk. Their first duty was to the students.

Last but not least, as the different stations were cleared, all traces of the evacuation needed to be swept away—footsteps, hoof marks, wheel marks, spills, etc. No traces could be left that would guide the enemy and show them where the villagers were headed.

This massive effort had to be completed within sixty hours, leaving twelve hours to get all the people and their possessions, including the animals, out of the compound (illus. 29). Then, they would have twenty-four hours to get as far away from the compound as possible. With so many people, there could be no forced march. Relying on the tunnels, the hemp highway, their alternate species, and the skills they had developed from childhood, they must disappear like ghosts into the forest, leaving little or no sign of where they went. Only the hooves of animals should be seen and, even then, only by an experienced scout.

Illus. 29. A Race against Time.

CHAPTER 49

A Change in Tactics

Fighting Fire with Fire

With the evacuation of the southeastern villages underway, Master Titus knew that nothing would bar Cassius's march across the grasslands. *This won't do,* he thought to himself. So he marshaled his security forces, bolstered by many capable adults, to meet Cassius east of the ridge in the grasslands—not so far east that they couldn't beat a hasty retreat to the ridge. There, they would meet their enemy with the goal of slowing their advance. To minimize their losses, Erwina's forces would give way—hopefully, gradually—back to the ridge, which they would ascend quickly. The cover and higher ground offered by the ridge would be to their advantage. "If we see any sign of a dragon, we will fight fire with fire," he told Madam Kavarova. "We will set the grasslands ablaze. The flames should spread quickly through the dry grasses. Westerly winds will whip up a wall of flames and speed the fire's descent upon Cassius's forces. Then, Cassius will be forced back or, at least, forced to find another way around"—or so he hoped.

If Erwina's forces were pushed back and forced to retreat beyond the ridge—which Master Titus considered entirely possible—then they would have to descend, reach the river, and get across it before Cassius's army reached the top of the ridge. He told Master Salinas, "Your crews will need to keep the boats and barges on the eastern bank ready to ferry Erwina's forces back to the western bank. Then, you will need to destroy all watercraft. If we are overwhelmed and you see Cassius's forces cresting the ridge, destroy any craft you do not need to get your people back to the western shore. Once you achieve the western shore, alert the compound and join up with the evacuation." Although the river would delay Cassius's advance, it would pose no barrier to a dragon, assuming he still had one. If he did, there was no way to know if he would send his dragon ahead or hold it back until he crossed the river.

Much to the consternation of Master Titus and Matron Kavarova, Ruwena had joined the forces that would meet Cassius on the grasslands. She would not be dissuaded from her decision. She also kept a promise she made to herself. When it came time to cross the river, she transformed into a falcon and flew over it.

The Initial Encounter

When Cassius first set forth, he met no resistance from Biogenics. Although this surprised him at first, he quickly decided that Biogenics was deferring to his greater might. Their spies had reported on the vastness of his army, and Biogenics was afraid to stand against him. From that assumption, Cassius made another quantum leap. Having already dismissed any resistance Erwina could offer, he thought he could sweep across Erwina's territory unopposed.

As had been the case with H'Aleth, Cassius did not expect an effective resistance. It didn't occur to him that Erwina's people might have learned something from the destruction of their sister House. "Erwina is nothing more than a few rustic outlying villages with a single large village devoted to education and to keeping historical records," he told his lieutenants. This part of his assessment was quite accurate. Cassius also thought of Erwinians only as educators, genealogists, and archivists—no more prepared for battle than his villagers. He assumed that such a lifestyle precluded any ability to mount an effective fighting force. In this assessment, he was quite mistaken. Consequently, Cassius was unprepared to meet defenders skilled in the military arts. Little did he know that the Erwinians would suffer few, if any, casualties against his first wave.

Both Cassius and Erwina proceeded in accordance with their respective strategies. Erwina's forces crossed the river and the ridge to meet Cassius's army on the grasslands of southeastern Erwina—about ten miles east of the ridge. As suggested once before, however, it is often prudent to build flexibility into one's plans.

Unwilling Conscripts

Cassius drove the villagers forward, as one would drive cattle to the slaughter, forcing them to advance toward the Erwinians. "Kill any *H. sapiens* or hominid attempting to run away," he ordered. Thus, these poor people were being forced to fight in self-defense. Erwina's defenders could see this was happening. These were the beings Ruwena wanted to save. Erwina's fighters were faced with a deadly dilemma, trying to figure out how to avoid harming or killing the villagers while still defending themselves. Although they could easily subdue them, Erwina did not have the resources needed to capture and imprison a large number of combatants—even temporarily.

Ruwena added to the quandary by moving far off to the southwestern side of the battlefield and away from it. From there, she called to the villagers in their language now that she was once again in their midst. "Come to me. Come this way!" she shouted as she signaled for them to come to her. Then, still in the language of the villagers so they would understand, she turned and called to Erwina's fighters, "Do not attack these people." She then repeated her orders in the common language so Erwina's defenders would understand as well.

Initially, the villagers were confused and did not know what to do. Most of them had no desire to fight. They were afraid to go forward, and they could not go back. Ruwena called to them again. "Leave your weapons on the ground and come this way." Each command she repeated in the common language for Erwina's fighters to hear. When Erwina's forces held back, a few of the villagers began to move toward Ruwena. They discarded their weapons, in the hope they could avoid being killed. When those that turned toward Ruwena were not attacked, many others began to follow them.

As most of the first wave left the battlefield and drew near Ruwena, Cassius was stunned. His initial plan of engagement was dissolving before his eyes. For a moment, Cassius and Ruwena could see each other clearly. His distinctive features were unmistakable. Ruwena knew at once he was the hominid whose wounds she had treated long ago. She wondered, *does he remember me?* At one time, Cassius would have remembered her very well. Now, there was no recognition of her—not even a hint of familiarity.

A Swirl of Tactics

Cassius was livid. In his fury, he cast aside his battle plan and unleashed his second wave. The majority of his forces he sent against Erwina, including his archers and cannons. First, he sent forth the aegyopteras to distract Erwina's forces. They were followed by hominids and animal hybrids designed to fight aggressively. These creatures would tear apart anyone or anything they encountered. Behind these forces he sent his *H. transformans*, who could transform into apex predators. Finally, he sent forth his lyvulfons to sweep down upon Erwina's defenders.

Cassius also sent a volley of cercopithuruses, lupucercopiths, lupuserojas, and crocutalupoids against the villagers and the human female who had called to them. Since the villagers had thrown down their weapons, there would be little they could do to fend off any attack. Once the villagers were wiped out, those forces would be in a position to attack the Erwinians from behind their flank while the remainder of his forces mounted a frontal attack.

When the villagers realized that Cassius had unleashed his forces against them, they started running away in earnest. Erwina's defenders saw this too. Master Titus deployed a small squad of archers who raced to intercept the attack on the fleeing villagers. Many years of practice and experience as scouts had honed their skills. These archers served the villagers and Ruwena well. Many creatures were brought down. This only fueled Cassius's fury. He promptly deployed one of his lyvulseroptera against the archers and the villagers.

No one from Erwina or Biogenics had ever seen such a creature. It was a large and clearly corrupted animal. As it seemed to amble forward, it drooled a substance from its mouth that immediately began disintegrating anything it touched—including the creatures the archers had killed or wounded. The struggles of the wounded were quickly silenced. Clearly, the creature's saliva was a destructive and deadly poison.

When Ruwena espied Cassius's creatures headed her way, she knew that neither she nor the villagers would be able to fend them off. In deploying the archers, Master Titus had slowed the creatures' advance. In turn, this tactic depleted some of his defenders, which were already in danger of being crushed by an overwhelming number of Cassius's human and hybrid forces. Faced with what could be a disaster for Erwina as well as the villagers, Ruwena knew what she must do. She had expected it and had prepared for it, but must retreat from the fight to transform. This was one change she could not do quickly.

Watchful Waiting

All the while, Biogenics had been following Cassius's movements from a discreet distance. When they saw the extent of his army in general—and the lyvulseropteras in particular—Commander Elisar decided, "We will sit out this battle for a while and wait for Cassius and Erwina to exhaust their resources." Even if Cassius won the fight, which was likely, he still would have lost many of his creatures.

This strategy also would give Biogenics the opportunity to see what the lyvulseropteras could do and the best way to kill them—if Erwina's forces could kill one. The people of Erwina, many of whom had fled from H'Aleth, were capable fighters. Unless Cassius could trot out another dragon, Erwina would not give up without a fight.

CHAPTER 50

Dragon!

Everyone was stunned when a red dragon appeared off the southwestern flank of Erwina—not far from where Cassius's villagers were fleeing. It seemed to come out of nowhere. The people who had immigrated from H'Aleth recognized it at once. The amber-red color of its scales and the streaks of gold on top of its head and back were unmistakable characteristics of *Dragonis rubra*. The dragon had no horns, so it was either a juvenile male or a dragoness of modest size.

Had the people fleeing from the southwestern villages disturbed the red dragons in their mountain retreats? Had the clash of forces raised their attention and brought one—and possibly others—to the fray looking for prey? They would soon know. Erwina's squad of archers and the villagers were directly in its path.

A Surprise Attack

Cassius was as surprised as everyone else; however, he was delighted that his treacherous villagers and a few of Erwina's forces were about to be decimated by a dragon. Not so. The dragon took flight, flew over the villagers and Erwina's forces, and immediately strafed with its fire the creatures Cassius had set against the villagers.

The dragon's fire killed or forced back most of the hybrids, except for the lyvulseroptera. It had tucked itself under its scales and withstood the brief strafing. When the lyvulseroptera reemerged, it spat wildly at the dragon, only to miss and see its venom destroyed by dragon fire (illus. 30).

371

Illus. 30. En garde!

The now-wary dragon turned to face the creature as the lyvulseroptera moved farther away. As the dragon eyed the creature, it suddenly spat again. This time, it was a narrow miss. Although less than perfect, the lyvulseroptera's aim was much more focused the second time. The dragon immediately fired back, only to see its fire fall short. It was now clear that the range of the creature's spit, bolstered by its long neck, was greater than the range of the dragon's fire.

The creature was not out of the range of an archer's arrow. Although it had wings, it seemed unable to take flight and moved sluggishly. With the absolute destructiveness of the venom and the range the lyvulseroptera could reach spitting it, only the archers could engage it. None of the others or their alternate species could get close enough. Although the archers' arrows reached their target, the creature did not go down. Its outer covering of thick scales served as a coat of armor. This explained why the lyvulseroptera did not take flight and sweep over the villagers. Nonetheless, the archers' arrows drew the creature's attention. The dragon took advantage of its distraction and attacked it. The dragon's breath and fire engulfed the creature and eventually consumed it—scales and all.

On Deadly Ground

Ruwena had used her fire to counter the onslaught by Cassius's creatures. Although she had destroyed the forces sent against the villagers, it was not enough. Cassius sent forth even more of his creatures as pawns. He could afford it. He need only wait until the dragon's supply of fire was depleted—and it was. Although the Ruwena's attack on the lyvulseroptera was successful, it had taken all her remaining fire to destroy it. There would be no more until a sufficient quantity of its constituents could be produced by the glands that supplied it.

Thus, Cassius was not dismayed. He had more than one lyvulseroptera, and he released the others he had brought. "Let the dragon take on another lyvulseroptera, if it can," he fumed. "I have more than enough to destroy Erwina's pitiful defense."

The lyvulseropteras appeared to be indiscriminant regarding when or where they spewed forth their venom. This was well-known to Cassius's human forces. Consequently, they kept a wide berth between themselves and the lyvulseropteras. They knew what the creatures could do and dared not get within their range. They allowed the lyvulseroptera to advance well ahead of them and destroy as many of the enemy as possible. In doing so, they had to be careful to avoid any place where the creature had spat or drooled. These precautions limited their effectiveness as a fighting force and diminished their influence on the battle. The lyvulseropteras effectively prevented Cassius's human forces from driving forward in a direct onslaught against Erwina's defenders. Nevertheless, his archers and cannons could still inflict considerable damage.

Cassius's thought processes had never considered the influence the lyvulseropteras would have on his own forces. Their effect, however, did not go unnoticed by Erwina's master strategists. Both Master Titus and Matron Kavarova noted the discretion with which the human members of Cassius's army kept their distance. "Look how his troops avoid stepping anywhere the lyvulseropteras have trod," said Master Titus. "Watch the behavior of some of the animals too," added Matron Kavarova. The thoughtfulness with which several animals also avoided the lyvulseropteras' tracks identified them as *H. transformans* in their alternate species. The animal hybrids and genetically engineered creatures were not so astute. Many of them did not know to avoid stepping where the creature had drooled. Any that came in contact with the venom were struck down by the poison as it was absorbed through their feet or paws.

Retreat

With the deployment of Cassius's remaining forces, including the lyvulseropteras, Erwina's forces had to fall back. They might well be annihilated if they did not do so. They had already suffered losses at the hands of Cassius's archers and cannon fire, and an overwhelming number of hybrids were about to overtake them. They had no countermeasures to bring down the lyvulseropteras. Their only hope of defending themselves was to retreat to the ridge.

Master Titus and Matron Kavarova had noted the clumsy gait of the lyvulseropteras and their inability to fly. These creatures were too unwieldy to get through the heavy brush and the dense forest of the ridge. Given its steep ascent, they might not be able to climb it at all. A retreat to the ridge might well stop them from being effective as a weapon; however, it would not stop Cassius's other forces.

Once the ground troops moved past the lyvulseropteras (at a discreet distance), their advance would quicken considerably. As they did so,

Erwina's archers would have the high ground and could bring them down with greater accuracy at a shorter range. Some could scale the trees and target the hybrids. Any attempt to bring cannons up the ridge would prove difficult; however, it might not be necessary. The cannons need only be in range to fire on the eastern side of the ridge. If any attempt was made to bring the cannons up the ridge, Erwina's archers could target the men and beasts manning the cannons.

Since Cassius had not produced a dragon of his own to engage the red dragon, Master Titus signaled his lieutenants to fall back to the ridge in an apparent rout. Once they had reached about halfway up the eastern side, some archers could ascend into the trees while others remained on the ground. Given the steep slope of the ridge, even the archers on the ground would have an advantage. Other defenders would disappear into hidden caves and other hideouts on the ridge and wait until Cassius's forces had moved past them. Then, they could mount an attack from the rear. The Erwinians had anticipated a retreat and had planned for it. Hopefully, this strategy could buy their people at least another hour to evacuate.

Erwina's plan, however, did not include rescuing hapless villagers, some of whom might also have difficulty getting up the ridge due to their deformities. It also did not include a red dragon, whom Master Titus and Matron Kavarova now strongly suspected was Ruwena. Firstly, it had appeared abruptly and only after Ruwena had disappeared—not the first time an animal appeared suddenly when Ruwena went missing. Secondly, both Master Titus and Matron Kavarova were certain Ruwena would not abandon villagers. Yet without fire, she would not be able to overcome the swarm of hybrids headed toward her and the villagers. Those forces included another lyvulseroptera.

Perhaps the lyvulseroptera could be stopped—or at least delayed—by fire from another source. Master Titus was certain setting the grasslands afire would delay Cassius's other forces from advancing. The risk was the shifting winds, which would change the fire's direction. The red dragon's fire had shown that the winds were not blowing steadily in any one direction. Depending upon how the winds shifted, the fire could turn on the villagers, who might not be able to flee from it. In a truly disastrous turn of events, the wind could turn the fire on Erwina's defenders and spare Cassius's army. In any case, the red dragon could fly out of danger.

Matron Kavarova led their remaining forces back toward the ridge. She would command the battle from there. Master Titus stayed behind with a few of his scouts and archers. He would wait as long as he could before setting fire to the grasslands. Once the last of Erwina's forces began ascending the ridge, he would set the grasslands ablaze. By that time, Cassius's forces may have overrun the villagers. If not, the villagers might have some chance to outrun the fire depending upon their abilities.

A Holding Action

Ruwena saw Erwina's forces starting to fall back. The small group of archers that had interceded earlier were falling back too. This was just as well. She knew she would not be able to defend them or the villagers again until she could generate fire. She turned her attention back to the enemy forces headed toward her and the villagers. The villagers might be able to outrun the lyvulseroptera, but not Cassius's other creatures. Although she could still fight the hybrids, their sheer numbers might overwhelm her or trap her until she was within range of the lyvulseroptera's spit or the archers' arrows. Her scales would not withstand the destruction of the lyvulseroptera's venom, nor could they withstand an arrow sent with the force a strong bowman could generate. As yet, Cassius had not redeployed any of his archers against her.

Meanwhile, Ruwena had felt her saliva start to flow again. She had regained enough of her fire to attack the hybrids and drive them back temporarily. Much to her distress, it was not nearly enough to destroy the lyvulseroptera, and her fire was soon spent again. Ruwena had used her fire only once before this battle, when she cremated her mistress. In no way did that effort test her limits. Now she has learned that her ability to generate fire did have limits. Unfortunately, the time to be judicious in its use had passed.

Still, some attackers hesitated and advanced slowly. The hominids were not quite sure of the dragon's ability—or lack thereof—to generate fire. They would let the lyvulseroptera and hybrids find out. More importantly, they were not about to get in front of the lyvulseroptera. The hybrids continued to forge forward despite losses from the lyvulseroptera's poison. Since they were bred or engineered in isolation, they could not work as a team or a pack. A few who reached the dragon first were struck down by its fangs, claws, and tail. This outcome slowed the attack of the other hybrids at the front. Even so, the forward movement of hybrids in the rear pushed those in front toward the dragon.

Without her fire, Ruwena had no effective means to fight off a surge of hybrids unless she strafed them from the air. Doing so would put her at greater risk from Cassius's archers. Yet the sheer number of hybrids threatened to bring her down anyway unless she flew away from the battle.

Ruwena was certain that she would not prevail over her attackers without intervention from a force more powerful than she. In a blind act of desperation, she turned toward the northern mountains. With all the force she could muster, she cried out in the manner of dragons, "Cassius!"

Master Titus could see the dragon turn and face the north. He saw no fire, nor did he hear the dragon's call. He could see a mass of Cassius's hybrids advancing toward the villagers, who had resumed running away. Only the red dragon stood between the villagers and their attackers. Master Titus signaled to the small group of archers who had aided the villagers. They, too, could see the villagers' situation and turned back to intercede once again.

Erwina's archers had no idea why the red dragon had attacked Cassius's forces and not their own. Perhaps Cassius had committed some grievous act against the dragon in the past. Nevertheless, the group ran toward the villagers and flanked the dragon. They did so knowing full well that they could not withstand the onslaught without reinforcements. With Erwina in retreat, there would be none. They could only hope that the red dragon would regain its fire and force the hybrids back.

With the exception of Master Titus, all the Erwinians who had remained behind, including the archers, could transform into wolves or foxes. They could reach top speeds of thirty to forty-five miles per hour to outrun a grass fire. As a bighorn mountain sheep, Master Titus could reach a speed of twenty miles per hour. If spurred by high winds, a grassland fire can burn almost as fast. So if he set fire to the grasslands, he and the other Erwinians who stayed behind could outrun the fire if it turned their way. Most of the villagers would not.

CHAPTER 51

Unexpected Alliances

Commander Elisar had watched the conflict with considerable interest and had observed several valuable pieces of tactical information. Not the least of these was a way to destroy the lyvulseropteras—dragon fire. Elisar presumed the dragon belonged to Erwina. *How did they acquire one?* he wondered. Unfortunately, Biogenics did not have a dragon of their own. Apparently, neither did Cassius. Surely, if he still had one, he would have set it against the red dragon. A red dragon is no match for a Great Gray dragon.

A Waiting Game

Cassius had deployed all his remaining forces against Erwina and the dragon. There were none left to protect his rear. The main component of his forces were devoted to attacking the Erwinian fighters who were now in full retreat—with one singular exception. Erwina's commander Master Titus was not retreating with his forces. He and a few archers were staying behind. *What is he waiting for?* Commander Elisar asked himself. Those few soldiers would not withstand Cassius's attack, and they were not poised to defend the dragon. Other archers were serving that purpose, and they were too few.

For all practical purposes, the lyvulseropteras and the hybrids were leading Cassius's army and holding up the advance of Cassius's remaining forces. Even though they were following behind, most of their attention was focused on the ground immediately in front of them. *For good reason,* Elisar had to admit. Once Cassius's archers and cannon gunners could find safe ground, they could fire their weapons. If Biogenics attacked Cassius's rear, the lyvulseropteras would not be in a position to lead the fight against them. Still, as Biogenics forces advanced, they, too, would have to exercise the same precautions as did Cassius's forces. In fact, if Cassius were to send back any of his fighters to defend against Biogenics, both armies would be tiptoeing through the grasslands.

The red dragon possessed the only weapon that could destroy the lyvulseropteras. If Biogenics were to prevail in this battle, they needed the dragon to stay alive, regain its fire, and somehow not turn on them. There was urgency in this matter. The dragon would not remain alive long without its fire. It was being assaulted by a branch of Cassius's forces, including another lyvulseroptera. The few archers deployed to defend it would soon be overwhelmed, as would the dragon.

Commander Elisar realized his forces could not sit out this battle after all. He changed his strategy to accommodate the present state of affairs. He, too, decided on a two-pronged attack and issued orders for his forces to engage at once.

The Enemy of My Enemy

Commander Elisar immediately dispatched two *H. transformans* couriers—both red foxes—at top speed in an end run around the battlefield. One he sent around the northern edge to intercept Matron Kavarova, who was leading Erwina's forces in retreat. The other courier he sent around the southern edge, between the dragon and the retreating villagers, to intercept Master Titus. Both messages said the same thing: *We are coming to defeat Cassius. If you agree not to fire on us—dragon included—we will come to your aid as allies. Advise at once.*

Neither courier was assured a safe path to their destination. Hopefully, an attack from the rear would distract Cassius's troops away from the routes the couriers would take. Commander Elisar knew that one or both might not reach Erwina's commanders. If detected, both could be cut down by either Cassius's or Erwina's forces. If Cassius captured or killed them, he would acquire the communique and take warning. Then any hope of surprising him would be lost. Consequently, Commander Elisar decided to launch Biogenics's forces without waiting for a reply. Erwina's commanders were astute. They would discern immediately that Biogenics was attacking Cassius. Their concern would be whether or not their own forces would be next if Biogenics was able to defeat Cassius.

In fact, when Master Titus saw a sudden influx of fighters surging forward into the grasslands, he thought they represented a major influx of reinforcements for Cassius. This promptly triggered a decision to set fire to the grasslands. He was on the verge of doing so when Rachel called to him.

"Wait!" she shouted. "Those archers are not shooting at us. They are attacking Cassius's troops. Some have broken off and are taking aim at the hybrids that are attacking the dragon and the villagers." She turned to Master Titus. "Who are these people?" she asked.

Master Titus knew of only one other entity that maintained a standing army. "Biogenics," he answered. Then the question of Biogenics's intentions was raised in his mind. He sent one of his scouts to alert Matron Kavarova. That part of their strategy would remain unchanged. Once her forces reached high ground on the ridge, they would turn and attack Cassius's forces. Master Titus would wait to set fire to the grasslands until he could wait no longer.

Soon afterward, a red fox with a leather pouch strapped to its back raced up to him. When Master Titus read the message, he thought to himself, *The enemy of my enemy is my ally—if only temporarily.* His response was immediate. *Agreed—provided you will not turn upon us, if we win the day against Cassius. Advise at once.* Once again, the fox was dispatched back to Commander Elisar. Then Master Titus sent a courier of his own to Matron Kavarova. *Biogenics has attacked Cassius. They wish to be allied with us. Stand and fight as long as you can. Retreat when you must.*

Cassius was engaged now on two fronts. He did indeed mount a counterattack against Biogenics. He might not have any more lyvulseropteras to set against them; however, he had many cannons and a plentiful supply of hybrids. He redeployed several of his cannons toward his rear and ordered a large portion of his hybrids to turn back and attack Biogenics. *After all, Erwina's forces are scattered and running away,* he thought. *They have only a few archers and a spent dragon left in the fight.* This notion proved to be a costly misapprehension.

As soon as Matron Kavarova received Master Titus's message, she sent word throughout her remaining forces. "Take the fight to Cassius!" The battle was rejoined; however, there was still no means to counter the lyvulseropteras. The red dragon itself was embattled and unable to come to their aid.

Biogenics had sent some of their fighters to attack the hybrids converging on the dragon. Those fighters soon found themselves surrounded by a portion of the hybrids that Cassius had redeployed to the rear. Now they, too, desperately needed reinforcements. Yet no one from their own armed forces could come to their aid. They were fully engaged with Cassius's army. The best that they and Erwina's archers could do was hold back Cassius's forces as long as possible in the hope that the dragon would regain its fire.

CHAPTER 52

Form and Fury

Ruwena's cry had not fallen on deaf ears. The air carried it into the nether regions of the northeastern mountain range, where it echoed and reached the aeries of the Great Gray dragons. Most were alerted by the tone and sound of distress in the dragoness's cry but did not understand what it meant. It was not from one of their kindred, and it was a word they did not know.

Cassius

One dragon, however, recognized it instantly. He took flight immediately and was joined by two others of his clan. The two realized he was responding to the same cry they had heard. The fierce determination they sensed in their comrade and the rapid acceleration of his flight speed was enough to tell them that he was on a deadly mission. His mate had understood it as well. As much as she longed to join him, the dragoness could not. Although mobile and able to fly, she remained too disabled to attain the speeds that her mate would reach—and she had two young chicks to tend.

The aeries of the gray dragons were in the northeastern mountains to the east of the ridge and about three hundred miles from the grasslands of Erwina. At his top speed, it would take the gray dragon over an hour to reach the battlefield. The cry he heard was a desperate one. The dragon knew he might not arrive in time to render aid. Nevertheless, with grim determination, he pushed the limits of speed he could achieve. Although his companions could not keep up, they could travel fast enough to track his wake and continue to follow.

When the gray reached the battlefield, it appeared to be in complete disarray. At first, he couldn't tell who was fighting whom. It didn't matter. He was after Cassius. He spotted the red dragon immediately, along with a horde of creatures converging on it and a singularly bizarre creature facing off with it. The horde he recognized as creatures belonging to Cassius. He had seen them in the village where his mate had been kept captive. The red dragon—clearly the one whose call he had heard—was struggling to keep them at bay. The other strange creature he did not recognize. He noticed that the red dragon was trying to keep its distance from that one. The gray suspected that it belonged to Cassius too.

During the battles between the three armies, no one had been watching the skies looking for another dragon. Without knowing how, both Cassius and Biogenics assumed that the red dragon belonged to Erwina. So it didn't even occur to any of the commanders that another one might appear. At the same time, only Master Titus and Matron Kavarova were certain the dragon was Ruwena. With the battle joined, all attention was focused on the battlefield.

So when a Great Gray dragon suddenly appeared soaring over the battlefield, everyone was caught off guard again. All three armies on the main battlefield abruptly ceased their attacks—almost frozen in time—as they watched the gray dragon hover briefly. Once again, they assumed the gray was a predator. Perhaps he had heard the sounds of the fighting and had come seeking prey. None dared to move lest they draw its attention.

Suddenly, the gray went into a steep dive toward the red dragon. Master Titus and Matron Kavarova were horrified. *He is going to attack the red dragon!* they both thought. Ruwena would be lost, and they could do nothing to prevent it.

Not so. With his powerful fire, the gray strafed the creatures attacking the red dragon, including the lyvulseroptera. It was enough to wipe out the hybrids that fell under his fire. Unfortunately, it was too brief to kill the lyvulseroptera. Once again, the latter had tucked its head and neck beneath its armored plumage and survived the strafing.

Now Master Titus knew why Ruwena had turned to the north. She had called to the gray dragons for their help. *Where did she come to know a Great Gray dragon?* wondered Master Titus. *If I get out of this alive, I'm going to sit her down and find out.*

Then, Master Titus saw the gray turn and circle the main battlefield. The three armies were still—waiting to see what it would do next. The gray was searching for Cassius—the one entity he knew was his enemy. He found him quickly. Cassius's form stood out above all the rest of the combatants on the field—human, animal, or hybrid. Despite his deformity or perhaps because of it, he was a striking figure to behold. The gray dragon landed not too far away and turned to face Cassius.

Cassius knew this dragon. Somehow, despite his dementia, he remembered challenging it. Although he could not remember why, he sensed that he had prevailed over the dragon. In defiance, he stood apart from his forces and challenged the dragon to single combat. In his enraged state, he attempted to transform once again into his most fearsome alternate species, the wild boar. He no longer recognized that he was already trapped in it—half man, half boar. He never considered that a wild boar could not withstand a dragon's fire. The stress of battle and his fury must have activated within him some capability to transform. Those not too far away could see a change occurring in his features and his form. It was enough to complete Cassius's descent into madness. With a guttural roar, he charged the dragon (illus. 31).

The gray dragon waited. Cassius's fate was already determined. He was simply racing to meet it.

As the gray reared back to rain his fire upon Cassius, Cassius suddenly stumbled and fell to the ground. His roar was blended with a scream. He had run across the ground over which the lyvulseroptera had drooled and had stepped in its venom. His booted foot and hoof were being eaten away. When he fell, it was into another pool of the lyvulseroptera's drool. Now the flesh of his arms and chest was disintegrating.

The gray dragon was inclined to let Cassius suffer. His mate had suffered greatly at his hands. Then he heard the red dragoness call to him. "He was not always like this," she said. "Do not let him suffer this way."

The gray recognized the voice. He remembered the child and the old woman who had cared for his mate and recalled their efforts to free her. He complied with the dragoness's request, and Cassius was no more. Not even his ashes remained.

Illus. 31. Form and Fury.

The gray then surveyed the rest of the battlefield. Once again, Commander Elisar had carefully withdrawn from it. He saw no need to engage with a gray dragon whose fire was far from spent. While the dragon's attention was focused on Cassius, Erwina's forces also withdrew back toward the ridge. The archers who had flanked the red dragon transformed into their alternate species and quickly blended into the grasslands as they headed back to rejoin their comrades at the ridge.

Both Erwina and Biogenics had sufficient opportunity to retreat out of the main battlefield. So also did the human component of Cassius's army. The hybrids, including the lyvulseropteras, knew nothing of gray dragons and automatically charged at him. The gray had no difficulty dispatching them, including the remaining lyvulseropteras. This action served to distract him away from the retreating forces. By the time he was finished, the battlefield had cleared. The Great Gray dragon had won the day.

Scattered around the field of battle were the dragoness, Master Titus with his scouts (who had stayed with him despite his order to retreat), and the villagers who were huddled some distance away. Once again, the dragoness called to the gray, "All who remain here are my friends or villagers who were oppressed by Cassius and also suffered at his hands. Thank you for saving us."

"It was a promise I made to myself," the gray replied. "As soon as I heard you, Cassius's fate was sealed. My mate now has two chicks. Thanks to you and your mistress, my line will continue."

"I have one more request," spoke the dragoness.

The gray looked at her. "What would the Mistress of H'Aleth have me do?" he asked.

Ruwena was surprised by the way he addressed her. Still, she replied, "Set fire to the battlefield. Destroy all traces of the poison the lyvulseropteras spat and drooled upon the land. Your fire will cleanse it and allow it to grow back again."

The gray complied and returned to the dragoness. "Farewell, H'Ester of the House of H'Aleth. Perhaps one day we will meet again, and my clan will come to know you as we once knew others of your clan." The gray then turned away and, after a brief, lumbering gallop, lifted off to return to the mountains. His comrades, who had caught up with him, joined him in the return flight. They had not joined the gray in the attack. This was definitely his fight. They had been present only to back him up.

Meanwhile, Matron Kavarova had ordered Erwina's forces to continue across the ridge to the river. She had stayed behind, anxiously watching and waiting. If the gray dragon turned on everyone, she would have to report the deaths of Ruwena, Master Titus, and the scouts who stayed on the field. Hopefully, the gray would not pursue them across the ridge or the river. As she watched the proceedings on the field, she was relieved when the gray flew away—and then shocked when she saw two more join him in flight.

The dragoness also took flight and landed again some distance away. Madam Kavarova suddenly realized that she may have been injured and unable to continue flying. She transformed into a gray wolf and raced back to meet up with Master Titus. Master Titus spoke with Matron Kavarova privately, "The red dragon and Ruwena are one, as we suspected. She is all right and has simply moved away to transform back to human form."

As Ruwena rested to resume her native form, she wondered if her mistress had told the gray dragoness who they were. *It would not have been like her to reveal our identities,* she thought to herself. *So how does a Great Gray dragon know who I am?* Ruwena covered as much of her torso as her smock could accommodate and slipped into a deep sleep. When she awoke the next day, Master Titus and Matron Kavarova were waiting a short distance away. Their forces had returned to Erwina. A few scouts remained behind to keep watch and to man the barge that would carry them across the river.

Oh no, Ruwena thought to herself, but she was too tired to transform into anything else. When they reached the western bank of the river, scouts with horses were waiting to accompany them back to the compound. Matron Aquina had rescinded her evacuation order, and most of the villagers were headed home.

A New Home

Shortly thereafter, Biogenics and Erwina met to forge a truce. Both parties agreed not to attack each other. Biogenics ceded H'Aleth's former territory to Erwina. This was done with the understanding that, if the House of H'Aleth were restored, it would be a party to the treaty as if it had been sitting at the treaty table. They did not know that H'Aleth's Mistress was seated at the table and, indeed, was a party to it. Form IV students were also in attendance. This provided them with a field exercise in developing alliances, treaties, and agreements.

Both parties also agreed to keep watch over the Cassius Foundation. Cassius might have been defeated, but the Foundation remained. Its new leadership would not forget their defeat, nor would they forgive Biogenics's role in it. There would be no truce with the Cassius Foundation. There was no doubt it would rebuild itself and try again to reassert its domination.

Under Erwina's auspices, Ruwena invited the villagers who had fled from Cassius to stay in H'Aleth's territory. As Matron Aquina had thought, it was the younger Erwinians eager for a new adventure who provided most of the support in establishing a village. They helped their new neighbors build houses as they are built in Erwina's grasslands. When the first village was finally built, it did serve as an outpost.

Evan, who had been stationed at the northeast outpost, soon joined Ruwena. It wasn't long before they were wed.

Over time, the Erwinians taught the villagers how to grow and harvest grains and strawberries. They brought egg-laying hens and showed the villagers how the hens' eggs could be a continuous source of food. In doing so, they taught the villagers the value of keeping and caring for the hens—not eating them.

The Erwinians also demonstrated how the villagers could trade their products—grains, strawberries, eggs—for other products made in Erwina's villages. In this manner, they would be able to sustain themselves. The Erwinians also taught the villagers to observe native wildlife. The animals can alert them to danger and should not be killed unless one of them attacked a villager. Later, the villagers would learn that many of these animals were scouts.

Dr. Jozefa and Dr. Stuvidicus would rotate coming to the new village to treat injuries and illness. Gregor provided therapy for any human-hybrid deformities and disabilities amenable to treatment. In turn, many of the hybrids were willing to give samples of their DNA to Gregor's geneticists. Thus, Gregor discovered a wealth of information about the outcomes of manipulating genes—expected and unexpected.

As Ruwena had anticipated, the villagers were eager to defend their new home and to set watch on Cassius's territory. Ruwena encouraged some of them to visit their old villages. "Let the villagers know that there is a place they can go for a better life—a place they could call home," she told them. Once again, the House of H'Aleth would become be a safe haven.

This brought one of Biogenics's wishes to fruition. Cassius's resources were being depleted as more and more *H. transformans* and hominids left Cassius villages and immigrated to H'Aleth.

Finally, the young Erwinians and the hominids worked together to build a new manor. The ruins of the old manor were designated a monument to the people who died defending the first House of H'Aleth.

Ruwena kept her adopted name among her friends and those who had always known her as Ruwena. To the villagers, she was known as H'Ester, Mistress of the House of H'Aleth. Thus, with the support of her sister Houses, H'Ester fulfilled the task her mistress, H'Ilgraith, had laid upon her. The House of H'Aleth was restored.

EPILOGUE

A pair of red foxes—a male (Evan, Master of the House of H'Aleth) and a female (Ruwena, Mistress of the House of H'Aleth)—were sitting together atop a grassy knoll. After a while, they both departed together and resumed their patrol over their territory. Just as the female's great-great-grandparents had done long ago, the two foxes kept a careful watch on the skies, listened for sounds, and sniffed for scents that indicated creatures not native to the region had entered it. If any evidence was detected, the male would investigate it on the ground while the female transformed into a Cooper's hawk and followed him in the air. In this manner, they worked together to find and identify the strangers. Both knew that danger would never be far away. Eventually, their House would come under siege again.

Appendix A

Genealogy of the House of H'Aleth

The Sister Lineage

Founders

Edvar H'Aleth Sr.

Lineage: Unknown. Head of the House of H'Aleth.

Description: A tall man of strong build, with pleasant features, brown hair, and brown eyes.

Transforms within *Canidae*.

Alternate species: Gray wolf, red fox.

Biography: Married to Ruth. After an attempted abduction of Ruth and one of their daughters, they moved with their extended family to a remote location with a few scattered villages. These villages were independent and not under the yoke of either Biogenics or Cassius. They settled on unclaimed land, where they built a new home and reestablished gardens and grainfields. They were soon joined by friends and neighbors to whom they sent word that *H. transformans* were neither persecuted nor pursued in the new territory. Over many years, other *H. transformans* who were being threatened by Cassius or Biogenics found surcease in the House of H'Aleth.

Ruth H'Aleth (ped. 6)

Lineage: Unknown. Designated the founder of subsequent lineages that can transform across both mammalian and avian families.

Description: A slender woman of slight build, with pleasant features, dark-brown hair, and amber eyes.

Transforms across mammalian and avian classes, including *Canidae, Felidae, Lontra, Falconidae, Accipitridae, Strigidae.*

Alternate species: Gray wolf, gray fox, cougar, lynx, river otter, peregrine falcon, Cooper's hawk, long-eared (woodland) owl.

Biography: Married to Edvar H'Aleth and first Mistress of the House of H'Aleth. With her husband, she established a territory that offered sanctuary to *H. transformans* and anyone fleeing from oppression by the Cassius Foundation or Biogenics Corporation. She had two sons and three daughters. All three daughters—H'Anna, H'Ophelia, and H'Elena—and their subsequent female progeny who were $2X^T$ could transform across multiple families. Her daughters became the first Sisters of the House of H'Aleth. She died of old age and did not see the destruction of her House.

Children of Edvar and Ruth H'Aleth (Second Generation, Male and Female, in Order of Birth)

Edvar Jr. (X^T, Y)

Lineage: Firstborn son of Edvar and Ruth.

Description: Favored his mother in build and features.

Transforms within *Canidae* family.

Alternate species: Gray wolf and red fox.

H'Anna ($2X^T$)

Lineage: Second child and first daughter of Edvar and Ruth.

Description: A slender woman, tall, with light-brown hair, and greyish-brown eyes.

Transforms across across mammalian and avian classes, including *Canidae, Felidae, Falconidae,* and *Strigidae,*

Alternate species: Red fox, gray fox, cougar, peregrine falcon, great horned owl.

Biography: As Ruth's first daughter, H'Anna established the standard by which she, her sisters, and all subsequent Sisters of the House of H'Aleth would be prepared to defend themselves, their family, and their House and be prepared to lead the House of H'Aleth. Thus, H'Anna and her sisters received the same level of instruction and training as did their brothers. In addition, Ruth mentored her daughters as they learned to transform from one alternate species directly into another alternate species and do so in midair (for avian species) and in the water (all species).

H'Ophelia ($2X^T$)

Lineage: Third child and second daughter of Edvar and Ruth. Mother of H'Elvinia and H'Assandra and great-grandmother of H'Ester.

Description: Favored her mother in form and features; however, she had auburn-red hair and amber eyes.

Transforms across mammalian and avian classes, including *Canidae, Felidae, Falconidae, Strigidae.*

Alternate species: Red wolf, gray fox, cougar, peregrine falcon, long-eared owl.

Biography: In retrospect, H'Ophelia was another matriarch of the House of H'Aleth. It was through her line that descendants of Ruth continued through the *maternal* line (ped. 7).

H'Elena ($2X^T$)

Lineage: Fourth child and third daughter of Edvar and Ruth and mother of H'Ilgraith and H'Umara.

Description: Favored her father in features, the tallest of her sisters, slender, with brown eyes.

Transforms across mammalian and avian classes, including *Canidae, Felidae, Accipitridae, Strigidae.*

Alternate species: Gray wolf, red fox, lynx, Cooper's hawk, great horned owl.

Biography: Two of her children, H'Umara and Edwin, became advocates of the rational use of genetics to support members of *H. transformans.* Her son Edwin became an advocate for the judicious use of genetic engineering and joined the House of Gregor when it was formed. This established a sound relationship between the House of H'Aleth and the House of Gregor. When his sister H'Umara married into the House of Erwina, H'Elena joined forces with Ruth to forge the tight bonds that developed among the three Houses.

Edmond (X^T, Y)

Lineage: Fifth and last child, second son of Edvar and Ruth.

Description: Favored his father in build and features except for having dark-red hair. He was as tall as H'Elena and taller than his brother.

Transforms within *Canidae* family.

Alternate species: Red wolf, gray fox.

Grandchildren of Edvar and Ruth H'Aleth (Third Generation, Female Offspring Listed Only, in Alphabetical Order)

H'Assandra (2X^T) (ped. 7)

Lineage: Daughter of H'Ophelia.

Description: Tall, statuesque, with auburn-brown hair and brown eyes.

Transforms across mammalian and avian classes, including *Canidae, Felidae,* and *Accipitridae.*

Alternate species: Gray wolf, red fox, lynx, red-tailed hawk, and golden eagle.

Biography: A Sister in the House of H'Aleth and eligible to become Mistress. With the death of Ruth, she stepped aside, allowing her niece H'Ossana to assume the role of Mistress. H'Assandra did not flee when H'Aleth was attacked. At over eighty years of age, she elected to stay and defend her House. She sent her granddaughters H'Alicia and H'Onora to Erwina, thereby preserving her line. Her son and daughter-in-law remained with her. They were killed there when a Great Gray dragon attacked the manor.

H'Elvinia (2X^T) (ped. 7)

Lineage: Daughter of H'Ophelia and mother of H'Osanna and H'Eleanora.

Description: Medium height, with light-brown hair and brown eyes.

Transforms across mammalian and avian classes, including *Canidae, Felidae, Lontra, Falconidae, Accipitridae, Strigidae.*

Alternate species: Red fox, gray fox, cougar, river otter, peregrine falcon, Cooper's hawk, long-eared owl.

Biography: A Sister in the House of H'Aleth and eligible to become Mistress. She was killed with her sister H'Assandra and her daughter H'Ossana defending their House.

H'Ilgraith [hil-*grāy*-ĭth] (2X[T])

    Lineage: Daughter of H'Elena and granddaughter of Edvar and Ruth

    Description: Tall, thin, with brown-black hair and dark-brown eyes

    Transforms across mammalian and avian classes, including *Canidae, Mustelidae, Felidae,* and *Strigidae.*

    Alternate species: Gray fox, badger, lynx, and great horned owl.

    Biography: A Sister in the House of H'Aleth, she escaped the destruction of H'Aleth. As the eldest of two surviving Sisters, she became Mistress of the House of H'Aleth in exile—a title she could never acknowledge. She raised H'Ester, daughter of H'Eleanora and the next Mistress of the House of H'Aleth, from infancy. H'Ilgraith kept H'Ester's heritage a secret to protect her until she came of age, was in command of her abilities to transform, and was prepared to reestablish the House of H'Aleth. H'Ilgraith died before she knew she had accomplished her task.

H'Umara [hu-*mar*-a] (2X[T])

    Lineage: Daughter of H'Elena and granddaughter of Edvar and Ruth

    Biography: H'Umara trained as a physician at Gregor. Through her experience at Gregor, she became a proponent of genetic counseling with selective breeding for the purposes of maintaining lineage (without inbreeding) and strengthening a genetic profile (to decrease risk of genetic diseases). When she married her husband, she joined his House, the House of Erwina, where she served as chief physician. This strengthened the sound relationship among the three Houses of H'Aleth, Gregor, and Erwina.

Great-Grandchildren of Edvar and Ruth H'Aleth (Fourth Generation, Female Offspring Listed Only, in Alphabetical Order)

H'Eleanora [*hĕl*-ĕ-an-*or*-ah] (2X[T])

    Lineage: Second daughter of H'Elvinia and mother of H'Ester.

    Description: Favored her grandmother H'Ophelia, tall and slender with dark-brown hair and amber eyes.

    Transforms across mammalian and avian classes, including *Canidae, Felidae, Cervidae,* and *Strigidae* families.

    Alternate species: Red fox, cougar, white-tailed deer, long-eared owl.

    Biography: As a Sister, she was eligible to become its Mistress. She died from complications of childbirth. Before her death, she tasked H'Igraith to raise and protect her infant daughter, whom she named H'Ester.

H'Osanna (2X^T)

Lineage: First daughter of H'Elvinia.

Description: Favored her grandmother H'Ophelia, slender with dark-brown hair and brown eyes.

Transforms across mammalian and avian classes, including *Canidae, Felidae, Lontra, Falconidae, Accipitridae, Strigidae.*

Alternate species: Red fox, cougar, river otter, peregrine falcon, Cooper's hawk, golden eagle, long-eared owl.

Biography: Born into the House of H'Aleth, she was a direct descendant of Ruth and a Sister. With the deaths of Ruth and H'Eleanora, she was eligible to become Mistress of the House of H'Aleth. She assumed this role when her aunt H'Assandra, who was nearing eighty years of age, stepped aside. H'Osanna's husband and two sons stayed with her to defend H'Aleth and were killed there. Her grandchildren, including her granddaughter H'Isabella, fled to Erwina with their mother before H'Aleth was attacked. Like her cousins H'Alicia and H'Onora, H'Isabella was a Sister of the House of H'Aleth through the *paternal* line.

Great-Great-Grandchildren of Edvar and Ruth H'Aleth (Fifth Generation, Female Offspring Listed Only, in Alphabetical Order)

H'Alicia (2X^T)

Lineage: Granddaughter of H'Assandra and a Sister of the House of H'Aleth through the *paternal* line.

Description: Favored her mother, medium height with blond hair and blue eyes.

Transforms across mammalian and avian classes, including *Canidae, Felidae,* and *Accipitridae.*

Alternate species: Gray wolf, gray fox, lynx, red-tailed hawk, and golden eagle.

Biography: A Sister in the House of H'Aleth, she was sent to the House of Erwina with her sister H'Onora. Her parents remained at H'Aleth to defend their House and were killed there. With the deaths of their parents, H'Alicia and H'Onora were accepted into the House of Erwina as were all other children of H'Aleth whose parents were lost.

H'Ester (Ruwena) (3X^T)

Lineage: Daughter of H'Eleanora and great-great-granddaughter of Ruth through the *maternal* line.

Description: Favored her mother, H'Eleanora, slender with dark-brown hair and amber eyes.

Transforms across multiple mammalian and avian classes including *Canidae, Felidae, Falconidae, Strigidae, Lontra, Dragonensis.*

Alternate species: Gray wolf, red fox, cougar, peregrine falcon, Cooper's hawk, long-eared owl, river otter, red dragon.

Biography: One of two surviving descendants of Ruth through the maternal line after the destruction of H'Aleth. She became Mistress of the House of H'Aleth in exile after the death of H'Ilgraith. With the support of the House of Erwina, she reestablished the House of H'Aleth. She married Evan of the House of Erwina, who then became Master of the House of H'Aleth. Her daughters H'Arianna and H'Edwina continued the maternal lineage of Ruth.

H'Onora (2X^T)

Lineage: Granddaughter of H'Assandra, daughter of H'Assandra's son and a Sister of the House of H'Aleth through the *paternal* line.

Description: Favored her grandmother, tall with auburn-brown hair and grayish-brown eyes.

Transforms across mammalian and avian classes, including *Canidae, Felidae,* and *Accipitridae.*

Alternate species: Red wolf, gray fox, lynx, red-tailed hawk, and golden eagle.

Biography: Fled to the House of Erwina with her sister just days before H'Aleth fell.

Ped. 6. Pedigree for Sisters of House of H'Aleth

Ped. 6. Pedigree for Sisters of the House of H'Aleth

Key to Pedigree Chart

Female with no transforming chromosome (X,X)	Male with no transforming Chromosome (X,X)
Female with one transforming chromosome (X,X^T)	Male with one transforming chromosome (X^T,Y)
Female with two transforming chromosomes (X^T,X^T) (2X^T)	Male with two transforming chromosomes (2X^T,Y)(trisomy)
	Female with three transforming chromosomes (3X^T) (trisomy)

Marriage or coupling

Descendants

HS = *Homo sapiens*

Ped. 7. Pedigree for Descendants of H'Ophelia

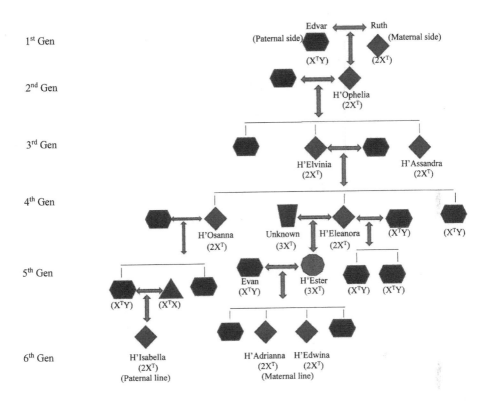

Ped. 7, Descendants of H'Ophelia

2nd Gen

3rd Gen

4th Gen

5th Gen

6th Gen

Key to Pedigree Chart

Female with no transforming
chromosome (X,X) (HS)

Female with one transforming
chromosome (X,X^T) ◄

Female with two transforming
chromosomes (X^T,X^T) (2X^T) ◆

Male with no transforming
Chromosome (X,Y) [HS]

Male with one transforming
chromosome (X^T,Y) ⬡

Male with two transforming
chromosomes (2X^T,Y)(trisomy)

Marriage or coupling ↕

Descendants ↔

Female with three transforming
chromosomes (3X^T) (trisomy X^T) ⬤

HS = *Homo sapiens*

Appendix B

A Sound Education

The House of Erwina had agreed to focus on education for the children and youth of all the Houses. Here, children would learn more than the rules of transformation. There were many other subjects that helped prepare them for life in their world. Representatives of all three Houses agreed that language, mathematics, sciences, history, ethics, vocational training, physical fitness, and readiness were essential for a sound education. They felt that these areas of study would provide their children with the knowledge and skills needed to sustain themselves in their community and help preserve it. Thus, the initial emphasis was on literacy, arithmetic followed by mathematics, and vocational education and training. All three Houses provided resources to build a schoolhouse that would provide dormitory space, classrooms, a library, and laboratories.

Most children started attending school at the age of five. Children sent from the other Houses often came to Erwina at four years of age. This gave them ample time to adjust to their new surroundings, learn their way around the compound, meet the people who would be their teachers and their classmates, and learn the House rules for Erwina, in general, and the schoolhouse, in particular.

Children were taught to read, write, and do arithmetic when they began formal schooling. Before that time, children of Erwina were expected to learn at home to speak their language (everyday use), recite all letters of the alphabet and recognize each letter, and count to at least thirty and recognize numbers one through ten when written. Children who came from other houses at an early age had the opportunity to gain these skills by attending preschool at age four.

Virtually every adult member of Erwina (eighteen years of age and above), regardless of where they lived, was expected to assist younger members achieve a sound and practical education. Even if villagers were not teachers in the schoolhouse, they were expected to proctor, mentor, tutor, and provide informal instruction or training to any students they encountered. Every village could expect students to come for some kind of field exercise or expedition. Even though the students would be accompanied by one or more faculty members from the school, all adults were expected to engage with the students.

Curriculum

The school year was divided into three terms and two summer practicums or one internship (table 5). Each term was eleven weeks in duration, which included ten weeks of instruction and one week of exams. There was a three-week interval between each term for students to travel to their home village and visit with their families. In addition, there were two two-week breaks, one immediately after the spring term and one just before the fall term to allow students to return home. Prior to the start of summer sessions, one week was set aside for the summer games. There were two summer sessions of four weeks each (practicums) or one eight-week session (internship). Practicums and internships could be done in home villages or regions with approval of the faculty and the availability of a preceptor or mentor in the home village.

Table 5. The School Year

Table 5. The School Year	
School year terms	Duration in weeks
Fall term	11
Fall vacation	3
Winter term	11
Winter vacation	3
Spring term	11
Spring break	2
Summer games	1
Summer sessions	8
Practicums (2)	4 each
Internship	8
Summer break	2

The curriculum (tables 6 through 9) for each form was a mixture of formal classroom presentations and associated practice sessions, supervised field experience, and independent practice in a setting of the student's choice. Field experiences for students in Form I were limited to the compound. For Form II students and above, the experience could be gained in any location within Erwina's region of influence as long as a qualified mentor was available. Only Form IV students were allowed to gain experience in a remote site beyond Erwina's region of influence (e.g., scouting expeditions).

The sciences were emphasized along with vocational training. All three Houses had agreed this course of study would best meet their needs given the social and geopolitical environments in which they lived. Consequently, with the exception of music (mathematics), sketching and painting (botany, biology, geography, glassmaking), and graphic drawing (design and construction), the arts were largely missing. Students were encouraged to pursue these and other areas of study as they had time and opportunity (which they didn't).

Faculty members at Erwina designed a formal program of study for children, starting at age five to young adults up to age sixteen. Their studies included basic education (e.g., reading, writing, arithmetic, and mathematics), knowledge of the biologic sciences (including biology, botany, biochemistry, and genetics), environmental sciences (e.g., geography, hydrology, geology, climatology, inorganic chemistry), and courses in research, governance, and ethics.

Students did not sit in a classroom all day. Approximately one-half of their school day during fall and spring terms was devoted to didactic classes, while the other half was dedicated to gaining practical experience. Practicums and field expeditions allowed students to gain experience in the actual setting and practice what they learned in the classroom. Form I students used their experiences to hone their senses, learn about their environment, and develop manual dexterity. Form II and Form III students continued to expand their knowledge, learn new skills, develop their dexterity, and become competent and independent. Although all students were encouraged to complete Form IV, some needed to return to their villages at the end of Form III. Students who wanted to develop leadership skills, become scouts, or matriculate to Gregor were required to complete Form IV.

Specific transformation classes were developed to prepare both *H. sapiens* and *H. transformans* students for the process of transformation. In these classes, they learned how to transform, the risks associated with transformation, and how to avoid the latter. Many field expeditions in Forms I and II exposed students to animals into which they might someday transform. Once students learned the animals' natural behaviors, these behaviors would seem less foreign to them when they first transformed. Field expeditions in Form III allowed those that could transform an opportunity to practice in field settings.

Vocational training and internships were provided in multiple arenas including mechanics, hydraulics, construction and engineering, manufacturing and forging, agriculture, forestry, animal husbandry, and the management of natural resources. These courses provided students with the knowledge to work in almost any area of productivity at Erwina. Field internships provided students with an opportunity to develop their skills and gain experience in these areas. Subsequently, they would have both the knowledge and the experience to choose the area where they would most like to work (or second most, depending upon manpower requirements).

A few advanced courses prepared students for specialization in a particular area, including research, medicine, and genetics. These courses were intended largely for those students who would continue their study in these arenas at Gregor.

In Form IV, students completed their education and prepared to work in their chosen arenas. In junior year internships, students became proficient in performing tasks and operations undertaken by the areas in which they will work. In senior year internships, students learned to manage these operations. By the time students graduated from the schoolhouse, their transition into the workforce was seamless.

All students engaged in physical fitness activities. Athletics and martial arts programs as well as sporting events (e.g., soccer, track and field, gymnastics, etc.) taught the skills and techniques for both survival and defense. These activities also prepared *H. transformans* students for the physical characteristics and maneuvers often encountered in their alternate species.

Students advanced through the curriculum as they become more astute and practiced. They were allowed to advance at their own rate based on intellectual ability, self-discipline, and demonstration of proficiency in required skills. The majority of students tended to advance with their fellow classmates in their Form.

Evacuation Exercises

Like H'Aleth, Erwina had no standing army. Its limited defenses could buy only so much time. Thus, it was critical that both students and adults have the knowledge, skills, and judgment to use the resources available to them. Evacuation exercises were scenario-based challenges in which students were obliged to use their skills and knowledge to escape danger. They were designed to both develop and test students' abilities to respond to danger. All students were expected to participate, including novice Form I freshman and sophomores. They needed to learn as quickly as possible what to do in a disaster. Their lives and those of others depended upon it.

These exercises were conducted every year at a randomly selected time. Students were not notified in advance that an alarm was actually an exercise. The scenarios students faced were designed to be as realistic as possible. They would vary with the type of danger posed (natural, manmade, corrupted creature, etc.), the direction from which the danger would come, and the obstacles presented to the students, which never failed to include transformed faculty members. Students must escape from danger by navigating any combination of tunnels, hemp-rope networks, low-lying rocky escarpments, nearby caves, and other resources. These exercises and the summer games were the only times that faculty, as role players, were allowed to transform into their alternate species to threaten a student.

The exercises usually occurred in early light before sunrise or at dusk shortly after sunset when natural light is low. Students were not allowed to light their way unless conditions would be unsafe. Certified *H. transformans* students were allowed to transform into their alternate species provided conditions warrant the transformation and there is sufficient time to transform safely. Given shadowy conditions, faculty and staff and Form IV students were widely dispersed to watch the students' performance, provide a safety net, and role-play as predators or enemies to spook a student or catch an unwary one.

Faculty evaluated the outcome of the exercise based on assessment of technical skills in traversing a route of escape, success in evading an enemy or predator, success in reaching the end of the exercise, and students' judgment and decision-making used during the exercise. Students were not to engage an enemy or a predator unless they have no other option for escape. This would be the case in a real disaster or attack. The students' duty was to help one another escape and evade capture. In an actual attack, Form IV students and any students skilled in archery could use their weapons to aid their escape and avoid capture.

Core Scenario and Expected Outcomes

Faculty and staff alert the students of an imminent danger.

Students should shutter all windows and muster quietly for an evacuation. In the event of an enemy attack, students should not raise any visible or audible alarms in order to avoid alerting the approaching enemy that it has been spotted or where students may be found.

Adults (faculty and staff) assemble a defensive force and leave the compound to intercept the threat. (In reality, the faculty and staff go to their assigned positions around the compound to watch and intercept the students.)

Students devise an appropriate plan of action. This includes identifying potential routes of escape, maintaining surveillance, mustering younger students, and assigning proctors to guide and reassure them. They establish watch posts, if indicated.

Students should evacuate the schoolhouse in a timely manner and in a direction away from the approaching danger. They are expected to evade capture, with more experienced students protecting younger students. (The faculty make sure this is easier said than done.)

In the event of an enemy attack, the students should evacuate by the tunnels to minimize any sign or sound of their escape. Students are expected to know which tunnels to use and how to get to them.

Students are expected to modify their strategy to avoid capture. Older more experienced students are expected to adjust their escape route(s) in response to obstacles put in the students' way.

All students are expected to adhere to the House rules.

Sporting Events

Although not mandatory, sporting events were incorporated into the program of study. Athletics served multiple purposes. During the long school year, they provided a release for pent-up energy. They also provided physical exercise to maintain skills and endurance. During the summer, the competitive nature of the games enticed students to hone the skills they might need, both as humans and in their alternate species, in a setting that minimized the risk of injury. Finally, every sport was selected to give students the skills and stamina they would need to escape from danger. There were no blood sports in Erwina. Native wild or domestic animals were not involved in any of the games. Moving targets in an archery competition were artificial.

Faculty encouraged all students from Form I junior year and above to compete in an event of their choice and provided guidance regarding which event(s) a student may select. To minimize the risk of injuries, students were not allowed to participate in an event if they lacked sufficient skill in that event. Form I freshmen and sophomore students were expected to watch and learn—and root for their favorite individual or team—in anticipation of the time when they would be allowed to compete.

With the exception of rescue swimming (an individual event) and soccer (a team event), the rest of the sports had both individual and team events. Faculty with expertise and recognized skill in an event served as judges. Form IV students with similar qualifications also served as judges.

Competitors (students) are matched based on age, height, weight, and level of skill as appropriate for the skill involved. Consequently, the majority of competitions were among students within one or two years of each other. Thus, most competitions occur within a Form, although the seniors in a lower Form could compete with freshman in the next Form. Faculty and Form IV seniors served as referees. Students and other Erwinians not participating in a given event were encouraged to root for the individual or team of their choice; however, they were not allowed to advise them. The outcome of the games were judged based on criteria established for a given activity (box 12).

Box 12. Criteria for Judging Events.

Criteria for Evaluating Evacuation Drills and Predator-Prey Games

1. Selecting the route(s) of escape.
2. Adapting and changing the plan when route of escape is blocked.
3. Dividing and merging with other teams or individuals, as conditions warrant.
4. Selecting when to transform (safely) and what alternate species to select (appropriate to environment and situation).
5. Ability to distinguish hazardous from nonhazardous situations in the scenario.
6. Response to hazards introduced in scenario (including transformed faculty).
7. Support and protection of other participants are encountered in exercise.
8. *Students are not to engage the enemy or a predator unless they have no other option for escape.*

Box 12

The *H. transformans* students did not transform into their alternate species during standard sporting events. Students were forbidden to compete to determine which student can transform into what and how fast. First and foremost, transformation was not a game. Students were reminded that a rapid transformation can result in an incomplete or aborted transformation with permanent malformations and disfigurement— provided the student survives. Secondly, *H. transformans* students would have an unfair advantage over the *H. sapiens* students.

Table 6. Curriculum for Form I

Learning Objectives

1. Basic knowledge that prepares the student to continue learning independently (reading, writing, arithmetic)
2. Basic knowledge that prepares the student to live independently (animal and plant species, care of farm animals, raising crops, seasons, weather patterns, energy sources)
3. Basic knowledge that prepares the student to avoid and survive danger (safety measures, purifying water, swimming, gymnastics, horseback riding)

Year/Term	Fall	Winter	Spring
Freshman (age 5)	Reading and writing I	Reading and writing II	Reading and writing III
	Arithmetic I (adding numbers up to two columns)	Arithmetic II (subtracting numbers up to two columns)	Arithmetic III (adding and subtracting more than two columns)
	Identification of native mammal species in the region with field experience within perimeter	Identification of native bird species in the region with practicum in aviary and within compound perimeter	Identification of native small reptiles and amphibians with practicum at the pond and stream
	Identification of common wild berries and nuts native to the region with field experience within perimeter	Identification of common vegetables with practicum in botanical garden	Identification of common flowers native to the region with practicum in flower garden and field experience within perimeter
	Sources of energy and their use—solar with field observations	Sources of energy and their use—wind with field observations (weather permitting)	Sources of energy and their use—water with observations at the watermill and stream
	Protocol and etiquette in the classroom (schoolhouse and classroom rules)	Safety measures I—reporting strangers, a fire, a strange animal, etc. and following directions in evacuation.	Propriety and decorum in the manor house (formal manners with practice in afternoon teas)
	Athletics—swimming (no diving)	Athletics—swimming (no diving)	Athletics—horseback riding
	Athletics—horseback riding	Athletics—basic gymnastics	Athletics—basic gymnastics

411

Year/Term	Fall	Winter	Spring
Sophomore (age 6)	Reading and writing IV (including grammar, spelling, and punctuation)	Reading and writing V (including grammar, spelling, and punctuation)	Reading and writing VI (including grammar, spelling, and punctuation)
	Arithmetic IV (multiplying by a single number)	Arithmetic V (multiplying by two or more numbers)	Arithmetic VI (dividing by a single number)
	Common weather events and their patterns I—fall and winter (snow, sleet, ice, freezing rain) and seasonal changes with observations, when applicable	Sources of energy and their use—steam power with observation in steam generators and facilities where energy is needed 24 hours/day	Common weather events and their patterns II—spring and summer (heat, humidity, thunderstorms, tornados, hurricanes, and seasonal changes with observations
	Identification of common fruits with practicums in grapevines, grove trees	Processing fruits with practicum in the winery	Sources of energy and their use—manpower and animals with field observations
	Telling time I—via sun dial and sun position in the sky (summer sun)	Telling time II—via the bell towers and sun position in the sky (winter sun)	Telling time III—of the month by moon phases
	Safety measures II—Identification of poisonous plants (e.g., mushrooms) and animals (e.g., frogs, snakes) with field experience	Safety measures III—sheltering in place, securing dormitory rooms and windows with practicum in dorm classroom and tunnels	Identification of common herbs (nonmedicinal) with practicums in herb garden and rectory
	Athletics—swimming (no diving)	Athletics—swimming (no diving)	Athletics—horseback riding
	Athletics—horseback riding	Athletics—basic gymnastics	Athletics—basic gymnastics

Table 6 (continued)

Year/Term	Fall	Winter	Spring
Junior (age 7)	Reading and writing VII (including essays)	Reading and writing VIII (including short papers)	Reading and writing IX (including short stories)
	Arithmetic VII (dividing by two or more numbers)	Arithmetic VIII (solving multiple arithmetic equations)	Arithmetic IX (solving multiple arithmetic equations)
	Raising grains (wheat, rye, oats, etc.) with field experience	Processing grains with practicum in granary and gristmill	Raising fruit and nut trees (apples, peaches, etc.) with practicum in tree nursery and field experience
	Care and feeding I—native small mammal species with field experience to open fields, forests, and small streams	Care and feeding II—native amphibian and reptile species with practicum in aviary, vet clinic, and field experience (weather permitting)	Care and feeding III—native small bird species (not raptors) with aviary practicum and field experience
	Raising vegetables with practicums in the vegetable and botanical gardens	Processing vegetables with practicum in the rectory	Safety Measures IV—dos and don'ts around wild animals
	Water sources—freshwater streams, river water, salt water, aquifers, estuaries with field experience	Distilling and purifying water with practicum	Identification of rocks and minerals with lab and field experience
	Athletics—horseback riding	Athletics—swimming and diving	Athletics—horseback riding
	Athletics—intermediate gymnastics	Athletics—intermediate gymnastics	Athletics—intermediate gymnastics

Table 6 (continued)

Year/Term	Fall	Winter	Spring
Senior (age 8)	Reading and writing (technical documents)	Reading and writing (technical documents)	Preserving and storing documents with practicum in the archives
	Care and feeding IV—farm birds (e.g., ducks, geese, chickens, etc.) with practicum and field experience	Care and feeding V—farm working animals (e.g., dogs, cats, horses, etc.) with practicum and field experience.	Care and feeding VI—ranch/range (e.g., cows, goats, sheep, etc.) with practicum and field experience.
	Raising grapes with field experience in the vineyards	Processing grapes and fruits with practicum in the winery	Raising nut trees (e.g., pecan, oak, walnut, etc.) with and field experience.
	Safety measures V—navigating in darkness (tunnels, caves, compound)	Arithmetic X (ratios, proportions)	Safety measures VII—accurate observation and reporting
	Nutrition I—types of nutrients (protein, carbohydrates, fats) and their uses	Nutrition II—nutritional value of foods	Nutrition III—meal planning and preparation with practicum in rectory
	Safety measures VI—suppressing small fires with practicum	Preparation of potions I—types of potions	Preparation of potions II—measuring portions and calculating doses
	Athletics—swimming and diving	Athletics—swimming and diving	Martial arts—mental and emotional discipline with basic maneuvers
	Athletics—horsemanship	Athletics—intermediate gymnastics	Athletics—horsemanship

Table 6 (continued)

Table 7. Curriculum for Form II

Learning Objectives
1. Basic knowledge that prepares the student to develop practical skills for daily living (gardening, potions, candle making, sewing)
2. Basic knowledge that advances the student's ability to live independently (botany, biology, geology)
3. Basic knowledge that prepares the student to care for younger children
4. Basic knowledge of geographic regions outside Erwina and their implications (geography, cartography)
5. Basic knowledge of the process of transformation and transforming safely
6. Basic knowledge that prepares the student for self defense

Year/Term	Fall	Winter	Spring
Freshman (age 9)	Mathematics I	Mathematics II	Mathematics III
	Regional geography I—northwestern regions and its implications with field expeditions	History of the three Houses	Regional geography II—southwestern regions and its implications with field expeditions
	Cartography I—reading and following directional signs with practicum (NW region)	Geology I—geologic formations and their implications with field expeditions	Cartography II—reading and following directional signs with practicum (SW region)
	Botany I—seed and flowering plant species with field experience	Gardening I—nurturing seedlings with practicum in the botanical garden	Gardening II—herbs with practicum in herb garden
	Identifying and distinguishing edible and nonedible wild plants with field practicum	Potions III—soups with practicum in the rectory kitchen	Gardening III—vegetables with practicum in vegetable garden
	Night-sky watching (fall/winter constellations)	Astronomy I—solar system, planet and satellite orbits, solar and lunar eclipses	Night-sky watching (spring/summer constellations)
	Athletics—track and field	Athletics—intermediate gymnastics	Athletics—track and field
	Martial arts—level I	Martial arts—level I	Martial arts—level I

415

Year/Term	Fall	Winter	Spring
Sophomore (age 10)	Biology I—mammalian species with field experience	Biology II—avian species, including raptors with practicum in the aviary, falconry, and field experience	Biology III—insects (pollinators, edible/nonedible, biting/stinging, disease bearing) with field expedition
	Botany II—tree species with field experience	Potions IV—soaps with practicum in the laundry	Botany III—aquatic plant species (ponds, rivers, oceans)
	Sewing I—stitches and mending with practicum	Sewing II—measuring, designing, cutting patterns, and making new clothes from patterns with practicum	Sewing III—collecting, preparing materials (cotton, wool), spinning, and weaving with practicum
	Family matters I—growth and development of infants and young children (toddlers)	Family matters II—caring for infants and young children (toddlers) safely	Geology III—surveying for coal and coal tar with field expeditions
	Regional geography III—northeastern regions and its implications with field expedition	Geology II—industrial rocks and minerals and their uses with lab and field experience	Regional geography IV—southeastern regions and its implications with field expedition
	Cartography III—reading and following directional signs with practicum (northeastern region)	Preparation of candles from beeswax and preparing hurricane lamps	Cartography IV—reading and following directional signs with practicum (southeastern region)
	Athletics—swimming and diving	Athletics—intermediate gymnastics	Athletics—the hemp highway
	Martial arts—level II	Martial arts—level II	Martial arts—level II

Table 7 (continued)

Year/Term	Fall	Winter	Spring
Junior (age 11)	Geography of Biogenics territory and border regions	History of Biogenics Corporation and Cassius Foundation	Geography of Cassius territory and border regions, including H'Aleth
	Biology IV—fish (in rivers, lakes, ponds) with practicum in fishery and pond	Basic first aid with CPR, laboratory and practicum in the medical infirmary	Biology V—reptiles, amphibians (in rivers, lakes, ponds) with field expeditions
	Soils I—types and their implications for agriculture with field expeditions	Potions VI—infusions, essential oils, salves, with practicum	Soils II—types and their implications for hydrology with field expeditions
	Potions V—preparation of inks, dyes, and stains	Preparation of paper with practicum in archives	Preparation of parchment with practicum in archives
	Family matters III—supervising younger children (ages 5–8) at home with practicum	Family matters IV—changes associated with puberty	Family matters V—supervising younger children (ages 5–8) in the field with practicum
	Preparation of reeds and grasses for wicker with practicum	Woodworking I—sanding and polishing with practicum	Woodworking II—preparing and applying stains with practicum
	Athletics—rock climbing / scaling	Athletics—basics of repelling	Athletics—rock climbing / scaling
	Martial arts—level III	Martial arts—level III	Martial arts—level III

Table 7 (continued)

Year/Term	Fall	Winter	Spring
Senior (age 12)	Flora and fauna I—grasslands and plains with field expeditions	Advanced first aid with practicum in the medical infirmary	Flora and fauna II—river valleys with field expeditions
	Botany IV—medicinal herbs and berries	Potions VII—topical antiseptics with practicum in the lab	Maintenance and repair of irrigation systems
	Biology VI—basic human anatomy with laboratory	Transformation I—basic rules with observation of transformations	Transformation II with practicum under faculty supervision
	Woodworking III—assessing and repairing furniture	Woodworking IV—measuring, cutting, and assembling furniture	Veterinary first aid with practicum in vet clinic
	Family matters VI—mentoring, tutoring, and providing support	Biology VII—basic cell biology	Maintenance and repair of farm equipment
	Making pottery with practicum in the armory	Glassmaking with observation in the armory	Brickmaking with practicum in the armory
	Rμηεîc I (elective)	Rμηεîc II (elective)	Rμηεîc III (elective)
	Athletics—boating (rowboat, canoe)	Athletics—rescue swimming (in a pool)	Athletics—boating (rafting on quiet waters)
	Martial arts—level IV	Martial arts—level IV	Martial arts—level IV

Table 7 (continued)

418

Table 8. Curriculum for Form III

Learning Objectives

1. Advanced knowledge that advances the student's ability to live independently and productively (agriculture, animal husbandry, forestry, climatology)
2. Basic knowledge of architecture, architectural design, and construction (graphic arts, masonry, tunnels, caves, geometry)
3. Basic knowledge of engineering (mining, electricity/magnetism, applied mechanics, hydrology, algebra, calculus)
4. Basic knowledge of sanitation and maintenance of sanitation fields
5. Basic knowledge of business matters (accounting, manufacturing, logistics)
6. Basic knowledge of physics and astronomy
7. Basic knowledge of weather patterns and weather emergencies
8. Basic knowledge of genetics and genealogy and their implications
9. Advanced knowledge of potions (medicinal potions)
10. Advanced knowledge of transformation and its complications
11. Basic knowledge of social anthropology (anthropology, sociology, psychology)
12. Knowledge and application of logic and ethical principles
13. Knowledge of principles and practices of scouting and surveillance

Year/Term	Fall	Winter	Spring
Freshman (age 13)	Agriculture I—farming (reaping and storage) with field experience	Architecture I—structure, form, and function with laboratory	Agriculture II—farming (sowing and planting) with experience
	Animal husbandry I—farm animals with field experience	Stone working—chiseling and sculpting with laboratory	Animal husbandry II—ranch/range animals (field experience)
	Biology VIII—basic human physiology with laboratory	Transformation III—adverse reactions and emergency care	Architecture II—basic building construction with practicum
	Forestry I—hardwood/deciduous trees with field expeditions	Mathematics IV—geometry	Forestry II—fruit/flowering trees with field expeditions
	Potions VIII (part 1)—medicinal recipes with laboratory	Potions VIII (part 2)—medicinal recipes with laboratory	Potions VIII (part 3)—medicinal recipes with laboratory
	Climatology I—fall and winter weather patterns with practicum	Climatology II—emergent conditions (drought, floods, fires, etc.)	Climatology III—spring and summer weather patterns with practicum
	Runeic IV (limited enrollment, with permission from faculty)	Runeic V (limited enrollment, with permission from faculty)	Runeic IV (limited enrollment, with permission from faculty)
	Athletics—activities based on student's need and preference	Athletics—activities based on student's need and preference	Athletics—activities based on student's need and preference
	Athletics—wrestling	Athletics—wrestling	Athletics—wrestling

Year/Term	Fall	Winter	Spring
Sophomore (age 14)	Architecture III—masonry (building with stone, brick, and mortar) with field experience	Architecture IV—construction of wood, wicker, and sod homes with field experience	Architecture V—basic tunnel construction with field experience
	Graphic arts I—sketching architectural designs with practicum	Graphic arts II—developing architectural designs and plans	Graphic arts III / architecture V—implementing plans with practicum
	Business I / mathematics V—business math	Business II—accounting	Forestry III—tree husbandry (grafting and growing trees) with practicum in tree nursery and field experience
	Flora and fauna III—mountain terrains with field expeditions	Construction of hemp ropes and ladders with practicum (laboratory)	Construction of byways (using hemp ropes and ladders) field experience
	Quarrying rocks and ores with field exercise	Historic preservation I—paper and parchment with practicum in archives	Historic preservation II—art and artifacts with practicum in library
	Genetics I—basic concepts (functions of genes and chromosomes) with laboratory	Genetics—pedigrees with practicum, taking family history, and preparing family pedigree	Genetics II—common causes of genetic disorders with laboratory
	Athletics—activities based on student's need and preference	Athletics—activities based on student's need and preference	Athletics—activities based on student's need and preference
	Athletics—boxing	Athletics—boxing	Athletics—boxing
	Boating—regatta (quiet river waters) (elective)		Kayaking (cascade level 0) (elective) (required for scouts)

Table 8 (continued)

Year/Term	Fall	Winter	Spring
Junior (age 15)	Flora and fauna IV—caves and caverns with field expeditions	Biology IX—exotic species (dragons, duck-billed platypus, etc.)	Architecture VI—cave construction with practicum expanding bat cave
	Hydrology I—lakes and streams with field experience	Hydrodynamics II—ground water, aquifers, flooded caverns	Hydrology III—rivers and waterfalls with field expeditions
	Scouting and surveillance I—summer and fall with field expeditions	Scouting and surveillance II—preparing, presenting, and analyzing surveillance reports with practicum	Scouting and surveillance III—winter and spring with field expeditions
	Plumbing—construction and maintenance with practicum	Biology X—basic microbiology	Sanitation with practicum in sanitation fields
	Mathematics VI—algebra I	Mathematics VII—algebra II	Chemistry I—general chemistry
	Principles of manufacturing	Logistics and supply with practicum	Ethics I—principles of ethics
	Athletics—basic archery	Athletics—basic archery	Athletics—basic archery
	Athletics—kayaking (cascade rapids level I) (elective) (required for scouts)	Athletics—river rescue swimming (restricted, by permission from faculty only) (required for scouts)	Athletics—kayaking (cascade rapids level II) (elective) (required for scouts)

Table 8 (continued)

Year/Term	Fall	Winter	Spring
Senior (age 16)	Flora and fauna V—inland waterways with field experience	Potions IX—inorganic solutions (e.g., acid, alkaline, fluorescent, etc.)	Hydrology IV—construction, maintenance, and management of dams
	Mathematics VIII—calculus I	Engineering I—electricity and magnetism with lab	Engineering II—applied mechanics with practicum
	Astronomy II—galaxies and other cosmic phenomena	Physics I—energy, mass, motion, and gravity	Physics II—*Stella Ignis*, the formation and death of stars
	Statistics	Demographics with field experience in population surveillance	Epidemiology with field experience in injury/illness surveillance
	Principles of logic	Ethics II/transformation IV—ethical considerations (breeding, genetic engineering, hybrids, etc.)	Ethics III—business ethics (cost benefit versus cost effectiveness)
	Anthropology—origin and evolution of human societies	Sociology—ethnicity and culture of human societies	Psychology I—normal human and animal psychological states and associated behaviors
	Art and architecture—wood sculpting (elective)	Art and architecture—stone sculpting (elective)	Art and architecture—landscaping and terracing (elective)
	Athletics—intermediate archery	Athletics—intermediate archery	Athletics—intermediate archery
	Martial arts—staff fighting	Martial arts—staff fighting	Martial arts—staff fighting
	Kayaking—cascade level III (elective, qualified students only) (required for scouts)		Kayaking—cascade level III (elective, qualified students only) (required for scouts)

Table 8 (continued)

Table 9. Curriculum for Form IV

Learning Objectives

1. Basic knowledge of governance (civics, government)
2. Advanced knowledge of transformation and its complications
3. Advanced knowledge of social behavior (psychology)
4. Advanced knowledge of scouting and surveillance
5. Knowledge of offensive and defensive strategies and tactics
6. Preparation for graduate education at Gregor (organic and biochemistry, comparative anatomy, potions X and XI, plant/environmental toxicology, advanced genetics)
7. Develop expertise in field of practice (advanced internships)

Year/Term	Fall	Winter	Spring
Junior (age 17)	Flora and fauna VI—mountain ranges[a] with expanded field experience (restricted, by permission from faculty)	Mathematics—calculus II	Flora and fauna VII of coastal plains[a] with expanded field experience (restricted, by permission from faculty)
	Business III—establishing a business	Business IV—managing a business	Business V—contracts
	Governance I—civics and principles of leadership	Governance II—rules and regulations	Governance III—policy and politics
	Psychology II—human and animal grieving and loss	Psychology III—common dysphorias (e.g., depression, anxiety)	Potions X—soporifics (restricted, by permission from faculty only)
	Chemistry II—organic chemistry[b] (elective)	Biology XI—comparative anatomy[b] (elective)	Chemistry III—biochemistry[b] (elective)

Year/Term	Fall	Winter	Spring
	Internship	Internship	Internship
	Internship	Internship	Internship
	Internship	Internship	Internship
	Athletics[c]—activities based on student's needs and preferences	Athletics[c]—activities based on student's needs and preferences	Athletics[c]—activities based on student's needs and preferences
	Kayaking[a] (cascade rapids level III, restricted, by permission from faculty only)	Martial arts—swordsmanship (restricted, by permission from faculty only)	Kayaking[a] (cascade rapids level IV, restricted, by permission from faculty only)
	Mountaineering (restricted, by permission from faculty only)		Mountaineering (restricted, by permission from faculty only)

Table 9 (continued)

Year/Term	Fall	Winter	Spring
Senior (age 18)	Scouting and surveillance IV—northeast region with expanded field experience[a] (restricted, by permission from faculty only)	Genetics III[b]—mutagens and mutation (restricted, by permission from faculty only)	Scouting and surveillance[a]—southeast territory with expanded field experience (restricted, by permission from faculty only)
	Plant toxicology[b] (laboratory, field expedition)	Research—principles and practices of qualitative and quantitative research	Explosive armaments (restricted, by permission from faculty only)
	Strategy—defense	Strategy—offense	Tactics with field exercise
	Environmental toxicology (laboratory, field expedition)	Potions XI[b]—toxins (restricted, by permission from faculty only)	Governance IV—alliances, treaties, and agreements
	Advanced internship	Advanced internship	Advanced internship
	Advanced internship	Advanced internship	Advanced internship
	Athletics[c]—activities based on student's needs and preferences	Athletics[c]—activities based on student's needs and preferences	Athletics[c]—activities based on student's needs and preferences
	Athletics—kayaking[a] (cascade rapids level IV, continued, restricted, by permission from faculty only)	Martial arts—swordsmanship (restricted, by permission from faculty only)	Athletics—kayaking[a] (cascade rapids level V, restricted, by permission from faculty only)

Table 9 (continued)

Notes

[a] Required for those pursing scouting

[b] Required for those pursing genetics or medicine at Gregor

[c] Expertise in archery, swimming, sprinting, long-distance running, and martial arts required for those pursuing scouting

APPENDIX C

Dragonensis dragonis

Class: Mammal
Family: Dragonidae
Genus: *Dragonensis*
Species: *Dragonis*

Animals are classified as mammals according to four primary characteristics. These are (1) being warm-blooded, (2) having hair or fur, (3) having three middle ear bones, and (4) nursing offspring with milk. The common ancestor of the mammalian clade dates back to the mid-Jurassic period.

There are three broad classifications of mammals. They are

1. monotremes (prototheria), which lay eggs to produce their young (duck-billed platypus, spiny anteater, dragons);
2. marsupials (metatheria), which produce very immature young and rely on pouches to complete their development (e.g., kangaroos, koalas, opossums, etc.); and
3. placentals (eutheria)—all other mammals—which rely on placentas, which connect blood supplies of both the mother and fetus to support the fetus in the womb (*in utero*).

Dragons are egg-laying mammals and, therefore, belong to the monotremes. Their bodies have a protective layer of overlapping plates (gray dragons) or scales (red dragons, arctic dragons) composed of structural proteins and a bony matrix that protects their underlying skin. The topmost layer of their skin has a leathery texture, which provides strength and elasticity and is a protective barrier against the environment. It is covered by a coat of very fine dark downy hair, which cushions the plates and scales and prevents them from rubbing against the skin. Although dragons are homeothermic, the lanugo also offers insulation against the harsh cold winds and temperatures encountered at the higher altitudes and in the high mountain regions they inhabit.

Dragons have a head, neck, and body size proportionate to their length. The head has an angular shape with a protruding snout. Adult male red dragons have horns similar to antlers (illus. 32). All species have upper and lower jaws armed with razor-sharp teeth. The neck is large, muscular, and capable of turning the head almost 190 degrees side to side.

The eyes are positioned on either side of the face to allow for stereoscopic vision and wide peripheral vision. Between the degree of neck rotation and their peripheral vision, they can see behind each shoulder; however, they cannot see directly behind their back. They have the long-distance vision of a raptor. Dragons have no external ears; however, they do have an auditory canal, which transmits sound to the middle ear. They have exquisite hearing and a very good sense of smell.

Most dragons have the reputation of breathing fire. This is a misconception. Dragon fire is not generated from breathing. There are two pairs of glands, one pair on each side of the dragon's throat: an incendiary and a salivary gland. The combined secretions from these glands are the source of the dragon's fire. A dragon can spew fire while in flight, with all four legs on the ground, or while raised in an upright position on its back legs. This allows the dragon to use its most effective weapon with maximum flexibility. It should be noted, however, that most of the components of the incendiary glands require substances that must be produced by these glands via some physiologic mechanism. Thus, the supply of these mixtures can be exhausted faster than they can be replaced.

Illus. 32. Red Dragon (male).

By:

The males, which tend to be larger, have a broader chest and back. Both males and females have back legs that are relatively short and stocky (in proportion to their size) in order to support their weight when rearing upright. They are armed with thick, heavy claws. The front legs are longer and more slender and are armed with long talon-like claws for gripping and holding prey.

Dragons' wings are broad, with large scallops that taper toward the wing tips. The wings extend from the shoulder—analogous to the wings of raptors. The skin of the wings is composed of the same leathery (keratinized) outer layer of skin as the rest of the body. The red and gray dragons have no scales or plates on their wings. Hence, in extreme weather conditions, these dragons must seek shelter and keep their wings folded against their bodies. In contrast, the arctic dragons have thin, waterproof scales on their wings. The lanugo on dragons' wings is longer, and it both insulates the wings and acts like feathers. Minute muscles in the skin raise and lower the hairs. Although the skin offers some degree of weather-proofing against rain, the lanugo does not and it can become saturated. This limits the conditions in which the red and gray dragons can fly.

Dragons prefer to launch into flight from a high cliff face or escarpment. Red dragons, with their slighter build, are able to lift off directly from the ground. Although gray and arctic dragons can do the same, it is difficult for them to do so from a standing position. A running start helps, but it is not their finest moment. They look like super-sized albatrosses.

Dragon tails are muscular and tapered like the tail of a river otter. It is used as a rudder during flight and for balance while on the ground when raising up to an erect position. When standing on all four legs, the dragon can use its tail like a whip. They can use it to help them tread shallow water, as well. Red and gray dragons, however, are not known for their swimming skills. Hence, they do not land in deep water (at least, not by choice). Although arctic dragons do not swim per se, they can fold their wings tightly against their bodies, close their nostrils, and execute a plunge dive to capture fish and other prey. The dive is relatively shallow and begins to curve almost immediately upon entry. So the arctic dragon must execute a precision dive to capture its intended prey. Their precision is due, in part, to their ability to detect an electric field and determine in what direction it is headed. The speed of the dive provides enough momentum to allow the dragon to resurface and resume flight. The wing compression is so tight that the scales overlap and protect the underlying laguno from becoming wet.

Contrary to popular belief, dragons are social animals and live in extended family clans. Usually, there is a lead male and female pair (alpha). Breeding is not limited to the dominant pair. Dragons live in cooperative, communal arrangements in which all members of the clan participate in caring for both the young and the old, hunting and foraging for food, defending their territory, and protecting each other.

Like many other mammals (including humans), dragons are quite intelligent. They can solve problems and use tools. They can use both their strong jaws and talons to pick up objects (e.g., rocks, branches) to build a structure (e.g., a barrier or a nest) or tear one down. They can join with other members and use their powerful wings to generate wind or to create a barrier against it. Frigid gales often blow through the northeastern and arctic terrains, so the males will encircle a nesting site while the females tuck their eggs or chicks under their wings and up against their bodies for warmth. Dragons also recognize the danger imposed by fire. Yet they will build a pyre of dead branches and brush among barren rocks and create a fire for warmth.

Dragons also have language. Although they do not have speech as humans know it, they have vocalizations that they use to communicate among themselves. Most of these are below the threshold of human hearing or may sound like deep rumblings. It is uncertain if this is due, in part, to the large incendiary and salivary glands on both sides of the throat or the thickness of their vocal chords or both. These rumbles carry for miles and can be heard by other dragons far away. It is one way they can keep in contact with each other when they are separated by long distances. In the mountains, their rumblings reverberate off granite walls and echo in the canyons. Since dragons possess echolocation, they can follow the sound to locate its source (e.g., a lost fledgling). They also have phonographic memory and can recognize individual voices.

Dragons can learn other languages and are reputed to be able to communicate with humans telepathically. This is another misconception. Dragons can modulate the frequency of their vocalizations in a manner that corresponds to syllables—only at a lower frequency. Once the sound waves strike a human's ear drum, they are transmitted and interpreted by the auditory center of the brain as human speech. Dragons do have the ability to focus their sound projections to only the ear(s) of the individual(s) with whom they wish to communicate. This latter feature and the low frequency of their vocalization have led to the misconception that dragons use telepathy.

Female dragons have mammary glands. When newborn dragons first hatch, they are capable of using their claws to climb onto the mother's chest and underbelly to suckle her milk and to get onto her back for transport. They are fully ambulatory at one to two months of age, are introduced to a meat diet after three to four months, and are weaned after four to six months. By nine months, they are using their wings to take long hops, which help them keep up with the mother on the ground as well as strengthen their wing muscles. At twelve months, they are able to sustain flight and fly at lower speeds than fully grown adults. Once dragon offspring are mobile, both male and female members of the clan take care of them. Older adolescents (two to three years old) tend to the nursery while both young adults (three to five years old) and mature adults hunt, guard, and defend the clan and its territory.

The notion of capturing a dragon—even a baby dragon—is out of the question. These creatures are generally elusive and remote. The gray dragons live high in northern mountain ranges (below the tundra), where the terrain is virtually inaccessible. They rarely come into the forested areas below except to hunt. The red dragons inhabit the southwestern mountains and high forests. Both species build their nests among the higher crags—and often within caves—where predators cannot reach vulnerable offspring. The arctic dragons range throughout the arctic and subarctic regions. All species of dragons have astounding flight capability and can defend their young by their ability to rain fire down upon any attacker from almost any direction.

Although omnivorous, dragons prefer a predominantly meat diet; however, they will consume fruits, nuts, and occasionally fish. They do not graze on vegetation, and they don't eat insects. If plagued by the latter, they simply roast them—literally.

Supplemental Notes and Citations

Characteristics of Mammals
Mammals are homeothermic. They are capable of maintaining a stable internal body temperature regardless of variable temperatures in the external environment (thermoregulation). They have middle ear bones (ossicles)—the

malleus (hammer), incus (anvil), and stapes (stirrup). Sound waves strike the tympanic membrane (eardrum), which reverberates against the ossicles. The ossicles, in turn, amplify the force of the sound waves as they are transmitted to the inner ear (Fontana and Porth, 2009). They have mammary (milk) glands, which are specialized glands in female mammals that produce milk for the young (e.g., breasts or teats). Finally, they have a common ancestor—two or more different species descending from the same ancestor. Fossils of all three mammalian classes have been found dating back over 160 million years.

Mammalian Characteristics of Dragons

Dragons have plates and scales similar to structures found in other mammals: e.g., the armadillo, with plates comprised of dermal bone and horn, and pangolia, with scales composed of keratin (Chen et al., 2011; Yang et al., 2013). Keratin is a fibrous structural protein that protects the outer layer of skin. It is also a component of hair, feathers, nails, horns, and hoofs. Collagen is the main fibrous structural protein found in connective tissue. It provides structural support, strength, and connectivity (e.g., scaffolding for tissues; ligaments, which connect one bone to another; and tendons, which connect muscle to bone).

The bony matrix is a framework of minerals (e.g., calcium phosphate, calcium carbonate) enmeshed with collagen fibers. Other minerals such aluminum, magnesium, and potassium may be present as well. Trace amounts of other minerals allow for different shades of color, especially in the scales of the red dragon (e.g., iron for red and brown, azurite for blue, malachite for green, etc.).

There are several sublayers of skin. The epidermis is the outermost layer of skin, and it has layers of dead keratin cells (keratinocytes). Keratinized skin is much thicker. Lanugo is a layer of fine, soft hair covering the body of the fetus after about sixteen weeks' gestation. Although usually shed before birth, lanugo may still be seen in newborns.

The arrector pili, minute muscles in hair follicles embedded deeper in the skin, are also present in humans (Simandl, 2009). When they contract, hair is raised upward. With the scant amount of body hair in humans, however, their actions may go unnoticed.

The tympanic membrane is a thin membrane that vibrates freely when sound waves strike it. The vibrations are transmitted via the nerve impulses to the brain for processing and interpretation. In *H. sapiens*, the temporal lobe (Wernicke's area) of the brain receives and processes the impulses from the auditory nerve and forwards them to other areas of the brain for interpretation.

Electroreception is the detection of electric fields caused by muscle contractions. Note: The duck-billed platypus, another monotreme, also has this capability.

Dragon-Specific Characteristics

Dragon fire is the result of a mixture of compounds excreted by a pair of glands in the back of a dragon's throat. One member of the pair, the incendiary gland, contains a mixture of carbon and hydrogen (a hydrocarbon), a mixture of sulfur and oxygen (sulfur trioxide), and nitrogen—all natural compounds. Each incendiary gland is paired with a salivary gland that contains saliva (99% water). The paired incendiary and salivary glands are located adjacent to each other. When both glands contract simultaneously and expel their contents, the sulfur trioxide reacts explosively with the water in the saliva to ignite the hydrocarbons. The dragon is already breathing out (exhaling) forcefully when this reaction takes place. When the nitrogen in exhaled air (75% of exhaled air) combines with oxygen (to form dinitrogen trioxide), its explosive nature sustains the reaction for as long as the dragon exhales. Note: A dragon's breath is exhaled aerosolized secretions from the incendiary gland alone. Its golden hue is due to the sulfur contained in the incendiary gland.

Dragon speech consists of vocalizations similar to those found among elephants, who generate low frequency sounds, which they modulate depending upon the meaning they wish to convey (Stoeger et al., 2012).

Dragon Species (app. F)

Great Gray dragon (*Dragonis fuscus*) is the largest dragon, so named for its drab-gray to charcoal-colored scales without marking. It inhabits northern and northeastern mountains and forest ranges below the frost line.

Red (golden) dragon (*Dragonis rubra*) is the smallest dragon, so named for its very colorful amber-red scales with streaks of gold on top of its head and back. It inhabits southern and southwestern mountains and forests.

Arctic dragon (*Dragonis alba*) is a medium-sized dragon that is smaller than the gray. It is white except for gray coloring on top of the head, back, and top of the wings. It inhabits the arctic and subarctic regions of Gregor.

Appendix D

Shelter in the Boar's Den

In building a shelter at the Cassius village, the old woman used stones of all sizes, as long as she and the child could lift and carry them. The largest stones formed the base of the shelter, followed by layers of progressively smaller stones. She instructed the child to prepare a mortar of thick mud mixed with small twigs and the stalks of dried grasses, both of which had been broken into small pieces. She used this mixture inside and outside and between the stones that would form the walls of the shelter. The child's smaller fingers could push the mortar between the stones. Once the mortar was allowed to dry over several days, it set with the stones firmly embedded in it.

For the roof, the old woman layered tree branches for structural support, building the branches up a little higher in the middle so the roof would slope downward from the center. Then, she and the child searched the surrounding forest area for mats and patches of thick moss. They dug these up with about an inch of soil and arrayed the patches of moss onto the branches until the roof was covered. Over time, the mat would coalesce and form a solid and nearly waterproof barrier (illus. 33).

Illus. 33. Shelter in the Boar's Den.

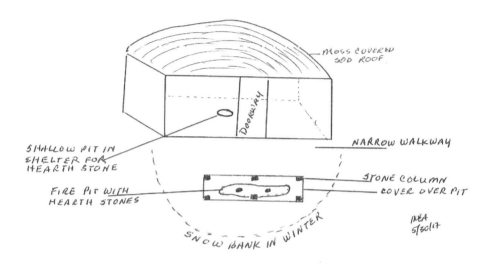

The fire pit was long and narrow, with room for two larger but moveable hearthstones that, once heated, would radiate their heat for a period of time. Thus, while one of the hearthstones was giving off heat inside the shelter, the other one would be in the pit heating up under the fire. When ready to swap the two stones, the old woman would put the cooled stone from the hut in the vacant spot at one end of the pit and transfer the fire and its ashes over to its location. When cooled enough to move, the heated stone could be moved into the hut.

With the child helping her, the old woman erected three stone pillars about three feet high along the pit's length on both sides. As she had done for the shelter, she used larger stones at the base followed by layers of progressively smaller stones and sealed them with mortar to hold them in place. Then she pulled up several dead hardwood bushes, overlapped them with one another, and used stones to flatten them into a tightly intertwined mat of branches somewhat longer and wider than the pillars beside the pit. She covered this trellis in several layers of the same mortar that she used to build the pillars. Once it had dried completely, the structure was rigid. The trellis would not burn if cinders reached it. She placed it atop the pillars so that it extended beyond the diameter of the shallow pit on all sides. Then she placed a large stone on top of the trellis at each pillar. In this manner, the pit sheltered the fire from wind, and the trellis sheltered it from rain.

APPENDIX E

Selected Medicinal Plants

Aloe vera—anecdotal reports suggest it soothes wounds; however, there is insufficient evidence to support wound healing. Safe to use as a topical agent.

Basil, essential oil—thought to have antiviral, antibacterial, antifungal, antiparasitic, antioxidant, and anti-inflammatory properties. See also *oregano*.

Belladonna (nightshade)—deadly poison. All parts of the plant are poisonous. Used as a pain reliever and sedative, it can cause hallucinations and delirium.

Camphor, essential oil—topical anesthetic, derived from wood of camphor tree via steam distillation.

Dandelion greens—may have some antioxidant effects. Leaves are nutritious and may be eaten as a green leafy vegetable or steeped in water to make dandelion tea.

Foxglove (digitalis) *leaf*—highly toxic compound. May help reduce the symptoms of heart failure and slow heart rates that are too fast. Can cause worsening of heart failure and induce a heart rate that is too slow or very irregular or both which may lead to death.

Lippea alba—may have sedative effects.

Menthol—a topical alcohol derived from the peppermint plant. Cools the skin and used for topical analgesia, as a topical antiseptic, and for relief from itching.

Oregano, essential oil—insufficient evidence to support any medicinal benefits. It is thought to have antiviral, antibacterial, antifungal, antiparasitic, antioxidant, and anti-inflammatory properties.

Peppermint oil—insufficient evidence to support any medicinal benefits. Peppermint tea is thought to have beneficial effect in alleviating nausea.

Psilocyabin—restricted compound (mycotoxin). A hallucinogenic substance that alters perceptions. May cause euphoria, intoxication, dissociation, and an altered sense of time.

St. John's wort—conflicting evidence of effectiveness in treating depression. It has significant drug interactions and can decrease the effects of several other drugs including selected anticancer drugs, warfarin, some oral contraceptive pills, and others.

Valeria roots—inconsistent evidence of effectiveness in inducing sleep. No single active compound identified to induce sleep. Several of the plant's chemical constituents combined may have a sedative effect.

Zizyphus (jujube)—limited evidence indicating it may be effective against many bacteria that infect wounds.

Appendix F

Alternate Species

Alternate Mammalian Species

Foxes (Canidae)

General characteristics—small omnivores. Speed ranges from thirty to forty miles per hour depending upon species. Senses—keen eyesight that is sensitive to movement, exquisite sense of hearing, sense of smell similar to dogs. Sociable, family oriented, and live in family groups. Bite force sufficient to break small bones in their prey. Prey—small mammals, birds, reptiles, amphibians, fish, insects, and will scavenge from other kills; fruits, vegetables, berries, seeds. Predators—large carnivores (cougars, wolves, bears). Red and gray foxes range throughout territories of Biogenics, Cassius, H'Aleth, and Erwina.

Red Fox (Vulpes vulpes)

The red fox has a luxurious red coat, sometimes with brown or orange tones. It is the largest of the fox species and has a long bushy tail. It can run at speeds up to thirty miles per hour.

Gray Fox (*Urocyon cinereoargenteus*)

The gray fox has a coat of various shades, predominantly gray with a mix of white and black. It is the second largest fox and has a long tail. It can run at speeds up to thirty-five to forty miles per hour and can climb trees and swim.

Arctic Fox (*Vulpes lagopus*)

The artic fox has a brownish-gray coat in summer, which becomes a luxuriant thick white coat in winter. It has a long bushy tail. Its highly sensitive hearing enables it to hunt prey (mostly small mammals) under snow cover. Additional fur on paws provide insulation from cold and additional traction on slippery surfaces. It is a good swimmer.

Wolves (*Canidae*)

General characteristics—apex predators and carnivores. They are endurance runners trotting at about five miles per hour for long distances. They can reach speeds of about thirty-five to forty-five miles per hour in a burst of speed over a short distance. They have the strongest bite of any canine species. They have an exquisite sense of smell, acute hearing, and keen eyesight sensitive to movement. They are very social and usually live in packs. Wolves range throughout the territories of Biogenics, Cassius, H'Aleth, and Erwina.

Gray (mountain) Wolf (*Canis lupus*)

The coat of the gray wolf comes in various shades, predominantly brown, gray, and black or a mix. It is the largest species of wolf with an average weight of eighty to one hundred pounds. It has a bite pressure about four hundred pounds per square inch, which can crush large bones.

Red Wolf (*Canis rufus*)

The red wolf has a grayish-black coat with reddish-brown tones. It is somewhat smaller than gray wolf.

Arctic Wolf (*Canis arctos*)

This wolf has a brownish-gray coat in summer, which turns white in winter. It is somewhat smaller than the gray wolf. It ranges throughout Gregor's territory.

Bears (Ursidae)

General characteristics—omnivores. Brown and black bears range throughout territories of Biogenics, Cassius, H'Aleth, and Erwina. They can sprint for short distances at twenty-five to thirty miles per hour. They have keen near vision and can see in color; however, their distance vision is much less acute. Their visual field is about 120 degrees (similar to humans), and they have a very good sense of smell and acute hearing. Their preferred ranges are mountains and forests.

Brown Bear (*Ursus arctos*)

The coat of the brown bear ranges in color from light cream to black. It is predominantly brown, gray, and black. It is the second largest bear, reaching eight feet or more when standing upright. It has a bite force of 850 pounds per square inch.

Black Bear (*Ursus americanus*)

The black bear has a dark-brown to black coat. It is smaller than a brown bear and may reach five to six feet tall when standing upright. Its bite force is approximately six hundred pounds per square inch.

Deer (Cervidae)

General characteristics—herbivores. These animals run over short distances at speeds ranging from thirty to forty-five miles per hour depending upon the species. They can leap over barriers eight to twelve feet high depending upon the width of barrier. They are good swimmers. They have acute vision supplemented by eyes on both side of their narrow face, which provide wide visual field of about three hundred degrees. They have an exquisite sense of smell and acute hearing augmented by the shape of their ears, which funnel sound. They range in woodlands and grasslands throughout the territories of Biogenics, Cassius, H'Aleth, and Erwina.

White-Tailed Deer (*Odocoileus virginianus*)

These deer have a reddish-brown coat in summer and a gray-brown coat in winter. They are a midsize deer. The stags have antlers.

Mule (Black-Tailed) Deer (*Odocoileus hemionus*)

These deer also have a reddish-brown coat in summer and a gray-black coat in winter. They are larger than the white-tailed deer. The stags have antlers.

Elk (Red Deer) *(Cervus elaphus)*

These deer are brown to gray colored with shades of red in summer and gray in the winter. They are among the largest of the deer family. The stags have branching antlers.

Cats (Felidae)

General characteristics—apex predators and primarily carnivores. Cats are primarily sprinters with speeds ranging from thirty to fifty miles per hour depending upon species. They have large eyes with acute vision adapted to low light and peripheral vision of 280 degrees. They have an acute sense of smell and hearing. Their large paws and hind legs provide agility. Cats can swim and may go into water after prey; however, most would rather not. They range in grasslands, plains, and woodlands throughout the territories of Biogenics, Cassius, H'Aleth, and Erwina.

Cougar *(Puma)*

The coat of the cougar is usually a variation of tan. It may have silver to reddish hue. It is a large cat, slightly smaller than northern wolves. It can reach top speeds of forty to fifty miles per hour. Its bite force is 350 pounds per square inch. Cougars prefer to range in mountainous and lightly forested areas.

Lynx (*Lynx rufus*)

The lynx has a thick brownish-gray fur with black markings on its back, head, and tail. It has a white underbelly with black markings. The tail has a black tip. It has tufted ears, and its large furry paws can act as snowshoes in winter. It is a medium-sized cat and smaller than the cougar. It can reach a top speed of about thirty miles per hour and is skilled in climbing trees.

Jaguar (*Panthera onca*)

The jaguar's spotted coat ranges from tan (with spots clearly visible) to almost completely black (spots visible if close enough). It is the largest cat with a short and stocky build, and it is more powerful than a cougar. It is skillful in climbing and a very good swimmer. Its bite force is seven hundred pounds per square inch.

Dragons (Dragonensis) (app. C)

General characteristics—apex predators and omnivores. They are the mammalian equivalent of a raptor. Instead of feathers, however, they are covered with keratin plates or scales. Depending upon the species, they can reach a soaring speed of 150 to 220 miles per hour with diving speeds of 200 to 300 miles per hour. Their ground speed ranges from fifteen to twenty-five miles per hour. Their fire can reach twenty-five to forty feet, and the temperature of dragon fire ranges from 1,600 to 2,200 degrees Fahrenheit (roughly the equivalent of a blast furnace). They have high-resolution vision, which allows them to see prey up to two miles away, acute hearing, and very good sense of smell. Their prey consists of mammals (any size), large birds, and large reptiles. They also eat fruits, vegetables, and berries. They are very social and usually live in clans.

Great Gray Dragon (*Dragonis fuscus magna*) (illus. 8)

Gray dragons are the most powerful of the three most common species of dragon. Shades of gray to charcoal color and no markings give it a drab appearance despite handsome features. The darker color also allows greater absorption of sunlight in cooler climates. Coloring blends in well with their habitat and allows dragons to meld into the mountainside as if part of it. They can remain very still for prolonged periods and, in this manner, essentially become invisible to the human eye. They are covered with thick keratin plates on the dorsal surfaces of their bodies. Their ventral surfaces are covered by plates, which are lighter in both thickness and color.

Gray dragons are the largest of the three species of dragon. Their body size is twenty to twenty-six feet, not including tail; the head and neck are an additional six to eight feet; and the tail adds eighteen to twenty-four feet. Their wingspan is forty to forty-six feet, with a soaring speed of 180 to 240 miles per hour and a diving speed of 200 to 250 miles per hour. Their size makes lifting off from the ground cumbersome and often requires a running start. The distance their fire reaches is thirty-five to forty-five feet. They have a bite force of 1,200 pounds per square inch. Their range is the northern and northeastern mountains and forests of Erwina and Biogenics.

Gray dragons have no predators. Humans can kill them if they have weapons that can penetrate the dragons' thick scales from a range that lies outside the range of its fire.

Red (golden) Dragon (*Dragonis rubra*) (illus. 32)

Red dragons are the smallest of the three most common species. They are very colorful with an iridescent reddish-brown color mixed with some gray, and there are gold tones on the head and back. Their scales are thinner and lighter than those of the gray dragon. They reflect sunlight, which helps cool them during summer in warmer climates. The scales typically cast an amber-red color with streaks of gold on the top of the head and back. Different combinations of mineral salts offer additional colors—iridescent streaks of blue and green may be seen, especially when reflected by light. They are stunningly beautiful both on the ground and in flight.

Red dragons are twelve to seventeen feet tall at the shoulders standing on all four legs. Their body length is fourteen to twenty feet (not including head, neck, and tail), the head and neck add an additional six to eight (not including horns), and the tail an additional twelve to sixteen feet. They are lighter, more slender body makes them faster and more agile than the gray dragon. They can take off from ground level without difficulty. Wingspan is thirty-two to thirty-eight feet. They have a soaring speed of 160 to 220 miles per hour and a diving speed of 250 to 300 miles per hour. Their fire reaches twenty to twenty-five feet, and their bite force is 500 pounds per square inch. Males are distinguished by their curved horns which begin to develop when they are ten to twelve years old; females have no horns.

Red dragons were nearly hunted to extinction by humans for their colorful scales until H'Aleth established a program protecting them. After the destruction of H'Aleth, they remained endangered and were rarely seen. They ranged in southern and southwestern mountains and forests, extending into grasslands of H'Aleth and Erwina.

Arctic (white) Dragon (*Dragonis alba*)

These dragons have gray coloring on top of the head, back, and top of wings to absorb radiation from the sun. They are almost pure white on the chest, underbelly, and under the wings. They are covered with relatively thin scales that compress tightly for diving. As the second largest dragon, they are smaller than the gray dragon. They are sixteen to eighteen feet tall at the shoulders standing on all four legs. Their body length is eighteen to twenty-four feet (not including head, neck, and tail), the head and neck add an additional eight to ten feet, and the tail an additional sixteen to eighteen feet. Their wingspan is thirty to forty-two feet. Their soaring speed is 150 to 180 miles per hour, and their diving speed 230 to 260 miles per hour. Their fire reaches thirty to forty feet. They have a bite force of 850 pounds per square inch. They range through arctic and subarctic regions of Gregor. Arctic dragons have no known predators.

Other Mammals

Badger *(Mustelidae)*—Omnivore

The badger's coat is a brownish-black coat with distinctive alternating white and black bands on its head and face. It has huge claws on the fore feet used for digging and can dig faster than any other species and excavate a burrow within minutes. It can run at fifteen to twenty miles per hour. It is a powerful and aggressive animal and can fend off predators successfully from its burrow. Although badgers can swim, they avoid doing so, if possible. Normally nocturnal, they will forage during the day. They are solitary animals. They range throughout grasslands and prairies of H'Aleth and Erwina.

Boar, Wild (*Suidae, Sus scrofa*)—Omnivore

The wild boar has a grayish-brown to black long-haired coat. It is built like a battering ram with a relatively large head that blends into a short thick neck and large trunk with relatively thin legs. Its snout has long canines that extend four to five inches and curve outward to the side, resembling tusks. Both males and females have tusks. The boar can shift about one hundred pounds using its tusks and its massive head, neck, and shoulder muscles. Its size varies depending upon availability of food in its environment. Its sense of smell is very good as is its hearing. Its eyesight is good during the day, but relatively poor in the dark. Its charging speed is about thirty miles per hour. Its range is the grasslands primarily in the southwestern regions of H'Aleth and Erwina.

Goat, Mountain (*Bovidae*)—Herbivore

The mountain goat has a wooly long thick white coat. Both males and females have long pointed black horns. Flexible pads within hooves provide traction and agility in mountainous terrains. It ranges in the high mountain regions of Erwina to subalpine and alpine regions of Gregor.

Horse, Domesticated (*Equidae*)—Herbivore

Horses have variable colors (white, brown, black) with short to long hair and thick coats depending upon breed with a characteristic long mane and tail. They can trot at ten to fifteen miles per hour, gallop at about thirty miles per hour, with short bursts of speed up to about forty to fifty-five miles per hour. They range throughout the territories of Biogenics, Cassius, H'Aleth, and Erwina.

Raccoon *(Procyonidae)*—Omnivore

The raccoon has a grayish dark coat with characteristic rings around their eyes ("bandit" face) and a ringed tail. It is nocturnal and usually solitary, may share territory with other raccoons of the same gender. They have excellent night vision, very good sense of smell and touch. It can use forepaws like hands (five slender fingers, no opposing thumb). It ranges in forests, coastal marshes, grasslands, and mountains throughout the territories of Biogenics, Cassius, H'Aleth and Erwina.

River Otter *(Lontra canadensis)*—Aquatic Mammal, Carnivore

The river otter has dark-brown water-repellant fur, webbed feet, and characteristic "mustache" whiskers. It has good eyesight and hearing and a keen sense of smell above water. It can hold its breath underwater for nearly eight minutes. It ranges throughout territories of Biogenics, Cassius,

H'Aleth, and Erwina wherever streams, lakes, wetlands, estuaries, marine environments, and other waterways have vegetation to provide cover and an adequate food supply.

Sheep, Mountain (big horn) (*Ovidae*)—Herbivore

Bighorn sheep have thick gray-white coats. Males have huge curved horns, while the females have much smaller horns. A charging ram can reach a speed of twenty miles per hour.

Wolverine *(Mustelidae)*—Omnivore, Primarily Carnivore

The wolverine's coat is black on the top of its back and extremities with grayish silver on top of its head and along both sides. It has relatively poor eyesight; however, it has acute hearing and smell. Its claws are designed to grip surfaces, and it is a good climber. Its top running speed is thirty miles per hour. It is very aggressive and solitary.

Alternate Avian (Raptor) Species

General characteristics of raptors—they have large eyes for their size with high-resolution vision that allows them to magnify and see prey from a hundred feet up to two miles away, depending upon the species. They have sharp hooked beaks for rending prey and sharp curved talons with a powerful grip to both kill and carry prey. Females are larger than males.

Owls (Strigidae)

General characteristics—these raptors are typically nocturnal. They have the largest eyes designed for low light and a head rotation of over 180 degrees. They have broad wings for slow, silent flight and maneuverability.

Great Horned Owl

This owl is one of largest owls. Its plumage is reddish brown, grayish black on its back, with a brown breast with black and white bars, and tufted ears. Its flight speed is twenty to forty miles per hour. Its range is throughout territories of Biogenics, Cassius, H'Aleth, and Erwina.

Long-Eared (woodland) Owl

This is a medium-sized owl with dark tufted ears; grayish-brown banded plumage on its back, wings, and tail; and white breast feathers with black bands. These birds normally inhabit forests in the southeastern territories of H'Aleth and Erwina.

Hawks (*Accipitridae*)

General characteristics—these raptors are active mostly during the day. They have color vision. They typically prey on other birds in flight.

Cooper's Hawk

This hawk is smaller than the red-tailed hawk. Its body feathers are blue-gray on its back and head with brown on its breast. It has a long narrow tail rounded at end. It has flight speeds of twenty to fifty-five miles per hour. Its range is through woodland areas of Biogenics, Cassius, H'Aleth, and Erwina.

The Cooper's hawk is very adept at flying though trees, even in a heavily wooded area. Its broad wings and long tail allows it to maneuver among dense woods at high speeds. This ability allows it to prey on other birds dodging through trees in an effort to escape it. The hawk is also known to fly low at high speeds to hide from its prey, then abruptly soar high and dive down upon it in a sneak attack.

Red-Tailed Hawk

The red-tailed is the largest hawk. Its body feathers are darker brown with red tail feathers in the middle of its tail. It can reach speeds of twenty to forty miles per hour and up to 120 miles per hour in a steep dive. It ranges across open country throughout territories of Biogenics, Cassius, H'Aleth, and Erwina.

Falcons (*Falconidae*)

General characteristics—among the fastest birds in flight, with flying speeds about 130 to 140 miles per hour and diving speeds up to 250 miles per hour in order to catch other birds in flight. They can soar on updrafts to search for prey. Distance vision is almost two miles.

Peregrine Falcon

This falcon has grayish to blue-black plumage on its head, back, and wings with gray-banded white breast and legs. It ranges throughout territories of Biogenics, Cassius, H'Aleth, and Erwina.

Prairie Falcon

This falcon has brown to light-tan plumage on its back and white breast feathers with dark markings. Its range is the southwestern territories on plains and grasslands.

Eagles (*Accipitridae*)

General characteristics—with the exception of some vultures, the eagle is the largest and most powerful raptor. They are considered an apex predator. Like other raptors, females are larger than males.

Golden Eagle *(Aquila chrysaetos)*

This eagle has gold feathers atop a dark-gray plumage on its back and head. It is one of the largest eagles, although it is smaller than the bald eagle. Its flight speed is twenty-eight to thirty miles per hour when soaring. It can glide up to 120 miles per hour, and its diving speed is 150 to 200 miles per hour. It ranges throughout open and forested territories of Biogenics, Cassius, H'Aleth, and Erwina.

Osprey *(Pandionidae)*

Often mistaken for an eagle, osprey have mostly white plumage speckled with gray-brown bands on wings. They range anywhere (except artic regions) there are ponds, rivers, lakes, and coastal waterways.

Additional Species Used in Hybrids

Baboon (*Cercopithecinae*)—Omnivore

This is a highly social nonhominoid primate with thick gray, brown, and black fur. It has a long muzzle with long canine teeth and powerful jaws. Its top running speed is forty-five miles per hour.

Hyena *(Hyaenidae)*—Carnivore

The hyena is a highly social animal with thick gray to brown hair with black markings. It has a stocky build with front legs longer than back legs and a canine muzzle with powerful jaws. Its top running speed is forty-five to fifty miles per hour.

Vulture, Griffon (*Gyps fulvus*)

This bird has grayish-brown to black feathers with a white head and neck ruff (not to be confused with bald eagle). It has a wingspan of seven and one-half to eight and one-half feet. Its average soaring speed is twenty to twenty-five miles per hour.

Appendix G

Life in Erwina

Almost everything Erwinians needed to live either had to be hewn from stone and wood, found in forests and streams, or grown and harvested. Hence, they relied heavily on crops they could grow and on animal husbandry. Many Erwinians kept milk cows or goats to supplement their diet with milk and milk products. Most had chickens to provide them with eggs; however, some relied on ducks or geese as a source of eggs. Nearly all Erwinians kept vegetable and herb gardens that provided a significant portion of their largely vegetarian diet. They planted flowers that would attract pollinators—bees, butterflies, humming birds—to their gardens and flowering fruit trees. Some also kept honeybees in hives to collect the honey. Each region also had wildlife that enjoyed the same food sources. Often, there was competition between the villagers and the wildlife regarding which one would get to the harvest first.

Natural Resources

Southern Erwina was largely an agricultural region. Grains formed a major component of Erwinians' diet. In the southeastern and southern villages, the climate and soil supported growing wheat, rye, and barley. In order to camouflage their presence, these grasses would be widely scattered among other prairie grasses. Although this maneuver obscured the presence of a nearby village, it also took longer to harvest the grain. Villages farther to the south and southwest could grow cotton and oats. In contrast, villages to the north and northeast could not grow grains in great quantity. They would harvest wild berries and edible mushrooms from the forest in their region

Most of the southeastern villages were sparsely populated with trees. They would have a few shade trees and, perhaps, a small grove of apple or pecan trees. This, too, was deliberate. Once H'Aleth was lost, Erwina's southeastern villages became the ones closest to Cassius territory and most likely to come under attack. If this happened, their trees along with their houses would likely be destroyed. It was important to keep the loss of resources to a minimum. The southwestern villages were much farther away, and so were their fruit trees. There, the groves of orange, peach, pear, and pecan trees were quite large. The northeastern villages could grow apple and black walnut trees.

Oaks were abundant just about everywhere across Erwina and produced volumes of acorns, which are a source of nutrition for both humans and animals. There were even a few beechnut and hickory nut trees scattered throughout the northeastern forests—and the scouts knew exactly where to find them. The nut trees and more than a few fruit trees also supported wildlife in the regions—often to the frustration of the villagers.

Village Life

Most village homes were single story with three to four rooms—a common living area with a small hearth (often unvented), possibly a small extension for a kitchen area, one or two bedrooms, and a small bath. Most were constructed with thatch, comprised of straw and dried grasses, and covered with sod to blend in with their environment. A few were constructed of wood or stone, depending upon the materials available nearby or imported from other villages.

Each village had a main house, which was the largest structure in the village (illus. 34). Typically, it was a single-story building, usually constructed of wood or stone. It had six to eight rooms including one large meeting area, which shared a large vented hearth with a kitchen on the other side. This was where the villagers customarily met with each other and with people from other villages.

Illus. 34. An Erwinian Main House.

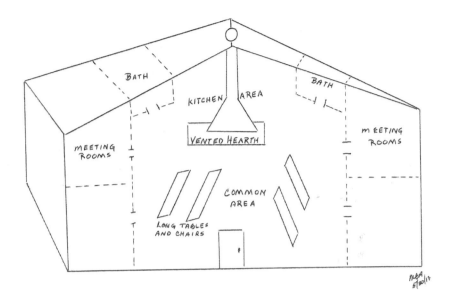

The main house would keep a fire whenever one was needed. Many homes used thatch in their construction, so a fire was not kept in them. When a source of heat was needed in these homes, the hearths were used to keep hearthstones, which could be heated in the main house. Most hot meals were served in the main house, where they could be eaten or taken home.

The main house also served as the business center for the village, where trades for the exchange of goods and services were conducted with people from other villages within and beyond Erwina's borders.

Although all villages were self-sustaining, there were differences in what each village had to offer. Depending upon soil and climate, villages would grow foods, raise farm animals, and produce products that other villages did not have. Villages located near grasslands and prairies could harvest the stalks of grasses or reeds from nearby streams. Their fibrous material could be soaked and then woven into various designs to make wicker products such as baskets of all shapes and sizes, furniture including chairs, and other household items. There was a high demand for wicker products across all the villages. Broken-down wicker products were used for fuel.

Villages in the south that tended sheep or grew cotton had spinning wheels and looms for making cloth and clothes. These were in high demand also.

A few villages made candles. Beeswax and tallow were the two most common sources. Those villages that farmed bees would make candles from beeswax. Those that had farm animals could make candles from tallow derived from the fat of any animals that had died. These differences formed the basis of trade and allowed a wider variety of diet and habitation than what might otherwise have been available. Thus, village inhabitants could exchange their products for others not readily available in their region.

Most villages had a small outdoor marketplace. Most of the setup for the market the villagers would bring with them. Most would bring a table, while others would display their wares (e.g., furniture) on the ground. Depending upon where the village was located and the prevailing weather at the time, villagers might join together to set up a tent or have a canopy.

Travel to and from villages was common. People from one village would travel to another and bring their products to trade. Children traveling with their parents and students attending school at the compound would travel to other villages to put new knowledge to work, practice their skills, and gain real-world experience. In the absence of roads, these trips also taught the students how to find each village.

Energy Sources

In Erwina, there were five common sources of energy—sun, wind, water, fire, and steam. Energy resources varied depending upon the season and where people lived. Wood, tightly bundled dried grasses, and coal provided the fuel for fire—especially during winter months. Most of the outlying villages in the southern regions relied predominantly on wind as a power source, supplemented by fire and coal. Few villages in the southern regions were close enough to a rapidly flowing river to use waterpower. In contrast, the compound and northeastern outposts had access to both wind and water as sources of power. The use of steam-powered generators was restricted to the compound, the largest village in Erwina; however, they were quite common in Gregor.

Fortunately, the southern regions of Erwina tended to have relatively mild weather with occasional blasts from a winter storm. This limited the amount of fuel needed at most times of the year. Most of the warmth during winter came from hearth rocks. Villagers could bring their hearth rocks to the main house and baste them in the fire of the hearth. Then, the villagers would take the heated rocks back to unvented hearths in their homes, where the rocks would radiate heat until they cooled. Hearth rocks could be rotated—as some were heating up in the main house, others would be giving off heat in the home. During periods of severe winter cold, the villagers would shelter inside the main house and huddle around both sides of the hearth fire—especially at night. Small animals would be brought inside as well. Larger animals would be brought to the tunnels deep underground. Someone was assigned to shepherd the animals at all times.

Most of the materials used for a fire came from the grains grown in southern villages. The husks and stems would be compressed and bound tightly together into very dense bundles of varying sizes. These bundles could be used to fire a hearth or oven. Erwinians rarely cut down trees for fuel. Most wood for burning was gleaned from the ground or harvested from a dead tree. Many of the fruit and nut trees had brittle limbs, and forest floors in the northeast provided an ample supply of wood—especially after summer and winter storms. If a tree needed to be harvested to build or repair an existing structure or make tools, then any wood not needed for these purposes could be burned for fuel. In these cases, the wood would be shared with other villages. Those homes with vented stone hearths or ovens could also burn coal from the northern regions of Erwina. Due to its sulfur content, which has the potential for creating sulfuric acid (H_2SO_4) and toxic fumes, use of coal was usually limited to wintertime.

The compound was the one location that needed a twenty-four-hour supply of energy. It was remote and nestled close to the northern mountains. It housed two steam generators that produced electricity. Even there, the most common source of light was sunlight during the day and either a fire or candles in hurricane lamps after nightfall.

There was one other source of fuel for light, and its location was a closely guarded secret. There were petroleum seeps hidden in the southwestern mountains. Faults among layers of shale allowed the petroleum to ooze upward and form shallows pools. Where shaded, the petroleum remained in a liquid form. Pools exposed to the hot summer sun would form tar pits. Paraffin could be derived from the coal tar to make candles. More importantly, however, torches could be made. Villagers would make staffs of wood with one end covered in a thick layer of cotton cloth. This end would be dipped in petroleum, soaking the cotton. Then the cotton end would be covered in coal tar and allowed to dry. This latter step would be repeated several times until there was a thick coating of tar. When lit, these torches would burn for at least an hour. Most of these torches were stored in caves and caverns to provide light in places were sunlight could not reach. A few would be kept in each village for emergency lighting. They were not used unless needed. When burned, they released hydrocarbons and their heat could damage some of the formations found in caverns. No torches were kept in a tunnel. The only light allowed in tunnels was a candle contained within a hurricane lamp.

Defensive Measures

Erwina's villages were few and widely dispersed throughout its regions. Preventing a potential enemy or spy from knowing where to find the villages was crucial to their safety. Hence, there were no roads connecting any villages to give direction to an enemy or abet an enemy's advance. If someone wanted to go from one village to another, he or she would have to know how to get there.

Unlike the compound, there were no bell towers in the villages to ring out a warning. The height of the towers would make them a beacon for any attacker. Should an enemy succeed in reaching a village, at least one building in every village was equipped for shelter and defense. After the destruction of H'Aleth, however, people knew that this would not be enough. Once an alarm was raised or a surprise attack occurred, the people of these villages would need to evacuate. Someone had to escape to warn the other villages. It was likely that many villagers would be lost trying to hold off attackers while others fled.

So over time, they built a network of interconnecting tunnels constructed deep underground that connected the main house with individual homes. Some of the tunnels extended long distances beyond the borders of the village. These tunnels were designed to be evacuation routes in the event of an attack. They provided the villagers with a means of escaping unseen—essentially abandoning their village—should dragon fire rain down upon them. Thus most village houses tended to be clustered around the main house to afford easy access to it and to the tunnel system.

Tunnels between buildings were relatively short and needed no shoring beyond a layer of mortar to keep dirt from shedding off the walls. Longer tunnels, usually those leading to an exterior evacuation point, required shoring at intervals. Wood could not be used for this purpose. Dragon fire could still reach inside a tunnel, and wood burns. Hence stone walls and arches strengthened with mortar were built into the walls of these tunnels at measured intervals. Even in total darkness, those evacuating could count how many arches they had passed and know where they were in the tunnel.

Dim light from stairwells, ramps, and other entryways would filter a short distance into most tunnels. The midsection of any tunnel would be pitch-black without light from a hurricane lamp. Thus, tunnels reinforced with stone walls had a small inset built into each wall. Each inset housed a hurricane lamp, one or two candles, and a small box of matches. These items could be used in an emergency or if a candle burned too low or its flame blew out.

Some tunnel systems became quite extensive and intricate. In some cases, they led directly to caverns where additional supplies could be stored. They also served as convenient avenues to move from one building to another—especially in bad weather or severe winter cold—and provided underground shelters to harbor people and animals in the event of a severe storm or a tornado.

Flight Plans

Erwina's leadership had devised a disaster plan, which could be modified by each village based on the resources it had and where its people would most likely go. The default disaster on which the plan was based was an attack by Cassius with his dragon. The plan included both harboring in tunnels and fleeing through them and then overland to a remote location. Each village would have to determine how much in the way of supplies they could carry with them and in what direction to flee. The plan also called for the villagers to prepare nonperishable supplies that they would need to survive, provided they escaped alive. These supplies would be packed and stored where they could be gathered up quickly in the event of an attack.

A southwestern village would likely flee farther south or west, possibly into the southwestern mountains. A southeastern village might flee to the southwest and join those villages in flight, or they might flee northwest to join up with the main compound and/or the northeastern outpost.

A northeastern village most likely would flee into the northeastern mountains, where they could disappear into the caverns. Flight to Gregor would only be possible during summer months.

Once an evacuation was underway, people would need to move at a brisk pace and be able to run, if necessary. Villagers who were *H. transformans* and had come of age could transform into their alternate species provided that species offered speed of flight and camouflage. Villagers who were *H. sapiens* and *H. transformans* children who had not come of age or were not yet proficient in transformation would need to flee on foot or horseback (if the village had horses) or ride any transformed species that could carry them. The use of horse-drawn wagons might not be fast enough to flee an attacker. If some form of rapid flight was not available for those who could not transform, then many children who had not come of age could be killed along with the adults trying to protect them. For this reason, young children spent most of their lives in school at the compound, where there was greater safety and where they would receive lessons in horseback riding as Form I freshman.

Erwina's Natural Barriers

The ridge was an ancient mountain range connected on its northern end to another younger range that curved southward. The ridge had eroded away over the eons. It and the river beyond it stood between the grasslands and its largest village, the compound, which served as Erwina's seat of government. The river, which also coursed north to south, had carved a valley beside the ridge. This effectively increased the height of the ridge on its western side so that it was much taller than its eastern side although its slope was more gradual. Although now passable, the ridge's rocky terrain and dense forest could still hinder men and their wagons, especially those carrying heavy weapons of war.

The Ferveo River was a major natural barrier between Erwina's central territory and Cassius. It originated in the northern mountains. As the river gained momentum and was fed by other mountain streams, it gained considerable speed and size. A steep grade resulted in a high flow rate. The river's rocky bed was the source of several rapids along the way. At one point, an ancient earthquake had created an expanse of deadly rapids. These rapids were marked by violent and extremely dangerous cascades with steep drops and by complex narrow channels riddled with outcroppings—the narrows. These conditions made the rapids impassable. Past the narrows, the river cascaded over a slip fault to form an enormous waterfall.

The energy from the waterfall provided even more power to the river flowing beyond it. The river, with its rapid current, was more than strong enough to sweep away men and their machines if one did not know where and how to cross it. The rapids above the narrows could destroy any weighted vessel, although a kayak could pass through them if an experienced paddler were guiding it. After the river spilled over the cascading falls, it split into two branches. The eastern branch continued its tumultuous course south into the foothills as the ridge continued its drop. The western branch took a more leisurely path through the western prairie. At one time, lands farther to the east of the river and the ridge had been a part of H'Aleth.

The northern mountains were a broad range of peaks that extended east to west across Ewina's northern border. It lay between Erwina and the territory claimed by Biogenics, and it served as a barrier between them, except on its northeastern border. The highest peak was twelve thousand feet. Glaciers could be found at the top of it. Its high mountain passes had snow even in summer. At lower levels, mountain mist limited visibility in the passes that were not snowed in. A dense forest of pine and hardwood trees were on its flanks. This was one of Erwina's natural barriers. To cross this range, one had to know where and when to cross and what travails to expect. Men and other creatures could get through the forest, but not their machines, at least not before cutting down trees to make way.

There were many caves and limestone caverns under these mountains. Scouts stored equipment and supplies in several of them so they could shelter in them, if necessary. They used some of the larger caverns as passageways to move through the mountains and shorten an otherwise much longer trek.

On the far side of the mountain range lay a deep gorge carved by a rapidly flowing river. Once it passed through the mountains and entered Erwina's territory, it became known as the Ferveo River.

Appendix H

The Compound

Buildings within the Courtyard

1. The manor house served as an entry point for everyone coming into the compound. Family members met their relatives and friends upon arrival at the compound. Visitors (which were rare) were received and greeted. Security was present to hear what everyone had to say or report. It also housed administrative offices and served as a meeting house where trades and other agreements could be negotiated.

2. The schoolhouse supported all formal classroom and laboratory instruction. Practicums and field experiences were held at the site of operation. Students were housed in dormitories on the upper floors of the main building. Classrooms and laboratories were located in the east and west wings. Faculty offices and conference rooms were on the main floor. The first cellar housed the laundry, dressmaker, and tailor locations and provided storage room. The second and deepest cellar served as a shelter in the event of an emergency and had multiple connections to the tunnel system.

3. The library was attached to the rear of the schoolhouse for the convenience of faculty and students, especially students ages four to five, who were not allowed outside the schoolhouse without an older student or adult escorting them. It also housed the art and

artifacts that represented significant events in the history of the three Houses.

4. The archives served as the repository of all records generated by Erwina and sent to Erwina by H'Aleth and Gregor, including pedigrees and copies of all research conducted by H'Aleth and Gregor. It also housed the facilities for making paper and parchment.

5. The H'Aleth natural history and research center conducted epidemiological research on the number of *H. transformans*, their alternate species, and their Mendelian pattern of inheritance. It also housed the museum of natural history.

6. The medical infirmary had clinics, a medical laboratory, and a small hospital. The staff treated common illnesses and injuries and mishaps of transformation. It also provided classrooms for training in first aid and the medical arts. Students' first attempt at a transformation were conducted there in case of an adverse event.

7. The gymnasium housed swimming pools and provided space for gymnastics, a boxing ring, martial arts, and swordsmanship. Its athletic field hosted archery, soccer, and track-and-field programs. This was where students and faculty alike trained, honed their skills, and played sports (e.g., soccer). It also supported competitive sports during the summer games.

8. The rectory was where the dining halls for Forms I–II and Forms III–IV and private dining rooms for faculty and staff were located. It also housed kitchens for preparing meals, canning foods, and student practicums.

9. The faculty quarters provided small apartments for faculty and their guests.

10. The botanical garden initially was a nursery for seedling plants including flowers, vegetables, grasses (grains), and trees. It was expanded subsequently to include plants that require a climate-controlled environment and those that cannot survive a freeze or cold weather.

Buildings beyond the Courtyard

11. The winery provided for the processing of grapes and other fruits for jams, jellies, juices, and fermented beverages.

12. The armory (illus. 30) supported building or repairing equipment and making weaponry. Craftsmen forged swords, fashioned arrow- and spearheads, made shields, and sculpted stones for use in construction. The armory also maintained ovens for firing bricks, pottery, and glass and provided space for artisans to make glass and pottery.

13. The falconry was an indoor and outdoor facility for nesting and roosting of all species of raptors. It provided an environment for the convalescence and rehabilitation of injured raptors until they could be released into the wild and maintained those that could not be released. Staff provided training for students, falconers, and falcons.

14. The aviary was an enclosed and partially covered facility for birds who were native to the region and are not raptors. These birds had to be kept in a separate environment since many of them were prey species for raptors. Staff trained some species of birds to serve as couriers.

15. The vet infirmary supported medical clinics and a small hospital for treating injuries in most classes of animals, both wild and domestic. It had large enclosures for rehabilitation of animals prior to release back into the wild or to service.

16. The stables and paddock provided housing for horses and mules. Staff trained both horses and riders.

17. The boathouse supported stowage and outfitting for rowboats, dinghies, canoes, kayaks, barges, and fishing gear. Staff provided training in use of each of these craft and taught boatmanship.

18. The fish hatchery supported predominantly bass and trout, which would be released into streams. Students learned about different types of fish. When released, the fish supported the food chain for many native species. There were canal locks on either side of the fish hatchery to control the flow of water past the fish hatchery, especially when fish were being released into the stream.

19. The barn provided housing for goats and milk cows when not grazing in the pasture.

20. The henhouse and barnyard provided secure housing for laying hens and chicks with an enclosure to protect them from foxes and other predators. Many mature chicks that would become laying hens were given to the outlying villages so they could have eggs as a food source.

21. The granary and gristmill with the waterwheel sifted and ground a variety of grains. Its operations supported instruction in mechanics.

22. A bat cave was located close to the forest's edge between and behind the armory (building 12) and the falconry (building 13). It provided a haven for native bats and supported instruction in excavation of tunnels and construction of caves.

Points of Interest

The Gardens

There were several flower gardens, especially around the manor house. The early spring flowers included pansies, hellebores, snowdrop anemones, grape hyacinths, crocuses, and forsythia. As they were fading, late spring flowers were beginning to bloom—lilac bushes, irises, daffodils and day lilies, tulips, azaleas, rhododendrons, and hostas. Soon the spring flowers would be joined by flowers that thrive in the summer sun—roses, hydrangeas, gardenias, peonies, gladiolas, tiger lilies, dahlias, marigolds, black-eyed Susans, lavender, asters, and gaillardias. Finally, in the fall, asters and chrysanthemums closed out the season.

The herb garden consisted of chives, oregano, mint, rosemary, and thyme. Other cooking herbs raised in this garden included basil, marjoram, saffron, dill, fennel (which also attracts butterflies), ginger, horseradish, garlic, and tarragon. Other villages might have a different combination of herbs in their gardens, so the villagers would trade with one another for those herbs and spices they did not have.

The vegetable gardens supported a vast array of leafy greens, roots and tubers, beans and peas, gourds and squashes, cauliflowers and cabbages, and many more. They were harvested at different times of the year and some all through the summer season. Some vegetables, such as corn, were brought to Erwina from other villages.

The Archives

The archives were a treasure trove of genealogy. Pedigrees from all the Houses were stored there. Thus, current and prospective genealogists had family history at their fingertips. This treasure and its secrets were closely guarded. If either Biogenics or Cassius ever learned of its existence, neither would hesitate to invade Erwina to acquire it.

The archives also housed the only center for the production of parchment and paper. Parchment was made from animal skins—specifically, goats, sheep, and cows—taken from any herd animals that had died of natural causes. Villages that fostered these animals would send the skins to the archives, where they were processed and rendered into parchment. First, all the animal's hair must be removed. Then, the skin must be soaked in water until it is softened so that it can be stretched very thin. Once softened, it must be stretched as tightly as possible on a wooden frame. It must not be allowed to wrinkle. Once it is dried, a perfectly smooth wooden roller is rolled over the surface under pressure to ensure the skin is smooth. A thin dusting of chalk may be rolled into the skin to improve the absorption of inks and dyes.

Paper was made from fibrous material including grasses, reeds, and vegetable stalks. Other sources included cloth (e.g., old robes, clothes, bedding, etc. that were threadbare) and used paper documents (e.g., student notes, written communiques, etc.) that did not need to be archived or housed in the library.

All pedigrees and any research deemed critical for documenting the origin and nature of *H. transformans*, including genotypes, were recorded on parchment. Even though its preparation was cumbersome, it was much more durable than paper. Bound paper was used to record any other documents that would be kept permanently, including textbooks and instructional materials.

The Rectory Kitchen

The kitchen was enormous. It was by far the largest room in the rectory. Its size rivaled all the dining rooms combined. It had a vented hearth and six ovens set inside its walls. A vast array of utensils lined the walls and were stacked in cupboards and drawers. Every manner and variety of tools to measure and mix something was in that kitchen. Drawers under the counter tops held utensils of every conceivable size—measuring spoons, mixing spoons, ladles, wooden and glass spatulas, knives for cutting and chopping, mortars and pestles for grinding, and tableware. Cupboards held iron pots, pans, double boilers, skillets, kettles, glass molds, mixing bowls, and dinnerware. Cupboards also stored ingredients that were not picked fresh every day. Long and short tables were spread about the center of the kitchen for preparation of foods.

There were plenty of brooms, mops, and buckets in the broom closet. There was an abundance of aprons, caps, towels, and tablecloths in the linen closet.

Adjacent to the main kitchen, there was a separate smaller kitchen for student practicums in preparing and cooking foods.

The Armory

Next to the schoolhouse, the armory was the second largest building in the compound (illus. 35). It was built like a huge barn. It accommodated forges for molten iron and glass, anvils for shaping metal, ovens for firing pottery, blowpipes and pottery wheels, and space for machinists and craftsmen and women to work. It offered a vast amount of storage space for materials and supplies, equipment being repaired, and products made there. A loft provided extra storage space and access to the roof. There were two steep narrow ladders leading to the loft—one on the left side of the back wall and one on the right side of the front wall.

Illus. 35. The Armory.

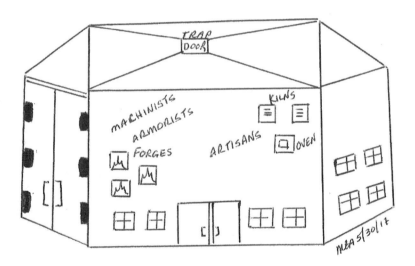

There was a trapdoor in the ceiling, which led to the roof. Ladders hung from the ceiling on either side of the trapdoor. They were held up by ropes and pulleys. The tops of the ladders were fixed to the ceiling. When raised, these ladders were secured to the ceiling by ropes, which tied onto hooks embedded in both sidewalls. When released, the ends of the ladders dropped down to the floor of the loft at an angle.

The armory needed plenty of ventilation. It had a back door of normal size and configuration, which faced the forest, a wide barn door in the front facing the infirmary, and silo doors on the side facing the winery, which could open up completely to allow large pieces of equipment to be moved in and out. It had six windows spread across the back wall, four large windows on the side facing the falconry, and two large windows on either side of the front barn door. When the windows were open, they allowed for full ventilation, even if the silo and barn doors were closed. Workers had virtually an open-air setting if the barn and silo doors were open as well. The trapdoor to the roof would siphon smoke out if the windows and doors needed to be shut.

The armory had to accommodate several industries and a large workforce. Armorists could fire iron to forge metal frames (e.g., for farm machinery) and make weapons. They could forge swords, shields, and knives. Although the armorists could forge steel from iron and coal, this was resource intensive. Iron ore had to be heated to high temperatures in ovens specifically designed to separate iron from other contaminants in the ores. When coal (or charcoal) was added, the two melded together to form steel. Since Erwina did not mine ores, the only coal available was what could be found close to the surface. Hence this resource was limited, which, in turn, limited the production and use of steel. Consequently, only those who demonstrated mastery in the use of a particular weapon were allocated one made with steel.

Spears and arrowheads and their respective wooden staffs and bows, axes and hammerheads and their wooden handles, chisels, and stone knives could be created by hand. Skilled craftsmen made these tools sleek and very effective. They also made wooden shields reinforced with coats of stone dust applied in successive layers. This made the shields more resistant to splintering and fracture from a blow. An iron sword of poor quality could shatter against these shields. Bows and arrows were plentiful, which allowed students to take archery lessons. Students also trained with wooden staves without spearheads. Those that demonstrated exceptional proficiency were allowed to enroll in sword fighting with permission from the faculty.

Windmills and Waterwheels

Windmills are usually built in wide open spaces. Although this would have been ideal, it was unwise in Erwina. Such structures erected in open territory would be a beacon for an enemy and readily targeted. Instead, windmills were embedded in a clearing created inside a cluster or copse of trees. There, the windmill would have access to the wind and have enough room for its blades to rotate. Often, these clearings were made by a dead tree that had fallen. In these cases, the trunk of the fallen tree would be used for the post, which would help disguise the windmill from the ground level. It also provided nesting sites for a wide variety of wildlife including birds and small mammals.

The post would be set deep into the ground to provide stability. The blades were designed using mats made from reeds or blades of grass. These would catch the wind and flutter as the blades rotated. When embedded with other trees, the blades would look like leaves from a distance. The blades were mounted on a swivel in such a manner that they could be rotated manually to accommodate wind direction. Thus, putting the windmill within a group of trees not only helped hide its presence but also protected it from wind damage. If a nearby tree was damaged or dying, it would be cut down before it could fall down. This provided a source of wood, protection for the mill, and a potential pole for another windmill.

Rotation of the windmill's blades drove gears, which in turn drove a mechanical device such as a gristmill. Where possible, these gears and devices were housed in a structure that was also built deep underground and around the main pole. In this manner, the gear house and gristmill would be hidden from view. They were vented by wooden or metal piping to ground level. These openings were protected by a cap and were camouflaged.

Waterwheels required a supply of briskly flowing water. Depending upon its location, a vertical waterwheel was positioned directly over a brisk stream to catch water as the stream flowed past. If near a rapidly flowing river, water from the river would be diverted into a natural or man-made channel. In either case, a gate across the water source was needed to control the flow—especially under flood conditions.

Of necessity, watermills and their associated structures (e.g., a gristmill) had to be built above the ground. Water damage and flooding was too great a risk to build them underground. Thus, waterwheels were more common in the northeast, where they could be obscured by forests and be built adjacent to nearby streams and rivers.

The Pond

The pond, located beyond and to the south of the barnyard [building 20], was a large freshwater pool supplied by a small underground stream, which coursed through it. It was supplemented by rainwater during the spring and fall seasons. The pond and nearby marshes supported a wide variety of wildlife.

Turtles and snakes were the most common reptiles seen in the pond. Amphibians including tadpoles (which live in the water until they become frogs), snails, crayfish, newts, salamanders, and leeches were plentiful. There were fish such as largemouth bass, blue gills, sunfish, and minnows, including zebrafish. There were even freshwater mussels (a mollusk). Insects such as dragonflies, water striders, and mosquitos were common inhabitants around the pond and surrounding marshland.

Migrating birds often landed in the area on their travels, including geese and ducks. A few pairs of mallards were permanent residents. Finally, small rodents such as shrews, voles, and muskrats had their burrows near and even under the pond. Like beavers, the opening to a muskrat's den is underwater.

A variety of plants inhabited the marshy areas around the pond. The sedge plant was the most common. Sedges have relatively tall stems that provide cover for frogs and other small amphibians and rodents. There were patches of flowering plants such as iris around the pond. The pond itself had a patch of water lilies, whose leaves and flowers float on the surface.

A small dam was located upstream of the waterwheel and granary [building 21]. When opened, the additional flow through the stream past the granary could backfill the pond with fresh water if its level fell too low. The operations of the dam and the watermill supported instruction in hydrodynamics.

Defensive Measures

Erwina's leadership had devised an evacuation plan, which would go into effect if the compound or a village were beset by an enemy or a natural disaster. It could be modified by each village based on the resources it had and where its people would most likely go. The default plan was based on an attack by Cassius with his dragon. The plan called for the villagers to excavate a tunnel system where villagers could harbor from dragon fire and flee through them to escape from the village. Then they could travel overland to a remote location. Each village would have to determine how much in the way of supplies they could carry with them and in what direction to flee. Nonperishable supplies would be packed and stored where they could be gathered up quickly in the event of an attack. The tunnels could serve as a depot for some of these supplies.

The Tunnel System

Deep beneath the compound was an intricate tunnel system (illus. 12). It was designed and built to maximize options for anyone to evacuate quickly regardless of their location. Each building in the compound was connected to at least two, if not three, other buildings. Some extended beyond the perimeter to allow escape under cover of the forest.

The system was like a maze, especially the branches coming off the schoolhouse. There were no maps to guide an invader. Students, faculty, and staff had to learn which tunnel went where and be able to navigate them in darkness. Invaders would be lost in the system, even if they carried lanterns or torches. Defenders would not be lost and could use the tunnel system to ambush invaders from virtually any point in the compound.

The Mound

The mound was a largely man-made structure built and camouflaged to look like a natural ridge in the local terrain or like the extension of an existing rock formation. It extended well beyond the visible confines of the village. Its height ranged from eight to twelve feet high and varied with the terrain.

The design of the mound and its camouflage was intended to be an impediment to humans and their machines of war and force invaders away from the compound as they traveled to find a way through it. It would not be an impediment to any humans who could transform into animals that could readily vault or scamper over it. If cannons ever made their way across the Ferveo River, cannon fire could create a breach in the mound;

however, it would also unleash a landslide of rocks that would likely bury the cannon and anyone near it.

Scouts would check the mound often throughout the day and night looking for places where it had been disturbed. This was quite common. Deer could vault over this formation easily. Other animals scampering over the mound might disturb its top; however, they rarely did much damage. Before repairing it, scouts would examine the damage for any indication it was caused by something other than a local denizen. If in doubt, they would follow the tracks of the being that caused the disturbance; however, they were not always successful in doing so. Cougars and lynx rarely disturbed the ground and left few tracks.

The Hemp Highway

The hemp highway was a system of strong fiber ropes and ladders that were draped and intertwined throughout the lower and middle branches of the forest canopy where they were secured. The combination of ropes, ladders, and branches created a throughway in the canopy that people could traverse through the forest without ever going onto the ground. If an individual's alternate species was small and light enough and able to climb trees (e.g., raccoon, badger, fox, lynx and cougars), then it could escape via the hemp highway as well. Defenders could use the ropes and ladders to achieve a position in the canopy, where they could conduct surveillance or ambush an intruder. Training in gymnastics and practice using the highway developed the skills students and adults needed to move through the trees.

Appendix I (Part 1)

The Schoolhouse

There were three wings branching off from the main building. The east and west wings housed the classrooms, laboratories, and workrooms used by both faculty and students. The east wing classrooms and laboratories were supplied with equipment to support the courses taken by Forms I and II students. The west wing was supplied for the courses taken by Forms III and IV students. The third wing extended from the back of the building. It was three stories high and housed the library.

The first floor had offices for the faculty, a large and a small conference room, reading rooms, and a front parlor as one entered the school. The top four floors of the main house were the dormitories. Each floor houses the students that belong to a particular Form.

Form IV students resided on the fifth floor. They were the oldest and most experienced students. In an emergency, they would be expected to help all others evacuate the building before they evacuated themselves. Form III students and Form II students resided on fourth and third floors respectively. Form I students, the youngest and most vulnerable during an evacuation, resided on the second floor. They had the fewest steps to navigate in an evacuation.

The Commons

The commons (illus. 36) was a large lobby area where all students from the form could meet and intermingle. It had wicker chairs, tables, and often a couch. Each commons had a large hearth where students could warm up, heat food and beverages, and heat hearth rocks for their rooms. The hearths on every floor shared the same chimney flue, which helped sustain the heat from one floor to the next. It was common for students to gather around the hearth itself—especially on a cold winter's evening. A hand pump supplied fresh, potable water for students to drink or use in cooking and bathing. All students who visited the commons were expected to keep it clean and tidy.

Illus. 36. The Commons.

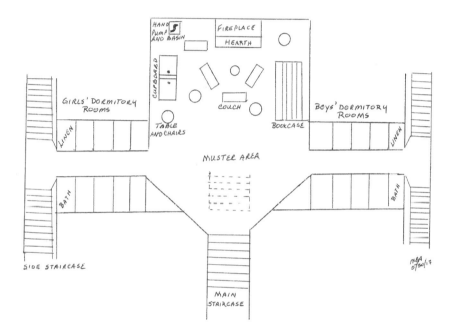

All floors shared a common staircase at the far end of each dormitory hallway. These staircases offered an alternate route to each floor and descended into the cellars beneath the main house and each of the wings, including the library. The first cellar housed the laundry and other services. It was also used to store classroom and laboratory supplies, furniture, building equipment, sports equipment, and a wide variety of other articles that needed to be stowed somewhere. The second deeper cellar was reserved for shelter and/or evacuation. Supplies for a siege and defense of the school were kept there.

The Library

The library had an enormous collection of books and manuscripts to support both students in their studies and faculty in their research. It also housed many of the books and manuscripts once held at H'Aleth. As people evacuated H'Aleth before the attack, they brought as many texts and manuscripts as they could carry. The library also housed books from Gregor. The staff there had several of their texts reprinted at Erwina so that they would be available in Erwina's library as well. This included copies of genetics references that Erwina's own researchers and geneticists might need. Students who planned to study genetics or medicine at Gregor would have these texts to help them prepare for future studies.

The library also housed resources that were not written. These included large documents generally kept rolled up: atlases, building schematics and diagrams, and expansive sketches and pictures. At the request of Master Titus, most of these were kept locked up for security reasons. They revealed a great deal about the structures in the compound and about Erwina's defenses. The library also served as a preserve for paintings, sculptures (mostly wood), and memorabilia that were deemed important to the history of the House and were strongly representative of their society. They learned the value of such things when H'Aleth was destroyed. The library did not keep the reports of research and pedigree analyses. These were kept secured in the archives.

Most books and manuscripts were sorted by category, then by subject, and then by title. The library staff maintained two sets of files for every item in the collection—one by title and one by author. Master Hectavian [hĕk-*tā*-vē-an], the chief librarian, and his staff were available to assist students and faculty in locating a reference.

Student Quarters

Most of the furniture in the room was made of wood except for the wicker chairs (illus. 13). Each student had a bed. Beside the bed was a small bedside table with a hurricane lamp, a small carafe (for water) with a lid, a single drawer, and a shelf at the bottom, which held the student's own washbasin. Two students would share a dresser and a closet. There was sufficient room at the end of each bed to put a small trunk or chest containing a student's personal items. A wooden chest stored clean bedding including blankets, comforters, and other items that could be used by students, especially during the winter.

All the windows could be opened or shuttered from the inside. There was ample room on either side of the double window to have a bedside table and/or chairs on both sides.

Personal bathing was usually done in the dormitory room, where a curtain could be pulled around each bed for privacy. Water from the hand pump in the commons was always cold. This could be quite refreshing during hot summer months. In winter, however, the water would need to be heated in a kettle over the hearth fire. Students bathed with plain water unless soap was needed to clean hair, scalp, or skin. This was often the case for students who had practicums involving animals or working outside.

Appendix I (Part 2)

The Laundry Room

In theory, the laundry room was organized to support an orderly sequence of activities for sorting, washing, drying, ironing, and folding laundry. The laundry staff would assist the students in Form I. Students in Form II and above were expected to accomplish their tasks without assistance. Girls and boys washed their laundry separately, so each group had their own designated day. The remaining days were reserved for faculty and staff.

Madam Gannett kept a watchful eye on the amount of soap and water students used. Clothing that was only lightly soiled would need little, if any, soap. If there was any clothing that was contaminated by blood or chemicals from the lab or any other potentially hazardous material, she and her staff would decontaminate and clean these items separately or destroy them in the fire.

The laundry room was set up like an assembly line with stations arranged in a logical progression around the room (illus. 37). First inside the doorway on the left, along the front wall, there were long tables for sorting dirty clothes (station I). Next to them, along the left-hand wall, were square tables for returning wicker baskets used to carry dirty laundry (station II). The hearth was also on the left-hand wall. To the left of the hearth, there was a hand pump for getting clean water (station III). Adjacent to it was a square stone-topped table where students could pick up and return kettles used for heating their wash water on the hearth (station

IV). There was a rack over the hearth for heating kettles of water and irons. To the right of the hearth were two more square tables with several washbasins stacked on them (station V). While water was heating in the kettles, students would fetch two basins for laundering their clothes. These basins were larger than those used in students' room for bathing.

Illus. 37. The Laundry Room.

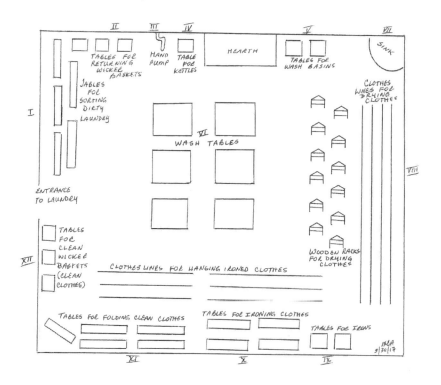

In the middle of the room were large tables with cutouts for rinse and washbasins (station VI). Here, students washed and rinsed their laundry. In the corner beyond the hearth, there was a large sink for pouring out water used in laundering (station VII). Along the back wall and protruding into the room, there was a multitude of wooden racks on which students could hang their clothes to dry (station VIII). Alternatively, clotheslines were strung all around the back and right-hand side of the laundry, where students could hang clothes that would not fit on the racks (e.g., long robes). A few lines also passed over and above the hearth for laundry that needed more heat to dry. Beyond the clothes racks, against the right-hand wall, there was another square stone-topped table where students could pick up and return irons used to press their clothes (station IX). Next to them were several long stone-topped tables for ironing clothes (station X).

Nearing the doorway to the laundry room, on the right-hand side, there were more long tables for folding and stacking clean clothes (station XI). Next to them, to the right side of the doorway, were more square tables with clean wicker baskets that students could use to carry their clean laundry back to their rooms (station XII).

During most times of the year, when it wasn't raining, laundry could be hung outside on the racks and dried by the sun. During the winter, both clotheslines and racks had to be used inside. Students could dry their clothes on a clothes rack in their room at any time; however, any items borrowed from the laundry had to be returned by the next morning when other people would need them.

Appendix I (Part 3)

The Potions Laboratory

The potions laboratory was located on the third floor on the Form III/IV side of the schoolhouse. It was quite large to accommodate workstations for several students (illus. 38), wall-mounted shelves with every manner and type of ingredient arrayed on them, and a hearth. Jars and boxes of herbs, flowers, leaves, roots, mushrooms, berries, and minerals filled almost every inch of shelf space. Except for the restricted agents, most of the ingredients used in any potion could be found on these shelves.

The recipe books for Potions I–VII were available on the shelves as well. The recipe books for medicinal potions and potions using toxic or corrosive agents were kept locked up with the restricted agents. Recipe books were signed out to each enrolled student and returned at the end of the term.

There were eight workbenches—four on each side of the room. Each workbench supported two workspaces. Each workspace had a hollowed-out place to hold a mixing bowl or kettle and a limited amount of space on each side to keep utensils. Each workspace also had a drawer. Each pair of workstations shared a shelf to hold ingredients, such as small bowls, a recipe book, or any other items students could cram on it. Although each student was expected to have his or her own workspace, there was enough room at each workstation to allow two students to share a workspace together, if necessary.

Illus. 38. The Potions Lab.

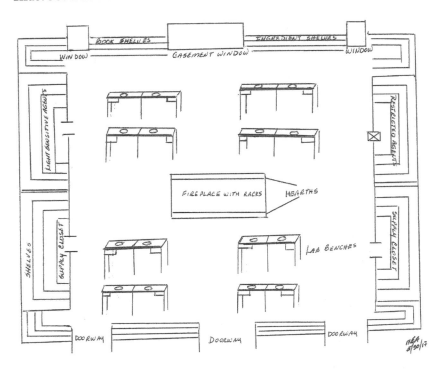

The tabletops for the workbenches consisted of a slab of heat-resistant granite shaped and smoothed by the stone workers in the armory. The granite was covered by a half-inch layer of stone dust mixed with mortar, which was allowed to harden. This construction made the workbenches very heavy, and their tops were fireproof and resistant to most spills. Highly alkaline or highly acidic solutions could erode the mortar and stone, respectively, and damage the tops. Students used heavy gloves and tongs for transporting containers with these solutions or lifting heated containers.

An ample walkway separated the four stations on the right from the four on the left. There was ample space between the workbenches as well. This space minimized the risk that students would bump into one another while transporting potions or ingredients. An open hearth lay between the second and third pair of workbenches. It held an active fire only during class sessions. Its location allowed students easier access to the fire if a potion needed to be heated. It had racks for students to place kettles and bowls for heating water and potions.

There were three unlocked supply closets with shelves and drawers. One kept a variety of supplies the students might need in the preparation of a potion (e.g., basins, pots, ladles, measuring spoons, and other utensils). Another supply closet had cloth aprons, padded mittens, and protective equipment (leather aprons, leather gloves, goggles, and masks) that students used, as needed, to prepare a recipe. A third closet held ingredients that were sensitive to light or heat. A fourth closet held the restricted ingredients, and it was locked.

The doors to the lab were wider than usual to allow for rapid egress in case of a fire or an explosion of fumes in the lab. Large windows on the outside wall opened wide to support ventilation in the lab.

Appendix J

Faculty and Staff in the House of Erwina

(In Alphabetical Order)

With few exceptions, members of the faculty were designated as madam or master. Those members who were head of specific operational elements in the compound were designated as chief. Many of the latter were dual hatted as both faculty and chief of operations and were often called upon to provide formal instruction in the schoolhouse. Hence, they were addressed as master or madam also. Whether stationed in a remote village or in the compound, Erwinians with specialized knowledge and expertise were considered adjunct faculty and, as such, carried the title of master or madam.

There were no mistresses at Erwina. The designation of matron was reserved for those women of the faculty who could trace their lineage directly back to Ruth. Had they been in the House of H'Aleth, these women would have been called Sisters. Some would have been eligible to become Mistress of that house. To distinguish the House of Erwina from the House of H'Aleth, these descendants of Ruth chose to be known as matrons of the House of Erwina. The head matron of Erwina was the equivalent of the Mistress of the House of H'Aleth. All other female members of the faculty were addressed as madam.

Master Androv [an-drŏf] (X, Y)—head tailor and shoemaker, chief business manager.

Subjects taught: Sewing III (with Madam Fredericka); business I / mathematics V (business math, with Madam Carawan), II (accounting), III (establishing business), IV (managing business), V (contracts); logistics and supply; and principles of manufacturing.

Provided vocational training and supervision of students rotating through the tailor shop to learn leatherworking, making clothes and hats, and repairing shoes.

Biography: Born into the House of Erwina, descendant of a lineage of *H. sapiens.*

Head Matron Aquina [a-*qui*-na] (2X^T)—head of the House of Erwina

Subjects taught: Propriety and decorum in the manor house; family matters VI (mentoring); governance I (civics), II (rules and regulations), III (policy and politics), IV (alliances, treaties).

Biography: Born into the House of Erwina and a descendant of Ruth.

Transforms across *Canidae*, *Felidae*, and *Falconidae* families. Alternate species: Red fox, gray wolf, lynx, peregrine falcon.

Madam Bernarda [bur-*nar*-da] (X, X)—assistant dean, liberal arts; dormitory supervisor for Form I.

Subjects taught: Reading and writing in the common language I–IX, safety measures III (sheltering, with Master Titus), Rμηεîc I–VI.

Biography: Born into the House of Erwina, descendant of a lineage of *H. sapiens.*

Madam Borislav [*bor*-is-lof] (X, X^T)—chief geographer and cartographer.

Subjects taught: Regional geography I (northwest), II (southwest), III northeast), and IV (southeast); cartography I (northwest), II (southwest), III northeast), and IV (southeast).

Biography: Born into the House of Erwina; descendant of an Erwinian lineage of *H. transformans.*

Transforms within *Canidae* family. Alternate species: Red fox.

Madam Carawan [*cāre*-a-wăn] (X, X^T)—chief statistician.

Subjects taught: Arithmetic I–IX; mathematics I, II, III, IV (geometry, with Master Heroditus),

V (business math, with Master Androv); algebra I, II (with Madam Kendarra); calculus I, II (with Master Vikarov); potions II (measuring portions and calculating doses, with Master Gaius); statistics.

Biography: Born into the House of Erwina, descendant of an Erwinian lineage of *H. transformans*.

Transforms within *Canidae* family. Alternate species: Gray fox, gray wolf.

Master Chernavich [*churn*-a-vĭch] (X^T, Y)—chief heraldist and armorist.

Subjects taught: Swordsmanship (with Madam Kavarova).

Provided vocational training and supervision of students rotating through the armory in the forging of ironworks.

Biography: Born into the House of Erwina, descendant of an Erwinian lineage of *H. transformans*.

Transforms within *Ursidae* family. Alternate species: Black bear.

Master Crocius [*crō*-ce-us] (X^T, Y)—chief, northeast outpost.

Subjects taught: None.

Provided vocational training and supervision for students interning as scouts and in directing operations at an outpost.

Biography: Born into the House of Erwina, descendant of an Erwinian lineage of *H. transformans*.

Served as a scout for thirty-five years. Scouted all regions of Erwina, eventually focusing on the northeast territory and Biogenics.

Transforms within *Ursidae* family. Alternate species: Brown bear.

Madam Davidea [dah-vĭ-*dē*-ah (X, X^T)—chief arborist.

Subjects taught: Forestry I (hardwood/deciduous), II (fruit/flowering), and III (grafting).

Provided vocational training and supervision for students interning in forestry.

Biography: Born into the House of Erwina, descendant of an Erwinian lineage of *H. transformans*.

Transforms within *Cervidae* family. Alternate species: White-tailed deer.

Master Ferronas [fer-ōn-ăs] (X^T, Y)—master gardener.

Subjects taught: Identification of common flowers; identification of common vegetables; gardening I (seedlings), II (herbs), and III (vegetables).

Biography: Born into the House of Erwina, descendant of an Erwinian lineage of *H. transformans*.

Transforms within *Mustelidae* family. Alternate species: Badger.

Madam Florenza [flōr-ěn-za] (X, X)—chief archivist.

Subjects taught: Preserving and storing documents (with Master Hectavian); historic preservation I (paper/parchment), II (art/artifacts, with Master Hectavian); genealogy (pedigrees, with Master Mikalov).

Provided vocational training and supervision for students rotating through the archives as they conduct searches, prepare pedigrees, and participate in the preparation of parchment.

Biography: Born into the House of Erwina, descendant of a lineage of *H. sapiens*.

Madam Fredrika [frěd-rē-ka] (X, X^T)—head seamstress.

Subjects taught: Sewing I (mending), II (patterns), III (designing, with Master Androv), IV (cloth materials), and V (spinning and weaving); graphic arts I (sketching, with Master Heroditus); logistics and supply (with Master Androv).

Provided vocational training and supervision of students rotating through the dressmaking shop and making clothes from patterns.

Biography: Born into the House of Erwina, descendant of an Erwinian lineage of *H. transformans*.

Transforms within *Canidae* family. Alternate species: Red wolf.

Master Gaius [gī-us] (X^T, Y)—assistant dean, potions master.

Subjects taught: Potions I (types of potions), II (calculations and measurements, with Madam Carawan), III (soups, with Madam Ranicova), IV (soaps, with Madam Gannett), V (inks, dyes, and stains, with Master Ignatius), VI (preparation of infusions, essential oils, and salves, with Matron H'Umara), VII (topical antiseptics, with Master Stuvidicus), VIII (medicinal with Matron H'Umara), IX (inorganic, with Master Ignatius), X (soporifics/hypnotics, with Matron H'Umara and Madam Ocala), XI (toxins, with Matron H'Umara and Madam Ocala); environmental toxicology; safety measures VI (small fires, with Master Titus and Master Ratorovic).

Biography: Born into the House of Erwina, descendant of an Erwinian lineage of *H. transformans*.

Transforms within *Canidae* family. Alternate species: Gray fox, gray wolf.

Madam Gannett [*gan*-net] (X, X^T)—head laundress.

Subjects taught: Potions IV (soaps, with Master Gaius).

Provided vocational training and supervision for students in the proper care and cleaning of different materials, including their own clothing.

Biography: Born into the House of Gregor and married into the House of Erwina.

Transforms within *Cervidae* family. Alternate species: Caribou.

Master Hectavian [hĕk-tā-vē-an] (X, Y)—chief librarian.

Subjects taught: Preserving and storing documents (with Madam Florenza); historic preservation I (paper/parchment, with Madam Florenza), II (art and artifacts).

Provided vocational training for students retrieving research material and texts from the library and in the protection and storage of perishable materials including artwork.

Biography: Born into the House of Erwina, descendant of a lineage of *H. sapiens*.

Master Heroditus [her-ŏd-ĭ-tus] (X^T, Y)—chief architect and master builder.

Subjects taught: Stone working and sculpture; geometry; architecture I (form and function), II (basic building), III (masonry), IV (homes), V (tunnels, with Madam Kendorra), VI (caves, with Madam Phillius); construction and maintenance of plumbing; graphic arts I (sketching, with Madam Fredericka), II (architectural designs), and III (implementation).

Biography: Born into the House of Erwina, descendant of an Erwinian lineage of *H. transformans*.

Transforms into *Ursidae* family: Alternate species: Brown bear.

Matron H'Umara [*hu*-mar-a] (2X^T)—chief physician at Erwina.

Subjects taught: Family matters IV (changes associated with puberty); potions VI (preparation of infusions, essential oils, and salves), VII (medicinal: parts 1, 2, 3), IX (toxins, with Master Gaius and Madam Ocala); botany IV (medicinal herbs, with Madam Ocala); transformation I (basic rules); biology VIII (human physiology); transformation III (treatment of complications); biology X (microbiology); chemistry III (biochemistry); psychology III (dysphorias).

Biography: Born into the House of H'Aleth, a direct descendant of Ruth and a Sister.

Transforms across mammalian and avian classes: *Canidae*, *Felidae*, *Lontra*, *Falconidae*, *Accipitridae*, *Strigidae*. Alternate species: Red fox, cougar, river otter, peregrine falcon, Cooper's hawk, golden eagle, long-eared owl.

Master Ignatius [ig-*nā*-cē-us] (X^T, Y)—chief geologist and chemist.

Subjects taught: Identification of rocks and minerals; industrial rocks and minerals and their uses; geology I (formations), II (industrial minerals), and III (coal); potions IV (preparation of inks, dyes, and stains and use of minerals); chemistry I (general), II (organic), III (biochemistry, with Matron H'Umara); minerology; environmental toxicology (with Madam Ocala).

Biography: Born into the House of Erwina, descendant of an Erwinian lineage of *H. transformans*.

Transforms within *Cervidae* family. Alternate species: Elk (red deer).

Master Iranapolis [ir-ăn-*a*-pōl-ĭs] (X^T, Y)—martial arts.

Subjects taught: Martial arts levels I, II, III, and IV (with Madam Kavarova); wrestling, boxing.

Biography: Born into the House of Erwina, descendant of an Erwinian lineage of *H. transformans*.

Transforms within *Suidae* family. Alternate species: Wild boar.

Master Janislov [*jan*-ĭs-lof] (X^T, Y)—chief agriculturalist.

Subjects taught: Raising and processing grains; raising fruit and nut trees; raising and processing vegetables; soils I (types and implications for agriculture), II (implications for hydrology, with Madam Kendorra); agriculture I (reaping), II (farming); landscaping and terracing.

Biography: Born into the House of Gregor, descendant of a Gregorian lineage of *H. transformans*.

Transforms within *Canidae* family. Alternate species: Artic wolf. During the winter, he travels to Gregor to work in botanical gardens.

Master Josephus [jōs-ĕ-fŭs] (X^T, Y)—researcher, natural history and research center.

Subjects taught: Ethnicity and culture, anthropology, sociology, research principles and methods.

Biography: Born into the House of Erwina, descendant of an Erwinian lineage of *H. transformans*.

Transforms within *Bovidae* family. Alternate species: Mountain goat.

Dr. Jozefa [jō-zĕ-fă]—physician, northeast outpost and Gregor.

Subjects taught: None at Erwina.

Supervises medical students and interns rotating to Erwina.

Biography: Born in to the House of Erwina, descendant of an Erwinian lineage of *H. transformans*.

Schooled in medicine and genetics at Gregor. He specializes in the genetics of corrupted creatures and their outcomes. He often visits the northeast outpost because of the number of sightings in that region.

Transforms across *Cervidae* species. Alternate species: White-tailed deer.

Matron Kavarova [ka-var-*o*-va] ($2X^T$)—specialist, martial arts.

Subjects taught: Martial arts I–IV (with Master Iranapolis); archery; strategy I (defense), II (offense, with Master Titus); tactics (with Master Titus); and swordsmanship (with Master Chernavich).

Biography: Born into the House of H'Aleth, descendant of Ruth and a former Sister, married into the House of Erwina and moved there before the destruction of H'Aleth.

Transforms across *Canidae, Felidae,* and *Strigidae* families. Alternate species: Gray wolf, gray fox, cougar, great horned owl.

Madam Kendorra [ken-*dor*-a] ($2X^T$)—chief engineer.

Subjects taught: Sources of energy II (wind, with Master Leonid), III (water, with Master Leonid), IV (steam), and V (man and animal power, with Madam Varanitova and Dr. Stuvidicus); algebra I, II (with Madam Carawan); soils II (implications for hydrology, with Master Janislov); hydrology I (lakes/streams), II (hydrodynamics), and III (rivers/waterfalls, with Master Leonid), IV (dams, with Master Heroditus); engineering I (electricity/magnetism), II (applied mechanics).

Biography: Born in to the House of Erwina, descendant of an Erwinian lineage of *H. transformans.*

Transforms across *Canidae and Felidae* families. Alternate Species: Gray wolf, lynx.

Master Leonid [*lē*-o-nĭd] (X, Y)—chief meteorologist.

Subjects taught: Sources of energy I (solar, with Master Vikerov), II (wind, with Madam Kendorra), and III (water, with Madam Kendorra); common weather events I (fall, winter), II (spring, summer); water sources; distilling and purifying water; climatology I (fall and winter), II (emergent conditions), III (spring and summer).

Biography: Born into the House of Erwina, descendant of a lineage of *H. sapiens.*

Madam Lindenova [*lĭn*-dĕn-*o*-va] (X, X^T)—chief, natural gistory and research center.

Subjects taught: Epidemiology, demographics, logic.

Biography: Born into the House of Erwina, descendant of an Erwinian lineage of *H. transformans;*

Transforms within *Cervidae* families. Alternate species: Mule deer.

Madam Merena [mer-ā-nah] ($2X^T$)—specialist, swimming and diving.

Subjects taught: Swimming (all styles); diving (platform and springboard).

Biography: Born into the House of Erwina, descendant of an Erwinian lineage of *H. transformans;*

Transforms across *Canidae* and *Felidae* families. Alternate species: Gray fox, jaguar.

Master Mikalov [*mĭk*-ă-lŏf] (X^T, Y)—chief geneticist at Erwina.

Subjects taught: Genetics I (functions of genes and chromosomes), II (genetic disorders, with Madam H'Umara), III (mutagens and mutations); genealogy (pedigrees, with Madam Florenza).

Biography: Born into the House of Gregor and moved to Erwina, descendant of a Gregorian lineage of *H. transformans.*

Transforms within *Cervidae* family. Alternate species: Caribou.

Madam Morenavik [mor-*ren*-a-vik] (X, X^T)—chief equestrian (spouse of Headmaster Morenavik).

Subjects taught: Horseback riding, care and feeding of animals V (farm working animals, with Master Navarov), horsemanship.

Provided supervision and vocational training for the care and training of horses.

Biography: Born into the House of Erwina, descendant of an Erwinian lineage of *H. transformans*.

Transforms within *Equidae* family. Alternate species: Horse.

Headmaster Morenavik (X^T, Y)—dean, schoolhouse.

Subjects taught: Epidemiology, logic.

Biography: Born into the House of Gregor, descendant of a Gregorian lineage of *H. transformans*.

Transforms within *Cervidae* family. Alternate species: Mule deer.

Madam Nadina [na-*de*-na] (X, X)—gymnastics instructor.

Subjects taught: Gymnastics (all levels).

Provided supervision and vocational training in care and maintenance of gymnastic equipment and use of the hemp highway.

Biography: Born into the House of Erwina, descendant of a lineage of *H. sapiens*.

Master Navarov [*năv*-ar-ŏf] (X^T, Y)—chief veterinarian, doctor of veterinary medicine.

Subjects taught: Care and feeding animals V (farm working animals, with Madam Morenavic), veterinary first aid, comparative anatomy.

Biography: Born into the House of Erwina, descendant of an Erwinian lineage of *H. transformans*.

Transforms within *Canidae* family. Alternate species: Gray fox, red wolf.

Master Nemenicus [nĕ-*men*-ĭ-cus] (X^T, Y)—chief ichthyologist (study of fish) and herpatologist (study of amphibians).

Subjects taught: Identification of small reptiles and amphibians; care and feeding II (native small reptiles and amphibians); biology IV (fish), IV (reptiles and amphibians, with Master Pastorov).

Biography: Born into the House of Erwina, descendant of an Erwinian lineage of *H. transformans*.

Transforms within *Cervidae* family. Alternate species: Mule deer.

Madam Ocala [o-*sa*-la] (X, X^T)—chief botanist.

Subjects taught: Identifying wild berries and nuts; identifying common (nonmedicinal) herbs; identifying edible from nonedible wild plants; identifying poisonous plants and animals (with Master Pastarov); botany I (seed/flowering), II (trees), III (aquatic), IV (medicinal herbs and berries, with Matron H'Umara); identifying and distinguishing toxic and poisonous plants; plant toxicology; environmental toxicology (with Master Ignatius); potions IX (toxins, with Matron H'Umara and Master Titus); scouting and surveillance V (southeast region, with Master Titus).

Biography: Born into the House of H'Aleth, descendant of another lineage of *H. transformans.*

Transforms within *Procyonidae* family. Alternate species: Raccoon.

Master Pastorov [*păs*-tor-ŏv] (X^T, Y)—chief biologist and zoologist.

Subjects taught: Identification of native mammal species; identifying poisonous plants and animals (with Madam Ocala); care and feeding I (native small mammals); safety measures IV (wild animals, with Master Titus); biology I (mammalian), II (avian, with Master Xavier), III (insects), IV (fish, with Master Nemenicus), V (reptiles/amphibians), VI (human anatomy, with Dr. Stuvidicus), VII (cell biology), VIII (human physiology, with Matron H'Osanna), IX (exotics, with Madam Phillius), X (microbiology), XI (comparative anatomy, with Master Stuvidicus); flora and fauna I (grasslands/plains, with Madam Ocala), II (river valleys, with Madam Ocala), III (mountains), IV (caves and caverns, with Madam Phillius), V (inland waterways), VI (mountains, extended survey), VII (coastal plains extended survey, with Madam Ocala).

Biography: Born into the House of Gregor, descendant of a Gregorian lineage of *H. transformans.*

Transforms within *Ursidae* family. Alternate species: Polar bear. He often travels to Gregor where he also serves chief biologist and zoologist.

Matron Patrina [pa-*trē*-nah] (2XT)—supervisor, Form II dormitory supervisor.

Subjects taught: Protocol and etiquette in the classroom; safety measures V (in the dark, with Madam Phillius).

Biography: Born into the House of H'Aleth, a direct descendant of Ruth, and a Sister. She was raised at H'Aleth. She moved to Erwina with her son only a few days before H'Aleth was attacked. Her husband remained to defend their House and died there.

Transforms within *Canidae, Felidae, Falconidae,* and *Mustelidae.* Alternate species: Gray wolf, cougar, prairie falcon, wolverine.

Madam Phillius [fĭl-ē-us] (X, X^T)—chief chiroptologist.

Subjects taught: Flora and fauna of caves and caverns (with Master Pastorov); safety measures V (in the dark, with Madam Patrina); biology IX (exotics, including bats).

Biography: Born into the House of Erwina, descendant of an Erwinian lineage of *H. transformans.*

Transforms within *Bovidae* family. Alternate species: Mountain goat.

Madam Ranicova [ran-ĭ-cō-va] (X, X^T)—chief nutritionist.

Subjects taught: Nutrition I (types of nutrients), II (nutritional values), and III (meal planning); potions III (soups).

Biography: Born into the House of Gregor, descendant of a Gregorian lineage of *H. transformans.* She moved to Erwina to teach in the schoolhouse.

Transforms within *Pagophilus* family. Alternate species: Harp seal.

Master Ratorovic [ră-*tor*-o-vĭk] (X^T, Y)—head chef, director of the rectory kitchen.

Subjects taught: Safety measures VI (small fires, with Master Titus and Master Gaius).

Provided vocational training and supervision for students rotating through the rectory in the preparation of meals including cooking and presentation.

Biography: Born into the House of Gregor, descendant of a Gregorian lineage of *H. transformans.*

Transforms within *Bovidae* family. Alternate species: Mountain goat.

Master Salinas [sal-*en*-us] (X^T, Y)—boat master.

Subjects taught: Boating and boatmanship.

Provided vocational training and supervision for students rotating through boating (all forms) and in maintenance and repair of boats and boating equipment.

Biography: Born into the House of Erwina, descendant of an Erwinian lineage of *H. transformans*.

Transforms within *Canidae* family. Alternate species: Gray fox.

Dr. Stuvidicus [stu-*vĭ*-dĭ-cus] (X^T, Y)—physician.

Subjects taught: Sources of energy (manpower, with Madam Kendorra); distilling and purifying water; basic first aid; potions VII (topical antiseptics); biology IV (human anatomy), XI (comparative anatomy with Master Pastorov); transformation II (limitations, adverse reactions); psychology I (human/animal, with Mastor Pastorov), II (human/animal grief/loss, with Mastor Pastorov).

Biography: Born into the House of Erwina, descendant of an Erwinian lineage of *H. transformans*.

Transforms within *Cervidae* family. Alternate species: White-tailed deer stag.

Master Titus [*tī*-tus] (X^T, Y)—chief of security, chief safety officer.

Subjects taught: Safety measures I (reporting), II (poisonous plants/animals, with Madam Ocala and Master Pastarov), III (sheltering, with Madam Bernarda), IV (wild animals, with Master Pastorov), V (darkness, with Madam Patrina and Madam Phillius), VI (small fires, with Master Gaius and Master Ratorovic), and VII (accurate observation); geography of Biogenics territories with implications; geography of Cassius territories with implications; scouting and surveillance I (summer/fall, with scout interns), II (reporting), III (winter/spring, with scout interns), IV (northeast region, with Master Crocius), and V (southeast region, with Madam Ocala); strategy I (defense, with Madam Kavarova), II (offense, with Madam Kavarova); tactics (with Madam Kavarova); explosive armaments (with Master Vikarov).

Biography: Born into the House of Erwina, descendant of an Erwinian lineage of *H. transformans*.

Transforms within *Ovidae* family. Alternate species: Big horn mountain sheep.

Matron Trevora [tre-*vŏr*-a] (2X^T)—associate dean.

Subjects taught: History of the three Houses; history of Biogenics Corporation and Cassius Foundation; ethics I (principles of ethics), II (ethics of transformation, with Matron Aquina), III (business ethics, with Master Androv).

Biography: Matron Trevora ($2X^T$) was born into the House of H'Aleth. She was a direct descendant of Ruth through H'Anna and a former Sister in the House of H'Aleth. Although once eligible to be its Mistress, Matron Trevora relinquished that role when she married into the House of Erwina. She and her husband (X^T, Y) had two children: a son (X^T, Y), who became a geneticist and moved to Gregor, and a daughter ($2X^T$), who married back into the House of H'Aleth and died there. Thus, even though Matron Trevora had been a member of Erwina for nearly twenty years, she still had a very strong kinship with H'Aleth. Matron Trevora became a widow when her husband was killed in a landslide triggered by an earthquake under the northern mountains. She was approaching seventy years of age when she first encountered Ruwena in an outpost village.

Transforms across *Canidae*, *Felidae*, *Cervidae*, and *Falconidae* families. Alternate species: Red wolf, lynx, mule deer, and peregrine falcon.

Madam Varanitova [var-an-ĭ-*tōv*-a] (X, X^T)—chief, animal husbandry

Subjects taught: Sources of energy and their use V (animal power, with Madam Kendorra); care and feeding IV (farm birds, with Master Xavier), V (working farm animals, with Madam Morenavic and Master Navarov), and VI (ranch/range animals); animal husbandry I (farm animals), II (ranch/range animals).

Biography: Born into the House of Gregor, descendant of a Gregorian lineage of *H. transformans*.

Transforms within *Canidae* families. Alternate species: Artic fox, artic wolf. During the winter, she would work in veterinary clinic at Gregor and conduct surveillance on artic species.

Master Vikarov [*vik*-ar-ov] (X^T, Y)—chief astronomer and physicist.

Subjects taught: Sources of energy I (solar energy, with Master Leonid); telling time I (sundial), II (bell towers), III (moon phases); night-sky watching I (fall/winter), II (spring/summer); astronomy I (solar system), III (galaxies); physics I (energy, mass, gravity), II (*Stella ignis*); calculus I, II (with Madam Carawan); explosive armaments (with Master Titus).

Biography: Born into the House of Erwina, descendant of another lineage of *H. transformans*.

Transforms within *Ovidae* family. Alternate species: Bighorn sheep.

Madam Wallenexis [wal-ĕn-*ex*-is] (X, X^T)—chief enologist and master winemaker.

Subjects taught: Identification of common fruits, processing fruits with practicum, raising and processing grapes.

Provided vocational training and supervision for students rotating through the winery in the preparation of jams, jellies, and juices from various fruits, including techniques for long-term storage.

Biography: Born into the House of Erwina, descendant of another lineage of *H. transformans*.

Transforms within the *Canidae* family. Alternate species: Red wolf. She was a redhead also.

Madam Wilhelmina [wil-hel-*min*-a] (2X^T)—associate dean, chair of curriculum forum, dormitory supervisor for Form III.

Subjects taught: Family matters I (growth/development), II (caring for infants), III (supervising children at home), IV (puberty), V (supervising children on expeditions), VI (mentoring, with Matron Aquina); ethnicity and culture; research principles and practices.

Biography: Born into the House of Erwina, descendant of an Erwinian lineage of *H. transformans*.

Transforms across *Canidae* and *Cervidae* families. Alternate species: Gray fox, mule deer.

Master Xavier [zā-vē-ĕr] (X^T, Y)—chief falconer and ornithologist (study of birds), doctor of veterinary medicine.

Subjects taught: Identification of native birds; care and feeding III (native small birds, not raptors), IV (farm birds, with Madam Varanitova); biology II (avian species, including raptors); falconry.

Provided supervision and vocational training in the care, management, and training of raptors.

Biography: Born in the House of H'Aleth, remote descendant of Edvar and another lineage of *H. transformans*.

Transforms within *Canidae* family. Alternate species: Gray wolf.

Master Yacobon [yak-ō-bŏn] (X, Y)—chief carpenter.

Subjects taught: Preparation of weeds and grasses for wicker; woodworking I (sanding/polishing), II (staining), III (repairing furniture),

IV (making furniture); construction of hemp ropes, ladders, and byways; wood sculpting.

Provided vocational training and supervision for students rotating through the woodworking shop to learn skills in repairing and making different types of products with wood and wicker.

Biography: Born into the House of Erwina, descendant of a lineage of *H. sapiens*.

Appendix K (Part 1)

Individual Students

(In Alphabetical Order)

Children who had lost both parents at H'Aleth were raised as sons and daughters of H'Aleth in the House of Erwina. This was done in remembrance of their House. Although their structural home was the schoolhouse, they were raised by the community and had full run of the compound within its perimeter. Every family in the main compound served as their surrogate parents.

Form II Senior Year Cohort (excluding Ruwena, née H'Ester)

Avelynda [*a*-věl-*ĭn*-da] (2X^T)
  Born into the House of Erwina, descendant of an Erwinian lineage of *H. transformans*.
  Transforms within *Canidae* family. Alternate species: Red fox.

Deven (X, Y)
  Born into the House of Erwina, descendant of an Erwinian lineage of *H. sapiens*.

Erik (X^T, Y)
    Born into the House of Erwina, descendant of an Erwinian lineage
of *H. transformans.*
    Transforms within *Procyonidae* family. Alternate species: Raccoon.

Ervan (X^T, Y)
    Born into the House of Erwina, descendant of an Erwinian lineage
of *H. transformans.*
    Transforms within *Bovidae* family. Alternate species: Mountain goat.

Henrik (X^T, Y)
    Born into the House of Erwina, descendant of an Erwinian lineage
of *H. transformans.*
    Transforms within *Cervidae* family. Alternate species: Mule deer.

Javier (X^T, Y)
    Born into the House of Erwina, descendant of an Erwinian lineage
of *H. transformans.*
    Transforms within *Mustelidae* family. Alternate species: Badger.

Marianna (X, X^T)
    Born into the House of Erwina, descendant of an Erwinian lineage
of *H. transformans.*
    Transforms within *Canidae* family. Alternate species: Gray fox.

Qwincy (X, Y)
    Born into the House of Erwina, descendant of an Erwinian lineage
of *H. sapiens.*

Salwen (X^T, Y)
    Born into the House of Erwina, descendant of an Erwinian lineage
of *H. transformans.*
    Transforms within *Ursidae* family. Alternate species: Black bear.

Samiya [sam-ī-ya] ($2X^T$)
    Born into the House of Erwina; descendant of an Erwinian lineage of
H. transformans and a distant relative of Ruth via the paternal line.

497

Transforms across *Felidae* and *Cervidae* families. Alternate species: Lynx, white-tailed deer.

Savannah ($2X^T$)

Born into the House of Erwina, descendant of an Erwinian lineage of *H. transformans*.

Transforms within *Canidae* family. Alternate species: Gray wolf.

Biography: Both of her parents lived and worked in Erwina. They had four children of which Savannah was the oldest. Consequently, she learned at any early age to care for her younger siblings and watch over them. Savannah became Ruwena's mentor during Ruwena's first year at Erwina. Subsequently, they became and remained close friends.

Other Students

Galan (X^T, Y)

Born into the House of Erwina, descendant of an Erwinian lineage of *H. transformans*.

Transforms within the *Ursidae* family. Alternate species: Black bear.

Galan was a Form IV senior during the predator-prey games.

Raphael (X^T, Y)

Born into the House of Erwina, descendant of an Erwinian lineage of *H. sapiens*.

Biography: Form IV student who led a group of Form I students during the unannounced evacuation drill.

Sala (X, X^T)

Born into the House of Erwina, descendant of an Erwinian lineage of *H. transformans*.

Transforms within the *Canidae* family. Alternate species: Red fox.

Sala was a Form IV senior during the unannounced evacuation drill. She also accompanied Madam Davidea on a field trip to plant trees, where she provided security and proctored the students. When a hybrid creature tried to attack one of the students, Sala interceded and killed the animal.

Stefan (X^T, Y)

Born into the House of Erwina, descendant of an Erwinian lineage of *H. transformans*.

Transforms within the *Cervidae* family. Alternate species: Elk (red deer).

Biography: Stefan was a Form IV student and was on a summer internship in the medical clinic when he met Savannah. Stefan subsequently went to Gregor to study medicine. He and Savannah married during his second year at Gregor. Savannah moved to Gregor until Stefan finished his studies, then they both returned to Erwina. Stefan later served as a physician providing care to the hominids who immigrated to H'Aleth when it was reestablished.

Appendix K (Part 2)

Family-Naming Conventions

House of H'Aleth

The first names of female children were often a variation of Ruth in memory of the mistress of the House of H'Aleth. This was especially true of firstborn female offspring. In addition to Ruth, commonly used names included Ruanna, Rulinda, Ruthalyn, Ruthanne, Rutilda, and Ruwena. These were followed by Rosalyn, Rose, Roseanne, and Rowena. Similarly, the first names of firstborn male children were often a variation of Edvar. Commonly used names were prefaced by *Ed* and included Edwin (also a common name in the House of Erwina), Edward, Edmard, and Edmond.

For female offspring who could trace their lineage directly back to Edvar and Ruth, their first names traditionally were prefaced with an *H'* and were often the only name used (e.g., H'Eleanora, H'Ilgraith, H'Ester, etc.). This convention readily distinguished those members who were Sisters of the House of H'Aleth and were eligible to become its Mistress (app. B, pedigrees 6 and 7).

Those members of H'Aleth who fled to Erwina and Gregor often maintained these naming conventions in honor of their kinsmen and women. With the last of the Sisters thought lost at H'Aleth, the use of the *H'* prefix ceased save for those who already bore it.

House of Erwina

The first names of native born Erwinians often included or ended with *-van*, *-ven*, *-vin*, *-wan*, *-wen*, and *-win*. When used as suffixes, these names identified most children as born into the House of Erwina. The first names of firstborn male children were often a variation of *Erwin* and were often prefaced with *Er*. In addition to Erwin, commonly used names included Ervin, Erven, or Ervan. These variations were a plague upon the faculty when they had multiple students so named in the same class. The names of firstborn female offspring often began with an *E* (e.g., Elena, Evelyn, etc.)

Many Erwinians derive their lineage from the House of H'Aleth. Thus, both the House of H'Aleth and the House of Erwina selected names starting with an *E* for both genders. Hence, there was considerable overlap in naming conventions.

House of Gregor

This House was founded by Dr. Wilhelm Gregorovich and Dr. Suzanne Ivanova Gregorovich, a husband-and-wife team of geneticists who believed in the judicious use of genetic engineering. They shortened the name to Gregor. Their descendants could be identified by surnames that included the suffixes *-ov*, *-ova*, *-vik*, and *-vich* (e.g., Master Janislov, Master Morenavik, Madam Ranicova, etc.).

Other Surnames

Other surnames reflect those who joined one of the three Houses as immigrants from another region and other families. Most but not all these were *H. transformans* who had fled from Biogenics and Cassius. There were many *H. sapiens* as well who were sympathetic to the plight of *H. transformans* and might have been persecuted for it.

Appendix L

Erwinian Scouts

(In Alphabetical Order)

Regardless of where they were born—H'Aleth, Erwina, or Gregor—scouts were almost always graduates of the schoolhouse. They often served as preceptors for students on field expeditions, and some served as adjunct faculty for the schoolhouse.

Alan (X^T, Y)—scout, north and northeastern and arctic regions.
    Born into the House of Erwina, descendant of an Erwinian lineage of *H. transformans*.
    Transforms within *Canidae* family. Alternate species: Arctic fox, gray wolf.
    Biography: during the winter, Alan traveled to Gregor and served as a scout in the high north.

Barrow (X^T, Y)—scout, south and southwestern regions.
    Born into the House of Erwina, descendant of an Erwinian lineage of *H. transformans*.
    Transforms within *Canidae* family. Alternate species: Red wolf.

Evan (X^T, Y)—scout, north and northeastern regions.

Born into the House of Erwina, descendant of an Erwinian lineage of *H. transformans*.

Transforms within *Canidae* family. Alternate species: red fox, gray wolf.

Biography: Evan was a Form III senior during the evacuation drill. He was a scout during the summer trip to the northeast outpost, where he rescued Ruwena. Evan met Ruwena again on her second trip to the northeast outpost. He was nearly killed when he overpowered a hybrid wolf. He became Ruwena's beau during that trip.

Both Evan's mother, Edrea ($2X^T$), and his father, Will (X^T, Y), were scouts at the northeast outpost and loved it. His mother's alternate species were gray wolf and red fox. His father's alternate species was gray wolf. Evan was sent to Erwina at age four for schooling; however, much of his experience was gained at the northeast outpost on visits to his home. Since both parents were scouts, he learned scouting techniques at a very early age. He also learned the value of being patient and became a steady and careful observer. Thus, Evan was already an experienced scout before ever taking the scouting and surveillance classes at Erwina. The faculty recognized his accomplishments and tasked him to serve as coleader with other faculty members on the student expeditions. This freed up a faculty member or another scout who would otherwise have been assigned. When his father died, his mother moved to the compound and lived out her life there. She continued to serve as a scout and later served as a mentor and guide on student scouting and surveillance expeditions.

Rachel ($2X^T$)—scout, south and southeastern regions.

Born into the House of H'Aleth and a remote descendant of Ruth via the paternal line (ped. 8).

Transforms across *Canidae*, *Felidae*, and *Accipitridae* families. Alternate species: Red wolf, red fox, lynx, and red-tailed hawk. She was one of the few Erwinians who could transform across canine, feline, and avian species.

Biography: Rachel had flaming-red hair—a gift from her parents of a recessive variant of a gene for red hair color (the MC1R gene on chromosome 16). This gene codes for a protein that stimulates the production of a specific form of melanin. In order to display this phenotype, Rachel had to be homozygous for the gene. This same gene was active in her alternate species, the red fox and red wolf.

Rachel's mother ($2X^T$) was a researcher at H'Aleth studying *H. transformans.* Her mother's alternate species were red wolf, red fox, and lynx. Her father (X^T, Y) was an architect and engineer at H'Aleth and served as a scout. His alternate species was a red wolf. Her parents had sent her to school at Erwina at five years of age. When Cassius attacked H'Aleth, both her parents stayed to defend it and were lost. Thus, Rachel essentially grew up in Erwina, which became her home and her House.

Rachel was skilled in the martial arts, including swordsmanship. She also keen eyesight (a gift of her raptor genes) and was highly skilled in archery. She had opted to become a scout in the southeastern region of Erwina where her alternate species—red wolf, red fox, lynx, and red-tailed hawk—were a good fit with the environment there. She was tasked to give Ruwena archery lessons before Ruwena went on her second trip to the northeast outpost.

Warren (X^T, Y)—scout, north and northeastern regions.

Biography: born into the House of Erwina, descendant of an Erwinian lineage of *H. transformans.*

Transforms within *Ursidae* family. Alternate species: Brown bear.

Warren was a scout when Ruwena went to the northeast outpost for the second time. He responded to her cries as a Cooper's hawk when Evan, as a wolf, was badly injured in a fight with a hybrid wolf. He also came to Galan's rescue when he dueled with Master Chervavich (a black bear) during the predator-prey games.

Ped. 8. Lineage of Rachel.

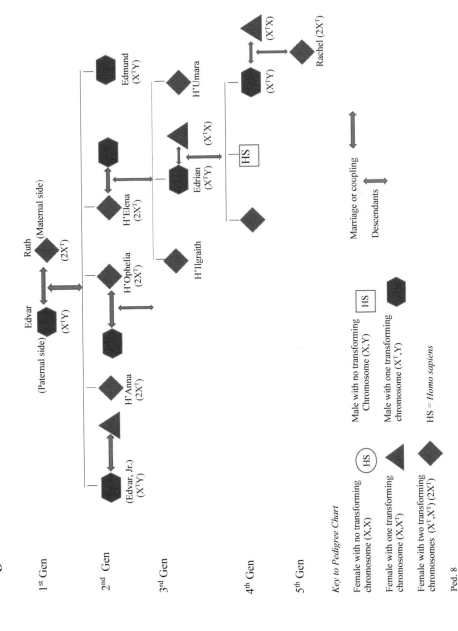

1st Gen

2nd Gen

3rd Gen

4th Gen

5th Gen

Edvar (Paternal side)   Ruth   (Maternal side)

Edvar (X^{T}Y)

Edvar, Jr. (X^{T}Y)

H'Anna (2X^T)

H'Ophelia (2X^T)

Ruth (2X^T)

H'Elena (2X^T)

Edmund (X^{T}Y)

H'Ilgraith

Edrian (X^{T}Y)

HS

(X^{T}X)

H'Umara

(X^{T}Y)

(X^{T}X)

Rachel (2X^T)

Marriage or coupling

Descendants

Key to Pedigree Chart

Female with no transforming chromosome (X,X)   HS

Female with one transforming chromosome (X,X^T)

Female with two transforming chromosomes (X^T,X^T) (2X^T)

Male with no transforming Chromosome (X,Y)

Male with one transforming chromosome (X^T,Y)   HS

HS = *Homo sapiens*

Ped. 8

505

Appendix M

Hybrid Creatures

Hybrids are humans and animals in which the genes of one species are mixed with those of one or more other species. In a human hybrid, the base genome is human with animal genes added. The names of corrupted humans end in *–id* or *–oid* and reflect the human base genome mixed with other animals (e.g., cercolupoid). In a hybrid animal, the base genome belongs to one animal with other animal genes added.

When the results of a hybridization are disastrous, the resulting entity is considered corrupted. The majority of these corruptions are the result of genetic experimentation. A corrupted human may also result from an incomplete or aborted transformation.

These creatures are not inherently monsters. They are humans and animals who were genetically altered and bred by the Cassius organization in general and by one malicious human in particular whose own physique was corrupted.

Human–Animal Hybrids

Cercolupoid [cer-co-*lu*-poid]—genes of a baboon (*cerco-*) and wolf (*lup-*) spliced into the genome of a human (*-oid*), who underwent forced transformation with disastrous results and no ability to restore human form. These creatures were one of Cassius's earliest and glaringly unsuccessful attempts to create an *H. transformans* hybrid via genetic engineering and forced transformation.

Cercopithursid [*cer*-co-*pith*-ur-sid] (illus. 6)—genes of a baboon (*cercopith-*) and bear (*urs-*) spliced into the genome of a human (*-id*), who was forced into a transformation that could not be reversed. Although his base genome is clearly human, this hybrid has fewer human features and more bear and baboon features than the serojabovid. These hominids were engineered specifically for purposes of performing hard labor in Cassius's villages and for serving as guards.

Crocutalupoid [*cro*-cu-ta-*lup*-oid] (illus. 11)—genes of a hyena (*crocuta-*) and wolf (*lup-*) spliced into the genome of a human (*-oid*). Similar to the cercopithursid, the base genome is clearly human with fewer human features and more hyena and wolf features. These hominids were engineered by Cassius specifically for purposes of hunting large prey, fighting an enemy, and guarding storehouses.

Serojabovid [ser-o-ja-*bōv*-id] (illus. 25)—genes of a boar (*seroja-*) and bison (*bov-*) spliced into the genome of a human (*-id*). This hominid was engineered specifically for purposes of performing hard labor in Cassius's villages. He was approximately six feet tall; had a large build (chest, arms, legs) with a humped back; large predominantly human head with some features of bison, especially nose, mouth, and chin; teeth broad and flat like that of an herbivore with upwardly curved canines that extended outside of the mouth (courtesy of boar genes); vestigial (small) bison horns on either side of head; and a thick layer of body hair.

Animal–Animal Hybrids

Aegyoptera [ā-gē-ŏp-tĕr-ah] (illus. 18)—genes of a bat (*-optera*) were spliced into the genes of a vulture (*aegy-*). This creature had the forehead and ears of a bat with the face and beak of the vulture. Its body size was much smaller than that of a pure vulture, with smaller wings, shorter legs, and smaller claws. It had feathered wings that were scalloped and vaguely resembled bat wings. Although it survived and could fly, Cassius considered it too small to be an effective weapon.

Cercopithursus [cer-ko-*pĭth*-ur-sus] (illus. 19)—genes of a baboon (*cercopith-*) spliced into those of a brown bear (*-ursus*). These creatures had the face and fangs of a baboon with the shape of a brown bear. It had the bear's heavier lower back legs and feet; however, it had the baboon's longer slender forearms, hands with opposing thumbs, and sharp long claws. It was bred to be aggressive and easily aroused.

Gryphon—a mythical beast with the body, tail, and hind legs of a lion and the head, wings, forelegs, and talons of an eagle. Note: Cassius was never successful in recreating the gryphon.

Hieractopera [*hī*-er-ac-*tŏp*-er-ah]—genes of a bat (*-topera*) were spliced into the genome of an eagle (*hierac-*) in an attempt to achieve a creature that resembled a dragon. The creature kept the head and talons of an eagle. Unfortunately, the skin of a bat's wings replaced the feathers of the eagle. The creature could still walk on the ground but not fly. If it could climb to a point high enough, it could launch into a controlled glide and attack its prey from the air.

Lupucercopith [*lu*-pu-*cer*-ko-pīth] (illus. 16)—genes of a baboon (*-cercopith*) spliced into genes of a wolf (*lupu-*) in an attempt to create an aggressive wolf-baboon hybrid to serve as a guard animal. This animal was bred to have the long snout and fangs of a baboon with the body and speed of a wolf. Its forelegs were longer than its back legs, and it had disjointed hips, resulting in hip dysplasia. This limited its speed and agility. Its upper canines, however, were very large and long—more closely resembling those of a saber-toothed cat.

Lupuseroja [*lu*-pu-ser-o-ja] (illus. 22)—genes of a boar (*-seroja*) spliced into genes of a wolf (*lupus-*) in an attempt to create an aggressive wolf-boar hybrid guard animal to protect storerooms, silos, and armories in Cassius's territory (mostly from the villagers). This animal was bred to have the snout and horns of a boar with the body and speed of a wolf; however, it had the shortened legs of the boar.

Lyvulfon [lī-*vul*-fon] (illus. 21)—in an attempt to recreate the legendary gryphon, genes of a vulture (*-vulfon*) were spliced into the genome of a lynx (*ly-*) in an attempt to achieve a phenotype similar to that of a gryphon. This creature of Cassius survived and could fly at speeds up to twenty-five miles per hour; however, it could not sustain flight over long distances. In hunting for prey, the lyvulfon would have to wait in a tree or on rocky ledge for its prey to get close enough to be snared.

Lyvulseroptera [*lī*-vul-ser-ŏp-ter-a] (illus. 28)—a lyvulfon with genes of viper (*-ser-*) and bat *(-optera)* spliced into it. Its head had the sharp pointed nose and ears of a bat and a bat's forehead. It had the eyes of the lynx and the tongue and fangs of a viper. It retained the beak of a vulture. It also had a long slender neck—akin to the body of a snake—by which it could maneuver its head nearly 360 degrees to the right or the left. It still had the hind legs and tail of a lynx and the forelegs and talons of the vulture. Its body was quite large, covered with thick scales (or plates), and bulky. Although it could lumber across the ground, its heavy bat-like wings were inverted and dragged on the ground, impeding its forward motion. It could not fly. Its body was too heavy and the wings too clumsy to lift the creature off the ground.

Ursuscro [ur-*sŭs*-crō] (illus. 26)—genes of a boar (*-scro*) spliced into the genome of a bear (*-ursus*) to create an especially aggressive creature. Cassius would set it loose on Biogenics—and anyone else who got in his way. This creature was engineered to kill anything it attacked. Cassius planned to use it as a weapon of war—especially against an *H. transformans* opponent whose alternate species was a bear. Cassius found he couldn't control it. The architecture of its brain was distorted, and the creature eventually went mad.

Varanhieracta [*var*-an-hī-ĕr-*ac*-tah]—genes of an eagle (*-hieracta*) were spliced into the genome of a Komodo dragon (*varan-*) in order to create a dragon that could fly. This creature had the head and torso of the Komodo dragon with feathers blended in among its scales, but no wings. Most importantly, all four legs had hollow bones that could not support it and shattered under its weight. It could not hunt and did not survive.

Viperoperidactyl [*vī*-per-o-perĭ-*dăc*-tyl] (illus. 15)—genes of a viper (*viperi-*) and a bat *(-opera-)* were spliced into the genome of an arboreal lizard *(-dactyl)* to create a venomous lizard that could climb trees, glide between trees or to the ground, and swim. It had physical features consistent with lizards that can glide from tree to tree except for a much larger body size. It had the head, body, and tail of a tree lizard with the tongue, fangs, and venom of a pit viper. It also had a membrane comparable to the folds of skin in a gliding tree lizard, except that they stretched between its forelegs and back legs and were attached to them similar to the wings of a bat. The membranes allowed it to glide between neighboring trees or look like leaf debris in a stream. This maximized its ability to camouflage or hide in trees and streams to ambush its prey.

GLOSSARY

actin—An essential component of a muscle fiber, which, along with myosin and other components, allows the muscle to contract.

adaptation—Changes in cell structure and/or organization in response to direct stimulation and/or changes in the environment.

adaptive changes—Are normal physiologic changes that enhance functionality and/or prevent loss of function.

additive (drug) effects—Occurs when two or more drugs with similar effects are taken together and each drug supplements the effect of the other(s) even though each drug may take different paths to achieve its effect.

adrenaline—Produced and secreted by the adrenal medulla, this hormone stimulates the function of the heart, increases blood flow and respiratory rate, and heightens alertness.

age-related gene activation—Preprogrammed time when selected genes are activated or stimulated.

aging—The process of growing older.

alternate species—The species into which an *H. transformans* can change. The individual may be able to transform into more than one animal provided his genome supports it.

amelia—Congenital absence or failure to fully develop part or all of one or more extremities.

aneuploidy—An abnormal number of chromosomes for a given species.

antiseptic—A salve or solution that inhibits and/or kills pathogenic organisms (e.g., bacteria, viruses, fungi).

apoptosis—Programmed (planned) cell death. This is a normal, orderly process for removing unwanted cells that are too old, too many, and/or no longer needed. The cells undergo natural cell death at the end of their life span. Eventually, the remains of the dead cell are removed by the immune system.

arrector pili muscles—Minute muscles in hair follicles embedded deeper in the skin that raise hair when they contract.

autophagy—A normal process in which dead cells and their components are broken down.

autosomes—Nonreproductive chromosomes.

biologic classification system (taxonomy)—Kingdom, phylum, class, order, family, genus, and species

biotransformation—The conversion of one agent into another by biochemical processes in the body. The liver is the primary organ that breaks down (metabolizes) foreign agents.

black-body effect—Absorbs all incident light (UV radiation), even through the clouds.

bone morphogenic protein—Growth factors that belong to the transforming growth factor beta group.

bony matrix—Framework of minerals (e.g., calcium phosphate, calcium carbonate) enmeshed with collagen fibers.

chromosomal microarray analysis (CMA)—Very very high resolution of genes arrayed on a chromosome. It can detect the abnormalities at the level of gene sequences.

chromosome—Large groups or sets of genes clustered together in a predetermined sequence and bundled together to form a single structure that compresses DNA into a relatively small area.

chromosome breakage—One or more breaks along the length of a chromosome.

chromosome pair—Each chromosome is matched with a second chromosome. One is from the mother and the other is from the father.

clade—A group of organisms that include all descendants with a common ancestor. Birds, dinosaurs, and crocodiles all have a common egg-laying ancestor.

class (taxonomy)—A group of organisms that have a common genetic background yet are genetically distinct from one another and thus have similar but distinct physical characteristics (e.g., mammals). Bacteria, reptiles, fish, dinosaurs, insects, mammals, birds, etc. all represent different classes within the animal kingdom.

clone—Artificial processes used to create genetically identical organisms.

coal—A black combustible rock made from carbon and a variety of other substances, including sulfur.

collagen—Main fibrous structural protein found in connective tissue. It provides structural support, strength, and connectivity.

collateral circulation—Development of new arteries (arteriogenesis) and capillaries (angiogenesis).

common ancestor—Two or more different species descending from the same ancestor.

coming-of-age—The age at which a child with a transforming X chromosome would have the capability to transform.

congenital anomaly—A structural or functional abnormality that forms during pregnancy (versus an inherited condition).

corrupted transformation—A defective transformation that results in grossly abnormal features and is usually fatal. It occurs when a transformation is abruptly stopped before its completion (aborted) or forced to progress too rapidly, causing missed steps in the process. It can also be caused by a merger of two incompatible genomes, an incomplete genome, and poor genetic engineering.

cortisol—Secreted by the adrenal cortex, this hormone has multiple metabolic functions and is a potent endogenous anti-inflammatory agent.

consanguinity—Breeding among closely related individuals.

counting—A reckoning by numbers; however, it may also be reflected in the ability to include or exclude objects, as if counting.

cyclopia—Presence of a single eye, associated with developmental (congenital) neural tube defects and trisomy 13 (chromosomal defect).

cytokinesis—The division of the cell after its nucleus has divided.

deontological ethics—The decision to act is based on a duty to do no harm or the least harm. The outcome is not used to justify the means.

DNA double helix—Two complementary strands of DNA are loosely bound to each other (for ease of separation) and twisted around each other along their length.

DNA fingerprinting—Analysis of differences in DNA sequencing.

DNA polymerase—A group of enzymes that can replicate an exact copy of a DNA strand then proofread and edit it for errors, making corrections along the way.

DNA ligase—An enzyme that (re)attaches DNA gene segments, including broken edges.

DNA methylation—Attachment of a methyl group (a biochemical agent) to a gene or gene segment in order to influences its expression (an epigenetic effect).
    hypermethylation—Associated with decreased activation of genes.
    hypomethylation—Associated with increased activation of genes.

DNA probe—A set of *complementary genes* for a *known* protein sequence which, when added to a solution containing the genes that actually code for that protein sequence, will form a paired DNA sequence.

DNA replication—The replication includes all the components of the DNA strand, including its backbone and the proteins supporting it (e.g., histones).

dosage—The amount of a substance (typically, a medicine) administered to achieve a specific effect.

dysplasia—Cell growth that results in abnormal changes to mature cells, often leading to a loss of the tissue's normal function.

dominant gene—In a heterozygous gene pair, the member of the gene pair that is expressed in the phenotype. See also genetic imprinting.

electroreception—Detection of electric fields caused by muscle contractions.

embryonic imprinting—Process whereby imprinted genes are established in the embryo (after fertilization) with the parent of origin for each imprinted gene also established.

eukaryote—Any organism comprised of cells that have a clearly defined nucleus containing distinct chromosomes.

endonuclease—An enzyme that can cut out a damaged DNA or RNA gene and repair the strand. It permits editing of a single base pair in a DNA or RNA strand.

energy metabolism—A cascade of biochemical reactions that converts glucose into energy (in the form of adenosine triphosphate [ATP]), which is used as fuel for cellular processes.

enzymes—Proteins that increase (catalyze) the rate of reaction between substances.

epidermis—Outer layer of skin. The outermost layer of skin, the stratum corneum, consist of layers of dead keratin cells (keratinocytes).

epigenetic effect—Nongenetic influence (e.g., environment, methyl groups) on the expression of a gene.

epigenetic factors—Nongenetic and typically biochemical substances that influence gene functions without altering the gene itself.

epigenetic influence—Nongenetic mechanisms that influence gene functions without altering the gene itself.
    placental effects—Some epigenetic effects are unique to the placenta.

epigenetic inheritance—A nongenetic substance attached to DNA that is passed on to progeny.

epigenome—The chemical agents within the genome that are attached to DNA.

eukaryotic cells—Cells that contain specialized organelles not found in more primitive organisms (prokaryotes), including a nucleus in which DNA is organized as chromosomes.

euploidy—The normal number of chromosomes in a cell for the species. There are forty-six for *H. sapiens*.

family (taxonomy)—Species that fall into the same class yet are still genetically distinct.

fetal alcohol spectrum disorders—Adverse effect of alcohol on brain development resulting in growth retardation and cognitive and behavior deficits.

fluorescence in situ hybridization (FISH) analysis—Detects much smaller submicroscopic rearrangements and deletions than conventional karyotyping can detect.

form—The level of schooling in which a child is enrolled. Typically, this corresponds to the students' age group, which may be subdivided. Each group constitutes a cohort.

founder—The individual (or gene) in which a characteristic was first seen, which was inherited subsequently by offspring.

gene—The basic building block of genetic matter (a set of three nucleosides).
    coding genes—Genes that dictate a physical component used in building a biologic structure (e.g., an amino acid).
    noncoding genes—Genes involved in regulating function of other genes.

gene activation—Turning on a gene or gene sequence.

gene conservation—Useful genes and gene sequences that have been handed down from a common ancestor and reused in multiple animals.

gene deactivation—Turning off a gene or gene sequence.

gene editing—The ability to manipulate the genome by amending gene sequences: e.g., via use of clustered regularly interspaced short palindromic repeats (CRISPR), which can excise a sequence.

gene expression—The ability of a gene to exert a visible effect.

gene mapping—Identification of genes and their location on chromosomes.

gene mutation—A spontaneous (random) or induced (man-made) change to genetic material.

gene pair—Genes arrayed in the same location along their sister chromosomes.

gene sequencing—Identification of the order in which genes occur that support a specific function.

gene splicing—Insertion of one or more genes into an organism's genome.

gene therapy—Using genes to prevent or correct a disease caused by an underlying genetic defect.

gene typing—Identifying the genetic makeup of a particular individual or organism.

genetic adaptation—Changes in genetic composition that allows an individual to adapt to his/her environment.

genetic admixture—Genetic variability that is introduced through progeny that arise from two unrelated parents.

genetic code—A set or series of nucleotides that determine what type of protein will be made.

genetic counseling—Consultation with geneticists and/or medical professionals with expertise in genetic diseases and their inheritance.

genetic engineering—The use of natural and man-made agents to modify genetic code.

genetic homology—Gene sequences that are conserved and reused among nearly all classes within the animal kingdom and even a few across kingdoms; genes with a shared ancestry.

genetic imprinting—An epigenetic process that silences one gene, allowing the other gene to be expressed.

genetic polymorphism—Naturally occurring variations in the structure of a gene. Two different versions of the same gene may be paired together.

genome—The total gene compliment of an individual organism.

genotype—An individual's overall genetic composition, whether or not it is expressed as an observable characteristic.

genus (taxonomy)—Groups of species whose genomes are very similar yet remain distinct: e.g., the genus Homo includes the species *H. habitus, H. erectus, H. neanderthalensis,* and *H. sapiens.*

glucocorticosteroids—Hormones (cortisol and related compounds) released in increased amounts during stress states.

growth factors—Direct cell growth, proliferation, and differentiation into specific cell types and regulate a variety of cellular processes.
   bone morphogenic protein—Growth factors that belong to the transforming growth factor beta group.
   transforming growth factor β (TGFβ)—A superfamily of morphogens and growth factors directly involved in the cell growth, development, proliferation, differentiation, and apoptosis.

growth hormone—An anabolic hormone stimulates growth and maturation of tissues.

hemoglobin—An essential component of a red blood cell required for it to carry oxygen to tissues.

heterozygous gene pair—Each member of a gene pair has a variation on its genetic code.

hominins—Classification for related species of humans, e.g., *H. sapiens, H. australopithicus, H. erectus,* etc.

homologous gene pair—The chromosomes from each parent are aligned so that each gene from the mother is matched with the corresponding gene from the father. The genes may or may not be exactly alike; however, they should have the same function.

homologous structures—Common ancestry for physical characteristics that have evolved to support different functions (e.g., wings of bats and arms of primates, both of which are mammalian).

homozygous gene pair—Both members of a gene pair have *exactly* the same genetic code.

hormones—Biochemical agents that exert an effect on living cells, including stimulating growth (trophic signal) and/or stimulating other activities.
adrenaline—Produced and secreted by the adrenal medulla, this hormone stimulates the function of the heart, increases blood flow and respiratory rate, and heightens alertness.
cortisol—Secreted by the adrenal cortex and has multiple metabolic and anti-inflammatory functions.
estrogen—Secreted by the ovaries and responsible for the development of the female reproductive system and corresponding female characteristics.
follical stimulating hormone—Produced and secreted by the anterior pituitary gland and stimulates the development of both ova and sperm.
growth hormone—Secreted by the pituitary gland and stimulates growth and maturation of tissues.
insulin—Secreted by the pancreas and stimulates the uptake and utilization of glucose.
prolactin—Secreted by the pituitary gland and stimulates the production of breast milk.
testosterone—Secreted by the testes and responsible for the development of the male reproductive system and corresponding male characteristics.
thyroxin—Secreted by the thyroid gland and stimulates cells to increase their metabolic activity.

hormonal triggers—Hormones are produced in response to internal and external factors and likely to be involved in either triggering and/or supporting transformation.

homeothermic—Capable of maintaining a stable internal body temperature regardless of variable temperatures in external environment (thermoregulation).

hybrid—A genetically engineered human-animal or animal-animal blend of two or more species, which were intended to have characteristics that met certain expectations or specifications.

hypermethylation—Associated with decreased activation of genes.

hypertrophy—An increase in functional cell size resulting in an increase in the size of functioning tissue (not the number of cells).

hypomethylation—Associated with increased activation of genes.

hypothalamic amenorrhea—Suppression of ovulation via central nervous system control mechanisms.

hypothermia—A body temperature that drops to a dangerously low level and may become too low to sustain life.

incidence—The number of new events (e.g., disrupted transformations) occurring within a given period of time.

infusion—A process of steeping leaves, herbs, seeds, fruits, and other plants in hot water (e.g., steeping tea leaves) to extract substances from the plants into the water (also called the infusion).

insulin—Secreted by the pancreas, this hormone stimulates the uptake and utilization of glucose.

integrase—An enzyme that helps insert genetic code. In *H. sapiens*, it is an enzyme used by the HIV virus to embed its genetic code into a human DNA strand. There are several drugs that treat HIV infection by inhibiting the action of this enzyme.

intelligence—A polygenic, multifactorial trait approximately 50% of which is attributed to genetics.

intracellular operations—Physical and biochemical actions occurring within the cell.

in vitro fertilization—Set of procedures in which ova and sperm are collected, the ova are fertilized, and a fertilized ovum is implanted into the uterus.

in vivo—Activity that occurs in a living organism versus those occurring under nonliving conditions (e.g., in a test tube).

karyotype—The number and appearance of chromosomes as seen under a microscope.

karyotyping—Examines the number and characteristic of chromosomes, detects large chromosome abnormalities.

keratin—A fibrous structural protein that protects the outer layer of skin. It is also a component of hair, feathers, nails, horns, and hoofs.

keratinocytes—A type of skin cell that changes its cellular structure to form a protective barrier for the skin.

keratinized skin—A much thicker equivalent of the stratum corneum.

Klinefelter's syndrome—The male receives two X chromosomes from the mother (an XXY genotype).

language—Usually associated with meaningful combinations of words or sounds.

lanugo—In *H. sapiens*, it is a layer of fine, soft hair covering the body of the fetus after about sixteen weeks gestation. Although usually shed before birth, lanugo may still be seen in newborns.

life expectancy—The length of time an organism is expected to live based on age, condition, and species.

life span—The length of time or duration an organism actually lives.

liver enzymes—Responsible for both the production and/or metabolism of an enormous range of substances.

inducers—Agents that lead to an *increase* in the number of enzymes, which, in turn, *increases* rate of metabolism of a particular agent. In most cases, this means that the agent is *degraded faster* and, therefore, becomes *inactive sooner.*

inhibitors—Agents that lead to a *decrease* in the number of enzymes, which, in turn, *decreases* rate of metabolism of a particular agent. In most cases, this means that the agent is *degraded more slowly* and, therefore, is *active longer.*

maladaptive changes—Pathologic changes that are usually the result of disease or lead to dysfunction or disease.

malignant transformation—A genetic change in a cell that permits unrestricted growth.

mammary (milk) glands—Specialized glands in female mammals that produce milk for the young (e.g., breasts or teats).

mechanical forces—Internal or external actions can cause changes in shape, pattern, and differentiation.

medical pedigrees—Tracing of family members who have or have had a disease (if known).

melatonin—Substance derived from tryptophan. In *H. sapiens*, it is thought to exert an anti-inflammatory effect as well as help induce sleep.

Mendelian inheritance (simple)—A straightforward pattern of inheritance based on the concept of dominant versus recessive genes.

messenger RNA (mRNA)—A subtype of RNA that serves as an edited copy of a segment of DNA for use in the assembly of a protein. In mRNA, uracil is substituted for thymine found in DNA.

metabolic pathway—A sequence of biochemical reactions leading to a biologic outcome (e.g., energy production).

The one carbon metabolic pathway is used by many biochemical reactions and is a major supplier of methyl groups.

metamorphosis—Radical change of an organism into an altogether different shape, form, and function; transformation in a living organism.

metaplasia—Replacement of one cell type by another cell type not normally found in that tissue, which changes the character and function of the tissues affected.

methyl group—Contains one carbon atom bound to three hydrogen atoms (CH_3). This molecule is found in many organic compounds.

middle ear bones (ossicles)—The malleus (hammer), incus (anvil), and stapes (stirrup).

mitochondria—Subcellular organelles that are found in all eukaryotes and provide approximately 95% of a cell's energy requirements via metabolic pathways (oxidative phosphorylation) that are totally dependent on the availability of oxygen.

mitosis—Division of cell's nucleus once the cell's DNA has been replicated. This is a crucial step in the process whereby certain types of nonreproductive cells divide, thereby making identical copies (clones) of themselves.

monosomy—One member of a chromosome pair is missing.

morphogenesis—Gradual changes in structure, form, and function as an organism grows and develops into its final adult form.

morphogens—Chemical substances, including hormones and growth factors, which exert control over growth, development, and morphogenesis.

mosaicism—Situations in which some cells have a variation on the normal complement of DNA. Different cells within the same individual have different numbers of chromosomes.

moulage—Artificially recreated injuries used to simulate actual injuries during training and/or drills.

multifactorial—Genes can be affected by multiple external factors (e.g., environmental), including those that can cause mutations (e.g., radiation, chemotherapy, etc.).

mutagen—An agent known to cause and/or increase the frequency of mutations.

mutation—A change in the DNA sequence of a gene, which could have no effect, be beneficial, or be harmful.

myosin—An essential component of a muscle fiber, which, along with actin and other components, allows the muscle to contract.

neural tube defects—Failure of the neural tube to close during embryonic development.

neurotransmitters—Chemical agents that can excite, quiet, or soothe nerves.

nidus—Meaning nest or breeding site, it is the cluster of cells from which structures of the body develop.

noncoding genes—Genes involved in regulating function of other genes.

nuclear receptor transcription factor—A class of proteins that interact directly with the DNA of a cell to regulate the expression of genes.

oncogenes—Promote growth (e.g., the *ras* gene). Mutation of a single oncogene can affect a change (autosomal dominant).

operons—Gene sequences that code for enzymes that control whether or not a gene is used.

ovum—An egg (plural is ova).

pair substitution—One gene pair is replaced by another.

parent of origin—The parent who donated the gene that is being expressed.

pedigree—Diagram or chart showing family lineage.

penetrance—The extent to which a specific genotype is expressed in an individual's phenotype.

phenotype—An individual's observable manifestations (physical characteristics) of genetic composition.

phylogenomics—Evolutionary history of a group or organisms based on genetic profile.

plasticity—Ability of one type of cell to change into another type of cell and usually encountered in stem cells.

plates and scales—Hardened exterior surfaces comprised of dermal bone, horn, and/or keratin.

pleiotropic gene—A pleiotropic gene that can affect many unrelated physical traits and thus have multiple and varying effects on different organ systems. If a pleiotropic gene is mutated, it can result in a wide range of expressions downstream on different organ systems.

pleiotropy—The ability of the same gene to affect multiple phenotypes in very different ways.

pluripotency—The ability to differentiate into any cell type (e.g., stem cells).

point mutation—Occurs at the individual gene level.

polygenic—Phenotypic traits that are affected by different genes, usually at different locations. Each gene exerts an additive effect on a trait.

precocious puberty—Early onset of puberty with completely normal development.

prevalence—The *total* number of events (e.g., disrupted transformations) present at any given time.

probability—The likelihood (or chance) than something will occur.

prolactin—Secreted by the pituitary gland, this hormone stimulates the production of breast milk.

psychosis—Disorder of perception, emotion, memory, and judgment leading to disordered thinking and loss of touch with reality.

puberty—The age at which production of reproductive hormones begins.

radiation—Ionizing radiation (e.g., x-rays, gamma rays) can induce genetic changes including gene mutations and chromosomal rearrangements.

recessive genes—In a heterozygous gene pair, the member of the gene pair that is not expressed.

recombinase—An enzyme that reattaches genes and chromosomes.

regulatory genes—Noncoding genes that control the activity of other genes. They direct if, when, how, and where coding genes are activated or inactivated. Examples include promoter genes that activate a gene sequence and repressor genes that suppress a gene sequence.

remodeling (bone)—Refers to the normal turnover of bone constituents and the process of repairing injured bone.

reverse transcriptase—An enzyme that can reverse engineer one form of genetic material into another form.

ribonucleic acid (RNA)—A single strand of genes that are a complimentary form of DNA. There are multiple subtypes depending upon the function the RNA is to perform.

ribosomal RNA (rRNA)—A subtype of RNA that serves as an interpreter between mRNA and tRNA.

ribosomes—A combination of proteins and rRNA designed to build proteins.

RNA polymerase—A group of enzymes that act on DNA to produce a complimentary copy (mRNA) of the gene sequence to be used in the production of the desired protein. It isolates and separates the desired segment of DNA genes and then makes a copy of them.

Sanger sequence—Can detect point mutations (single gene mutations), which cause genetic disease.

set point—Internal regulation that limits body/organ size.

single nucleotide polymorphism (SNP)—Most common type of genetic variation, it represents a difference in a single nucleotide (e.g., swapping C for T).
    SNPs provide the basis of genetic diversity both within groups and across populations.

single nucleotide polymorphism (SNP) microarray—Identifies long segments of homozygous genes with focus on identification of paired homozygous recessive genes, which could cause hereditary genetic diseases associated with inbreeding.

specialized cells—Cells that have differentiated to perform specific functions.

species—Any group of organisms that is genetically similar yet maintains a distinctive set of genetic and physical characteristics.

stem cells—Undifferentiated cells that can continue to reproduce themselves indefinitely or can develop and differentiate into any kind of specialized cell (totipotent stem cells).
    adult stem cells—Cells with a limited ability to regenerate and replace specific tissue types.

embryonic stem cells—Cells with an unlimited ability to reproduce and ability to change into any cell type the embryo needs (pluripotent stem cells).

pluripotent stem cells—Derived from totipotent stem cells (e.g., embryonic stem cells).

stress hormones—Hormones such as adrenaline, cortisol, glucagon, and others are released under acute or chronic stress.

sulfuric acid (H_2SO_4)—A strong acid that is highly corrosive.

suppression of ovulation—Conditions (e.g., severe stress) in which development of a mature ovum is inhibited.

tar (e.g., coal tar)—A thick black liquid that results from heating coal at extreme temperatures.

telomeres—Nucleotide sequences located at the end of a chromosome, which protect it from being damaged by repeated replications.

teratogen—An agent, typically toxins, that causes developmental defects and/or malformations in the embryo or fetus.

thyroxin—Secreted by the thyroid gland, this hormone stimulates cells to increase their metabolic activity.

tissue plasticity—The ability to become a different type of cell (plasticity) can lead to a different tissue type and affect phenotype.

transcription—Process of making an edited copy of a DNA gene sequence (mRNA) for use in the production of a protein.

transfer RNA (tRNA)—A subtype of RNA that retrieves the correct amino acid and assembles the amino acid in the sequence dictated by mRNA.

transformation—A radical change in structure, form, and function. When applied to living organisms, it is also known as metamorphosis.

transforming growth factor β (TGFβ)—a superfamily of morphogens and growth factors directly involved in the cell growth, development, proliferation, differentiation, and apoptosis.

translation—Process whereby mRNA directs the synthesis of a protein.

transmutation—A radical change in structure, form, and function usually applied to physics and alchemy.

transposable elements (TEs)—Small DNA sequences that can change their location in the genome in a cut-and-paste fashion.

traumatic brain injury (TBI)—Injury to the brain causing nerve damage and, possibly, affecting blood supply to the brain; damage could be limited to one or more small areas or be more global in extent.

trisomy—One pair of chromosomes has an extra member (e.g., Down syndrome [trisomy 21]).

trisomy X—A female has three X chromosomes (XXX genotype).

trophic signals—Chemical agents (e.g., hormones, growth factors) that promote cell growth, differentiation, migration (to their assembly sites), and survival.

tryptophan—A precursor of serotonin found in some foods and thought to help induce sleep.

tumor suppressor genes—Restrain growth (e.g., *BRCA1*/*BRCA2* genes). A change in both copies of the gene is required for expression (reflecting an autosomal recessive gene).

Turner's syndrome—Monosomy in which the Y chromosome or a second X chromosome is missing (45, XO genotype).

tympanic membrane—A thin membrane that vibrates freely when sound waves strike it.

utilitarian principles—The outcome is used to justify how it was achieved. The greater good can outweigh any harm.

viral vectors—Viral genetic material used to introduce or facilitate the introduction of foreign genes into a native genome.

visual field—An individual's range of vision in all planes when staring straight ahead.

vitamin—An essential biologic compound needed for normal growth and development.

whole exome sequencing—Specifically examines genes that code for protein synthesis, where most genetic defects are found.

whole genome sequencing—Looks at entire genome.

wicker—Plant materials (e.g., stalks, shoots, rushes, straw, etc.) soaked and then used to make products.

X chromosome—One of the two reproductive chromosomes that codes for female phenotype.

Y chromosome—The second reproductive chromosome that codes for male phenotype.

zygote—Fertilized egg, a result of merging of sperm and ovum.

REFERENCES

General References for Genetics

Beery, T. A., and Workman, M. L. (2012.) *Genetics and Genomics in Nursing and Health Care*. Philadelphia: F. A. Davis.

Booker, R. J. (2009.) *Genetics: Analysis and Principles*, 3rd ed. McGraw-Hill (Higher Education).

Carroll, E. W. (2009b.) Genetic control of cell function and inheritance. In: Porth, C. M., and Matfin (eds.), *Pathophysiology: Concepts of Altered Health States* (8th ed.), Chapter 6. Lippincott Williams and Wilkins.

Faulhaber, J.. and Aberg, J.A. (2009.) Acquired Immunodeficiency Syndrome. In: Porth, C. M., and Matfin (eds.), *Pathophysiology: Concepts of Altered Health States* (8th ed.), Chapter 6. Lippincott Williams and Wilkins.

Guyton, A.C., and Hall, J. E. (2006.) Genetic control of protein synthesis. In: *Textbook of Medical Physiology* (11th ed.), Chapter 3. Philadelphia: Elsevier/Saunders.

Jorde, L.B. (2014a.) Genes and genetic diseases. In: K. L. McCance, S. E. Huether, V. L. Brashers, V.L., and N. S. Rote, *Pathophysiology: The Biologic Basis for Disease in Adults and Children* (7th ed.), Chapter 4. St. Louis: Mosby/Elsevier.

Jorde, L.B. (2014b.) Genes, environment, and common diseases. In: K. L. McCance, S. E. Huether, V. L. Brashers, V.L., and N. S. Rote, *Pathophysiology: The Biologic Basis for Disease in Adults and Children* (7th ed.), Chapter 5. St. Louis: Mosby/Elsevier.

Porth, C. M. (2009.) Genetic and congenital disorders. In: Porth, C. M., and Matfin (eds), *Pathophysiology: Concepts of Altered Health States* (8th ed.), Chapter 7. Lippincott Williams and Wilkins.

Additional References

Preface

Carneiro, B. A., *et al.* (2016.) Is personalized medicine here? *Oncology* (Williston Park), 30(4), 293-303, 307.

Marson, F. A. L., Bertuzzo, C. S., Ribeiro, J. D. (2017.) Personalized or Precision Medicine? The Example of Cystic Fibrosis. *Front Pharmacol*, 8, 390. doi: 10.3389/fphar.2017.00390.

Warren, W. C., Hillier, L. W., Graves, J. A. M., Birney, E., *et al.* (2008.) Genome analysis of the platypus reveals unique signatures of evolution. *Nature*, 458, 175-183. doi: 10.1038/nature06936

Chapter 1.
No references.

Chapter 2. A New Species (Genes and Chromosomes)

Gabani, P., and Singh, O. V. (2013.) Radiation resistant extremophiles and their potential in biotechnology and therapeutics. *Appl Microbiol Biotechnol*, 97(3), 993-1004. doi: 10.1007/s00253-012-4642-7.

Hada, M., and Georgakilas, A. G. (2008.) Formation of clustered DNA damage after high-LET irradiation: a review. *J Radiat Res*, 49(3), 203-10.

Jayakumar, S., Pal, D., Sandur, S. K.(2015.) Nrf2 facilitates repair of radiation induced DNA damage through homologous recombination repair pathway in a ROS independent manner in cancer cells. Mutation Res, 779, 33-45. doi: 10.1016/j.mrfmmm.2015.06.007.

Konevega, L. V., and Kalinin, V. L. (2000.) Mutagenic effects of gamma-rays and incorporated 8-3H-purines on extracellular lambda phage: influence of mutY and mutM host mutations. *Mutat Res*, 459(3), 229-35.

Melott, A. L., B.S. Lieberman. B. S., C.M. Laird, C. M., *et al.* (2003.) Did a gamma-ray burst initiate the late Ordovician mass extinction? *https://arxiv.org/ftp/astro-ph/papers/0309/0309415.pdf.*

Pavlopoulou, A., Savva, G. D, Louka, M., *et al.* (2016, Jan-Mar.) Unraveling the mechanisms of extreme radioresistance in prokaryotes: Lessons from nature. *Mutat Res Rev Mutat Res,* 767, 92-107.

Raddadi, N., Cherif, A., Daffonchio, D. *et al.* (2015.) Biotechnological applications of extremophiles, extremozymes and extremolytes. *Appl Microbiol Biotechnol,* 99(19), 7907-13. doi: 10.1007/s00253-012-4642-7.

Rainey, F. A., Ray, K., Ferreira, M., *et al.* (2005.) Extensive Diversity of Ionizing-Radiation-Resistant Bacteria Recovered from Sonoran Desert Soil and Description of Nine New Species of the Genus *Deinococcus* Obtained from a Single Soil Sample. *Appl Environ Microbiol,* 71(9), 5225–5235. doi: 10.1128/AEM.71.9.5225-5235.2005.

Reddi, A. H. (2000.) Morphogenesis and tissue engineering of bone and cartilage: inductive signals, stems cells, and biomimetic biomaterials. *Tissue Eng,* 6(4), 351-359.

Sekhar, K. R., and Freeman, M. L. (2015.) Nrf2 promotes survival following exposure to ionizing radiation. *Free Radic Biol Med,* 88(Pt B), 268-74. doi: 10.1016/j.freeradbiomed.2015.04.035.

Shorey-Kendrick, L. E., Ford, M. M., Allen, D. C., *et al.* (2015.) Nicotinic receptors in non-human primates: Analysis of genetic and functional conservation with humans. *Neuropharmacology,* 96 (Pt. B), 263-273. doi: 10.1016/j.neuropharm2015.01.023

Soo, P., and Milian, L. M. (2001.) The effect of gamma radiation on the strength of Portland cement mortars. *J. Materials Science Letters,* 20, 1345-1348.

Thomas, C. C. (2009.) Gamma-ray bursts as a threat to life on earth. Dept. of Physicis and Astronomy, Washburn University. *https://arxiv.org/ftp/arxiv/papers/0903/0903.4710.pdf.*

Tisljar-Lentulis, G., Henneberg, P., Feinendegen, L. E, Commerford, S. L. (1983.) The oxygen enhancement ratio for single- and double-strand breaks induced by tritium incorporated in DNA of cultured human T1 cells. Impact of the transmutation effect. *Radiat Res*, 94(1), 41-50.

Vodak, R., Vydra, V., Trtik, K., Kapickova, O. (2011.) Effect of gamma irradiation on properties of hardened cement paste. *Materials and Structures*, 44(1), 101-107.

Warren, W. C., Hillier, L. W., Graves, J. A. M., Birney, E., *et al.* (2008.) Genome analysis of the platypus reveals unique signatures of evolution. *Nature*, 458, 175-183. doi: 10.1038/nature06936

William, K., Xi, Y., Naus, D. (2013.) A review of the effects of radiation on microstructure and properties of concretes used in nuclear power plants. NUREG/CR-7171. Division of Engineering, Office of Nuclear Regulatory Research, U.S. Nuclear Regulatory Comission.

Yu, L. Z., Luo, X. S., Liu, M., Huang, Q. (2015.) Diversity of ionizing radiation-resistant bacteria obtained from the Taklimakan Desert. *J Basic Microbiol*, 55(1), 135-40. doi: 10.1002/jobm.201300390.

Chapter 3. The X^T Factor (Genotype and Phenotype)

Bush, W. S., Oetjens, M. T., Crawford, D. C. (2016.) Unravelling the human genome-phenome relationship using phenome-wide association studies. *Nat Rev Genet*, 17(3), 129-45. doi: 10.1038/nrg.2015.36.

Champagne, F. A. (2013.) Epigenetics and developmental plasticity across species. *Dev. Psychobiol*, 55(1), 33-41.

Devlin, L., and Morrison, P.J. (2004.) Accuracy of the clinical diagnosis of Down's Syndrome. *Ulster Med J*, 73(1), 4-12.

Genazzani, A. D., Chierchia, E., Santagni, S., *et al.* (2010.) Hypothalamic amenorrhea: from diagnosis to therapeutic approach. *Ann Endocrinol* (Paris), 71(3), 163-9. doi: 10.1016/j.ando.2010.02.006.

Geraghty, A. C., and Kaufer, D. (2015.) Glucocorticoid Regulation of Reproduction. Adv Exp Med Biol, 872, 253-78. doi: 10.1007/978-1-4939-2895-8-11.

Kalantaridou, S.N., Makrigiannakis, A., Zoumaki, E., Chrousos, G. P. (2004.) Stress and the female reproductive system. *J Reprod Immunol*, 62(1-2), 61-8. doi: 10.1016/j.jri.2003.09.004.

Latham, K. E. (2015.) Endoplasmic reticulum stress signaling in mammalian oocytes and embryos: life in balance. *Int Rev Cell Mol Biol*, 316:227-65. doi: 10.1016/bs.ircmb.2015.01.005.

Liu, X.H., Dai, Z.M., Kang, H.F., Lin, S., *et al.* (2015.) Association of IL-23R Polymorphisms (rs6682925, rs10889677, rs1884444) With Cancer Risk: A PRISMA-Compliant Meta-Analysis. http://www.ncbi.nlm.nih.gov/pubmed/26717375.

Misra, M., and Klibanski, A. (2014.) Endocrine consequences of anorexia nervosa. *Lancet Diabetes Endocrinol*, 2(7), 581-92. doi: 10.1016/S2213-8587(13)70180-3.

Orio, F., Muscogiuri, G., Ascione, A., *et al.* (2013.) Effects of physical exercise on the female reproductive system. *Minerva Endocrinol*, 38(3), 305-19.

Ross, W. T., Grafham, D. V., Coffey, A. J., *et al.* (2005.) The DNA sequence of the human X chromosome. *Nature*, 434, 325-336.

Scheid, J. L., and de Souza, M.J. (2010.) Menstral irregularities and energy deficiency in physically active women: the role of ghrelin, PYY and adipocytokines. *Med Sport Sci*, 5, 82-102. doi: 10.1159/000321974.

Tsutsui, K., Ubuka, T., Bentley, G. E., and Kriegsfeld, L. J. (2012.) Gonadotropin-inhibitory hormone (GnIH): Discovery, progress and prospect. *Gen Comp Endocrinol*, 177(3), 305–314. doi: 10.1016/j.ygcen.2012.02.013

Whirledge, S., and Cidlowski, J. A. (2010.) Glucocorticoids, stress, and fertility. *Minerva Endocrinol*, 35(2), 109-25.

Whirledge, S., and Cidlowski, J. A. (2013.) A role for glucocorticoids in stress-impaired reproduction: beyond the hypothalamus and pituitary. *Endocrinology*, 154(12), 4450-68. doi: 10.1210/en.2013-1652.

Zdrojewicz, Z., Kowalik, M., Jagodziński, A. (2016.) Secrets of the red-headed. *Pol Merkur Lekarski*, 41(246), 306-309.

Chapter 4. First, Do No Harm (Ethics)

Araujo, T. F., Ribeiro, E. M., Arruda, A. P., *et al.* (2016.) Molecular analysis of the CTSK gene in a cohort of 33 Brazilian families with pycnodysostosis from a cluster in a Brazilian Northeast region. *Eur J Med Res*, 21(1), 33. doi: 10.1186/s40001-016-0228-7.

Busby, G. B., Hellenthal, G., Tofanelli, S., *et al.* (2015.) The Role of Recent Admixture in Forming the Contemporary West Eurasian Genomic Landscape. *Curr Biol*, 25(19), 2518-26. doi: 10.1016/j.cub.2015.08.007.

Carroll, E. W. (2009b.) Genetic control of cell function and inheritance. In: Porth, C. M., and Matfin (eds.), *Pathophysiology: Concepts of Altered Health States* (8th ed.), Chapter 6. Lippincott Williams and Wilkins.

Fernandez, J. R., Pearson, K., E., Kell, K. P. *et al.* (2013.) Genetic admixture and obesity: recent perspectives and future applications. *Hum Hered*, 75(2-4), 98-105. doi: 10.1159/000353180.

Ikehata, H., and Ono, T. (2011.) The mechanisms of UV mutagenesis. *J Radiat Res*, 52(2), 115-25.

Jorde, L.B. (2014a.) Genes and genetic diseases. In: K. L. McCance, S. E. Huether, V. L. Brashers, V.L., and N. S. Rote, *Pathophysiology: The Biologic Basis for Disease in Adults and Children* (7th ed.), Chapter 4. St. Louis: Mosby/Elsevier.

Lemmelä, S., Solovieva, S., Shiri, R., *et al.* (2016.) Genome-Wide Meta Analysis of Sciatica in Finnish Population. *PLoS One,* 11(10), e0163877. doi: 10.1371/journal.pone.0163877.

Yancoski, J., Rocco, C., Bernasconi, A, *et al.* (2009.) A 475 years-old founder effect involving IL12RB1: A highly prevalent mutation conferring Mendelian Susceptibility to Mycobacterial Diseases in European descendants. *Genet Evol*, 9 (4), 574-80. doi: 10.1016/j.meegid.2009.02.010.

Additional references:

Broni, J. V. G. (2010.) Ethical dimensions in the conduct of business: Business ethics, corporate social responsibility and the law. The "Ethics in Business" as a sense of business ethics. *International Conference on Applied Economics – ICOAE*, 795-821. *http://citeseerx.ist.psu.edu/viewdoc/download?*

Dondorp, W., DeWert, G., Pennings, G., *et al.* (2013.) ESHRE Task Force on ethics and law 20: sex selection for non-medical reasons. *Human Reprod*, 28(6), 1448-54. doi: 10.1093/humrep/det109.

Fulda, K. g., and Lykens, K. (2006.) Ethical issues in predictive genetic testing: A public health perspective. *J.Med.Ethics*, 32(3), 143-147. doi: 10.1136/jme.2004.010272.

Gershon, E. S., Alliey-Rodriguez, N., Grennan, K. (2014.) Ethical and public policy challenges for pharmacogenomics. *Dialogues Clin Neurosci*, 16(4), 567-74.

Kent, M., and Wade, P. (2015.) Genetics against race: Science, politics and affirmative action in Brazil. *Soc Stud Sci*, 45(6), 816-38.

Kohn, D. B., Porteus, M. H.. Scharenberg, A. M. (2016.) Ethical and regulatory aspects of genome editing. *Blood*, 127, 2553-2560. doi: https://doi.org/10.1182/blood-2016-01-678136.

Mandal, J., Ponnambath, D. K., Parija, S. C. (2016.) Utilitarian and deontological ethics in medicine. *Trop Parasitol*, 6(1), 5–7. doi: 10.4103/2229-5070.175024.

Omond, K. E. (2008.) Medical Ethics for the Genome World. *J Molecular Diagnostics*, 10(5), 377-381. doi: 10/2353/jmoldx.2008.070162.

Chapter 5. Predators and Prey (Patterns of Inheritance)

Brooker, R. J. (2009.) Extensions of Mendelian inheritance. In: Brooker, R.J., Genetics: Analysis and Principles (3rd edition). (Chapter 4). New York: McGraw-Hill.

Gayon, J. (2016.) From Mendel to epigenetics: History of genetics. *C R Biol*, 339(7-8), 225-30. doi: 10.1016/j.crvi.2016.05.009.

Habara, A., and Steinberg, M. H. (2016.) Minireview: Genetic basis of heterogeneity and severity in sickle cell disease. *Exp Biol Med (Maywood)*, 241(7), 689-96. doi: 10.1177/1535370216636726.

Hernandez, D. G. Reed, X., Singleton, A. B. (2016.) Genetics in Parkinson disease: Mendelian versus non-Mendelian inheritance. *J Neurochem*, 139, Suppl 1:59-74. doi: 10.1111/jnc.13593.

Chapter 6. Minor Details (Genetic Engineering)

Cheng, S. Y., Leonard, J. L., Davis, P. J. (2010.) Molecular aspects of thyroid hormone actions. *Endocr Rev*, 31(2), 139-170. doi: 1210/er.2009-0007.

Fogarty, C. E., and Bergmann, A. (2015.) The sound of silence: signaling by apoptotic cells. *Curr Top Devel Biol*, 114, 241-65. doi: 10.1016/bs.ctdb.2015.07.013.

Ranabir S., and Reetu, K. (2011.) Stress and hormones. *Indian J. Endocrinol Metab*, 15(1), 18-22. doi: 10.4103./2230-8210.77573.

You, L., Wang, Z., Li, H., *et al.* (2015.) The role of STAT3 in autophagy. *Autophagy*, 11(5), 729-39. doi: 10.1080/15548627.2015.1017192.

Chapter 7. Custom Designs (Manipulating genes)

Asaithamby, A., and Chen, D. J. (2011.) Mechanism of cluster DNA damage repair in response to high-atomic number and energy particles radiation. *Mutat Res*, 711(1-2), 87-99. doi. 10.1016/j.mrfmmm.2010.11.002.

Belancio, V. P., Deininger, P. L., Roy-Enge, A. M. (2009.) LINE dancing in the human genome: Transposable elements and disease. *Genome Med*, 1(10), 97. doi: 10.1186/gm97.

Britten, R. J. (2010.) Transposable element insertions have strongly affected human evolution. *Proceed of the Nat'l Acad Sci*, (107(4), 19945-48. doi. 10.1073/pnas.1014330107.

Brown, D. D., and Cai, L. (2007.) Amphibian metamorphosis. *Dev Biol*, 306(1), 20-23. doi: 10.1016/j.ydbio.2007.03.021.

Brown, N. J., and Hirsch, M. L. (2015.) Adeno-associated virus (AAV) gene delivery in stem cell therapy. *Discov Med*, 20(111), 333-42.

Craigie, R., and Bushman, R.D. (2012.) HIV DNA integration. *Cold Spr Harb Perspect Med*, 2(7), a006890. doi: 10.1101/cshperspect.a006890. [Integrase]

Daley, J. M., Kwon, Y., Niu, H., Sung, P. (2013.) Investigations of homologous recombination pathways and their regulation. *Yale J Biol Med*, 86(4), 453-61.

Faulhaber, J.. and Aberg, J.A. (2009.) Acquired Immunodeficiency Syndrome. In: Porth, C. M., and Matfin (eds.), *Pathophysiology: Concepts of Altered Health States* (8th ed.), Chapter 20. Lippincott Williams and Wilkins.

Fogg, P. C., Colloms, S., Rosser, S., *et al.* (2014.) New applications for phage integrases. *J Mol Biol*, 426(15), 2703-16. Doi: 10.1016/jmb.2014.05.014.

Gaj, T., Sirk, S. J., Barbas, C. F. III. (2014.) Expanding the scope of site-specific recombinases for genetic and metabolic engineering. *Biotechnol Bioeng*, 111(1), 1-15. doi: 10.1002/bit.25096.

Hille, F., and Charpentier, E. (2016.) CRISPR-Cas: biology, mechanisms and relevance. *Philos Trans R Soc Lond B Biol Sci*, 371(1707), pii: 20150496. doi: 0.1098/rstb.2015.0496.

Kim, G. J., Chandrasekaran, K., Morgan, W. E. (2006.) Mitochondrial dysfunction, persistently elevated levels of reactive oxygen species and radiation-induced genomic instability: a review. *Mutagenesis*, 21(6), 361-367. doi: 10.1093/mutage/ge1048.

Mills, R. E., Bennett, E. A., Iskow, R. C., Devine, S. E. (2007.) Which transposable elements are active in the human genome? *Trends Genet*, 23(4), 183-191. doi: 10/1016/j.tig.2007.02.006.

Mitsunobu, H., Teramoto, J., Nishida, K., Kondo, A. (2017.) Beyond Native Cas9: Manipulating Genomic Information and Function. *Trends Biotechnol*, 21. pii: S0167-7799(17)30132-4. doi: 10.1016/j.tibtech.2017.06.004.

Morales, M. E., Servant, G., Ade, C., Roy-Enge, A. M. (2015.) Altering genomic integrity: heavy metal exposure promotes trans-posable element-mediated damage. *Biol Trace Elem Res*, 166(1), 24-33. doi: 10.1007/s12011-015-0298-3.

Nayerossadat, N., Maedeh, T., Ali, P.A. (2012.) Viral and nonviral delivery systems for gene delivery. *Adv. Biomed Res.*, 1: 27, doi: 10.4103/2277-9175.98152.

Pluta, K., and Kacprzak, M. M. (2009.) Use of HIV as a gene transfer vector. *Acta Biochimica Polonica*, 56(4), 531-595.

Shen, S., Loh, T. J., Shen, H., *et al.* (2017.) CRISPR as a strong gene editing tool. *BMB Rep*, 50(1), 20-24.

Shuang, L., Yuanyuan, Y., Yan, Q., *et al.* (2017.) Applications of genome editing tools in precision medicine research. *Yi Chuan*, 39(3, 177-188. doi: 10.16288/j.yczz.16-395.

Suzuki, K., Ojima, M., Kodama, S., Watanabe, M. (2003.) Radiation-induced DNA damage and delayed induced genomic instability. *Oncogene*, 22(45), 6988-93. doi: 1038/sj.onc.1206881.

Tolarová, M., McGrath, J. A, Tolar, J. (2016.) Venturing into the New Science of Nucleases. *J Invest Dermatol*, 136(4),742-5. doi: 10.1016/j.jid.2016.01.02.1.

Vand Rajabpour, F., Raoofian, R., Habibi, L., *et al.* (2014.) Novel trends in genetics. Transposable elements and their application in medicine. *Arch Iran Med*, 17(10, 702-712. doi: 0141710/AIM.0012.

Yin, H., Kauffman, K. J., Anderson, D. G. (2017.) Delivery technologies for genome editing.

Nat Rev Drug Discov, 16(6), 387-399. doi: 10.1038/nrd.2016.280.

Chapter 8. The Three Houses (Pedigrees)

Brown, N. J., and Hirsch, M. L. (2015.) Adeno-associated virus (AAV) gene delivery in stem cell therapy. *Discov Med*, 20(111), 333-42.

Genetic Alliance: The New England Public Health Genetics Education Collaborative (GA-NEPHGEC). (2010a.) Genetic Counseling (Chapter 5.) *Understanding Genetics: A New England Guide for Patients and Health Professions*. Washington, D.C.

Genetic Alliance: The New England Public Health Genetics Education Collaborative. (2010b.) Pedigree and family history taking (Chapter 3). *Understanding Genetics: A New England Guide for Patients and Health Professions*. Washington, D.C.

Guerreiro, R., and Hardy J. (2014.) Genetics of Alzheimer's disease. *Neurotherapeutics*, 11(4), 732-7. doi: 10.1007/s13311-014-0295-9.

Hinton Jr., R. B. (2008.) The Family History: Reemergence of an Established Tool. *Crit Care Nurs Clin North Amer*, 20(2), 149–158.

Lynch, H. T., and Lynch, P. M. (2006.) Clinical selection of candidates for mutational testing for cancer susceptibility. *Oncology*, 20(14, Supplement 10), 29-34.

Rodriguez JL, Thomas CC, Massetti GM, *et al.* (2016.) CDC Grand Rounds: Family History and Genomics as Tools for Cancer Prevention and Control. *MMWR Morb Mortal Wkly Rep*, 65, 1291–1294. doi.org/10.15585/mmwr.mm6546a3.

Wattendorf, D.J. and Hadley, D.W. (2005.) Family history: The three-generation pedigree. *Amer Fam Phys*, 72(3), 441-448.

Chapter 9. Rafe (Genetic Pleiotropy)

Gratten, J. and Visscher, P. M. (2016.) Genetic pleiotropy in complex traits and diseases: implications for genomic medicine. *Genome Medicine*, 8:78 doi 10.1186/ s13073-016-0332-x.

Louvi, A., and Artavanis-Tsakonas, S. (2012.) Notch and disease: a growing field. *Semin Cell Dev Biol*, 23(4), 473-80. doi: 10.1016/j.semcdb.2012.02.005.

Paaby, A. B., and Rockman, M. V. (2013.) The many faces of pleiotropy. *Trends Genet*, 29(2), 66–73. doi: 10.1016/j.tig.2012.10.010.

Pasipoularides, A. (2015.) Linking Genes to Cardiovascular Diseases: Gene Action and Gene-Environment Interactions. *J Cardiovasc Transl Res*, 8(9), 506-27. doi: 10.1007/s12265-015-9658-9.

Price, A. L., Spencer, C. C., Donnelly, P. (2015.) Progress and promise in understanding the genetic basis of common diseases. *Proc Biol Sci.*, 282(1821), 20151684. doi: 10.1098/rspb.2015.1684.

Sivakumaran, S., Agakov, F., Theodoratou, E. *et al.* (2011.) Abundant pleiotropy in human complex diseases and traits. *Am J Hum Genet*, 89(5), 607-18. doi: 10.1016/j.ajhg.2011.10.004.

Solovieff, N., Cotsapas, C., Lee, P. H., *et al.* (2013.) Pleiotropy in complex traits: challenges and strategies. *Nat Rev Genet*, 14(7), 483-95. doi: 10.1038/nrg3461.

Zheng, W., and Rao, S. (2015.) Knowledge-based analysis of genetic associations of rheumatoid arthritis to inform studies searching for pleiotropic genes: a literature review and network analysis. *Arthritis Res Ther*, 17:202. doi: 10.1186/ s13075-015-0715-1.

Chapters 10-11.
   No references.

Bermejo-Sánchez, E., *et al.* (2011.) Amelia: a multi-center descriptive epidemiologic study in a large dataset from the International Clearinghouse for

Birth Defects Surveillance and Research, and overview of the literature. *Am J Med Genet C Semin Med Genet*, 157C(4), 288-304. doi: 10.1002/ajmg.c.30319.

Booker, R. J. (2009.) *Genetics: Analysis and Principles*, 3rd ed. McGraw-Hill (Higher Education).

Carroll, E. W. (2009b.) Genetic control of cell function and inheritance. In: Porth, C. M., and Matfin (eds.), *Pathophysiology: Concepts of Altered Health States* (8th ed.), Chapter 6. Lippincott Williams and Wilkins.

Craigie, R., and Bushman, R.D. (2012.) HIV DNA integration. *Cold Spr Harb Perspect Med*, 2(7), a006890. doi: 10.1101/cshperspect.a006890.

Daley, J. M., Kwon, Y., Niu, H., Sung, P. (2013.) Investigations of homologous recombination pathways and their regulation. *Yale J Biol Med*, 86(4), 453-61.

Faulhaber, J.. and Aberg, J.A. (2009.) Acquired Immunodeficiency Syndrome. In: Porth, C. M., and Matfin (eds.), *Pathophysiology: Concepts of Altered Health States* (8th ed.), Chapter 20. Lippincott Williams and Wilkins.

Jensen, R. B. (2013.) BRCA2: One small step for DNA repair, one giant protein purified. *Yale J Biol Med*, 86(4), 479-489.

Kuraoka, I. (2015.) Diversity of endonuclease V: from DNA repair to RNA editing. *Biomolecules*, 5(4), 2194-206. doi: 10.3390/biom5402194.

Orioli, I. M. (2011.) Cyclopia: An epidemiologic study in a large dataset from the International Clearinghouse for Birth Defects Surveillance and Research. *Am J Med Genet C Semin Med Genet*, 157C(4), 344-357. doi: 10.1002/ajmg.c.30323.

Sun, R., Liu, M., Lu, L., *et al.* (2015.) Congenital Heart Disease: Causes, Diagnosis, Symptoms, and Treatments. *Cell Biochem Biophys*, 72(3), 857-60. doi: 10.1007/s12013-015-0551-6.

Tolarová, M., McGrath, J. A, Tolar, J. (2016.) Venturing into the New Science of Nucleases. *J Invest Dermatol*, 136(4),742-5. doi: 10.1016/j.jid.2016.01.02.1.

Webber, D. M., MacLeod, S. L., Bamshad, M. J., (2015.) Developments in our understanding of the genetic basis of birth defects. *Birth Defects* Res A Clin Mol Teratol, 103(8), 680-91. doi: 10.1002/bdra.23385.

Chapter 13. *Unexpected Encounters*

See Appendix E for a description of plants purported to have medicinal properties.

Chapter 14.
No references.

Chapter 15. *Flight to Erwina* (Genetic Homology)

Fournier, D., Luft, F. C., Bader, M., *et al.* (2012.) Emergence and evolution of the renin-angiotensin-aldosterone system. *J Mol Med (Berl)*, 90(5), 495-508. doi: 10.1007/s00109-012-0894-z.

Goldsmith, J. R. and Jobin, C. (2012.) Think small: Zebrafish as a model system of human pathology. *J. Biomed. Biotechnol.*, 2012:817341. doi: 10.1155/2012/817341.

Manda, P., Mungall, C. J., Balhoff, J. P., *et al.* (2016.) Investigating the importance of anatomical homology for cross-species phenotype comparisons using semantic similarity. *Pac Symp Biocomput*, 21:132-43.

Nitta, K. R., Jolma, A., Yin, Y., *et al.* (2015.) Conservation of transcription factor binding specificities across 600 million years of bilateria evolution. *Elife*, 17:4. doi.10.7554/eLife.04837.

Ohta, Y., and Flajnik, M. F. (2015.) Coevolution of MHC genes (LMP/TAP/ class Ia, NKT-class Ib, NKp30-B7H6): Lessons from cold-blooded vertebrates. *Immunol Rev.*, 267(1), 6-15. doi: 1111/imr.12324.

Shorey-Kendrick, L. E., Ford, M. M., Allen, D. C., *et al.* (2015.) Nicotinic receptors in non-human primates: Analysis of genetic and functional conservation with humans. *Neuropharmacology*, 96 (Pt. B), 263-273. doi: 10.1016/j. neuropharm2015.01.023.

Wells, M. L., Hicks, S. N., Perera, L., Blackshear, P. J. (2015.) Functional equivalence of an evolutionarily conserved RNA binding molecule. *J. Biol Chem.*, 290(4), 24413-24423. doi: 10.1074/jbc.M115.673012.

Chapters 16-19.
No references.

Beaudin, A. E., and Stover, P. J. (2007.) Folate-mediated one-carbon metabolism and neural tube defects: Balancing genome synthesis and gene expression. *Birth Defects Res C Embryo Today*, 81(3), 183-203. doi: 10.1002/bdrc.20100.

Bian, E. B., Zhao, B., Huang, C., *et al.* (2013.) New advances of DNA methylation in liver fibrosis, with special emphasis on the crosstalk between microRNAs and DNA methylation machinery. *J. Cell Signal*, 25(9), 1837-44.

Burd, L., Roberts, D., Olson, M., Odendaal, H. (2007.) Ethanol and the placenta: A review. *J Matern Fetal Neonatal Med*, 20(5), 361-75. doi: 10.1080/14767050701298365.

Champagne, F. A. (2013.) Epigenetics and developmental plasticity across species. *Dev Psychobiol*, 55(1), 33-41.

Delcuve, G. P., Rastegar, M., Davie, J.R. (2009.) Epigenetic control. *J Cell Physiol*, 219(2), 243-50. doi: 10.1002/jcp.21678.

Duncan, E. J., Gluckman, P. D., Dearden, P. K. (2014.) Epigenetics, plasticity, and evolution: How do we link epigenetic change to phenotype? *J Exp Zool B Mol Dev Evol*, 322(4), 208-20. doi: 10.1002/jez.b.22571.

Fowler, A. K., Hewetson, A., Agrawal, R. G., *et al.* (2012.) Alcohol induced one-carbon metabolism impairment promotes dysfunction of DNA base excision repair in adult brain. *J Biol Chem*, 287(52), 43533-42. doi: 10.1074/jbc.M112.401497.

Green, B. B., and Marsit, C. J. (2015.) Select prenatal environmental exposures and subsequent alterations of gene-specific and repetitive element DNA methylation in fetal tissues. *Curr Environ Health Rep*, 2(2), 126-136. doi: 10.1007/s40572-105-0045-0.

Gupta, K. K., Gupta, V. K., Shirasaka, T. (2016.) An update on fetal alcohol syndrome – pathogenesis, risks, and treatment. *Alcohol Clin Exp Res*, 40(8), 1594-1602. doi: 10.111/acer.13135.

Guzzo-Merello, G., Cobo-Marcos, M., Gallego-Delgado, M., Garcia-Pavia, P. (2014.) Alcoholic cardiomyopathy. *World J Cardiol*, 6(8), 771-81. doi: 10.4330/wjc.v6.i8.771.

Hamm, C. A., and Costa, F. F. (2015.) Epigenomes as therapeutic targets. *Pharmacol Ther*, 151, 72-86. doi: 10.1016/j.pharmthera.2015.03.003.

Januar, V., Desoye, G., Novakovic, B., *et al.* (2015.) Epigenetic regulation of human placental function and pregnancy outcome: Considerations for causal inference. *Am J Obstet Gynecol*, 213(4 Suppl), 2182-96. doi:10.1016/j. ajog. 2015.07.011.

Jin, B., Li, Y., Robertson, K. D. (2011.) DNA methylation: Superior or subordinate in the epigenetic hierarachy? *Genes and Cancer*, 2(6) 607-617.

Jones, M. J., Goodman, S. J., Kobor, M. S. (2015.) DNA methylation and healthy human aging. *Aging Cell*, 14(6), 924-32. doi: 10.1111/acel.12349.

Kazanets, A., Shorstoya, T., Hilmi, K., *et al.* (2016.) Epigenetic silencing of tumor suppressor genes: Paradigms, puzzles, and potential. *Biochim Biophys Acta*, 1865(2), 275-88. doi: 10.1016/j.bbcan.2016.04.001.

Kalhan, S. C. (2016.) One carbon metabolism in pregnancy: Impact on maternal, fetal and neonatal health. *Mol Cell Endocrinol*. 435:48-60. doi: 10.1016/j. mce.2016.06.006.

Khalid, O., Kim, J. J., Kim, H. S., *et al.* (2014.) Gene expression signatures affected by alcohol-induced DNA methylomic deregulation in human embryonic stem cells. *Stem Cell Res*, 12(3), 791-806. doi: 10.1016/j.scr.2014.03.009.

Khandi, V. and Vadakedath, S. (2015.) Effect of DNA methylation in various diseases and the probable protective role of nutrition: A mini-review. *Cureus*, 7(8), 3309. doi: 10.7759/cureus.309.

Koukoura, O., Sifakis, S., Spandidos, D. A. (2012.) DNA methylation in the human placenta and fetal growth. *Mol Med Rep*, 5(4), 883-889. doi:10.3892/ mmr.2012.763.

Kruman, I. I., and Fowler, A. K. (2014.) Impaired one carbon metabolism and DNA methylation in alcohol toxicity. *J Neurochem*, 129(5), 770-80. doi: 10.1111/ jnc.12677.

Lee, H. S. (2015.) Impact of maternal diet on the epigenome during *in utero* life and the developmental programming of diseases in childhood and adulthood. *Nutrients*, 7(11), 9492-9507. doi: 10/3390/nu7115487.

Long, X., and Miano, J. M. (2007.) Remote control of gene expression. *J Biol Chem*, 282(22), 15941-5. doi: 10.1074/jbc.R700010200.

Luczak, M. W., and Jagodzinski, P. P. (2006.) The role of DNA methylation in cancer development. *Folia Histochem Cytobiol*, 44(3),143-54.

Marsit, C. J. (2016.) Placental epigenetics in children's environmental health. *Semin Reprod Med*, 34(1), 36-41. doi: 10.1055/2-0035-1570028.

Masarone, M., Rosato, V., Dallio, M., *et al.* (2016.) Epidemiology and Natural History of Alcoholic Liver Disease. *Rev Recent Clin Trials*, 11(3), 167-74.

McCance, K. L., and Grey, T. C. (2014.) Altered Cellular and Tissue Biology. In: K. L. McCance, S. E. Huether, V. L. Brashers, V.L., and N. S. Rote, *Pathophysiology: The Biologic Basis for Disease in Adults and Children* (7th ed.), Chapter 2. St. Louis: Mosby/Elsevier.

Mentch, S. J., and Locasale, J. W. (2016.) One-carbon metabolism and epigenetics: Understanding the specificity. *Ann N Y Acad Sci*, 1363, 91-98. doi: 10.1111/nyas.12956.

Merkle, C. J. (2009a.) Cellular adaptation, injury, and death. In: Porth, C. M., and Matfin (eds), *Pathophysiology: Concepts of Altered Health States* (8th ed.), Chapter 5. Lippincott Williams and Wilkins.

Mummaneni, P., and Shord, S. S. (2014.) Epigenetics and oncology. *Pharmacotherapy*, 34(5), 495-505. doi: 10.1002/phar.1408.

Nahon, P., and Nault, J. C. (2017.) Constitutional and functional genetics of human alcohol-related hepatocellular carcinoma. *Liver Int*. doi: 10.1111/liv.13419.

Natarajan, S. K., Pachunka, J. M., Mott, J. L. (2015.) Role of microRNAs in Alcohol-Induced Multi-Organ Injury. *Biomolecules*, 5(4), 3309-38. doi: 10.3390/biom5043309

Ning, B., Li, W., Zhao, W., *et al.* (2016.) Targeting epigenetic regulations in cancer. *Acta Biochim Biophys Sin* (Shanghai), 48(1), 97-109. doi: 10.1093/abbs/gmv116.

Pacchierotti, F., and Spanò, M. (2015.) Environmental impact on DNA methylation in the germline: State of the art and gaps of knowledge. *Biomed Res Int*, 2015, 123484. doi: 10.1155/2015/123484.

Park, L. K., Friso, S., Choi, S. W. (2012.) Nutritional influences on epigenetics and age-related disease. *Proc Nutr Soc*, 71(1), 75-73. doi: 10.1017/S0029665111003302.

Porth, C. M. (2009.) Genetic and congenital disorders. In: Porth, C. M., and Matfin (eds), *Pathophysiology: Concepts of Altered Health States* (8th ed.), Chapter 7. Lippincott Williams and Wilkins.

Resendiz, M., Chen, Y., Oztürk, N. C., Zhou. FC. (2013.) Epigenetic medicine and fetal alcohol spectrum disorders. *Epigenomics*, 5(1), 73-86. doi: 10.2217/epi.12.80.

Safi, J., Joyeux, L., Chalouhi, G. E. (2012.) Periconceptional folate deficiency and implications in neural tube defects. *J. Pregnancy*, 2012, 295083. doi: 10.1155/2012/295083.

Salih, M. A., Murshid, W. R., Seidahmed, M. Z. (2014.) Classification, clinical features, and genetics of neural tube defects. *Saudi Med J*, 35 Suppl 1, S5-S14.

Sarkar, D. K. (2016.) Male germline transmits fetal alcohol epigenetic marks for multiple generations: a review. *Addict Biol*, 21(1), 23-34. doi: 10.1111/adb.12186.

Selhub, J. (2002.) Folate, vitamin B12 and vitamin B6 and one carbon metabolism. J *Nutr Health Aging*, 6(1), 39-42.

Stolk, L., Bouwland-Both, M. I., van Mil, N. H., *et al.* (2013.) Epigenetic profiles in children with a neural tube defect: A case-control study in two populations. *PloS One*, 8(11), e78642. doi: 10.1371/journal.pone.0078462.

Su, X., Wellen, K. E., Rabinowitz, J. D. (2016.) Metabolic control of methylation and acetylation. *Curr Opin Chem Biol*, 30, 52-60. doi: 10.1016/j.cbpa.2015.10.030.

Ungerer, M., Knezovich, J., Ramsay, M. (2013.) In utero alcohol exposure, epigenetic changes, and their consequences. *Alcohol Res*, 35(1), 37-46.

Wright, R., and Saul, R. A. (2013.) Epigenetics and Primary Care. *Pediatrics*. 132 (suppl. 3), S216-S223.

Chapter 21. Protocol and Etiquette
No references.

Abdul-Raouf, N., Al-Homaidan, A. A., Ibraheem, I. B. M. (2012.) Microalgae and wastewater treatment. *Saudi J Biol Sci*, 19, 257-275.

Chater, K. F. (2006.) *Streptomyces* **inside-out: a new perspective on the bacteria that provide us with antibiotics.** *Philos Trans R Soc Lond B Biol Sci*, 361(1469), 761–768. doi: 10.1098/rstb.2005.1758.

Deller, S., Mascher, F., Platzer, S., *et. al.* (2006.) Effect of solar radiation on survival of indicator bacteria in bathing waters. *Cent Eur J Pub Health*, 14(3), 133-137.

Chapter 23. Proficiency and Potions (Genetic Polymorphism)

Andersson, E., Murgia, N., Nilsson, T., *et al.* (2013.) Incidence of chronic bronchitis in a cohort of pulp mill workers with repeated gassings to sulphur dioxide and other irritant gases. *Environ Health*, 12, 113. doi: 10.1186/1476-069X-12-113.

Guarnieri, M., and Balmes, J. R. (2014.) Outdoor air pollution and asthma. *Lancet*, 383(9928), 1581-92. doi: 10.1016/S0140-6736(14)60617-6.

Jangra, A., Sriram, C. S., Pandey, S. *et al.*, (2016.) Epigenetic Modifications, Alcoholic Brain and Potential Drug Targets. *Ann Neurosci*, 23(4), 246-260.

Karki, R. Pandya, D., Elston, R. C., Ferlini, C. (2015.) Defining "mutation" and "polymorphism" in the era of personal genomics. *BMC Medical Genomics*, 8, 37. doi: 10.1186/s12920-015-0115-z.

Lynch, T. and Price, A. (2013.) The effect of cytochrome P450 metabolism on drug response, interactions, and adverse effect. *Amer Fam Phys*, 76(3), 391-396.

Nebert, D. W., Wikvall, K., Miller, W. L. (2013.) Human cytochromes P450 in health and disease. *Phil Trans R Soc B*, 368: 20120431.

Quiñones, L., Roco, Á., Cayún, J. P., *et al.* (2017.) Clinical applications of pharmacogenomics. *Rev Med Chil*, 145(4),483-500. doi: 10.4067/S0034-98872017000400009.

van der Weide, J., and Hinrichs, J. W. J. (2006.) The Influence of Cytochrome P450 Pharmacogenetics on Disposition of Common Antidepressant and Antipsychotic Medications. *Clin Biochem Rev*, 27(1), 17–25.

Wall, T. L., Luczak, S. E., Hiller-Sturmhöfel, S. (2016.) Biology, Genetics, and Environment: Underlying Factors Influencing Alcohol Metabolism. *Alcohol Res*, 38(1), 59-68.

Zanger, U. M., and Schwab, M. (2012.) Cytochrome P450 enzymes in drug metabolism: Regulation of gene expression, enzyme activities, and impact of genetic variation. *Pharmacology and Therapeutics*, 138(1), 103–141. http://dx.doi.org/10.1016/j.pharmthera.2012.12.007.

Chapters 24-26.
No references.

Chapter 27. Zebrafish (Morphogenesis)

Abreu A, Tovar AP, Castellanos R, *et al.* (2016.) Challenges in the diagnosis and management of acromegaly: a focus on comorbidities. *Pituitary*, 19(4), 448-57. doi: 10.1007/s11102-016-0725-2.

Bellas, E., and Chen, C. S. (2014.) Forms, forces, and stem cell fate. *Curr Opin Cell Biol*, 31, 92-97. doi: 10:1016/j.ceb.2014.09.006.

Blanplain, C., and Fuchs, E. (2014.) Stem cell plasticity. Plasticity of epithelial stem cells in tissue regeneration. *Science*, 344(6189), 1242281. doi: 10.1126/science.1242281.

Borsos, M., and Torres-Padilla, M. E. (2016.) Building up the nucleus: nuclear organization in the establishment of totipotency and pluripotency during mammalian development. *Genes Dev*, 30(6), 611-21. doi: 10.1101/gad.273805.115.

Chen, D., Zhao, M., and Mundy, G.R. (2004.) Bone morphogenetic proteins. *Growth Factors*, 22(4), 233-241.

Daley, G. Q. (2015.) Stem cells and the evolving notion of cellular identity. *Philos Trans R Soc Lond B Biol Sci*, 370(1680), 20140376. doi: 10.1098/ rstb.2014.0376.

Dulak, J., Szade, K., Szade, A., *et al.* (2015.) Adult stem cells: hopes and hypes of regenerative medicine. *Acta Biochin Pol*, 62(3), 329-37. doi: 10.18388/abp.2015_1023.

Findlay, J. K., Gear, M. L., Illingworth, P. J., *et al.* (2007.) Human embryo: A biological definition. *Hum Reprod*, 22(4), 905-911. doi: 10.1093/humrep/del467.

Gordon, K. J., and Blobe, G. C., (2008.) Role of transforming growth factor-B superfamily signaling. *Biochim et Biophys Acta – Molec Basis of Dis*, 1782 (4), 197-228. doi.org/10.1010/j.bbadis.2008.01.006.

Kajdaniuk, D., Marek, B., Borgiel-Marek, H., Kos-Kudla, B. (2013.) Transforming growth factor β1 (TGFβ1) in physiology and pathology. *Endokrynol Pol*, 64(5), 384-396. doi: 10.5063/ep.2013.0022.

Mehlen, P., Mille, F., Thibert, C. (2005.) Morphogens and cell survival during development. *J. Neurobiol*, 64(4), 357-66. doi: 10.1002/neu.20167.

Melcer, S., and Meshorer, E. (2010.) Chromatin plasticity in pluripotent cells. *Essays Biochem*, 48(1), 245-62. doi: 10.1042/bse0480245.

Merkle, C. J. (2009a.) Cellular adaptation, injury, and death. In: Porth, C. M., and Matfin (eds), *Pathophysiology: Concepts of Altered Health States* (8th ed.), Chapter 5. Lippincott Williams and Wilkins.

Mitalipov, S., and Wolf, D. (2009.) Totipotency, pluripotency and nuclear reprogramming. *Adv Biochem Eng Biotechnol*, 114, 185-199. doi: 10.1007/10_2008_45.

Na, J., Plews, J., Li, J., *et al.* (2010.) Molecular mechanisms of pluripotency and reprogramming. *Stem Cell Res Ther*, 1(4), 33. doi: 10.1186/scrt33.

Nana, A. W., Yang, P. M., Lin, H. Y. (2015.) Overview of Transforming Growth Factor β superfamily involvement in glioblastoma initiation and progression. *Asian Pac J Cancer Prev*, 16(16), 6813-23.

Peng, L. H., Tsang, S. Y., Tabata, Y., Gao, J. Q. (2012.) Genetically-manipulated adult stem cells as therapeutic agents and gene delivery vehicle for wound repair and regeneration. *J Control Release*, 157(3), 321-30. doi: 10.1016/j.jconrel.2011.08.027.

Scacchi, M., and Cavagnini F. (2006.) Acromegaly. *Pituitary*, 9(4), 297-303.

Seymour, T., Twigger, A. J., Kakulas, F. (2015.) Pluripotency genes and their functions in the normal and aberrant breast and brain. *Int J Mol Sci*, 16(11), 27288-301. doi: 10.3390/jims161126024.

Stachowiak M. K., Stachowiak E. K. (2016.) Evidence-Based Theory for Integrated Genome Regulation of Ontogeny--An Unprecedented Role of Nuclear FGFR1 Signaling. *J Cell Physiol.*, 231(6), 1199-218. doi: 10.1002/jcp.25298.

Tabata, T., and Takei, Y. (2004.) Morphogens, their identification and regulation. *Development*, 131, 703-712.

Terranova, C., Narla, S. T., Lee, Y. W., *et al.* (2015.) Global Developmental Gene Programing Involves a Nuclear Form of Fibroblast Growth Factor Receptor-1 (FGFR1). *PLoS One*, 10(4), e0123380. doi: 10.1371/journal.pone.0123380.

Zhou, Q., Li, L., Zhao, B., Guan, K. L. (2015.) The hippo pathway in heart development, regeneration, and diseases. *Circ Res*, 116(8), 1431-47. doi: 1161/circresaha.116.303311.

Chapter 28. From Caterpillar to Butterfly (Metamorphosis)

Champagne, F. A. (2013.) Epigenetics and developmental plasticity across species. *Dev. Psychobiol*, 55(1), 33-41.

Chen, D., Zhao, M., and Mundy, G.R. (2004.) Bone morphogenetic proteins. *Growth Factors*, 22(4), 233-241.

Crowther-Radulewicz, C. L. (2014.) Structure and function of the musculoskeletal system. In: K. L. McCance, S. E. Huether, V. L. Brashers, V.L., and N. S. Rote, *Pathophysiology: The Biologic Basis for Disease in Adults and Children* (7ᵗʰ ed.), Chapter 41. St. Louis: Mosby/Elsevier.

Evans, R. M., and Mangelsdorf, D. J. (2014.) Nuclear Receptors, RXR, and the Big Bang. *Cell*, 57(1), 255-66. doi: 10.1016/j.cell.2014.03.012.

Gokhale, R. H., and Shingleton, A. W. (2015.) Size control: the developmental physiology of body and organ size regulation. *Wiley Interdiscip Rev Dev Biol*, 4(4), 335-56. doi: 10.1002/wdev.181.

Grimaldi, A., Buisine, N., Miller, T., *et al.* (2013.) Mechanisms of thyroid hormone receptor action during development: lessons from amphibian studies. *Biochim Biophys Acta*, 1830(7), 3882-92. doi: 10.1016/j.bbagen.2012.04.020.

Heisenberg, C-P., and Bellaiche, Y. (2013.) Forces in tissue morphogenesis and patterning. *Cell*, 153(5), 948-962. doi: http://dx.doi.org/10.1016/j.cell.2013.05.008.

Hernandez, S.E., Krishnaswami, M., Miller, A. L., Koleske, A. J. (2004.) How do Abl family kinases regulate cell shape and movement? *Trends Cell Biol*, 14(1), 36-44.

Kemper, K. E., Visscher, P. M., Goddard, M. E. (2012.) Genetic architecture of body size in mammals. *Genome Biol*, 13(4), 244. doi: 10.1186/gb4016.

Leevers, S. J., and McNeill, H. (2005.) Controlling the size of organs and organisms. *Curr Opin Cell Biol*, 17(6), 604-9. doi: 10.1016/j.ceb.2005.09.008.

Lui, J. C., and Baron, J. (2011.) Mechanisms limiting body growth in mammals. *Endocr Rev*, 32(3), 422-40. doi: 10.1210/er.2011-0001.

Poser, S. W., Chenoweth, J. G., Colantuoni, C., *et al.* (2015.) Concise Review: Reprogramming, Behind the Scenes: Noncanonical Neural Stem Cell Signaling Pathways Reveal New, Unseen Regulators of Tissue Plasticity with Therapeutic Implications. *Stem Cells Transl Med*, 4(11), 1251-7. doi: 10.5966/sctm.2015-0105.

Psaltis, P. J., Simari, R. D. (2015.) Vascular wall progenitor cells in health and disease. *Circ Res*, 116(8), 1392-1412. doi: 10.1161/circresaha.116.305368.

Reddi, A. H. (2000.) Morphogenesis and tissue engineering of bone and cartilage: inductive signals, stems cells, and biomimetic biomaterials. *Tissue Eng*, 6(4), 351-359.

Rosello-Diez, A., and Joyner, A. L. (2015.) Regulation of Long Bone Growth in Vertebrates; It Is Time to Catch Up. *Endocr Rev*, 36(6), 646-80. doi: 10.1210/er.2015-1048.

Rowold, D. J., and Herrera, R. J. (2000.) Alu elements and the human genome. *Genetics*, 108(1), 57-72.

Simpson, C. L., Patel, D. M., Green, K. J. (2011.) Deconstructing the skin: Cytoarchectural determinants of epidermal morphogenesis. *Nature Reviews Molecular Cell Biology*, 12, 565 580. doi: 10.1038/nrm3175.

Sirakov, M., Kress, E., Nadjar, J., Plateroti, M. (2014.) Thyroid hormones and their nuclear receptors: new players in intestinal epithelium stem cell biology? *Cell Mol Life Sci*, 71(15), 2897-907. doi: 10.1007/s00018-014-1586-3.

Sirakov, M., Skah, S., Nadjar, J., Plateroti, M. (2013.) Thyroid hormone's action on progenitor/stem cell biology: new challenge for a classic hormone? *Biochim Biophys Acta*, 1830(7), 3917-27. doi: 10.1016/j.bbagen.2012.07.014.

Stachowiak M. K., Stachowiak E. K. (2016.) Evidence-Based Theory for Integrated Genome Regulation of Ontogeny--An Unprecedented Role of Nuclear FGFR1 Signaling. *J Cell Physiol.*, 231(6), 1199-218. doi: 10.1002/jcp.25298.

Stanger, B. Z. (2008.) The biology of organ size determination. *Diabetes Obes Metab*, Suppl 4:16-22. doi: 10.1111/j.1463-1326.2008.00938.x.

Terranova, C., Narla, S. T., Lee, Y. W., *et al.* (2015.) Global Developmental Gene Programing Involves a Nuclear Form of Fibroblast Growth Factor Receptor-1 (FGFR1. *PLoS One*, 10(4), e0123380. doi: 10.1371/journal.pone.0123380.

Tumaneng, K., Russell, R. C., Guan, K. K. (2012.) Organ size control by Hippo and TOR pathways. *Curr Biol,* 22(9), R368-79. doi: 10.1016/j.cub.2012.03.003.

Wang, C., and Huang, S. (2014.) Nuclear function of Alus. *Nucleus*, 5(2), 131-137. doi: 10.4161/nucl.28005.

Chapter 29.
    No references.

Chapter 30. Chasing Dreams

Serres, L. (2012.) The preservation of parchment. Emporia State University at Denver. *http://lisaserresportfolio.weebly.com/uploads/8/2/4/1/8241619/parchment.pdf.*

Chapters 31–33.
    No references.

Chapter 34. The Scent of Flowers (Genetic Imprinting)

Jirtle, R. L., Sander, M., Barret,. J. C. (2000.) Genomic imprinting and environmental disease susceptibility. *Environ Health Perspect*, 108(3), 271-8.

Kalish, J. M., Jiang, C., Bartolomei, M. S. (2014.) Epigenetics and imprinting in human disease. *Int J Dev Biol*, 58(2-4), 291-298. doi: 10.1387/ijdb.140077mb.

Kappil, M., Lambertini, I., Chen, J. (2015.) Environmental influences on genomic imprinting. *Curr Environ Health Rep*, 2(2), 155-162.

Lawson, H. A., Cheverud, J. M., Wolf, J. B. (2013.) Genomic imprinting and parent-of-origin effects on complex traits. *Nat Rev Genet*, 14(9), 609-17. doi: 10.1038/nrg3543.

Marzi, S. J., Meaburn, E. L., Dempster, E. L., *et al.* (2016.) Tissue-specific patterns of allelically-skewed DNA methylation. *Epigenetics*, 11(1), 24-35. doi: 10.1080/15592294.2015.1127479.

Meng, H., Cao, Y., Qin, J., *et al.* (2015.) DNA methylation, its mediators and genome integrity. *Int J. Biol*, 11(5), 604-17. doi: 10.7150/ijbs.11218.

Monk, D. (2015.) Germline-derived DNA methylation and early embryo epidenteic reprogramming: The selected survival of imprints. *Int J Biochem Cell Biol*, 67, 128-138. doi: 10.1016/j.biocel.2015.04.014.

Moore, G. E., Ishida, M., Demetriou, C., *et al.* (2015.) The role and interaction of imprinted genes in human fetal growth. *Philos Trans R Soc Lond B*, 370(1663), 20140074. doi: 10.1098/rstlb.2014.0074.

Nguyen, C. M., and Liao, W. (2015.) Genomic imprinting in psoriasis and atopic dermatitis: A review. *J Dermatol Sci*, 80(2), 89-93. doi: 10.1016/j.jdermsci.2015.08.004.

Pacchierotti, F., and Spano, M. (2015.) Environmental impact on DNA methylation in the germline: State of the art and gaps of knowledge. *Biomed Res Int*, 2015, 123484. doi: 10.1155/2015/123484.

Pfeifer, K. (2000.) Mechanisms of genomic imprinting. *Am J Hum Genet*, 67(4), 777-87.

Sadakierska-Chudy, A., Kostrzewa, R. M., Filip, M. (2015.) A comprehensive view of the epigenetic landscape part I: DNA methylation, passive and active DNA demethylation pathways and histone variants. *Neurotox Res*, 27(1), 84-97. doi: 10.1007/s12640-014-9497-5.

Tycko, B. (2000.) Epigenetic gene silencing in cancer. *J Clin Invest*, 105(4), 401–407. doi: 10.1172/JCI9462.

Chapter 35.
No references.

Chapter 36. Ascent into the Clouds (Genetics of Intelligence)

Deary, I. J., Johnson, W., Houlihan, L. M. (2009.) Genetic foundations of human intelligence. *Hum Genet*, 126(1), 215-232. doi: 10.1007/s00439-009-0655-4.

Junkiert-Czarnecka, A., and Haus, O. (2016.) Genetical background of intelligence. *Postepy Hig Med Dosw* (Online), 13, 70(0), 590-8.

Logue, S. F., and Gould, T. J, (2014.) The neural and genetic basis of executive function: attention, cognitive flexibility, and response inhibition. *Pharmacol Biochem Behav*, 123, 45-54. doi: 10.1016/j.pbb.2013.08.007.

Plomin, R., and Deary, I. J. (2015.) Genetics and intelligence differences: five special findings. *Mol Psychiatry*, 20(1), 98-108. doi: 10.1038/mp.2014.105.

Chapter 36. Descent into the Depths (Ancestral Genes)

Cooper, K. L., and Tabin, C. J. (2008.) Understanding of bat wing evolution takes flight. *Genes Dev*, 22(2), 121–124. doi: 10.1101/gad.1639108.

Sears, K. E. (2008.) Molecular Determinants of Bat Wing Development. *Cells Tissues Organs*, 187, 6–12. doi: 10.1159/000109959.

Young, N. M., and Hallgrímsson, B. (2005.) Serial homology and the evolution of mammalian limb covariation structure. *Evolution*, 59(12), 2691-704.

Chapters 38-39.
No references.

Chapter 40. Heritage (Aneuploidy)

Afshan, A. (2012.) Triple X syndrome. *J Pak Med Assoc*, 62(4), 392-394.

Berletch, J. B., Yang, F., Xu, J., *et al.* (2011.) Genes that escape from X inactivation. *Hum Genet*, 130(2), 237-45. doi: 10.1007/s00439-011-1011-z.

Devlin, L., and Morrison, P.J. (2004.) Accuracy of the clinical diagnosis of Down Syndrome. *Ulster Med J*, 73(1), 4-12.

Eichenlaub-Ritter, U. (1996.) Parental age-related aneuploidy in human germ cells and offspring: a story of past and present. *Environ Mol Mutagen*, 28(3), 211-36. doi: 10.1002/(SICI)1098-2280(1996)28:3<211::aid-em6>3.0.CO;2-G.

Gribnau, J., and Grootegoed, J. A. (2012.) Origin and evolution of X chromosome inactivation. *Curr Opin Cell Biol*, 24(3), 396-404. doi: 10.1016/j.ceb.2012.02.004.

Jorde, L. B. (2014a.) Genes and genetic diseases. In: K. L. McCance, S. E. Huether, V. L. Brashers, V.L., and N. S. Rote, *Pathophysiology: The Biologic Basis for Disease in Adults and Children* (7th ed.), Chapter 4. St. Louis: Mosby/Elsevier.

Loane, M., Morris J. K., Addor, M. C., *et al.* (2013.) Twenty-year trends in the prevalence of Down syndrome and other trisomies in Europe: impact of maternal age and prenatal screening. *Eur J Hum Genet*, 21(1), 27-33. doi: 10.1038/ejhg.2012.94.

MacLennan, M., Crichton, J. H., Playfoot, C. J., Adams, I. R. (2015.) Oocyte development, meiosis and aneuploidy. *Semin Cell Dev Biol*, 45, 68-76. doi: 10.1016/j.semcdb.2015.10.005.

Migeon, B. R., Pappas, K., Stetten, G., *et al.* (2008.) X inactivation in triploidy and trisomy: the search for autosomal transfactors that choose the active X. *Eur J Hum Genet*, 16(2), 153-62. doi: 10.1038/sj.ejhg.5201944.

Otter, M., Schrander-Stumpel, C. T., Curfs, L. M. (2010.) Triple X syndrome: a review of the literature. *Eur J Hum Genet*, 18(3), 265-71. doi: 10.1038/ejhg.2009.109.

Pessia, E., Makino, T., Bailly-Bechet, M., *et al.* (2012.) Mammalian X chromosome inactivation evolved as a dosage-compensation mechanism for dosage-sensitive genes on the X chromosome. *Proc Natl Acad Sci USA* 109(14), 5346-51. doi: 10.1073/pnas.1116763109.

Rocca, M. S., Pecile, V., Cleva, L., *et al.* (2016.) The Klinefelter syndrome is associated with high recurrence of copy number variations on the X chromosome with a potential role in the clinical phenotype. *Andrology*, 4(2), 328-34. doi: 10.1111/andr.12146.

Sato, H., Kato, H., Yamaza, H., *et al.* (2017.) Engineering of Systematic Elimination of a Targeted Chromosome in Human Cells. *Biomed Res Int,* 2017:6037159. doi: 10.1155/2017/6037159.

Tartaglia, N. R., Howell, S., Sutherland, A., *et al.* (2010.) A review of trisomy X (47,XXX). *Orphanet J Rare Dis,* 11, 5, 8. doi: 10.1186/1750-1172-5-8.

Visootsak, J., and Graham, J. M. Jr. (2006.) Klinefelter syndrome and other sex chromosomal aneuploidies. *Orphanet J Rare Dis,* 24 (1), 42. doi: 10.1186/1750-1172-1-42.

Chapter 41. Fragments (Genetic Testing)

Bettinger, B., and Wayne, D. P. (2016.) Geneological applications for mtDNA. In: Bettinger, B.T., and Wayne, D. P., Genetic Geneology in Practice (chapter 4). National Genealogical Society special topics series (NGS special publications no. 120).

Benn, P., Cuckle, H., Pergament, E. (2013.) Non-invasive prenatal testing for aneuploidy: current status and future prospects. *Ultrasound Obstet Gynecol,* 42(1), 15-33. doi: 10.1002/uog.12513.

Bentley, D. R., Balasubramanian, S., Swerdlow, H. P., *et al.* (2008.) Accurate whole human genome sequencing using reversible terminator chemistry. *Nature,* 456(7218), 53-9. doi: 10.1038/nature07517.

Botkin, J. R., Belmont, J. W., Berg, J. S. (2015.) Points to Consider: Ethical, Legal, and Psychosocial Implications of Genetic Testing in Children and Adolescents. *Am J Hum Genet,* 97(1), 6-21. doi: 10.1016/j.ajhg.2015.05.022.

Budowle, B., and van Daal, A. (2008.) Forensically relevant SNP classes. *Biotechniques,* 44(5), 603-8, 610. doi: 10.2144/000112806.

Carroll, E. W. (2009b.) Genetic control of cell function and inheritance. In: Porth, C. M., and Matfin (eds.), *Pathophysiology: Concepts of Altered Health States* (8th ed.), Chapter 6. Lippincott Williams and Wilkins.

Kemper, K. E., Visscher, P. M., Goddard, M. E. (2012.) Genetic architecture of body size in mammals. *Genome Biol,* 13(4), 244. doi: 10.1186/gb4016.

Ochiai, H. (2015.) Single-base pair genome editing in human cells by using site-specific endonucleases. *Int J Molec Sci*, 16(9), 21128-37. doi: 10.3390/ijms160921128.

Peters, D. G., Yatsenko, S. A., Surti, U. (2015.) Recent advances of genomic testing in perinatal medicine. *Semin Perinatol*, 39(1), 44–54. doi:10.1053/j.semperi.2014.10.009.

Peters, D. T., and Musunuru, K. (2012.) Functional evaluation of genetic variation in complex human traits. *Hum Mol Genet*, 21(R1), R18-23. doi: 10.1093/hmg/dds363.

Samuelsson, J. K., Alonso, S., Yamamoto, F., Perucho, M. (2010.) DNA fingerprinting techniques for the analysis of genetic and epigenetic alterations in colorectal cancer. *Mutat Res*, 693(1-2), 61-76. doi: 10.1016/j.mrfmmm.2010.08.010.

Sato, M., and Sato, K. (2013.) Maternal inheritance of mitochondrial DNA by diverse mechanisms to eliminate paternal mitochondrial DNA. *Biochim Biophys Acta*, 1833(8), 1979-84. doi. 1016/j.bbamcr.2013.03.010.

Vega, R. B., Horton, J. L., Kelly, D. P. (2015.) Maintaining ancient organelles: Mitochondrial biogenesis and maturation. *Circ Res*, 116(11), 1820-34. doi: 10.1161/circresaha.116.305420.

Chapter 42. Mistress and Matron (Genetics of Longevity)

Franzke, B., Neubauer, O., Wagner, K. H. (2015.) Super DNAging-New insights into DNA integrity, genome stability and telomeres in the oldest old. *Mutat Res Rev Mutat Res*, 766:48-57. doi: 10.1016/j.mrrev.2015.08.001.

Jones, M. J., Goodman, S. J., Kobor, M. S. (2015.) DNA methylation and healthy human aging. *Aging Cell*, 14(6), 924-32. doi: 10.1111/acel.12349.

Milman, S., and Barzilai, N. (2015.) Dissecting the Mechanisms Underlying Unusually Successful Human Health Span and Life Span. *Cold Spring Harb Perspect Med*, 6(1), a025098. doi: 10.1101/cshperspect.a025098.

Moskalev, A. A, Aliper, A. M., Smit-McBride, Z., *et al.* (2014.) Genetics and epigenetics of aging and longevity. *Cell Cycle*, 13(7), 1063-77. doi: 10.4161/cc.28433.

Oeseburg, H., de Boer, R. A., van Gilst, W. H., van der Harst, P. (2010.) Telomere biology in healthy aging and disease. *Pflugers Arch,* 459(2), 259-68. doi: 10.1007/s00424-009-0728-1.

Pan, M. R., Li, K., Lin, S. Y., Hung, W. C. (2016.) Connecting the Dots: From DNA Damage and Repair to Aging. *Int J Mol Sci,* 17(5), pii: E685. doi: 10.3390/ijms17050685.

Pusceddu, I., Farrell, C. J., Di Pierro, A. M., *et al.* (2015.) The role of telomeres and vitamin D in cellular aging and age-related diseases. *Clin Chem Lab Med,* 53(11), 1661-78. doi: 10.1515/cclm-2014-1184

Shadyab, A. H., and LaCroix, A. Z. (2015.) Genetic factors associated with longevity: a review of recent findings. *Aging Res Rev,* 19:1-7. doi: 10.1016/j.arr.2014.10.005.

Shay, J. W. (2016.) Role of Telomeres and Telomerase in Aging and Cancer. *Cancer Discov,* 6 (6), 584-93. doi: 10.1158/2159-8290.CD-16-0062.

Chapter 43.
No references.

Chapter 44. On Patrol (Copy Number Variations)

Campbell, I. A., Shaw, C. A., Stankiewicz, P., Lupski, R. R. (2015.) Somatic Mosaicism: Implications for Disease and Transmission Genetics. *Trends Genet,* 31(7), 382–392. doi: 10.1016/j.tig.2015.03.013.

Mishra, S., Whetstine, J. R. (2016.) Different Facets of Copy Number Changes: Permanent, Transient, and Adaptive. *Mol Cell Biol,* 36(7), 1050-63. doi: 10.1128/MCB.00652-15.

Rocca, M. S., Pecile, V., Cleva, L., *et al.* (2016.) The Klinefelter syndrome is associated with high recurrence of copy number variations on the X chromosome with a potential role in the clinical phenotype. *Andrology,* 4(2), 328-34. doi: 10.1111/andr.12146.

Vattahil, S., and Scheet, P. (2016.) Extensive Hidden Genomic Mosaicism Revealed in Normal Tissue. *Am J Hum Genet,* 98(3), 571-8. doi: 10.1016/j.ajhg.2016.02.003.

Zhang, F., and Lupski, J. R. (2015.) Non-coding genetic variants in human disease. *Hum Mol Genet*, 24(R1), R102-10. doi: 10.1093/hmg/ddv259.

Zilina, O., Koltsina, M., Raid, R., *et al.* (2015.) Somatic mosaicism for copy-neutral loss of heterozygosity and DNA copy number variations in the human genome. *BMC Genomics*, 16, 703. doi: 10.1186/s12864-015-1916-3.

Chapter 45. The Lyvulsoptera (Genetics of Dementia and Psychosis)

Boss, B. J. (2014.) Disorders of the central and peripheral nervous systems and the neuromuscular junction. In: K. L. McCance, S. E. Huether, V. L. Brashers, V.L., and N. S. Rote, *Pathophysiology: The Biologic Basis for Disease in Adults and Children* (7th ed.), Chapter 14. St. Louis: Mosby/Elsevier.

Cohn-Hokke, P. E., Elting, M. W., Rijnenburg, Y. A., van Swieten, J. C. (2012.) Genetics of dementia: update and guidelines for the clinician. *Am J Med Genet B Neuropsychiatr Genet*, 159B(6), 628-43. doi: 10.1002/ajmg.b.32080.

DeRosse, P., Malhotra, A. K., Lencz, T. (2012.) Molecular Genetics of the Psychosis Phenotype. *Can J Psychiatry*. 2012 Jul; 57(7), 446–453.

Jonas, R. K., Montojo, C. A., Bearden, C. E. (2014.) The 22q11.2 deletion syndrome as a window into complex neuropsychiatric disorders over the lifespan. *Biol Psychiatry*, 75(5), 351-60. doi: 10.1016/j.biopsych.2013.07.019.

Jorde, L.B. (2014b.) Genes, environment, and common diseases. In: K. L. McCance, S. E. Huether, V. L. Brashers, V.L., and N. S. Rote, *Pathophysiology: The Biologic Basis for Disease in Adults and Children* (7th ed.), Chapter 5. St. Louis: Mosby/Elsevier.

Pasch, S. K. (2009.) Disorders of thought, mood, and memory. In: Porth, C. M., and Matfin (eds.), *Pathophysiology: Concepts of Altered Health States* (8th ed.), Chapter 53. Lippincott Williams and Wilkins.

Loy, C. T., Schofield, P. R., Turner, A. M., Kwok, J. B. (2013.) Genetics of dementia. *Lancet,* http://dx.doi.org/10.1016/ S0140-6736(13)60630-3.

Serrano-Pozo, A., Frosch, M. P., Masliah, E., Hyman, B. T. (2011.) Neuropathological alterations in Alzheimer disease. *Cold Spring Harb Perspect Med*, 1(1), a006189. doi: 10.1101/cshpperspec.

Shively, S., Scher, A. I., Perl, D. P., Diaz-Arrastia, R. (2012.) Dementia resulting from traumatic brain injury: what is the pathology? *Arch Neurol*, 69(10), 1245-51. doi: 10.1001/archneurol.2011.3747.

Takahashi, L. K. (2014.) Neurobiology of schizophrenia mood disorders, and anxiety disorders. In: K. L. McCance, S. E. Huether, V. L. Brashers, V.L., and N. S. Rote, *Pathophysiology: The Biologic Basis for Disease in Adults and Children* (7th ed.), Chapter 18. St. Louis: Mosby/Elsevier.

Toth, M. (2015.) Mechanisms of non-genetic inheritance and psychiatric disorders. *Neuropsychopharmacology.* 40(1), 129-40. doi: 10.1038/npp.2014.127.

Washington P. M., Villapol, S., Burns, M. P. (2016.) Polypathology and dementia after brain trauma: Does brain injury trigger distinct neurodegenerative diseases, or should they be classified together as traumatic encephalopathy? *Exp Neurol*, 275 Pt 3, 381-8. doi: 10.1016/j.expneurol.2015.06.015.

Chapters 46-52.
    No references.

Appendix A Dragonensis dragonis

Chen, I. H., Kiang, J. H., Correa, V., *et al.* (2011.) Armadillo armor: mechanical testing and micro-structural evaluation. *J Mech Behav Biomed Mater*, 4(5), 713-22. doi: 10.1016/j.jmbbm.2010.12.013.

Fontana, S. S., and Porth, C. M. (2009.) Disorders of hearing and vestibular function. In: Porth, C. M., and Matfin (eds), *Pathophysiology: Concepts of Altered Health States* (8th ed.,) Chapter 55. Lippincott Williams and Wilkins.

Simandl, G. (2009.) Structure and function of the skin. In: Porth, C. M., and Matfin (eds), *Pathophysiology: Concepts of Altered Health States* (8th ed.), Chapter 60. Lippincott Williams and Wilkins.

Stoeger, A. S., Heilmann, G., Zeppelzauer, M., *et al.* (2012.) Visualizing Sound Emission of Elephant Vocalizations: Evidence for Two Rumble Production Types. *PLoS One*, 7(11), e48907. doi: 10.1371/journal.pone.0048907.

Yang, W., Chen, I. H., Gludovatz, B., *et al.* (2013.) Natural flexible dermal armor. *Adv Mater*, 25(1), 31-48. doi: 10.1002/adma.201202713.

Ambrosy, A. P., Butler, J., Ahmed, A. *et al.* (2014.) The use of digoxin in patients with worsening chronic heart failure: reconsidering an old drug to reduce hospital admissions. *J Am Coll Cardiol*, 63(18), 1823-32. doi: 10.1016/j.jacc.2014.01.051.

Araújo, A. M., Carvalho, F., Bastos, Mde. L., *et al.* (2015.) The hallucinogenic world of tryptamines: an updated review. *Arch Toxicol*, 89(8), 1151-73. doi: 10.1007/s00204-015-1513-x.

Barton, D. L., Atherton, P. J., Bauer, B. A. (2011.) The use of Valeriana officinalis (Valerian) in improving sleep in patients who are undergoing treatment for cancer: A phase III randomized, placebo-controlled, double-blind study (NCCTG Trial, N01C5). *J Support Oncol*, 9(1), 24-31. doi: 10.1016/j.suponc.2010.12.008. Valerian. https://ods.od.nih.gov/factsheets/Valerian-HealthProfessional/

Baser, K. H. (2008.) Biological and pharmacological activities of carvacrol and carvacrol bearing essential oils. *Curr Pharm Des*, 14(29), 3106-19.

Cash, B. D., Epstein, M. S., Shah, S. M. (2016.) A Novel Delivery System of Peppermint Oil Is an Effective Therapy for Irritable Bowel Syndrome Symptoms. *Dig Dis Sci*, 61(2), 560-71. doi: 10.1007/s10620-015-3858-7.

Chen, W., Vermaak, I., Viljoen, A. (2013.) Camphor--a fumigant during the Black Death and a coveted fragrant wood in ancient Egypt and Babylon- a review. *Molecules*, 18(5):5434-54. doi: 10.3390/molecules18055434.

Farco, J. A., and Grundmann, O. (2013.) Menthol--pharmacology of an important naturally medicinal "cool". *Mini Rev Med Chem*. 13(1), 124-31.

Firouzi, R., Shekarforoush, S. S., Nazer, A. H. (2007.) Effects of essential oils of oregano and nutmeg on growth and survival of Yersinia enterocolitica and Listeria monocytogenes in barbecued chicken. *J Food Prot*, 70(11), 2626-30.

Friedman, M. (2014.) Chemistry and multibeneficial bioactivities of carvacrol (4-isopropyl-2-methylphenol), a component of essential oils produced by aromatic plants and spices. *J Agric Food Chem*, 62(31), 7652-70. doi: 10.1021/jf5023862.

Griffith, R. E., and Maisch, J. M. (1874.) A Universal Formulary: Containing the Methods of Preparing and ... https://books.google.com/books?id=w8EwAAAAYAAJ.

González-Castejón, M., Visioli, F., Rodriguez-Casado A. (2012.) Diverse biological activities of dandelion. *Nutr Rev*, 70(9), 534-47. doi: 10.1111/j.1753-4887.2012.00509.x.

Gutierrez, J., Barry-Ryan, C., Bourke, P. (2008.) The antimicrobial efficacy of plant essential oil combinations and interactions with food ingredients. *Int J Food Microbiol*, 124(1), 91-7. doi: 10.1016/j.ijfoodmicro.2008.02.028.

Halberstadt, A.L, and Geyer, M. A. (2011.) Multiple receptors contribute to the behavioral effects of indoleamine hallucinogens. *Neuropharmacology*, 61(3), 364-81. doi: 10.1016/j.neuropharm.2011.01.017.

Hashemi, S. A., Madani, S. A., Abediankenari, S. (2015.) The Review on Properties of Aloe Vera in Healing of Cutaneous Wounds. *Biomed Res Int*, 2015:714216. doi: 10.1155/2015/714216.

Hennebelle, T., Sahpaz, S., Gressier, B., et al. (2008.) Antioxidant and neurosedative properties of polyphenols and iridoids from Lippia alba. *Phytother Res*, 22(2), 256-8.

Jędrejek, D., Kontek, B., Lis, B., *et al.* (2017.) Evaluation of antioxidant activity of phenolic fractions from the leaves and petals of dandelion in human plasma treated with H_2O_2 and H_2O_2/Fe. *Chem Biol Interact*, 262, 29-37. doi: 10.1016/j.cbi.2016.12.003.

Mehriardestani, M., Aliahmadi, A., Toliat, T., Rahimi, R. (2017.) Medicinal plants and their isolated compounds showing anti-Trichomonas vaginalis- activity. *Biomed Pharmacother*, 88, 885-893. doi: 10.1016/j.biopha.2017.01.149.

Nahas, R., and Sheikh, O. (2011.) Complementary and alternative medicine for the treatment of major depressive disorder. *Can Fam Physician*, 57(6), 659-63.

Patel, T., Ishiuji, Y., Yosipovitch, G. (2007.) Menthol: a refreshing look at this ancient compound. *J Am Acad Dermatol*, 57(5), 873-8. doi: 10.1016/j.jaad.2007.04.008.

Schütz, K., Carle, R., Schieber, A. (2006.) Taraxacum--a review on its phytochemical and pharmacological profile. *J Ethnopharmacol*, 107(3), 313-23.

Sharopov, F. S., Satyal, P., Ali, N. A., *et al.* (2016.) The Essential Oil Compositions of Ocimum basilicum from Three Different Regions: Nepal, Tajikistan, and Yemen. *Chem Biodivers*, 13(2), 241-8. doi: 10.1002/cbdv.201500108.

Shukla, A., Garg, A., Mourya, P. (2016.) Zizyphus oenoplia Mill: A review on pharmacological aspects. *Advance Pharmaceutical J*, 1(1), 8-12. http://www.apjonline.in/uploaded/p2.pdf.

Silva, F. S., Menezes, P. M., de Sá, P. G., *et al.* (2016.) Chemical composition and pharmacological properties of the essential oils obtained seasonally from Lippia thymoides. *Pharm Biol*, 54(1), 25-34. doi: 10.3109/13880209.2015.1005751.

Suntres, Z. E., Coccimiglio, J., Alipour, M. (2015.) The bioactivity and toxicological actions of carvacrol. *Crit Rev Food Sci Nutr*, 55(3), 304-18. doi: 10.1080/10408398.2011.653458.

Index of Genetic Terms